Miracles *can* happen...if you only **believe.**
And love is the greatest miracle of all....

In *The Miracle Man,*
a woman desperate for a child
but despondent about love finds the answer
to both her prayers...in the form of the
U.S. marshal who washes ashore at her feet.

In *When You Call My Name,*
a man whose life was saved by a transfusion
finds himself linked to the woman whose blood he
now shares—in more ways than just the obvious....

And in *Shades of a Desperado,*
night after restless night a woman is
kept awake by dreams of a hard-edged outlaw
straight out of the Old West—until she meets
the man of her dreams...in real life!

SHARON
SALA
Believe

Silhouette® Books

Published by Silhouette Books

America's Publisher of Contemporary Romance

SILHOUETTE BOOKS

ISBN 0-373-20191-5

by Request

BELIEVE

Copyright © 2001 by Harlequin Books S.A.

The publisher acknowledges the copyright holder of the individual works as follows:

THE MIRACLE MAN
Copyright © 1995 by Sharon Sala

WHEN YOU CALL MY NAME
Copyright © 1996 by Sharon Sala

SHADES OF A DESPERADO
Copyright © 1997 by Sharon Sala

Visit Silhouette at www.eHarlequin.com

Printed in U.S.A.

CONTENTS

Dear Reader,

I was so pleased to learn that Silhouette has decided to reissue three of my most-talked-about stories. Each, in its own way, is unique, and yet there is also a special connection between them.

The Miracle Man is about a woman with remarkable strength and courage, whose femininity is overlooked by her family until a federal marshal named Lane Monday comes into her life. It's a story of love and acceptance, and one of which I'm very proud.

When You Call My Name is a sequel to *The Miracle Man*, but also deals with a woman named Glory Dixon whose psychic abilities have ostracized her within her own community. It isn't until a stranger named Wyatt Hatfield comes into their lives that they learn what a gift they have in her.

Shades of a Desperado is one of my all-time favorites. The story came to me in a dream. It was so real that I woke up gasping for breath, convinced that I had just died. If you've ever lost a loved one and had to live with regrets of what had never been said, then this book will speak to your heart.

If you believe in love—if you believe that love never dies—then these stories are for you.

I can be reached at P.O. Box 127, Henryetta, OK, 74437, or by e-mail at sharonsala@romanticfiction.com.

Sharon Sala

THE MIRACLE MAN

This book is dedicated to the belief in miracles and miracle workers everywhere. To the doctors, nurses, caregivers and EMTs. To men and women of the cloth. To all the men in law enforcement who daily put their lives on the line, and to everyone who believes.

And especially to the miracle workers who have impacted upon my life: Dennis Dukes, EMT: Kathy Orr, EMT; RaeAnne Berry, EMT; Dr. Frank Howard, Dr. Robert L. Talley, Dr. Ross Pope, Dr. Michael Goddard and Dr. Don Mace. Also a belated thanks to retired doctors John G. Rollins, M.D., and Jake Jones, M.D., and to the late Dr. Ned Burleson, as well as the late Dr. Kirk T. Mosley, who was always there when I needed him.

Chapter 1

The small, twelve-seater airplane assigned to the United States Marshal's Office sat on a runway at the Tallahassee airport. As armed guards watched from the runway, a nondescript blue van pulled up and began emptying its deadly cargo.

Three men, marked by prison uniforms, leg irons and shackles, filed out of the van with little fuss. Hog-tied by more than the bonds of the criminal justice system, they had nowhere to go but up the ramp and into the waiting plane where they were placed in seats.

Emmit Rice muttered belligerently as he shifted his six-foot-five-inch, three-hundred-pound bulk toward two of the three seats at the front of the airplane.

Oversize handcuffs circled his massive wrists, and the shackles and leg irons, compliments of the Federal Correctional Institution in Tallahassee, Florida, rattled when he came to an abrupt stop at the seat and landed with a grunt. He glanced up and then glared at the marshal who was waiting patiently for him to settle.

"What the hell are you looking at?" he muttered.

For the past fifteen years, Lane Monday had served as a United States marshal. So a disgruntled prisoner, even one the size of a small tank, was nothing new to him.

Lane grinned, then ducked out of habit to keep from bumping his head as he maneuvered his own six feet six inches into the bulkhead of the plane. His answer, as well as the slow appraisal that he gave Emmit Rice, were telling.

"What am *I* looking at? Not much," he said, and stifled another grin when Emmit Rice's face flushed in anger. It was probably one of the few times in his life, Lane mused, that Emmit Rice had been reduced in size, as well as strength, by little more than a look.

Rice snorted and stretched his massive body into as much space as he possibly could. It was an intimidating gesture that he knew usually netted results. But the cool, assessing stare that the big marshal gave him was proof that intimidation was not going to work. Not on Lane Monday.

Monday was more than a match for him in height. And while he had nowhere near the bulk of Emmit Rice, he had a powerful body to back up the gun that he carried.

And it was Lane Monday's size alone that had been the reason for his recall from a much-needed vacation. Someone had to escort Emmit Rice from the Federal Correctional Institution in Tallahassee, Florida, to the one in Lexington, Kentucky. Who better than a man who could look Rice in the eye and come away grinning?

The last man to board the plane was the other marshal, Bob Tell. "Buckle up, boys. Better safe than sorry." Bob laughed at his own joke as he did a last-minute check of the prisoners and their restraints.

One of the prisoners laughed with him. The other two, Rice included, neither smiled nor looked at the man who thought he was a comic. Their eyes were fixed upon the mass of man who stood between them and freedom, wearing a cold blue stare and a gun on his hip.

"Time to check guns," Bob said, opening the lid of a

strongbox and holding it toward Lane, while he kept an eye on the prisoners who were watching the proceedings with entirely too much interest.

Monday slid his weapon out of its holster and dropped it into the lockbox as Bob followed suit, pocketing the key before stowing the box in the cockpit.

It was standard procedure to check guns before taking off. The last thing a lawman wanted was to be overpowered by a prisoner and have his own weapon taken away and used on an innocent bystander—or on himself.

Finally the plane was airborne, and there was nowhere to go but down. It was then that the air within the cabin seemed to settle, and two of the prisoners even dozed while Bob sat watch.

But Rice didn't sleep. His small, green eyes were firmly fixed upon the marshal who'd had to turn sideways to get his shoulders through the door.

Lane Monday didn't budge from the position that he'd taken when the plane had lifted off. He knew all too well how desperate the man was he'd been assigned to transport.

Emmit Rice was a lawman's nightmare. He was a lifer with nothing to lose. Regardless of what else he might do, he'd already lost everything that mattered but his life. And the way he looked at living behind bars, his life was already lost.

And then they flew into the storm and everything changed, including the hand that fate had dealt them.

Although it was still hours before nightfall, the clouds that had arrived, seemingly from nowhere, were pitch-black. In the space of a heartbeat, the plane appeared to go from day into night as it flew right into the mouth of a storm. Lightning flashed outside the plane, momentarily illuminating the sky.

"Son of a bitch," one of the prisoners muttered, ducking his head from the brilliant flash of electrical energy.

In seconds, Bob was on his feet and heading for the cockpit while Monday stayed put, bracing himself against the bulkhead with both feet outspread and his arms above his head, riding out the air pockets with grim-lipped determination. He'd been in some bad spots before and gotten through them fine. But something told him that this time might be a different story.

"We're gonna crash! We're gonna crash!"

Prisoner DeVon Randall was losing control. His voice had elevated three octaves as, wild-eyed, he stared around the cabin, trying to free himself from the seat in which he was bound.

Emmit Rice glared at Randall, hating him for verbalizing what they all felt. He would not have admitted his fear under penalty of death, but he was afraid the little man might be right.

"Calm down, Randall," Monday said.

His order to the prisoner went in one ear and out the other. The man was chained—and in hysterics. The combination could prove lethal for them all. Then Bob burst out of the cockpit and nearly ran Monday down.

"Damn, Monday. This is bad. We've got to prepare the men in case of—"

He never finished what he was saying. Blinding light, followed by a loud crack, sent both lawmen to their knees. The plane bucked and the cabin momentarily went dark. When the lights flickered back on, Bob was scrambling for the keys in his pocket and heading for the three prisoners, pinned in their seats by shackles and leg irons.

"Help me," Bob shouted. "We're going down, and they'll die for sure if they can't get out."

Monday hesitated for a moment. It was instinctive. Letting these three loose, even inside a plane in danger of crashing, was taking chances that he didn't want to consider. But leaving them as they were was the same as shooting them where they sat.

"I want my gun back," Monday growled. Bob nodded, hurrying to retrieve their weapons.

When his gun was safely back in its holster, Monday

headed for Emmit Rice. He was, after all, the reason that he'd come.

Nearly nose to nose with the big marshal, Rice stared up into a cold blue gaze and swallowed. He wanted to be able to threaten him; he needed to reassert himself and his territory. But he was too damned afraid of crashing and burning to give much thought to the hard warning that was evident in Monday's eyes.

"Don't even think about it, and assume the position," Monday warned as he put the flat of his hand squarely in the back of Rice's head and pushed.

Rice obliged by ducking his head between his knees. Not for the first time, he wished that he didn't have so much belly to get around. It would have been easier to brace himself for the crash if he could have gotten lower in the seat.

"Tell, buckle up!"

Monday's warning coincided with the second bolt of lightning that hit the plane. The sound of his voice was lost in the thunder and the second wave of darkness that ensued.

Monday felt the floor of the plane tilt. *Oh, hell, not down.*

But his plea went unanswered, and his heart followed the angle of the plane as he braced himself for the impact that was bound to come. Once again, lightning flashed, and he had a moment's impression of Emmit Rice lying unconscious against the bulkhead between the cockpit and the seating area.

"What the...?" Monday muttered as he staggered with the pitch of the plane.

When he'd last checked, Rice had been buckled in his seat. Now that he was out, Monday figured that Rice had been planning to try something. Although the man was obviously unconscious, he frowned at the thought of Rice on the loose and slipped a pair of handcuffs out of his pocket. If Rice tried to escape, the prisoner was going to have to take him along when he did it.

Purposefully, Monday fastened one bracelet of the handcuff around his own wrist, then waited for the plane to steady before heading for Rice. When Rice revived, he was going to have more company than he might have wanted. Being cuffed to a lawman was going to put a big kink in his plans for escape.

Bob Tell's expression, and those of the now-chained prisoners, became grotesquely illuminated from the blue-white flash of lightning, which gave them all a deathly appearance. Monday grimaced and wondered if he looked the same. Then the plane lurched unexpectedly into a sharp downward angle, and everything, including his thoughts, went out like the lights as the plane hit the ground.

Blinding rain stung Lane's face and eyelids. It was his first indication that he was still alive. Thunder rumbled overhead, grinding through the air like a runaway train. He flinched at the sound, and then groaned when the small movement caused him pain.

The scent of fuel was strong. Even through the deluge, sparks arced from the wreckage with frightening irregularity. He knew that it was only a matter of time before what was left of the plane exploded.

"Bob? Bob? Where are you, man? Answer me!" Lane shouted, then waited, praying for his partner's voice to come out of the darkness. When he shouted again and still received no answer, he tried to get up, then cursed when he found himself unable to move.

My God, don't let me be trapped.

His stomach turned at the thought of surviving the crash, only to burn alive. If he was going to die, he would choose his own method of exit. A bullet was definitely an easier way to go than burning. His hand shook as he reached for his gun and then came away empty.

"Damn."

The gun was missing from its holster. When his panic had subsided, his training kicked in, and he began to assess where he was by feel alone.

It was with no small amount of relief that he realized he could feel his feet and legs. Even the sharp, burning pain up his thigh was a welcome antidote to his initial fear that he'd been paralyzed. At this point, pain was the lesser of two evils.

He tried, unsuccessfully, to move again, and only then did he realize his predicament as he felt fabric and metal beneath his fingertips. Something large and heavy had him pinned to the ground.

Lightning once again shattered the darkness, streaking across the night sky like a flame running up a fuse.

"Son of a..."

Lane inhaled and tried not to panic at what the momentary burst of light had revealed. At least now he knew why he hadn't been able to move. He was pinned in the wreckage by a section of seats...and DeVon Randall's body. Instinctively, he traced the shape of Randall's face down to his neck, searching for pulse. There was none.

Using his massive upper-body strength, Lane pushed until the seats gave. Randall's lifeless body followed, and finally Lane was free. He crawled to his feet in blinding pain, then staggered, losing his center of gravity as another streak of lightning flashed across the sky.

But this time, in the swift flash of light, in spite of his nausea and disorientation, he saw the rest of what there was to see. Bob Tell lay sprawled atop the other prisoners. Lane didn't have to touch them to know that they were all dead. It was a well-known fact that no one lived with their head on backward.

Rain continued to hammer down on Lane's face and body. Sparks continued to fly. The smell of burning fuel became stronger and stronger. *He had to get out. Now!* He turned, then staggered, and as he did, metal clanked against metal, and he felt the dangling handcuff at the end of his wrist.

It was then that he remembered Rice. He was the only prisoner as yet unaccounted for. The last time he'd seen him, Rice had been lying unconscious against the bulkhead of the plane.

But Emmit Rice was nowhere in sight, although Lane told himself that the man could easily be under any part of the wreckage. Lane tried to take another step, when a sharp pain rocketed through his leg, sending him to his knees. The plane was a time bomb waiting for the right spark, and he'd just realized that he couldn't walk. Never one to let a small thing stop him, he began to crawl, searching for a way out.

He was less than twenty yards from the plane when the first explosion came, rocking the ground on which he crawled and sending burning debris straight up into the air, only to shower back down around him like shrapnel. The empty holster around his waist hampered his movements, and he quickly unbuckled it and then continued to drag himself out of harm's way.

There was no time to worry about missing prisoners or burning bodies. All Lane could do was get as far away from the fire as possible.

Just when he thought he was out of danger, the ground gave way under him. He went headfirst off the ledge and into the flood-swollen waters of the ravine below. For the first time in his life, he wished that he'd been born a runt. Then he would never have been on this godforsaken flight.

A short time later in the fading light of dusk, he surfaced, gasping for air and cursing to keep from passing out from the pain. A log struck him in the back, and he bobbed with the impact, then turned and grasped it as if it were a long-lost lover. He was barely afloat. Barely alive.

Antonette Hatfield gave the new strand of wire on the north pasture fence a final twist, then cursed beneath her breath when the shiny barb poked her knuckle.

"If I had a man, *he* would be out here melting in this damned heat and I would be home doing something better. Like tending to a house and raising my babies."

But her complaint was an old one, said only out of habit and not real dismay.

Antonette had long ago given up expecting Mr. Right to appear on her doorstep. For some reason, she kept scaring the good ones away. It had occurred to her that her size, nearly six feet tall and generously proportioned with womanly curves and valleys, might have had something to do with it. That and the fact that she had no tolerance for fools seemed to send a lot of men packing.

The few who had lingered over those two hurdles had never made it past the knowledge that she had seven brothers who would take great pride in hurting them—badly—should they cross the line of proper behavior. Her brothers considered it their responsibility to see "Toni" suitably wed. Better, they thought, that she become an old maid, than bring someone into the family who didn't belong.

At her present age of twenty-nine, she had even given up her dream of marrying Mr. Wrong. What she wanted now— and what she would settle for at the drop of a hat—was a baby. Granted, it took one to get the other, but the way she looked at it, the mister could take himself off to greener pastures any old day, as long as he left her with child before he did it.

While she was daydreaming, a warning rumble of far-off thunder made her look up.

A storm was brewing.

Thankful that she had this job nearly finished, she leaned back against the seat of her all-terrain vehicle and pulled open the top of her water jug. The ice had melted long ago, but the water was wet and fairly cool, and for the time being settled the hungry grumble in her belly as it went down.

The sultry, late-evening air had already molded her clothes to her body. And while she'd started the day with her long hair twisted haphazardly on top of her head like a thick brown nest of curls, heat and work had sent it tumbling down around her face and neck.

Sweat stung her eyes. She absently swiped at it with the back of her forearm, then thought of iced tea and a clean change of clothes, and began gathering up leftover fencing material. Ignoring the impulse to return it as orderly as it had been loaded, she cast one last look at the gathering storm and began tossing the fence posts and wire into the back of the small, low-sided wagon she was pulling behind her ATV.

The thick Tennessee woods in which she lived had few paved roads, and even fewer that were graveled. Raising cows, corn and hay, with eight children thrown in for good measure, were all that Anton and Lissy Hatfield had ever done. But Lissy had been dead for years, and all seven of her sons had married and moved away from home. Four months ago, Anton Hatfield had joined Lissy, leaving their baby alone to care for the family farm.

That "baby," Antonette, was stronger than most men, and her being nearly six feet tall had little to do with it. She was still the youngest, and she bore, on a daily basis, the constant, unsolicited advice of her neighbor, Justin, who also happened to be her oldest brother.

Beyond the hills thunder rumbled. Toni looked up and frowned. She wanted a bath, all right, but not the kind that accompanied thunder and lightning. Anxious to beat the on-coming storm, she tossed the last of her tools into the wagon and jumped on the ATV.

She was miles from home. And pulling this load, it would take her a good twenty minutes to get to safety. She squinted, assessing the buildup of storm clouds now evident over the treetops, and made a bet with herself that she would be wet before she got home.

The ATV roared to life. Moments later, Toni was speeding past her new quarter mile of fence, racing storm clouds toward the home that sat high on a hill above Chaney Creek.

A couple of miles down the road, she came to a sliding halt in a cloud of dust. Some of her fence posts had bounced from the back of the wagon onto the ground, forcing her to stop and go back for them.

"I don't know why I'm hurrying," she grumbled to herself. "There's no one at home to care whether I'm late, wet, or both."

Feeling a little sorry for herself and aching through her shoulders from the long day of stringing barbed wire, she stomped back to her ATV and slipped it into gear. Rain or not, she would take her time about getting home.

By the time she reached Chaney Creek, the sky was as black as the inside of a devil's heart. Thunderheads rolled with increasing intensity as the wind within them continued to blow. The quickening breeze lifted the thick, loose hair from Toni's neck as she contemplated the load in her wagon against the steep hill ahead of her. She would have to go very slow to save what was left of her posts. Carrying them up the hill by the armload didn't appeal to her at all, not even if she were physically strong enough to do so.

Before she had made any decision, the rains came. All at once and without the warning of a few early droplets to let a body know that it was time to run. Toni sighed and lifted her sweaty face to the torrent, letting Mother Nature cool her weary body.

She looked back at the wagon again and then once more at the steep path leading to her home. Her decision had just been made for her. She might succeed in getting the ATV up the hill, but in this downpour, she also might not. The hill was mostly red clay, and when it got wet, it was, as her brother Justin always said, "slick as snot."

She parked beneath the overhang of a large spreading oak just as a tremendous explosion rent the air. Stunned by the intensity of the sound, she jumped out from under the massive branches before a fork of lightning could find its way to this tree and fry her along with it. Squinting against the oncoming darkness and the downpour of rain in her face, she looked at the rim of the next hill and saw a huge, orange ball of fire spiral into the sky.

"Good Lord. Lightning must have struck something awfully big."

Reassured by the fact that her home was in the opposite direction, Toni started to run.

The path was slick, just as she feared it would be. Her shirt and jeans were plastered to her body. Had any of her past, fair-weather suitors gotten a glimpse of the generous curves she normally kept hidden beneath nondescript clothing, they might have been tempted to give her one more try. But they weren't and she was alone and running like hell in the near dark toward the hill above Chaney Creek.

Lightning flashed again. This time it was close. Too close. Toni froze in place. In shock over the near miss, and momentarily blinded by the flash, her vision cleared only to present her with another, more frightening dilemma than being caught in a storm. Someone had fallen into Chaney Creek and was being swept downstream.

"Oh, my God!" Toni pivoted on the path and ran down the hill toward the flooded waters of the creek, unable to believe her eyes. "Hey! Hey! I'm here! Swim this way! I'll help you."

But the man gave no indication of having heard her. And the closer he came, the more convinced she was of his distress. Only the upper portion of his body was above water. His arms were wrapped around a piece of log that bobbed in the foaming water like a float on a fishing line. It was all that kept him afloat. His eyes were closed. He moved only where the water took him. It was obvious to Toni that if he survived, it would not be under his own steam. With no thought for her own safety, she waded into Chaney Creek after him.

Normally, the creek would have had a hard time wetting her ankles, but the rains were heavy, and the runoff from the hills above had increased the trickle in the creek bed to a torrent. Now when she ran into the water, she was at once knee-deep in a current that nearly swept her off her feet. In spite of the rain that continued to pour, the roof of her mouth went dry from fear. One misstep and she would be as lost as the drifting man, unless she was careful.

Moving faster, but choosing her position with care, Toni waded into the path of the oncoming man and his half-submerged log, readying herself for the grab. It should have been simple, really, for a woman as strong as Toni Hatfield. Any one of her brothers would have bragged about her physical ability as they would of an equal's, but that bravado didn't take into account the now waist-high water, or the size of the man and the log.

With her arms outstretched and her legs braced against the impact, she caught both man and log and was instantly swept off her feet by the blow.

She went under as swiftly as she'd entered Chaney Creek. Water went up her nose and in her eyes as she struggled to right herself. She had strength and stubbornness on her side, not to mention the fact that she'd grown up playing in every twist and turn of this old creek. Water or no water, Toni Hatfield was in familiar territory. She reached up, connected with cold flesh and wet wood, then pulled herself from under the water by sheer determination.

It was almost completely dark. The only light that Toni could count on now was the intermittent flashes of lightning that briefly brightened the sky. But the man was too big to miss, and the water too deep and too swift to fight. And yet fight she did.

Unwilling to give up, Toni wrapped her arms around the man and the log and started treading water, riding with the current as she swiftly calculated how fast and how far they were being swept downstream. Lightning flashed again, and Toni went weak with relief. She recognized the huge, over-hanging limbs of the tree just ahead. It was the big willow above the outcrop of rock that she often stood upon to fish.

If she could only steer herself and her cargo toward the side, she might have a chance. The outcrop had to be just below the surface of the water. It would be the foothold that she needed to save them both.

Just when she thought she had made it, the log bobbed, then hit something with such force that Toni was almost thrown free.

"No, damn it, no!" she screamed. Frustration and fear were battling neck and neck as she struggled to stay afloat. But the moment she shouted, she instinctively shut her mouth before she swallowed too much water.

Sheer strength and muleheaded determination kept her from

releasing the man and his buoy. But with the impact came the realization that she was holding on to more than a body. The groan that she'd heard had not been her own. He was still alive!

Toni reacted without taking time to think, aiming the log toward the bank. When the outcrop of rocks bumped her shins, sending shafts of pain rocketing to the roots of her teeth, misery had never been so welcome. She scrambled for a firm foothold, churning water and scraping what skin was left on her palms, as she grabbed at the low-hanging limbs with her right hand, while clutching the man with her left.

Lightning streaked across the sky. Thunder followed. Rain pelted her body, while the floodwaters once again rushed up her nose and into her throat.

"Turn it loose," she screamed, trying to make the man release the log that had kept him alive so far. He didn't respond; he had a death grip on the broken stub and was in no condition to think of alternatives.

Toni groaned as her wet hands kept slipping on his cold, slick clothes and skin. "Oh, my God, I'm going to lose him."

And then something floated past and blessedly jammed them both firmly against the creek bank. It was all the edge that Toni needed. She crawled onto the submerged ledge and slipped her hands beneath his armpits and pulled. It was the unexpected movement that slid the man's hand free of the stub.

With a grunt, Toni fell backward onto the bank with the man in her arms. Halfway out of the flooded creek, she lay unmoving, with the back of his head against her cheek. And when he groaned again, she started to shake.

Okay, mister, you're out. Now, what in the world am I going to do with you?

Only one thing came to mind. She had to find a way to get him up the hill and into her house, or he would drown faceup in the downpour as surely as he'd chanced drowning in the flood.

She rolled him over onto his belly and pulled him the rest

of the way up the bank, then waited for the next lightning flash to tell her where she was.

When it came, she groaned. The water had taken her a good quarter of a mile from where she'd parked the ATV. Toni leaned down until her mouth was against the curl of his ear.

"Don't move," she said, convincing herself that he could hear. "I'm going to get help."

She got to her feet. Ignoring the tremble in her legs, she navigated the trees along the bank. No more than five steps from where she'd started, she turned and looked back just to make sure he was still there. Even in the dark, even in the downpour, the size of him was impossible to overlook.

"My God," she muttered. "How did I just do that?"

But no one answered, and when she turned, her eyes were focused on the path in front of her.

Chapter 2

It was so dark beneath the trees that she could barely make out the path. Toni gripped the handlebars on the ATV with stubborn force and squinted, wishing that the headlights on her vehicle were brighter and stronger. Although she had lived here all of her life, she found herself now losing her bearings and knew that it was panic that had her so rattled. No one had ever depended upon her for their life, or on her ability to find her way through the woods at night.

It was only after the headlights on the ATV caught the shape of the man's body that Toni realized she'd been holding her breath.

"Thank God, he's still there," she muttered.

She slipped the vehicle into park, then left it running with the headlights centered on his body. Her legs shook as she dismounted the four-wheeler as she would a horse. The wagon she pulled was now empty; the fencing equipment had been left behind beneath the tree where she'd first parked.

Toni gauged the distance from the empty wagon to the man and groaned beneath her breath. She was going to have to drag him again, and as tired as she was, and as big as he appeared, even a yard would be too much. Her hair was matted and cold against the back of her neck, and her clothes stuck to her body with muddy persistence. But she knew her discomfort was nothing compared to his state. She'd come this far with him, it was too late to give up now.

The rain had all but stopped. The wild blast of wind from the passing storm was down to a mere whistle through the trees, but the roar of the flooded creek still echoed in Toni's ears. Lingering horse tails from the storm clouds drifted across the sky, baring the half-moon and its weak glow for added light by which to see. She knelt by the man she'd dragged from the water and ran her hand across his forehead, then gently down the side of his face. He was so cold and too still.

The features of his face were cast in repose as he lay flat on his back with his arms out, unmoving. Toni shuddered. It was too close to the expression that her father had worn just before they had shut the lid on his casket.

"Mister, can you hear me?"

No answer. Not even a groan. That fact alone was enough to send a shiver of worry across Toni's senses. There was no way of guessing how long he'd been in the water, or even how he'd gotten there. The blood on his face looked black in the moonlight, and seeped from a cut somewhere in his scalp, running down his forehead and across one closed eyelid. Even in this half-light, he looked blue with cold.

"Okay. I did this once, I can do it again."

She slid her hands beneath his armpits and started to pull him toward the now-empty wagon. Without the buoyancy of water to aid her in moving him, his deadweight was almost impossible to budge.

But Toni had been told all of her life that she was a "big girl," and that big girls didn't need any help, they could do anything. And so, because she believed that she could, she did.

She maneuvered what she could of him into the wagon, then collapsed in a heap upon the ground and contemplated

the fact that while he *was* in the wagon, there was an awful
lot of him left hanging over the sides. It seemed impossible
to consider, but he looked even bigger in there than he had
on the ground.

His shirt and jeans were torn, and only half of his jacket
was still on his body. The backs of his knees lay across the
wagon's shallow sides, leaving the lower half of his legs and
his feet to dangle down to the ground. One of his arms was
jammed against his side, but the other was over his head and
limply aimed toward the ATV. Try as she might, there was
no way that all of him was ever going to fit, and she had yet
to negotiate the steep hill leading to her house. The thought
made her shudder.

"Okay, mister. We're going to take a little ride. And while
I'm a damned good driver, if I say so myself, I suggest you
hang on. The first step is a doozy."

Her attempt at humor was lost upon the unconscious man.
He didn't even flinch when she slipped the ATV in gear and
began to wind her way back through the trees toward the path
that led up to her house.

True to her fears, the "slick-as-snot" path had them moving sideways as often as moving forward, but eventually, Toni
made it. When she reached the top of the hill and saw moonlight reflecting off the rooster weather vane on the roof of her
house, she breathed a quiet sigh of relief.

The front porch of her house had two steps. Toni took the
ATV and her wagonload of man straight up both.

Unloading the man was much easier than loading him had
been. She simply unhooked the wagon and let it tilt. He rolled
onto the porch without so much as a thump.

"Sorry," Toni muttered, although he didn't seem to hear
or care whether she made an apology or not. She stepped over
his prone body, opened the front door and turned on the lights.
At least now she would have light by which to maneuver. Just
a little farther, and she would have him safely inside, out of
the night and the inclement weather.

Once again, Toni assumed the position and pulled. He slid

easier on the porch planks than he had on the wet ground. Three hefts and one agonizing grunt and she had cleared his long legs of her front door before slamming it shut.

Moments later, Toni was on the phone in the hall, calling for help. Unfortunately, she didn't even have a dial tone with which to argue.

"I should have known." She replaced the receiver and hoped that the sinking feeling in the pit of her stomach had nothing to do with the man's ultimate destiny. The phones and electricity in the area always lost power during storms like this one. "But at least I have light."

No sooner had the words come out of her mouth than the lights flickered and died. If it hadn't been so tragic, she thought, it might have been funny. But Toni had no way of knowing how badly this man was hurt, and the last thing she wanted was to have dragged a dead man up the hill and now be stuck with him for the night.

Water squished in her tennis shoes as she felt her way along the hall toward the kitchen. With a flashlight and two candles in hand, Toni headed back to the living room and the man sprawled upon her floor.

Candlelight was supposed to be romantic, not traumatic, but that was exactly what Toni felt when she knelt at the big man's side.

"Please don't be dead," she begged.

Her voice was just above a whisper as she touched the side of his neck, searching for a pulse. When it jumped beneath her fingers, she fell back on her heels, sighing with relief.

She needed an extra pair of hands, another someone to hold the flashlight so that she could better see what she was feeling. And what she felt was man—a whole lot of man. From the breadth of his shoulders to the width of his chest. Hard and wide, but cold and wet.

When he shivered beneath the brush of her fingers, she breathed a littler easier. Any sign of life was better than the lack of response that she'd had from him so far.

"I should get a blanket," she told herself as she traced the length of his arms, telling herself it was to test for injuries, when she knew full well she was daunted by the man's size.

It was when she pushed his jacket aside to feel his rib cage for possible broken bones that she sensed his focus returning. His head jerked, and he inhaled long and deep as his fingers clenched and reclenched in slow motion.

Toni shuddered, mesmerized by the latent power in him. It was like watching a volcano building for an eruption. He groaned, and lifted his left arm. Candlelight reflected off the circle of metal dangling from his wrist.

Handcuffs! She'd fished a man out of the flood who'd been handcuffed!

"Oh, Lord, what have I done?" Toni tumbled backward in shock. If she hadn't been so stunned, she might have crawled away in time to prevent what happened next. But she was and she didn't and it happened anyway.

Toni gasped. For a man who had been all but unconscious only moments ago, he moved awfully darned fast. Before she could blink, he grabbed her by the arm. Raising himself onto one elbow long enough to prove who was boss, he hit the open end of the handcuff against her wrist and squeezed.

The click was loud. Metallic. Ominous. Toni looked down in disbelief at what the man had done, then watched as he swayed precariously on his elbow before passing out with a thump.

"Oh, my God." Toni looked, but couldn't believe what she was seeing.

He'd handcuffed them together!

She yanked, and succeeded only in hurting her wrist. When she tried to crawl away from him, she went no farther than the length of his arm.

"Oh, my God!" Saying it a second time still had not conjured up any heavenly helpers. Her shock gave way to rage. "Damn you. Let me go! You repay me for saving your worthless life by doing this? Let me go!"

Not only didn't he answer, but she wasn't even sure he was

still breathing. This was bad. Really bad. She was handcuffed to a man who could be anything—even dead.

Dismayed by the possibilities, Toni crawled as far away from him as possible, relishing the fact that his elbow thumped on the floor with a rather sharp thud when she gave the cuff a vicious yank.

She sneezed. Her lower lip quivered as she tried not to cry. Big girls didn't cry. But no girl, no matter how big or small, wanted to be bound to the unknown as Toni was. Either he came to and did her harm, or he died, and she found herself arm in arm with a corpse.

She stared, then glared. All of her compassion for him was gone. But as she watched him, to her utter dismay she saw a single tear roll out the side of his eye and down into the hairline above his ear.

"Ah, God, help me," Lane whispered, unaware that he'd even spoken.

The whisper was soft, almost inaudible. But Toni heard it just the same, and she bit her lip as she considered the fact that this man, whoever he was, had called on a higher power for help. That had to mean he was one of the good guys, didn't it?

She leaned forward. Just a little. It was a move that she shouldn't have made. As quickly as before, without opening his eyes, the man reached up, then pulled her down. Now, not only was she bound to him by a metal bracelet, but her neck was firmly caught between the crook of his elbow and the wall of his chest.

"Snufabch."

Toni's curse was muffled and as weak as the candle's glow above her head. She had a worm's-eye view of the floor, as well as the tear on his shirt pocket. From her new angle, she had only two options. Either she struggled until she hanged herself, or she lay still and hoped that he would turn her loose as suddenly as she'd been caught.

While she was cursing the mysteries of fate, wondering if she had enough guts to search his pockets for a key to unlock the cuffs, the candles had the grace to burn out. She was literally in the dark. What remained to be seen was whether it was man or monster that she had fished out of Chaney Creek.

Antonette Hatfield had wished all of her life for a man, one that would take her in his arms when they went to bed and only reluctantly turn her loose when it was time to get up.

This wasn't exactly what she'd had in mind.

The only thing pertinent to this mess with regard to her dream was the fact that he *was* a man. In every sense of the word.

During the long and miserable night, she had been under him, on top of him and beside him. And during that time, she'd learned a few facts about the fish that she'd landed, as well as some shocking facts about herself.

It felt as though he weighed a ton. After the initial shock of having his weight upon her body, and further adjusting her breathing to it so that she would not be smothered, she hadn't minded nearly as much as she knew she should. Without her assent, she'd been dragged on top of him in the most intimate of positions, under him in a frightening and demanding manner and beside him in an "up close and personal" view of his neck and chin. And in every possible, miserable position, the man held fast to her body.

Not only hadn't she been able to put an inch of distance between them, but even in semiconsciousness, he'd found a way to fit her curves to his valleys and vice versa, until Toni knew the man's shape as well as she knew her own. It was daunting to know that when they were body to body, face-to-face, the tips of her toes were still inches above the ankle area of his boots. She knew the size of…everything…about him. And yet, she didn't even know his name.

More than once during the night, when she should have been screaming in panic, she'd actually felt safe. As big as he was, she'd expected to be crushed bone by bone.

And she always knew when he slid from one dream into

the next, because the texture of his touch would drastically change. He didn't actually hurt her, but if she survived this mess, she knew she would have bruises in places she couldn't even see.

Dawn broke over a calm sky. Toni awoke with a numb left arm, nose to nose with the bluest eyes that she'd ever seen. That they were wide and colored with pain and confusion didn't seem to matter, not when she wanted a bathroom and a change of clothes worse than anything she'd ever wanted in her life.

"Oh, my God, are you still here?" she muttered, halfway between hope and sleep that it had all been a bad dream.

But her disgust was nothing compared to the shock that Lane Monday felt when he had come to only moments earlier and found himself in possession of someone other than his prisoner, Emmit Rice.

That the someone was female and looked mad as hell, had yet to sink in. He was more amazed that he was still alive.

"Get off of me," Toni groaned, flexing the fingers in her lifeless hand and wondering if they would ever be the same.

Lane jerked in response to the demand, then gritted his teeth as the room rocked and pain left him flat on his back, too breathless to speak.

Toni sat up, staring coldly at her other half and willing herself to look formidable. But she felt like hell and suspected that formidable was too much to expect.

Lane groaned, then clasped his head with both hands. He wasn't prepared for the woman who came flying across his chest with the action.

"What in the hell are you trying to do, lady?"

If he didn't already have a dozen bumps and bruises and one particularly ugly-looking gash she could vaguely see through the tear in his jeans, she would have given him an answer he wouldn't have liked.

She rolled off of him, then held up her arm without speaking, letting the chain that bound them speak for itself.

Lane stared, first at the handcuffs that bound his wrist to hers, then up at the fury on her face.

"How…?"

"You did it." Her answer was starkly succinct.

"When…?"

"Last night."

Her chin jutted mutinously. Lane had seen mad on a woman plenty of times, but never quite this pronounced.

"Why did I…?"

"I've been asking myself that same question for hours," Toni said, then scooted back as far as she could before she continued. "What I came up with does not make me happy. I've been asking myself why a man would be wearing handcuffs to begin with," Toni muttered. She looked away, unwilling to let him see her fear.

Lane frowned, then winced as the motion sent pain all the way to his back teeth before he managed to speak.

"I'm a lawman. I've got a key."

Toni glared. "I would love to see it. I haven't gone to the bathroom since before eight o'clock yesterday evening."

Lane flushed, then forgot that they were still connected, once again yanking her on top of him when he started to dig through his pocket. But the only hand to get anywhere near his pockets—and his manly parts—was hers.

"Will you *please* quit doing that?"

The woman's voice was barely above a snarl. The hiss burned the side of his cheek as he stared up into eyes that reminded him of the underside of a burned cookie. They were dark, and brown, and looked hot as hell.

"Sorry," Lane said. "I can't reach that pocket with my free hand. You'll have to use yours."

Toni's eyebrows arched and her face flushed. She'd wanted a man. She'd even prayed more than once for one to be delivered unto her. But this was not what she'd had in mind.

"You want *me* to—"

The image of Bob Tell's broken neck, and the last sight he'd had of the plane and the prisoners, made his stomach roll. And because he was sick and in so much pain, his words were sharper than he'd intended.

"Damn it, woman, I don't know how this happened, but I have more things to worry about than your sense of propriety."

Toni jammed her hand into his front pocket, stuffing it as far as it would go. She ignored everything in her quest for the key that would get her out of this hellish mess. But there was too much of him to ignore, and the key was nowhere to be found.

"It isn't there," she hissed again.

"Oh, God." Lane's head dropped to the floor with a thump. "Try the other pocket, lady. Please. One of us has got to be a man about this, and I'm not in any position to volunteer for the job."

At that moment, Toni hated him. She didn't want to be a man about anything. But fate, and the fact that she was taller than most, hadn't given her much choice.

To her growing dismay, the other pocket yielded exactly what the first one had. Nothing.

"It's not there, either," she said, then yanked her arm up, ignoring the pain that racked his face when she did.

"It has to be," Lane said, closing his eyes, and trying not to think about turning her over his knee. Damn, he needed to get to a phone.

"Not if you never had one," Toni said. "Not if you were the prisoner instead of the lawman."

Lane grew still. For the first time since he'd awakened, he realized how frightened she must be. He opened his eyes and stared up into her face. His voice was low, but the promise was there if she would only hear it.

"Lady, I swear to God, I am not a criminal. I am a United States marshal. And I need like hell to get us loose." The walls tilted, and he closed his eyes to keep from getting sick by the motion.

Toni sighed. She had no other choice. Whether she believed

him or not was moot. They were connected in body, if not in spirit.

"Good grief," she mumbled. "Like I don't need it as badly as you?" She crawled to her knees and leaned over him. "If I helped you, could you stand?"

Lane sighed, then inhaled slowly. He couldn't remember the last time someone had offered him a shoulder, or anything else to lean on.

"I don't know, lady, but I'm damn sure willing to try."

Because of their combined size, going through doorways side by side was impossible. And as luck had it, there were two doors between them and the kitchen. By the time they staggered into the room, both of them were reeling from the effort.

Lane felt sick down to the toes of his boots. The room kept spinning. Pain racked him. More than once, he'd felt his leg buckle and knew that it was solely due to this woman's gutsy determination that he did not fall flat on his face.

"Just a little farther," Toni coaxed. "I need to get to my tool drawer."

Lane gritted his teeth and complied, his left leg dragging with every step.

A few minutes later, he was seated at a table, his forehead resting in the crook of his free arm, hoping that the room would stand still. But he feared that wasn't going to happen as long as this damnable woman kept hammering on the handcuff chain with muleheaded determination.

With each blow of the tool, his ears buzzed and his head pounded. She might as well be using the hammer on him, instead. It couldn't possibly hurt any worse.

"Oh, shoot," Toni muttered beneath her breath. "It keeps slipping."

Lane reacted before thinking. He yanked the hammer from her hand and tried not to see the fear that spread across her face when he raised it above his head. She looked as if she expected him to hurt her with it right there and then.

He pulled until the chain that bound them was on the edge

of the table. "Don't move," he warned, swinging the hammer with every ounce of strength he had left.

The chain and the table broke simultaneously. Frozen by the image of what lay before her, Toni gawked at her table lying broken on the floor, its legs upturned like a dead possum, then she staggered backward in shock.

To hell with the table, she thought. She and the man were no longer bound. She bolted from the room. Seconds later, she'd shut herself in the bathroom, leaving the man with the hammer to his own devices.

Relief came as she quickly washed her face and swiped her hair from her face. She would kill for a bath and a change of clothes, but first things first. There was a big, strange man in her house. If he was a criminal, she would know soon enough.

Toni came out of the bathroom much slower than the way she'd gone in. When she walked back into the kitchen, the man was nowhere in sight.

"Hey?" she called, then waited for an answer that didn't come.

She found him in the hall, using the wall for a leaning post and wearing a disoriented expression on his face as he kept trying to talk into a phone that had no power.

Toni took it from his hand and listened, then replaced it on the cradle.

"Phone's still out," she said.

"Ah, damn."

The soft complaint put her off guard. But when he turned and started toward her with the hammer still clutched tightly in his other fist, she screamed, then bolted for the living room.

Oh, my God, I was right. He's going to kill me!

The front door was stuck. Tight. It had been sticking every time it rained for more than twenty-nine years, but that was not a fact that Toni was ready to deal with right now. She was just at the point of going headfirst out a window and taking chances on cutting her own throat, when he staggered into the room with a blank look on his face.

"What the hell is wrong with you?" Lane growled, and

then slid down the side of the wall because he could no longer stand.

Toni saw her chance and yanked open the closet near the front door. It had once served as a closet for all the Hatfield children's coats and hats. Now it was simply full of junk.

"Oh, God, oh, God! It's here somewhere, I just know it," Toni muttered, digging through the mess with shaking hands.

When her fingers closed around the cool metal barrels of her daddy's double-barreled shotgun, she yanked it free, spun around and aimed as smoothly as if she'd done it a thousand times.

"Drop that hammer," she ordered from across the room. When he did not comply, she came a little closer, thinking she could intimidate him with the yawning holes of the twin barrels.

Lane blinked. Once. Twice. His vision cleared enough to see that she had drawn down on him. In spite of his misery and pain, he started to grin.

Toni froze. The small smile had done things to his face that she hadn't expected. There were matching grooves on either side of his mouth that she knew, in his youth, had been dimples. The twinkle in his eyes was obvious, even through the misery of his drawl.

"If you're gonna shoot, you might want to knock the mud daubers' nests out of the barrels first, or it could blow up in your face."

She gawked at him, then turned the barrels up. Both were plugged tighter than her daddy's jug of whiskey.

"Oh, for Pete's sake," she said, and turned the gun down toward the floor.

"No, lady, for mine. Please get me to a phone. I have to report a plane crash and too damn many victims."

The misery in his voice was impossible to miss. A flashback of the explosion that she'd witnessed just as the storm hit last night made her shudder. Had that been his plane going down? Dear Lord, had she been an unwitting witness to people's deaths?

"Oh, no," Toni whispered. "I'm sorry. So sorry."

The gun slid out of her hands and onto the floor. She kicked it aside as she knelt at his feet. Gingerly, she took the hammer from his hand and saw the shock on his face when he realized he still held it.

"You *are* for real, aren't you?" Toni asked.

Lane groaned. "I'm about as real as it gets, lady. Now help me up again. We've got to get to a phone."

Toni shook her head. "If what you say is true, you're not moving unless it's in an ambulance. I can't carry you to my pickup, and you can't walk. Besides, your leg is bleeding badly. I need to get it stopped before I go for help."

She got to her feet.

"Where are you going?" Lane asked.

"To get some scissors and cut those clothes off of you. I can't fix your injuries unless I can see where they are."

Lane gritted his teeth once again. But this time, there was force in his words as well as his grip when he stopped her departure by grabbing her ankle.

"Lady, you would be well-advised not to cut anything off of me, unless you don't mind seeing me buck naked."

Toni shook off his hand and took several hesitant steps back. "I don't get it," she said.

Lane swallowed a rush of water that bubbled up his throat. If he didn't lie down somewhere fast, he was going to either throw up or pass out.

"Look at me. I'm willing to bet that there aren't four clothing stores in the state that would have clothes to fit me. If you want something off, I'll help. But for God's sake, don't tear up any more of it than has already been."

"Oh."

If Toni had been in a mind to doubt, the width of his shoulders and the length of his legs were a vivid reminder of the truth of his words.

Long minutes later, Toni had all but dragged him into her father's room just off the hallway and was helping him off with his clothes.

"Damn, damn, damn."

It was all Lane was able to say as Toni pulled off his other boot. His head hurt like the devil, and his leg was a mess. He just hoped to hell that nothing was broken. There was a long rip in the leg of his Levi's and blood all over the place. Whatever was down there couldn't be good.

"I'm sorry," Toni muttered.

Lane blinked. It was the only indication that he acknowledged her apology. "I'll unbuckle and unzip. You pull."

His order went in one ear and out the other when his hands went to the belt at his waist, then unzipped the fly of his Levi's. Toni's mind boggled at what he was about to reveal.

After last night, she'd already felt every bulge and bone on his body. But feeling was one thing, seeing was another.

"Pull, damn it. I'm so close to passing out, it doesn't even matter," Lane said, his voice breaking on the last word. Sweat beaded across his upper lip as the room spun again.

Refusing to admit how intimidating he was, Toni grabbed hold of the cuffs of his jeans. As best he could, Lane lifted himself from the bed when she pulled. The jeans slid down his hips and legs without a hitch, leaving him bare below the waist, except for a very revealing pair of cotton briefs.

I won't look. Good Lord, what's wrong with me? The man is in pain and all I can do is stare at his...

"Oh, my God, your leg."

Lane cursed beneath his breath. Hearing the shock in her voice made him almost afraid to look, but he did. Expecting to see bone sticking out of flesh, or at the least, a knot beneath the muscles that bespoke fractures, he was faintly relieved to see that it was only a gash. Granted, the wound ran from the middle of his upper thigh to just below his knee.

"It's just a cut. Give me something to make a pressure bandage, then go for help," he said.

"What if you pass out? You could bleed to death before I get back," Toni countered.

"Lady, if you don't quit talking and start moving, I'm going to bleed to death, anyway."

She flushed. Once again, her lower lip slid slightly out of position. Her brother Justin called it a pout. Toni considered it nothing more than an expression of disgust.

She packed his wound with all the bandages that she had, then after fastening them on his leg with several white towels, she leaned back and sighed. There was nothing else she could do for him here. If he bled through these towels, then nothing was going to stop the flow.

He was so pale around the mouth, and he'd grown so quiet that Toni feared he might have lost consciousness again. Before she thought, she brushed a lock of thick black hair away from his forehead and leaned over to whisper in his ear. "I'll hurry," she said. "Don't give up."

She hadn't expected him to answer, let alone hear her. But before she could straighten up, she found herself staring down into a well of blue so pure it almost made her cry.

"Lady, I don't know the meaning of the word."

She gasped and straightened, then an odd thing happened. For the first time since she'd fished him out of Chaney Creek, they connected. She smiled. And he smiled back.

Chapter 3

Minutes were precious, but she wasted no more than necessary as she changed her shoes. Her clothes she could bear, but the sand in her wet sneakers was rubbing her feet raw.

Anxiety for the man in her bed gave way to relief as she saw the new red pickup pulling off the road and into her driveway.

"It's Justin. Thank God," she muttered, and ran out the door to meet him.

"You won't believe what I did last night," she said, waving her arms above her head and talking with every step. "And I need to borrow your truck."

"I came to see how you weathered the storm," he said. "And I don't mind if you borrow my truck, but what's wrong with yours?"

Before she had time to answer, Toni saw the smile slide off of her brother's face.

Justin looked over his baby sister's shoulder to the porch beyond. He grabbed Toni by the arm and yanked her around to face him, his eyes blazing. "Antonette Hatfield, just what the hell *did* you do last night?"

His question coincided with the discovery of the handcuff that was still locked around her wrist. If she hadn't been in such a panic, she might have considered getting nervous.

Toni groaned beneath her breath as her brother yanked her about. She didn't have to ask what had sparked his fury, she could see for herself. Her "fish" was standing on the front porch, and except for the "brief" cotton briefs and the matching half of her handcuff, he was as bare as God had made him.

"You wouldn't believe it if I told you," she said, and spun out of his hands. "Stay with him. For God's sake, put that bandage back on his leg before he bleeds to death. My phone is out, so I'm going into Chaney for an ambulance."

Toni grabbed the pickup keys from Justin's hand and, moments later, was on her way to the neighboring town, leaving Justin to deal with the stranger she'd left behind.

Then anger slid out of Justin Hatfield as quickly as it had come, as he took a longer look at the big man on the porch. He saw beyond the obvious to the bruises and the horrible cuts that had started to weep a steady stream of red.

"Hey, buddy." Justin caught Lane just before he staggered off the porch. "Let's get you back inside. Then you can explain why you're naked as a jaybird in front of Antonette."

Everything was confusion inside Lane's head, but one thing had connected. Now he had a name to go with that mule-headed woman and her big dark eyes. Her name was Antonette.

"My head hurts," he muttered, vaguely remembering being put to bed. He didn't remember getting out of it, but when he found himself in the hallway of a strange house, trying to find a door, instinct had led him toward the sounds of voices. "I was a...I need to...to make a call."

Justin grunted with effort as he tried to navigate the staggering man back through the doorway. "Come on, big fellow.

As soon as I get you back in bed, you can call everyone in town.''

Lane shuddered as darkness began to envelop him. He never even felt the softness of the mattress at his back, or the gentle way in which Justin Hatfield replaced the bandages that he'd mindlessly removed. Blessedly, he was out for the count.

Toni sat in the hallway near the emergency room of Chaney Clinic and listened to the low rumble of voices beyond the curtains. She would give ten good acres of land to know what they were saying, but she knew that wasn't going to happen. She was a woman. It didn't matter that he was *her* piece of Chaney Creek flotsam, or that she'd fished him out of the flood with great danger to herself. All of a sudden, she didn't belong.

"So, what else is new," Toni muttered to herself. She'd spent her entire life knowing that she didn't quite fit in.

Loose hair tickled the back of her neck, and she remembered that she had yet to brush it. Grooming would have to wait, but she *could* redo the clasp holding it away from her face. With that thought in mind, she lifted her hands toward the back of her neck, and in doing so, caught the dangling edge of the handcuff chain in her hair.

"Good grief."

When she tried to free herself, she succeeded only in tangling it more. From the way that it felt, she would have to pull the spot bald to get herself loose.

"Damn," she muttered, and wondered how long she could fake holding her head without looking ridiculous.

"Here now, Toni girl. Let me do that."

Sheriff Dan Holley's voice was familiar, but she hadn't been expecting him. Then she remembered the stranger's claim about being a lawman and wondered if he might have been telling the truth.

"Don't fidget, girl, just be still, and I'll have you loose in a jiffy."

Toni gritted her teeth and closed her eyes. It would seem

that she was doomed to experience humiliation upon humiliation.

To her great relief, the sheriff easily freed the chain from her tangles, then unlocked the cuff that encircled her wrist.

"Thank you, Dan," she said, and was equally grateful that he hadn't bothered to ask her how she'd come to have it on there in the first place.

When the handcuff fell loose in her lap, the emotion that swamped her should have been relief, but that wasn't what she felt as her last link to the man behind the curtain had been severed. It was loss.

"What are you doing here?" Toni asked.

"Got a fax this morning. You know, those things are a real wonder, and that's a fact. You get hooked up to a phone just right, and you can get everything over them things, even pictures."

Toni sighed. It took Dan Holley forever to get to the point.

"What does that have to do with why you're here?"

"Oh, that. Well, it seems a U.S. marshal's plane went down somewhere over the Smokies."

"What was it carrying?" Toni held her breath, waiting for the answer.

"Two marshals, three prisoners and two pilots." Dan Holley slid a finger beneath his hat and scratched, then settled the hat back in place without mussing his hair. "Don't suppose that fellow you brought in had any ID on him?"

Toni shook her head.

Dan Holley grinned. "Didn't think so. Heard he didn't have on much of anything when the ambulance got to your house." He glanced down at the handcuff, then back up at her. He'd made his point.

Toni flushed and then glared. It was hell living in the same town in which you'd been born. Everyone knew everyone else's business.

"He's been hurt pretty bad," she said, ignoring his teasing. "He has lots of bad cuts and bruises. Something could even be broken. It's all he can do just to stand up."

"Heard he's big. Real big," the sheriff said.

Toni rolled her eyes. "You aren't telling me anything new. I didn't think I would ever get him out of the water, let alone myself."

Holley frowned. He picked up Toni's hands and turned them palms up, then whistled slowly at the raw, chafed areas across the center.

"What do you mean you pulled him out of the water? What in blazes were you doing in there to begin with? Chaney Creek is still in flood stage."

Toni shrugged. "I went in after him."

Dan Holley's mouth dropped. Before he had time to respond, the curtain parted and the attending physician in charge came out.

Toni caught a glimpse of bare leg, bare torso, a curve of stubborn chin, and then the curtain fell back in place. She shuddered. There had been an awful lot of gauze and bandage on what little of him that she'd seen.

"How's he doing, Doc?" Holley asked.

Dr. Bennett saw the handcuff lying in Toni's lap. "If you don't mind, Sheriff, I would appreciate your removing the other half of that thing from my patient."

The sheriff slipped through the curtain with the key in hand. Because of his occupation, he'd often used his voice authoritatively. It carried well. Toni listened intently, hoping to finally hear something important regarding her stranger's condition, but she heard nothing beyond a soft chuckle and the sound of metal falling onto tiled floor.

Moments later, Dan Holley came out and dropped the other half into her lap. He grinned. "Want a souvenir?"

"I want some answers," Toni grumbled. "Was he able to tell you his name?"

"He didn't have to," Holley said. "Along with that fax, we got pictures of all who were aboard. There were two men of nearly equal size on that plane. One was Emmit Rice, a criminal bound for the federal correctional facility in Lexington, Kentucky. The other was U.S. Marshal Lane Monday. You got lucky, girl.''

Toni felt herself going limp. ''Are you saying he's the marshal?''

Dan Holley nodded. ''Got himself quite a reputation as a hard-nose, too. But I guess that's what it takes to get his kind of job done.''

''Oh, my.'' It was all Toni could think to say. But her thoughts were another thing altogether. *His name is Lane. Lane Monday.*

Then the curtain parted, and Toni stood. The air stilled around her. Voices and people faded until she forgot that they were there. She forgot everything, and everyone, except the man lying on the bed. His eyes were closed, his face in repose. She started toward him, and when she did, his eyes popped open as if he sensed the approach of someone new, and Toni found herself staring down into pain-filled eyes that were so blue they looked translucent.

''How are you feeling?''

Lane started to nod, and then reconsidered the movement when pain rocked the back of his neck. He licked his lips and decided that it would hurt less to talk.

''Better.''

Sheriff Holley gave Toni's shoulder a companionable thump as Justin moved to the foot of the bed.

''You've got Toni to thank for pulling you out of that flood,'' Dan said. ''I still don't know how it was accomplished. You're a big ol' boy, and that's a plain fact.''

Justin's laugh was short. ''Shoot, nothing's too big for Toni. She can take care of herself and anything else that comes along. She's as strong as an ox.''

Lane blinked. *She?* He was getting confused. And when the woman he knew as Antonette paled and turned away, he knew that somehow the words had hurt her. Maybe this Tony fellow meant something to her.

Toni's voice was a couple of octaves below shrill. ''Thank

you for reminding me, Justin. You really know how to make a woman feel special.''

Disgusted with herself for letting them know that the words had hurt, she hunched her shoulders against the humiliation she felt, and stalked away from the bed and out into the hallway while blinking back tears.

Why did her brothers see fit to remind her on at least a weekly basis that, as a woman, she was too tall, too strong and altogether too capable for a man to feel needed? She sighed, then leaned against the wall and contemplated her shoes. If that was what people who loved her really thought, then it was no wonder she was close to being an old maid. To a stranger, she must be just shy of a geek.

''What the hell did I say?'' Justin asked as he watched Toni's angry flight, and ran a hand through his hair.

Sheriff Holley shrugged. ''You sort of belittled her part in saving this man's life, that's what you did,'' Holley growled. ''Damn it, Justin, she didn't just throw some rope around him and haul him out of the water as if she were landing a damned fish. She told me that she went into the flood after him. Hell's bells, you fool, your sister could have drowned trying to save this man.''

Justin paled, but it was nothing to the shot of adrenaline that raced through Lane's system. Before the sheriff could think to move, Lane had him by the wrist.

''I thought you told me someone named Tony pulled me out of the water.''

The sheriff nodded. ''I did. That's Toni with an *i*, not a *y*.'' He pointed over his shoulder with his thumb. ''Antonette Hatfield might be on her birth certificate, but she's been Toni as long as I've known her.''

''My sweet Lord.'' Lane couldn't believe what he was hearing. Unaware of the sheet he was wadding in both hands, he stared out the doorway through which the woman had disappeared. ''That little bitty thing pulled me out of a flood?''

Justin grinned. ''Oh, Lord, you really did get a lump on

your head. You've got to be seeing things to think Toni is little.''

Lane almost glared at the smirk on the man's face. ''Mister, I don't remember your name, but I do remember who and what I am. I'm six inches over six feet tall. The last time I weighed myself, the scales only went up to two-fifty, and the needle went off the mark. You add that to deadweight and the force of a flood, and I don't know how the hell she did it. From where I stand, when I'm standing, she doesn't look that big to me.''

In the hallway, Toni gasped. She'd left the room, but she hadn't gone so far as to be unable to hear what was being said. If she hadn't overheard it with her own ears, she wouldn't have believed it was true.

Lane Monday had stood up for her. He'd even chastised Justin for making fun of her size. No one had ever done that for her. Suddenly the experience became too much to bear. She hid her face in her hands and bolted for the ladies' room. There was no way on earth she wanted anyone to see her cry.

Minutes later, while drying her hands and face, she heard Justin's voice outside the ladies' room door.

''Toni, Toni, are you in there?''

She yanked open the door and gave him what she hoped was a cool, disdainful stare, noting with some satisfaction that he seemed worried.

''What do you want?''

''I'm sorry, honey.''

Toni refused to relent. ''For what?'' she asked. ''For thinking I'd spent a wild night in handcuffs with a naked man, or for calling me a moose in front of God and everyone, then laughing about it? Exactly which *thing* are you apologizing for?''

''Well, hell. I damn sure didn't call you a moose.''

Toni rolled her eyes. ''Your apologies stink, Justin. I hope you're better at telling your wife you're sorry than you are at telling me.''

Before he could answer, Toni stalked away, her head held high, her shoulders straight.

"Damn woman," he muttered dryly.

Toni returned to the emergency room just as the doctor was issuing orders that Lane Monday didn't seem to like.

"Look, Mr. Monday, I know, as you just reminded me, that nothing is broken and that your concussion is mild, but you have numerous stitches in several places. They have to be tended. And you strained ligaments in your knee. At this point, you cannot take care of yourself without help. You really should be admitted to a hospital, at least for a few days. I recommend the one in Knoxville. It's closest and will give your leg time to heal."

Lane's chin jutted mutinously. "I lost a good friend in that crash, as well as two, maybe three, prisoners who'd been given over to our care. Until I know that Emmit Rice is dead, I won't rest. I'm praying that the S.O.B. burned with the plane, or is floating facedown somewhere in a river, but we have no way of knowing that until the bodies at the crash site are identified. I'm not lying flat on my back while people do my job for me, and that's a damned fact."

"He can stay with me."

It was hard to say who was most shocked, Toni for saying it, Justin for hearing it, or Lane for considering the offer.

"Now see here, Toni—"

"Shut up, Justin. You've already said enough to me and about me for one day. Look at him, for God's sake. He's flat on his back and in pain. And look at me! I'm the *moose* who can take care of herself, remember? Exactly when do you expect him to jump my bones, while he's crawling from his bed to mine, bleeding all the way?"

Justin flushed.

Dan Holley reentered the room and walked unwittingly into the argument. "I just got off the phone with your superiors," he told Lane. "They said to tell you they're real sorry about Bob Tell, and very glad that you're all right, and not to worry about anything except getting better. They're sending people to go over the crash site. They'll coordinate with the FAA, and we'll have this wrapped up in no time."

"I may be missing a prisoner," Lane warned. "He was the only one I didn't see before I got out of the wreckage. Emmit Rice is dangerous. If you find him alive, don't assume he'll go quietly. He'll die before he's recaptured, and he'll take someone with him when he goes."

Holley frowned. "His rap sheet is on my desk. I know the type."

"You don't know Emmit Rice. He doesn't take hostages, and he leaves his victims in pieces."

"Oh, my God." Toni felt the room beginning to spin.

"Grab her," Justin shouted. "She's going to faint."

The help came from an unexpected source. Lane rose onto his elbow and caught Toni as she staggered.

"Hey, lady, don't go out on me now," he said gently.

With the low rumble of his voice, the room settled, along with Toni's stomach. His hand was warm, his grip firm. She stared first at it, then at him, then swallowed twice before she could speak.

"I don't faint."

He smiled, and Toni's heart fell all the way to her toes.

"I imagine I knew that," Lane said.

Toni took a deep breath. "Well, are you going to take me up on my offer, or do you want to recuperate here?"

"I think that if you're willing to take me and all this on, then I would rather be with you." When he realized how that sounded, he felt obliged to add, "It would put me closer to the on-site investigation."

Toni nodded. She'd known what he meant. At this point in her life, there was no way she would assume a man could possibly have a romantic interest in her. Besides, she reminded herself, she wasn't looking for romance, not anymore. What she wanted was a family. It took a man to get a baby, and there was a lot of man on the bed.

She gave him a long look. Now that she knew he was a socially acceptable person and not the missing prisoner, he might be the answer to her prayers. That is, if he had no personal attachments....

Then she heard herself asking, "Do you want us to notify your wife, or significant other?"

Toni's question was simple, and not entirely unexpected. Yet somehow, Lane sensed a desperation in the polite request. Answering her question hurt. Saying aloud a truth that he had spent five years trying to accept wasn't easy. He lay back on the bed and looked up at the ceiling. If he didn't have to see their faces, maybe it wouldn't be so hard to say.

"I don't have a wife. Not anymore. And there are no others, significant or otherwise."

It took all she had not to smile. Her relief was so overwhelming that she missed the grimness around his mouth as he spoke.

"Well, then that's that." She gave the doctor a straightforward look. "You'll have to give me instructions for his care. What I can't do, Justin can."

Justin didn't waver under her look. "Sure thing," he said. "Always ready to help a good man out."

With this act, Antonette Hatfield's fate was set in motion.

By the morning of the next day, the Hatfield farm was crawling with police, FAA investigators, men with bloodhounds and several local hunters who were familiar with every nook and cranny of the Smoky Mountains surrounding Toni's home.

She went about her chores as if there were no one there. But when she went inside her home, there was no way to ignore the man whose presence permeated every inch of space.

She came in the back door and winced as it slammed behind her, hoping that Lane hadn't been asleep. If he had, he probably wasn't now. The sound was still echoing through the house.

"Shoot," she muttered as she went to the kitchen sink to wash her face and hands. "Only four months since Daddy died, and I've already lost all of my manners. Momma would have had my hide for slamming doors.''

The water ran swift and cool beneath her fingers as it sluiced her heated skin. For early May it was very hot and the day was so humid that her clothing had become stuck to her body in the first five minutes she'd been outside. Unaware of how revealing the damp clothes were against her skin, she washed, then dried her hands, while absently considering what she might fix Lane to eat.

The crutches thumped with every swing of his arms, but Lane's socks-clad feet made no sound as he moved from the bedroom where he'd been resting, in search of Toni. She didn't seem like a stranger, and he wondered if it was because of the life-and-death situation in which they'd become entwined. Then he knew that was a foolish thought, because he had little to no memory of anything except waking up in the wreckage and then crawling off the edge of a cliff. What he did remember vividly was waking up handcuffed to a mad-as-hell woman.

He still wondered how that had happened, and stifled a smile. Man alive, but his Toni could work up a snit faster than anyone he'd ever known. When he realized he'd just thought of her as *his*, he staggered into a wall and bumped everything that hurt.

''Oh, damn,'' he groaned, and propped himself up with the crutches until the stars dancing beneath his eyelids stopped spinning.

Toni heard him coming up the hallway, followed by the groan and the curse. She was out of the kitchen before he could think to hide his pain.

''What do you think you're doing? You already broke my table and now you're aiming at my walls.'' She slipped an arm beneath his shoulder and let him rest upon her instead of on the awkward crutch.

When Lane was able to talk, he looked down to speak, but got lost instead in the study of her face. Apart, not one of her features was particularly unique. But the accumulation of them upon her face, coupled with her statuesque body and fiery temperament, made her unforgettable.

Her eyes were so dark that he had to strain to discern the pupils from the irises. Her nose was not too long and not too short, a perfectly straight nose for a straightforward woman. But there were freckles scattered across the bridge that he suspected she would not like to be reminded of. Her eyebrows and lashes were dark, a perfect match to the thick, almost chocolate-colored hair, and her mouth was full, just shy of voluptuous. Just like her body. At that thought, he shuddered. There was quite a lot of woman in his arms.

"I'm sorry," he said, unable to think of anything else to say.

"You know that you shouldn't be up," she reminded him.

"You've been up since daybreak," he countered.

"That's different. I wasn't in a plane crash. I didn't try to drown myself in Chaney Creek. I didn't—"

Lane put a finger across her lips, shocking himself as much as her by his action. "Oh, but, lady, I think you did just that," he said softly. "You saved my life, at great risk to your own, I might add. How do you think that makes me feel?"

Toni could only shake her head. She had no idea how he felt. But at that moment, she could have given lessons on lust. Everywhere she touched, she felt muscle. Everywhere she looked, she saw a brown, firm expanse of skin. And beyond the obvious attraction of so much man and so little time, Toni felt a sense of loss. She wished those clear blue eyes were darkening with passion for her, and not his own pain.

"I think you probably feel like hell," Toni said.

"I think you're right," Lane replied, then sighed.

"Do you want to lie back down?"

"No. In fact, hell, no," Lane growled. "What were you about to do?"

"Fix us some lunch."

"Can I watch? You can tell me what's going on outside. It makes me crazy knowing that everyone is involved in my business except me."

For a long moment, they stood arm in arm within the confines of the cool, dark hallway, assessing the possibilities that lay between them. But when it came down to fact, there was nothing between them. Not really. Two days ago, neither of them had known the other existed. Today, one of them had the other to thank for a life.

"Come with me," Toni said. "You can sit in Daddy's chair. He used to watch me work before he got so sick he couldn't sit up anymore."

As she helped him down the hall and into the kitchen, Lane silently absorbed the textures of her sadness, and wondered how long she'd been alone here on her farm.

Pillowed by the old recliner in the corner of the kitchen, he was forced to let her help him. It disgusted him greatly that he couldn't even lift his own leg onto the extended footrest.

As she cradled his foot, the muscles in her bare arms corded, and for the first time he was forced to consider her strength. She wasn't bulky like a man would be, but when she moved, the muscles rippled delicately beneath her skin like ribbons upon water. He liked how it made her look. He liked how she made him feel. If only they had met under different circumstances—when he was strong on two feet and not flat on his back—he might like to test the waters between them in other ways.

But he lived in Florida, and she was here in Tennessee. The city in which he lived was hectic, and his job was often a reflection of the uglier side of humanity. On the farm, her life was simple, almost sedate. Fate had thrown two people from two different worlds together. There was no way a relationship between them would ever work, and he had no will to even attempt one. He thought of Sharla, and the image of her petite features and short, flyaway blond hair came and went within his mind's eye. He thought of his wife's smile—and then of the pain that she had endured before she died.

Forget it all, he told himself. *Toni has no place in my life.* With that thought firmly settled in his mind, Lane looked

out the window at the circus of vehicles and people beyond
the walls of her house.

"Is this making you nuts?" He meant the mess outside,
but she'd taken it another way.

Toni turned. "What? Having you here? Of course not. I'm
glad for the company."

The moment she'd said it, she wished that she hadn't. It
made her sound pitiful, and she wasn't a pitiful sort of person.
She was resourceful. She should know; she'd been told so by
her family all of her life.

"How long since your father died?"

Toni's hand stilled on the potatoes that she'd been peeling.
Her emotions were well in hand by the time she turned to
answer.

"Just over four months. Sometimes it seems like only yesterday, other times…" She shrugged. "Other times it seems
like I've been by myself forever."

"I know there must be times when you're lonely, but don't
you ever feel afraid?"

The smile on her face was too wide, the glitter in her eyes
too bright. "Of what? In case you haven't noticed, I'm a very
big girl. I can take care of myself."

Lane frowned. This wasn't the first time that he'd heard
her put herself down. He sighed. Hell, from what he'd heard
out of her brother Justin, her family had probably been doing
it to her for years. She was simply echoing what she'd heard
all of her life.

"You may be taller than some, but I don't know where you
get off thinking that makes you less of a woman, lady. From
where I sit, it only makes you more."

Toni's eyes widened and her mouth went slack. A faint
flush slid across her cheeks and up into her hairline. She could
feel the heat of her blush under her skin, as surely as the man
on the other side of the room who was already under it. Then
she eyed his bandages and the gray pallor on his face and
knew that he was way too hurt and sick for what she was
thinking.

"It's time for your medicine."

The minute she said it, Toni knew how inane she must have sounded. He'd paid her a dazzling compliment, and all she wanted to do was knock him out with pain pills. She needed more than her head examined.

Lane grinned. "Doping me up won't change a thing, Antonette."

She glared. "If it will shut you up for a while, it's worth it." She ignored his smirk and turned with relief as Justin entered the kitchen with a bang.

"I just talked to Dan Holley," he said.

"Who?" Lane asked, certain that the name was one he should remember, yet unable to think where he'd heard it.

"The sheriff," Toni said. "He took the handcuff off of you in the hospital, remember?"

Lane nodded, then hid a grin when he saw Toni's blush. He would give a lot to know exactly how that had occurred, and what exactly had happened afterward.

Justin frowned and got back to the story that he'd been about to tell. "Sheriff Holley says that old Sam Sumter left home again. I swear, that sorry excuse for a man leaves every time his wife has another baby. Their latest can't be more than a month or two old. If he doesn't like to feed them, why in hell do they keep having them?"

Toni frowned. It wasn't right. People like Livvie Sumter had babies they didn't want, and she wanted one she couldn't have. The world was not a fair place.

"Where does he go?" Lane asked.

Toni shrugged. "Who knows? The pitiful thing is that he always comes back, and Livvie Sumter keeps having babies."

Justin snorted. "Right. But while he's gone, every farmer within ten miles of the Sumter place will come up short on anything that isn't tied down."

Lane frowned. "Why?"

"Because Samuel Sumter has eleven, maybe twelve, children and they're hungry," Toni said. "Sometimes, they take something they can sell for money to buy food. Other times, they steal the food outright. About a year before Daddy died, we lost a cow. Never did find it. We figured that the Sumter boys took it for the milk. I didn't have the heart to send Dan Holley out to check.''

Outside, a car horn honked as a man shouted. Justin frowned. "I haven't seen such a mess outside since the day of Momma's funeral," he grumbled.

Toni sniffed, then turned back to her potatoes. "It's not on your front porch, so I don't see why you're squawking."

Justin glared. "Even if you hated it, you wouldn't tell me so because then you wouldn't be able to argue about it."

Lane grinned. Although brother and sister seemed in constant disagreement, it was obvious that they were close. It was especially obvious to Lane when Justin gave him a long, assessing look.

"So, feeling any better?" he asked. "I see you're able to get about."

"A couple of other marshals will be spending the night here for a while, Justin," Toni stated. "They've already been here with their luggage, so you can wipe that look off of your face. God forbid that I might spend the night alone with a man."

"Well, hell, Toni, I don't remember hearing myself say anything about where you spend your nights, or who with."

She turned away from the conversation and dumped the potatoes into the sink, then washed and cut them up before dropping them into a pan to boil. While both men tried not to look at her, or at each other, Toni got Lane's medicine.

She didn't speak as she dropped the pills into his hand, then shoved a glass of water beneath his nose.

"What's that?" Justin asked as the lawman made a face.

"Knockout pills. She's trying to shut me up," Lane said, and stifled a grin by tossing the pills to the back of his throat and chasing them with the drink of water.

"I hate both of you," Toni said mildly, and walked out of

the kitchen before she said anything else that she would later regret.

Justin looked miffed. Lane grinned. It was an odd ending to a hell of a day.

Chapter 4

Toni stared down the long garden rows and stretched the aching muscles in her back, wishing that she'd had the foresight not to plant so many rows of peas. But the long pods of purple-hulls had been her father's favorite.

"I don't know what I was thinking." She had planted them long after her father's death.

Even if she ate peas all year long, she would never be able to eat them all. The only thing she could do was call upon her two brothers who lived nearby. Their wives would be glad for the chance to pick the patch; feeding their hungry families was a never-ending job.

The muted sounds of voices carried over the evening air, permeating her solitude. She sighed. This was the third day since the crash, and the authorities still weren't finished with the investigation. It was getting late. They must be quitting for the day, she thought.

She glanced at her watch. Nearly four and a half hours had passed since everyone from the FAA to the coroner's office had filed through her front yard. The crash had been ruled an accident due to the weather. Surely this investigation would end soon.

She thought of Lane and wondered where he was. He'd been resting when she left the house. But if she knew Lane Monday, he wouldn't be flat on his back when they brought what was left of his friend out of the hills.

She hefted the bushel basket of peas onto her hip and started toward the house. Minutes later, with the peas sitting in the shade of the back porch, she entered the kitchen, pausing only long enough to wash the purple stain from the pea pods off of her fingertips.

"Lane?"

Her voice rang clear throughout the house, but an echo was her only answer. Where had he gone? She began drying her hands on her denim shorts as she headed toward the front door.

She looked out and could see him at the far end of the yard, and in the thick of things, right where she'd expected him to be. All she could see was his back, but she could tell by the set of his shoulders and the stillness with which he stood, that the impact of what was taking place had hit him hard.

His crutches were by the steps where he'd obviously dumped them in frustration. They were too short for his height, but they were the longest ones in town that had been available for rent. The jeans he was wearing were the ones that he'd had on when she found him. They had been laundered, but Toni had purposely not mended the tear in the left leg of his Levi's to accommodate the bandages over his stitches.

As she stared across the yard, she couldn't help noticing that blue jeans suited him better than most of the men she'd known and decided that it had something to do with his long legs and the way the fabric cupped his backside. His blue, long-sleeved shirt hung loose upon his shoulders. Untucked and unbuttoned, the tail flapped gently in the hot summer breeze as he watched the proceedings going on before him.

Toni frowned as he wiped a hand across his face. She

hoped that he was only sweating. If she saw him cry, she would not be able to keep her heart at the distance it needed to stay. Already, she had become more emotionally involved with him than she'd intended. It wouldn't pay to care for the man she'd chosen as a means to an end.

He turned at the sound of her footsteps crunching on the graveled path, and the last straw in her resistance crumbled. She'd never seen so much pain on a man's face in her life.

When he saw who it was, he turned away without speaking, yet Toni knew that it wasn't because he hadn't cared about his partner, but because he cared too much.

She stood beside him without speaking, resisting the urge to hold his hand as the search crew carried what was left of five men through the clearing toward the waiting vehicles from the coroner's office.

One black bag followed another, pitifully small and weightless. Somewhere within them were the remnants of two prisoners, two pilots and one good cop. Yet, after crashing, then burning, what more would there be?

It was impossible for Lane to put into words what he felt. He sensed Toni's concern, and while he appreciated her presence, he could not trust himself to speak. His shoulders hunched against the sight of the five black bags. *Why wasn't I killed, too?* he wondered.

Therein lay the crux of his misery. He hadn't been able to get beyond that question. One thought after another had followed it, but it always came back without an answer.

The worst of it was that there was no reason for his survival. Upon impact, he and Emmit Rice had not even been strapped into a seat. By every rule and caution known to man, they should have been the first to die.

There should have been one more body at the crash site. And because there wasn't, Lane would not rest until Emmit Rice was found. Officially, Rice was listed as missing and presumed dead.

Hell, they are all dead...except me.

"Your leg is bleeding."

Lane jerked, startled by the sound of a human voice, after he'd been so lost in watching the parade of death passing by. He'd actually forgotten that she was still beside him. Toni's quiet voice held no censure, only compassion, but his bitterness had to go somewhere, and because she was the only one around, it fell to her to suffer his rage.

"Tell it to them," he said harshly, and pointed toward the body bags before he turned and stalked back toward the house.

Tears blurred her sight, but not so much that she couldn't see him dragging his injured leg as he hobbled over the graveled path on his bare feet.

Knowing that he wasn't ready to hear it, Toni waited until he was out of earshot before she muttered, "It's not your fault, you know."

She ignored the impetus to follow and assure him further. Instead, she turned away, unable to watch him leave. She didn't want to feel compassion, or give in to the urge to throw her arms around him and comfort him. She needed to feel separate from him in order to do what she'd decided upon.

Last night, in the midst of a sleepless and lonely vigil, Toni Hatfield had come to a life-altering conclusion. She didn't know how, and she didn't know when, but she wanted Lane Monday to be the father of the child she so longed to bear. And she kept telling her heart that she didn't care that he would come and go in her life without notice. What he left behind would, for her, suffice. If she wasn't destined to know the love of a good man, so be it. But there was no handwriting on the wall that said she couldn't have a good man's child.

That was what Toni kept telling herself as she watched the last vehicle drive away. A stray lock of her hair slipped out of its clip. Toni gave it a halfhearted swipe as she turned toward the house, ignoring a painful shaft of conscience. She couldn't afford to care about a man who would be leaving in a matter of days. She had the rest of her life to live without him when he was gone. With that thought in mind, she started up the hill.

"Miss Hatfield, wait up," a voice said.

Toni turned and looked back down the hill. Coming toward her were the two other men from Lane's office who had arrived the night before to coordinate the investigation. Along with a stack of papers and an armful of cameras, they had brought a suitcase full of Lane's clothes. Someone had had the foresight to recognize the situation that a man his size would be in.

Bill Reese and Chuck Palmer were ordinary-looking men. The only thing that set them apart from just anybody on the street were the U.S. marshals' badges that they carried. From the looks on their faces, they had been affected by the situation as deeply as Lane had been.

"You both look as if you would trade your last dollar for a bath and something cold to drink. Am I right?" she asked.

The men looked at Toni, then at each other. Chuck Palmer managed an uneasy chuckle as Bill Reese spoke.

"Yesterday when you offered to let us stay here with Lane, I knew you were one-in-a-million. Now we find out you're a mind reader, as well. Just lead the way, pretty lady. We're right behind you."

Toni flushed. Pretty lady, indeed.

"Lane's not in a very good mood," she warned as they neared the porch. "He's fighting a lot of hurt from both directions. Right now, I would hate to guess what hurts more, his heart or his leg."

Reese sighed. "Coming up a body short in the investigation doesn't sit well with us, either. We've got searchers and dogs in the hills, checking for any sign of Rice, but we're pretty sure that he drowned in the same flood that nearly got Lane. It's simply a matter of waiting for the body to surface, and it will. As for Lane being sad, well, he and Bob Tell were real close friends and had been ever since Lane's wife died," he said.

Toni stumbled and paled, but the men behind her never noticed.

"Watch that first step, it's loose," she muttered, and hoped that it covered her shock.

Lane had told her that he'd been married, but she'd assumed he was divorced. Knowing that his wife had died instead changed a lot of things. He might not be as receptive to what she'd planned as she'd hoped. What if he was still grieving? What if the idea of making love with another woman was repugnant to him?

"How long has he been a...when did she die?" Toni asked.

Reese frowned thoughtfully and then looked at Palmer for assistance. "At least four or five years, don't you think?"

Palmer nodded. "At least. Monday's two years younger than I am, and I just turned forty. He was in his early thirties when it happened. Yeah, that would be about right."

Toni nodded while she made mental calculations. Four or five years. Surely he'd passed the celibate part of grief by now. If he hadn't, all of her plans would be futile. The cold, abstract calculation of what she was planning made her feel guilty as hell. But the last man she'd counted on had broken her heart. She'd long since given up on being loved by a man. She was past counting on anyone but herself.

"When you're ready, supper will be waiting," Toni said.

Both men hurried past her on their way to their rooms, anxious to remove the stench of death from their clothes and their memory.

Lane heard them come into the house. Their voices carried down the hall and into his room. He rolled over on his back and closed his eyes, hating himself for the way that he'd lashed out at Toni. It was a miserable thing to do to the woman who'd saved his life.

And yet, he couldn't get the sight of those body bags out of his mind.

"Damn it, Tell, that wasn't the way it was supposed to happen," he groaned.

His stomach lurched as he fought back a wave of emotion. Like Bob Tell, Lane had contained no illusions about his job.

Being a sheriff had always held more than the normal share of risks. Every lawman faced the possibility of being shot in the line of duty, maybe even dying in such a manner. But the senseless act of nature had been unexpected, and because of that, oddly more difficult to accept.

Outside his door, the sound of Toni's laughter was soft, but unmistakable. One of the men, probably Reese, had obviously cracked a joke. Lane knew Reese was good at making strangers feel comfortable.

He wondered if Toni's eyes had crinkled at the corners as he'd seen them do before. Or if she'd turned away to return to her work with a lingering smile on her face. And the moment he thought it, he wondered why he cared. What was happening to him? Why was he becoming so fixated upon Toni Hatfield's every movement? She was a good woman, maybe even a special woman. But that was as far as it went.

He rolled to the side of the bed and sat up, trying to make sense out of what he was feeling.

"This connection I feel with her must be because she saved my life." He combed his fingers through his hair in frustration and wished for things he could not have. "That's got to be what it is. I don't have a personal desire to get mixed up with a woman again. Damn it, I don't!"

Yeah, Monday, say it often enough and you might even convince yourself, he thought, pulling himself to his feet.

The stitches in his leg pulled as his muscles contracted. He winced, savoring the pain; he felt he deserved that and much more. What was a little pain compared to the devastating sense of loss that the families of those crash victims would suffer? His pain would pass, but their loss would be with them forever. And Lane knew about loss in a big way.

When Sharla had died, he'd wanted to die with her. Month after month, he'd waited for the breath to leave his body as ruthlessly as it had left hers. But it hadn't, and over time, the feeling had passed. He was proof that life did go on, maybe not as fulfilled as before, but breath was drawn, years passed and the pain faded, leaving a void where his heart had once been. That void was not going to be filled, not if Lane had anything to say about it. He had loved once. He wasn't about to go through the pain of loving and losing again.

But while he wasn't ready for emotional entanglements, the apology he owed Toni was past due. He'd had no reason to lash out at her when it had been himself with whom he'd been angry. Shame sent him out of his room and in search of the woman who had borne the brunt of his pain.

He found her on the back porch. He stood in the kitchen and looked out the screen door, absorbing the serenity of the scene before him.

The evening shadows that stretched across the yard were long and pencil thin, a reminder that the day was near its end. The porch-swing chain gave an occasional squeak, warning its occupant not to fall asleep. A half-empty basket of peas sat nearby, while Toni shelled from the bowl in her lap.

Toni's repose as she worked was so much a part of the scene that Lane hesitated to interrupt. Her long, nimble fingers bent, stripped, then emptied the supple, purple pods of their bounty, spilling the dark-eyed little peas into the bowl with constant regularity. Her purple-tinged fingertips bore the mark of her labor, while a small pile of empty pods accumulated at her feet.

The screen door squeaked as Lane pushed it open. Startled, Toni turned sharply at the sound, causing a dark abundance of curls to spill from her loose topknot of hair. The tendrils fell against the back of her neck, then fluttered in the soft evening breeze, giving her face an unusually fragile, feminine look. Lane saw beyond the richness of her hair to the shadows in her eyes, and hated himself for being the cause.

"If it didn't hurt so much to bend, I would kneel at your feet," he said.

Her pulse jerked, then steadied. From the tone in his voice, she guessed that he'd come to apologize.

"I would settle for a helping hand instead," she said, and gave him a judging glance before scooting over on the porch swing to make room.

Lane sighed as his guilt lifted. Just that small, telling look and a gentle smile from a woman he hardly knew, and the knot in his belly was gone. He wondered what else she might remove if given half a chance, and then the minute he thought it, he willed the thought back to hell where it belonged. He didn't need this kind of trouble. But, if he was going to help shell peas, he did need a bowl. When she handed him hers, he wondered if she also read minds.

Blue was her favorite color, but Toni wondered if she would ever again be able to see it and not think of Lane Monday's eyes. She looked at him and forgot what she'd been about to say, so she handed him the bowl in her lap instead.

Reflex made him grab for it, and when their hands touched, Toni jerked back and then jumped to her feet, suddenly anxious to put some space between herself and the future father of her child.

"Do you know how?" she asked.

Lane grinned. That was a loaded question if he'd ever heard one. And being the man that he was, he couldn't resist the urge to taunt.

"Do you really want me to answer that, lady?"

The flush on Toni's face went from pink to red before she found her voice. "I meant shelling peas, and you know it."

She glared as he grinned.

"Maybe you'd better demonstrate," Lane said. "Do a couple for me. I'll watch and learn." And when Toni bent over to do just that, his deep voice rumbled in her ear. "I'm a quick study and really good at just about everything."

Her hands trembled, but she wouldn't have bolted for all the trees in Tennessee. This was her land, her home, her back porch, for Pete's sake. Why should she let some overgrown oaf make her act like a silly schoolgirl?

"Maybe so," Toni said shortly. "But you don't float worth a darn."

Lane couldn't think of a thing to say in response to her less-than-subtle reminder that she'd saved him from drowning. He looked down at the bowl in his lap, then at her long, slender hands deftly working their magic on the pea pods, and he tried to imagine them holding his head above water, and pulling his limp and all-but-lifeless body from the flood.

"You aren't paying attention," she warned, and was rewarded by a grin before he refocused on what she was doing.

It looked as simple as unzipping a zipper, but something told him that it had probably taken her years to perfect the skill. And when she laughed at his effort, he knew he'd been right.

"You'll get the hang of it…eventually," she said. "You're a quick study. Remember?"

Not wanting her to leave, Lane caught her hand, then turned it over palm up, and studied the perfect shape and hidden strength.

Toni's stomach tilted, and her pulse raced as she looked down. As big as she was, his hand dwarfed her own. Just thinking about his body covering hers in the same manner made her sick with guilt, and she realized that what she was planning to do might be too cold-blooded to consider.

No matter how badly she wanted a child, she was finding it more and more difficult to face the idea of lying down with this man and taking something from him that he might not be willing to give.

There's always artificial insemination. Her stomach turned at the thought. Now she was back to square one and a lonely, empty life unless she was able to talk this man into her bed.

The ball of his thumb traced the center of her wrist, testing the pulse that pounded beneath.

"Toni, I'm sorry about this afternoon. I hated not being a part of the search team, and I wanted someone to tell me they found Emmit Rice's body in the wreckage. Watching them carry Bob Tell out instead was hard. I took my hurt out on you. It was uncalled-for, and unforgivable, especially after all you've done for me, but I'm asking you to forgive me all the same."

The blue in his eyes had softened to a dusky gray. The tone of his voice had gone from sexy to serious. Resisting him was impossible; giving up her dream even more so. She wondered if it could be done. She pulled back her hand, unwilling to let him learn too much about how she felt.

"I knew why you said it," Toni said. "I didn't take it personally." And then she grinned, unaware that bitterness colored her smile, as well as the rest of her response. "I learned that lesson the hard way a long time ago. A man rarely means what he says, at least not to me."

She stood abruptly, causing the porch swing to tilt. "Supper in thirty minutes. I'll finish the peas later. Go visit with your friends or something. You don't owe me anything, Lane Monday. I did what I did because I don't think before I act, not because I wanted something in return. And don't you ever say I did."

The back door slammed as she disappeared into the house, and he wondered where the hell that had come from. All he'd done was try to apologize for being rude and offer to shell a few peas.

He sighed. *Try to figure out what goes on in a woman's head and a man will go crazy.*

He looked down at the bowl in his lap, then frowned and picked up a pea. By God, he wasn't going anywhere until he'd shelled this bowl of peas first.

The night air still held the heat of the day. Although the air conditioners hummed softly inside the house, Toni couldn't bear another minute of being cooped up within these walls. Lane had his friends to keep him company, she'd already changed the bandages on his leg, and the last pea had been shelled and stored in the cooler. There should be no further need of her services from anyone or anything, at least not today. She slipped out the back door, careful not to let the hinges squeak. She was tired of pretending that she didn't care.

Just when she'd gotten used to being unneeded, all of this had happened. When everyone left, she would have to adjust to loneliness all over again. But tonight, she wished for something more than a job to keep her busy. She wished for companionship, even for love. But because there was no one there to hold her, she hugged the porch post instead, closing her eyes and leaning her forehead against the cool, smooth wood in weary defeat.

It smelled of paint and the fainter, but more enticing, scent of wisteria. The vine was nearby, running up the trellis and falling down around the edge of the back porch like a lavender ruffle. The thick, sweet scent made Toni think of her mother. Next to her eight children, the vine had been her mother's pride and joy.

Toni opened her eyes and lifted her head, gazing intently into the dark, cloudless sky. The new moon gave off no glow, and the stars seemed too far away to even twinkle. She had more company inside her house tonight than she'd had since the day of her father's funeral. But she'd never felt so alone…or so lonely.

"Toni."

Startled by the sound of Lane's voice, she caught her breath, thankful that the night hid her face from his all-seeing eyes. "What?"

"Are you all right?" he asked softly.

"Of course. Was there anything you needed?"

Her answer was casual, but the tone of her voice was not. During the day, something had changed between them, and although Lane wasn't in the habit of trying to placate a woman's whims, something about this one kept getting under his skin. Maybe it was because she tried so hard not to need anyone. And maybe it was something else he wasn't ready to face. Whatever it was, Lane couldn't leave her, or well enough, alone.

"Why do you keep answering a question with a question?" he asked.

Because it's safer. Because you won't want to hear what I really want to say.

"Sorry. I wasn't aware I did that. I suppose that's what comes of answering to no one but myself."

Lane shoved his hands into his pockets and ignored the thrust of pain to his thigh.

"All through supper, you seemed...bothered. If it's something we've done, I wish you would say so. This whole business has probably uprooted every routine you ever had. It won't be long before we're out of here, and then your life can get back to normal."

Normal? My life will never be the same.

Toni laughed, but there was no joy in the sound. Lane didn't have to look to know that there were tears in her eyes.

"You're probably right," Toni said. "I never did get through fixing that north fence." She started past him into the house. "I'll see if the men want any more cobbler. It's never as good the second—"

"Toni..."

She paused. A faint light from within the house cast shadows on his face, once again reminding her that this man was only passing through her life. She sighed and swallowed a lump in her throat.

"Don't," she said softly. "In a few days, you'll be gone. Whatever it is you're about to say, you would later regret."

She walked away, leaving Lane alone on the porch with the night and his thoughts.

I may have some regrets, lady, but they won't include you. Never you.

He followed her into the house. Without thinking, he locked the door behind him, as if it were his own house. Like the woman, the farm had already claimed its place in his heart. What, he wondered, would his apartment in Tallahassee be like when he returned? Would his footsteps echo from room to room? Would he pace the floor at night, longing for the sound of her voice and a sight of her smile, or would she fade with the memory of it all?

"Hellfire," Lane muttered, and bypassed the trio in the kitchen who were sharing the last of supper's dessert. "You know where you belong, Toni Hatfield. You're as much a part of these Tennessee hills as the trees that cover them. If I could be as certain as that, I would know more than I do right now.''

Breakfast was on the table when Justin Hatfield walked into the house without knocking, just as he'd done for all the years that he'd lived there. ''I see you finally got the table fixed,'' he said, eyeing the crack on the top and the edges of plywood showing on the sides that Toni had used as patches.

Toni cocked an eyebrow as a greeting. Her brother acted as if he owned the place. As the eldest in the family, she supposed it was his right, although he'd married and moved away years ago.

''Have a biscuit and a cup of coffee, Justin. Maybe they'll give your mouth something else to do besides yap.''

Justin grinned.

Lane eyed Toni's brother, then the table, and shrugged. He still didn't remember a damn thing about the whole episode except waking up handcuffed to the maddest woman he'd ever seen. Already a veteran of several meals at the patched-up table, he wisely shifted his plate to the end that didn't rock and slid into the nearest chair before someone else beat him to it.

Reese and Palmer took one look at the steaming plates of eggs and sausage, the basket of hot biscuits and the jars of jelly, and groaned.

''I may never go home again,'' Reese said. ''Toni girl, you're going to make some lucky man the best darned wife in the state.''

The smile was halfway to ready on Toni's face when Justin snorted, and then laughed aloud.

''She would make a better man,'' he said. ''Say, Toni, that reminds me of why I came. Someone knocked down your mailbox. You better put it back up before the mail carrier comes around.''

Toni froze. It was nothing more than what she'd heard from her brothers nearly all of her life, but to have it thrown in her face in front of three near strangers was almost more than she could bear. Her shoulders were stiff, her expression blank as she set the coffeepot on the table.

"Eat while it's hot," she said softly. "I'll be back later." Without looking back, she walked out of the room.

Lane froze. He couldn't believe what he'd just heard. Reese and Palmer took one look at their buddy's face and started talking at once, obviously aware that if someone didn't change the subject, Justin Hatfield might find himself on the outside looking in.

"I can't believe you said that," Lane said.

Justin froze, the biscuit halfway in his mouth.

"Said what?" he mumbled around a mouthful of buttery crumbs.

"You know what," Lane said, dragging himself to his feet, then leaning across the table until he was only inches away from Justin's nose. "You don't want to make me hurt you, do you?"

The biscuit broke into pieces and fell from his fingers as Justin stared back. "Hell, no," Justin said, leaning forward until they were nose to nose. "But I would like to know why you're so damned mad before we start throwing punches."

Lane inhaled. He couldn't believe it, but it seemed as if Justin really didn't get it.

"You've got about three seconds to clear out of this kitchen and go fix what you sent your sister to do, or so help me God, I'll…"

Justin gawked, then jerked as if he'd actually been punched. "But Toni always fixes the—"

"She shouldn't have to," Lane said. "She's a woman, for God's sake. Doesn't anyone around here see that besides me?"

Reese and Palmer stared regretfully at their plates of sausage and biscuits and got to their feet. "We'll do it," they said in unison.

"It's the least we can do for our room and board," Reese added.

Lane's eyes never left Justin's face, and the longer he

looked at him the colder they got. Finally, he shook his head once and grinned. It was enough.

"No, boys, finish your breakfast like Toni said. I think Justin was already on his way out the door, weren't you, buddy?"

Justin gave Lane a considering look and then nodded. "I think you may be right," Justin said, and took a biscuit with him as he left.

Lane dropped into the chair and shifted his leg so that he didn't have to bend it to reach his plate.

"Reese, pass the eggs, please, and don't eat all of the biscuits. Save Toni some. She should be here any minute."

Less than five minutes later, Lane's prophecy was proven true as Toni entered the kitchen. As usual, her unruly curls were already on the move. A slight smudge of dust shadowed the upper thrust of her right breast, and she wore a matching handprint on the thigh of her blue jeans. Her eyes were wide and slightly shell-shocked as she went to the sink to wash up.

She would have given a year of her life to know what had been said after she'd left. But whatever it was, Lane's expression was as unreadable as Justin's had been when he'd taken the posthole digger from her hands and sent her back to the house with a terse command.

She slid into the empty chair and picked up her fork before she had the guts to look up at the men who were staring at her, waiting for her to make the first move.

Thankfully, Lane took the initiative. "Want some eggs, Antonette?"

Toni took the bowl that Lane offered and spooned clumps of fluffy yellow egg onto her plate without thought.

"How about some sausage, and maybe a biscuit?" Reese added, and elbowed Palmer to pass Toni the jam.

She took what was offered, then stared down at her plate, unable to take a bite. Shame and embarrassment overwhelmed her. What must they be thinking?

"Like the man said, you'll make a hell of a wife."

Lane's voice echoed over and over in her ears, drowning out everything except the hammer of her heartbeat.

Chapter 5

By noon Toni's embarrassment had eased, but she still couldn't bring herself to ask Lane what he'd said that had sent Justin to the mailbox and her back to the house. And she hadn't received any information from Justin, either. When the mailbox was fixed, he'd crawled into his truck and driven away without further explanation, leaving no clue to his unusual behavior except for the telling glance he'd given Lane Monday before he'd left.

Now, with lunch out of the way and Reese and Palmer checking on the searchers who were dragging the river downstream for Rice's body, Toni had hours before supper and plenty to do. If it rained again, the grass might green up in the lower pasture, and she could end one chore by not having to hay. But except for the thunderstorm several days earlier, the spring had been unusually dry, and hay still had to be fed to the cows.

Toni headed for the barn with work gloves in her hand, wishing instead that she were going to the creek to swim. But while the water was slowly receding, it was still unfit for any recreational dip. In any case, she had no desire to prance around on the creek bank in front of a dozen strangers.

So work it would have to be. She backed her pickup truck toward the hay bales stacked at the north end of the barn, then got out and started tossing them, one after the other, into the bed of the truck.

A half hour later, she shifted the last bale into place, then jumped down, tossing her work gloves into the driver's seat as she walked past. Her blue jeans stuck to her legs, and her old long-sleeved shirt was thin from years of wear. Although she knew that T-shirts and shorts would have been cooler apparel, she also knew that handling hay would have been impossible against all that bare skin. She would trade hot for scratched and itchy any day.

Before she drove up to the pasture to feed the cows, she wanted to check on Lane and get herself a drink. She came out of the barn on a run, and ran face first into the second button down on Lane Monday's shirt.

"Oh!" She grabbed her nose and staggered, seeing stars as the unexpected thump brought tears to her eyes. If it weren't for Lane's quick reaction, she would have fallen backward in the dust.

He caught her as she stumbled, but the grin that he'd been wearing died as she tore out of his arms and pushed him away.

"Don't touch me," she grumbled, still holding her nose, and then couldn't believed what she'd said.

Her shock was nothing compared to the anger that swamped him. He cursed beneath his breath to keep from shouting.

"You can get that indignant expression off of your face right now, lady. I was only trying to keep you from falling on your butt," he said, then started back to the house, forgetting as he did, why he'd come in search of her in the first place.

"Oh, good grief, why did I do that?" Toni moaned. She was shocked by her own behavior and by what she'd said. "Lane! Please wait."

Her shout stopped his progress, but the touch of her hand on his arm was the magnet that turned him around.

"What?" he muttered. "And don't tell me you left something out, because you were pretty damned clear to me."

"I'm sorry," she said. "I didn't mean to react like some stupid, fainting female. You just startled me, that's all."

"Females who faint aren't necessarily stupid, Antonette," he said shortly. "And I came to tell you that Justin called. He wants you to call him back as soon as possible."

Choosing to ignore his assessment of womanly attributes, she frowned at the message instead. "Did he say why?"

Lane shrugged. "Just something about missing chickens and dead dogs."

"Good Lord," she said, more than a little startled, and looked toward the barn. The hay would have to wait. This definitely took precedence over her chores.

They started toward the house together, and Lane could tell that she was torn between trying to slow her gait to his and the need to find out what was wrong at her brother's place.

"Don't wait on me," Lane said. "I'll get there when I get there."

She went from walk to run in three seconds flat, and when her long, shapely legs went from step to stride, Lane forgot to follow. He was too lost in watching the beauty of her body as it moved. She was as graceful and lithe as a gazelle, and in spite of her aggressive, independent tendencies, about as shy. He'd already noticed that when Toni got nervous, she slipped into a bossy mode that could make a man nuts.

"What am I thinking?" he muttered. "She's already made me nuts, and I've only been here four days."

With that thought came the knowledge that soon he would have to leave. As easy as it would be to stay in the quiet and comfort of these green Tennessee hills, he couldn't stay here forever. He had a job, friends, people who counted on him. And as soon as he thought it, he knew that when it came time to go, he would be leaving a part of himself behind that had nothing to do with gratitude for his life being saved. Toni

Hatfield and her Smoky Mountains had insinuated themselves into his heart as quietly as a sigh in the wind.

He entered the house in time to see Toni drop into a chair, the phone pressed against her ear like the lifeline that it was to the world outside her home. And then he frowned in response to the growing expressions on her face that looked to be a mixture of dismay and despair.

"How many?" Toni asked, and missed seeing Lane's frown deepen. "When did it happen? Is that Bobby crying?"

She bit her lip and pressed her hand to her belly in response to the shaft of sympathetic pain. She could hear the child's sobs, even though Justin had claimed that the boy was in another room. Her heart ached for the child's sorrow, and she wished that she were there to give him a hug.

Without thinking, Lane walked up behind her and slipped a hand across her shoulder. It was instinctive, just a comforting gesture he might have given to anyone in a similar situation. But the moment he touched her, Lane felt her tense like a skittish colt. He sighed, then moved away, wondering as he did, how this woman had ever gotten a date. And then he turned back and stared.

She was twenty-nine. He knew, because she'd announced it one morning at the table as firmly as if she'd asked him to pass the salt. Remembering, he could almost say that she'd thrown the information out like a gauntlet, as if daring him to make something of the fact that she was alone and unmarried and, to all intents and purposes, well on her way to being an old maid.

He snorted beneath his breath. Antonette Hatfield was as unlikely an old-maid prospect as the possibility of his becoming a midget. But something told him that if he was a betting man, he could make money guessing the number of times this woman had gone out with a man who was not her kin.

"Oh, Lord, Justin, I'm sorry," Toni said. "Yes, thanks for calling. I'll be careful, but I got rid of the chickens when Daddy died, remember? And I'll keep watch on the livestock." She sighed, then hung up the phone.

''Honey, what's wrong?''

Lane was so fixed upon seeing a smile come back into those dark chocolate eyes that he hadn't even heard himself call her by an endearment.

But Toni heard. She saw and took note of everything concerning this man who'd washed down Chaney Creek and into her life. And she knew that if she wasn't careful, he would take the heart out of her when he went home. She shrugged and spread her hands in a defeated gesture as if she couldn't believe what she was about to say.

''This morning, while Justin was over here, something or someone got into their chickens. He thinks it might have been the Sumters stealing food.''

Lane frowned, but thought little of it. This was, after all, mountain country. Keeping animals was bound to hold some risks, even from ne'er-do-well neighbors.

''That's too bad,'' he said. ''Is Bobby one of Justin's boys? I heard you ask why he was crying. Were some of the chickens his pets?''

Toni looked up, then quickly away. She didn't want to see his sympathy.

''Yes, he's Justin's oldest. He's just past ten. And no, they weren't his pets.''

She frowned, then walked to the window overlooking her front yard, parting the curtains to glance out before she spoke again. Her voice trembled and her stomach kept rolling. But not in disgust. It was fear that held her thoughts. In all the years that thefts had been blamed on Sumters, not once had anything like this ever happened. She could hardly bring herself to say it.

''Something killed Bobby's dog, too.''

She spun, and the lace curtains fell into place behind her like a bridal veil. As he stared at her, Lane caught his breath and then forget to take another, so shocked was he by the image that flashed through his mind. But it wasn't Toni that he'd seen when she'd turned around. Just for a moment, he would have sworn that it was Sharla's face that he saw—

Sharla, silhouetted by the lace. It took everything he had to get back to the conversation and away from the vision that Toni had unwittingly inspired.

He inhaled slowly, relishing the burst of oxygen into his starving lungs, then wiped a shaky hand across his eyes. He had to get back to the matter at hand.

"Would those Sumter kids do something like that?" Lane asked.

Toni frowned, then shook her head. "Justin thinks so, but for some reason, I don't."

"Why not?" he asked.

"Brownie was a redbone." When she saw the puzzled expression on his face, she added, "That's a breed of hunting dog, and the Sumters live for hunting and dogs. I don't think they would randomly kill one like that."

"They would have taken it with them, right?"

She nodded. "I would have guessed it was some animal that killed Brownie, but Justin said that there was hardly any blood on or around the dog, and no footprints that he could see. A wildcat would have cut a dog that big to shreds before it died, the same way a wolf would have done. There would at least have been wounds from a fight. And, the chickens were out and running all over the yard. Justin didn't even know how many were missing until he began to put them up."

Something within Lane started to surface. His lawman instincts had kicked in. There were some more questions he wanted to ask. "Surely the missing chickens are out there. Maybe they just flew off and are somewhere up a tree."

"Maybe," Toni said, "but chickens can't fly far, usually no more than a few yards." She shrugged and looked away.

Lane could see that she didn't buy his theory, either, and truth be known, he didn't think much of it himself.

"So how did the dog actually die?" Lane asked.

Toni turned. Lane felt her fear from across the room.

"A broken neck."

"Well, damn," he whispered, and this time the thought bubbled again. A little harder. A little longer.

"I've got to go feed the livestock," she said, starting out the door. "If you want to watch television or read, feel free to look through Daddy's things. I haven't been able to pack them away." Her lip quivered. "At least not yet."

"Where were you going?" Lane asked, remembering the pickup with its load of hay.

"To the back forty. I have ten, cow and calf pairs. I like to feed the mamas more when they're nursing than the cows that range. It's been so dry this spring that the grass is short. I've been supplementing their pasture grass with hay."

"I'm going with you."

Toni looked startled. She knew her mouth was open, but she couldn't seem to help it. The last time someone had followed her at work, it had been her father. And he'd simply been telling her what to do, not actually helping to get it done.

"I don't need any help," she said. "You can't lift because of your stitches and bad knee, and I'm strong as an—"

"Antonette, in spite of my aches and pains, I am not the man with whom you should be arguing strength."

She couldn't help it, but her gaze went straight to his broad shoulders and massive chest beneath the soft plaid shirt he was wearing. Finally, she looked up and caught his cold, blue glare as he continued.

"I said, I'm going with you. You have no business roaming all over these damned mountains alone, especially after what happened at Justin's. What if it's a bear that's the culprit, for God's sake? Do you want one to walk up on you while you're babying those cows?"

She paled. She hadn't thought of that possibility. There *were* still places in the mountains that were wild and unfettered. And something big *had* broken the dog's neck. A swipe of a bear paw would just about fill that bill.

Determined not to show how deeply his warning had affected her, Toni shrugged. "Okay, okay. I'm sure it's no big deal, but you can come if you promise not to be a back-seat driver. I don't like to be told what to do.''

Lane grinned. "Now why am I not surprised?" he drawled, and pulled a piece of straw out of her ponytail as she started past him.

Toni glared, then stomped out the door, refusing to admit, even to herself, that she was darned glad he was behind her all the way.

She fed the cows without incident, and with little argument from Lane, other than his telling her she shouldn't be lifting all that weight. She'd made fun of his concerns, but secretly cherished the thought that he believed she could actually have a fragile bone in her body. If she had one, she had yet to discover its location. But for the time being, she was perfectly willing to let Lane keep his fantasies about her. If he thought she looked weak and helpless, then God love him for being a fool. He was the first man who had ever told her she was too little to do something.

It was when they started back to the house that Lane's perception of Toni took a sharp right into shock.

"I need to stop here a minute," Toni said, parking beneath the trees that lined the dirt path. "I'm missing a good hammer and I think I may have lost it the night of the flood."

Lane's attention piqued. That would be the night she'd pulled him out of Chaney Creek. "Where are you going to look? There has got to be at least a thousand trees between here and the house."

The pickup door slammed behind her as she started down the incline.

"Oh, I know where to look," she said over her shoulder. "It's either where I dumped the fencing materials when I went back for you, or where I loaded you onto the wagon."

"I want to see."

She paused and turned. The expression on his face made her shiver, but not with fear. Anticipation threaded through her system, reminding her that the tension between them did not run on anger, but on interest.

"So come," she said. "But watch where you walk. It's downhill most of the way. You don't want to pull out your stitches."

No, I damn sure don't, he thought, and then sighed when he saw that she was waiting on the path for him to catch up. He should have known that she would be ready, if necessary, to offer another shoulder to lean on.

Toni girl, how am I going to manage the rest of my days without you telling me what to do? And without you to catch me if I fall?

"It's not here," she said after carefully searching beneath the trees where she'd parked the night she'd seen him caught in the flood. "I'm going farther downhill. You may want to wait here. It's almost a quarter of a…" His glare ended her advice and sent her down the hill with him only steps behind.

"Tell me," Lane said when he figured she'd cooled down enough to talk to him again.

"Tell you what?" she asked.

"About that night."

She shrugged. "What's to tell? You already know I'd been fixing my fence. I was on the ATV, and luckily for you, pulling a wagon." She paused and looked back. "You know, the one that's in the backyard near the garden."

Lane nodded.

"When I saw the storm coming, I tried to hurry. But the wagon was full of posts and wire, and the mud was too thick to get up much speed. By the time I got to the foot of the hill, it was raining pretty hard. I left the ATV because I was afraid I might get stuck going up the hill. I would rather be wet than stuck in red clay, any day."

"And…" He urged her to continue.

"And…I heard an explosion and thought lightning had struck something and set it on fire." She paused, then turned to look at him when she continued. "I still can't believe that what I saw was you...falling out of the sky...and men dying. It still gives me nightmares just thinking about it.''

Lane was surprised. ''I didn't know that you saw the plane crash,'' he said.

''Well, I didn't know what I saw, either, until you told me differently. All I saw was an orange ball of fire above the trees.'' She shuddered, then looked away as she resumed her walk, afraid that he'd seen too much.

''So, what did you do then?'' he urged.

''I started to run. I didn't want the lightning to strike me, too. That's when...''

She got quiet. Lane knew what came next. But he hadn't heard it from her. The sheriff had volunteered that information and everything else he'd learned about Toni's part in saving his life.

Lane caught up with her, and when she wouldn't stop, he grabbed her by the arm. She had no choice but to give in to his silent demand. She turned and looked up at him.

''Why did you go in after me?'' he asked.

She swallowed around a lump in her throat. It was hard to look at the face of a man who had come to mean far too much to her for her own peace of mind.

''Because you couldn't get out any other way,'' she said. ''Come on. It's going to get dark unless we hurry. I won't be able to look for the hammer.''

Because I couldn't get out any other way.

The simple statement was deceiving. What she'd done had taken more than nerve. It had taken a stronger spirit and a braver heart than most men would have had.

Lane started walking, one foot in front of the other, barely noticing his sore leg. Going down was easy; coming up was going to be hell. But he wouldn't have missed this trip with Toni Hatfield for anything.

A few minutes later, she stopped and started walking in a circle, her eyes down to the ground as she searched for the missing hammer. Lane kept walking until he came to the edge of the hill overlooking the ravine and stared down into the steadily flowing stream that was Chaney Creek.

Debris from the flood was still caught in the tree roots that sprouted from the creek bank high above the water. A watermark was still visible, and would be for several days until the heat had dried it back to its normal shade of dirty red. A couple of feet from where he was standing, a sharp overhang of rock shaded several square feet of creek beneath. Lane stared, unable to fathom what had happened here…in a storm…in the dark.

"It's not here, either," Toni muttered, stomping to the edge of the ravine, then absently staring over to the other side. She pointed. "Look. That side of Chaney Creek is the back edge of Justin's place. He bought it right after—"

"My God!"

Lane took her by the shoulders and made her look at him. He couldn't get past the thought of what she'd done. His fingers dug into the soft skin of her shoulders until he felt muscle and bone, and still she seemed too fragile to have pulled them both out of a flood.

"What's wrong?" Toni asked. "Did you hurt your leg?" She started to kneel to see if blood had seeped through the bandage and into the denim of his jeans. "I knew this was too far for you to—"

He yanked her to her feet. "Don't kneel at any man's feet, Antonette. If there's any kneeling to be done, I should be the one doing it. This has to be where it happened, but I've got to know. How in hell did you get us out?"

He turned her toward the creek, and then couldn't make himself let her go. It was as if he was suddenly afraid she might fall. And as he held her close against him, she felt his body pressing against her backside like a wall.

She closed her eyes to see more clearly within her mind the night…and the storm.

"I think it was all due to a streak of lightning and a big streak of luck." She leaned over and pointed to the rock below. "I knew that outcrop of rock was there, and I counted on being able to get a foothold." She turned and laughed, remembering what had come next. "Even with that, we still almost drowned. I couldn't get you to turn loose of that log you were holding."

Her chuckle seemed out of place next to his shock. How could she laugh at nearly losing her life to save his?

He lifted her hands and turned them palms up, rubbing a thumb in the center of each as if testing their strength. Unable to voice his thoughts, all Lane could do was lift them reverently to his face.

He pressed one, then the other to his lips, and when he did, Toni Hatfield forgot the promises she'd made to herself about not caring for this man. She forgot that she'd all but given up thoughts of babies and motherhood. And when he wrapped his arms around her and held her clasped against his chest, Toni wanted to cry.

Why did I have to meet you when it's too late for you to care? she thought.

One big hand cradled her head, while the other rested low around her waist. She was trapped as neatly as if she were in a vise, and yet she had never felt this cared for or this safe in her life.

"As long as I live, I will never be able to say thank you enough," Lane said softly, and cupped her face with his hands. "You, Toni Hatfield, are one hell of a woman."

He leaned down.

Toni saw his intent. She could have objected. She could have moved. She did neither. Instead, she stood and waited for the world to stop, and when his mouth slid across her lips, then centered perfectly on hers, she found that it was her heart that had stopped.

Lane expected her to resist, and when she didn't, he was not prepared for the soft, open invitation she made when their lips connected.

He felt her tremble and heard her sigh, but when she shifted slightly beneath his touch and then slipped her hands onto his waist to steady herself, he lost sight of what he'd started to do.

It was supposed to be a simple thank-you, accompanied by a light, friendly kiss. But the woman who stood within the circle of his arms was accepting more than he'd meant to give.

Lane groaned, and when Toni took one step forward, his hands slid off of her shoulders and down her back, drawing her deeper into the kiss of no return. He vaguely remembered thinking that this couldn't go on, then Toni's arms slid around his waist and locked behind his back.

He remembered little of what came afterward beyond a few undeniable facts. Her skin was softer than he'd expected. Her breasts fit his body contours to perfection, and he'd never wanted to be inside a woman this badly in his entire life. But that wasn't going to happen, not if he had anything to do with it. He couldn't repay a lady like Antonette by using her body in a fit of lust. Not even if she seemed willing.

He gave up their connection with painful regret as he tore his mouth from hers; then he closed his eyes and rested his chin on the crest of her head.

"Ah, damn," he said softly as he rubbed his hands up and down the middle of her back in a gentling motion. "I'm sorry, Toni. I didn't mean to let that go so far."

Toni's heart shattered. He was sorry? It was the last thing she'd wanted to hear him say. She ducked her head and tried to laugh as she pushed herself out of his arms. In her mind, things hadn't gone nearly far enough.

"Forget it," she said shortly, and hated herself for the bitterness that she heard in her voice. "It was just a kiss. And you're not the first man I've known who's handed one out, then moved on to something better."

"That's not what I…"

He could have saved his excuse for Sunday morning, because Toni was already walking away. And, if he read her reaction correctly, she thought that he'd quit from lack of passion. Guilt overwhelmed him. He'd known her self-esteem was low, but this was ridiculous.

She thinks I stopped because I got bored? Lord have mercy. What does that woman see when she looks in a mirror? Doesn't she know that she's beautiful?

He groaned and started uphill, telling himself that he deserved every ache that came with the trip. He hadn't gotten himself into this kind of condition with no chance of relief since high school. And, to be honest, he wasn't sure how it had happened from just one kiss. As a rule, he had more control over his emotions than this. But that was before he'd taken the back door into Tennessee, and then been fished out of Chaney Creek like a sack of unwanted pups.

He ate supper alone, standing at the counter and chewing his sandwich while he watched her from the kitchen window as she worked. The weeds in her garden were suffering the consequences of what had transpired between them. She wielded the hoe with frightening irregularity, as if one false swipe and someone's head might fall instead of the uprooted weed.

"My stitches will be out in two more days and then I'm gone. How do I make this right before I go?" Lane muttered to himself as he gave up pretending to eat. Toni wouldn't even look at him, never mind talk to him. He didn't know how to make things right between them again.

But Lane had a streak of stubbornness that was almost as big as he was. He dumped his sandwich on the counter and headed for the door. "Damn her hide, she's going to listen to me or else."

He stomped outside and never realized that his leg hardly hurt at all. He was healing, and at the same time, still suffering from an attack of misplaced indignity.

"Antonette!"

Toni paused and turned. From the look on Lane's face as he came toward her, the massacre of weeds would have to wait. She'd seen mad on her brothers' faces so often that she recognized anger on sight. It had something to do with the jut of male chin, lower lip and a glower across the forehead. She sighed. As tired as she was, dealing with a wounded ego was going to play hell with her manners.

"You shouted?"

He flushed, then made an effort to lower his voice several octaves before he spoke again. "I've already said I'm sorry that I overstepped the bounds of friendship you've shown me. I wish to hell that it hadn't happened. I like watching you smile. I like sharing a meal with you. But I don't like feeling like Jack the damn Ripper. Can't we please go back to square one?"

A rush of pleasure came and went so fast that she almost forgot it had ever happened. It was what he'd said after "sorry" that had hurt the most. And it was because he would soon be gone that she had the nerve to say what was in her heart.

"That's just fine, Mr. Monday. I'm glad I give good service. I'm glad you find my manners pleasing to your taste. And while I don't feel threatened by your presence in any way, shape or form like I might with Jack the damn Ripper, I do resent the hell out of hearing that you wished you hadn't kissed me."

Unintentionally, she leaned closer. Lane was stunned by the depth of anger in her eyes.

"I, personally, was enjoying it when you got an attack of conscience, or guilt or whatever men call it when they don't want to leave any strings behind."

"I didn't mean that I didn't—"

"Didn't you just say you wished it hadn't happened?"

He swallowed and nodded. At this point, answering her was impossible. He might be bigger, but she could outbalk a mule.

"And you want to go back to square one?" she asked.

He sighed and nodded again. Finally they were getting somewhere.

She smirked. "I hope that doesn't include the handcuffs. I would hate like hell to spend another night on the floor tied to you." She handed him the hoe. "Oh, and I don't think my table is up to another parting of the ways, so let's just agree to disagree on this, and drop the subject altogether. What do you say?''

''I give up.''

''What?''

Lane sighed and shrugged, then used the hoe for a cane as he started trudging up the row toward the house.

''I can't outtalk you, Antonette. And half the time, I don't know what you're thinking, so I give up. I hurt your feelings and didn't mean to. I'm sorry. I'm sorry. I'm sorry.''

''Apology accepted,'' she said softly, and anxiously awaited his reaction.

He hadn't expected an answer, so when it came, he wasn't ready for the flash of relief that settled in the pit of his stomach. He stopped, looked down at the dirt beneath his feet and grinned wryly before wiping the smile off of his face. He turned to face her.

''You're a hard woman, Antonette Hatfield.''

She nodded. ''It's a hard life, Mr. Monday.''

''That it is, lady. That it is.''

He held out a hand. Moments later, Toni's fingers slid across his palm and threaded through his. She looked up, gauging his reaction to their reluctant connection.

''It's getting dark,'' she said.

He lifted his head and smelled the air, then squinted toward the blaze of colors on the horizon. ''Want to sit on the porch for a while and watch the sunset?''

Toni was thankful for the shades of dusk that hid her sudden tears. She would give a year of her life to be able to spend the rest of it with this man…on some porch…watching life and sunsets pass them by. But she was going to have to settle for a couple of days' worth instead.

''I suppose,'' she said. ''At least we don't have to shell any more peas. Justin's wife, Judy, and my brother David's wife, Laura, will be over tomorrow to pick the patch.''

Lane rolled his eyes and pulled her gently out of the garden. ''More family?''

She nodded.

He grinned. "Reese and Palmer won't be back until late tonight, so let's get dibs on the swing before company comes."

His smile was easy, his tone of voice gentle. The lines on either side of his cheeks deepened from the smile. It made him seem younger, more innocent. At that moment, Toni forgot everything ugly that had happened during the day, including the harsh words that had come between them.

Toni's steps were lighter as she followed in his wake, their hands still connected in a way that their bodies could not.

"You don't have to hurry," she told him. "The porch swing isn't going anywhere. Besides, it's a long time until morning."

The blue in his eyes turned black with emotion. Her warning put thoughts in his mind that had no business being there. He could think of several good ways to get through a night, and all of them needed a woman like Toni to make them work. But they weren't going to happen. Toni kept herself and her emotions as distant as the state in which he lived, and considering all of the facts, that was as it should be.

"Don't remind me," Lane said, pulling her up the steps and into the swing. Before Toni had time to make something more out of what he'd said, he added, "My stitches come out the day after tomorrow."

"It will be all right," she assured him. "I'll go with you." Absently, she reached over and patted his uninjured thigh, before closing her eyes and letting the swing take her places her thoughts dared not go.

Lane couldn't look at her. And he damn sure wouldn't touch her. If he did, he would ruin everything that he'd spent the afternoon trying to fix. But he couldn't get over her easy, gentle assurance that he would not suffer alone.

Dear God, if only I dared hope that might be true, I would never leave this woman.

But old wounds and painful losses kept Lane's thoughts

and wants to himself, just as Toni cherished her dreams to herself. And because of those reasons, the two of them watched the sunset in silence, wishing for things that couldn't be.

Chapter 6

Kids ran wild across the yard, climbing trees, running down hills and adding high-pitched shrieks of delight to the hysteria brought on by being together. While their mothers picked the bounteous overflow from her garden, Toni sat on the front-porch swing. She kept one eye on her nieces and nephews' riotous behavior, and another on the youngest member of the Hatfield clan, three-month-old Lucy, who belonged to Justin and Judy.

The baby's tiny head was covered with a downy layer of soft, brown curls. Her small nose wrinkled in sleep, and her rosebud lips pouted, then sucked in a reflex motion as Toni shifted her from one shoulder to the other.

Toni inhaled the sweet scent of baby powder and line-dried clothes as she patted Lucy's diapered bottom in rhythm to the rocking of the swing. With children in the yard, and one in her arms, her life seemed nearly complete.

And then, Lane Monday walked out of the barn and started toward the house. The absence of a limp was noticeable, as was the length and breadth of the man himself. Toni clutched

Lucy a little tighter and tried not to notice, or even care, that his big body moved like a well-oiled machine.

A ball rolled near Lane's feet. He laughed, and tossed it back to the children at play, and for a moment, Toni pretended that this was her world, and the man coming toward her was a permanent fixture in it.

The baby whimpered, and without missing a beat, Toni set the swing back in motion with the tip of her toe, pushing off like a bird taking flight.

Pat, pat on the baby's bottom. Back and forth in the old porch swing. The rhythm felt right, and as old as Time. A mother rocking a child to sleep.

And then Judy Hatfield came around the house with a weary smile and a bushel of peas, and set it near the porch. Her sister-in-law, Laura, followed with her bushel.

"We're through," Laura called. "Hey, kids, put away the toys and go wash. We've got to go home."

Grumbles and groans could be heard all around, but the children did as they were told.

"Bet you thought I would never get done," Judy said, and lifted the baby from Toni's arms, missing the empty look that swept over Toni's face as she did. "The peas are great. I'll put the kids to shelling when we get home, and Justin can baby-sit later while I put them up."

Toni's heart felt as empty as her arms. She looked down at the sleeping baby and wanted to cry. "I could keep Lucy longer if you needed to—"

"No way," Judy said. "Laura and I have already imposed upon you long enough by asking you to watch this wild bunch."

"It wasn't an imposition," Toni said softly, unaware that Lane saw all of what she felt and was trying to hide. "I like taking care of the kids, especially the babies," she said, and brushed a baby curl behind Lucy's ear, just so she could feel the silky softness one more time.

"Judy's right," Laura said. "Every time we have a family get-together, you wind up playing nursemaid to all the little

Hatfields, instead of enjoying the day with the rest of us.''
Then she groaned and rolled her neck. ''Tonight, I will ache
in places I didn't know I had.''

Laura batted her eyes and giggled as she tucked a loose
blond curl beneath her headband where it belonged. She was
small and plump and David Hatfield doted on her.

You don't understand what a real ache is, Toni thought.
The children are why I enjoy the day. But she kept the thought
to herself, as she did everything that was dear to her heart.

Lane stood to one side and watched. He didn't understand
Toni's pain, but it was obvious to him that she was hurting.
And because it hurt him to see her sad, he took the oppor-
tunity to break into the conversation.

''Ladies, if you would tell me where to put your baskets,
I'll set them in your cars.''

Judy and Laura gave Lane a considering look, as if trying
to imagine this man and their socially inept sister-in-law together.

''I'll get them,'' Toni said, and ran to the edge of the house
where the women had set them down.

She picked one up and was about to drag the other, when
Lane walked up behind her, took them out of her arms and
hefted one onto each hip.

''No you don't. You do too much and lift too much as it
is. I'll do it,'' Lane said, and ignored Toni's frown.

Two at one time would have been more than a normal-size
man could have handled. Lane had them balanced on his hips,
one beneath each long arm as if they were nothing.

''If you can find an empty spot in the car, you can put mine
anywhere,'' Laura said, giggling, and headed for her car to
open the trunk with Lane right behind her. Her less-than-
subtle reference pointed to the fact that four of the six children
loading into cars were hers.

''Be careful,'' Toni called. ''Remember your stitches.''

Lane loaded the baskets, then turned. There was a soft
smile on his face and a deeper one in his eyes. ''My hands

and arms do not have stitches, Antonette. And after tomorrow, neither will my leg. You fuss too much. I'm fine."

Toni was at a loss for what to do or say while he loaded the baskets into the cars. All she could do was watch while the joy in her morning disappeared.

Because Lane and the children had otherwise occupied her thoughts, she missed seeing the all-knowing look that Judy and Laura exchanged. It was an "Aha!" look if ever there was one.

As Lane deposited the last basket in her car, Judy apologized. "Toni is right. We forgot that you've been through so much. You seem so strong and healthy, we just—"

"I'm fine," Lane said. "Toni's just trying to keep me in one piece long enough to ship me out."

"Oh, wait," Toni said, then darted back into the house. Seconds later she was back with a half-empty bottle in her hand. "Lucy's milk. She went to sleep before she finished it all."

Judy smiled as Toni stuck the bottle into the baby's bag. "The little squirt's been doing that lately, then waking up an hour or so later squawking for more. I swear she's going to be as hardheaded as her daddy."

"We're off. Thanks for the peas," Laura shouted, waving as she drove away.

Judy echoed the sentiment, then drove away, leaving Toni and Lane alone in the yard.

"I always feel like I've been in the eye of a whirlwind when the kids leave," Toni said, and didn't know that her chin quivered as she watched them drive away. "But I wouldn't trade them for anything. I would keep them all if their mothers would let me."

"Toni?"

"What?" she asked, still lost in the memory of what it had felt like to hold the baby against her breast.

"Why aren't you married?"

Pain, followed by anger, made her lash out. "Why aren't

you?'' she countered, satisfied by the startled expression on his face.

"*I* was," Lane said, and wished he'd never started this.

"Don't you ever want to remarry? Maybe raise a family?"

The expression on Lane's face went blank. Toni didn't know what she'd said, but something had struck a serious nerve in him.

"I will not father any children, and that's a damned fact," he said bitterly.

Toni was shocked. She would never have believed Lane to be the type to dislike children. Matching his defiant answer with a defiance of her own, she spoke before she thought. "If I could, I would have a hundred. Children are wonderful. They're the most loving, honest people I know."

Lane grew cold, from the inside out. He didn't see the angry tears in her eyes, or hear the tremble in her voice. Memories as painful as the wounds healing on his body were making him sick. He saw nothing but the memory of Sharla in a pool of blood and the way she'd looked when the life had gone out of her eyes.

"Then you should have gotten married and had a dozen," he muttered, wishing to hell that this conversation had never started.

Hurt and angry at learning that he held disdain for what she most wanted out of life, she spoke the truth before she thought. "No one ever asked me," she said, and then paled and walked away before she saw the sympathy on his face, hating him for making her admit the fact.

The shock of her statement yanked him out of his bitter memories. He knew by the set of her shoulders that his thoughtless statement had hurt her as deeply as if he'd struck a blow to her heart. He would give anything to be able to take back what he'd said. But it was too late. The damage had already been done.

"What in hell is wrong with the men around here, anyway?" he muttered, and followed her into the house, unwilling to let what he'd said fester between them. "Toni?"

He was not surprised when she didn't answer. She'd probably had enough of men and their stupidity to last her a lifetime. But Lane wasn't the type to give up, so he went from room to room until he found her in the kitchen...ignoring him.

It took everything he had not to focus on her long bare legs and shapely backside, encased in frayed denim cutoffs. Her pink T-shirt was soft and old, and he knew that if she turned around, the outline of her bra and the defiant push of her breasts beneath could make a man forget his manners. And while he would have liked to undo her braid and dig his fingers into the tangles so deep that he would be forever caught, he knew that it wasn't smart to let lust get in the way of why he'd come in search of her.

"Look," he began, "I've never been good at saying I'm sorry, but that doesn't mean I can't admit when I'm wrong. I was way out of line out there. I would like to think you'll forgive me and just chalk it up to a bad day."

Toni turned. His apology was welcome, and oddly, unexpected. She should have been happy to know that he'd cared about her enough to at least clear the air between them. But she was too upset about something else to do much more than nod.

"It's fine," she said. "Forget it."

Lane took a deep breath and resisted the urge to shake her. "It's not fine, Antonette, and we both know it. I said some things I shouldn't have and I—"

"My pie is gone."

Her remark was so unexpected that Lane forgot what he'd been about to say. "What do you mean, your pie is gone?"

She shrugged and pointed. "Just what I mean. I took an apple pie out of the oven just before Judy and Laura arrived, and put it out back to cool. It's gone." She sighed. "The boys probably took it and ate it while their mothers weren't looking. I don't really care, but I would like to know where my pie pan is. It's one of my favorites."

"I could look around for you," Lane offered. "They

couldn't have gone far with it. Maybe it's in the barn or out behind your machine shed."

Toni sighed and dropped into a chair. "It doesn't matter to me," she said. "It's just that you won't have dessert today, and I would lay odds that three little boys will have a belly-ache before the afternoon is over."

Lane grinned, aware that what he was about to say would get a rise out of Toni. "I can give up dessert for a day, even several if I have to, but why are you blaming the boys? There were several little girls out there, too."

"Because the girls don't like to get dirty. They wouldn't have eaten a pie with their fingers even if someone had tried to make them. I know my nieces...and my nephews. Believe me, it was the boys."

"Are you going to call their mothers?" Lane asked.

Toni looked up, then quickly away. There was too much tenderness in his expression to face. "No way. Favorite aunt-ies do not snitch. At least, not over missing pies."

Lane bent down and covered her hands with his own. "Toni, look at me."

The touch of his hands was bittersweet. He gave so little, and she wanted so much more. But she bit her lip and com-plied. She had, after all, no other choice. There was no way she could let him know how much she'd come to count on his daily presence in her life.

"What?"

Lane sighed. Her name was Antonette, but someone should have called her Defiance instead. "Are you going to say it?" he asked.

"Say what?" It was a dumb question. She knew what he wanted to hear. It was just so hard to say the words, because acknowledging what he'd said about children was like the death of a dream.

"That I'm forgiven for hurting your feelings."

Toni sighed. "You're forgiven."

Lane laughed, but it was a harsh, unhappy sound. "Damn, Toni, don't overdo the sentimentality on my account."

Her gaze was level, her voice calm. "I can't afford senti
mentality, Lane. I am a self-assured woman, remember?"

What I remember is the pain in your voice, lady. I hear
what you say. But do you hear yourself saying it?

The thought was impossible to voice, because however
badly he might wish to do so, he was in no position to change
one single aspect of Toni Hatfield's personal life. He'd al
ready given happiness a try and been cut off at the heart for
the effort. He didn't have enough guts to repeat the pain.

"So, what are you going to do?" he asked.

Toni pushed herself up from the chair. "Call the doctor
and confirm your appointment."

"Appointment?"

"You've got a checkup coming and stitches to be re
moved."

"Trying to get rid of me, are you?" It was a poor joke that
fell flat between them.

Toni paused in the doorway, looking strangely elegant in
spite of her T-shirt and shorts. Her chin tilted and her eyes
darkened with defiance.

"Does that mean you're not anxious to leave?" she asked.

He flushed. How could he answer that and not hurt her
worse than he'd already done? He chose to remain silent.

Unbeknownst to him, his silence hurt her even more. But
she would be damned if she let him know that.

"That's what I thought," Toni said. "There's a casserole
in the refrigerator. Heat what you want in the microwave. I'm
not hungry anymore."

All six feet six inches of his body went numb. He knew he
kept breathing, though, because the pain around his heart had
not gone away. But he couldn't have moved or spoken to save
his life. If he didn't get the hell out of Tennessee soon, he
was going to ruin both their lives.

There was a note on the table, and Toni was nowhere to
be found. If he hadn't sat down on that sofa, he wouldn't

have dozed off. He hated this lingering weakness and would be heartily glad when his full strength finally returned.

"How could she disappear without my hearing her leave?" Lane muttered, picking up the note and then frowning. "Eleven o'clock tomorrow. Not even a 'Dear Sir' or 'go to hell.'"

He tossed the note back onto the table. That, he supposed, was the confirmation of his appointment time; the lack of everything else had to be the sum of what his departure meant to her. Absolutely nothing.

He sighed and ran a hand through his hair in frustration. How did she expect him to act? They'd known each other less than a week. Granted, the circumstances surrounding their meeting had been more dramatic than most. And it was true that you get to know a person real fast when you spend the night handcuffed together. That was a fact that Toni could claim. His situation was a little bit different, though. He had the feeling that if he could remember it, too, then he would be a lot better off.

How, he wondered, did that old Chinese proverb go? If you save a man's life, then he will be in your debt forever?

That didn't help his guilt. So he owed her his life, but that didn't mean he had to give up the rest of it for her, did it? Surely she hadn't expected him to just toss off fifteen years of law enforcement and try farming, Tennessee-style.

"What the hell am I doing?" Lane asked himself. "She hasn't asked a damned thing of me. Why am I reading so much into what she doesn't say?" But there were no answers forthcoming, and no tall, dark-eyed woman to deny what he thought.

Lane walked outside to the back porch and looked up into the hills beyond the house. A haze hung above the treetops, filtering the heat of the sun just enough to give the less cautious a dangerous burn. He stood at the edge of the top step, gazing intently into the tree line, watching for something, anything, that might tell him where Toni had gone. He heard nothing, and saw nothing but a lone turkey buzzard riding the air currents far above the house.

As he watched, it dawned on him that this was part of her everyday life. She came and went to suit herself, and she knew that when she came home, no one would be standing on the porch watching and waiting for her to arrive.

A slow, sick feeling settled near the center of his belly. Now that he'd met her, how could he leave, knowing that she would be alone? He'd seen the longing in her eyes for more than life had seen fit to give her. He'd sensed the emptiness with which she lived, although she would have been the first to deny it, especially to him.

"Ah, lady, why did this have to happen? You deserve a whole man, not one who's been crippled by life."

But admitting that he wanted to stay would be admitting the reason why. And Lane Monday wasn't ready to face the fact that he was falling for the woman who had saved his life.

"I'll get back to Tallahassee and this *thing* that I feel between us will fade," he told himself.

Relieved to see her coming out of the trees, Lane knew that he'd been lying. To himself, and to her, ever since the day that they'd met. He didn't want to leave Toni Hatfield, but he would. And it would be one of the hardest things he'd ever had to do. Maybe even harder than the day he'd buried his wife.

And then he realized that Toni was running and he forgot to breathe. He could tell by the way she was moving that something was wrong.

The last thing Toni had expected to find when she left the house was a dead calf. And she knew that she wouldn't have found it for days if the mama cow had not kept bawling.

She'd heard it earlier when Laura and Judy were in the garden and she was on the porch with the baby, but she'd thought little of it. Cows bawled all the time.

But later, after confirming Lane's appointment, she'd stepped outside to get a breath of fresh air, hoping to clear away the misery of knowing that he would soon be gone. The first thing she'd noticed was the distant, but steady, bawl of a cow. Without thought, she'd struck out across the back lot, heading for the repetitive sound.

She'd gone farther than she'd meant to on foot. If she'd known she was going to go this far away from the house, she would have taken the ATV. But the longer she'd walked, the sillier it would have been to turn around and go back to get the vehicle. Any minute now, she expected to find the cow and see that she'd worried for nothing.

But that hadn't been the case.

When she walked into the clearing and saw the cow in the corral on the opposite side, she sighed.

"Well, bossy, how did you get yourself stuck in there?" she muttered.

And then the cow lifted her head and bawled again. Toni could see that her udder was tight and swollen with milk. It was clear that the calf hadn't nursed at all during the day. It was then that Toni had started to worry. It was odd that the cow had gotten herself caught inside the corral, but even stranger that the calf was not right there, on the other side of the fence, bawling to get in to its mama.

"I'm coming, girl," Toni said softly, and started walking across the pasture.

The cow lowed again. Toni imagined she heard sadness in the cry, although she knew that it was just her sympathetic heart working overtime again.

"Do you hurt, girl?" Toni asked as she neared the cow. "It'll be all right. We'll get you out of there and find your baby for you, and you'll be good as gold."

Her hand was on the gate when she saw the calf at the edge of the trees. She'd expected it to be nearby. But she hadn't expected to find it dead, or in its present condition.

The left hind leg was gone from the carcass. She knelt and held her breath against the gory sight, needing to see, yet unwilling to touch.

It hadn't been dead for long. The blood was still red and

fairly fresh, although the edges of the wound were already starting to curl and dry. If she could only see the…

"Oh, God!"

She jumped to her feet and staggered backward before slowly turning in place. She searched the surrounding tree line with a sharp gaze. The calf's throat had been cut. Someone, rather than something, had killed it. And it was then that she realized the leg hadn't been torn from the body; it had been butchered instead.

"Damn, damn, damn," she muttered, thinking of the Sumter family and the missing father. This was worse than before. She could understand starvation, but she could not suffer wanton waste. If they were hungry, then why on earth hadn't they taken the entire calf?

A sense of profound violation crept into her soul. Someone had come onto her property and taken something belonging to her, something that had depended upon her for food and care. Rage for that injustice overwhelmed her. She doubled her fists and resisted the urge to scream. And the moment she thought it, she felt a different sense of urgency. What if they were still here? That might explain why the calf was dismembered. Maybe they'd heard her coming and been frightened away from finishing the job.

The cow lowed and moved toward the back of its pen. Toni paused in the act of turning around and cocked her head just a bit toward the tree line.

But she saw and heard nothing. And that was when her anxiety turned to fear. Subconsciously, she'd noticed what her conscious self had not; there was a complete and overwhelming absence of sound. Not a bird. Not a bug. Not one thing was moving, not even the cow she'd just put in the pen. It stood, with its head lifted and ears up, looking into the woods behind her. The flesh crawled beneath her hair. It felt as though someone were blowing on her neck. She shuddered and clenched her fists, trying to regain some of her earlier anger.

She told herself that she was imagining things. Then something popped behind her, a familiar sound she'd heard all of her life. It was the sound of twigs breaking beneath the steps of someone's feet.

"Oh, no, they're still here," she gasped, and remembered that Samuel Sumter's three oldest boys were in their twenties and nearly as big and worthless as their daddy.

She turned in the direction of her house. Lane was near. Only minutes away. But she had the terrible feeling that he would still be too far to help her.

Without looking back, she bolted from the corral, ran across the clearing and deeper into the woods, dodging trees and jumping rocks as if her life depended upon it, certain that they were coming after her.

She ran until her legs were shaking and her heart hammered in her eardrums. She ran until the stitch in her side was in danger of becoming a real pain, and she never looked back to see if she was being followed.

She was out of the trees and coming down the hillside toward the house when she saw Lane moving toward her. Unaware that he'd already sensed she was in trouble, Toni wanted to shout, to somehow warn him that someone might be in pursuit, but there was no breath left in her body to talk, only enough to run. Until she ran straight into his arms.

Lane caught her in midstep, bracing himself against the impact of her flight. He wrapped his arms around her shoulders and held her fast against him. Even through the pounding of his heart, he felt her trembling and heard her trying to catch her breath enough to speak.

"Back there...in the woods...dead."

"Shh," he whispered, soothing her gently with the touch of his hand until he sensed that she was calm enough to make sense.

And then he realized what she'd said. Dead!

"Toni, calm down, honey. I've got you. Whatever it is, you're safe now. Take deep breaths and calm down so you can tell me what's wrong."

The pain in her side ripped across her belly. "Oh, Lord,"

she moaned, and jerked out of his arms before she doubled over, grasping her knees to keep from passing out.

Seeing her in this condition made him crazy. He needed to know what was wrong, and she was in such bad shape that she could scarcely breathe, let alone talk.

"Are you all right?"

She groaned and nodded, and as she realized that she really was all right, she began to feel foolish. She'd reacted like a silly female, jumping to conclusions just because she *might* have heard footsteps in the woods. She hadn't even looked to see. She'd simply assumed. Embarrassed by her behavior, there was no way she could tell Lane what she'd feared.

"Thank God," Lane muttered. Ignoring the dry pull of healing stitches beneath his blue jeans, he knelt at her side and cupped her face, brushing her hair away from her forehead and out of her eyes with one hand, while he cradled the back of her head with the other. The sight of tiny scratches swiftly turning red across her cheeks angered him. "Toni, sweetheart, listen to me. Did someone try to hurt you?"

"No," she gasped, leaning her forehead on her knees, intent on not passing out. "Just mad," she said, and then motioned for him to be patient. When she could, she would get it all out.

But Lane was not a patient man. "Mad at who?"

She shrugged. How could she say who when she hadn't really seen anyone, only heard what she thought to be footsteps in the woods behind her?

"Wait. Wait a minute. Then I'll talk," she said, still gasping.

Lane had no choice but to wait, all the while seething at the thought of what had made Toni so angry.

Chapter 7

When she could talk without gasping, Toni groaned and then held up her hand. "Help me up," she said, wincing as Lane pulled her to her feet. "Good grief, I won't be able to walk tomorrow."

"Damn it, lady, I've run out of patience. Start talking. What happened up there?"

Toni sighed. All things considered, it seemed silly. She suspected that she'd scared herself more than anything.

"I went to check on a cow," she told him. "All afternoon I kept hearing her bawl. I thought maybe she'd lost her calf."

Lane frowned. "Why didn't you tell me where you'd gone? I was worried." The look she gave him was measured and cool, almost as if to ask, why should you care?

"I was fine. I'm always fine."

He resisted the urge to shake some sense into her and wisely kept his mouth shut, waiting for her to continue.

"Anyway, I found the cow locked in the corral up in the back pasture. I thought she'd accidentally shut herself in until

I found the calf. Someone had killed it. I think they were butchering it when I came up.''

Lane grabbed her by the shoulders, pinning her in place with his grip and the blaze in his eyes. His voice was barely above a whisper. ''Are you telling me that you walked up on someone out there in the woods?''

She shrugged. ''Not exactly. I thought I heard something in the woods and when I saw the calf, I just assumed it was the Sumters.''

''Even so,'' Lane said, ''thieves don't like witnesses, Toni. The crime they're committing is called rustling. I don't know what the penalty is for that in Tennessee, but I would venture to say it's more than the thief is willing to pay.''

She shivered, then tried to laugh. ''I made a big deal out of nothing, Lane. It's not like this hasn't happened before. But damn it, if they were hungry, why didn't they take the whole calf? Why were they hacking it up piece by piece instead of carrying it off before they butchered it?'' She frowned, and kicked the dirt with the toe of her shoe. ''Even if they were hungry, I hate waste.''

Lane spun around and headed for the house.

''Where are you going?'' Toni asked. When he didn't answer, she ran to catch up.

''Hey! I asked you where you're going.''

''I can't believe you even have to ask,'' he muttered, and hit the back door with the flat of his hand, pushing it open as if it were nothing more than a piece of paper.

Toni followed him into the hallway, and when he picked up the phone and asked the operator to connect him with the sheriff's office in Chaney, she took the phone from his hand.

''I can do that myself,'' she said, and turned her back on him so that he couldn't see the nervousness on her face when she retold her story.

Even now, she could feel the danger that she'd sensed, and she wondered why her reaction had been so strong. The Sumters were capable of stealing, but nothing else—of that she was certain. Then why, she asked herself, if I'm so right, do I feel certain that I just outran the Grim Reaper?

Lane paced, waiting for Dan Holley to arrive. Toni tried to pretend all was well, but it was extremely difficult to concentrate on the mending she had in her lap when her fingers kept trembling too much to hold the needle.

"When he gets here, I'm going out to the hills with you," Lane said.

Toni frowned. "It's a long way from the house. Are you sure your leg is up to it?"

Lane spun around. "Stop it!" he said, hating the fact that he was shouting at her. "Stop using my welfare to dodge the issue we have here, lady. My leg is fine. If it hurts tonight, then it hurts. It's not going to fall off just because I walked too far."

"You don't have to yell," she muttered. "I'm not deaf."

"Maybe not, but you're the most muleheaded woman I've ever known."

Toni's lower lip jutted mutinously. She glared, and received a similar look in return. The situation was saved by Sheriff Holley's arrival. When Justin pulled in behind him and parked, Toni could do nothing but mutter. "Oh, good grief, just what I need, more men to tell me what to do."

She inhaled, then counted to ten before opening the door. There was no other way to get through what was about to occur.

Lane heard what she'd said, although he was pretty certain that she hadn't meant him to. He considered her quiet complaint and then frowned.

Looking at the situation from her point of view, it probably did seem unfair. On the one hand, everyone assumed she could take care of herself and left her alone without help or company to do just that. On the other hand, let some trouble occur, and advice came from every corner, telling her how to mind her own business.

Hindsight was sometimes an unfortunate thing. It left a person with the memory of having made a big error in judgment, and no way of changing the past. Lane knew now that he should have asked Toni what she intended to do, instead of charging to the rescue. But taking over was a habit too deeply ingrained within him for him to stop without a reason.

However, he reminded himself, there was always tomorrow, then he stopped short at the thought. Tomorrow he would get his stitches out. The day after that, he would be gone. For him, there was no tomorrow. At least not where Toni was concerned.

"Damn it to hell," Lane muttered, jamming his hands into his pockets to keep himself from putting them through a wall.

But cursing gave him no satisfaction or relief. There was nothing he could do but play out the hand that life kept dealing; right now, that meant retracing Toni's steps into the hills. And, he reminded himself, taking backup.

He'd lost his gun during the plane crash, but thanks to Reese and Palmer, he now had another one. He'd never been on duty without one, and so he wore the gun out of habit. When he stepped out onto the porch and unconsciously took a stand behind the woman on the steps, it felt right to be armed. Without knowing, his heart had done what his mind had refused to accept. He was already behind her...all the way.

Toni leaned against the corral and watched the men combing the area where she'd found the calf.

The animal was gone now. Somehow, she wasn't surprised. *I knew there was someone in the woods, and I was right. It had to be the Sumters after something to eat.*

"Calf's gone," Justin reaffirmed, then leaned against the corral beside his sister. "Damn those Sumters, anyway. Someone ought to run them plumb out of the country, or lock them up for life, whichever comes first."

Toni frowned. Men's attitudes about things differed greatly from women's. There was no doubt about it. The way she looked at it, using energy on hate was wasted when a more viable solution to the Sumter problem could be found, such as relocating Samuel's family to a city where the younger children could go to school regularly, and where the older ones could find work. However, logic and reasoning did not necessarily go hand in hand with Justin's sense of justice.

"Yes, Justin. I know that the calf is gone."

"Are you going to press charges?" he asked.

"Against whom? I didn't see anyone. I can't blame someone on suspicion alone."

He hit the post with the flat of his hand. "That's stupid," he said. "You know who did it. You're just too damned softhearted to say so."

Toni leaned forward until she and Justin were eye to eye. "That's just it, Justin, I don't know who did it. No more than you know what happened to your chickens and Bobby's dog. Did you press charges against the Sumters for that?"

He flushed and looked away. "Judy wouldn't let me."

She rolled her eyes. "Thank God for the sanity of women. She saved you from making a bigger fool of yourself than normal."

Before more than words could fly, Lane stepped between the two and put his hand on Toni's shoulder. "You were right about being followed out of here. We saw a set of footprints that ran parallel to yours. Whoever it was didn't follow you long, but he did follow you."

Toni shuddered. The thought of being pursued made her sick.

"Thank God those young whelps of Sumter's changed their minds," Justin said. "If you hadn't come up here by yourself, none of this would have happened."

Toni snorted softly. "What on earth is wrong with you, Justin? The calf was still dead, whether I found it or not. At least I saved the cow and called the law, which is more than you did when your dog was killed."

Sheriff Holley walked up in time to hear the last of what Toni had just said. He frowned as he poked his notebook into his shirt pocket. "What's this, Justin? Someone killed your dog?"

"And made off with some of his chickens," Lane added, then walked out of the argument to stare thoughtfully into the tree line, trying to imagine someone watching Toni from some concealed vantage point.

Something about this didn't feel right. And he thought of his missing prisoner. Even though they claimed that the Sumters were just harmless and hungry, the fact that Toni had been followed was contrary to someone's simply thieving. Stalking a victim was the approach an attacker would take. Someone who intended further harm would follow, whereas a sneak thief would run in the opposite direction in frantic flight, hoping to get away from the scene of the crime. Surely, he thought, Dan Holley could check this out and warn the Sumter family against further trespassing. He needed assurance that it was actually the Sumters who were responsible.

"We're ready to go," Toni said.

The sound of her voice startled Lane. He hadn't even heard her walk up. He turned, and when he saw the weariness in her eyes, he reached out and took her hand in his.

"You got lucky today, honey," he said softly. "Please don't take any more unnecessary chances. Until this mess with your neighbors is put to rest, don't go anywhere on foot, okay?" When she frowned and started to argue, Lane's voice softened. "I'm not telling you, I'm asking. Okay? I don't want to get a phone call from someone one day telling me that you've disappeared."

Her eyes widened as she worried the edge of her lower lip between her teeth. Lane hated seeing the look of shock on her face, knowing that he'd been the one to put it there.

"I didn't mean to scare you. I just want you to be careful. I care about your welfare, Toni Hatfield, just like you cared about mine. Understand?"

She nodded. *Oh, Lane, I understand all too well. You feel an obligation, and I want a commitment instead.*

"Come on," he said, giving her hand a tug. "Let's get

back to the house. Reese and Palmer should be back by now. I want to talk to them before they leave tomorrow. Maybe they have news about the search for Emmit Rice's body. That's one identification I would willingly make.''

She nodded, and for the moment she was willing to let someone else make some decisions. The day had gotten seriously on her nerves.

"Toni, I'm going to talk to Livvie Sumter," the sheriff said. "I know you're not pressing charges, but she's still got to know that I won't stand for any more of this going on in my county."

Lane and Toni walked hand in hand out of the clearing, leaving Sheriff Holley and Justin to follow close behind. Once they arrived at their vehicles, the sheriff and Justin drove off. But not before Toni caught the scowl her brother sent her as he directed his gaze to her and Lane's clasped hands.

Within a few minutes of returning to the house, Toni found herself alone with Lane. Reese and Palmer had not returned. Memories of her flight into Lane's arms, and the way that he'd held her, kept colliding with the facts. And the facts were that he'd simply acted the way a friend would have by comforting her in a time of stress and that he'd meant nothing by it. Acceptance of that truth was what would get her past the next few days. She looked everywhere and at everything except him, and hated that she felt out of place in her own home.

Lane didn't know what was wrong, but if history had anything to do with it, it was bound to be something that he'd done.

"Lady, if you don't stop fiddling and pacing, you're going to run us both up a wall."

She blushed and looked away, then without thinking took down her hair, intent on putting it back up again, only in a more sedate fashion. The trek up the hill, then back down again, had played havoc with her constantly unruly curls.

With her arms raised above her head, the thrust of her breasts against her shirt was unmistakable and impossible to ignore. Lane gritted his teeth and told himself to look away.

And he might have been able to do that if she hadn't dropped the elastic band for her hair on the ground.

"Shoot," she muttered, then bent over to look at the floor, trying to locate the band that seemed lost against the pattern on the rug.

Lane would have offered to help, but he couldn't find the will to move away from the sight of all that hair falling down around her shoulders, or the way her jean shorts had suddenly conformed to her rear when she'd bent down. He had a sudden wish to see her standing before him wearing nothing but the smile on her face, and then he shuddered and walked out of the room before his body gave him away.

When she wandered through the kitchen moments later, he had his lust well under control. It had even crossed his mind to offer to help her fix the evening meal, until he turned, looked into her eyes and got lost in the memory all over again.

He was staring, and it made her nervous. In the past, when men had looked at her too long, they'd inevitably found fault with something about her. Because of that, she turned away and missed seeing the blatant look of want that spread across Lane Monday's face.

"I'm going to fix pork chops," she said. "If you have an objection, speak now or forever hold your peace."

"Whatever you fix will be fine," he said. "I'm going to go outside now."

He walked out after that odd remark, leaving Toni standing in the kitchen with no explanation for his behavior other than what she'd already assumed.

I must look awful, she thought. *And earlier, I clung to him like cockleburs. He probably thinks I'm going to do it all over again and embarrass him.* She'd made him uncomfortable. That had to be it.

Tears pricked at the backs of her eyes. But Toni swiped them away and headed for the cabinet to take down a bowl. Crying over impossibilities was a waste of time and effort. Why should she care what Lane Monday thought about her? In two days he would be gone.

But the longer she peeled and stirred and cooked, the louder the voice inside her cried out. *When he leaves, it will be too late to try having a baby. Do something, Toni, before it's too late.*

"But how?" she moaned. "How do I entice a man to make love with me when he can't even stand the sight of my face?"

"Those sure are good pork chops, Toni," Reese said as he helped himself to another without waiting for an invitation.

"They're going to keep dragging the river, aren't they?" Lane asked. The need to hear positive information about the fate of Emmit Rice was eating Lane up. He had no interest in food.

"We're dragging everything, including our tails between our legs," Palmer replied, and dipped a second helping of mashed potatoes onto his plate before passing the bowl to Reese.

Toni propped her elbows on the table and rested her chin in the palms of her hands. Her dark eyes went from one man to the other, gauging their interest in what was going on at the table as opposed to what had gone on during the continuing search. Lane hadn't eaten anything, and the other two men couldn't talk for eating. What a day this had been.

"Hell, Lane." Reese flushed as he remembered the lady's presence and grinned at Toni before continuing. "Excuse my language, but we may never find Emmit Rice, and you know it. That was a hell of big flood, and that creek empties out into one long river."

Lane stared down at the half-eaten food on his plate and tried to imagine never knowing Emmit Rice's fate. It didn't sit well with him at all.

"Okay," he muttered, tracing a pattern on the tablecloth that Toni had spread to hide her patchwork on the broken table. "I know that, but I don't like it. How about if we call back the men and the dogs and have them take a second run-through in the hills. Maybe see if they can come up with any new—"

"What the hell's wrong with you?" Reese dropped his fork in his plate and leaned back in the chair, his expression just shy of disbelief. "If the searchers came up empty three days ago, why would you think they would find something now? What is it you're not saying?"

Lane couldn't look at Toni when he said it, but he couldn't live with himself unless it was out in the open. He had to admit his worst fear aloud.

"I'm not saying anything specific," Lane told him. "But until I see Emmit Rice's body, I'm not going to believe that he's dead."

"Why not?" Palmer asked, sounding stunned. "It's nothing short of a miracle that you survived. There is no earthly indication that Emmit Rice crawled out of that plane ahead of you. Damn it, Monday, you heard me tell you yesterday that they're not even sure who's in what bag. They're still trying to make positive identifications."

Toni's chin slipped from her hand as her eyes grew rounder. Her mouth slackened, and her slow, unsteady gasp was all the indication they needed that this conversation should have been saved for somewhere other than the dinner table.

She knew the men were staring at her; she could feel their sympathetic looks. They'd spoken about human beings as if their remains were just pieces of meat. With that thought, she looked down at the pork chops, then back up at the men, and knew that she was going to have to leave the table. She held her breath and got to her feet. She needed some air. Now. The images that Chuck Palmer had just conjured were too vivid to ignore.

"Well, hell, Palmer. While you were at it, why didn't you just pass around the pictures you took at the scene for our viewing enjoyment?" Lane growled, then watched with regret as Toni slipped from the room.

Palmer shrugged. "Sorry. I didn't think. I sometimes forget that she's not one of us. Besides, she's so competent and cool, I didn't figure it would bother her."

Lane pushed back his chair and stood. "Why the hell not? She's a woman, and a civilian, to boot. The ordinary housewife is not usually faced with this sort of conversation."

"She's not a housewife," Palmer muttered.

And she'll never be ordinary, Lane thought. *But she damn sure ought to be someone's wife.* He left Reese and Palmer and went to find Toni.

Someone's wife. Someone's wife...but not mine. "Oh, damn," Lane muttered.

Caring wasn't part of the plan. It was supposed to be: Remove stitches. *Find a way to say goodbye to Toni Hatfield.* Pack my bag. *Remember why loving the second time around isn't wise.* Get on the plane. *Don't think about the woman I'm leaving behind.* Put the episode behind me. *But not in this lifetime.*

He caught her on her way out the front door. "Toni, I'm sorry we upset you."

She turned. Framed by the doorway and the dusky evening shadows in the yard behind her, she watched as Lane moved toward her from across the room, and felt the world growing smaller with every heartbeat. He was so big that he dwarfed everything and everyone around him. And yet the look on his face was full of regret and tenderness. Her breath caught on a sob. That tenderness was going to be her undoing.

Lane heard the catch in her breath, and regretted the fact that, once again, they had caused her distress.

"Palmer wasn't thinking." He shrugged. "Or better yet, that's exactly what he was doing, thinking aloud. Only not about your feelings. He should have been more careful."

His hand cupped her face, intending to give comfort. But when her fingers traced the shape of his hand, he forgot what he'd been about to say. All he saw was the look of horror in her eyes.

She didn't mean to, but when he'd touched her, instinctively she'd returned the gesture. They had talked about death in the same breath as they'd complimented her on the pork chops, allowing no more consequence for one than the other.

She didn't understand how they could separate their feelings from their work. Something like that would destroy her, just like the crash that had nearly destroyed Lane Monday. It was that thought which made her reach out, needing to feel proof of the life he'd come so close to losing.

And what better way to feel life than to touch the center of its existence. Toni's fingers went from his hand toward his chest. Her gaze was centered on the place above his rib cage where she knew his heart continued to beat. Her fingers shook, her legs trembled, but she needed to feel the life he'd so nearly lost.

"It could have been you." Toni closed her eyes and sighed as the rock-hard rhythm of his heart vibrated against the palm of her hand. "Thank God that it wasn't."

Lane almost didn't hear her words. Her voice seemed broken, barely above a whisper. And when her hand flattened against the wall of his chest, splaying across his heart, the look on her face nearly broke his heart.

He wanted to hold her but knew that would be a mistake. He needed to take away her pain, but instead he faced the fact that he would not always be around for her next pain, or the next.

"Have mercy," he groaned, unable to move.

Toni blinked, then shuddered and looked up. The muscles in his face appeared to have been chiseled from stone. His mouth was grim; his eyes narrowed against revealing too much emotion. She felt the heat from his body on her palm, and knew a sense of loss so profound that she could not speak. Instead, she simply dropped her hand, shook her head and walked out the door, leaving Lane to do as he chose.

What he wanted to do was follow her into the night and claim the woman and her heart without further delay. What he did was walk away. He'd seen too much of the woman she was to be able to hold her, then let her go. And let her go he must. For there was a line in their relationship that he must not cross…could not cross…and still hope to survive.

Toni knew when she walked off the porch steps that Lane

would not follow. She'd seen the expression on his face go blank and felt him shut off his emotions as plainly as if she'd been slapped.

"Why can't I get this right?" she muttered, unaware of the tears streaming down her cheeks. "Why am I so stupid? I know I disgust him, and yet I keep setting myself up for these falls."

She laughed, but stopped when it came out a sob. Instead, she lifted her face to the starlit sky. "Help me," she whispered. "Just until he's gone. Then I promise I will help myself."

A breeze lifted the curls from her neck, then cupped the fabric of her shirt to her body like a jealous lover. Crickets sounded in the nearby grass while a whippoorwill cried in a nearby tree. Down the ravine she heard a cow bawl, then a calf answer. Weak yellow light spilled out in squares from the curtained windows of her house and onto the dark ground below it like butter on burned toast. Familiar sights, familiar sounds. And Toni felt as if she were dying.

She buried her face in her hands and knew that she would never feel as empty as she felt at this moment, barren of everything in life that mattered. No man, no child, no life except her own. She felt the tears on her face, and at that moment, hated as she'd never hated before.

She hated herself for having been born, and every male that she'd ever known for not being man enough to see past the surface to the woman she was beneath.

"That does it," she muttered, and swiped angrily at the tear tracks. "I've never been a weak, sobbing female, and I'm not going to start now. Especially over a man. But, by God, I will take from him what I can get."

In that moment, new determination was born. If the opportunity came to use Lane Monday to father her child, she would—with no regrets. He'd made it perfectly clear that she wasn't his type, and that was okay. At least, it would be when she could think of him without tears and anger. But she had two more nights to find a way to make this happen, to find a way to make him want her. God willing, the chance would come, and with the chance, the child.

It had to.

Chapter 8

"Well, Mr. Monday, I'd say you're as good as new. Your bruises are nearly gone and your leg is healing on schedule. I'd say you're about ready to fly the coop."

"Oh, hell, Doc. Smile when you say the word *fly,*" Lane said, and surprised himself by being able to poke fun at what had happened to him.

From her seat in the waiting room, Toni heard Lane's laughter. She didn't know what had amused him, because nothing was funny to her. The loss of his stitches had finally cut the strings connecting him to her. Now there was no longer a reason for him to stay, and facing that fact was getting harder and harder for Toni to accept.

Why did I have to like him? Toni thought, and blinked back tears as she looked at her lap rather than let anyone see how she felt. *It isn't fair.*

She sighed. Her dream of having Lane's child was exactly that, a dream. How was she possibly going to set her plan in motion? *All I have is tonight. Short of throwing myself into his bed like a fool, it's over.*

The weight around her heart settled a little heavier. She knew that he was anxious to get home, and why shouldn't he be? He'd left his home over a week ago, expecting to be back that same day, and instead, wound up the sole survivor of a devastating plane crash.

While she was trying to regain a sense of self and dignity, the door to the examining room opened, and Toni instinctively looked up as Lane and Dr. Bennett emerged.

All they had done was remove some stitches, but Lane Monday walked out as if someone had removed the weight of the world from his shoulders. He moved with the confidence of a man who could whip snakes, fight bears and love a woman to the point of insanity. At that moment, Toni hated him for not loving her.

The smile on Lane's face froze as he looked at Toni. Her eyes were shimmering with unshed tears.

All of his joy at being pronounced fit and whole slowly died as he realized it also meant leaving her. Yes, he wanted to be well. And yes, he needed to be back in full swing in the department. He was good at what he did and took pride in that fact. But he hadn't counted on becoming attracted to the woman who had saved his life. Grateful, yes. In lust and near love, no.

"Take care, Mr. Monday," Dr. Bennett said, shaking Lane's hand.

"If you're ever in Tallahassee, give me a call. I'll save you a place beneath a palm tree and an extra-cold long-neck to go with it," Lane told the man.

The doctor grinned and gave him a thumbs-up before disappearing into the next examining room as Lane turned back to Toni. She looked like a child ready to cry. He would have liked nothing better than to put his arms around her and hug the sadness away, but the little he knew about women told him not to react to her mood unless she gave him permission.

"I'm ready when you are," he said.

Toni stood. *Ready? I will never be ready to tell you goodbye.*

When she walked past him and out the door without giving him time to play the gentleman, Lane suffered the slight in quiet. If he wasn't mistaken, he'd just received permission to react. He caught the door before it slammed shut in his face.

"Just what I like, a woman who speaks her mind," he said under his breath, and followed her to the sidewalk.

"Do you want to talk about it?" he asked as they neared her pickup.

When she would have ignored him, he grabbed her arm and then stopped, halting her momentum while he waited patiently for her to respond. Finally she had nowhere to look but at him.

"About what?" she asked.

"About whatever it is that's bothering you."

"Why, Marshal, whatever makes you think anything is bothering me?"

The sarcasm in her voice was impossible to miss. If he let himself, he could remember other times during the past week when he knew she would have let their relationship go farther than friendship. Lane had always been the one to call a halt, or refuse to take the next step toward changing it. And yet, for him, there was no other way. If Toni was resentful, he would have to live with that fact, because he couldn't live with himself knowing that he'd lied to a good woman by making promises he had no intention of keeping. And that was what moving their relationship beyond friendship would be. A lie.

"I don't know," he drawled. "Maybe it was the frown on your face, or it could have been the tears in your eyes that gave you away."

If someone had dropped a rock down her throat and into her stomach, it wouldn't have made any bigger impact than his accusation had.

"I wasn't crying," she muttered, and yanked her arm from his grasp.

"I didn't say you were crying, Antonette. I said that you

had tears in your eyes. If you want, we can pretend they were never there.''

She looked up at him and smiled wryly. ''Just like a man. It's easier to ignore things than to confront them, isn't it, Lane?''

Oh, damn, I think that I was right. She does hold it against me for being the one to hold back. But before he could think of how to respond, Sheriff Holley shouted at them from across the street.

''Hey, you two, wait up.''

Toni sighed, uncertain whether she felt relief or aggravation for the interruption. It was probably just as well that they'd been interrupted. Their conversation had nowhere to go but down.

''Don't think you're off the hook. This isn't finished between us,'' Lane growled as the sheriff jumped the curb and came huffing to a halt in front of them.

Finished? That's where you're wrong, Lane Monday. You can't finish something that never got started.

Toni did the best she could to hide her despair, but it was difficult. The feeling she had of impending doom was overwhelming. She wasn't off the hook and knew that better than he did. She was intent upon taking a part of this man from him, and keeping it when he left. That thought, and the fact that she didn't know how to make it happen, were killing her. She was dying by degrees; she just didn't know it yet.

And then the sheriff spoke up and ended her mental suicide. ''Hey, Toni, I'm glad I saw you two coming out of the doctor's office,'' he said. ''It saves me a trip out to your place.''

''Why?'' she asked. ''Have you learned something new about my calf?''

Holley shrugged. ''It's all in how you want to look at it.''

''How about from every angle?'' Lane said, then knew when Toni glared at him that he'd probably overstepped his bounds by insinuating that the sheriff hadn't done a thorough job.

Holley responded with a whoop of laughter. "Man, I like your style," he said. "You don't mess around, do you, boy?"

Lane had to grin. It had been years since anyone had had the nerve to call him boy. He'd outgrown the title long before he should have, simply because of his size.

"No, sir, I don't suppose I do," he replied. "So, what's up? Why were you coming to Toni's?"

It might have been the way Dan Holley didn't quite look her in the eye when he spoke, but Toni got the distinct impression that he wasn't entirely comfortable with what he was about to say.

"I talked to Livvie Sumter about her boys."

Before Toni could comment, Lane, as usual, took over the conversation and set her impatience on simmer all over again.

"Well, thank God," Lane muttered. "I hope to hell you told her to keep them off of other people's property, and I hope you told them the next time they think about frightening someone like they did Toni, they'll have to answer to an authority other than their mother."

Dan pursed his mouth as he worried the day-old whiskers on his chin. "That's just it," he said. "Those three oldest boys of hers, the ones who usually commit all the thievery, are gone. Livvie says they're in Nashville on a construction job." He shrugged, then looked Lane straight in the eye. "That part of her story checks out."

Toni watched a nerve jumping in Lane's cheek. Why did he keep worrying this thing to death? Unfortunately for all concerned, Samuel Sumter's children were not the only ones in the area capable of stealing.

"And?" Lane urged.

"She says Samuel's missing."

This time, Toni took the lead in the conversation and threw her hands up in disgust. "But, Dan, that's not news. He leaves her each time she has a baby, and we all know it. So it was probably Samuel who killed my calf, and not his boys. I'll bet if you look real hard, you'll find where he's camping. He's probably sulking because Livvie has to devote her attention to a new baby and not him. I think the man's a skunk.''

Dan grinned. ''I know what you think, Toni. You've made that perfectly clear more than once to anyone who will listen.''

Her eyes flashed, then darkened, while the sheriff smiled. Above everything else, she despised condescension. And when Lane's hand slid across her shoulder in companionable silence, he might as well have patted her on the head and said ''good dog,'' while he was at it, because that was exactly how she took it. It was, for Toni, the spark that lit her fuse.

''What's that for?'' she said, pushing his hand from her shoulder. ''And don't pretend to be on my side about anything, okay? I don't need to be babied. I can take care of myself. If I tell you Samuel Sumter probably stole my calf, then why can't I be right? Do you have any other suggestions that make more sense?''

His surprise turned to hurt, but was hidden by the lowering of his lashes. Then a flash of how unfair she was being to him turned it all to anger as he resisted the urge to shake her silly.

''Damn it, Toni, there is no my side or your side. You're the most aggravating, irritable female I've met in years. You would fry the hair off a cat and then wonder where it had gone. I touched your shoulder, not your butt. And believe me, it won't happen again.''

He turned away without giving her time to argue as he refocused his attention on the sheriff.

Toni was furious with herself and with Lane. She was taking all of her disappointment out on a man who didn't deserve it, but for the life of her, she couldn't seem to stop.

''Darn man,'' she muttered. Unwilling to stay and listen while they continued to ignore her presence, she went to the pickup and missed hearing the rest of the conversation.

Lane heard her mumble, and would have liked nothing better than to bend her over his knee. It took everything he had to concentrate on what he needed to ask. He wouldn't—

couldn't—leave Toni alone on her farm without knowing all
there was to know.

It was that instinct alone that made him a good lawman
and a formidable enemy. Willing himself not to watch her
walk away, he gave the sheriff his full attention.

"Reese and Palmer left this morning, so I'm out of touch
with the downriver search for Emmit Rice's body. Are there
any reports?" Lane asked.

Holley frowned. "No. But I assure you that when and if I
get one, you'll be one of the first to know what it says." He
squinted slightly as he tilted his head to get a better look at
Lane's face. "You know what?"

"What?" Lane asked.

"I think something's going through that bulldog mind of
yours that you aren't telling me. Are you of a mind to share?"

Lane shrugged. Saying anything before all the facts were
in was not his way. "There's nothing to tell," he said. "I'm
just checking every aspect of this mess before I leave."

"And when would that be?" he asked.

"Tomorrow," Lane said, squinting his eyes to gaze at the
jet trail in the sky overhead. It was easier than facing what
he'd just said.

"So if you hear anything, give me a call," Lane continued.
"You have my number at the office."

"I'll do just that," the sheriff said, then walked away.

Lane crawled into the passenger side of the pickup and
slammed the door behind him. A long, silent minute passed
without any sound or movement from either one of them. And
then they both chose the same instant to say their piece.

"I'm sorry..."

They spoke in unison, then stopped at the same time. The
coincidence of their mutual apology was too odd to ignore.
Toni sighed and leaned back in the seat while Lane grinned.

"You first," she said, and tried to ignore how small the
interior of the cab felt with him taking up over half the seat.

"Lady, you won't catch me in that again," Lane told her
with a chuckle. "No way. Ladies first."

She grinned in spite of her determination not to give him an inch. *Oh, damn you, Lane Monday. How can I stay mad and protect my heart if you keep behaving like this?*

"I overreacted. I'm sorry," she said, and knew it sounded grudging, but it was the best that she could do without throwing her arms around him and begging him to stay.

"Apology accepted," he replied, wanting her to look at him, but he could tell by the way she kept biting her lower lip that she wasn't about to do that. "I shouldn't have yelled at you. And I didn't mean to hurt your feelings about anything."

Toni wanted to cry. Her feelings were so miserable that an apology was never going to be enough to take away the pain. But from Lane, it was all she was going to get.

"You're forgiven, too," she said.

"Well, thank God," Lane muttered, and tried not to resent her halfhearted apology. That was his thanks for behaving like a gentleman, a sore-as-a-boil woman who wouldn't give him the time of day.

But when she neither moved nor made an effort to start the engine, he didn't have the guts to ask her why. If she had another purpose for coming to town besides bringing him to see the doctor, she was going to have to reveal it herself.

Toni was sick with anxiety. The thought of tomorrow was agonizing. Lane had consumed exactly seven days of her life, and when he left, he would be taking her heart with him. And while she had faced his rejection too many times to hope that he might actually care for her, she was having difficulty giving up her dream of bearing this man's child.

How do I ask him? How does a woman say…sleep with me and give me a baby.

Toni groaned, then hit the steering wheel with the flat of her hand, aware that as she did, Lane visibly jerked in reflex to the action.

"So, how does your leg feel?" she asked as if she hadn't just made her frustration clear.

Lane gawked. That was, without doubt, the most inane

question she'd asked him since they'd met. He knew good and well that the state of his leg was not what was on her mind at the moment.

"It feels fine," he said. *Unlike you, I might add.* But he wisely kept the postscript to himself.

She gritted her teeth, then nodded. "Good. That's really good, I'm glad."

Lane turned to face her. "Toni..."

It was more a warning than a question. She knew he wasn't buying her conversational feint any more than she was.

"If you're through here, we may as well head back home. I've got all sorts of chores," she told him.

He sighed, then turned to look out the window. She wouldn't say what she was thinking, and he'd already made up his mind to keep his feelings for her to himself, so there was no point in dwelling on what each of them was unwilling to say.

"Fine. It'll give me time to pack," he said. "I hope when Reese and Palmer took off this morning, they left me their rental car as they'd promised. Otherwise, I'll have to beg another ride from you tomorrow when it's time for me to leave."

It was the wrong thing for him to have said.

Damn you! Damn you, Lane Monday. All you can think about is leaving!

With an angry twist of her wrist, Toni turned the ignition key and brought the engine to life, gunning it, backing up and then slamming the gears into drive before Lane had time to react. When they turned the corner that led out of town on less than four wheels, he braced himself with his hands against the dashboard and growled.

"I hadn't planned on being airborne quite this soon."

Toni reacted, but not in the way he'd expected. No sooner had he said the words than her foot hit the brake. She pulled over to the side of the road, got out of the pickup and walked around to the passenger's side without looking up. She opened his door.

"You drive," she said quietly. "I don't think I feel so good."

"Damn it, Antonette, don't do this. Not to me, or to yourself."

It was then that she looked up. Her expression was bland, her voice low and controlled. Only her eyes, dark and nearly blinded from pain, gave her away.

"I don't know what the hell you're talking about," she said quietly. "I'm doing nothing except asking you to drive."

He swore and scooted across the seat. When she crawled into the spot he'd just vacated, he would have sworn that he saw her hand linger on the place where he'd just sat. But when he looked again, he decided he must have been mistaken. She was busy buckling up her seat belt and digging into her purse.

They made the rest of the drive home in total silence.

Toni went about her chores like a woman in mourning. Lane watched from a distance as she checked on the livestock, then wisely gave her space when they'd returned to the house. While he suspected that she harbored feelings for him, he had no way of knowing that.

And that was the death of her dream for a child. It was, for Toni, over. She didn't know how to flirt, and she knew that she didn't have the guts to just ask him for sex. There would be no time left for happenstance to intervene because tomorrow he would be gone.

By nightfall, she had slipped into an "ignore the devastation and it will go away" mood.

She might be fooling herself, but she wasn't fooling Lane. Her misery, like his, was visible. One had only to look at the set of her jaw, or the stance that she took when she believed no one was around, as if she were bracing herself for a mortal blow, to know that she was hurting.

As for Lane, his agony was of a different sort. He'd already faced the fact that he was drawn by more than debt to the woman who'd saved his life. He'd held her and kissed her. He'd tasted woman and wanted more.

Tonight would be their last night together. While it was only their second night alone in the old farmhouse, it was going to be the longest eight hours of his life.

Sleeping wasn't an option. He needed to maintain his determination to leave her as intact as the day that they had met. The thought of pursuing intimacy with her was overshadowed by his admiration for her as a woman. He could not take what she offered and give nothing back. And nothing was all that he had to give.

And so they sidestepped each other all evening, and laughed uneasily at things that were not funny, and when it came time to go to bed, they parted without saying goodnight. It was far too close to saying goodbye.

Toni lay on her side, dry-eyed and aching, and clutched the sheet beneath her chin as she rolled herself into a ball.

I will not cry. I will not cry.

When she tried to smooth out the sheet and get some sleep, she realized that it was nothing but a wad, and yanked it off of the bed in a fit of anger, throwing it onto the floor before falling flat on her stomach across the bed, daring herself to rest.

In spite of the air conditioner humming in the window, her nightgown felt hot and stuck to her skin in limp persistence. She untwisted it, then flopped around some more, trying to find a comfortable spot.

Before she knew it, she'd rolled from her bed and torn the offending gown over her head, sending it to the same place that she'd sent her sheet. The floor. But the moment cool air hit her skin, she shuddered. It was too much like a man's breath upon her body to bear.

"Damn you, Lane Monday," she groaned, and threw herself back onto the bed, naked as the day she was born. "Damn you for not being worthless enough to use me. Damn you for having morals. Any other man would have been at this door days ago, whether he liked me or not, just because he could."

She closed her eyes, doubled her fists and resisted the urge to cross the hall on her own. But she would not stand naked before a man who did not want her, no matter what. Bearing the rejection from that encounter—and she was certain that there was bound to be one—would be impossible for her to endure.

And so she lay, and finally slept while Lane fought devils of his own.

Since the crash, his body had healed in so many ways. Seven days had passed and he was almost as good as new. And yet the scars he still bore from his first wife's death were as sore as they'd been five years ago. He couldn't get past the thought of loving like that, then losing again. It had nearly destroyed him. Lane knew himself well enough to realize that he would not survive a similar loss a second time.

And while common sense might dictate that falling in love did not go hand in hand with dying, Lane's heart was too scarred to trust what his mind might say. All he could do was hope to hell that morning came before he lost all sense of reason and took what he knew Toni would give.

The sun was up, which was more than could be said for Lane or Toni. It was the telephone that woke them, and sent them dashing into the hall on reflex to answer.

It was hard to say who was more stunned, Lane for seeing her wearing nothing more than a robe that she held together with the clutch of one hand, or Toni for having to endure one last sight of all that man wearing nothing but a pair of white cotton briefs.

"The phone's ringing," Lane said as he realized that answering a phone in a house that didn't belong to him was overstepping his bounds.

Toni's voice shook as she turned away. "I hear it," she muttered, and yanked the receiver on the fifth ring.

"Hello!"

"Toni, this is Dan Holley. Did I wake you?"

She didn't answer, couldn't answer, because Lane was on

his way back into his room, probably to get a pair of pants, and she was too busy watching him leave.

"Toni?"

She jerked, and then stared at the receiver. She'd forgotten that it was in her hand. "What?" she asked.

"If Lane is up, I would like to speak to him. I have some news he's been waiting for."

Toni pressed a finger across her lips to keep them from trembling before she spoke. She took a deep breath, and when she was certain that she had her emotions well under control, she spoke. "He's up. Hang on." She let the phone drop on the table without saying goodbye to Dan.

"It's for you," she shouted in the direction of Lane's room, and then went back into her room, slamming the door behind her.

Lane left his room and grabbed the phone, then balanced it against his ear with his shoulder as he finished buttoning his jeans. He didn't have the guts to get caught that near-naked around Toni Hatfield again. The next time, he would not be able to walk away.

"This is Monday," he said.

Dan Holley spoke. "They pulled a rather badly decomposed body out of the Pigeon River right after daylight this morning."

Lane felt a grin coming. He'd waited a week to hear this news. And the fear that he'd refused to name began to disappear. At least this part of his worry was over.

"Thank God," Lane said, and leaned against the wall.

"They're doing an autopsy as soon as possible," Dan told him. "Although down here, that may take anywhere from a week to a month. But it was a white male, and he was big. Really big."

"It's Rice. It has to be. He's the only whale we have on the missing-persons list."

Dan laughed aloud. "There sure wasn't any love lost between you two, was there?"

Lane closed his eyes, and thought of the hatred that he'd

seen on Rice's face. "No. He was bad all the way through. I can't say I'm sorry he's dead." He paused, pushing himself away from the wall to stare at the door between him and Toni before he thought to add, "Sheriff, thank you for calling. And when you get it, I'd like a copy of the autopsy report to close out my file."

"It's already yours," Dan said. "Have a safe flight."

Lane nodded as the line went dead. The sheriff hadn't needed a response to his request for Lane to have a safe flight. They both knew all too well how difficult it would be for Lane to take that first step onto a plane, and how much Lane was counting on a smooth, uneventful trip.

And then Toni's door opened. She stood, waiting for him to confirm the bits and pieces of what she'd overheard. But he was looking at her too intently for her peace of mind, and so she spoke first.

"They found him, didn't they?"

Lane nodded. "It looks like it," he replied.

"That's good," Toni said. "It's been bothering you, hasn't it?" And when she saw the way he was studying her face and the way her clothes fit her body, she prodded him back to the conversation at hand. "Not finding Emmit Rice, I mean."

Lane nodded again, and thought that if he looked hard enough, he would remember how long her legs were, hidden beneath her well-worn jeans, or how the fullness of her breasts coerced the knit on her shirt to give way.

The nervous swipe of her hand across her hair made him remember how thick and soft the curls were to the touch. And when she gave him a nervous look, he got the full force of eyes so dark that they seemed black.

"A lot of things have been bothering me since the crash. That was one of them."

Now! Say something now! But Toni couldn't find the words. Lane walked back into his room to finish dressing, and the moment was lost.

"Stupid," she muttered beneath her breath, and stalked toward the kitchen to prepare breakfast. "It was a stupid thought. I can't ask it, and that's that."

But the idea wouldn't go away, and Toni had to face the fact that her dream hadn't died a full death. It was still lingering in her mind. Obviously, she was reluctant to give up what life it still had.

Lane was halfway through his second cup of coffee when Toni put down her spoon, replaced the lid on the jelly and pinned him with a bottomless gaze and a question he couldn't ignore.

"Are you packed?" she asked.

He froze with the cup against his lip. It hurt to hear the words, but the look on her face was more difficult to bear. He set the cup down without taking a drink, then folded his hands in his lap to hide the fact that they shook. It was nearly time to leave and he hadn't reconciled himself with the knowledge that when he awoke tomorrow, he would be thousands of miles away from Toni Hatfield and Chaney Creek.

"No," he said.

"You don't want to miss your plane," she reminded him, and began stacking dishes into the sink.

Oh, yes, I do. But he didn't say it. Instead, he stood and walked from the room without further comment. He didn't have it in him to debate.

When she could no longer hear his footsteps, she went limp and grabbed on to the sink for support.

"Oh, God," she pleaded. "Just get me through this."

Half an hour later, she was still saying prayers and begging for a reprieve that hadn't come. And Lane was walking toward the door with suitcase in hand, a well and whole man compared to the one she'd dragged into her house during the night of the storm.

"Take care," she said. "Drive safely."

He turned at the doorway, almost hating her for being able to maintain composure now when his was nearly nonexistent.

And then he looked into her eyes and saw that her misery so nearly matched his own that it made no difference.

"Come here," he said, and held out his arms.

She didn't mean to, but resisting his offer was too difficult. With a soft sob, and then a quiet sigh, she walked into his embrace and settled her cheek against his chest. It was like being wrapped in steel, then cushioned by the promise of gentleness waiting.

"I will miss you, even though you are one bossy man," Toni said, trying to make a joke out of it, but failing miserably.

Lane tightened his embrace and felt her willingly readjust herself to the lack of space. Just as with everything else she did, she gave without asking for anything in return. And yet, if she were to ask a favor, he knew what it would be. *Just don't say it, love. Don't say what I see in your eyes.*

"I'll miss you, too," he told her. "More than you'll ever know. And I don't know how I'll ever be able to thank you for saving my life."

Toni went still. Even her heart forgot to beat. This was it. He'd given her an opportunity that she couldn't ignore. What he did when she asked was another thing entirely. But at least, she told herself, she would have made the effort.

"I do," she said.

He grinned and moved back far enough to see her expression. He should have known that she would still be trying to take control. It was the Toni he knew and loved.

Loved? Impossible! Where had that thought come from? *I haven't fallen in love with her, damn it!* he thought. But the shock of his realization was nothing compared to what she said next.

"You could make love to me. Just once. Just for fun."

Chapter 9

She kept talking because she knew that the silence that was bound to ensue would destroy her. She'd seen the shock on his face and felt the tension in his body increase tenfold.

"It's no big deal," she said, trying to smile. "Everyone does it, all the time. It's what they call recreational sex, right?"

Oh, hell, Lane thought. *How do I answer and not lie? My God, I would like nothing more than to take you to bed, woman. But walking away afterward might kill us both.* He heard himself mouthing a platitude that even he didn't believe.

"Now, Toni, you haven't thought this through. You're not the kind of woman to have casual sex."

"Oh, but I have thought it through," she said brightly. "And I'm not a virgin, you know. I've already tried it. Sex, I mean. Twice. In high school. It wasn't much, but I thought I might give it another chance."

There was too much effervescence in her voice. She could hear it and hated that it almost sounded like begging. *Damn you, Lane. Either tell me no, or shut the door.*

My God! She tried it twice? Lane pondered in awe.

The implications were nearly staggering. She was as near to a virgin as a woman could be and still call herself experienced. Lane fought the urge to take her in his arms. As badly as he wanted to comply with her wishes, doing so would only end up hurting them both. And then something occurred to Lane that he figured would end this conversation before it brought them to their knees.

"I don't have any protection with me."

Toni swallowed a lump in her throat. The last obstacle in the conversation had just been broached. It was up to her to get past it without giving away her intentions.

"Oh, that! I'm prepared to handle that on my own." She held her breath, hoping that he would assume what most men would, that she was taking, or using, something that would prevent pregnancy. What she'd meant, though, was that she was prepared to handle whatever came of their union on her own.

Damn you, woman. When will you stop? I haven't got it in me anymore to say no.

"I don't think I've ever had a better offer," Lane said, and cupped her face with his hands, branding her cheeks and mouth with short but gentle kisses that said what he could not.

Toni laughed through her tears. She knew it had been a long shot, but she'd been willing to give it a try. Now there was only one thing she could do to save face—for herself as well as for him.

"But you'll pass, right?" She laughed again, and spun out of his arms, certain that if he touched her again, she would start screaming and never stop. "It's no big deal," she said. "It was just an idea. I thought if you were willing, I would get in a little practice for the next man I fish out of Chaney Creek. But…" She shrugged. "As my daddy used to say, 'that's life.'"

Lane hurt for her in so many places that he wasn't sure he would be able to walk away. The tears in her eyes were vivid.

The laughter on her lips was a sham and he knew it. How had he let this happen?

"You aren't a woman for one-night stands, Antonette. You deserve better, and you deserve a better man than me. Don't give up on yourself. You're a hell of a woman."

"Thank you, Mr. Monday. You're the first man to say so, but I'm sure you won't be the last. Take care, and drive safely."

She shut the door in his face before it was too late to hide her shame, and did not watch as he drove away.

As Lane drove, the miles passed without notice. He was vaguely aware of obeying traffic signals and the laws of the road, but all he kept seeing was the pain on Toni's face. And all he could feel was the way she'd spun out of his arms with a smile on her face that he didn't believe.

That memory blended with the past into a collage of the days and nights that he'd spent under her roof and under her care and attention, until he couldn't separate the good from the bad. He couldn't remember her laughter, for seeing the tears he'd left in her eyes. He couldn't remember a single thing that had given her joy, for thinking of what had hurt her.

Sick with guilt, he kept remembering the way her brother had belittled her womanly traits, as well as the times that Lane, himself, had told her no, or turned her away, when every indication she'd given had said that she wanted more. What must she think of herself if every man who knew her took and took, but was unwilling to give?

"That was damned noble of me," Lane muttered as he continued driving toward the Knoxville airport and the airplane that would ultimately take him home. "But just what did I prove? And worse yet, what did my behavior prove to her?"

He swerved to miss a dog that had run across the road, swearing as he came to a shaky halt at the side of the road. Either he got his focus back on the trip, or he would wind up

going home the same way that Bob Tell and the rest of the
passengers and crew of the plane had done. In a body bag.

Just once. Just for fun.

With one eye on the time and the other on the intermittent
cars on the road, Lane tried to ignore the haunting voice and
pulled back into the traffic flow, doing everything that he
knew how to do to concentrate on driving, not on the woman
he'd left behind.

I've tried it twice. It wasn't much.

He groaned. How could a woman get to be twenty-nine
years old and stay that…the only word that came to mind was
untouched? And as soon as he thought it, he knew the answer.
He'd been a witness to the reason more than once himself.

She'd been the baby of her family, the one who had stayed
behind to care for the aging parent while everyone else had
moved away, married and set up separate households of their
own. She'd been insulated from social contact by life itself.
Add to that the constant feedback from one brother, maybe
more, who'd reminded her continuously that it was her size
and her capability that were the worthy traits, not the fact that
she smelled good, had soft skin and a pretty face.

"Then I come along, after God knows how many other
men who'd shunned her," Lane mumbled, "full of myself
and with all the right answers for all the wrong reasons and
finished the job that they'd started."

He laughed bitterly, then stopped, startled by the ugliness
of the sound within the quiet interior of the car.

Practice for the next man who comes along.

"Like hell!"

It was hard for a man like Lane to face the fact that he
didn't want her practicing on anyone but him. Then how did
he reconcile his decision to remain unfettered by emotional
relationships to the fact that he wanted to make love to Toni
Hatfield in the worst possible way?

In his mind there was only one logical answer. He owed
her. The least he could do was pay his damned debt. And
maybe in so doing, get her out of his mind once and for all.

With that thought fixed firmly in his mind, he drove onto the shoulder of the road, and when the way was clear, headed back the same way that he'd come. Back to Chaney.

Back to Antonette.

It was nearly dusk when he turned down the long, winding road leading to her house. A red haze hung over the treetops, and the sun was all but hidden by the gathering clouds. It was fitting. He'd arrived on the day of a storm. He'd come back to her in the same fashion.

His stomach twisted, a nervous reaction to the fact that she just might pull that mud-dauber-packed shotgun on him again and this time pull the trigger. Why hadn't he thought about what this could do to her before returning to the scene of what might be a crime?

But he was too close to walk away, and too much in need to ignore the pull of knowing that the woman he wanted was only yards away on the other side of four walls.

He parked, then headed for the house with single-minded intent. He was as hard eyed and focused as he'd been on the day that they'd loaded three federal prisoners into a plane on a runway in Tallahassee, and almost as nervous as he'd been until he'd learned of Emmit Rice's demise.

He cleared both steps in one leap and made it to the front door in two. Without knocking, he hit the door with the flat of his hand, relishing the sharp bang it made against the wall before swinging shut behind him.

The sounds he heard in the back of the house suddenly stopped. He knew that she'd heard the door. If he'd frightened her, it was nothing compared to the way that he felt, waiting for her to appear. But when she came into the room, the expression on her face said it all.

She'd thought that it was Justin. It was always the way he entered the house. Loudly. Without knocking. So she wasn't prepared for the shock, or the man who was waiting for her.

"What happened?" she whispered, then started to shake. If he'd come back because he'd forgotten something, she was going to make a bigger fool of herself than she already had. "Did you forget something?"

He took off his jacket, unbuckled his gun and tossed them both on the chair near the door before he started toward her.

Toni didn't know whether to run backward or into his arms. The look on his face was one she'd never seen before.

"Yes, lady, I did. Something very important."

Oh, my Lord, Toni thought. *Now I'm going to have to endure this goodbye all over again.*

"Damn you, Lane, why did you come back?" She knew her voice was shaking, but she couldn't have steadied it to save her soul.

Lane stopped just inches away from her face. Even from where he stood, he could see her fear and feel her shaky breaths on his face.

"I came to pay a debt. And I came to make love to a woman. Just once. Just for fun."

Her expression faltered, but her stance never wavered. And when he started to touch her face, she stepped away, then turned, never looking back to see if he would follow.

Lane shook from the top of his head to the toes on his feet. It took all that he had to follow her down the hall. The leggy saunter and easy sway of her body beckoned him as no word ever could. He'd seen her acceptance, and knew that whatever deeper reason she'd had for asking, she would truly be satisfied with what he could give. Just once. Just for fun. If she could live with it, then surely to God, he could, too.

When he entered her room, she was taking off her clothes. From where he stood, he could see her fingers shaking. She was trying so hard to do this right.

"Don't, baby," he said softly. "Let me. It's part of the fun. Remember?"

She sighed, then dropped her hands to her sides. She didn't know beans about fun and remembered little of her other two times. They'd been with a boy; Lane was a man. As she watched him coming toward her from across the room, she wondered if she was woman enough to hold him. Even for one night. Even for fun.

"I'm scared, you know," she said.

Lane grinned and slid his arms around her, for the moment making no move to undress her any further. It was just like Toni to get straight to the point. What other woman would admit her fears as readily—or vocally—as she did? At the thought, he wondered if he had the guts to do the same.

"I know," he said, and kissed her temple, just above her right ear. She shuddered within his embrace and Lane sighed. "So am I, baby. So am I."

It was the best thing he could have said to her. At least on this level, they were even.

"What do I do next?" she asked. "Something for you...or to you? Or do I—?"

"Let's try something new," he said, and felt her stiffen in his arms. "I don't know if you're up to it, but I can guarantee that it'll make things better."

She bit her lip, hoping that he couldn't see her fear. Something new? She didn't even know the old stuff. But she'd been the one to ask, so it was now up to her to play along. And she wouldn't think of her deception. He thought she was protected from pregnancy. He thought it was for fun. Let him think what he wanted. She would take what she got, and be thankful for the chance.

"What is it that you want me to do?" she asked.

Lane lowered his head. Just before his lips centered on hers, he whispered, "Stop talking."

She almost smiled, and then his mouth descended and removed the last sane thought in her head.

Lane knew from the moment his arms went around her that there was no turning back. She was so much woman for a lot of man, and he didn't know where to start. But when he cupped her bottom, pulling her closer against his groin, then deepened the kiss they were sharing, he knew where to start.

She sighed, then shuddered, and leaned against the wall of chest before her, giving him all of her weight and anything else he might want. They'd shared a kiss before, but there had never been the promise or the passion as there was in this one.

His lips were firm, but his touch was tender, and when his hands cupped her hips and ground her against his obvious need, Toni's legs went weak at the thought of being one with this man and then giving him up without complaint. She'd prayed for a man to give her a child; hoping for more would be pushing her luck. So when he rocked against her hips in a beckoning motion, she followed along because she could not resist.

Lane broke the kiss with reluctance, moving his hands from her hips to her waist and then up. When they came to rest beneath the weight of her breasts, she moaned in spite of herself. She wanted more, so much more, and she wanted it now.

"Lane," she whispered. "Touch me, please. Pretend that you—"

"No more talking, remember? And, darlin', whatever I do, whatever we share, there will be no pretense. Not between us. Not ever. I do what I do out of want. I want to make love to you…with you. Never doubt that, or me."

Joy filled her heart. A sob wanted release, but there was no time because Lane had moved from her breasts to her shirt and was finishing what she had begun.

"Sweet," Lane groaned when she spilled from her bra into his hands. "You are so beautiful, lady. So very, very perfect."

His last word was a whisper against her skin as his head descended. When his mouth replaced his hands, and he began to settle small, searching kisses across the curve of her breasts, Toni's legs went out from under her.

"I don't think I can stand," she said, and felt weightless when he lifted her into his arms and laid her upon the bed.

"It doesn't matter," he said. "What we're about to do is better this way."

Her eyes widened as she watched him descend, and she was reminded of their first night together, handcuffed upon the floor. That night, she'd spent on top and then beneath this man with less results and far less pleasure than what she knew she was about to receive.

"You were well worth the wait," she whispered, and lifted her arms to pull him down.

He didn't know what she meant, and was too far-gone to care. Within the space of a minute, their clothes were on the floor. There was no room for anything else on the bed except the man and the woman who occupied it.

Somewhere between the door and the bed, the unhurried pace had gone out of the act. There was nothing left between them but a driving need to complete their union. And as badly as Lane wanted to be inside of her, he would not make the move until he'd watched and felt this woman come apart in his arms. Only then would he take what she'd offered. He'd come back to her in order to give.

Time ceased for Toni. There was nothing and no one in her world except the man who had taken command of her, body and soul. His touch was a plea that he didn't have to voice. When he urged, she followed, giving herself up to his skill and the need that he invoked.

His skin became slick with perspiration, his body hard with want. Yet his hands were strong and sure, skilled and gentle at teasing Toni into a mindless need she could not control. He watched her burn through a blue haze as he shook with desire. He'd seen her eyes grow black from passion, her lips go slack from shock. And when she'd arched uncontrollably beneath his circling fingers, he knew a kind of joy he'd thought he would never feel again. It was the pleasure of giving to someone special, to someone he loved.

"Oh! What are you...?" Toni gasped, and clutched his arms as something deep within her belly started to coil.

"Shh," Lane whispered, and increased the intensity of his caress. "Let it happen, darlin'."

Toni fought it. This wasn't the way it was supposed to be. She needed him with her. She was afraid to go alone.

"No," she cried. "Please, Lane, no! Not without you."

But it was too late to stop and too sweet to deny. She gave herself up to the fire and lost sight of everything but the spiral of heat that shattered low, then spread throughout her body in a constant, shimmering release.

"Oh, my darling," she moaned, and covered her face with her hands.

"Don't, baby," he said, and moved her hands with a gentle sweep of his arm. "It's not over yet. Make room for me. I need a place to come in."

Tears burned her cheeks as she shifted, and then he went from beside her to inside her, and she thought that she would faint from the joy. When he began to move in a powerful, rocking thrust, she held him fast with her arms and her heart, and took what he gave without promises or love. Because it was just once. Just for fun.

She met him thrust for mindless thrust, kiss for burning kiss. And when he shattered within her, she held him fast and tight and never minded that he saw her cry.

And then it began to rain.

Just once. That had been all that she had hoped for. Yet twice more before morning, Lane took her body, wholly and without reservation, loving her to glorious distraction and leaving more of himself behind than he knew, while storm clouds rumbled overhead. Yet each time they loved, Toni knew in her heart that all they were sharing was passion. There was no future and no whispered lies being said between them in the dark.

It was, for Toni, enough. She'd had him for one night. It was more than she'd ever dreamed. If God was willing, Lane would leave a piece of himself behind when he left. If not, she would survive because she had to.

But for Lane, the night had held a different kind of resignation. He'd given away something he'd never meant to share. He'd not only made love, but he'd fallen the rest of the way in love with a woman he refused to keep.

When the last kiss and the last drop of passion had been

spent between them, they slept, wrapped within each other's embrace, and dreamed of things that were not meant to be.

And when morning came, Toni awoke with the knowledge that the earth outside had been replenished, while she'd been drained of everything except despair.

She was alone in the bed and knew the reason why. There would be no reckless search through a house that she already knew would echo with emptiness, no frantic cry for a man who could not answer the call of his name. Lane had done what she'd asked, and more. He'd paid his debt a thousand-fold, and his last thought had still been for her. At least this time, she'd been spared the goodbye.

By noon Lane was boarding his plane in Knoxville, weary in more than body. His steps were slow and heavy like the beat of his heart. The flight attendant smiled, but Lane didn't notice her. The man in the seat next to him spoke, but Lane didn't hear him. When he buckled his seat belt, he realized that his hands were trembling and that he didn't even remember making the drive from Chaney to the airport in Knoxville. All he could see was the way that Toni had looked when he'd walked out of her room.

She'd slept curled on her side, with one arm flung out, as if searching for a man who was already gone, and the tracks of her tears were still drying upon the curve of her cheeks.

"Oh, God," he muttered, and covered his face, wondering if he was going to be haunted by her and that image for the rest of his life.

The attendant paused at Lane's seat. Her hand was soft upon his shoulder, her voice low and pleasant in his ear. And he resented her and every woman present for not being Toni Hatfield, and he hated himself because it was his own fault that it was not so.

"Are you all right?" the attendant asked. "If you're sick or need some assistance, all you need to do is ask."

He shuddered, then closed his eyes and leaned back against the seat. "I'm not sick. I'm fine. I'm as fine as I'm ever going to get," he muttered, and had the satisfaction of hearing her drift away to the next passenger.

Hours later, the plane landed and Lane entered the airport a sadder and wiser man than the one he'd been a week earlier. He'd survived a plane crash only to find that he might not survive crashing into Toni Hatfield's heart.

Two things happened within days of everyone's departure that did nothing but remind Toni of what she'd lost. The first, a bouquet of flowers from Palmer and Reese, came with a knock on her door. It was enormous, the message on the card a sparse opposite. It simply read, "Thanks for everything."

She wanted to laugh, but the corners of her mouth couldn't make the shape.

"You're welcome," she muttered to herself, and set the flowers in the center of her table, trying not to notice the wobbly legs. It reminded her of why they rocked. Lane had broken it, just as he'd broken her heart. Both had survived, but neither would ever be the same.

The next surprise came hours later when it was nearly evening. She watched from the window as a delivery truck, bearing the name of a well-known furniture store in Knoxville, lumbered up her driveway and parked in the yard. She'd watched, unsuspecting of anything except perhaps that she would have to direct them to another residence.

"Is this the Hatfield residence?" the man asked.

Toni nodded. "Yes, but I think you've got the wrong Hatfield. I didn't order any furniture."

The man looked down at his order sheet and frowned. "Are you Antonette Hatfield?"

An odd warning started in the pit of her stomach. He wouldn't. "Yes," she said.

He nodded. "Then we have the right place. Boys, bring it in. And watch the doorway. I don't deliver scratched goods and that's a fact."

All she could do was watch. There were no words to voice what she felt as they started inside her house with their load.

"Lady, where do you want this?" someone asked.

Tears choked her, making speech nearly impossible. All she could do was lead the way. The deliverymen followed her into the kitchen and set their cargo down next to what they were about to replace.

"Want us to put the old one somewhere else, lady?"

She pointed toward the back porch. It would have to do for now. She couldn't think past the sight of the round top and the rich, dark, shiny color of the cherrywood table.

When they carried out the old table, she watched through teary eyes, staring at the patched underside and uneven legs as it cleared the doorway with little room to spare. Its removal was as symbolic of his departure as the actual one had been. The final link with Lane was gone.

When the last of the six new chairs was in place, the men stood back, admiring what Toni could not face.

"Looks real nice in here," the man said. "Hope you enjoy it." He was starting out the door when he patted his pocket in remembrance. "Shoot! I nearly forgot. This came with it."

He handed her the card, then ushered his helpers out the door. Moments later, Toni was alone, suffering the scent of new wood and high gloss and wondering when her life had gotten so off track. She had only to remember that it had begun with a storm…in the night…on the crest of a wave…and in the arms of a man who hadn't looked back when he'd left.

Her fingers trembled as she opened the card. It was the first time that she'd seen Lane's handwriting, but she would have known it anywhere. It was as large and decisive as the man who'd written it. He'd written:

Dear Toni,
    I can't fix everything I broke, but I can try. Take care of yourself and remember what we shared.
                                                          Lane

Not Love, Lane. Just Lane. It was more than she'd expected and still not enough.

"What I wanted from you, mister, was not tables and chairs."

She sat down, testing the shape of the chair against the curve of her hip and back, then folded her arms upon the shiny surface and hid her face from the sight. She prayed for the day when his loss would be easier to bear, and prayed also that there might possibly be a little something of him within her that he had left behind.

Chapter 10

It had been the longest week of Lane's life. And in those seven days since his return, the perennial tropic beauty of Tallahassee had, for him, lost its appeal. He drove the streets through the maze of traffic, unaware of the sidewalks bounded by elegant, swaying palms, ignoring the constant throng of females of every size, shape and color who were on a constant search for the man of their dreams.

He was in the midst of a single man's paradise, and wished instead for tall green mountains with smoky caps, quiet mornings and narrow country roads, and a tall, independent woman who gave new meaning to blue-jean shorts and old, faded shirts.

Lane Monday was home, but he was homesick for Toni Hatfield and her Tennessee hills. He'd caught himself in the act of calling her number so many times during the past seven days that he had nightmares of doing it in his sleep and not being able to stop until it was too late. He knew that if he heard her voice, if he made a connection one more time, he wasn't certain he had it in him to tell her goodbye again.

She'd claimed a place in his heart that he hadn't meant to give up. But making love with her had been a far step from happily-ever-after. She was a woman who deserved a husband and a houseful of children. She needed a family as loud as the one in which she'd grown up, not a man haunted by old ghosts and with no hope for a future except one filled with heartache and disappointment.

For her, as well as for himself, he wouldn't let himself care.

"Hey, Monday! You have a call on line three."

Lane frowned at the interruption as he picked up the phone. He was in the middle of a sentence, and halfway through the report on his desk, so changing trains of thought was a distraction he didn't need.

"This is Monday."

"Naw, it's not, boy. It's Thursday, but who am I to quibble about days of the week when I've got myself a hatful of trouble."

Lane grinned when he heard the laconic drawl of Dan Holley coming across the wire. "Hello, Holley. I don't suppose you called me this early in the morning for any good reason," he said. "And what seems to be the trouble?"

"I don't know any easy way to say this, Monday, so here goes. I got the autopsy on the body we fished out of the Pigeon River this morning. It wasn't Emmit Rice."

Lane's gut twisted. This wasn't what he'd expected or wanted to hear, and it set a whole series of what ifs circling in his brain.

"Who the hell was it?" Lane asked.

"Samuel Sumter."

The skin crawled on the back of Lane's neck. "Then that means…"

"That's not all," Holley said. "The pawnshop in town was robbed sometime last night."

Lane didn't want to hear this sitting down. Something told him that if he did, his legs might not be able to hold him up when he left, and he'd already made a mental plan for departure before Holley had finished talking. The chair squeaked, then rolled backward as he ejected himself to an upright position.

"What was stolen?" he asked, and he could hear the disgust in the sheriff's voice as he answered.

"Guns and ammunition. Not a good way to start a day, is it?"

Lane closed his eyes against the news, but there was no way to deny what he suspected. "Damn."

"That about summed up my opinion, too, boy. I don't suppose I have to ask if—"

"Notify every law enforcement agency in the area to be on the lookout for a man answering Emmit Rice's description. I'll handle the fax information from here." As he spoke, he thought of Toni alone on her farm and got sick to his stomach. "Every resident within a ten-mile radius of Chaney should be notified to be on the alert. Set up checkpoints on all the roads and highways leading out of the area. It sounds to me like someone is planning to make a move."

"That's just about what I expected you to say," Holley replied. "It's already in the works. I'll let you know what—"

"You won't have to let me know anything. I should be there in three or four hours, give or take a few."

"What are you gonna do, hitch a ride with Superman?"

"Something like that," Lane said. "Look for me when you see me coming."

Three and a half hours later, a helicopter set down in the field behind the Chaney city hall. A big, long-legged man emerged from the cockpit, ducking when he ran beneath the spinning rotor.

Lane Monday was back.

Toni walked the length of fence that stretched up the back pasture, placing the last of the metal clasps on the angle-iron posts that would hold her new four-strand barbed-wire fence in place. Down the hill, she could hear the clank of metal against metal as Justin loaded the fencing equipment into the back of his truck.

Working side by side with her brother had been an odd experience. She didn't know whether or not she was going to be able to deal with being told, once again, what to do and how to do it, but she knew who she had to thank for Justin's help. It was Lane. And it had all begun the day that she'd gone out to repair her mailbox.

She could still remember the high flush of color on Justin's cheeks as he'd yanked the posthole digger from her hands and sent her back to the house, when only moments earlier it had been his suggestion that she repair the broken mailbox post herself.

She sighed, and mentally shut herself off from the pain of thinking about the man she'd pulled out of Chaney Creek. It did no good to dwell on what might have been. For Toni, her might-have-been had come and gone and she was right where she'd been before the crash had occurred.

Sweat ran beneath Toni's shirt, tunneling along her spinal column in a sticky, persistent track. But she didn't notice, or if she did, she didn't care. The job was over. The fence was complete. She dropped the sack of leftover clips in the toolbox and slid into the passenger seat of Justin's truck without comment, then let her head fall back with a weary thump.

"Hot one, isn't it, Toni?" Justin asked.

She nodded. "It's been hotter," she said softly, and rolled down the window as Justin started to move.

"Want me to turn on the air conditioner?" he asked.

She shook her head. "No need. I'll just get hot all over again when we get out to unload."

He sighed. "Judy said for me to bring you home for lunch when we were through."

Toni smiled and then did what was, for her, an unusual thing. She patted her brother on the leg and then leaned over and kissed him on the cheek as he pulled up to the barn.

"I appreciate your help, Justin. Really I do. But tell Judy thanks, but no, thanks. As soon as I clean up, I've got to go into Chaney. The cows are out of salt, and I want to pick up some cubes and sweet feed for the steers.''

Toni noticed Justin's shock. She couldn't remember the last time that she'd done something so out of character as to kiss her brother. It was such a female move that obviously he didn't know how to respond.

They exited the truck and began to unload.

"Just so you know," he muttered, "you're always welcome.''

She paused in the act of lifting a near-empty spool of wire and rested her arms upon the fender as she gazed across the truck bed at Justin. A Madonna-like smile changed her features from intense to introspective.

"I know that, Justin. It's late. Go on home and get your food before Judy throws it, and you, out to the hogs.''

He did as he was told, and minutes later, Toni made the hot, dusty walk from the barn to her house alone. Within the hour, she was clean, cool and on the way to Chaney when she remembered that she still hadn't eaten.

"I'll get something in town," she told herself, and kept driving, her eyes on the road before her, because concentrating on what was going on inside her head might make her insane.

When Toni drove into Chaney and parked her pickup in the alley near the loading dock of Dobbler's Feed and Seed rather than on the street, she missed seeing a big man exit the sheriff's office with Dan Holley and then get into Dan's car.

After leaving the store, Toni went to the café downtown, and was patiently waiting for her order to arrive, unaware of the chain of events that had already taken place that morning in town. If she had paid attention to the babble around her, she would have heard all sorts of comments flying fast and furious about the theft at the pawnshop. But she wasn't listening to the murmurs around her, as much as to the replay of memories inside her head.

The echo of Lane's voice in her ear as they'd made love had not gone away. Neither had the feel of his lips upon hers, or his hands tracing the shape of her body before he took control of her mind. All she had to do to bring the memories back was simply close her eyes and let go of everything but the sound of his name.

Lane.

The blaze of blue from his eyes and the breadth of his shoulders as he lowered himself inside her would be forever in her heart. For a giant, he'd been gentle beyond belief. His first and last thought had been for her. She sighed, and bit her lip to keep her chin from trembling. Crying in front of the customers of the Inn and Out Café would not be smart.

"Do you want catsup with your fries?"

Toni jerked to attention, brought rudely back to the present by the food that the waitress had slid under her nose. She looked down. The hamburger was thick, hot and shiny with grease, as were the fries.

"Catsup?"

Toni couldn't think what to say. It was impossible to go from making love to Lane to an overdose of cholesterol and not be confused.

The waitress sighed. Obviously, the woman was too weary from the noon rush to be patient any longer. She repeated her question in a short staccato chain of words.

"Catsup, Toni! Do you want catsup?"

"No. No, thanks. I don't want any catsup." *I want Lane Monday.*

Toni kept her last request to herself.

Four farms and thirty minutes later, the sheriff turned from the main road onto the driveway leading up the hill to Toni Hatfield's farm. The residents that they'd been notifying had reacted with varying degrees of alarm and alternating decisions. One man had even started packing up his wife and children to take them into Knoxville to his mother's home until the problem in the area was solved. But Lane knew that when Toni was notified, she wouldn't be going anywhere. He could already imagine how her chin would jut, and her eyes flash.

"Hmm," Holley said as he pulled into the yard and parked in the front of Toni's house. "I don't think she's home."

Lane got out and started toward the porch, although he'd already come to the same conclusion. Her red-and-white pickup was missing from its parking place in the hallway of the barn.

Lane knocked on the front door, and then turned the knob. He cursed when the door swung open to his touch.

"Damn it," he muttered as Dan followed him onto the porch. "She doesn't even lock the door when she leaves."

Dan shrugged. "Not many do out here. Haven't had much reason to... before now, that is."

"I'm going to leave her a note," Lane said. "I'll tell her to call the station for details, but for now, I don't want her in the dark about what's going on."

Holley nodded, then dropped into the porch swing while Lane entered the house. He was struck by the realization that the essence of Toni was everywhere. A pair of her tennis shoes was sitting beside the living room couch. Her hairbrush was on the hall table, and one dirty sock was in the hall, as if she'd dropped it on the way to the wash.

He bent down and picked it up. At least he knew where that went, he thought, then tried to focus on his mission as he headed for the kitchen where he knew she kept a notepad and pen for making grocery lists. He tossed the sock onto the washer and tried to think of what to write. But he kept seeing her alone in this house, and then remembered the calf that she'd found and her nephew's dog with a broken neck. The mischief had gone from missing chickens to stolen guns and ammunition. The way Lane saw it, someone had been holed up in these hills, stealing from the land and the people who lived on it, recuperating and readying himself to make a run. With the theft of the guns and ammunition, all clues led him to believe that the person was ready to move out. Although the thought was repugnant, gut instinct told him that it was Emmit Rice.

"If I could live through the crash, then, by God, so could he," he muttered, and started writing his note.

The message was brief. He could imagine Toni's shock when she read it, especially since he'd signed his name. But it was for her own good, and the good of the people, that he'd come back. Not, he kept reminding himself, because he wanted to see her one more time. Not because he couldn't get the feel of her body and the memory of her scent out of his mind. He was a U.S. marshal doing his duty. Nothing more. Nothing less.

When he stepped onto the porch, it was just in time to see a familiar pickup pulling into the driveway. He stifled a grin at the glare of the man who crawled out from behind the wheel and stalked toward the house.

"What the hell are you doing back?" Justin demanded.

Lane grinned. "Good to see you, too, Justin."

Justin flushed, then glared.

"We were on our way to your place next," the sheriff said. "Just as well we caught you. It'll save us some time."

Justin looked startled, as if realizing that someone else was with Lane Monday. "What's going on, Dan?" Then he looked around at the yard, staring intently toward the barn where Toni's truck ought to be. "And where the hell is my sister? It's nearly four o'clock. She should be back from town. Has something happened? Has she had a wreck? Is that why you're all—"

"Whoa," Dan said, and started off the porch. "It's nothing like that, boy. Settle down."

He quickly proceeded to tell Justin exactly what they had been telling everyone in the area regarding the thefts and who they believed was perpetrating them.

Justin went pale. He thrust his hands into his pockets, then yanked them out and combed them through his hair instead, giving him a slightly startled appearance when the strands stuck up in all directions.

"She wouldn't come eat lunch with me and Judy," he said. "She said she needed to get stuff in town. She was leaving for Chaney as soon as she cleaned up."

Lane hated the way his gut twisted. It was too reminiscent of the instinct he had that something was already wrong and he had yet to find out what.

"Go call," he ordered, and had the satisfaction of seeing Justin react toward him in a positive manner. "You know where she was going. Find out when she left, okay?"

Justin bolted into the house while Lane and Dan waited on the porch. A few minutes later, he came back more anxious than when he'd gone in.

"She got feed. I talked to the man who loaded it. They said she was going to the café. I checked. She left there over an hour and a half ago. I even called home on the chance that she'd gone there to see the baby before coming back. She's crazy about kids, you know." Sweat beaded across his upper lip as he seemed to be considering where else she might have gone.

"Did you tell your wife to be on the lookout for strangers and to lock the doors?" Dan asked, and was rewarded with a nod from Justin.

Lane tuned out the thought of Toni and babies and frowned. There was no need dwelling on what could never be when he needed to be focusing on the issues at hand. And while he wasn't one to jump to conclusions, he also wasn't going to waste time waiting to see what happened.

Lane's hand slid beneath his jacket, feeling for his gun. It was an instinctive safety test, a lawman's gesture that he'd performed many times. And then he stepped off the porch and started toward the patrol car.

"Are you coming?" Lane asked the men.

"Where to?" Justin countered.

"To look for Toni. Where else? It takes exactly fifteen minutes to get from here to Chaney. She might have had engine trouble. She might have a flat. Whatever it is, I'm going to see for myself."

He couldn't let himself think of Toni lying beneath him, giving and giving, while he took and took, and then imagine her in danger. They would find her and then they would all have a good laugh.

"Hurry up," Lane muttered as the sheriff opened the door of the patrol car.

Dan obliged by sliding into the driver's seat as Lane began to fold himself inside the small car. Lane didn't have to look back to see if Justin Hatfield followed. Even inside the car, he could hear the gravel flying as the pickup tires spun out on the driveway. He didn't blame Justin for being concerned. The day had started out bad; there was no reason to assume it was going to get better anytime soon.

Toni's meandering thoughts came to an abrupt halt as the familiar *flap, flap, flap* of a flat tire could be heard upon the blacktop road.

"Well, great," she muttered, and pulled her pickup to the side of the road before getting out.

It couldn't have been a worse time or place to have a flat. This was the only stretch on the entire road home that had no shade, and she had a load of feed in the back. It would be hot and heavy work, jacking up the bed and replacing the tire. And, what made it even worse, her spare tire was on a rack underneath the truck bed.

With a muffled curse, Toni grabbed the key from the ignition, flopped flat on her back, then scooted beneath the bed of the truck, quickly unlocking the spare. Moments later, she was hard at work, doing the thing that she knew best how to do. Cope.

Emmit's two-week growth of beard itched. He scratched it and cursed beneath his breath, unwilling to investigate the itch too closely. It could be fleas. It could be poison ivy. It could be both. He'd encountered both during his time in hiding. But it was of no consequence to Emmit Rice. He had needed a place to heal, and he'd found it.

The first day after the crash had been hazy. He remembered waking up in the wreckage, surprised that he was still alive, then staggering up into the hills. He had no idea where he'd gone or how he'd gotten there. And it had been much later before he realized how lucky he'd been to have escaped during the storm. The rain had washed away virtually every trace of his flight from the area.

He hadn't known that the one-room shack he'd found up in the hills was Samuel Sumter's own getaway place until the big man had walked up on him in the yard. Emmit had never considered trying to talk his way out of the encounter, not after he saw the way the man had eyed his bright orange prison coveralls or the remaining leg iron he had yet to remove.

All it had taken was a swing of the hammer that he'd stolen out of a neighboring barn, and the man had dropped like a felled ox. It had been a simple matter to pull the body to the creek and then toss it into the current. He had considered it a point of luck that the creek had still been in flood stage; otherwise, the searchers he'd seen combing the hills might have found the man's body long before, and Emmit would have lost valuable healing time in trying to hide.

Most of his forays for food had centered on the neighboring farms and their livestock, and had taken place during the day, when many were gone on errands or out in the fields at work. His most daring exploit had been into a house while two women were working in a nearby garden. He still laughed, remembering the pie that he'd filched from the back porch while no one was the wiser.

Emmit had known from the first that he was going to get away. He considered it divine intervention that he had survived and then escaped without detection. And he had run, with no thought of his fellow prisoners or the lawmen who might, or might not, have had a chance to live had he stopped to help.

His cuts had healed, leaving an ugly track of scars as serious proof of his injuries. Long gashes that had been in desperate need of stitches had sealed themselves over and then run with infection before finally coming to a halt. The raised scars that were left behind ran the gamut of his face and body like thick red worms, some still bearing scabs. Emmit Rice could have cared less. It was nothing more than an added disguise for him, a man who because of size alone had a difficult time hiding his presence.

But now he considered himself healthy enough to move out of the area. The searchers were long since gone. He'd laughed, watching them drag the flooded creek, as he'd crawled back up the hill to hide.

But he was ready to move. All he needed now was a means of escape. And like everything else that had happened since he'd crawled out of the wrecked plane, it appeared to him like magic in the form of a red-and-white pickup that was parked on the side of the road.

There was only one problem. When he had left the concealment of the trees in which he stood, he had a good hundred yards to cover, without being seen, just to get to where the pickup had stopped. And while he was debating how to accomplish that, the driver solved his problem when she turned her back on his location and began to change a flat.

"Just one more lug nut," Toni muttered to herself, and reached into the hubcap near her knee where she'd tossed them earlier.

Sweat ran into her eyes; her hands were filthy; her nose itched, and she wanted a drink of water. She was miserable.

"Hey there, honey. Are you about done?"

Startled by the sound of a man's voice, her first thought was that he could have at least come a little earlier and helped. And then she stood and turned. She had a vague impression of a huge ham-fist swinging toward her chin, then oblivion.

* * *

When the sheriff's car turned the curve, Lane breathed a sigh of relief. Toni's pickup was on the side of the road. Even from here he could see the elevated rear.

"There she is," Dan said. "Looks like she had herself a flat tire."

But Lane's relief died within seconds as he saw a flash of dirty orange and a hulk of a man pulling an unconscious woman to the opposite side of the pickup. Instinctively, his hand went to his gun.

"Call it in," Lane said harshly. "It's Rice. He's got Toni."

Holley's hand was on the radio before the patrol car came to a stop, and by the time he started relaying the message, Lane was already out of the car. He was crouching behind the half-open door, shouting an order to surrender to a man who didn't know the meaning of the word, as the dust they'd outrun slowly caught up and settled upon them.

"No!" Justin screamed as he ground his vehicle to a halt just behind the sheriff's car, then started to get out.

"Stay down, you fool," Dan shouted. "He's armed."

"But he's got my sister," Justin yelled.

And he's got my lady, Lane thought as his finger tightened on the trigger of the gun he had aimed at Emmit Rice's head.

"Give it up, Rice. Let her go," Lane ordered and shifted the sight of his gun to follow the erratic movement of Emmit's upper body.

"Get back, you son of a bitch, or I'll break her neck," Rice yelled, unable to believe who had pulled a gun on him. The last time he'd seen that man, he'd been dead underneath DeVon Randall and a section of seats. What had he done? Resurrected himself?

Lane didn't blink. His arm was rock steady, his finger taut and ready to pull.

"Let her go," Lane repeated, and fought back a wave of fear. He couldn't let himself think about the woman in Rice's arms. She was a hostage, an unknown. He couldn't let himself remember her laugh, and her eyes or the way she'd gone weak at his touch.

''Like hell! You get back, and I mean now! I'm in charge here! You do what I say or the woman dies,'' Rice roared.

''Let her go!'' Lane said once more, swallowing back the bile rising in his throat.

Rice laughed. His head tilted in amusement as he shifted his squeeze hold on the woman's neck just to prove that he could.

A barrage of images flashed through Monday's mind. A dog with a broken neck. A calf with its throat slashed and gaping. Toni, limp and unmoving, as Rice held her to his chest like a shield.

''Toni! Can you hear me?'' Lane shouted.

''Help is on the way,'' Dan told him, and shifted to a less compromising position at the back of the patrol car.

''Help will be too damned late,'' Lane growled. He knew this man. He'd seen his rap sheet. There were no survivors of encounters with Emmit Rice.

''You get back, and you get back now,'' Rice shouted, and waved the gun that he was holding toward Toni's head. ''Move, or I blow her brains out. It makes no difference to me, Monday, and you damn well know it!''

''Dear God, no!'' Justin groaned.

''I'm taking her with me,'' Emmit shouted, and started toward the door on the passenger side. ''You give me safe passage and I promise I'll…''

Lane's thoughts froze on the word *promise*. Emmit Rice didn't know the meaning of the word. Suddenly Lane stood, his decision made as he offered himself as a target to the man with the gun.

Dan Holley saw Lane's movement and followed to cover him.

Lane shouted. ''Rice! Let her go!''

Startled by the shout as well as the lawman's unexpected movement, Rice inadvertently jerked, then turned as he aimed at Lane's chest. Just a fraction. Just enough.

The gun bucked in Lane's hands, and a loud, reverberating roar echoed over and over at the once-quiet roadside where a woman had been fixing a flat. The gun in Emmit's hand discharged in return. But it was only a reflex, and the bullet went into the ground, because Emmit Rice had died the moment the bullet from Lane's gun had hit his brain. He went down, taking Toni with him. Within a heartbeat of the shot, three men were running toward the other side of Toni's truck.

Lane reached her first and tore her out of Rice's grasp.

Don't let this be happening, Lane thought as his hands traced her face and body. *Don't let it be too late!*

This was not the first time that he'd touched Toni's body in such an intimate manner, but now he wanted to feel a heartbeat, not the catch in her breath as their bodies joined. And when he found her pulse, coupled with the slow, uneven groan that slipped out of her mouth, he knew a moment of total joy unlike anything that making love could have brought him.

"Thank you, God." It was all he could say.

He lifted her into his arms and carried her away from the remnants of the man who'd nearly ended her life.

"You damn fool!" Justin grabbed at Lane's shoulder, trying to pull his sister from Lane's embrace. "You might have killed her."

"I *might* have," Lane said, and then looked back at the man on the ground. "But he *would* have. Emmit Rice did not take hostages. He took victims, and left them in pieces for their families to bury."

Justin blanched, then watched, unable to move as Lane carried Toni a short distance away.

"Let it go, Justin," Dan said as sirens could be heard coming down the road. "He did the right thing, and it saved Toni's life."

Chapter 11

Toni shifted in Lane's arms.

"What happened?" she mumbled as her hand moved toward her jaw and the pain that she felt there.

What happened? I nearly lost you, lady. But the thought did not fit the decision that Lane had already made. He couldn't lose something that he'd already given away.

Lane caught her fingertips before they centered upon the swiftly darkening bruise and held them to his lips without caring how it might look to the gathering crowd. All he could think of was the living, breathing woman that he held who had survived the ordeal. He had no way of knowing how long she'd been in Rice's clutches, or what she'd had to endure, but at this point, he didn't care. She was alive.

"You're safe, baby," Lane said softly.

Toni's heart thumped erratically as she blinked to clear her vision. She knew that voice. She recognized the touch.

"Lane? Is that you? How did you..." Toni jerked, and started to fight her way out of his arms. "There was a man!" she cried. "He came up from—"

"He's gone. It's over. He can't hurt you again," Lane said, and felt satisfaction from the knowledge.

Justin knelt, and without asking, pulled his sister from the lawman's embrace. "Come here, sis, don't be afraid. You're safe now."

Toni let herself be traded from one man's arms to the other's because it was not in her at the moment to think straight. But when Lane had turned her loose and walked away, she knew a bit of her heart had gone with him.

Lane had given her up to Justin because he had no right to object, but it was a cold, empty feeling that he took with him as he returned to the scene of the crime. There were things to be done that only he could do, and the one that satisfied him the most was giving a positive identification to the man who was lying in a spreading pool of blood.

"Justin, where did you come from, and better yet, where did they?" Toni shuddered, staring around in dismay at the gathering of people and cars.

"God, Toni, I thought you were dead."

Toni vaguely remembered seeing the man's fist and then everything going dark. It could just as easily have been a permanent "lights out" for her. She had never realized before how fast a person could die.

"It seems that Lane Monday wasn't the only man who survived the plane crash," Justin informed her. "The body the authorities fished out of Pigeon River wasn't Emmit Rice, after all. It was old man Sumter. They're speculating that Rice was responsible for the thievery." He shuddered and clutched his sister tightly. "We figured he was trying to steal your pickup for a getaway. He was going to take you with him as a hostage."

"Oh, my God!"

Toni wouldn't let herself think of what might have been. Suddenly, she was very glad that she'd been unconscious. Having to deal with remembering something like this might have taken a while to get over.

"How did they stop him?"

Justin bowed his head. "Monday did it. He saved your life."

Toni's heart leapt in her chest. It was a strange and telling thing to know that she now drew breath because of another person's actions. *Now I know how he felt,* she thought.

"Justin, help me up," she said, and started to struggle to her feet.

"No, Toni! The ambulance should be here any minute. Let them check you out first and see if—"

"I have a sore jaw. Nothing more. The dirt on me was already there before he came. I was changing a flat. Now damn it, Justin, help me up!"

Justin sighed. "Just be careful," he warned, but she was already gone, walking through the heat and dust toward the tall, dark-haired man who was standing in the center of the nearby crowd.

Toni's legs were shaky, but her need to get to Lane was strong. She hadn't expected to see this man ever again, and now, to have it happen like this was almost too much to bear. When he'd left last week, in her mind, they had been even. She'd saved his life and he'd granted her a last request.

They were an unlikely couple with an impossible situation between them. He had more than made it plain to her that he didn't want entanglements, and as hard as it had been to accept, she'd taken from him what he was willing to give and told herself it was enough. Yet why, she wondered, did fate keep throwing them together? What good could ever come from the pain of continual parting?

But the knowledge that she could see him, be with him, even if it was only for a short space of time, was worth more sleepless nights, because Lane Monday had stolen a piece of her heart.

"Lane."

In the middle of a crowd, in the middle of a sentence, Lane froze. The soft sound of his name on Toni's lips sent him spinning around as the people surrounding them blurred out of focus. All he could see was her face and those eyes, dark and compelling, asking more of him than he was willing to give.

He looked over the heads of the people around him, searching for Justin, for the paramedics, someone... anyone...to explain why she was not under someone's care. And then she touched his arm and it was too late to stop the flow of feelings that swamped him. He could no more stop himself from touching her than he could have ceased taking his next breath. His palm cupped her cheek, and gentleness was in every nuance of his touch and voice.

"What are you doing up, lady? You should be lying down taking it easy. You've had a hell of a scare."

She covered his hand with her own and shook her head. "I'm not the one who got scared. I got off easy. I don't remember a thing after a swinging fist until I heard your voice."

"Ah, God." He pulled her into his arms and crushed her against his chest. "I was nearly too late," he said, and let himself go as he started to shake.

Toni wrapped her arms around his waist and allowed herself the fantasy that this was where she belonged. His heartbeat was rapid beneath her eardrum. His clutch seemed desperate as he held her fast. She pretended it was more than relief with which they embraced.

"This time it was you who saved my life," Toni said. "I don't know how to say thank you, but I..."

The words died on her lips. A sensation of having already been in this place, saying these words, made her head spin as a wave of embarrassment sent a rapid flush to her cheeks.

Lane went still. Only days ago he'd been saying the same thing to her. And the memory of what she'd asked was uppermost in his mind as he tilted her face to his and stared long and hard into her eyes. Could he? Should he?

"I do," he said, and felt her shock even though she did not move.

Dear Lord, Toni thought. *Please let this be what I think.*

"You do? What?" she asked.

"I know how you can say thank you."

She closed her eyes and swallowed. If she was wrong, there would be no way to get out of the shame of letting him know that she cared too much. She opened her eyes. When she looked up, she was staring into a wall of blue fire.

"What are you saying?" she whispered.

He tried to smile, but it got lost in his pain. "Once more…just for fun?" he whispered, and kissed the corner of her mouth.

"Toni! The ambulance is here," Justin said, grabbing her arm as he demanded her attention.

Startled by the interruption, Lane stepped back and resisted the urge to punch Justin Hatfield in the nose.

Toni didn't argue. She was too busy trying to assimilate the implications of what Lane had asked. *Oh, God, if I do this again, will I have the strength to pretend it doesn't matter when he leaves?*

She answered her own question when she suddenly stopped, then turned and looked back to Lane, who was still watching her.

"I suppose there will be all kinds of paperwork," she asked, and knew it was the last thing he might have expected her to say.

"A fair amount, I suppose."

She nodded. "It will probably take at least a day or so, won't it?"

Lane's eyes widened. Suddenly he knew where she was leading, but he couldn't help himself, or hide his expression of shock. She was going to say yes.

"At least," Dan Holley added, overhearing and answering for Lane as he walked up. "It's good to see you up and walking, girl," he said, and patted her gently on the arm. Then he grinned. "And you had better believe there'll be paperwork. Local reports, state reports and federal forms that I don't even want to consider. I've already got this man a room at the Smoky Mountain Motel. He's not budging from Chaney until he has dotted the last *i* and crossed the last *t*.''

Toni nodded without looking at Lane again, but it hadn't been necessary. In his mind it was what she hadn't said that counted. She hadn't told him goodbye.

Toni wished that she were in her own home this evening, instead of under the caring, watchful eye of Justin and enduring the noisy romp of family running in and out of the house. Her thoughts were on Lane and what he'd asked. And she knew good and well that she'd complied simply by asking about his location. Inwardly, they read each other all too well. It was what they couldn't say aloud that was making all of this so difficult.

Justin pretended to be reading a paper, but Toni knew that he hadn't missed one of her fidgets since bringing her home. But her family was simply going to have to worry, because there wasn't anything she could say or do to help. It was going to take time for them to learn how to accept that the ugliness of the outside world had come into their small, rural community and changed their perception of safety forever.

As for herself, she'd already come to terms with losing more than a woman deserved to bear. For Toni, all she had left was her life. Her parents were gone. The man she'd foolishly fallen in love with was leaving her again. She had nothing but years stretching ahead of her. Single, lonely years, unless...

She took a deep breath and rose from her chair, unwilling to let hope get in the way of consequences. She and Lane had made love, but for all the wrong reasons. She'd wanted something from him that he wasn't willing to give, and had taken something he didn't know that he'd left. It remained to be seen whether anything would come of their union, but one thing was clear. Baby or not, she would never forget Lane Monday.

A tiny squeak, followed by a rather loud cry, was all the impetus that Toni needed to pick Lucy up from her crib.

She clasped the baby close against her, loving the feel of downy hair brushing against the skin on her neck. "What's wrong, little girl? Is there too much noise for you to rest?"

Judy walked over and gave her baby's rump a comforting pat. "Noise is the last thing that bothers her," she said. "It's probably my fault. I've done nothing but cry all evening. I'm sure she senses the unrest. Here, let me have her. I'll rock her a while. Maybe that will calm her down."

Reluctantly, Toni gave up her niece, and turned toward the door, unwilling to stay inside another moment under her brother's scrutiny.

"Where are you going?" he asked.

Toni sighed, pausing in the doorway. "Outside, Justin. Only outside. I need some space. Okay?" Without waiting for his permission, she walked out, closing the door firmly behind her as indication that company was not invited.

The next morning, when the sun was barely over the horizon, Justin walked out of the house in time to see Toni loading her overnight bag into her pickup.

"Where are you going?" he asked. "You haven't even had breakfast."

Toni hugged her brother's neck. "I'm going home, Justin, where I belong. I want my own bed. I need to check on the livestock. I want to eat a bowl of cereal in peace without looking to see if you're watching me eat."

He flushed. "I didn't mean to...I just wanted to make sure that you were..." He sighed and ran a hand through his hair. "Oh, shoot, Toni. You know what I mean."

She grinned as two of his children burst out the front door in a fit of shrieks and joy at the sight of a new day.

"And you know what I mean," she said.

He looked over his shoulder at the noise, then shrugged and answered her smile with one of his own. "I guess I do," he said. "It *is* hard to get over a headache in this house."

She cried all the way home, thinking of the quiet that awaited her, wishing it were not so.

* * *

Lane put down his pen and hung up the phone. There was nothing left to be done but wait for tomorrow and leave the same way that he'd come. It was amazing how well law enforcement agencies could work together when called upon to do so. He'd been through a number of cases where the difficulty in the job came not from the crime itself, but from having to fight for the right to do his job and not step on someone else's territory and toes.

Tomorrow.

The word was, in itself, an abomination. If she didn't come tonight, he wouldn't see her again. He'd promised himself that much. She deserved to be able to make the choice. And while he'd found himself and his thoughts wandering far too often toward a tall, dark-eyed woman and the way she fit in his arms, he couldn't—wouldn't—let himself forget Sharla, or the way that she'd died.

Remember the disbelief on her face. Remember her pain...and the blood. Remember, you fool, that it was all your fault.

Lane shuddered and buried his face in his hands. How could he forget? He didn't need to be reminded that she'd died because of him. What he needed to remember was the vow that he'd made when it had happened. Never again. Never again.

"Are you finished?" Dan asked.

Lane lifted his head. *Probably, and I just don't know it.* But he didn't say it, and thankfully, the sheriff did not remark on the lonely expression in Lane Monday's eyes.

"I am now," Lane said, and handed the stack of files to Dan. "I do reports, but I don't do files." He grinned to soften his remark. "Besides, I don't know where you want them."

Dan took them and tossed them on his desk. "Time enough for filing tomorrow. Come on, man. I'm treating you to the biggest steak dinner Knoxville has to offer."

The thought of food made him sick. "I think I'll pass," he said. "I'd rather grab a sandwich and an early night. The chopper should be here by daybreak tomorrow."

Dan nodded as he extended his hand. "Monday, we've had one hell of a ride the past two weeks, from pulling you out of Chaney Creek to sending Rice home in a body bag. I can't say that I'm sorry this is over. My fishing is way behind schedule as it is."

Lane smiled back and took the handshake that the sheriff offered. "Take care, Holley, and remember my invitation."

"Yeah, right. Palm trees. Cold long-necks." He grinned as he walked away.

And I would trade every damn one of them for a long night with a sweet woman named Antonette, Lane thought.

Moments later he was gone, retracing the path that he'd worn between the Smoky Mountain Motel and the sheriff's office in Chaney. Hours later, he was inside the room with his back to the wall, watching a door that he feared wouldn't open.

It was almost dark. Toni paced her living room floor, telling herself that she was simply asking for heartache, and then reminding herself what she would get in return. What was a little heartache compared to the joy of making love with Lane? How could it hurt to give it one more try?

"All right, mister. It can't possibly hurt me any more than it has already," she muttered as she grabbed her purse on the way out the door. "Besides, I pay what I owe." And she owed him her life.

Minutes later, the silence of the night was broken by the sound of her truck as she drove away, and then all was quiet on the hill above Chaney Creek.

Four cabins sat in a neat, straight row, facing away from the main street of Chaney. Four distinct little bungalows that had been built during the late fifties when it was "cute" to have awnings on every window. Little, white, one-room houses with green shingles and shutters and small picket fences.

The Smoky Mountain Motel was not doing a booming business. Three of the bungalows were dark and shuttered. It was the one on the far end with the light that drew Toni like a moth to a flame, pulling her closer to a fire that she knew could destroy her, if she let it.

Her truck's engine was barely running above idle as she coasted to a quiet stop near the edge of the mini-picket fence in front of Lane's bungalow. When she killed the engine and slipped the key into her pocket, she had a moment of anxiety, wondering if she was making a mistake, and then knew that the only mistake would be in leaving. For her, the decision had already been made.

But having come, it did not stop her legs from shaking, or make her heartbeat slow down. It didn't make it any easier to knock, and then stand and wait for him to appear.

But when he opened the door, blocking the opening with his size and intensity, the look on his face was of such overwhelming relief that she knew she had not been the only one in fear. When Lane stepped silently aside to allow her to enter, she did so with a graceful finality that was not lost on the watching man.

Toni took his silence as what it was intended to be, filling her mind with the sight of this man to remember when he would be gone.

"Ah, God, lady. You know how to make a man weak. I didn't think you would come."

Moments later, she was in his arms. *I didn't know how to stay away,* she thought, and then thought became impossible.

Lane couldn't get past the fear of yesterday when they had come around the curve in the road and he'd seen her in Emmit Rice's arms. So limp. So still. The experience made her presence here now that more precious.

"Are you all right?" he asked as his hands traced the path of her spine down to the curve of her hips. "Maybe we shouldn't be doing this after what you went through yesterday."

Toni smiled through her tears. "Oh, no, Lane. That's exactly why we should. Yesterday, I realized how easy it was to die. Tonight, I want to remember what it feels like to live."

How easy it is to die. My God, my lady, if you only knew.

"I want you to make love to me again, Lane Monday. One more time."

Her chin quivered and she hid her face against his chest when he whispered against her cheek, "And just for fun."

If that was all it was to him, so be it.

But when their clothes fell away, and they met in each other's arms, what came next was not in the name of fun. Their clasp was as urgent as the heat between their bodies, their breaths as short as the fuse on Lane's control. Gentleness and foreplay had no part in the fierceness with which he took her to his bed and buried himself inside her. There was nothing left but an overwhelming need to forget everything and everybody except the now in which they lived.

Cognizant thought had come and gone, leaving Toni weak and helpless to everything but the need to meet Lane's every demand. His weight came hot and heavy upon her as he thrust between her legs, using the skill of his sex to tell her what he could not say. That he wanted. That he needed. That he loved. That he would leave.

And when the wild, unfettered spiral of pleasure began to unwind low in her belly, and when his mouth was on her lips and his hands beneath her hips, she felt a splintering joy and at the same time a rage that this was over before it had ever begun.

Lane thrust a final time, then shook from the effort as he died a slow death in her arms. It would be justice if he did, he thought, and a fitting place in which to go.

"Ah, lady. You take my breath away," he whispered, and rained kisses across her face and neck, tasting her tears upon his lips.

Their foreheads touched in mutual understanding and agreement for what had transpired. Their bodies had joined, but it was their souls that had met. Yet, for Lane, there were no words to be said to change what was.

Twice more before morning, they awoke. Once it was Lane who turned to her in desperation. And once it was Toni who rolled over and on top of him, taking him into her before he'd opened his eyes. But the pleasure was too brief and the ending incomplete. They had made love, but could not say the words, leaving Toni feeling cheated and Lane with a burden of guilt.

But it was only one more time...and just for fun.

The sky outside was turning gray, losing the shadows of night at an alarming rate. Toni had only a matter of minutes in which to leave before the early risers of Chaney caught her in the act.

She dressed without conscious thought, pulling on clothes simply because leaving this room naked was against the law. But in effect, she had already stripped herself, heart and soul, for the world to see. Loving a man who made no promises was as revealing as it got.

She turned at the doorway. Her lips twisted bitterly as she faced the pain of losing this man once again to a life in which she had no place or part.

"We're even, Lane Monday. Fly safe and fly high. I won't be around next time to save you."

Moments later, she was gone, unaware that he had been awake from the start, listening to the careful, quiet manner in which she'd dressed, absorbing every breath she'd taken and each step that she'd made away from him. But it had been her parting remark that he knew he might not survive.

"Next time, sweet lady, I won't even care," he muttered, and rolled himself out of the bed.

Within the hour he was airborne, up in a flurry of dust and dry grass, above the green cover from the treetops below, back to a place where there were no foggy-top mountains or narrow dirt roads leading to a quiet country farm above a place called Chaney Creek.

Chapter 12

First you get mad, then you get even.

Toni had heard that old saying all of her life. But how, she wondered, could she be mad with anyone except herself? Not once during the two weeks that she'd known Lane Monday had he ever misled her, or given her reason to believe he would do anything other than what he'd done, and that was to leave.

As for getting even, they had more or less parted on that note. She'd saved his life. He'd saved hers. He'd sent her a new dining room set to replace the one that he'd broken. Everything was as nearly normal in her life as it had been before he came. Now there was nothing left for Toni to do but get on with the business of living. How to do that without the tender presence of her towering giant would remain to be seen. She didn't really have a plan. It was going to have to be dealt with one day at a time.

By the time the first letter came, she had numbed herself with a mindless routine of constant, daily work after which, each night, she would fall into an exhausted, dreamless sleep.

So when she saw the Florida postmark, and the broad, even strokes on the envelope spelling her name, she wasn't prepared for the pain that came from reconnecting with him, even if it was long-distance and through the mail.

"Just let me out at the mailbox," Toni said as her brother David slowed down to make the turn into the driveway.

"Surely not here?" her sister-in-law Laura asked. "You'll have to carry your groceries up the hill to the house."

Toni unwound herself from the seat, unloading a niece and nephew from each knee as she exited the car. "It's just one sack, and I can always use the exercise. Thanks for the lift," she added, and waved goodbye to the rambunctious crew who had given her a ride home from town.

Thanks to a blown gasket, her pickup would be in the garage for at least another week. She was at the mercy of whichever family member was heading her way and would be willing to take her with them. This morning it had been David and his wife, Laura, as well as all four of their children. The ride had not been monotonous.

She hefted the sack of groceries to her hip and retrieved the handful of mail from the box, absently sorting through the stack before starting toward home.

The serenity of the Tennessee hills should have been balm to an empty heart. Towering pines, thick stands of oak, elm and hickory abounded. Along the road, clumps of brown-eyed Susan and wild white daisies grew, adding a splash of color to the green-and-brown palette that was the setting for her home.

With each step that she took, the dust poofed softly around her shoes, coating the clean white canvas with a dusty red shadow. Her blue jeans were nearly new and swished sharply with each stride. Her white shirt had started out crisp and freshly ironed, but now bore the brunt of a morning in town, and wrestling children from front seat to back during the ride home.

Butterflies danced above the heads of wildflowers, bright,

flighty droplets of color that added life and spark to the land-scape. But Toni didn't see all this, and even if she had, she would not have been able to appreciate the almost perfect beauty of the land around her. She was too numbed by a Florida postmark and the implications of the letter's arrival.

She didn't know how she got inside the house. It was only after she took the pages out of the envelope that she realized she was in the kitchen and sitting in her daddy's old chair. Holding her breath against the shock of connection, she began to read.

Dear Toni,

I know that we said it before, but I had to say thank you again. Every day I look at myself in the mirror and realize that I owe my life to you. I hope that you are well. I think of you often and wish you all the happiness in the world. You deserve all that life has to give, and so much more.

I will never forget you.

                                                    Lane

She looked up from the letter, staring blindly out the open doorway as the pages crumpled beneath her fingers. Her face was pale, her lips compressed as her nostrils flared in quick anger.

"So you wish me the best, do you, Lane? Thank you so much for the bland sentimentality. A drugstore greeting card couldn't have said it better!"

Angry with herself for having hoped for something more than a bread-and-butter thank-you note, she wadded the letter and tossed it into the trash.

"That's what I get for getting my hopes up," she muttered, refusing to give way to tears. "Why won't I ever learn?"

She tore into her grocery sack, tossing cans into cabinets and slinging her carton of milk into the refrigerator as she berated herself for the hope that she'd let spring.

"This is it, Toni. Your roll in the hay with a lawman is all you're going to get out of life...and it was more than you expected."

She laughed to keep from crying, but there was no humor, only bitterness, in the sound.

And because she hurt with the days that continued to pass, she lashed out at those around her until everyone, including Justin, began to give her a wide, careful berth. She rarely answered her phone, and when she did, was short to the point of rudeness, no longer willing to listen endlessly to Laura's latest tale of the children's antics. The shopping trips that Judy offered were quickly turned down without explanation. Toni hadn't retreated from life, but she had taken a serious look into regrouping. Rearranging her attitude had to help her get through the pain. It just had to.

Lane's days were long, but his nights were longer, endless, hot summer nights in a cool bed with nothing but a pillow to hold. No sweet sigh in his ear. No soft gasp of breath against his lips as he dreamed of making love to Toni.

He had believed that the letter he'd written thanking her for everything one last time would put a knot in the line connecting him to Toni Hatfield. It should have, but it did not.

Foolishly, he'd watched his own mail for days and then weeks, hoping for a simple return note that might echo his own sentiments. Something—anything—that would bind them together again.

But it hadn't happened, and he tried to accept that it was all for the best. He didn't need to prolong something that had no hope of growing. In his mind, he'd already ruined Sharla's life to the point that it had caused her death. He wasn't about to risk his sanity and another woman's life, not even for love.

And then one day he picked up the phone at work and found himself dialing Toni's number. By the time it rang seven times, he'd regained enough control of himself to disconnect, and thanked his lucky stars that she hadn't been in the house to answer.

What, he thought, would he have said if she'd answered? He had no idea, but the question wouldn't go away, and he couldn't let go of wondering what might have been.

But, he'd done it! It *had* happened. He'd dialed her number and the world had not come to an end. He'd made an attempt to contact her that hadn't interrupted the flow of traffic or initiated another impasse between heads of state. For that reason, it made calling the second time that much easier. And that time, when he still did not get an answer, he told himself it was just as well.

Two days later, without considering his reasons, he bought an answering machine and had it sent Federal Express to Chaney, Tennessee, before he could change his mind. By the time the package was on its way to Toni, he'd convinced himself that what he'd done was only for her own good. In this day and time it only stood to reason that she needed to stay in communication with other people. She was a woman alone in a fairly secluded area. Emmit Rice hadn't been the only bad man in the world.

Convinced that he'd done nothing out of turn, he settled back into a routine and waited. He didn't realize that what he'd done, he'd done to stay in touch with her. It was, quite literally, a "reach out and touch someone" gesture that would have made the phone companies proud.

If Toni's Hereford bull hadn't gotten out and into old man Warner's pasture and serviced four of Warner's purebred Angus cows before it was removed, Toni might have been in a better frame of mind when the delivery van came up her driveway. But she'd already had to apologize to Silas Warner and commiserate with him about the loss of money he might suffer from having calves born of something other than their registered Angus status.

And this morning, for the second time in a week, she'd overslept. Add to that the worn-out, run-down feeling that had dogged her every step for the past few days, and you had a woman who was not in a receptive frame of mind for the deliveryman or the package that he carried to her door.

''Now what?'' Toni muttered as she raced to answer the abrupt knocking on her front door.

''Miss Antonette Hatfield?''

She sighed, then slumped against the doorframe at the sight of the uniformed man bearing a small, but suspicious-looking package.

Her fourteen-year-old nephew Harry, who was her brother Arnie's son, and who lived in Nashville, had taken it upon himself to give the names of every member of his family to a computer company in the hopes of winning some fly-by-night video prize. Harry was already in trouble with his father and two of his uncles because of the stunt. And while Toni had heard of this only through the family grapevine, she wondered if she was about to become victim number three. If this was a free-for-ten-days-or-send-it-back-with-no-charge deal, she was not going to be happy knowing that she was now on some con artist's mailing list, and Harry would probably be grounded for life.

''Miss Hatfield? You are Antonette Hatfield, aren't you?''

She peered over his clipboard to the package in his hand, but couldn't see anything other than a bunch of upside-down labels and codes that she wouldn't have been able to understand had she seen them upright.

''Yes, I'm Toni Hatfield.''

''Package for you,'' he said, and handed her the clipboard. ''Sign here, please.''

She did as he asked, and watched the dust in the driveway settle long after he was gone, realizing as she closed the door how suspicious she'd become since nearly losing her life. Emmit Rice may have missed his target when he'd failed in taking her hostage, but he'd taken something precious just the same when he had died. She no longer assumed that she was safe, and *trust* wasn't just a word, but a thing to be treasured.

''So, Harry. What wonderful prize have I just won, and how much is it going to cost me to claim it?''

The small smile she'd been wearing as she tore into the wrapping died on her lips with the card that fell on the floor at her feet. Once again, the shock of seeing that broad, dark slash of handwriting bearing her name seemed a mockery in the face of his absence.

"What now?" she muttered, and then stared at the obvious. "An answering machine? What on earth can he be thinking...?"

The card said it all.

Dear Toni,

    Just to make sure you are still all right, I tried several times to call you. You kept missing my calls and I realized how isolated you are out there. The instructions for hooking this up are simple. Take care and maybe we will make a connection another time. My address and phone number are enclosed.

Lane

"He tried to call?" She let out a shout of anger, but no one heard. "What, pray tell, could he possibly have to say to me that he hasn't already said?"

She glared down at the answering machine, still packaged inside its box, then headed for the kitchen, muttering beneath her breath with every step that she took.

"I don't need to be checked up on, and if I'd wanted one of these...these...things, I would have bought it myself. My God! The nerve of the man! He's worse than Justin. Next thing I know, he'll be sending me a pager so that he can keep track of my whereabouts!"

She scribbled a scathing retort that she chose not to reread, afraid that if she did, she might relent and be nicer to him than he had a right to expect, then stuck it to the outside of the box. Paper flew and string knotted as she wrapped and taped and cursed all manner of men for their hard heads and small minds.

"When he left, he gave up any right he might have had to worry about me," she said, walking to the bathroom where she washed her face and yanked a brush and then a comb through her hair. "And why would I want to call him? What on earth would I possibly say?" She snorted and ignored the furious glaze of tears shimmering across her eyes. "Maybe he's expecting a 'next time you're in the neighborhood come on by' invitation. I suppose he's ready to have a little more *fun.*"

Although it was nearly suppertime, and the cows would be coming down the lane anytime now to be fed, Toni hauled herself and her "gift" out to her pickup, thankful that her vehicle was now in good repair, and tore down the driveway in a flurry of drying leaves and red dust. If she hurried, she would just about make it to the post office before it closed for the day.

Having had one hellish day at work had done nothing for Lane's peace of mind. Traffic was snarled, the weather was hot and he'd had dreams last night that he couldn't forget. They had ranged from the first moment he'd opened his eyes and found himself face-to-face with a dark-eyed angry woman to seeing her unconscious in Emmit Rice's arms. During what was supposed to have been a good night of rest, his emotions had run the gamut to the point of exhaustion. He'd gotten up tired, gone to work mad and was now coming home to a lonely, solitary apartment.

But, he reminded himself, it was what he wanted, and then reworded that message within his own mind. No, he didn't necessarily want it, but it was what he had to do, for her sake as well as his own.

When he saw the Tennessee postmark on the package in his apartment mailbox, he realized that the response he'd been hoping to get wasn't coming. This one was as unorthodox as the woman who'd sent it. Not only did he get his answering machine back, but the note that came with it set him back on his heels.

I kept the table you sent because you broke mine. After all, fair is fair. But frankly, Mr. Monday, I believe that we've traded about all there is to trade between us. Like lives, a roll in the sack, etc. You get the picture.

Unless you have something more to say to me than what's already been said, I don't see the need for further communication. You came and went through my life like the flood that went down Chaney Creek.

We owe each other exactly nothing, which under the circumstances, is probably for the best. I do not need a man who does not need me.

What totally irked Lane was the fact that she'd referred to him as "Mr. Monday," and the way that she'd signed the note.

Sincerely. She'd signed the damned letter, Sincerely, Toni Hatfield.

He was all but shouting as he dropped the answering machine into a trash can and tossed the note in after it, then pivoted and picked it up again, rereading the last two sentences, trying to make sense out of the ambiguous remark.

"What the hell does she mean...under the circumstances...probably for the best...do not need a man who does not need me? I never said she needed a man. Hellfire! All I did was send her a damned answering machine!"

And then all the anger in him died. He had just answered his own questions. "Under the circumstances" was simple. He was here. She was there. Whatever happened to her from now on was none of his business, and he'd made that point perfectly clear by leaving her. After all, it had been "just for fun" between them. It was what she'd wanted, wasn't it?

As for the "doesn't need a man who didn't need her," she was right. What possible good could he do her? He'd shown her what he needed and wanted by walking out on her after the first time they had made love without so much as a good-bye. And he'd let her go the second time with more of the same. What Toni needed was a man who was able to stand by her, not an emotional cripple like him.

"Ah, God, lady," he said softly as he folded her letter and put it in a drawer. "I didn't mean to…"

He couldn't even finish his own sentence, because Lane himself didn't know what he'd meant. All he knew was that his days and nights were being haunted by two women. One that he'd killed, the other that he'd left behind.

That night, for the first time in more than five years, he shut himself in his apartment with a fifth of whiskey and drank himself into oblivion, because facing what he had done was an impossible, unbearable task.

The same night, many miles and mountains away, Toni felt pain and knew that it was not all her own. And when morning came, bringing a bright, new day, she could not find it anywhere within herself to care.

That came later, on the morning that she'd overslept for the umpteenth time in as many weeks and then rolled out of bed just in time to throw up. Only after the calm in her belly had resumed did it occur to her to wonder why she'd been sick. And when realization dawned, so did Toni Hatfield's hope for salvation. She'd lost her man, but if she was right, she would be having his child.

"No, Justin, I don't need company just to drive into Knoxville," she argued, and wished for the hundredth time that she hadn't bothered to tell him that she was going. She shifted the phone to her other ear as she gauged the time against driving distance. If she hurried, she would just about make her appointment, and the last thing she needed was her eldest brother at her side when she found out for sure that she was about to become an unwed mother.

"Look, I've made the drive a jillion times before and you never cared. What's the big deal now?"

Justin sighed heavily. "I didn't mean to imply that you needed help, sis. I was just remembering…" He stopped suddenly. "Never mind. If you want to, you can call before you leave Knoxville. That way, you'll simply be safeguarding yourself. Understand?''

Toni relented. He was right. And she was being too touchy only because she didn't want or need anyone's advice about what she'd learn.

"I'm the one who should be saying I'm sorry," she said. "I appreciate knowing someone is around who cares whether I live or die. It may as well be you. I'll call you before I leave Knoxville. I promise."

Every breath that Toni took as she drove toward Knoxville was a prayer that what she suspected would be so. And although she could have bought a pregnancy test kit in Chaney, it would not have been wise to do so. The inevitable would be revealed in time. For now, keeping the secret to herself seemed the best possible option.

She didn't even mind as much as she usually did when the doctor's nurse asked her to disrobe for her examination. What was a little embarrassment compared to what she could gain?

"Well, Mrs. Hatfield, I believe congratulations are in order. You are going to be a mother," Dr. Cross told her a scant fifteen minutes later.

"Miss." Toni corrected him absently.

Her heart was too full to care that his face had reddened slightly.

"I'm sorry," he said, and glanced at her chart, noting her age and that this would be her first. "I didn't mean to imply—"

Toni smiled. "Don't be sorry," she said, and clasped her hands in her lap to keep them from shaking. "This baby is nothing less than an answer to a prayer."

He smiled. "Is the father going to be in the baby's life at all?" he asked.

The smile froze on her face. "Not likely," she said shortly. "But I have seven brothers. If I need a male role model, I have more than enough."

He laughed. "I'm a member of a rather large family myself.

I think I know what you mean. A little can go a long way, right?''

"Right," Toni echoed, and tried not to think of Lane Monday. Not now. He didn't belong in this joy, because he hadn't wanted to belong in her life.

"At first I'll need to see you only on a monthly basis. The closer you come to term, the closer your checkups will be. My nurse will give you a handful of literature. Read it all. Ask me questions next month. If you have any problems, and I do mean *any*, call me, day or night. Got that?''

She nodded.

"I don't know what you do for a living, but I want you to get plenty of rest, eat right and give up any strenuous activities. Exercise is good. Overdoing it is not.''

"Since my father's death, I rent out my farmland, but I still raise cattle," Toni said. "From time to time, I do lift heavy things. Bales of hay, sacks of feed…that sort of stuff.''

He frowned. "I don't recommend you push yourself so hard anymore.''

She shrugged. "So I'll hire help.''

"Good girl," he said. "Ask my nurse to make your next appointment, and I'll see you next month. Okay?''

Toni stood, and then impulsively hugged him just because she could.

"Thank you, Doctor,'' she said, and grinned when he blushed again.

"Don't thank me," he said. "I'm just the bearer of the news. Thank the man who made you this happy.''

That, my dear doctor, is impossible. We've burned more than bridges between us.

"Then that would have to be God for answering my prayer.''

The doctor grinned. "You're not going to try and convince me that this was an immaculate conception or anything like that?" he teased.

"Hardly," Toni responded. *I would say it was closer to a*

careful deception. "See you next month," she said, trying not to let her elation show as she left.

But it was impossible to ignore her joy. It had lasted all the way home, and she was halfway through her evening meal when the phone rang and she remembered that she hadn't called Justin to tell him she was leaving Knoxville.

Certain of the caller's identity, she answered on the second ring and was apologizing before she'd given him a chance to speak.

"I'm sorry. I'm sorry. I'm sorry," she said, her voice light and full of laughter, waiting to hear her brother's disgusted remark.

Lane forgot what he'd been about to say. He hadn't expected to hear such happiness from her. He closed his eyes, picturing the expression on her face and trying not to think of who had put such joy in her voice.

"No, Toni, I'm the one who's sorry," he said softly. "I overstepped so damned many boundaries with you that it makes me sick. Forgive me, lady. Then maybe I can forgive myself."

Toni froze, and before she could think, before she could react to the shock of hearing his voice, he hung up the phone.

"Oh, my God," she whispered, feeling behind her for a seat before she fell to the floor instead. "Lane? Lane, is that you?"

There was nothing but a dull buzz and an empty silence, and she heard it clear through to her soul. She hung up the phone, then buried her face in her hands. Fate had to be laughing up its sleeve at this coincidence.

On the day that she'd learned she was pregnant, the father of the child called and expressed regret for everything that had passed between them. If she had needed a sign to let her know she'd made the right decision to keep her news to herself, then she'd just gotten it. In big, loud, clear tones and compliments of the telephone.

Chapter 13

A new peace settled within Toni's heart. It came with the acceptance of what life had given her, and from knowing that she had the will to endure whatever negative response she might suffer. The happiness she felt for the forthcoming child far outweighed whatever else might occur.

Her family saw her change and she knew they did not understand. They only knew that the angry, semireclusive woman that she'd been was gone, and for that they seemed grateful. Toni realized that they would never have imagined, not even in their wildest dreams, that independent, do-it-myself Toni was going to become a mother. Or that she had done so under the grayest of circumstances. Deliberate deception was not something they would have ever associated with straightforward Antonette.

As for herself, Toni didn't care or worry about anything except her health and the welfare of the baby that she carried inside of her. She let the hot, lazy days of summer pass her by with little fuss, and she did what she needed to do without pushing the limits of her endurance.

Hiring a semiretired widower named Abel Morris to help her with the heavy work had been a stroke of genius. He was so thankful for the chance to be busy again, he nearly begged her for chores.

It was a time of passage that was doomed to an all-too-brief sojourn in her life. Inevitably, her family would have to be told, preferably before they saw for themselves the changes that her body was already undergoing. But for now, she waited, and cherished the life that was growing within her, and tried not to care that the man who was responsible for it all was unaware of what he'd done.

All fall Toni had put off the inevitable. The telling of her blessed event was going to produce a family uproar and she knew it. She'd practiced her speech so many times in so many different ways that it had gotten to be her own private joke.

Once, Justin had even teased her by commenting on the fact that in her old age and solitary state, she had started talking to herself, and recommended that she get a house cat rather than the barnful of half-wild felines that roamed the hay rafters. She had laughed in his face. A cat? The joke was almost too good to keep to herself, but she'd done it just the same.

But in her fifth month, and on the latest trip to her obstetrician, she'd done something that she couldn't hide with loose clothing and jackets. She bought a baby bed, and then a high chair and a stroller. Before she knew it, the bed of her pickup was fully loaded with cardboard boxes and packing crates, all marked "Some Assembly Required."

Not only was she going to need expert help, but someone was going to have to help her unload.

"Maybe I should just call everyone and ask them to bring a screwdriver and come over," Toni muttered, arguing with herself as she exited the highway from Knoxville onto the

ounty road leading to Chaney. "Sort of let them figure it all
ut for themselves."

She glanced over her shoulder, peering through the window
o make sure that her load was still safely intact behind her.
'Or, maybe I could just show up in their front yards for a
isterly visit and let each brother draw his own conclusions
s to what I'm hauling."

Then she groaned and shifted uncomfortably on the seat,
eminding herself that she was being silly. Something this
nonumental could not be told in such a cavalier fashion.

"Goodness, baby," she whispered, and patted the gentle
well of her belly to apologize for complaining. "Who would
ave thought that carrying a little thing like you would make
verything else in my body ache?"

Yet her sense of fair play and unwillingness to deal with
n all-out brawl within the family warned her that she had
nly one outlet.

"I'll tell Justin and let him deal with everyone else," she
lecided aloud, and waved at the sheriff as she sailed through
own, hoping that Dan Holley was thinking about fishing and
not what she had in the back of the truck.

Seeing the sheriff brought another lawman to mind, one
she kept trying to forget. The memory of Lane should have
faded. It had been almost five months since she'd seen him,
and in those five months the Smoky Mountains had undergone
as drastic a change as she had. But her memories of him were
as vivid as the night she'd dragged him from the flood.

Sometimes during the day when she was lost in some mun-
dane job, with her mind on one thing, her hands on another,
the old farmhouse would creak and she would turn, expecting
to see Lane come walking into the room. The disappointment
that came next was always startling, and she hated herself for
being so weak.

And late at night, when finding a comfortable place in her
bed was next to impossible, she would remember the feel of
his arms cradling her and the solid thud of his heartbeat
against her ear, and she would cry from the loss of it all.

Lost in thought, she turned into her driveway in a cloud of dust, scattering the covering of autumn-hued leaves that had fallen near the road. She drove the pickup like a red-and-white arrow, streaking up the driveway and moving aside all that lay in her path.

And that was how Justin saw her as he came out of the barn, her pickup racing just ahead of the dirt and the leaves. He grinned and dumped the tools in the back of his truck and started toward the house to help her unload.

"Oh, God," Toni groaned. Whether she liked it or not, her Waterloo was at hand.

She crawled out of the pickup and stood, leaving the cab between them as Justin neared the front yard. From where she stood, she could see the expressions on his face as they changed. He'd went from greeting to gawking, and when he leaned over the truck bed and shifted one box to read what was written on the side, then another, then another, he looked up at his sister with an expression that she didn't want to face.

"What in the world have you done, Toni? Lucy doesn't need any of this stuff. The stuff we already have is going to last through her baby years just fine."

Toni exhaled slowly, then counted to ten. He thought that she'd bought these things as a gift for his own baby. It figured. He would never expect her to need anything like this for herself.

"They aren't for Lucy," she said. "They're for me."

The look in his eyes said it all. Shock turned to disbelief and then to overwhelming rage. He dropped the box that he'd been holding and walked around the truck like a man in a daze. His eyes never left her face until he turned the corner of the truck bed. At that point his gaze went straight to her belly. Toni watched his eyebrows arch and his mouth go slack.

He cleared his throat several times before he spoke. "I don't believe it!"

"Believe what, Justin? That I could possibly be pregnant, or that I didn't tell you?"

"Why didn't you say something to me sooner, sis? No matter what the son of a bitch said to deny it, I would have made damn sure he owned up to what he did to you!"

Toni felt weak. This was exactly the attitude that she'd expected Justin to have. And when he saw her sway, he grabbed her to keep her from falling and led her to the house.

"Come inside, honey," he said as he opened the door and led her into the living room. "Sit down before you fall down. We'll decide what to do as soon as you're feeling better."

Toni sighed and stifled a smile as she sat down. It was so like Justin to assume that she needed someone to tell her what to do.

"I've already decided what I'm doing, Justin. I would think that it was fairly obvious. I made my decision the day I found out I was pregnant. I'm having my baby and thanking God that I can."

"I'm not going to insult you by asking who the father is, because this is nothing more than what I feared might happen when you took that bastard Monday in. I told Judy he would take advantage of you. I'll break his damned neck if he doesn't get himself down here and marry you."

This was where it was going to get rough. But Toni didn't have it in her to lie, or to let Justin keep maligning a man who was as ignorant of the facts as he himself had been until only moments ago.

"He did not take advantage of me, Justin. In fact, it was just the opposite. He was nothing but a gentleman the whole time he was here."

Justin frowned and threw up his hands in frustration. "Don't try to protect him. You didn't get like this by yourself. He lied to you, and now you're paying the consequences." He headed for the telephone in the hall.

"No!"

She was shouting as she bolted from her chair and yanked Justin's hand from the phone before he could make the call.

Toni's mouth was grim, her eyes dark with fury. For the moment, she had her brother's full attention.

"Now you listen to me, and you listen good! You aren'
going to like this, but it's the truth. And so help me God, i
you do something without my consent, I'll never, and I mea
never, speak to you again!"

Justin went pale. "But, sis, why would you—?"

"Shut up and listen to me! Just once, will you listen?"

He bowed his head and waited. He seemed to understan
that he had no other choice.

"Lane Monday never said he loved me. He never told m
a thing to lead me to believe he would do anything other tha
leave when he was well enough to travel. He did not mak
unwanted advances. Why should he? I'm not the kind o
woman a man wants to marry."

"What do you mean…you're not the kind of woman a ma
would marry?"

She spun toward him, her laughter as sharp and brittle a
the lines around her mouth.

"Do you see any men lined up at my door? Have you *eve*
seen them standing in line for a date with me? No! I don'
think so. It's fairly obvious to me that men don't want som
big moose to take to bed when they could have a beautiful
feminine lady instead."

"Oh, my God." He buried his face in his hands. "I'm
sorry, so sorry. We did this to you. We didn't mean it, Toni
I swear to God. You're as pretty as any girl I've ever seen.
can't believe you think that you're not."

Her laughter was short and just below a snort of disbelief.

"I will be thirty years old before this baby is born. I have
never been proposed to. I have never even had someone try
to take advantage of me. How do you think that makes me
feel?" And before he could answer, she told him. "It makes
me feel like a failure, Justin. In fact, as a woman, I *am* a
failure. But by God, as a mother, I will be just about perfect.
So don't you dare go and ruin what has happened to me. As
far as I'm concerned, it's a gift from heaven, not something
of which I should be ashamed."

"I don't get it," he persisted. "If the man was such a gentleman, then how did this happen?"

Toni's chin went up. Her eyes blazed with a light that Justin didn't dare dispute.

"Because I asked him to sleep with me. And I got pregnant because I took no precautions...on purpose." She leaned closer until they were eye to eye. "Do you understand what I mean? Is that plain enough for you?"

"I can't believe that in this day and time a man with his background would just blindly sleep with a woman without taking precautions of his own, or at least ask about them."

Toni's voice faltered, but her gaze did not. "He didn't ignore it. He asked me if I was protected. I didn't exactly lie to him, but I also didn't tell him the truth. I purposely let him believe it was safe."

She'd said all she was going to say about an incident that was her own painful, personal memory, then spun toward the door.

"Where are you going?" he asked.

"To the pickup. I have things to unload. I'm hiring painters next week and redoing the bedroom next to mine. I think I'll paint the walls green like my Tennessee hills, and have Marcy Simmons, the high school art teacher, do a mural. Maybe I'll have her add some trees and birds to it, too, sort of like an American jungle, if you know what I mean. What do you think?"

Justin's mood was a shadow of its former belligerence. "I think you don't need to hire the painters. David and I will paint the damned walls green. We'll paint them black and blue if it will make you happy. Just let me help." And then he added, "Damn it, sis, I need to help."

Tension slipped out of her stance as quickly as it had come. She smiled, then stood aside to hold back the door.

"Okay," she said. "And just because I love you, I'm going to let you have the privilege of dealing with 'some assembly required.'"

She heard him groan as he passed, but it didn't matter. The

worst was over. Saying it aloud hadn't been easy, but no
nearly as difficult as she'd expected it to be. And as for th
rest of the family, the grapevine and the telephone would d
the rest. They could think what they chose, and say what the
must, as long as they kept the news to themselves. The las
thing she needed was for someone to mind her business an
tell Lane Monday that he was going to be a father. She knew
her brothers. They would all bow to Justin's decisions, jus
as they had during their growing-up years.

That is, all of them except Wyatt. The youngest Hatfield
male and only four years older than Toni, he'd been a rebe
from the day he'd learned how to walk. If anyone would in
terfere, it would be Wyatt. But Toni knew her younger brothe
would never get the chance to put in his two cents. He'
walked off the family farm on his eighteenth birthday, joine
the marines and went off to "see the world," as the poster a
the recruiting station had promised.

Yes, Toni didn't know when they'd be seeing Wyatt Hat
field again.

"Is the turkey about done, Aunt Toni?"

Bobby Hatfield's plaintive cry was nothing more than a
echo of the same lament that she'd heard from every othe
hungry mouth awaiting the arrival of "the bird."

"Almost, sweetie," she said, softly. "Go wash, and tel
your cousins to do the same." She ruffled his short, dark hai
before sending him scooting with a pat on the rear.

The heat from the old, roomy kitchen was near to intense
Just like the marathon baking it had just endured. Pies i
sundry shapes and scents lined the sideboard while hot rolls
fresh from the oven, mounded the breadbaskets at either end
of the table.

Toni eyed the feast critically and knew that she would be
glad when this day was over. Volunteering to hostess thi
annual event had been done without thinking of the back
breaking chores that would accompany it. Thankfully, the
army of able sisters-in-law had done more than their fair share

of adding to the Thanksgiving repast, but the effort had taken its toll on her.

"Is it done?"

Toni turned and grinned at Justin, who hovered at her elbow with a hungry look that matched the one his son had been wearing.

"Like father, like son. And yes, it's done."

"I'll lift it out for you," he said, taking the pot holders from her hands.

She willingly gave up the chore. Bending was difficult enough these days without bringing a twenty-five-pound turkey, hot from the oven, up with her as she stood.

"Let me finish for you," Judy offered as she sidestepped two other helpers to get to the bird that needed to be transferred to the platter.

Toni sighed, smiled and moved aside for the time being, allowing them to interfere because it made her family feel as if they were helping her cope. But the truth be known, she was coping pretty well on her own.

She wandered to the kitchen window overlooking the front yard, and smiled to herself as she watched the yardful of children at play.

Next year...or maybe the next when the baby is a little older, he, or she, will be out there, too.

Her vision blurred as she looked into the future, imagining that she could almost see the dark little head and the short, baby steps of a toddler wobbling about, investigating every rock and leaf in its path.

And then her world and everything in it suddenly came back into focus as she saw a black sports car pull up and park among all the other vehicles and the tall, dark-haired driver start toward the house.

His stride was laconic. She knew if she were closer, she would be able to see devils dancing in the soft brown depths of eyes just like her own.

"Oh, my God," she gasped, and headed for the door.

"What is it? Did one of the children get hurt?" Justin wa.
right behind her before she got out the door.

"It's Wyatt!" she cried. "Wyatt came home for Thanksgiving!"

Toni, still graceful even in the latter stages of pregnancy
bounded from the back porch and started toward him across
the yard, dodging kids and footballs with every other step
"Wyatt! Wyatt! Welcome home!"

"Well, well," he muttered, grinning. "My, how things
have changed."

He caught her in midflight and swung her off of her feet
and up into the air, completely disregarding her condition as
well as the shock on everyone else's face.

"Be careful, Wyatt!" Justin shouted, then breathed a sigh
of relief when his brother finally put Toni's feet back on earth.

One after the other, Wyatt hugged and greeted, pounded
backs and kissed cheeks.

"Come back inside," Toni finally said. "You're just in
time to carve the turkey."

Everyone began filing back into the house, but Wyatt
caught Toni's hand and tugged it in a teasing gesture, speaking softly to her alone.

"Honey, I think you should let your husband carve the
turkey. I haven't had the pleasure yet, but if I were the man
of the house, I would be expecting to do the honors myself,
especially on Thanksgiving."

Toni stopped. When she turned to face him, the shock had
all but disappeared from her eyes.

"Justin didn't tell you, did he?" she asked.

Wyatt frowned. "Tell me what?"

Toni sighed, unaware that she absently rubbed her belly in
a protective gesture, then started to explain. "There is no man
of the house, Wyatt. I'm what you might call an unwed
mother. And before you get all indignant, you need to know
that it's by choice. That's also all you need to know. Get it?"

It was hard to explain the rage that settled deep in his belly.
It didn't even make sense for him to care when he'd all but

abandoned the entire family for the better part of twenty years. But something about the way that Toni held herself apart from the words, as if she had faced the truth of her condition without facing the pain, told him that it wasn't all right, and he wasn't about to put up and shut up as she expected.

He pulled her into his arms and hugged her. "You always were a hardheaded, prissy little thing," he said gruffly. "I can see some things never change." He stepped back. "So where's that bird in need of a trim? I'm hungry as hell, and so glad to be home that I don't even care if I eat off the tail."

Toni grinned. "I was never prissy, not one day in my entire life. If I had been, I would have been better off."

Wyatt pondered the oddity of her remark all during dinner and long into the night after everyone else had gone home. What Toni didn't know, and what Wyatt hadn't decided until he'd set foot back on Tennessee soil and seen the condition his family was in, was that he wasn't going anywhere. At least not yet.

His life had gone to hell in a hand basket, but there was no reason for his sister to wind up the same way. He would find out what he needed to know and then fix it.

Living through holidays had always been rough for Lane, and this year had been no different. A child of foster homes and faceless pretend-parents, he'd only truly known family life after marrying Sharla. The short time that they had been together, he'd gotten a taste of what it meant to have someone else who cared. When she died, the hole it had left in his life was even bigger and emptier than the one he'd had before they'd met.

On the job he was always the man who volunteered to do holiday duty. It was no sacrifice on his part to show up at work because he had no one at home. In fact, it had helped him to get through the loneliest parts of the year.

But when Thanksgiving rolled around this year, he found himself thinking of Toni and that wild brood of Hatfields he'd met, and he could only imagine what dinner would be like in that household. It would be full of laughter and love, leaving a warmth deep inside a man that had nothing to do with the heat from a fire.

The want that came with the sound of her name and the memory of her face still amazed him. He should have been over a woman who he had never really claimed. The memory of the passion that they had shared should have faded.

Should have, but had not.

And yet when the need to reconnect with her came, it was always followed by a silent warning to himself that he couldn't get involved with another woman. All he had to do was think of what he'd done to Sharla and then transpose that horror and fear onto Toni's face. It was enough to put a damper on the fiercest of needs.

"Monday! Phone for you! Line two!"

The voice snapped him out of his reverie. Lane spun in his chair and picked up the phone. "This is Monday."

"This is Wyatt Hatfield. We haven't had the pleasure, but I'm—"

Lane sat upright. "You're one of Toni's brothers, aren't you? I remember her talking about you." And then a shot of adrenaline surged. Why should this man be calling? "What's wrong? Has something happened to Antonette?" he asked, unaware that his voice had come out sounding like a growl.

"Yes, you could say that," Wyatt drawled.

"What happened? Damn it, man, get it said!" *Oh, God,* Lane thought. *I didn't know it would hurt this bad to say her name.*

"It's a little hard to explain over the phone," Wyatt said. "And if the truth was told, she would take the hide off of me for calling you. But if you're half the man everyone said you are, you'll come out and see for yourself."

"Lord! Don't call me long-distance and then give me some mystic bull. What the hell is wrong with Toni?"

"I've said more than I should. But no one made *me* promise not to tell."

"Tell what?" Lane asked, and knew when every man in the office turned and looked at him that he'd just shouted into the phone at the top of his lungs.

The line went dead in his ear.

"Son of a bitch!"

He slammed the receiver onto the cradle and bolted up from the desk.

"Damn it to hell!"

He stuffed a stack of papers into a file and then tossed them on Palmer's desk as he stomped past.

"What's wrong?" Palmer asked, and then held up his hands to ward off the blow he felt coming. "Don't mind me," he muttered, and picked up the file Lane had tossed. "I'd be more than happy to finish it for you. Thank you so much for asking me first."

The door banged behind Lane, and then all was silent in the room as the officers stared at one another in shock.

Chapter 14

Lane left Tallahassee in a blaze of sunlight and arrived in Tennessee on a cold winter chill. It was the first snow of the season. Two weeks before Christmas and the light dusting on the ground was still not enough to make a decent-size snowball, although to give them credit, every child in Chaney that Lane had passed seemed bent on trying to do just that.

"Chaney hasn't changed. I just pray to God that neither has anything or anyone else."

Lane wouldn't even pretend to guess what the phone call from Toni's brother had been about. There were too many ominous implications to wonder. But the fear was real that had carried him from his apartment to the airport, and then across miles and through states on the road back to her.

And all he could feel was the cold sweat that came with the sound of her name, and the memory of a line going dead in his ear. If this was nothing serious, he was going to punch Wyatt Hatfield in the nose. But if it mattered…

He took a turn in the road, passing the place where he'd

killed Emmit Rice and in so doing had saved Toni's life; he
didn't even remember to look.

"When I see her face, then it will be all right," he reassured himself, and had to be satisfied with that thought.

The driveway loomed. He took the curve high and fast, his
eyes on the rooftop visible above the treetops, and on the silly
rooster weather vane that marked the spot where Toni lived.

Toni spun at the knock on the front door, then rolled her
eyes as she wiped her hands on a towel. Wyatt must have
locked himself out, although she couldn't imagine how or
why. She smoothed her hands down the front of her plaid
shirt and brushed a smear of flour off the leg of her jeans.

Carrying a baby hadn't changed what she wore, only the
style. She'd traded her 501 Blues for maternity denim, but
she was still the same dark-haired, chocolate-eyed woman
with more hair than she could manage. Older but wiser, and
only a little bit rounder, she wore her pregnancy with grace.

"What did you do, lock yourself out?"

The laughter died on her lips as she stared in openmouthed
shock at the man across the threshold. She had the intense
urge to slam the door in his face before it was too late, but
knew that it already was.

She looked into his eyes, saw the shock and a stark wave
of horror slide across his expression, and wished Wyatt to
hell and back for what he had done. And she knew it was
Wyatt who had caused this from the look he wore as he came
up the steps behind him.

"Oh, my God," Lane muttered.

He stepped across the threshold unaware of the man behind
him and started backing Toni across the room, his arms reaching out to her in a beseeching manner that she kept trying to
elude.

"Oh, Lord! Toni, baby...you shouldn't have...you don't
understand, you can't..."

He couldn't think past praying, nor could he find the words

to say what needed to be said. And when he did, they came out all wrong.

I shouldn't have? I can't? Toni needed to scream, but she settled for a sarcastic remark instead. "What do you mean, I can't? I already have, Mr. Monday."

"Toni, Toni, what in hell have you done?"

The accusation was as sharp as a knife thrust beneath her heart. It rang in her ears long after Wyatt had entered the room and closed the door after him.

"Nothing that concerns you," Toni said. "And why, may I ask, have you come at this late date in our…association?"

Lane shook his head and wiped a hand across his face. "I got a call. Someone said you were…I thought you'd been hurt or worse. I came as quick as I…" He spun, suddenly aware of someone standing there.

Wyatt leaned against the wall with the nonchalance of a man who knew he was in the right. "You would be Lane Monday, am I right?"

"You son of a bitch," Lane muttered. "You scared me half to death."

Wyatt grinned. "You came, didn't you?"

Toni shook from shock and rage. At that moment she hated both men. Wyatt for interfering, and Lane for reacting exactly as she'd feared and not as she'd dreamed.

"Why don't you two take your disagreement outside," Toni said. "I don't feel like mopping up blood."

Lane turned to face her, completely blocking out every thought except what he'd just learned.

"Why didn't you tell me?" he groaned, and tried once again to take her into his arms.

Toni pushed his hands away and glared through her tears. "Probably because it was none of your business, and because I knew you would react exactly as you did. I don't need pity. Thanks to an interfering family, I have all that I need."

Lane paled. His hands shook, and the room tilted. He had a momentary vision of Sharla's face contorted in excruciating pain, and then he remembered the blood and the way in which life had drained from her eyes. He groaned.

"Oh, God, not again. Not again."

Wyatt frowned. "What do you mean, not again? Are you trying to tell us you've done this before? Gotten some woman pregnant and then walked out on her without so much as a thank you, ma'am?"

Toni gasped. "Wyatt, I told you it was all my doing! You shouldn't have interfered. He didn't make promises, and I didn't ask for any."

"You can't have this baby," Lane said quietly, and wondered if he could die from a broken heart.

Toni thought that she was prepared for everything, but to hear this man telling her that she should terminate a pregnancy she had prayed for made her weak with shock.

"How dare you?" she accused, and cradled her belly as if to protect the child from the sudden appearance of a demon. "How dare you ask me to kill my own—"

"Oh, God," Lane groaned, grabbing her hands from her stomach and pulling her fiercely into his arms. "That's not what I meant, honey! That's not what I meant! I meant, you won't *physically* be able to have it. If you try, it will kill you. It happened before. It will happen again." Ignoring her protests, he buried his face against the heat on her cheek and wished that he'd drowned in the flood. "I can't be responsible for another woman's death. So help me God, I just can't."

Toni froze. She heard what he said, but it didn't make sense. The only thing certain was the true depth of Lane Monday's fear, because he was coming apart in her arms.

"You're crazy," she said, and tried to tear herself away. "I'm fine. The baby is due in a couple of months. Everything is, or was, perfect until you showed up. I'm sorry Wyatt frightened you, but you need not worry that I'll make any demands on you. I know you didn't want me, and I learned to accept that, but I want this baby. It's mine," she said, and finally succeeded in pushing him away.

Didn't want you? How did our signals get so messed up?

he wondered. Yet listening to her talk, he felt that he knew. What he'd meant as caution, she'd felt as rejection. He groaned beneath his breath. It was time for explanations.

"I weighed eleven pounds when I was born," Lane said.

Wyatt whistled softly between his teeth, eyeing his sister's belly. "Damn."

"After my wife, Sharla, got pregnant, they told her she would have to have a cesarean delivery because the baby was going to be so big."

"Lots of women have those," Toni said.

"She went into labor at seven and a half months while I was out of town. All sorts of complications happened before they found her. I got to the hospital in time to watch her die in my arms."

"That's not your fault," Toni argued.

But Lane couldn't—wouldn't—hear the truth in what she said, even though it was an echo of what the doctor had told him that fateful day. If he'd been a different man…a normal-size man…his wife and baby would not have died, and that was a fact. The memories were making him shake, but he couldn't seem to stop. He took Toni by the arms and all but shook her as he spoke.

"I stood in her blood, watching her trying to have a baby that was too damned big for her, and you stand here telling me it's none of my business! Like hell, lady! Like hell!"

"Oh Lord," Toni whispered, and unintentionally cradled herself again. "I'm sorry, Lane. I didn't know. I swear I didn't know."

She inhaled slowly, choosing her words carefully, hoping that she could make him understand. "You don't realize it, but you aren't thinking clearly. You're letting something that happened a long time ago color your judgment of an entirely different situation. Look at me! I'm as big as a horse, and as healthy, remember? That won't happen to me. I'll be fine. You don't have to worry."

Lane glared at her. *She would be fine!* He'd just spilled his guts about something that had haunted him every day of his life since it had happened, and she'd brushed it aside as old news.

"I don't intend to worry, because I'm not letting you out of my sight until this child is born," he said. And then he leaned forward, trying not to glare at the woman who was carrying his child. "And maybe not even then."

Toni's eyebrows arched. Her chin jutted. And in that moment, Lane knew how much he loved her, and how impossible it would be to make her believe it.

"You will marry me," he said.

"I will not."

"I'll find a judge. Being a lawman has its perks, and bypassing waiting periods is one of them. If you want anyone besides me present, you'd better start calling. As soon as the license is in my hands, you're mine, lady."

"I'm not yours," Toni retorted. "You didn't want me, remember? And I won't marry a man who doesn't love me!"

"Why the hell not?" Lane shouted back at her. "According to you, you went to bed with one!"

As it turned out, she had called no one to come and witness her humiliation other than the brother who had caused it all. Wyatt was present in a dishonorable position, relegated to the sidelines by a look from Toni that would have wilted a lesser man's nerve.

The minister shifted his Bible to a position nearer his eyeglasses and cleared his throat as he began the ceremony. "Dearly beloved, we are gathered here today to join this man and woman in holy matrimony. If there be anyone present who objects, speak now or forever hold your peace."

Lane increased the pressure of his hold on Toni's wrist and stared down into her eyes with a warning that she didn't dare ignore.

But her chin jutted just the same as she stared at him without blinking, daring him to utter one kind, sentimental word about this farce of a marriage.

Everything floated in and out of Toni's consciousness.

Words were traded with little emotion. Feelings were hidden well-deep inside, where no one could tell how moved she was by the moment, and how desperately she wished that this had been done in the name of love, not duty and fear. She kept reminding herself that this was for the baby's sake. That now, her child would know its father.

Lane's hand was strong and firm upon Toni's arm as he repeated his vows, but his thoughts kept jumping in and out of the past. And then his attention ricocheted sharply from the past to the present as he heard the preacher repeat his question.

"Mr. Monday, do you have a ring?"

Before Lane could answer, he heard Toni take a deep breath, and when she yanked her hand out of his, obviously overwhelmed by the entire ceremony, he took it as an indication that she was ready to bolt. Before he had time to think, the handcuffs that normally hung from his belt were in his hand. For a lawman used to restraints that corralled the unwilling, it had been an instinctive gesture. And considering their history, the move was highly appropriate. He popped one bracelet across her wrist, then calmly fastened the other one to his own.

"It's symbolic," he said shortly, ignoring the preacher's bugged eyes and Toni's shocked gasp. "Please continue."

The preacher nodded.

Wyatt started to laugh, but the look of disbelief on Toni's face and the warning that Lane gave him stifled his mirth.

"In lieu of the traditional giving of rings—" the preacher cast one last glance at the metallic binding upon their wrists "—I now pronounce that you are husband and wife. Mr. Monday, you may kiss your bride."

Lane exhaled on a slow, weary breath and looked at his new wife.

"You have no right," Toni said, hating herself for the tears running down her cheeks.

"I do now, Mrs. Monday," he said softly, and cupped her face with his hands and tasted the tears on her mouth.

Toni froze. Tenderness had no part in this day or the farce that they had enacted. But resisting this man had been impossible for her from the start. Today, in spite of her disappointment that it had all come to this, she could not resist the tug of his lips against her own, and her resolve softened just enough to return the kiss.

"My turn," Wyatt said, and started to swoop his sister into his arms when the handcuffs binding the pair together clanged against his waist and got in his way. "Do you mind?" he asked Lane, pointing to the cuffs.

Lane shrugged and unlocked the cuff. Toni's hand came loose at the same moment Wyatt took her in his arms.

"Congratulations, baby sister. You make a beautiful bride."

"I will hate you forever, Wyatt Hatfield," Toni muttered, and suffered his kiss.

"No, you won't," he said softly, and then turned back to the glowering groom. There was no jest in his voice as he spoke. "Monday, you are now in possession of the only sister we Hatfield boys have. We care for her greatly. If you hurt her, I will kill you, and that is a promise."

Lane wasn't impressed by the man or his threat. He saw past it all, but felt compelled to add a warning of his own. "Yeah, and if you ever scare me again like you did yesterday, there won't be enough left of you to do the deed."

Wyatt grinned. "Fair enough, brother," he said with a grin, and reached out to shake Lane's hand. "Welcome to the family."

Toni wouldn't let herself care about the pleasure that she saw on Lane's face when Wyatt embraced him, or the joy in his eyes when Wyatt had said, "Welcome to the family." Wyatt didn't have to live with the man. Her brother hadn't deliberately deceived someone for the chance to have a baby.

"I'll be leaving now," Wyatt said. "Take care, Toni. Have a great honeymoon."

She snorted lightly beneath her breath and then had to suffer the echo of his laughter long after he had gone.

"Where to now?" Toni asked.

"Home. I'm taking you home."

"To Florida?" Dismay was deep in her voice.

Lane shook his head and gently brushed a curl away from her face. "No, baby. You're the one with roots, not me. I'm taking you back where you belong."

It was the first good news that she'd had all day.

The house echoed with their footsteps as they entered, two silent people caught up in a web of their own doing, uncertain how to fix the situation that they now found themselves in.

Lane stood near the doorway, his gaze never wavering from Toni's face, gauging the pale line around her mouth against the flush across her cheeks.

"Do you want to lie down?"

She sighed. "Do you want something to eat?"

Lane tried a smile. "I asked you first."

Toni walked past him on her way to her room. She didn't have the energy to fight. Not today. Not anymore. She'd just gotten married to the father of her child, and knew that they were the least happy couple she'd ever seen.

Lane watched her go without venturing another word. What could he say that hadn't already been said? He picked up his bag, and followed.

Toni was sitting on the side of the bed about to pull off her shoes when Lane walked into her room and headed for the closet.

"What do you think you're doing?" she asked.

"Hanging up my clothes."

"Not in there!" she cried.

"Why not? I see no need in getting out of bed each morning, and then having to go to another room to dress." He unzipped the bag as if there were no argument and proceeded to unpack.

She'd never felt so helpless or frustrated in her life. It didn't seem to matter what she said to this man, he just kept bulldozing his way through her business as if she weren't there.

"You're not sleeping in here, either," she said, and resisted the urge to stomp her feet. They were too swollen for fits of pique.

"Yes, I am," Lane said. "This is marriage, Toni, not a horse trade where one tries to outdo the other." He dropped his bag and sat down beside her. "It may have happened for all the wrong reasons, but it's not going to continue that way. I made love to you because I wanted to, not because you think you talked me into it. All you did by getting pregnant was give me a damned good reason to break an old promise I'd made to myself. The mistake was not in making love. My mistake was that I did not take precautions with you. If I had been as responsible as you tried to be, this might not have happened to you."

"I don't believe you, you know. You did not love me then. You do not love me now." She bit her lip and told herself it wouldn't matter if she lied just this once. "Just like I don't love you," she said.

Even to her own ears, she knew that the lie didn't sound right, but she couldn't find it within herself to admit to him that she'd loved him ever since she'd found him in the flooded creek. It was humiliating to be the only one who cared.

"I don't care what you believe," Lane argued. "The truth is, I let you take all the responsibility of precautions and obviously they failed."

Oh, Lord, Toni thought. *They say that confession is good for the soul. I can't live with a man under these circumstances and let him think this baby was an accident.*

She took a deep breath.

"I did it on purpose," she said, staring at a corner of the carpet design to keep from looking at his face.

Lane didn't move—couldn't move. What she'd said had absolutely dumbfounded him. She couldn't possibly mean what he thought that she meant.

"Exactly *what* did you do on purpose, Toni?"

"Got pregnant."

"My God," he muttered, and got to his feet with a jerk,

staring at her as if she'd lost her mind. "Why? Why would you do that?"

She shrugged. "I wanted a family. But I knew no man would ever want to marry me. It was the only way I knew how to make one by myself."

"Bull!" He tilted her chin to his gaze. "I'm sick and tired of hearing you put yourself down."

"It's true, and we both know it. I wasn't pretty enough or woman enough, not even for you. You didn't want to make love to me. You only agreed to it after I asked."

"You still don't get it, do you?" Lane shouted. He was angry. With her, the situation, and even himself. He leaned toward her until they were nearly nose to nose. "My wife died because of me. Our child died because of me."

Toni felt his breath on her cheek. His voice shook with each word that he spoke. "And now there's you. I'm living through this hell all over again when I swore never to put another woman—or myself—in this position."

Toni pushed him away and stood. "You are obsessed with something that was never your fault," she argued. "And as for putting yourself through this again, remember this, mister. I didn't ask you to marry me. You brought *that* upon yourself."

She stomped out of the room, leaving anger in her wake.

It was nearly midnight. The floorboards creaked beneath Toni's feet as she rolled out of bed and headed for another trip to the bathroom. Being pregnant had its annoying drawbacks.

Minutes later, she was still up and wandering through the house, taking comfort in the familiar darkness and the safety within these walls. The baby turned within her belly, rolling so distinctly that she cradled herself and tried not to grunt as it settled with a plop.

"You can't sleep, either, can you, baby?" she whispered, and absently rubbed the mound of her stomach as she went to get a drink.

"Are you all right?"

The sound of Lane's voice startled her. She spun at the sink, clutching the glass between them like a talisman against something that she couldn't name as she peered through the shadows to the dark, bulky shape of the man in the doorway.

"I came to get a drink," she said shortly, and turned her back to him, afraid that he could see too much of what was in her heart.

He moved silently across the room on bare feet, wearing nothing but a pair of cotton briefs, and then stood behind her.

"Let me," he said, taking the glass from her hands and running the water long enough to let it cool in the pipes before filling the glass. He handed it to her, and as he did, traced the side of her arm, testing the surface of her skin. "Are you cold? I could turn up the heat."

Toni set down the glass with a thump. "Lane, if we're going to get through this together, you are going to have to get over this," she said. "I can get my own drink of water. If I'm cold, I have enough sense to do something about it. I do not bend, and I will not break."

He watched her like a hawk eyeing its prey, but did not speak. Toni glared through the shadows and then took a drink too quickly, coughing on the last gulp and hating him for making her appear so inept. She set the glass down on the counter with another thump.

"I'm going back to bed." When he started through the house behind her like a silent but persistent shadow, she couldn't resist a final dig. "I will be glad when this is over, and you can get back to your own business and leave me to get on with mine."

Lane stopped short. It was the first time since they had started this travesty of a marriage that he realized she thought it was going to come and go.

"No way, lady," he said shortly. "That's not the way this is going to work. I'm not here just until the baby is born. I'm here forever. The sooner you get used to that, the better off we'll both be."

Toni's heart raced. The surface of her skin suddenly felt cold and clammy as shock slid into her system. And while she tried to think of something to say, Lane walked past her and crawled back into the bed. But he wasn't alone long.

She ripped back the covers on her side of the bed and then crawled in on her knees. "What do you mean, you're here forever?"

"It's late. We'll talk tomorrow," he said, then reached up and pulled her down against him, moving her without her permission until she was safe and snug beneath the covers.

"Be still," he mumbled, when she would have resisted his embrace, and shifted his hand from her arm, letting it slide over her belly, then cupping the mound beneath with a tenderness that brought tears to her eyes.

"I hate you," Toni whispered, and knew that she lied.

"No, you don't, Antonette," he said softly. "It's yourself that you hate."

She lay still beneath his touch because she knew she had no choice. And she heard what he'd said because it was the truth. She did hate herself. For being less than a woman. And for practicing a deliberate deception.

Chapter 15

Within the first week of their marriage, Lane had tied up nearly every loose end of his life prior to Toni. His request for an extended leave of absence from his job had been received with shock by all who knew him, but granted nevertheless. He had sublet his apartment, transferred his bank accounts, both savings and checking, to the bank in Chaney, and yesterday his car and the rest of his clothes had arrived via two lawmen who had volunteered to bring it all out on the way to their annual hunting trip in Kentucky.

But he had yet to confront the balance of Toni's family or the doctor in charge of her care. The family would have to wait. Lane was determined that Dr. Cross tell him to his face that she was not in danger. Accompanying her to her next appointment was high on his list of things to do.

The phone rang sharply in the hall, breaking the quiet with a persistence that sent Toni scrambling to answer. She picked up on the fourth ring and was gasping for breath when she lifted the receiver to her ear. "Hello?"

"What's wrong?" Justin asked. "You sound like you're out of breath."

Toni leaned against the wall and pressed her hand to her chest, trying to slow down the rapid thump of her heartbeat.

"I am, you dolt," she said lightly. "I can't even walk without puffing, never mind running for the phone."

"You shouldn't be running," Justin said shortly. "You might fall."

Toni sighed. "Justin, for once, have pity on me and give it a rest. I hear caution on a daily basis now, you know."

"No, I don't know anything about what's going on over there anymore," he said, sounding slightly aggrieved.

"It's probably just as well that you don't," she muttered, and didn't realize that she'd spoken aloud.

She saw Lane out of the corner of her eye and tried not to stare. If he would only put on more clothes after his shower, she would be able to cope with his presence in a more dignified fashion. In her mind it wasn't seemly to be so ungainly with child, and still so in lust for the man who had fathered it. She kept waiting for her nesting instincts to replace the ones that had gotten her into this mess, but they were lost somewhere in the memory of making love to a gentle giant.

Lane watched her from the hallway, and thought that she grew more beautiful with every day. Hiding his feelings was difficult, but imperative. Telling her that she was loved before she believed that she was worthy was not a wise move. Not after all that had come and gone between them during the past week.

After a lifetime in sunny Florida, the shock of a Tennessee winter and the warm woman he held each night without possibility of loving was making him slightly insane. Coupled with that, each day he was reliving a hell on earth just by watching her body grow bigger with a child that he'd caused, a child that he still believed might kill her. He was not a happy man.

Toni turned away from the intensity of Lane's gaze and realized that Justin had stopped talking. She hoped that he had not been waiting for an answer to a question that she hadn't heard.

"So, Justin, other than a small dose of guilt, which, by the way, remind me to thank you for later, was there anything else you wanted me to know?"

"I was just making sure you had someone to take you to your doctor's appointment today. And," he added, "Judy wanted me to invite you…and the lawman…to come to dinner this weekend after church. Everyone will be here."

Toni wanted to say no, but there was really no point in delaying the inevitable. Her family already knew Lane as the man she'd saved from the flood, and who later had saved her life. But they had yet to meet him on personal ground as the newest member of the Hatfield clan. The implications of what might happen when they got together boggled, but she knew the time had come.

"I suppose we could," she said.

Lane paused in the doorway, wearing nothing but a towel and giving her a look that she didn't want to interpret. He was her husband in name only, but she still felt obligated to inform him of the invitation.

"Justin has invited us to dinner the day after tomorrow. Is there a reason why we can't go?"

Lane grinned at the flush on her face, letting his gaze rake her lush, pregnant curves from top to bottom, then shook his head slowly from side to side.

"Not one I can do anything about," he whispered for her ears alone.

Toni inhaled sharply and spun away from his taunting look. Why he kept flirting with her while she was in this…condition was beyond her comprehension. She'd always imagined that men would be turned off at the thought of hugging a whale. She hated pretense, and she was convinced that he was only being nice to her because he was a nice man, not because he really cared a damn about her. She had, after all, deceived him four ways from Sunday.

"We'll be there," she said. "And Lane's going to the doctor with me, so I don't need you to ride sidesaddle anymore."

"Well, if you ever need me, Judy and I are just a phone call away," he muttered, and hung up the phone.

Toni replaced the receiver with a sigh. Her brother was feeling rejected, but she didn't have time to pamper his ego, not when Lane kept putting himself in her direct line of vision.

"Aren't you ever going to get dressed?" she grumbled. "We'll be late for my appointment."

Lane grinned. "No, we won't. But just to make you happy…" He came so close to her that she could smell the scent of soap still fresh on his skin. "I'll go put on some clothes. I wouldn't want to make you mad." He leaned down and kissed the tip of her ear. "I like to keep my women happy."

"And you're very good at it, too, aren't you? Comes from extreme amounts of practice, I would assume."

She glared at him, almost begging him to deny what she'd implied, that he'd had so many women that he was highly adept at keeping them satisfied. But he did nothing but arch an eyebrow and stare intently at the curve of her lower lip.

"You're very beautiful when you're angry, did you know that?" He tilted her chin just enough to catch the light from the window behind him and knew that she was in shock by what he'd said. "It makes those little gold flecks in your eyes almost burn. And your nostrils flare, just like they do when you make love. It's a sexy thing to see, Antonette. I hope you know you're making me hurt all over."

Oh, my God. I can almost…almost believe he means that.

She slapped his hand away and pushed him toward the bedroom door. "Just put on some clothes and quit lying through your teeth. I don't need to hear all of this, and I damn sure don't believe it."

Lane groaned softly with want. Ignoring the pout on her mouth, he leaned down and kissed her, savoring the connection as deeply as if it had been their bodies and not their lips that had joined.

"But you will," he whispered as he reluctantly released her from the kiss. "One of these days you will believe everything I tell you." *If it isn't too late,* he thought. *If I haven't already killed you and we just don't know it.*

"I'll be ready in a few minutes." He ran a finger down the straight of her nose. "You know what? You don't have any more lipstick on, honey." He winked as he walked away.

Toni held the memory of that kiss and his wink long after they had ended, and reminded herself not to make so much of the lust that she'd seen in his eyes. It had to have been her imagination.

As usual, the doctor's office was crowded. Women in various stages of pregnancy sat or sprawled, as their conditions demanded, upon the waiting room chairs while herding their other offspring with weary eyes.

Lane tried to find a place for himself among this all-female show, but considering the location, and his size, it wasn't easy. His legs stuck out in the aisle, and his shoulders bunched as he tried to make himself as small as possible.

At this point in their lives, no matter what their marital status, these women were almost past appreciating the male of the species. But Lane Monday was a hard man to ignore, and so he suffered more than one speculative glance.

Toni checked in, quietly giving the receptionist the new information regarding her name change. But a half hour later when the nurse announced the name of Toni Monday, and the woman everyone had known during the past few months as Toni Hatfield stood, the women grinned.

"Way to go, girl," one woman said, and wiggled her eyebrows at Toni and appreciatively eyed Lane's long legs and backside as they passed.

"Good grief," Lane muttered, and sighed with relief as they bypassed the waiting room for an examining room instead.

Toni hid a grin. It was the first time in their entire relationship that she'd seen him ill at ease. She wanted to laugh at it all. At his unwarranted fears regarding the child. At the way fate had intervened with her plans. But she wouldn't laugh in the face of fate. Not anymore. She'd come to realize that she was no good at playing God with people's lives. She'd tried to have a child without the father's knowledge and look what had happened. She'd ruined his future as well as her future plans. She'd planned on being a mother, not a wife. In her mind the two had still not mixed.

"Just have a seat," the nurse said. "Dr. Cross will be with you shortly."

The moment that they entered the confines of the sterile-looking room, Lane started to sweat. There were too many ugly memories associated with baby doctors and hospitals for him to relax.

Toni recognized his agitation and suspected its cause. Instinctively, she sought a way to make his fears a little easier to bear.

"It will be fine," she said softly, and patted his arm without thinking that she'd initiated a contact she'd sworn not to make.

Lane covered her hand with his own, and then caught it to his lips, pressing a kiss on the palm of her hand before pulling his chair as close to hers as it could get.

"God, Toni, you just don't understand. You keep saying that I should look at you and know that you can handle anything. Well, look at me for a change. See me and know the truth. I'm so big, Toni. Maybe too big. I sire children just like me."

She shuddered and wanted to throw her arms around him. But that would be admitting to herself, as well as to him, that she couldn't do this alone.

"I certainly hope so," she said. "I always wanted a child with blue eyes."

Lane's eyes widened, and a slight smile spread across his face. "You are so damned hardheaded, aren't you?"

She shrugged, trying to think of an answer that was close to the truth; then the doctor entered the room and saved her from lying.

"Miss Hatfield, I see you're—"

"Mrs. Monday," Toni said, correcting him at the same instant that the doctor noticed Lane. "Dr. Cross, this is my husband, Lane Monday. And he seems to believe that I will die having this child."

The shock of her statement stayed with Dr. Cross as he watched the man unfold himself from the chair and then stand to shake his hand. He looked up, then up some more.

"Mr. Monday, it's a pleasure," he said, and waved for them to sit as he dropped onto his stool. "And what exactly is it that causes such fears? Your wife is as healthy a patient as I've ever had."

"I've already lost one woman I got in this condition, that's why," Lane growled. "Now, you tell me that it's not going to happen again."

"I don't understand," the doctor said.

"His first wife died trying to give birth. The baby was too big, and she didn't survive the shock of other complications. Because of his size, Lane blames himself."

"A common, but unfortunate, misconception," the doctor said. He smiled at Lane as if to ease his words. "You are definitely a big man. But all big men start out as small babies."

"Not always so small. I weighed eleven pounds when I was born," Lane said. "My first wife wife died trying to give birth to a seven-and-a-half-month preemie that weighed nearly ten pounds. Talk me out of this. I need to believe you," Lane said.

The doctor's eyebrows rose as he listened to the big man's shaky voice. "Look, Mr. Monday, during a woman's pregnancy and the ultimate act of birth, the only real thing a man can take credit for is the sex of the child. Whatever else happens during the pregnancy and birth process is the mother's and the doctor's business. You just sit back and wait for it all to happen. If there should be a complication, thanks to your warnings, we'll be well prepared. But I do appreciate knowing your family history. It will help me prepare for things I might not have foreseen.''

"I told you it would be fine," Toni said, and tried not to think of another woman dying without being able to give life to the baby that she and Lane had created.

"I will believe it when I see that baby and know that my wife is fine and not before then," Lane said stubbornly.

"I take it you wish to be in the delivery room," the doctor said.

"I have to be," Lane replied, taking Toni's hand as he spoke. "I need to see for myself that she will be all right."

He doesn't mean that the way it sounded, Toni told herself. *He doesn't really care about me on that level. It's just fear, and not love, that I hear in his voice.*

But the notion had still been set, and when the checkup was over and they were on their way home, Toni dozed with her head against his shoulder, and dreamed of a man and a baby and matching eyes of blue.

"You sure are big," a young Hatfield announced. "Are you a giant?"

Lane eyed the stair-stepped brood of children surrounding his chair, and tried not to grin. They were so serious that he felt they at least deserved his full attention.

"Nope," he said, and ruffled the dark brown hair of the nearest child. "Do I look like one?"

"Yes," they chorused, and then giggled.

"Well, you all look like little squirts to me. Are you?"

A small blond girl giggled. She was David and Laura's youngest, and the Sunday dinner that Lane was given to endure seemed destined to be a series of questions and answers. First from the grown-ups, now from their children.

"I'm not a squirt," the child said. "I'm Chelsea."

Lane laughed, and lifted the tiny child onto his lap. "Hello there, Chelsea. You sure are pretty. Just like your aunt Toni."

She nodded, apparently well aware of her worth in her family. "Did you really marry my aunt Toni?"

"Yes. Is that okay?"

"I guess so," she said, giving his face and hands special consideration. "You don't even have to stand on a chair to do the tree, do you?"

Even the adults who were trying not to listen laughed along with Lane at the little girl's reference to decorating the Christmas trees that stood in every Hatfield home. And it was fairly obvious, even to the babies, that Lane Monday did not stand on chairs to do anything.

Toni watched from across the room, wishing she believed Lane when he said that she was pretty, and wanting desperately to be the one sitting in Lane's lap, and not her niece. She was tired and aching, and sleepy beyond belief, and she could have used that broad strong shoulder to lean on.

Her spirit was still willing, but her body was giving out on her on a daily basis. At eight months pregnant, she completed daily tasks with slow deliberation, not wasting a motion or wanting to retrace a step.

She shifted in her seat, and then stood, bracing her back with her hand as she slipped from the room. Maybe if she could just find a quiet place to lie down for a minute, she would feel better.

It was instinctive, but the moment Toni left the room, Lane seemed to know it. It was as if she'd turned out a light behind her. The sense of loss was physical as his gaze lifted from the child in his lap to the people sitting and standing around the room.

He stood, making a game out of dumping the little girl on her head in the chair that he had just vacated, while he searched the room for a sign of his wife.

"Where did Toni go?" Lane asked.

Both Justin and David looked startled at Lane's obvious concern. "Why, she's right over..."

The chair was empty.

Lane walked out of the room without waiting for an answer
He would see for himself.

There were no empty beds. They were full of napping babies in various stages of development, from toddlers to crawl-
ers. The youngest baby, Lucy, claimed the baby bed for her
own.

Toni sighed and then smiled at the sight of the babies in
slumber. "I should have known better," she said, and then
turned and walked straight into Lane's outstretched arms.

"Oh!" she gasped, and would have staggered but for the
strong clasp of his hands upon her arms. "I didn't see you
there."

"But I saw you," he whispered, aware of sleeping children
and his weary woman, and held out his arms again. He
groaned beneath his breath when she walked into the hug
without complaint. Little by little, she was coming around. He
just had to have faith that she would finally realize what she
meant to him.

"Are you ready to go home?" he asked as he stroked the
back of her neck with a gentle, massaging touch. "You look
tired."

Toni leaned sideways against him, remembering a time
when their bodies fit much closer, and tried not to cry, although it was something that happened often these days.

"Yes, I am. Thank you for asking."

He frowned. "I don't need to be thanked for taking care
of what's mine."

Oh, Lane, if only I believed that you meant that. But the
only sign that she gave of how moved she was by his words
was to lay her head a little closer to the middle of his chest.
It felt safest to be closest to his heart.

She entered the living room beneath the shelter of his arm,
although from Toni's point of view, Lane was simply helping
her stay on her feet.

"What's wrong?" Justin asked when he saw how Toni was
leaning.

Lane answered for the both of them. "She's tired. We're going home. Thank you for dinner and the family welcome. She will call."

Toni didn't even bother adding to his comments other than sending a smile and a couple of kisses to a niece who demanded what she called "bye-bye sugars."

She wondered as they drove home if she dared let herself get used to someone making decisions for her. Having a broad shoulder and a warm body to lean on was a luxury she could get used to fast.

It was almost dark when Lane burst through the kitchen door, slamming it shut behind him, trying to outrun the cold gust of air that had been on his heels.

"I wondered where you had gone," Toni said nonchalantly, trying not to let him know that she even cared. She'd awakened from her nap to an empty house and realized how much she'd come to depend upon his presence for comfort.

"I was helping Abel feed the livestock," he said, stuffing his gloves into the pocket of his coat before hanging it on a peg by the door. "He says it's going to snow before morning."

Toni shrugged. The man that she'd hired months earlier to help her with the heavy work had taken a definite liking to Lane.

"If Abel says it will snow, then it wouldn't surprise me." And then she smiled at the thought of the Christmas tree in the living room and the presents tucked far underneath the spreading branches. "In six more days, it will be Christmas. It would be nice if we could have a white one."

Lane frowned at the thought of snow and ice. "I don't want to be stranded up here," he muttered, unaware that he'd thought out loud.

Tears stung Toni's eyes, and she turned away, unwilling to let him see that he could hurt her this badly, simply by admitting that he didn't want to be around her.

"I know I'm not the best company, but you asked for every bit of this, you know."

Lane groaned, caught her in his arms, then turned her to face him. "I didn't mean I didn't want to be stranded *with* you. I meant I didn't want *you* to be stranded, honey. When are you going to get it through your head that I want you safe?"

"And when are you going to stop making me crazy talking like I'm a doomed woman? How do you think that makes me feel, Lane? I've never had a baby before. I want this to be a positive experience, not one where I go in expecting to breathe my last gasp on a delivery table while you stand there pointing and saying 'I told you so.'"

Shame made him acknowledge the truth of her words, although he couldn't let go of his fear.

"You're right," he said quietly, and tilted her chin with his fingertip. "I'm sorry. I'm a jerk."

"I already knew that," Toni said, then looked away so that he would not see her smile.

"How can I make it up to you?" Lane asked, and nipped the lobe of her ear with his teeth before cupping her hips with the palms of his hands.

"Don't," Toni said, trying to twist out of his arms. "I'm ugly. You don't want to—"

"My God," Lane said, and shook from the need to make love to her. "How can you say that? Better yet, how can you think it, lady? Do you feel this?"

He grabbed her hand and slid it down the front of his jeans. It wasn't the zipper that bulged against her palm. Her eyes widened as he wrapped her in his arms and whispered against her cheek.

"I lie beside you and watch you sleep and think I've never seen a woman as beautiful. You smile and my damned legs get weak in the knees. I've loved you far longer than I had a right to. And I don't care anymore whether you believe me or not. I had what I thought was a really good reason to leave you behind. You, my hardheaded woman, have proved me wrong.''

''I don't believe you, you know,'' Toni whispered, and let his hands wander across her body because it felt too good to make him stop.

''Oh, hell, I know that,'' he muttered, and picked her up into his arms as if she didn't weigh an ounce.

''Where are we going?'' she asked.

''To bed. I want to show you something.''

''What?'' she asked.

''How many ways there are to make love without rocking the boat...and our baby.''

She gasped and unconsciously covered her belly with her hands. ''You can't actually mean you want to...that we can...'' She ducked her head and then closed her eyes when he laid her gently in the middle of the bed. She heard the rustling of clothing being removed and moaned softly. ''I don't want you to see me like this.''

''Why not, love, why not?'' he whispered. ''I'm willing to let you see me like this.''

Toni opened her eyes and couldn't tear her gaze away. He wore nothing but the jutting proof of his desire and a fire in his eyes that burned white-hot.

Her voice shook, but her gaze never wavered as she made a place for him on the bed.

''Oh, Lane, what was I thinking when I pulled you out of that flood?''

''If you weren't out of your mind then, I can assure you that before we're through tonight, you will be.''

''It snowed.''

''Good morning, love,'' Lane whispered as he walked up behind her, kissing the back of her neck before peering over her shoulder and out the window. ''Of course it snowed. Abel said it would, remember?''

Toni remembered a whole lot more about last night than

Abel's predictions. She'd never known a body could soar when weighed down with a burgeoning anchor.

"Oh!" she gasped, laughing when the baby kicked and rolled inside her like a tumbling pup. "Feel that! We're not the only ones awake."

Lane's eyes turned dark with emotion as Toni grabbed his hands and held them flat against the skin on her belly. But old memories got in the way of new joy, and he dropped his hands and turned away. As badly as he wanted to share Toni's joy, he was unable to let himself care. If he cared too much, it might jinx them all.

"Don't," Toni urged, pulling him back around and then stepping into his arms. "Don't be afraid for me or for your child. We're going to be fine."

And if you're not, I will not survive twice.

Chapter 16

The days rolled one into the other until finally Christmas arrived, bringing a false frivolity with it that had little place in the reality of their lives. The intensity of Toni's fears increased on a daily basis. Facing the fact that she loved Lane without hope of a lifetime together was unbearable. But she wouldn't let herself pretend that he would stay after the baby's birth. Once he saw that they were safe and that he had not been responsible for another woman's death, she fully expected him to leave.

And Lane watched her coming closer and closer to her time, and spent countless nights awake, watching for a sign of impending danger, praying that he would be able to prevent another tragedy from occurring. Life without the child that she carried would be heartbreaking, but life without Toni would be impossible to bear. All he could do was hope for the best and pray that they both survived.

And so they existed, day after day, not saying what was in their hearts, and pretending that nearly all was well.

* * *

Lane propped himself onto one elbow as he played with the tousled curls that lay across Toni's forehead, careful not to wake her as he kept watch. She slept without moving, weary from daylight to dusk from the burden of the child that grew bigger with each passing day.

It was instinct that made him feather his fingers across the swell of her belly, desperate for some kind of assurance that all was well within. But when the tiny kick of little feet and bumping elbows vibrated beneath his palm, he buried his face against her shoulder and shook with fear. So much life. So much danger.

Toni sighed, and rolled over on her back, unaware that the man with whom she lay was on sentry duty at her side.

Lane watched her eyelids flutter and knew that she was near to waking. When her arms stretched high above her head and she arched her back like a slumberous cat, he rolled over, grabbed the small box from the bedside table that he'd put there earlier, and leaned down and kissed her the rest of the way awake.

"Merry Christmas, love."

Unaware of the turmoil with which he'd spent the night, Toni rolled over in bed and then sat up, rubbing sleep from her eyes as Lane dropped a small package in what was left of her lap.

"What is this?" she asked.

"Your Christmas present. Open it."

"My hair," she muttered, and started swiping at the curls that had escaped their tie.

"Lady, you would drive a man crazy just to prove that you could," he growled. "I love your hair. I like it in knots. Open the damned present."

"I need to go to the…"

Lane groaned and rolled over onto his back. "Go," he said, and pointed toward the bathroom door. "I should have known better than to try to compete with Mother Nature."

Unable to wait for her return, he tore into the wrapping himself, and when she came out, hair combed, face washed, ready to open her gift, Lane met her at the door with it already in his hand. He spread her fingers and then slipped the ring onto her finger and didn't know that he was shaking until he took a breath.

"It's a sight better than handcuffs, don't you think?"

Tears blurred all but the glimmer of stones from her vision.

"Does this mean you're going to keep me?" she asked.

He groaned and then held her. "You don't listen very well, do you? I already told you I'm here forever."

"I don't know why you still care," Toni said. Guilt pricked her conscience on a daily basis, and this show of affection only made it worse. "I begged you to make love to me. Then I lied to you. I tricked you. I used you, Lane. You should hate me...why don't you?"

He sighed, and rubbed the small of her back where he knew that she always hurt.

"Beats the hell out of me, woman," he said softly. "All I know is I don't want to let you out of my sight."

"What about when this waiting is all over and I've had the baby?" Toni asked. "What will you do with your life then, Lane?" *What will you do with mine?*

"It will never be over for me," he whispered. "I'm always going to be waiting for you to come into a room and light up my life."

Toni sighed. She'd heard it before, but she needed to hear it again. Maybe if she heard it enough, she would really begin to believe.

"And you really don't mind that you had to transfer your job location?"

He grinned. "Naw...I'm sort of looking forward to it," he said. "For a lawman, one place is just about as good as another. I like the business and don't much care where it's done. Besides, I'm enjoying this time off. I've even learned enough about farming and ranching that Abel has stopped laughing at me."

She leaned against his chest and lifted her hand, tilting her fingers so that the brilliance from the circlet of gold and di-

amonds caught the rays of early-morning sun coming through
the bedroom window and reflected it back into her eyes.

"Do you like it?" Lane asked anxiously.

Toni smiled through her tears. "I love it." *And you. Maybe
one day I'll be able to say so without making a fool of myself.*

His grin said it all. Impulsively, Toni threw her arms around
his neck and did something he wasn't expecting. She kissed
him. Hard. With something close to desperation.

Their lips met. His were firm and slightly shocked; hers
were soft and warm, begging for an acceptance that she already had and just wouldn't believe.

"Ah, Toni girl, I love you so much." He wrapped her in
his arms. "How did I ever exist without you?"

She took his words to heart and pretended that it was so.
"Want some breakfast, or do you want to wait for lunch?"

They were going to Justin's for the holiday meal, and Toni
knew from experience that the feast would be endless.

"I don't want to wait for anything," he whispered, and
feathered kisses down the side of her neck.

She blushed. "Would you like your present now?"

"Please," he groaned, and took her back to bed.

It was only later that he opened his gift that she had hidden
beneath the tree. Compared to what they had shared in their
bed, it came in a distant second, but he would never tell her
so. Her joy in finding him a sweater that actually fit his long
arms and broad shoulders went a long way toward getting
him through the day with in-laws who watched his every
move, and the multitude of children who reminded him that
he and Toni would soon have one of their own.

Several inches of snow covered the ground. Icy spears
clung to the eaves of the house as well as to the tree branches
in the surrounding yard. New Year's Day had arrived with a
blast of fresh winter weather that they were just now coming
out from under. Two days earlier the roads had been nearly
impassable.

It was with relief that they had awakened this morning and

seen that things were starting to melt. Lane had gone to town for groceries, leaving Toni safely inside where it was warm, with no danger of slipping and falling and a promise to be back within the hour.

Only moments ago she'd heard the pickup pulling into the barn and breathed a sigh of thanksgiving that he was back. She felt off center, as if something approached from an unseen angle. And then the quiet within her erupted as her nephew, Bobby, burst through the back door in tears.

"Aunt Toni! Aunt Toni! You've got to come quick!"

The child's frantic cry was thick with fear. And the shock of seeing Justin's ten-year-old son come running into the kitchen with blood on his hands and face made her sick.

"Oh, my God! Bobby! You're bleeding! What happened? Did someone have an accident?"

And then everything faded out of focus. She saw the little boy talking, but she couldn't hear his words. Staggered by the shock of what was happening, she braced herself and leaned against the cabinet while a sharp pain rippled low across her back. "Oh," she groaned, and cradled her belly. It suddenly felt as if it had doubled in weight.

Lane jumped the steps and entered the house on a run, unaware that the shock on Toni's face was from pain, and not the sight of her nephew covered in blood. From the barn he'd seen Bobby coming through the trees and knew from the way he was running that something was wrong.

"What happened, son?" he asked, catching the child just as the child spun around and flung himself into Lane's arms.

"It's my daddy," he cried. "You've got to come. A tree fell on him. I can't get it off!"

"Dear God," Toni moaned, and pushed herself away from the cabinet. "Where is he?"

"We were cutting firewood down in the hollow beside the old spring. Daddy slipped on the ice just as the tree started to fall. He slid under it. I couldn't get it off of him. I tried and I tried to pull him out, but I couldn't."

"Bobby! Listen to me," Lane said. "You've got to calm

down so we can help your daddy. How long ago did this happen?"

Bobby choked, swallowing his sobs as he swiped at his face with both hands, streaking the blood even worse. Toni tried not to think of her brother and death in the same breath, but it was impossible.

"Just a little while ago," Bobby said. "Maybe fifteen minutes."

"Good," Lane said. "Now, was your daddy talking to you?"

"No," Bobby groaned. "He's all pale and I know he's cold. There's snow all over him."

Lane hugged the child and then knelt. "Can you show me where your daddy is?"

Bobby nodded.

Lane stood abruptly and turned to Toni, unaware that she bore the burden of two fears. He was all business.

"Honey, call the sheriff. Tell Dan that we need an ambulance and whatever rescue equipment the volunteer fire department has. I'm going with Bobby now. When the men get to the farm, tell them how to get to the spring."

She nodded, and bit her lower lip to keep from moaning. She was scared to death to be here alone. What if they were gone a long time? The baby was coming. She knew it. And then she looked at Bobby's face and her decision was instantly made. She could not sacrifice her brother's welfare for her own safety. If Lane knew what was happening to her, he wouldn't go and she knew it. He would wait for the sheriff to arrive and that might be the difference between Justin living and dying. Whatever was happening to her she would deal with after they were gone.

"Take the tractor and a log chain," she said. "There should be several in that empty granary next to the feed bin, and you should probably take the first-aid kit. I don't know what's in it, but you might be able to use something."

"I'll get it, Aunt Toni," Bobby cried. "I know where it is."

Toni clutched at Lane, willing some of his strength into herself as she wrapped her arms around his waist.

"Be careful," she whispered. "I don't know what I would do if anything happened to you, too."

Lane's heart leapt. He'd been waiting for weeks to hear her say something like this, and now to be unable to stay and pursue this declaration was painful. But for Justin's sake, it would have to wait.

"That goes double for me, lady," he said, and pressed a hard, hungry kiss against her mouth. "You take care of yourself and our baby. Don't do anything stupid, honey. Call Judy and tell her what happened, then call the rest of your family. Some of them will probably go to her, but make sure that someone comes to stay with you. I don't want you here worrying alone."

She nodded, and then they were gone. Her fingers shook as she dialed the phone. But it was not from fear. It was pain. Another spasm rolled across the muscles of her back, ripping through her senses as a reminder that this was only just starting.

When Dan Holley answered the phone, his voice was music to her ears.

"Chaney Sheriff's Office."

"Dan, this is Toni Monday. I need an ambulance out here fast."

Dan grinned. "Is it time, girl?"

She gritted her teeth. "You have no idea," she groaned, and leaned against the wall to brace herself for what she felt coming.

"Where's that big ol' husband of yours? I expected him to be the one making the call," he teased.

"Listen to me, Dan. I don't have much time," she gasped, and let the pain roll across her senses. "Justin's been hurt. I don't know how badly. All we know is that a tree fell on him while he and Bobby were cutting wood. Lane's gone back to the old spring below our place to try to help. We need an ambulance and all the rescue equipment you have."

"Oh, my God," Dan muttered. "Hang on, honey. We'll be there in a whistle."

She bit her lip to keep from crying. "And would you send a second ambulance for me while you're at it?"

Dan nearly dropped the phone. "Are you saying what I think you're saying?"

"I'm in labor. Lane doesn't know it. It just started, but it seems like the pains are already pretty severe."

"How far apart?"

"Maybe five minutes," Toni said, and hugged herself to keep from shaking. Doing this alone was scary business.

"I'm calling for a mediflight helicopter. Lane already told me about the difficulties you might face during delivery. There's no way an ambulance will get you safely to Knoxville in time, not if your pains are already that close."

"I don't care what you do," she cried, then doubled over. "Just hurry!"

"For once, make that big family of yours useful and get someone over there with you now!" he said, and hung up in her ear.

Seconds later she'd dialed another number. "Laura, this is Toni. We need help."

By the time she was through, Hatfields were in motion, but she didn't care. She was trying to get to a bed. Standing had become an impossible feat.

"There he is!" Bobby cried, and pointed toward the slough on the opposite side of the creek from where they stood.

Without wasted motion Lane shifted the tractor into low gear and proceeded across the frozen streambed. He stopped on the last level space of ground, aware that if he got any closer, he would be sliding down the incline and right into Justin's lap, which was exactly what they didn't need.

"Now if only we'd brought enough chain," he muttered. They had not.

"What are we going to do?" Bobby said, and started to

cry. "We can't pull the tree off of him. The chain's too short."

"Damn it," Lane said, then dumped the log chain, and slid down into the slough without giving himself time to think.

The snow felt like ground glass. It was icy and hard, and packed to the point that standing was next to impossible. Lane made the last few yards to the fallen tree on his rear. He knelt beside Justin, then felt on his brother-in-law's neck for a pulse.

"Thank God," Lane muttered when he felt the faint beat, then cupped Justin's face in his hand. "Justin! Can you hear me?"

Justin's eyelids fluttered. It was all the answer that Lane was going to get. He looked at his watch, gauging the time from when they'd left the house against the time that it would take the rescue squad to arrive, and he knew that they were looking at another thirty minutes at least.

He won't last.

Lane knew it as surely as he knew his own name. Justin was already in shock. And from what he could see of the wound on his leg, it was a wonder that he hadn't already bled to death. The cold was probably what had saved him, but it could ultimately be what killed him, too.

Lane stood up, then looked to the hill where the ten-year-old stood, frozen in horror by what had happened to his daddy.

"Bobby, get down here."

The child quickly obeyed.

"Here's what we're going to do," he said. "When I lift this tree up off of your daddy's legs, I want you to grab him by the boots and pull. Do you think you can do that? It's downhill enough that I think his own weight will help him slide out from under the tree if you can get him started."

Bobby's eyes grew round. He stared down at the immensity of the tree pinning his father to the ground, and then back up at the man towering above him.

"Can you do that?" Bobby whispered.

Lane's lips thinned with determination. "I hope to hell I can, son. Now come on. Say a prayer for your daddy, and one for me while you're at it. We're both going to need some extra help today."

Bobby gritted his teeth and sniffed back the last of his sobs.

"Yes, sir," he muttered, and bent down.

Lane cursed beneath his breath when he saw that Bobby Hatfield's hands spanned less than half the circumference of his father's work boots.

"Maybe you could get a better grip on his blue jeans instead," he offered, and nodded when he saw Bobby get a good, solid handful of denim in each fist.

"Good boy," he said, bending toward the fallen tree. "Now get ready. When I say pull, you give it all you've got."

The boy nodded, and when he looked up at Lane with all the trust in the world written upon his face, Lane recognized it as a look that Toni had given him more than once. The thought of what he had to lose gave him the courage to continue. But he was going to need more than courage to move the tree.

The bark was rough against his palms, the snow cold against his knees as he knelt. He had already decided that lifting the tree from a dead squat would be impossible, even for him. It left him with one option that involved great risk for him, as well.

There was just enough space near the root end for a man to crawl under. And if he was lucky, and didn't slip on the ice and the snow himself, there might be a way for him to lever the tree up enough for Bobby to pull his father out. To do it he would have to use the broad surface and great strength of his size and the back that God had given him.

Lane dropped to his knees.

"What are you doing, Uncle Lane?"

The quaver in the boy's voice was all the reminder that he needed to hurry, but it was what Bobby had called him that he would never forget. He didn't want to lose that respect...ever.

And then Justin moaned, and his eyelids fluttered open just as Lane centered the tree directly across the strongest part of his back.

"What the hell do you think you're trying to do?" he groaned, and pushed weakly at Lane's arm.

"Don't bite the hand that's about to free you," Lane ordered; then he grinned and winked at Justin, trying to alleviate some of the terrible tension of the moment.

"You're a stupid, crazy son of a bitch," Justin mumbled. "If it slips, we're both dead."

"Daddy, try not to move," Bobby said as tears rolled down his face. "It makes your leg bleed worse."

"Shut up and help your son when he starts pulling you out," Lane ordered. "Remember, Bobby, when I say pull, you yank for all you're worth."

"Yes, sir," Bobby said, and reaffirmed his grip on his father's jeans.

Before he could talk himself out of what he intended to do, Lane started to lift. The weight was at once unbearable and impossible to budge. He shifted his body lower down the trunk and closer to where Justin was pinned, then repeated the lift, letting most of the weight rest upon the broadest portion of his shoulders.

In spite of the cold, in spite of the ice and snow down the tops of his boots and inside his pockets, he started to sweat. He groaned and lifted himself a little bit higher, using his leg muscles now, as well as his arms, to lever himself higher and higher off of the ground.

A twig on a limb down the trunk snapped. And then another and another, and Lane knew that he must be moving something other than the snow beneath his hand and feet for the branches at the other end of the tree to start breaking.

"You're doing it! You're doing it!" Bobby shouted. "A little more, Uncle Lane. Just a little bit more."

Lane groaned again, and moved his knees a little closer to his chest, now using his full body weight as a lever against the end of the fallen tree. His muscles bunched, then tightened, then burned, and he knew he was nearly at the end of his strength. He couldn't look over at Justin and see the fear on his face. But he desperately needed to concentrate on something other than the ground slipping beneath his feet.

He cursed, shifted his weight once again and closed his eyes and thought of Toni.

"Damn it, move!" he cursed, and bunched every muscle in his body toward the weight upon his back, then tried to stand.

The branches that were holding it off the ground at the other end suddenly snapped, and Lane felt the tree beginning to give.

"Now, Bobby!" he shouted, readjusting his position so that the tree would not move with the pull of Justin's body. "Pull, son! Pull with everything you've got."

At first nothing happened. He heard the child's frantic sobs and desperate gasps for breath. He heard the scrape of snow as Bobby slipped and fell backward upon his rear. And then suddenly Justin was sliding out of his line of vision, and Lane blinked rapidly to clear his sight as sweat ran and burned into his eyes.

"He's out! He's out!" Bobby cried.

"Keep pulling him," Lane urged. "The tree might slide back over him when I let it go!"

Justin did what he could to help, digging his fingers into the snowpacked ground, trying to pull himself along. Then a miracle occurred. He started to slide.

"Let me go," he yelled, and waved his son aside as he tried to get as far away from the tree as possible.

"Let it go, Uncle Lane," Bobby cried, and ran in front of the tree until he was eye to eye with the big man who had just saved his father's life. "He's sliding down the hill by himself. The tree can't hurt him now."

"Get back," Lane groaned, and knew that he had nothing more than a few seconds in which to clear himself from the danger of being trapped as Justin had been.

With his last ounce of strength, he moved the bulk of his

lift from an upward motion to a backward one instead, then propelled himself forward, falling facedown onto the icy ground. Snow spewed up into the air as the tree belly flopped only inches from his heels, and Lane moaned, then rolled over on his back, gasping for breath, and staring up into the gray, winter sky, never so glad to feel cold in his entire life.

When he could breathe without pain, he lifted his head and looked over the tree and down the hill. Justin lifted his arm and waved. Lane started to return the favor, when he realized that Justin was not waving at him. He looked up at the crest of the hill. Help had arrived. And from the trail of blood Justin had left behind him in the snow when he'd slid out from under the tree, it was none too soon.

Dan Holley was first on the scene, followed closely behind by paramedics and a couple of men with chain saws.

"Doesn't look like we'll be needing the saws, boys," Dan said, and left Justin's care to the experts, while he knelt at Lane's side. He looked down at Lane and shook his head. "I have a feeling I just missed a hell of a show."

Bobby Hatfield appeared out of the crowd and threw his arms around Lane's neck. "You did it! You did it! You're the strongest man in the whole world, Uncle Lane."

Lane grinned and wrapped the boy in a warm but shaky hug. "You helped, Bobby. I couldn't have done it alone, and don't you ever forget it."

"You should have seen him, Sheriff Holley," Bobby said. "He just lifted that big ol' tree off of Daddy like it was nothing."

Lane fell back onto the snow with a weak laugh. "Had one of them faked out, didn't I, Dan? Did you hear him? Like it was nothing." He covered his face with his hands and moaned before rolling to a sitting position.

"Help me up," he said, lifting his hand for Dan to pull. "I've just about used up all there is in me."

Dan frowned.

"I sure hope you've got a little bit left, old son, because if things are still going like they were when I left your place, you're in the process of becoming a father.''

Lane was on his feet without aid in seconds. ''Lord,'' he muttered as he headed for the ridge where he'd left the tractor. ''Turn my back on her and look what she does.''

''I already called for a mediflight helicopter. I didn't think she could make the run to Knoxville, considering the facts.''

Lane stopped in midstride and turned. The look on his face was colder than the ground on which he was walking.

''What do you mean...considering the facts?''

Dan shrugged. ''She was already having pains five minutes apart when she called for an ambulance. If you hurry, you just might get to kiss her goodbye before the chopper lifts off.''

Lane was already running up the hill.

Chapter 17

Lane was coming through the trees below the house when the chopper set down in the backyard where the garden had been. He shoved the tractor into high gear and spun up the slippery slope and into the yard just as they carried Toni out the back door.

Running on legs that felt like rubber, he made it around the house and caught the stretcher just as the flight crew was about to lift it into the belly of the aircraft.

"Wait!" he shouted, and felt the air being sucked out of his body by the impact of the spinning rotor above their heads.

"Mister, there isn't any time left to wait," the paramedic shouted. "And there's no room for passengers."

Lane looked down into Toni's face, expecting to see fear, even accusations of abandonment flowing from her lips. She was gritting her teeth, but she was smiling through tears.

"Race you," she said, trying to laugh at the fact that she was going to beat him to the hospital by nearly an hour, and then caught her breath upon another pain.

"This is it, buddy. Kiss her bye-bye. We're gone."

Lane grabbed the man by the arm, pinning him to the spot with the intensity of his gaze as well as his brute strength.

"If it comes down to it," Lane shouted, "you tell that doctor to save my wife. No matter what else happens, you save her...for me."

Toni's pulse rocketed on a pain and a joy, all at the same time. *Save her for me. No matter what.*

And then his mouth was on her lips, and he swallowed her moan of pain and wanted to scream. When they pushed him away and the helicopter lifted off, he felt incomplete, bereft. Everything that mattered to him in this world was out of his hands and swiftly moving out of his sight.

Seconds later she was gone, and Lane was running back into the house for dry clothes and the keys to his car, scattering Hatfields in his wake like chickens.

"Here comes another one, Toni. Now push."

Dr. Cross's order came on the heels of a pain that had lifted Toni off of the bed. She hadn't needed his warning that the pain was on its way. She'd felt it coming a long time before he had.

"I'm pushing," she groaned, and gripped the sides of the bed to brace herself.

"More. More. Just a little bit more," he urged.

"No more," she said hoarsely, then shuddered and moaned and fell back onto the bed, weak and spent.

Time, for Toni, had ceased upon her arrival at the Knoxville hospital. There were no seconds ticking, minutes passing or hours flowing in the birthing room, only wave after mindbending wave of pain that seemed to have no end. No matter how hard she'd tried during the past hour, the baby hadn't budged. She could tell by the expression on Dr. Cross's face that he was beginning to be concerned. And while she couldn't read the monitors to which she was hooked up, even she knew when the numbers began to fall.

"We're losing pressure, Doctor."

The nurse's whisper was soft, but Toni heard the warning,

anyway. She moaned weakly as she felt the arrival of another wave of pain, then lifted herself onto her elbows and bit her lip to keep from screaming. There was no energy left in her to react to the pain, only what it took to survive the next spasm.

"This is it, girl," Dr. Cross urged, and pressed his hand in the middle of Toni's abdomen. "Come on, honey. You can do it."

It was the tiny blip registering a fading pulse and a waning heartbeat that gave her the impetus to give it one last try. She'd done the unforgivable in order to bear this child; she would do the impossible to keep it.

She gritted her teeth, braced herself and closed her eyes, concentrating on the contraction and the pressure, trying to follow it with her body. She would have this baby or die trying. Lane flashed into her mind with the thought, and in that moment, Toni knew that she couldn't afford to die. He would never forgive her.

"Oh, God," she groaned, and let herself go with the pain.

She never even heard the doctor's shout of approval, or her baby's first cry. She was out of hearing distance, lost in the blackness between unconsciousness and exhaustion.

And then she felt a weight upon her belly and instinctively clutched it in her arms. She opened her eyes and looked down just as the baby's head turned. Their eyes met, and for a fraction of a second, Toni swore that recognition passed between them…mother to child.

"Well, hello, sweet baby," she whispered, and ran her finger across the tiny face, feature by feature, unwilling to wait for the nurse to even clean the infant up. She'd waited entirely too long as it was to meet this child.

"It's a girl," the doctor said.

"Is she perfect?" Toni asked, cradling the tiny head within the palms of her hands as the doctor did a quick inspection.

Dr. Cross grinned. "Now if I say she's not, will you give me a head start before you take off my head?" And then he relented. "From the looks of things, I would say so." He lifted her from Toni's arms. "She needs to take a little trip, to get weighed in, blood-typed and such. And you need a breather, too. By the time you're both changed, you can have one hell of a conversation for all I care."

Toni frowned when the baby was lifted from her arms. "Do you promise to bring her right back?"

"I swear," he said. "But first things first."

Moments later the sounds of a baby's loud cry could be heard down the hall in the nursery.

"She's fine," the doctor cautioned. "It sounds like she just doesn't like having her face washed."

Toni frowned and then started to cry.

"Here now," Dr. Cross said. "You're supposed to be happy."

"I've just had a baby, and I don't know if my brother is alive or dead," she said, and sobbed a little bit harder.

"If you promise not to cry, I'll get you your answers. What do you say?"

Toni hiccuped and closed her eyes. She was too tired to argue. "I promise. Especially if you can find my husband in the process."

"That might take some doing, but I'll give it my best shot," the doctor said. Moments later she was alone except for the nurse who was quietly cleaning up.

Lane came off of the elevator on a run and met Dr. Cross coming down the hall. Their expressions were of mutual surprise.

"Just the man I was sent to find," Dr. Cross said with a grin.

Lane grabbed the doctor by the shoulders and tried not to shout.

"Where is my wife?"

"Room 301. They haven't moved her out of the birthing room yet, but..."

Lane left him standing there.

"As I was about to say, feel free to go in," Dr. Cross muttered, then continued on his way.

Lane was inside the room before it dawned on him that he hadn't even asked the doctor what had happened. And then he saw Toni, rolled over on her side away from him, her shoulders shaking with sobs, and he felt the floor going out from under his feet.

Oh, my God. Something bad happened. It was all he could think of to explain why she was crying.

"I'm sorry, sir," the nurse said. "She's not ready for visitors. Please wait outside."

"Toni? Sweetheart," he said, ignoring the nurse's behest.

Toni rolled over onto her back and held out her arms.

"I didn't think you would get here this soon."

He sat down on the side of the bed, and when her arms slid around his neck and she began sobbing against his chest, his heart froze. Breathing constricted until words became impossible to form.

"My God, sweetheart, I'm sorry. I didn't know. I didn't know. I wouldn't have left you if I had."

"Justin! How is Justin?"

"It's all my fault. Whatever happened, we'll get through it together. I love you, lady. With all my heart. Don't give up on me now. I couldn't make it without you in my life."

Toni tightened her hold around his neck. He wasn't making sense, but it felt so good to be holding him that she almost didn't care.

"Lane, what happened? Did Justin...is he okay?" Her voice trembled as she waited anxiously for him to answer.

"We can adopt a baby if you want. Hell, we can adopt ten. Just don't send me away."

"Have you lost your mind?" Toni sighed, and snuggled her nose a little deeper in the breadth of his chest. He smelled of after-shave and the starch that she'd used on his shirt and cold, fresh air, and she'd never been so glad to feel a man's arms around her in her life.

Her words finally penetrated. He leaned back enough to be

able to see her face, then kissed the corner of each of her eyes before moving to her mouth.

"I love you, Toni. I'm sorry I—"

"Lane, listen to me!"

He jerked. "What is it?"

"How is my brother? Is he okay?"

He leaned his forehead against her shoulder and sighed. "Oh, hell, I'm sorry," he muttered. "Yes, honey. We got him out. His leg didn't look good, but he's alive."

"Thank God," she said, and hugged him tight. "I knew that you could do it."

He cradled her face in his hands, searching for signs of despair that he could not see.

"Are you all right?"

"I need to sleep for a week, but I fear my sleeping days are over," she said.

"The baby…was it…did they have to…?"

Toni's eyes widened. Obviously he still didn't know that she'd safely delivered their child. And then the door opened behind him.

"See for yourself," she said, and pointed toward the nurse who was entering with a wiggling bundle in her arms.

Lane's head turned toward the door. He stood, a look of wonder upon his face, then stared in disbelief at the baby.

"You did it," he muttered.

"I suspect you helped," the nurse said sweetly, eyeing the mass of man before her. "Hold out your arms."

Lane did as he was told, and then staggered backward, using Toni's bed for a seat to avoid dropping them both onto the floor.

"Oh, my God," he whispered, and parted the tightly wrapped blanket.

"Now you've done it," the nurse admonished as the baby's hands began to flail in the air. "This one's a real live wire. She doesn't like to be still." She gave Toni a look of admiration. "And if she'd weighed a whit more than the ten pounds, two ounces that she came in at, she wouldn't be here."

For Toni the details and what ifs were over. She was too lost in the joy on Lane's face as the nurse walked out of the room.

"Say hello to your daughter."

He turned to Toni with tears shimmering across his eyes and shook his head, unable to speak.

The baby's mouth pursed, and just when she would have puckered and yelped, Lane's finger stroked the side of her cheek. Her mouth turned like a magnet toward the touch, instantly open in an instinctive search for sustenance.

"Wrong parent," Lane whispered, and bent down and kissed the baby's soft cheek.

Toni was moved to a fresh set of tears. "Do you want to name her?" she asked.

He nodded, then lifted the baby close, cradling her in arms so big against a chest so broad that she was almost lost in the vast amount of space. He looked down at the woman who'd given him the world.

"Since the day that we met, you have given me joy. Constantly...without asking for anything in return. Would you care if I named her Joy?"

Toni held out her arms for the baby. "Let me see if she looks like a Joy," she teased. She ran her hands lightly over the baby's head, loving the feel of soft hair and tender skin beneath her palm. "You look like a Joy. Do you feel like a Joy, little girl?"

The baby squeaked and wiggled. Toni grinned. "She says yes, thank you, she believes that she does."

Lane grinned through tears. "My days are numbered," he muttered, to hide his emotion. "I will be forever outvoted in a house full of women. What is a man to do?"

"Love us?"

Lane heard the uncertainty in her voice. Even now, after all they had been through together, she still doubted her ability to hold a man's love.

"I already do," he said solemnly. "You should know that by now, Antonette. Don't ever, and I mean ever, ask me that in such a doubting fashion again."

Toni sighed and lay back on the pillow, snuggling the baby closely against her side. She closed her eyes and thought of answered prayers and a future that she never thought she would have, and looked up to find Lane staring intently at her face.

"Lane?"

"What, sweetheart?"

"I don't know the words to thank you for all that you've done…for what you've given me."

Lane's eyes narrowed until Toni could see only slits of blue fire.

"I do," he said quietly.

Her eyes widened. Suddenly this conversation had a very familiar ring.

"You could tell me that you love me. Just once. Just for fun."

Emotions overwhelmed her. Of what he had given and given without hope of return. "I love you."

Lane sighed. He was so certain she wouldn't say it that he was already talking before her words sank in. "I'm not asking for much, you understand. It's no more than a man has a right to expect from the woman he expects to spend the rest of his life with."

"I love you very much."

"I've told *you* countless times that I love you. You can't…" He quit in the middle of a sentence. For a moment he couldn't think past the wonder of what he'd just heard. And then she smiled and patted the bed beside her, and he lay his head in the bare space between baby and breast and let her love encompass them all.

Toni threaded her fingers through his hair, loving the way the silky, dark strands parted at her touch.

"I hope Joy has your hair and eyes," she whispered, and felt his shoulders shaking beneath her hands.

Lane lifted his head. "Say it again, Toni. Tell me you love me."

"Of course I love you," she whispered. "I had to love the man before I would consider having his child. I just couldn't believe that he would love me back."

Lane's eyes widened in disbelief. "Are you telling me that you've been in love with me all along?"

Toni smiled, and lifted the baby into her arms. "Lesson number one, little girl. Men are dense."

Lane laughed aloud. "But we float pretty damned good," he said, reminding her of how they had met.

Toni grinned in return. "With absolutely no sense of direction," she added, her own reminder of how she'd saved him from the flood.

"That's what women are for," Lane whispered, his mouth aiming for her lips. "To keep us on the straight and narrow…forever and ever, till death do us part. Remember?"

The kiss was sweet, with a promise of years to come. When Lane broke the connection between them, he whispered one word that she instantly understood.

"Deal?"

Toni smiled. "Deal."

Epilogue

The morning glory that hung over the front-porch roof swung back and forth in the easy breeze like small blue bells with no sound. Sunshine dappled the yard between the spaces of shade where children ran, shrieking with excitement as they searched out the brightly colored eggs hidden earlier. Baskets already overflowing with chocolate bunnies and yellow marshmallow chicks had to make room for the Easter eggs that were being found.

It was Easter at the Monday homestead, and the Hatfields had come to dinner. But no one was eating. Those who weren't watching the frivolity in action were busy snapping pictures of the event, trying desperately to capture the expression of joy on each child's face when a new egg was discovered.

And Toni was right in the middle of it all with her baby on one hip and a basket full of eggs on the other, while the persistent breeze molded the skirt of her white cotton dress to her body.

"Smile for Daddy," she said, and jiggled Joy into a wide,

toothless smile while Lane aimed the camcorder in their direction.

Lane watched it all through the camera's eye, and he knew that if he lived to be a hundred, he would never see a more beautiful sight than what was before his eyes.

Marriage and motherhood had made a beautiful woman out of a pretty lady. Her face creased constantly in smiles, and she was never still. She wouldn't have changed a thing in her world if given the chance and he knew it. The knowledge that he held the hearts of two beautiful females in the palms of his hands was staggering. The baby adored him, and Toni's love bound them all. He was a man twice blessed.

"Uncle Lane, watch this."

In response to the shout, he turned, taking the eye of the camera with him, and found Bobby Hatfield centered within the frame, attempting to juggle three eggs.

Bright pink, brilliant blue and grass green eggs went up, then down, then fell at the boy's feet with a splat as he made a frantic grab for the last one and missed. Lane aimed the camera at the mess, then back up at the look of disgust on Bobby's face.

"You've got to have faster hands than that, boy," Lane teased, then laughed when a couple of barn cats headed for the disaster, already licking their whiskers at the unexpected feast.

While they were watching, the sheriff pulled his car into the driveway and parked.

Lane aimed the camera and caught the look of surprise on Dan Holley's face when he accidentally stepped on an egg hidden in the grass.

"Oh, shoot," Dan said, stopping to clean off his shoe. "These are my new boots."

"What do you suppose he wants?" Justin muttered as he limped up beside Lane.

"Here, you do the honors and I'll go find out," Lane said, handing Justin the camera.

"You're supposed to put them in a basket, not on the sides

of your feet," Lane said, and grinned when the sheriff rolled his eyes and lightly cursed beneath his breath.

"Fine thanks I get for coming out on a holiday," Dan said, handing Lane an envelope. "I found a Western Union man lost as hell on the other side of town. He was looking for your place. It was easier to bring this myself than to try and explain how to get here."

"Thanks," Lane said, then opened up the telegram.

HAPPY EASTER TO EVERYONE. STOP. KISS MY NEWEST NIECE FOR ME AND HUG MY SISTER. STOP. THANKS FOR PROVING ME RIGHT, LAWMAN. STOP. IF I CAN FIX MY WORLD THAT WELL, MAYBE I WILL COME HOME. STOP.

LOVE, WYATT

"Well, I'll be damned," Lane said. "The prodigal son might actually return one of these days."

"Must be from Wyatt," Dan said.

Lane nodded, then looked up at Toni in the middle of it all, and smiled. He had a lot to thank Wyatt Hatfield for. He hoped he *did* come back.

"You're just in time to eat," Lane said, and gave the squashed egg on Dan's boots another glance. "I think the egg hunt is nearly over."

Dan grinned. "No, thanks, but that's my cue to exit. You have a good day, now, you hear?"

Lane waved him off and then turned to see Toni coming toward him across the yard.

"Lane, you have a phone call. It's your boss. He called me darling and praised the latest picture of Joy that he'd seen and told me you never looked better." She made a face. "It sounds to me like it's a good thing I did the laundry yesterday. You'll be needing clean clothes for the trip."

Lane sighed and hugged her. "Maybe not. Here, Dan brought a telegram from Wyatt. You can share it with the clan while I get the phone." Then he held out his hands to the baby who was wearing a miniature bunny suit, complete with long pink ears and a tiny, white powder-puff tail. "Want to come with Daddy to talk to the bad man?"

Toni laughed, and watched with a happy heart as Joy willingly went from her arms to his with a drool and a smile and pink ears flopping. Father and daughter disappeared into the house as Justin walked up.

"What did Dan want?"

Toni handed him the telegram. "It was from Wyatt. You can read it. He said to tell everyone hello."

Justin quickly scanned the page, and handed it back with a rueful smile.

"He's right, you know. He read Lane Monday's intentions better than any of us. Thank God that he interfered. If it wasn't for Lane, you wouldn't be this happy, and I would be less of a man today."

Toni hugged her brother, then whispered softly in his ear. "I don't care what you look like, Justin, or how you walk. You will *never* be less of a man. You're just about the best brother a girl could have."

Justin grinned to hide how moved he was by Toni's praise.

"Well, hell yes, I'm the best. If you don't believe me, you can ask Judy."

Toni grinned and hit him on the arm. "You're awful," she said. "I've got to go see what that darned man wanted with Lane. I suspect duty is about to call."

She hurried across the yard, her long legs moving gracefully beneath the full skirt of her dress, and entered the house on the run. Lane met her at the door empty-handed.

"Where's Joy?" Toni asked.

"Laura took her. The kids wanted to have their picture taken with the Easter bunny. Joy seems to be it."

Toni grinned. The suit had been an inspiration. "When do you have to leave?" she asked, knowing Lane's assistance was needed on another assignment. His duties had been lessened, but her husband's expertise was still essential to some cases.

"Tonight."

Lane slid his hands around her waist and then lowered them until her hips were perfectly cupped in the palms of his hands. She moaned softly in his ear when he pulled her close against the thrust of his manhood.

"When will you be back?" she gasped, wishing that they were alone.

"Day after tomorrow."

She tried not to let her dismay show, but she hated to sleep alone and he knew it.

"I will miss you like hell," he whispered. "Can't you tell everyone to go home now? I want to make love to my wife."

Toni made a face, and wrapped her arms around his neck. "I don't think so," she whispered, and sighed when his mouth descended.

He tasted of baby powder and soap, and she knew that the last place his mouth must have been was on their baby's face.

"I love you, Lane," she said when his mouth had moved from her lips to her throat.

He stilled, and his arms tightened around her waist, crushing her to him until she found it difficult to breathe, but she did not protest. Being loved this much, by this much man, was something special. She would take all that he had to give her and still want more.

"I love you, too, Antonette," he whispered, and then he grinned. "I'll bet I'm the only man who can claim the luckiest day of his life was the day he nearly died."

Toni smiled, and leaned back in his arms, well aware that it placed their lower bodies in perfect but painful alignment.

"I might know where there's an empty hayloft," she said.

Delight was rich in his voice as he swept her off of her feet and twirled her around the room while the party went on outside without them.

"Are you asking me to take you to the barn and make love to you?"

Toni pursed her lips and cocked her head thoughtfully, giving him a cool, assessing look.

"I might be…but only just this once."

He laughed. "And just for fun?"

She wrapped her arms around his neck and blew lightly in his ear.

"Darling Lane, is there any other way?"

* * * * *

WHEN YOU CALL MY NAME

Once, in the middle of the night,
I heard my sister, Diane, call my name.
I sat alone in the dark, listening for hours
for the sound of her voice. It never came again.

I do not believe that death breaks the bonds of love.
And because of that, sometimes I still listen,
just to see if she will call for me again.
Diane, if you're listening, this book is dedicated to you,
and to the love that we shared.

Chapter 1

It's all your fault. You let me down...let me down.

Wyatt Hatfield shifted in his seat and gripped the steering wheel a little tighter, trying to see through the falling snow to the road ahead, doing everything he could to ignore the memories of his ex-wife's accusations. Shirley and his years with the military were things of the past.

This soul-searching journey he'd embarked upon months earlier was for the sole purpose of finding a new direction for himself. He'd fixed what was wrong with Antonette's life with little more than a phone call. Why, he wondered, couldn't he find a way to fix his own? And then he grinned, remembering how mad his sister had been when he'd interfered.

"At least I'm in her good graces now," he muttered, then cursed beneath his breath when his car suddenly fishtailed.

His heartbeat was still on high as he reminded himself to concentrate on the more pressing issues at hand, namely, the blizzard into which he'd driven. The windshield wipers scratched across the icy film covering the glass, scattering the snow in their paths like a dry, whirling flurry, while the heater and defroster did what they could to keep the interior of his car warm.

But as hard as he tried to concentrate on driving, her voice kept ringing in his ear, complaining that when she'd needed him, he was never there.

"Damn it, Shirley, give me a break," Wyatt muttered. "I was wrong. You were right. That should be enough satisfaction for you to let go of my mind."

The car skidded sideways on a patch of ice and Wyatt eased off on the gas, riding with the skid and sighing in relief as the car finally righted itself.

He'd made the wrong decision when he hadn't stopped back in the last town, and he knew it. Then the weather hadn't been this bad, and getting to Lexington, Kentucky, tonight had seemed more important then than it did now. To make things worse, because of the severity of the snowstorm, he wasn't even sure he was on the right road anymore. The weak yellow beam of the headlights did little to illuminate what was left of the road, leaving Wyatt with nothing more than instinct to keep him from driving off the side of the mountain.

And then out of nowhere, the dark, hulking shape of a truck came barreling around a curve and into the beam of light, slipping and sliding as Wyatt had done only moments before, and there was no more time to dwell upon past mistakes. It was too late to do anything but react.

Wyatt gripped the steering wheel, trying desperately to turn away from the truck gone out of control, but he knew before impact that they were going to crash.

"God help us all," Wyatt murmured, knowing there was no earthly way to prevent what was about to happen.

And then the truck's bumper and fender connected with the side of Wyatt's car. Bulk and weight superseded driving skill. Impact sent Wyatt and his car careening across the road and then down the side of the snowpacked mountain.

The last thing he saw was the picture-perfect beauty of lofty pines, heavy with snow and glistening in the head-lights of his car. Blessedly, he never felt the car's impact into the first stand of trees…or the next…or the next, or knew when it rolled sideways, then end over end, coming to a steaming, hissing halt against a fifty-foot pine.

He didn't hear the frantic cries of the truck driver, standing at the edge of the road, calling down the mountain and praying for an answer that never came.

The wind from the blizzard whistled beneath the crack in the windowsill across the room. Even in her sleep, Glory heard the high-pitched moan and unconsciously pulled the covers a little higher around her neck. She could hear the warm, familiar grumble of her father, Rafe, snoring. It signified home, protection and family. Directly across from Glory's room, her brother, J.C., slept to the accompaniment of an all-night music station. Mixing with the wail of the wind and the low rumble of an old man's sleep, the melodies seemed somehow appropriate. Glory's long flannel gown added to the cocoon of warmth beneath the mound of covers under which she slept. She shifted, then sighed, and just as her subconscious slipped into dream sleep, she jerked. There was no escape for what came next, even in sleep.

Eyes! Wide, dark, shocked! Red shirt! No…white shirt covered in blood! Blood was everywhere. Pain sifted, filtering through unconsciousness, too terrible to be borne!

Glory's eyelids fluttered and then flew open as suddenly as if someone had thrown open shutters to the world. She sat straight up in bed, unaware of the familiarity of her room, or the snow splattering against the windowpanes. Her gaze was wide, fixed, frozen to the picture inside her mind, seeing…but not seeing…someone else's horror.

White. Cold, so cold! Snow everywhere…in everything. Can't breathe! Can't see! Can't feel! Oh, God, don't let me die!

Glory shuddered as her body went limp. She leaned forward and, covering her face with her hands, she began to sob. Suddenly the warmth of her room and the comfort of knowing she was safe seemed obscene in the face of what she'd just witnessed. And then as suddenly as the vision had come upon her, the knowledge followed of what she must do next.

She threw back the covers, stumbling on the tail of her nightgown as she crawled out of bed. As she flipped the switch, her bedroom was instantly bathed in the glow of a pale yellow light that gave off a false warmth.

The floor was cold beneath her bare feet as she ran down the hall to the room where her father lay sleeping. For a moment, she stood in his doorway in the dark, listening to the soft, even sound of his snore, and regretted what she was about to do. Yet ignoring her instinct was as impossible for Glory to do as denying the fact that she was a woman.

"Daddy…"

Rafe Dixon woke with a start. He'd heard that sound in his daughter's voice a thousand times before. He rolled over in bed like a hibernating bear coming out of a sleep, and dug at his eyes with the heels of his hands.

"Glory girl, what's wrong?"

"We've got to go, Daddy. He's dying…and I've got to help."

Rafe groaned. He knew better than to deny what Glory was telling him, but he also knew that there was a near blizzard in force, and getting down off this mountain and into Larner's Mill might prove deadly for them all.

"But honey…the storm."

"We'll make it, Daddy, but he won't."

The certainty in her voice was all Rafe Dixon needed to hear. He rolled out of bed with a thump and started reaching for his clothes.

"Go wake your brother," he said.

"I'm here, Daddy. I heard."

J.C. slipped a comforting arm across his baby sister's shoulders and hugged her. "Was it bad, Sis?"

The look on her face was all he needed to know. He headed back down the hall to his room, calling over his shoulder as he went. "I'll go start the truck."

"Dress warm, girl," Rafe growled. "It's a bitch outside."

Glory nodded, and flew back to her room, pulling on clothes with wild abandon. The urgency within her made her shake, but her resolve was firm.

Minutes later, they walked out of the house into a blast of snow that stung their faces, but Glory didn't falter. As she was about to step off the porch, J.C. appeared out of nowhere and lifted her off her feet, carrying her through the snow to the waiting vehicle. She shuddered as she clung to his broad shoulders, still locked into the vision before her. And as she saw…she prayed.

"We're not gonna make it," the ambulance driver groaned, as he fought the steering wheel and the vehicle's urge to slide.

"Damn it, Farley, just quit talking and drive. We have to make it! If we don't, this fellow sure won't."

Luke Dennis, the emergency medical technician whose fortune it had been to be on duty this night, was up to his elbows in blood. His clothes were soaking wet, and his boots were filled to the tops with melting snow. The last thing he wanted to hear was another negative. They'd worked too long and too hard just getting this victim out of his car and up the side of the mountain to give up now.

"Come on, buddy, hang with me," Dennis muttered, as he traded a fresh container of D5W for the one going empty on the other end of the IV.

An unceasing flow of blood ran out of the victim's dark hair and across his face, mapping his once-handsome features with a crazy quilt of red. It was impossible to guess how many bones this man had broken, and to be honest, those were the least of Dennis's worries. If they couldn't get him back to the hospital in time, it was the internal injuries that would kill him.

"I see lights!" Farley shouted.

Thank God, Dennis thought, and then grabbed his patient and the stretcher, holding on to it, and to him, as the ambulance took the street corner sideways. Moments later they were at the hospital, unloading a man whose chance of a future depended upon the skills of the people awaiting him in-side.

Before he was a doctor, Amos Steading had been a medic in Vietnam. When he saw Wyatt Hatfield being wheeled into his ER, he realized he might have been practicing medicine longer than this patient had been alive. It hurt to lose a patient, but the younger ones were much harder to accept.

"What have we got?" Amos growled, lowering his bushy eyebrows as his attention instantly focused upon the injuries.

"Trouble, Doc," Dennis said. "Thirty-four-year-old male. Recently discharged from the Marines. He's still wearing his ID tags. He got sideswiped by a truck and went over the side of Tulley's Mountain. Didn't think we'd ever get him up and out. He's got head injuries, and from the feel of his belly, internal bleeding as well. From external exam, I'd guess at least four broken ribs, and, his right leg has quite a bit of damage, although it's hard to tell what, if anything, is broken. We had to saw a tree and move it off him to get him out of the car." He took a deep breath as the stretcher slid to a halt. As they transferred the victim to the gurney, he added, "This is his third bag of D5W."

Steading's eyebrows arched as he yanked his stethoscope from around his neck and slipped it into place. This man was bleeding to death before their eyes. Moments later, he began firing orders to the nurse and the other doctor on call.

"Get me a blood type," Steading shouted, and a nurse ran to do his bidding.

It was then that EMT Luke Dennis added the last bit of information about the victim, which made them all pause.

"According to his dog tags, he's AB negative," Dennis said.

A low curse slid out of Amos's mouth as he continued to work. Rare blood types didn't belong in this backwater town of eighteen hundred people. There was no way their blood bank was going to have anything like that, and the plasma they had on hand was sparse.

"Type it anyway," Steading ordered. "And get me some

plasma, goddamn it! This man's going to die before I can get him stable enough for surgery.''

The once quiet hospital instantly became a flurry of shouts, curses and noise. Luke Dennis stepped out of the way, aware that he'd done his job. The rest was up to the doc and his staff...and God.

He started back toward the door to restock the ambulance, aware that the night was far from over. It was entirely possible that more than one fool might decide to venture out in a storm like this. He just hoped that if they plowed themselves into the snow—or into someone else—they were nowhere near a mountain when it happened. But before he could leave, the outside door burst open right before him, and three people blew in, along with a blinding gust of snow.

Glory breathed a shaky sigh of relief. One hurdle crossed. Another yet to come. She burst free of her father's grasp and ran toward the EMT who'd stepped aside to let them pass.

''Mister! Please! Take me to the soldier's doctor.''

Dennis couldn't quit staring at the young woman clutching his coat. Her voice was frantic, her behavior strange, but it was her request that startled him. How could she know that the man they'd just brought in was—or at least had been—a soldier?

''Are you a relative?'' Dennis asked.

''No! Who I am doesn't matter, but he does,'' Glory cried, gripping his coat a little tighter. And then she felt her father's hand move across her shoulder.

''Ease up, Glory. You got to explain yourself a little, honey.''

She blinked, and Dennis watched focus returning to her expression, thinking as he did that he'd never seen eyes quite that shade of blue. In a certain light, they almost looked silver...as silver as her hair, which clung to her face and coat like strands of wet taffy.

She took a deep breath and started over.

''Please,'' she said softly. ''I came to give blood.''

Dennis shook his head. "I don't know how you heard about the accident, but I'm afraid coming out in this storm was a waste of time for you. He's got a rare—"

Glory dug through her purse, her fingers shaking as she searched the contents of her wallet.

"Here," she said, thrusting a card into the man's hands. "Show the doctor. Tell him I can help—that it's urgent that he wait no longer. The man won't live through the night without me."

As Dennis looked down at the card, the hair crawled on the back of his neck. He glanced back up at the woman, then at the card again, and suddenly grabbed her by the arm, pulling her down the hall toward the room where Steading was working.

"Doc, we just got ourselves a miracle," Dennis shouted as he ran into the room.

Amos Steading frowned at the woman Dennis was dragging into their midst.

"Get her out of here, Dennis! You know better than to bring—"

"She's AB negative, Doc, and she's come to give blood."

Steading's hands froze above the tear in the flesh on Wyatt Hatfield's leg.

"You're full of bull," he growled.

Dennis shook his head. "No, I swear to God, Doc. Here's her donor card."

Steading's eyes narrowed and then he barked at a nurse on the other side of the room. "Get her typed and cross-matched. Now!"

She flew to do his bidding.

"And get me some more saline, damn it! This man's losing more fluids than I can pump in him." He cursed softly, then added beneath his breath, fully expecting someone to hear and obey, "And call down to X ray and find out why his films aren't back!" As he leaned back over the patient, he began to mumble again, more to himself than to anyone else. "Now where the hell is that bleeder?"

There was a moment, in the midst of all the doctor's orders, when Glory looked upon the injured man's face. It wasn't often that she had a physical connection to the people in her mind.

"What's his name?" she whispered, as a nurse grabbed her by the arm and all but dragged her down the hall to the lab.

"Who, Dr. Steading?"

"No," Glory said. "The man who was hurt."

"Oh…uh…Hatfield. William…no, uh…Wyatt. Yes, that's right. Wyatt Hatfield. It's a shame, too," the nurse muttered, more to herself than to Glory. "He looks like he was real handsome…and so young. Just got out of the service. From his identification, some sort of special forces. It's sort of ironic, isn't it?"

"What's ironic?" Glory asked, and then they entered the lab, and the scents that assailed her threatened to overwhelm. She swayed on her feet, and the nurse quickly seated her in a chair.

The nurse grimaced. "Why, the fact that he could survive God knows what during his stint in the military, and then come to this, and all because of a snowstorm on a mountain road." Suddenly she was all business. "Stuart, type and cross-match this woman's blood, stat! If she comes up AB negative, and a match to the man in ER, then draw blood. She's a donor."

As the lab tech began, Glory relaxed. At least they were on the right track.

Three o'clock in the morning had come and gone, and the waiting room in ER was quiet. Rafe Dixon glanced at his son, then at his daughter, who seemed to be dozing beside him. How he'd fathered two such different children was beyond him, but his pride in each was unbounded. It just took more effort to keep up with Glory than it did J.C.

He understood his son and his love for their land. He didn't understand one thing about his daughter's gift, but he believed in it, and he believed in her. What worried him most was, who would take care of Glory when he was gone? J.C. was nearly thirty and he couldn't be expected to watch over his sister for the rest of his life. Besides, if he were to marry, a wife might resent the attention J.C. unstintingly gave his baby sister. Although Glory was twenty-five, she looked little more than eighteen. Her delicate features and her fragile build often gave her the appearance of a child...until one looked into her eyes and saw the ancient soul looking back.

Glory child...who will take care of you when I am gone?

Suddenly Glory stood and looked down the hall. Rafe stirred, expecting to see someone open and walk through the doors at the far end. But nothing happened, and no one came.

She slipped her fingers in the palm of her brother's hand and then stood. "We can go home now."

J.C. yawned, and looked up at his father. Their eyes met in a moment of instant understanding. For whatever her reasons, Glory seemed satisfied within herself, and for them, that was all that mattered.

"Are you sure, girl?" Rafe asked, as he helped Glory on with her coat.

She nodded, her head bobbing wearily upon her shoulders. "I'm sure, Daddy."

"You don't want to wait and talk to the doctor?"

She smiled. "There's no need."

As suddenly as they'd arrived, they were gone.

Within the hour, Amos Steading came out of surgery, tossing surgical gloves and blood-splattered clothing in their respective hampers. Later, when he went to look for the unexpected blood donor, to his surprise, she was nowhere to be found. And while he thought it strange that she'd not stayed to hear the results of the surgery, he was too tired and too elated to worry about her odd exodus. Tonight he'd fought the Grim Reaper and won. And while he knew his skill as a surgeon was nothing at which to scoff, his patient still lived because of a girl who'd come out of the storm.

Steading dropped into a chair at his desk and began working up Hatfield's chart, adding notes of the surgery to what had been done in ER. A nurse entered, then gave him a cup of hot coffee and an understanding smile. As the heat from the cup warmed his hand, he sighed in satisfaction.

"Did you locate his next of kin?" Steading asked.

The nurse nodded. "Yes, sir, a sister. Her name is Antonette Monday. She said that she and her husband will come as soon as weather permits."

Steading nodded, and sipped the steaming brew. "It's good to have family."

High up on the mountain above Larner's Mill, Glory Dixon would have agreed with him. When they finally pulled into the yard of their home, it was only a few hours before daybreak, and yet she knew a sense of satisfaction for a job well done. It wasn't always that good came of what she *saw*, but tonight, she'd been able to make a difference.

She reached over and patted her father's knee. "Thank you, Daddy," she said quietly.

"For what?" he asked.

"For believing me."

He slid a long arm across her shoulder, giving her a hug. There was nothing more that needed to be said.

"Looks like the snow's about stopped," he said, gauging the sparse spit of snowflakes dancing before the headlights of their truck.

"Who's hungry?" Glory asked.

J.C. grinned. "Wanna guess?"

She laughed. It was a perfect ending to a very bad beginning.

Back in recovery, Wyatt Hatfield wasn't laughing, but if he'd been conscious, he would have been counting his blessings. He had a cut on his cheek that would probably scar, and had survived a lung that had collapsed, a concussion that should have put him into a coma and hadn't, five broken ribs and two cracked ones, more stitches in his left leg than he would be able to count and, had he been able to feel them, bruises in every joint.

He could thank a seat belt, a trucker who hadn't kept going

after causing the wreck, a rescue crew that went above and beyond the call of duty to get him off of the mountain and an EMT who didn't know the meaning of the word *quit*. And it was extremely good luck on Wyatt's part that, after all that, he wound up in the skilled hands of Amos Steading.

Yet it was fate that had delivered him to Glory Dixon. And had she not given of the blood from her body, the cold and simple fact was that he would have died. But Wyatt didn't know his good fortune. It would be days before he would know his own name.

All day long, the sun kept trying to shine. Wyatt paced the floor of his hospital room, ignoring the muscle twinges in his injured leg, and the pull of sore muscles across his belly.

He didn't give a damn about pain. Today he was going home, or a reasonable facsimile thereof. While he didn't have a home of his own, he still had roots in the land on which he'd been raised. If he had refused to accompany his sister, Toni, back to Tennessee, he suspected that her husband, Lane Monday, would have slung him over his shoulder and taken him anyway. Few but Toni dared argue with Lane Monday. At six feet, seven inches, he was a powerful, imposing man. As a United States Marshal, he was formidable. In Wyatt's eyes, he'd come through for Toni like a real man should. There was little else to be said.

Outside his door, he could hear his sister's voice at the nurses' station while she signed the papers that would check him out. He leaned his forehead against the window, surprised that in spite of the sun's rays it felt cold, and then remembered that winter sun, at its best, was rarely warm.

"Are you ready, Wyatt?"

Wyatt turned. Lane filled the doorway with his size and his presence.

He shrugged. "I guess." He turned back to the window as Lane crossed the room.

For a while, both men were silent, and then Lane gave

Wyatt a quick pat on the back before he spoke. "I think maybe I know how you feel," Lane said.

Wyatt shrugged. "Then I wish to hell you'd tell me, because I don't understand. Don't get me wrong. I'm happy to be alive." He tried to grin. "Hell, and if truth be told, a little surprised. When I went over the mountain, in the space of time it took to hit the first stand of trees, I more or less made my peace with God. I never expected to wake up."

Lane listened without commenting, knowing that something was bothering Wyatt that he needed to get said.

"As for my family, I consider myself lucky to have people who are willing to take me in, but I feel so...so..."

"Rootless?"

For a moment Wyatt was silent, and then he nodded.

"Exactly. I feel rootless. And...I feel like leaving here will be taking a step backward in what I was searching for. I know it's weird, but I keep thinking that I was *this* close to the end of a journey, and now—"

Toni broke the moment of confiding as she came into the room.

"You're all checked out!" When Wyatt started toward the door, she held up her hand. "Don't get in too big a hurry. They're bringing a wheelchair. Lane, honey, why don't you pull the car up to the curb? Wyatt, are you all packed?"

Both men looked at each other and then grinned. "She was your sister before she was my wife," Lane warned him. "So you can't be surprised by all this."

Toni ignored them. It was her nature to organize. She'd spent too long on her own, running a farm and caring for aging parents, to wait for someone else to make a decision.

"Why don't I go get the car?" Lane said, and stole a kiss from his Toni as he passed.

"I'm packed," Wyatt said.

"I brought one of Justin's coats for you to wear. The clothes you had on were ruined," Toni said, her eyes tearing as she remembered his condition upon their arrival right after the accident. She held out the coat for him to put on. Wyatt slipped one arm in his brother's coat, and then the other, then turned and hugged her, letting himself absorb the care…and the love.

"Now all I need is my ride," Wyatt teased, and pulled at a loose curl hanging across Toni's forehead.

On cue, a nurse came in pushing a wheelchair, and within minutes, Wyatt was on his way.

The air outside was a welcome respite from the recirculated air inside his room. And the cold, fresh scent of snow was infinitely better than the aroma of antiseptic. Wyatt gripped the arms of the wheelchair in anticipation of going home.

Just outside the doors, Toni turned away to speak to the nurse, and Lane had yet to arrive. For a brief moment, Wyatt was left to his own devices. He braced himself, angling his sore leg until he was able to stand, and then lifted his face and inhaled, letting the brisk draft of air circling the corner of the hospital have its way with the cobwebs in his mind. He'd been inside far too long.

A pharmacy across the street was doing a booming business, and Wyatt watched absently as customers came and went. As a van loaded with senior citizens backed up and drove away, a dark blue pickup truck pulled into the recently vacated parking space. He tried not to stare at the three people who got out, but they were such a range of sizes, he couldn't quit looking.

The older man was tall and broad beneath the heavy winter coat he wore. A red sock cap covered a thatch of thick graying hair, and a brush of mustache across his upper lip was several shades darker than the gray. The younger man was just as tall, and in spite of his own heavy clothing, obviously fit. His face was creased with laugh lines, and he moved with the grace and assurance of youth and good health.

It was the girl between them who caught Wyatt's eye. At first he thought she was little more than a child, and then the wind caught the front of her unbuttoned coat, and he got a glimpse of womanly breast and shapely hips before she pulled it together.

Her hair was the color of spun honey. Almost gold. Not quite white. Her lips were full and tilted in a grin at something one of the men just said, and Wyatt had a sudden wish that he'd been the one to make her smile.

No sooner had he thought it than she paused at the door, then stopped completely. He held his breath as she began to turn. When she caught his gaze, he imagined he felt her gasp, although he knew it was a foolish thing to consider. His mind wandered as he let himself feast upon her face.

So beautiful, Wyatt thought.

Why, thank you.

Wyatt was so locked into her gaze that he felt no surprise at the thoughts that suddenly drifted through his mind, or that he was answering them back in an unusual fashion.

You are welcome.

So, Wyatt Hatfield, you're going home?

Yes.

God be with you, soldier.

I'm no longer a soldier.

You will always fight for those you love.

"Here comes Lane!"

At the sound of Toni's voice, Wyatt blinked, then turned and stepped back as Lane pulled up to the curb. When he remembered to look up, the trio had disappeared into the store. He felt an odd sense of loss, as if he'd been disconnected from something he needed to know.

Bowing to the demands of his family's concerns, he let himself be plied with pillows and blankets. By the time they had him comfortable in the roomy back seat of their car, he was more than ready for the long journey home to begin.

They were past the boundary of Larner's Mill, heading out of Kentucky and toward Tennessee, when Wyatt's thoughts wandered back to the girl he'd seen on the street. And as suddenly as he remembered her, he froze. His heart began to hammer inside his chest as he slowly sat up and stared out the back window at the small mountain town that was swiftly disappearing from sight.

"Dear God," he whispered, and wiped a shaky hand across his face.

"Wyatt, darling, are you all right?"

His sister's tone of voice was worried, the touch of her hand upon his shoulder gentle and concerned. Lane began to ease off the accelerator, thinking that Wyatt might be getting sick.

"I'm fine. I'm fine," he muttered, and dropped back onto the bed they'd made for him in the back seat.

There was no way he could tell them what he'd suddenly realized. There wasn't even any way he could explain it to himself. But he knew, as well as he knew his own name, that the conversation he'd had with that girl had been real. And yet understanding how it had happened was another thing altogether. He'd heard of silent communication, but this… this…thing that just happened…it was impossible.

"Then how did she know my name?" he murmured.

"What did you say?" Toni asked.

Wyatt turned his head into the pillow and closed his eyes.

"Nothing, Sis. Nothing at all."

Chapter 2

Clouds moved in wild, scattered patterns above the Hatfield homestead, giving way to the swift air current blasting through the upper atmosphere. The clouds looked as unsettled as Wyatt felt. In his mind, it had taken forever to get back his health, and then even longer to gain strength. But now, except for a scar on his cheek and a leg that would probably ache for the rest of his life every time it rained, he was fine.

Problem was, he'd been here too long. He leaned forward, bracing his hands upon the windowsill and gazing out at the yard that spilled toward the banks of Chaney Creek, while his blood stirred to be on the move.

"The grass is beginning to green."

The longing in Wyatt's voice was obvious, but for what, Toni didn't know. Was he missing the companionship of his ex-wife, or was there something missing from his own inner self that he didn't know how to find?

"I know," Toni said, and shifted Joy to her other hip, trying not to mind that Wyatt was restless. He was her brother, and this *was* his home, but he was no longer the boy who'd chased her through the woods. He'd been a man alone for a long, long time.

She could hear the longing in his voice, and sensed his need to be on the move, but she feared that once gone, he would fall back into the depression in which they'd brought him home. Her mind whirled as she tried to think of something to cheer him up. Her daughter fidgeted in her arms, reaching for anything she could lay her hands on. Toni smiled, and kissed Joy on her cheek, thinking what they'd been doing this time last year, and the telegram that Wyatt had sent.

"Remember last year…when you sent the telegram? It came on Easter. Did you know that?"

Wyatt nodded, then grinned, also remembering how mad Toni had been at him when he'd interfered in her personal life.

"In a few weeks, it will be Easter again. Last year, some-one gave us a little jumpsuit for Joy, complete with long pink ears on the outside of the hood. It made her look like a baby rabbit. The kids carried her around all day, fussing over who was going to have their picture taken next with the Easter Bunny."

Wyatt smiled, and when Joy leaned over, trying to stick her hand in the pot on the stove, he took the toddler from his sister's arms, freeing her to finish the pudding she was stirring.

Joy instantly grabbed a fistful of his hair in each hand and began to pull. Wyatt winced, then laughed, as he started to unwind her tiny hands from the grip they had on his head.

"Hey, puddin' face. Don't pull all of Uncle Wyatt's hair out. He's going to need it for when he's an old man."

Joy chortled gleefully as it quickly became a game, and for a time, Wyatt's restlessness was forgotten in his delight with the child.

It was long into the night when the old, uneasy feelings began to return. Wyatt paced the floor beside his bed until he was sick of the room, then slipped out of the house to stand on the porch. The moonless night was so thick and dark that it seemed airless. Absorbing the quiet, he let it surround him. As a kind of peace began to settle, he sat down on the steps, listening to the night life that abounded in their woods.

He kept telling himself that it was the memories of the wreck, and the lost days in between, that kept him out of bed. If he lay down, he would sleep. If he slept, he would dream. Nightmares of snow and blood, of pain and confusion. But that wasn't exactly true. It was the memory of a woman's voice that wouldn't let go of his mind.

You will always fight for those you love.

Eliminating the obvious, which he took to mean his own family, exactly what did that mean? Even more important, how the hell had that…that thing…happened between them?

Toni had told him more than once that he'd survived the wreck for a reason, and that one day he'd know why. But Wyatt wanted answers to questions he didn't even know how to ask. In effect, he felt as though he were living in a vacuum, waiting for someone to break the seal.

Yet Wyatt Hatfield wasn't the only man that night at a breaking point. Back in Larner's Mill, Kentucky, a man named Carter Foster was at the point of no return, trying to hold on to his sanity and his wife, and doing a poor job of both.

Carter paced the space in front of their bed, watching with growing dismay as Betty Jo began to put on another layer of makeup. As if the dress she was wearing wasn't revealing enough, she was making herself look like a whore. Her actions of late seemed to dare him to complain.

"Now, sweetheart, I'm not trying to control you, but I think I have a right to know where you're going. How is it going to look to the townspeople if you keep going out at night without me?"

He hated the whine in his voice, but couldn't find another way to approach his wife of eleven years about her latest affair. That she was having them was no secret. That the people of Larner's Mill must never find out was of the utmost importance to him. In his profession, appearances were everything.

Betty Jo arched her perfectly painted eyebrows and then stabbed a hair pick into her hair, lifting the back-combed nest she'd made of her dark red tresses to add necessary inches to her height. Ignoring Carter's complaint, she stepped back from the full-length mirror, running her hands lightly down her buxom figure in silent appreciation. That white knit dress she'd bought yesterday looked even better on than it had on the hanger.

"Betty Jo, you didn't answer me," Carter said, unaware that his voice had risen a couple of notes.

Silence prevailed as she ran her little finger across her upper, then lower lip, smoothing out the Dixie Red lipstick she'd applied with a flourish. When she rubbed her lips together to even out the color, Carter shuddered, hating himself for still wanting her. He couldn't remember the last time she put those lips anywhere on him.

"Carter, honey, you know a woman like me needs her space. With you stuck in that stuffy old courtroom all day, and in your office here at home all night, what am I to do?"

The pout on her lips made him furious. At this stage of their marriage, that baby-faced attitude would get her nowhere.

"But you're *my* wife," Carter argued. "It just isn't right that you…that men…" He took a deep breath and then puffed out his cheeks in frustration, unaware that it made him look like a bullfrog.

Betty Jo pivoted toward him, then stepped into her shoes, relishing the power that the added height of the three-inch heels gave her. She knew that if she had had college to do over again, she would have married the jock, not the brain. This poor excuse for a man was losing his hair and sporting a belly that disgusted her. When he walked, it swayed lightly from side to side like the big breasts of a woman who wore no support. She liked tight, firm bellies and hard muscles. There was nothing hard on Carter Foster. Not even periodically. To put it bluntly, Betty Jo Foster was an unsatisfied woman in the prime of her life.

Ignoring his petulant complaints as nothing but more of the same, she picked up her purse. To her surprise, he grabbed her by the forearm and all but shook her. The purse fell between them, lost in the unexpected shuffle of feet.

"Damn it, Betty Jo! You heard me! This just isn't right!"

"Hey!" she said, then frowned. She couldn't remember the last time Carter had raised his voice to her. She yanked, trying to pull herself free from his grasp, but to her dismay, his fingers tightened.

"Carter! You're hurting me!"

"So what?" he snarled, and shoved her backward onto their bed. "You're hurting me."

A slight panic began to surface. He never got angry. At least he never *used* to. Without thinking, she rolled over on her stomach to keep from messing up her hair, and started to crawl off of the bed. But turning her back on him was her first and last mistake. Before she could get up, Carter came down on top of her, pushing her into the mattress, calling her names she didn't even know he knew.

Betty Jo screamed, but the sound had nowhere to go. The weight of his body kept pushing her deeper and deeper into the mattress, and when the bulk of him settled across her hips, and his shoes began snagging runs in her panty hose, she realized that he was sitting on her. In shock, she began to fight.

Flailing helplessly, her hands clenched in the bedspread as she tried unsuccessfully to maneuver herself out from under him. Panic became horror as his hands suddenly circled her neck. The more she kicked and bounced, the tighter he squeezed.

A wayward thought crossed her mind that he'd messed up her hair and that Dixie Red lipstick would not wash out of the bedspread. It was the last of her worries as tiny bursts of lights began to go off behind her eyelids. Bright, bright, brighter, they burned until they shattered into one great, blinding-white explosion.

As suddenly as it had come, the rage that had taken him into another dimension began to subside. Carter shuddered and shuddered as his hands slowly loosened, and when he went limp atop her body, guilt at his unexpected burst of temper began to surface. He'd never been a physical sort of man, and didn't quite know how to explain this side of himself.

"Damn it, Betty Jo, I'm real sorry this happened, but you've been driving me to it for years."

Oddly enough, Betty Jo had nothing to say about his emotional outburst, and he wondered, as he crawled off her butt, why he hadn't done this years earlier? Maybe if he'd asserted himself when all of her misbehaving began, brute force would never have been necessary.

He smoothed down his hair, then wiped his sweaty palms against the legs of his slacks. Even from here, he could still smell the scent of her perfume upon his skin.

"Get up, Betty Jo. There's no need to pout. You always get your way, whether I like it or not."

Again, she remained silent. Carter's gaze ran up, then down her body, noting as it did, that he'd ruined her hose and smudged her dress. When she saw what he'd done to the back of her skirt, she would be furious.

"Okay, fine," Carter said, and started to walk away.

As he passed the foot of the bed, one of her shoes suddenly popped off the end of her heel and stabbed itself into the spread. He paused, starting to make an ugly comment about the fact that she was undressing for the wrong man, when something about her position struck him as odd. He leaned over the bed frame and tentatively ran his forefinger across the bottom of her foot. Her immobility scared the hell out of him. Betty Jo was as ticklish as they came.

"Oh, God," Carter muttered, and ran around to the edge of the bed, grabbing her by the shoulder. "Betty Jo, this isn't funny!"

He rolled her onto her back, and when he got a firsthand look at the dark, red smear of lipstick across her face and her wide, sightless eyes staring up at him, he began to shake.

"Betty, honey..."

She didn't move.

He thumped her in the middle of the chest, noting absently that she was not wearing a bra, and then started to sweat.

"Betty Jo, wake up!" he screamed, and pushed up and down between her breasts, trying to emulate CPR techniques he didn't actually know.

The only motion he got out of her was a lilt and a sway from her buxom bosom as he hammered about her chest, trying to make her breathe.

"No! God, no!"

Suddenly he jerked his hands to his stomach, as if he'd been burned by the touch of her skin. To his utter dismay, he felt bile rising, and barely made it to the bathroom before it spewed.

Several hours later, he heard the hall clock strike two times, and realized that, in four hours, it would be time to get up. He giggled at the thought, then buried his face in his hands. That was silly. How could one get up, when one had never been down? Betty Jo's body lay right where he'd left it, half-on, half-off the bed, as if he wasn't sure what to do next.

And therein lay Carter's problem. He *didn't* know what to do next. Twice since the deed, he'd reached for the phone to call the police, and each time he'd paused, remembering what would happen when they came. There was no way he could explain that it was really all her fault. That she'd ruined him and his reputation by tarnishing her own.

And that was when it struck him. It *was* her fault. And by God, he shouldn't have to pay!

Suddenly, a way out presented itself, and he bolted from the chair and began rolling her up in the stained bedspread, then fastening it in place with two of his belts. One he buckled just above her head, the other at her ankles. He stepped back to survey his work, and had an absent thought that Betty Jo would hate knowing that she was going to her Maker looking like a tamale. Without giving himself time to reconsider, he threw her over his shoulder and carried her, fireman style, out of the kitchen and into the attached garage, dumping her into the trunk of his car.

Grabbing a suitcase from the back of a closet, he raced to their bedroom and began throwing items of her clothing haphazardly into the bag, before returning to the car. As he tossed the suitcase in the trunk with her body, he took great satisfaction in the fact that he had to lie on the trunk to get it closed.

As he backed from the garage and headed uptown toward an all-night money machine, the deviousness of his own thoughts surprised him. He would never have imagined himself being able to carry off something like this, yet it was happening just the same. If he was going to make this work, it had to look like Betty Jo took money with her when she ran. With this in mind, he continued toward the town's only ATM.

As he pulled up, the spotlight above the money machine glared in his eyes. He jumped out of the car, and with a sharp blow of his fist, knocked out the Plexiglas and the bulb, leaving himself in the bank drive-through in sudden darkness. Minutes later, with the cash in his pocket, he was back in the car and heading out of town toward the city dump.

Ever thankful that Larner's Mill was too small-town in its thinking to ever put up a gate or a lock, Carter drove right through and up to the pit without having to brake for anything more than a possum ambling across the road in the dark.

When he got out, he was shaking with a mixture of exertion and excitement. As he threw the suitcase over the edge, he took a deep breath, watching it bounce end over end, down the steep embankment. When he lifted his wife from the trunk and sent her after it, he started to grin. But the white bedspread in which she was wrapped stood out like a beacon in the night. He could just imagine what would hit the fan if

Betty Jo turned up in this condition. He had to cover up the spread.

It was while he was turning in a circle, looking for something with which to shovel, that he saw the bulldozer off to the side.

That's it, he thought. All he needed to do was shove some dirt down on top. Tomorrow was trash day. By the time the trash trucks made the rounds and dumped the loads, she'd be right where she belonged, buried with the rest of the garbage.

It took a bit for him to figure out how to work the bulldozer's controls, but desperation was a shrewd taskmaster, and Carter Foster was as desperate as they came. Within the hour, a goodly portion of dirt had been pushed in on top of the latest addition to the city dump, and Betty Jo Foster's burial was slightly less dignified than she would have hoped.

Minutes later, Carter was on his way home to shower and change. As he pulled into his garage, he pressed the remote control and breathed a great sigh of satisfaction as the door dropped shut behind him.

It was over!

His feet were dragging as he went inside, but his lawyer mind was already preparing the case he would present to his co-workers. Exactly how much he would be willing to humble himself was still in the planning stage. If they made fun of him behind his back because he'd been dumped, he didn't think he would care. The last laugh would be his.

Days later, while Betty Jo rotted along with the rest of the garbage in Larner's Mill, Glory Dixon was making her second sweep through the house, looking behind chairs and under cushions, trying to find her keys. But the harder she looked the more certain she was that someone else and not her carelessness was to blame.

Her brother came into the kitchen just as she dumped the trash onto the floor and began sorting through the papers.

"J.C., have you seen my keys? I can't find them anywhere."

"Nope." He pulled the long braid she'd made of her hair. "Why don't you just psych them out?"

Glory ignored the casual slander he made of her psychic ability and removed her braid from his hand. "You know it doesn't work like that. I never know what I'm going to *see*. If I did, I would have told on you years ago for filching Granny's blackberry pies."

He was still laughing as their father entered the house by the back door.

"Honey, are you ready to go?" Rafe asked. "We've got a full morning and then some before we're through in town."

She threw up her hands in frustration. "I can't find my keys."

Her father shrugged, then had a thought. "Did you let that pup in the house last night?"

The guilty expression on her face was answer enough.

"Then there's your answer," he muttered. "What that blamed pooch hasn't already chewed up, he's buried. You'll be lucky if you ever see them again."

"Shoot," Glory muttered, and started out the door in search of the dog.

"Let it wait until we come home," Rafe said. "I've got keys galore. If you don't find yours, we'll get copies made of mine. Now grab your grocery list. Time's a'wastin'."

"Don't forget my Twinkies," J.C. said, and slammed the kitchen door behind him as he exited the house.

Glory grinned at her brother's request, then did as her father asked. As she and Rafe drove out of the yard, they could see the back end of the John Deere tractor turning the corner in the lane. J.C. was on his way to the south forty. It was time to work ground for spring planting.

Carter was playing the abandoned husband to the hilt, and oddly enough, enjoying the unexpected sympathy he was receiving from the townspeople. It seemed that they'd known about Betty Jo's high jinks for years, and were not the least surprised by this latest stunt.

As he stood in line at the teller's window at the bank, he was congratulating himself on the brilliance of his latest plan. This would be the icing on the cake.

"I need to withdraw some money from my savings account and deposit it into checking," he told the teller. "Betty Jo nearly cleaned me out."

The teller clucked sympathetically. "I'll need your account numbers," she said.

Carter looked slightly appalled. "I forgot to bring them."

"Don't you worry," the teller said. "I can look them up on the computer. It won't take but a minute."

As the teller hurried away, Carter relaxed, gazing absently around the room, taking note of who was begging and who was borrowing, when he saw a woman across the lobby staring at him as if he'd suddenly grown horns and warts. So intent was her interest, that he instinctively glanced down to see if his fly was unzipped, and then covertly brushed at his face, then his tie, checking for something that didn't belong. Except for her interest, all was as it should be.

Twice he looked away, thinking that when he would turn back, she'd surely be doing something else. To his dismay, her expression never wavered. By the time the teller came back, his impatience had turned to curiosity.

He leaned toward the teller, whispering in a low, urgent tone. "Who is that woman?"

The teller looked up as he pointed across the room at Glory.

"What woman?" she asked.

"The blonde beside that old man. The one who keeps staring this way."

The teller rolled her eyes and then snorted softly through her nostrils.

"Oh! Her! That's that crazy Glory Dixon and her father."

Dixon…I know that man. I hunted quail on his place last year with Tollet Faye and his boys.

The teller kept talking, unaware that Carter was turning pale. He was remembering the gossip he'd heard about the girl, and imagined she could see blood on him that wasn't really there.

"She fancies herself some sort of psychic. Claims that she can *see* into the future, or some such nonsense. Personally, I don't believe in that garbage. Now then…how much did you want to transfer?"

Carter was shaking. He told himself that he didn't believe in such things either, but his guilty conscience and Betty Jo's rotting body were hard to get past. He had visions of Glory Dixon standing up from her chair, pointing an accusing finger toward him, and screaming "murderer" to all who cared to hear.

And no sooner had the thought come than Glory uncrossed her legs. Believing her to be on the verge of a revelation, he panicked.

"I just remembered an appointment," he told the teller. "I'll have to come back later."

With that, he bolted out of the bank and across the street into an alley, leaving the teller to think what she chose. Moments later, the Dixons came out of the bank and drove away. He watched until he saw them turn into the parking lot of the diner on the corner, and then relaxed.

Okay, okay, maybe I made a big deal out of nothing, he told himself, and brushed at the front of his suit coat as he started back to his office. But the farther he walked, the more convinced he became that he was playing with fire if he didn't tie up his loose ends. Before he gave himself time to reconsider, he got into his car and drove out of town. He had no plan in mind. Only a destination.

The small frame house was nestled against a backdrop of Pine Mountain. A black-and-white pup lay on the front porch, gnawing on a stick. Carter watched until the puppy ambled off toward the barn, and then he waited a while longer, just to make sure that there was no one in sight. Off in the distance, the sound of a tractor could be heard as it plowed up and down a field. As he started toward the house, a light breeze lifted the tail of his suit coat.

He didn't know what he was going to do, but he told himself that something *must* be done, or all of his careful planning would be for nothing. If he was going to ignore the fact that Glory Dixon could reveal his secret, then he might as well have called the police the night of the crime, instead of going to all the trouble to conceal it.

Planks creaked upon the porch as it gave beneath his weight. He knocked, then waited, wondering what on earth he would say if someone actually answered. Then he knocked again and again, but no one came. He looked around the yard, assuring himself that he was still unobserved, and then threw his weight against the door. It popped like a cork out of a bottle, and before Carter could think to brace himself, he fell through the doorway and onto the floor before scrambling to his feet.

Now that he was inside, his thoughts scattered. Betty Jo's death had been an accident. What he was thinking of doing was premeditated murder. Yet the problem remained, how to hide one without committing the other. He stood in place, letting himself absorb the thought of the deed. And as he gazed around the room, his attention caught and then focused on the small heating stove in the corner.

It was fueled with gas.

He began to smile.

An idea was forming as he headed for the kitchen. His hands were shaking as he began to investigate the inner workings of the Dixons' cookstove. It didn't take long to find and then blow out the pilot light. As he turned on all the jets, he held his breath. The unmistakable hiss of escaping gas filled the quiet room.

With a sharp turn of his wrist, he turned even harder until one of the controls broke off in his hands. Let them try to turn that baby off, he thought, and hurried out of the kitchen.

Carter wasn't stupid. He knew that almost anything could ignite this—from a ringing telephone to the simple flick of a light switch when someone entered a room. And while he had no control over who came in the house first, he could at least make sure the house didn't blow with no one in it.

With his thumb and forefinger, he carefully lifted the receiver from the cradle and set it to one side. The loud, intermittent buzz of a phone off the hook mingled with the deadly hiss behind him.

Now that it was done, an anxiety to escape was overwhelming. Carter ran through the house and out onto the porch. Careful to pull the front door shut behind him, he jumped into his car and drove away while death filtered slowly throughout the rooms.

It was dusk. Dew was already settling upon the grass, and the sun, like Humpty-Dumpty, was about to fall beyond the horizon as Rafe Dixon drove into the yard and parked beneath the tree near the back door.

J.C. came out of the barn just as Rafe crawled out of the cab. Glory swung her legs out and then slid out of the seat, stretching wearily from the long ride. It felt good to be home. She couldn't wait to get in the house and trade her ropers for slippers, her blue jeans for shorts and the long-sleeved pink shirt she was wearing for one of J.C.'s old T-shirts. They went down past her knees, and felt soft as butter against her skin. They were her favorite items of clothing.

Their errands had taken longer than she'd expected, and she'd told herself more than once during the day that if she'd known all her father had planned to do, she wouldn't have gone. She leaned over the side of the truck bed and lifted the nearest sack into her arms.

"Right on time," Rafe shouted, and motioned his son to the sacks of groceries yet to be unloaded from the back of their truck. "Hey, boy, give us a hand."

J.C. came running. "Daddy! Look! I found another arrowhead today."

Both Rafe and Glory turned to admire his latest find. Collecting them had been J.C.'s passion since he'd found his first years ago. Now he was an avid collector and had more than one hundred of them mounted in frames and hanging on the walls of his room.

"That's a good one," Glory said, running her fingers over the hand-chipped edge, and marveling at the skill of the one who had made it. In spite of its obvious age, it was perfectly symmetrical in form.

"Groceries are gonna melt," Rafe warned.

J.C. grinned and winked at his little sister, then dropped the arrowhead into his pocket. He obliged his father by picking up a sack and then stopping to dig through the one Glory was holding.

"Hey, Morning Glory, did you remember my Twinkies?"

The childhood nickname made her smile as she took the package from her sack and dropped it into the one he was holding. But the urge to laugh faded as quickly as the world that began to slip out of focus.

Common sense told her that she was standing in the yard surrounded by those who loved her best, but it wasn't how she felt. She could barely hear her father's voice above the sound of her own heart breaking. Every breath that she took was a struggle, and although she tried over and over to talk, the words wouldn't come.

Struggling to come out of the fugue, she grabbed hold of the truck bed, desperate to regain her sense of self. Vaguely, she could hear her brother and father arguing over whose turn it was to do the dishes after supper. When sanity returned and she found the words to speak, they were at the back porch steps.

"Daddy! Wait," Glory shouted, as her father slipped the key in the lock.

Even from where she stood, she knew it was going to be too late.

"Hey, look! I think I just found your keys!" J.C. shouted, laughing and pointing at the puppy, coming out of the barn behind them.

It was reflex that made Glory turn. Sure enough, keys dangled from the corner of the pup's mouth as he chewed on the braided leather strap dangling from the ring.

And then it seemed as if everything happened in slow motion. She spun, her father's name on her lips as she started toward the house. In a corner of her mind, she was vaguely aware of J.C.'s surprised shout, and then the back door flew off the hinges and into the bed of the truck. The impact of the explosion threw Glory across the yard where she lay, unconscious.

When reason returned, the first things she felt were heat on her back, and the puppy licking her face. She groaned, unable to remember how she'd come to this position, and crawled to her knees before staggering to her feet. Something wet slid down her cheek, and when she touched it, her fingers came away covered in blood. And then she remembered the blast and spun.

She kept telling herself that this was all a bad dream, and that her brother would come out of the door with one Twinkie in his mouth and another in his hand. But it was impossible to ignore the thick, black coils of smoke snaking up from the burning timbers, marking the spot that had once been home.

Still unable to believe her eyes, she took several shaky steps forward.

"Daddy?" He didn't answer. Her voice rose and trembled as she repeated the cry. "Daaddee! No! No! God, no! Somebody help me!"

Something inside the inferno exploded. A fire within a fire. It was then that she began to scream.

Terror. Horror. Despair.

There were no words for what she felt. Only the devastating knowledge that she'd *seen* the end of those she loved most and had not been able to stop it.

She fell to her knees as gut-wrenching tears tore up her throat and out into the night. Heat seared her skin and scorched her hair as she considered walking into what was left of the pyre. All of her life she'd been separated from the crowd by the fact that she was different, and the only people who'd accepted and loved her for herself had been her father and brother. If they were gone, who would love her now?

And while she stared blindly at the orange and yellow tongues licking at what was left of her home, another image superimposed itself over the flames, and Glory found herself straining toward it, unable to believe what she saw.

A man! Walking through their house, running from room to room. She saw the backs of his hands as they hovered above the stove. Saw them twist…saw them turn…saw them kill. And then he ran, and all that she saw was the silhouette of his back as he moved out the door. The hair crawled on the back of her neck as a reality only Glory understood suddenly surfaced.

Oh, my God! This wasn't an accident!

It was a gut reaction, but she spun in fear, searching for a place to hide. In the dark, she stumbled, falling to her knees. Still in a panic to hide, she crawled, then ran, aiming for the dark, yawning maw of the barn door. Only when she was inside did she turn to look behind her, imagining him still out there…somewhere.

Why would someone want us dead? And no sooner had the thought come, than her answer followed. *It wasn't them. It was me who was supposed to die.*

She slipped even farther inside the barn, staring wide-eyed out into the night, unable to believe what her mind already knew. The guilt that came with the knowledge could have driven Glory over the edge of reason. But it didn't. She couldn't let her father and brother's killer get away with this.

But who…and why? Who could possibly care if she lived or died?

Instinct told her that it wasn't a stranger. But instinct was a poor substitute for facts, and Glory had none. The only thing she knew for sure was that she needed a plan, and she needed time.

There was no way of knowing how long she'd been unconscious, but neighbors were bound to see the fire and could be arriving any minute. A sense of self-preservation warned her that she must hide until she found someone she could trust. Within a day or so, the killer would know that two, not three people, had died in the fire, and then whoever had tried to hurt her would come looking again.

"Oh, God, I need help," she moaned, and then jumped with fright as something furry rubbed up against her leg. She knelt, wrapping her arms around the puppy's neck, and sobbed. "You're not what I needed, but you're all I've got, aren't you, fella?"

A wet tongue slid across her cheek, and Glory moaned as the puppy instinctively licked at the blood on her face. She pushed him away, then stood. Her eyes narrowed above lashes spiked with tears, her lips firmed, her chin tilted as she stared at the fire.

Daddy…J.C.…I swear on Mother's grave…and on yours, that I will find him. All I need is a little help.

No sooner had that thought come than an image followed. A man's face centered within her mind. A man who had been a soldier. A man who understood killing. A stranger who, right now, Glory trusted more than friends.

If I knew where you were, Wyatt Hatfield, I would call in a debt.

But the fantasy of finding a stranger in a world full of people was more than she could cope with. Right now she had to hide, and there was no family left alive to help her.

Except…

She took a deep breath. "Granny."

The puppy heard the tone of her voice, and whined softly from somewhere behind her, uncertain what it was that she wanted, yet aware that a word had been uttered it did not understand.

Granny Dixon's house sat just across the hollow as it had for the past one hundred years, a small shelter carved out of a dense wilderness of trees and bush. As a child, Granny had been Glory's only link with another female, and she had often spent the day in her lap, lulled by the sound of her voice and the stories she would tell.

Glory took a deep breath and closed her eyes, imagining she could hear her granny's voice now.

When you tire of them menfolks, child, you just come to old Granny. We women hafta stick together, now, don't we?

Her saving grace was that Granny Dixon's cabin was just as she'd left it. Its presence could be the answer to her prayer. She was counting on the fact that few would remember its existence. Rafe had promised his mother that he wouldn't touch or change a single thing in her home until they'd put her in the ground. In a way, Glory was thankful that Granny's mind was almost gone. At least she would be spared the grief of knowing that her only son and grandson had beat her to heaven.

And while the cabin was there, food was not. Glory made a quick trip through the root cellar, using the light from the fire as a guide, she ran her fingers along the jars until she found what she wanted. She came up and out with a jar of peaches in one hand and a quart of soup in the other. It would be enough to keep her going until she figured out what to do.

And then she and the puppy vanished into the darkness of the tree line. Minutes later, the sounds of cars and trucks could be heard grinding up the hill. Someone had seen the fire. Someone else would rescue what was left of her loved ones. Glory had disappeared.

Chapter 3

The scream came without warning. Right in the middle of a dream he could no longer remember. Wyatt sat straight up in bed, his instinct for survival working overtime as he imagined Toni or the baby in dire need of help. In seconds, he was pulling on a pair of jeans and running in an all-out sprint as he flew out of the door.

He slid to a stop in the hallway outside the baby's room and then looked inside. Nothing was amiss. He sighed with relief at the sight of the toddler asleep on her tummy with her blanket clutched tightly in one fist. She was fine, so Toni hadn't screamed about her. That meant...

Fearing the worst, he crept farther down the hall, praying that he wouldn't surprise a burglar in the act of murder, and wondering why on earth Lane Monday wasn't raising all kinds of hell in response to his wife's screams.

More than a year ago, Lane had taken down a man the size of a mountain to save his sister's life. He couldn't imagine Lane letting someone sneak up on them and do his family harm. Yet in Wyatt's mind, he knew that whatever had made Toni scream couldn't have been good.

The door was ajar so Lane or Toni could hear the baby if she cried. Wyatt pushed it aside and looked in. Lane was flat on his back and sound asleep, with Toni held gently, but firmly, within the shelter of one arm. Even from here, Wyatt could hear the soft, even sounds of their breathing.

"Thank God," he muttered, and eased out of their room the same way he'd come in, trying to convince himself that he'd been dreaming. *But it sounded so real.*

He made his way through the house, careful not to step on the boards that creaked, and headed for the kitchen to get a drink. He wasn't particularly thirsty, but at the moment, crawling back in that bed did not hold much interest. His heart was still pounding as he took a glass from the cabinet and ran water in the sink, letting it cool in the pipes before filling a glass.

The water tasted good going down, and panic was subsiding. If he stretched the facts, he could convince himself that his heart rate was almost back to normal. It was just a bad dream. That was all. Just a bad dream.

Wyatt.

"What?"

He spun toward the doorway, expecting Toni to be standing there with a worried expression on her face. There was nothing but a reflection of the outside security light glancing off the living room window and onto the floor.

Wyatt...Wyatt Hatfield.

His stomach muscles clenched, and he took a deep breath. "Jesus Christ."

Help me.

He started to shake. "This isn't happening."

God... Oh, God...help. I need help.

He slammed the glass onto the cabinet and stalked out of the kitchen and onto the back porch, inhaling one after the other of deep, lung-chilling breaths of cool night air. When he could think without wanting to throw up, he sat down on the steps with a thump and buried his face in his hands, then instantly yanked them off his face, unable to believe what he'd felt.

His hands were cold…and they were wet. He lifted his fingers to his cheeks and traced the tracks of his tears.

"I'm crying? For God's sake, I'm crying? What's wrong with me? I don't cry, and when I do, I will sure as hell need a reason."

But anger could not replace the overwhelming sense of despair that was seeping into his system. He felt weak and drained, hopeless and helpless. The last time he'd felt this down had been the day he'd regained consciousness in a Kentucky hospital and seen the vague image of his sister's face hovering somewhere above his bed.

He remembered thinking that he'd known his sister was an angel to have put up with so many brothers all of her life, but he'd never imagined that all angels in heaven looked like her. It was the next day before he realized that he hadn't died, and by that time, worrying about the faces of angels had become secondary to the mind-bending pain that had come to stay.

Out of the silence of the night, a dog suddenly bugled in a hollow somewhere below Chaney Creek. The sound was familiar. He shuddered, trying to relax as his nerves began to settle. This was something to which he could relate. Someone was running hounds. Whether it was raccoon, bobcat or something else that they hunted, it rarely mattered. To the hunters, the dogs and the hunt were what counted.

He listened, remembering days far in his past when he and his brothers had done the same, nights when they'd sat around a campfire swapping lies that sounded good in the dark, drinking coffee made in a pot that they wouldn't have fed the pigs out of in the light of day and listening to their hounds running far and wide across the hills and in the deep valleys.

He sighed, then dropped his head in his hands, wishing for simpler times, saner times. He wondered where he'd gone wrong. He'd married Shirley full of good intent, then screwed up her life, as well as his own.

And now this!

He didn't know what to think. He'd survived a wreck that should have killed him. But if it had messed with his head in a way they hadn't expected, then making a new life for himself had suddenly become more complicated than he'd planned.

Help. I need help.

He lifted his head, like an animal sniffing the air. His nostrils flared, his eyes narrowed to dark, gleaming slits. This time, he knew he wasn't dreaming. He was wide-awake and barefoot on his sister's back porch. And he knew what he heard. The voice was inside his head. He shivered, then shifted his gaze, looking out at the darkness, listening... waiting.

When the first weak rays of sunlight changed the sky from black to baby blue, Wyatt got to his feet and walked into the house. It had taken all night, and more soul-searching than he'd realized he had in him, but he knew what he had to do.

Somewhere down the hall, Joy babbled, and Toni laughed. Lane smiled to himself at the sound, buttoning his shirt on his way to the kitchen to start the coffee. He walked in just in time to see Wyatt closing the back door.

"Up kinda early, aren't you, buddy?" Lane asked, and then froze at the expression on Wyatt's face, grabbing him by the arm. "What's wrong?"

Wyatt tried to explain, but it just wouldn't come. "I need to borrow one of your cars."

Lane headed for the coffeepot, giving himself time to absorb the unexpected request, and wondering about the intensity of Wyatt's voice. Yet refusing him was not a consideration.

"It's yours," he said.

Measuring his words, along with coffee and water, Lane turned on the coffeemaker before taking Wyatt to task. "Mind telling me where you're going so early in the morning? This isn't exactly Memphis, and to my knowledge there's no McDonald's on the next corner cooking up sausage biscuits.''

"I've got to go," Wyatt repeated. "Someone needs me."

Lane's posture went from easy to erect. "Why didn't you say so? I'll help."

Wyatt shook his head. "No, you don't understand. Hell, for that matter, I don't understand. All I know is, last night while I was wide-awake and watching dark turn to day, someone kept calling my name."

The oddity of the remark was not lost on Lane, but trespassing on another man's business was not his way.

"Do you know where you're going?" Lane asked.

Wyatt eyed his brother-in-law, wondering if he would understand what he was about to say.

"I think, back to where it all started," Wyatt said quietly, remembering the woman outside of the hospital and the way he'd heard her voice…and she, his. He'd ignored it then. He couldn't ignore it any longer.

"Back to Kentucky?" Lane asked, unable to keep surprise out of his voice.

Wyatt nodded.

Wisely, Lane stifled the rest of his concerns. While he didn't understand what Wyatt was trying to say, he trusted the man implicitly. He swung a wide hand across his shoulder and thumped him lightly on the back.

"Then let's get you packed," Lane said. "It's an all-day drive."

Wyatt had been on this road before. Last winter. And with no destination in mind. This time, he knew where he was going. He even knew why. What he didn't understand was the pull that drew him down the road. The closer he came to the great Pine Mountain, the more certain he became that he was on the right track. He drove relentlessly, stopping only when necessary, compelled to reach Larner's Mill before nightfall. He couldn't get past the increasing panic he felt, or the fact that he was listening for a voice that had suddenly gone silent.

The sun was halfway between zenith and horizon when he pulled into Larner's Mill, but the relief he imagined he would feel was not there. In fact, the urgency of his quest seemed to have taken on darker overtones. An unsettled feeling had taken root in his belly, and try as he might, there was no rational explanation for the emotion, other than the uncertainty of his quest.

When he pulled into the parking lot of the small community hospital and got out, he found himself wanting to run. But to where? Instead, he took a deep breath and entered through the emergency room doors.

A nurse glanced up from a desk near the door. "May I help you, sir?"

"I want to talk to one of your doctors," Wyatt said.

She slipped a fresh page on a clipboard and held a pen poised above the lines.

"Your name?" she asked.

"Wyatt Hatfield," he said.

"And what are your symptoms?"

"I'm not sick. But I was here before. Last winter, in fact. I had a car wreck during a blizzard. I was…"

"I remember you," she cried, and jumped to her feet. "Dr. Steading was your doctor. You were the talk of the hospital for some time."

"Why was that?" Wyatt asked.

"You know," she said. "About how lucky you were to have had that donor show up when she did. With such a rare blood type, and the blizzard and all, there was no way we could access the blood banks in the bigger cities as we normally might have done."

The expression on Wyatt's face stilled as he absorbed the nurse's unwitting revelation.

"Yes, I suppose you're right. I am one lucky man." He gave her a smile he didn't feel. "So, could I talk to Dr. Steading? There are some things about the accident that I don't remember. I thought maybe he could give me some help.''

''I'll see,'' she said, and shortly thereafter, Wyatt found himself on the way through the corridors to an office in the other wing. When he saw the name on the door, his pulse accelerated. He knocked and then entered.

''Dr. Steading?''

Amos Steading arched one bushy eyebrow, and then stood and reached over his desk, his hand outstretched.

''You, sir, look a damn sight healthier than the last time I saw you,'' he said, his gravelly voice booming within the small confines of the office.

Wyatt caught the handshake and grinned. ''I suppose I feel better, too,'' he said.

Steading frowned. ''Suppose?''

Wyatt took the chair offered him, and tried not to show his uneasiness, but it seemed it was impossible to hide anything, including an emotion, from the grizzled veteran.

Steading persisted. ''So, did you come all this way just to shake my hand, or are you going to spit it out?''

Wyatt took a deep breath, and then started talking.

''I know I was in serious condition when I was brought in here,'' he said.

''No,'' Steading interrupted. ''You were dying, boy.''

Wyatt paled, but persisted. ''The reason I came is…I need to know if, in your opinion, I could have suffered any residual brain damage.''

Steading frowned. That was the last thing he expected to hear this man say. His eyes were clear and bright, his manner straightforward, and he'd walked into his office like a man with a purpose. None of this hinted at any sort of mental disability.

''Why?'' Steading asked. ''Are you suffering memory loss, or…''

Wyatt shook his head. ''No, nothing like that.''

''So…?''

"So, I want to know what exactly happened to my head," Wyatt growled.

"You had one hell of a concussion. I wouldn't have been surprised if you'd gone into a coma."

Wyatt started to relax. Maybe this would explain what he thought he'd heard. Maybe his head was still lost in some sort of fugue.

"But you didn't," Steading added. "After surgery, you pretty much sailed through recovery. There's a lot to be said for a young, healthy body."

"Damn," Wyatt muttered beneath his breath. One theory shot to hell.

This time, both of Steading's eyebrows arched. "You're disappointed?"

Wyatt shrugged. "It would have explained a lot."

"Like what?" Steading persisted.

The last thing he intended to admit, especially to a doctor, was that he was hearing voices. They'd lock him up in a New York minute. He changed the subject.

"I understand that I was given transfusions."

"Transfusion," Steading corrected. "And damned lucky to have that one. Whole blood made the difference. I'm good, but I don't think I could have pulled you through surgery without it, and that's the gospel truth."

"I'd like to thank the person who cared enough to come out in such a storm. If it wouldn't be against hospital policy, could you give me a name?"

Amos Steading's face fell. He rocked backward in his chair, and gazed at a corner of the ceiling, trying to find the right way to say the words.

"If that's a problem," Wyatt said, "I'll understand. It's just that I'm trying to make sense of some things in my life, and I thought that retracing my steps through that night might help."

"It isn't that," Steading finally said. "It's just that you're about a day too late."

Wyatt straightened. An inner warning was going off that told him he wasn't going to like this.

"That young woman...the one who gave you blood...she, along with her family, died sometime last night. I heard about it when I came in to work this morning."

Oh, God! Oh, no! Was that what I heard...the sound of someone crying out for help?

Wyatt's voice broke, and he had to clear his throat to get out the words. "How did it happen? Was it a car accident?"

"No, a fire at the home."

Wyatt shuddered, trying not to think of the horror of burning alive.

"Yes, and a real shame, too, what with her and her brother so young and all. That night when the EMT dragged her into the room where I was working on you, I remember thinking she was just a kid. Wasn't any bigger than a minute, and all that white blond hair and those big blue eyes, it's no wonder I misjudged her age."

It was the description that caught Wyatt's attention. He'd seen a woman who looked like that. A woman with hair like angel's wings, whom *he'd* mistaken for a girl until an errant wind had moved her coat, revealing a womanly figure.

He blanched, and covered his face in his hands. There was something else about that woman that had been unique, and only Wyatt was privy to the fact.

Somehow, when his guard had been down and his defenses weak, she'd insinuated herself within his thoughts. He didn't know how it had happened, but after what he'd just heard, he was firmly convinced that she'd done it again last night, presumably at the point of her death.

"My God," he muttered. Leaning forward, he rested his elbows upon his knees and stared at a pattern on the carpet until the colors all ran together.

"Sorry to be the bearer of such bad news," Steading said. "Are you all right?"

Wyatt shrugged. "I didn't really know her. It was her kindness that I wanted to acknowledge. It's a damn shame I came too late." And then he had a thought. "I'd like to see. Where she lived, I mean. Do you know?"

"Nope, I can't say that I do. But you could ask at the police department. Anders Conway could tell you."

Wyatt stood. "I've taken up enough of your time, Dr. Steading. Thanks for your help."

Steading shrugged.

Wyatt was at the door, when he paused and then turned. "Doctor?"

"Yes?"

"What was her name?"

"Dixon. Glory Dixon."

A twist of pain spiked, and then centered in the region of Wyatt's heart. "Glory," he repeated, more to himself than to the doctor, then closed the door behind him.

"Damn," Amos muttered. "In fact…damn it all to hell."

Wyatt navigated the winding road with absentminded skill. He'd gone over the side of one Kentucky mountain. It was enough. Remembering the directions he'd been given, he kept a sharp watch for a twisted pine, aware that he was to turn left just beyond it. As he rounded a bend, the last rays of the setting sun suddenly spiked through a cloud and the waning light hit the top of a tree. Wyatt eased off the gas. It was the pine. He began looking for the road, and sure enough, a few yards beyond, a narrow, one-laned dirt road took a sharp turn to the left. Wyatt followed it to its destination.

The clearing came without warning. One minute the road was shadowed and treelined, and then suddenly he was braking to a sliding halt as his fingers tightened upon the steering wheel, and his breath came in short, painful gasps.

"Dear God."

There was little else to say as he got out of the car and walked toward the blackened timbers. Yellow police tape was tied from tree to tree and then from fence post to the bumper

of what was left of a pickup truck—a vivid reminder that
death had occurred here.

The fact that the shell of a washing machine and dryer still
stood, while a house was gone, seemed obscene, too vivid a
reminder of how frail human life truly was. Smoke continued
to rise from several locations as cross beams and a stack of
something no longer identifiable smoldered. An unnatural heat
lingered in the cooler evening air.

Wyatt stuffed his hands in his pockets and hunched his
shoulders against the weight of despair that hung over the
area. Last night he'd heard a cry for help and had been unable
to respond, and yet when *he'd* needed help most, she had
come. The burden of his guilt was almost more than he could
bear.

"Ah, God, Glory Dixon. It *was* you, wasn't it? I am so, so
sorry. If I had known, I would have helped."

"Do you swear?"

Wyatt spun. This time the voice he just heard had been
behind him, not in his head. And when a young woman
walked out of the trees, he thought he was seeing a ghost. It
was her! The woman from the street!

He looked over his shoulder at the ruins, and then back at
her, unable to believe his own eyes. Suddenly, a puppy darted
out of the woods behind her and began pouncing around her
feet. Wyatt stared. He'd never heard of a ghost with a dog.

He stood his ground, fighting the urge to run. "Are you
real?"

Glory sighed, and Wyatt imagined he felt the air stir from
her breath. And then she was standing before him, and he
looked down and got lost in a silver-blue gaze. An errant
breeze lifted the hair from her neck and shoulders, and for a
moment, it seemed to float on the air like wings. Once again,
Wyatt was reminded of angels.

"Why did you come?" Glory whispered. "How did you
know?"

The sound of her voice broke the spell, and Wyatt blinked,
trying to regain a true focus on the world around him. Unable

to believe his eyes, he grasped a portion of her hair between his fingers. Although it was silken in texture, there was nothing unearthly about it.

"I heard you call my name," he muttered, as he watched the hair curl around his finger.

Glory gasped, startled by what he'd revealed, and stepped back. *Dear God, did I give him more than my blood? Have I given away part of myself?*

Then drawn by the horror she couldn't ignore, her gaze shifted to the pile of blackened timbers, and without warning, tears pooled and then tracked down her cheeks in silent misery. Wyatt groaned and opened his arms, and to his surprise, she walked into his embrace with no hesitation.

In his mind, holding her was like trying to hold sunshine. She was light, fragile, and seemed to sway within his arms with every beat of his heart. Her shoulders shook with grief, and yet her sobs were silent, as if the agony just wouldn't let go.

"I'm so sorry about your family," Wyatt said softly, and closed the gap between his hands until she stood locked firmly within his grasp. "But everyone's going to be so happy to learn that you survived. As soon as you're able, I'll take you back to town."

She went limp, and for a moment, he thought she was going to faint. Instead, it seemed more of a physical retreat. Sensing her uneasiness, he immediately turned her loose.

"I can't go back. Not yet," Glory said quietly.

Wyatt couldn't hide his surprise. "Why ever not?"

"Because this wasn't an accident. Because someone tried to kill me, and my daddy and brother suffered for it."

Before he thought, Wyatt had her by the arms. "What the hell do you mean, 'someone tried to kill me'? Are you saying that this fire was set?"

"At first it wasn't a fire, it was an explosion. The fire came afterward."

Unable to look at him, she turned away. He was bound to doubt. Everyone always did.

"Well, hell," Wyatt muttered. "Then you need to tell the police chief. He'll know what to do."

Glory spun, and for the first time since she'd walked out of the woods, Wyatt saw a light in her eyes and heard fire in her voice.

"No! You don't understand! They'll come tomorrow...or the next day...to go through the ruins. When they do, they're only going to find two bodies, not three. And then whoever it was that did this will try again. I need time to try and figure out what to do."

Wyatt frowned. "What do you mean, whoever did this? I thought you knew."

She shook her head.

"Then how do you know it wasn't an accident?"

Glory lifted her chin, silencing his argument with a piercing look he couldn't ignore.

"I *see* things. Sometimes I know things before they happen, sometimes I see them happen. But however my knowledge comes...I know what I know."

Wyatt took a deep breath. He knew for a fact that he'd been hearing some things of his own. Right now, it wasn't in him to doubt that she might...just might...be able to do more than hear. What if she could see? What if she was for real?

"Are you telling me that you're psychic?"

"Some people call it that."

Wyatt went quiet as he considered the ramifications of her admission.

"Why did you come to the hospital to help me?"

Her chin trembled, but her words were sure. "I *saw* your accident as it happened. I heard your cry for help...and because I could come, I did."

Daring the risk of rejection, Wyatt reached out and cupped her face with his hand. To his joy, she withstood his familiarity, in fact, even seemed to take strength from the comfort.

"How can I thank you, Glory Dixon?"

"By not giving me away. By helping me stay alive until I can figure out why...and who...and..."

"It's done. Tell me what to do first."

Again, she swayed on her feet. Wyatt reached out, but she pushed him away. Her gaze searched the boundary of trees around the rubble, constantly on the lookout for a hidden menace. Fear that she would be found before it was time was a constant companion.

"You need to hide your car. Maybe drive it around behind the barn, out in the pasture."

"Where are you…uh…?"

"Hiding?"

He nodded.

"When you've parked your car, I'll show you, but we need to hurry. There'll be no moon tonight, and the woods are dense and dark."

Wyatt headed for his car, and as he followed her directions through the narrow lanes, wondered what on earth he'd let himself in for. Yet as the beam of his headlights caught and then held on the beauty of her face and the pain he saw hidden in her eyes, he knew he didn't give a damn. She'd helped him. The least he could do was repay the debt.

A few minutes later, they walked away from the site, following what was left of a road overgrown with bushes and weeds. The air was already damp. Dew was heavy on the grass, blotching the legs of their jeans and seeping into the soles of their shoes. The bag Wyatt was carrying kept getting caught on low-hanging limbs, but Glory seemed to pass through the brush without leaving a trace. It would seem that her fragile, delicate appearance was deceiving. He suspected that she moved through life as she did through these trees—with purpose.

The pup ran between their legs, barking once from the delight of just being alive. He ran with his nose to the ground and his long, puppy ears flopping, yet a single word from Glory and he hushed.

Something silent and dark came out of a tree overhead and sailed across their line of vision. Instinctively, Glory threw up her hands and gasped. Wyatt caught her as she started to run.

"I think it was an owl," he said gently, and held her until she had calmed.

"Sorry," she said. "I'm not usually so jumpy. It's just that…" Tears were thick in her voice as she pushed herself out of his arms and resumed their trek.

Visibility was nearly zero, yet Glory moved with a sure sense of direction and Wyatt followed without question. Night creatures hid as the pair walked past, then scurried back into their holes, suddenly unsure of their world. Wyatt heard the rustling in the deep, thick grass, and even though he knew what it was that he heard, he couldn't prevent a shiver of anxiety. This was a far cry from the safety and comfort of the Tennessee home where he'd been recuperating. It reminded him too much of secret maneuvers he'd been on in places he'd rather forget.

He clutched at the bag over his shoulder and caught himself wishing it was a gun in his hands, and not a duffel bag. Twice as they walked, Glory paused, listening carefully to the sounds of the woods through which they walked, judging what she heard against what she knew should be there. After a time, she would resume the trek without looking back, trusting that because Wyatt had come, he would still follow.

Just when he was wondering if they would walk all night, they entered a clearing. Again Glory paused, this time clutching the sleeve of his shirt as she stared through the darkness, searching for something that would feel out of place.

The instinct that had carried Wyatt safely through several tours of duty told him that all was well.

"It's okay," he said, and this time he took her by the hand and led the way toward the cabin on the other side of the yard.

The night could not disguise the humble quality of the tiny abode. It was no more than four walls and a slanted, shingle roof, a rock chimney that angled up from the corner of the roof, with two narrow windows at the front of the cabin that stared back at them like a pair of dark, accusing eyes.

Glory shivered apprehensively, then slipped the key from

her jeans. As her fingers closed around it, she was thankful that her daddy had kept this one hidden at the cabin, or she would have been unable to get inside the night before.

Wyatt listened to the woods around them as she worked the lock, and when the door swung open with a slight, warning squeak, she took his hand and led him through with an odd little welcome.

"We're home," she said.

As he followed her inside, he had the oddest sensation that what she said was true.

Chapter 4

"Don't turn on the light."

Wyatt's fingers paused on the edge of the switch. The panic in her voice was too real to ignore.

"You're serious about this, aren't you?"

Glory nodded, then realized that in the dark, Wyatt Hatfield couldn't see her face.

"Yes, I'm serious. Please wait here. I have a candle."

Wyatt did as he was told. He set down his duffel bag and then closed the door behind him, thinking that the dark in here was as thick as the woods through which they'd just walked. Moments later, he heard the rasp of a match to wood, focused on the swift flare of light and watched a wick catch and burn. And then she turned, bathed in the gentle glow of candlelight. Once again, Wyatt was struck by her fragile beauty.

"Will the pup be all right outside?"

"Yes," Glory said. "Follow me." Wyatt picked up his bag. "This is where you'll sleep," she said, and held the candle above her head, giving him a dim view of the tiny room and the single bed. "I'm just across the hall in Granny's bed."

"Granny?"

"My father's mother. This was her cabin. She's all the family I have left." And then her face crumpled as tears shimmered in her eyes. "The only problem is, she's ninety-one years old and in a nursing home. Half the time she doesn't remember her name, let alone me."

As she turned away, Wyatt set his bag inside the room and followed her across the hall, watching as she set the candle on a bedside table, then ran across the room to check the curtains, making sure that no light would be visible from outside.

"Glory?"

She stilled, then slowly turned. "What?"

"Talk to me."

She understood his confusion, but wasn't sure she could make him understand. With a defeated sigh, she dropped to the corner of the bed, running her fingers lightly across the stitching on the handmade quilt, drawing strength from the woman who'd sewn it, and then bent over to pull off her boots. She tugged once, then twice, and without warning, started to cry quiet tears of heartbreak.

Wyatt flinched as her misery filled the tiny space. Without thinking, he knelt at her feet. Grasping her foot, he pulled one boot off and then the other before turning back the bed upon which she sat.

"Lie down."

The gentleness in his voice was her undoing. Glory rolled over, then into a ball, and when the weight of the covers fell upon her shoulders, she began to sob.

"He was laughing," she whispered.

Wyatt frowned. "Who was laughing, honey?"

"My brother, J.C. One minute he was digging through the grocery sack for Twinkies and laughing at something the pup had done, and then everything exploded." She took a deep, shaky breath, trying to talk past the sobs. "I should have been with them."

Wyatt cursed beneath his breath. Her pain was more than he could bear. He wanted to hold her, yet the unfamiliarity of their odd connection held him back. Slowly, she rolled over, looking at him through those silver-blue eyes while the skin crawled on the back of his neck.

"I was the first female born to the Dixon family in more than five generations. They say that my eyes were open when I was born, and that when Granny laid me on my mother's stomach, I lifted my head, looked at my mother's face and smiled. An hour later, my mother suddenly hemorrhaged, then died, and although I was in another room, Granny says that the moment she took her last breath, I started to cry. Granny called it 'the sight.' I consider it more of a curse."

Wyatt brushed the tangle of hair from her eyes, smoothing it from her forehead and off her shoulders. "It saved me," he said quietly.

She closed her eyes. A tear slipped out of each corner and ran down her temples and into her hair.

"I know." Her mouth twisted as she tried to talk around the pain. "But why couldn't I save Daddy and J.C.? Why, Wyatt Hatfield? Tell me why."

Unable to stay unattached from her pain, Wyatt slid his hands beneath her shoulders and lifted her from the covers, then into his lap. As he nestled his chin in her hair, he held her against him.

"I don't know the whys of the world, Glory Dixon. I only know the hows. And I swear to you, I will keep you safe until they find the man responsible."

It was the promise he made and the honesty with which it was said that gave her hope. Maybe together they could get it done.

I'm so glad he's here, Glory thought.

"I'm glad I came, too," Wyatt whispered.

Glory froze. Without realizing it, he'd read her thoughts and answered. And as she let herself draw from his strength, she faced the fact that she'd given more than just blood to this man. It seemed impossible, and it shouldn't have happened, but it was the only explanation that made sense.

A dog ran across the street in front of the car as Wyatt turned a corner in Larner's Mill, aiming for the local police department down the street. He knew where it was. He'd been there yesterday when asking directions to the Dixon home. The people were friendly enough, but he wasn't sure if one small-town police chief and two part-time deputies were going to be up to finding a killer. When they'd driven out of the yard earlier that morning, no one had even bothered to stop them and ask why they were near the scene. On the surface, they seemed geared more toward drunks and traffic violations than tracking criminals. He hoped he was wrong. As he pulled to the curb and parked, Glory's nervousness was impossible to ignore any longer.

"It's going to be all right," he said.

Her eyes were wide and on the verge of tears, her mouth set. He could tell she was hovering on the edge of panic.

"They're not going to believe me," she said, but when Wyatt slipped his hand over hers and squeezed, the fear receded.

"It doesn't really matter whether they believe you or not, as long as they proceed with some kind of investigation. Besides, don't forget Lane's coming."

Glory nodded, remembering their earlier phone call to Wyatt's brother-in-law.

"Having a U.S. marshal on our side isn't going to hurt," Wyatt added, then glanced down at his watch. "In fact, I'd lay odds that he'll be here before dark."

Glory bit her lip and then looked away.

"You have to trust me, girl."

She turned, and Wyatt found himself looking into her eyes and fighting the sensation of falling deeper and deeper into a place with no way out. And then she blinked, and he realized he'd been holding his breath. Muttering to himself, he helped her out of the car.

Glory took heart in the fact that as they walked through the door, he was right beside her all the way.

"God Almighty!"

Anders Conway jumped to his feet and stumbled backward as the couple came in the door. He'd been police chief of Larner's Mill for twenty-nine years, but it was his first time seeing a ghost.

Wyatt felt Glory flinch, and instinctively slipped a hand across her shoulder, just to remind her that he was there.

"Chief Conway, I came to report a murder," Glory said softly.

He was so shocked by her appearance that her remark went right over his head. "We thought you were dead," he said. "Where on earth have you been, girl?"

"Hiding."

"Whatever for? No one's gonna hurt you."

Glory looked to Wyatt for reassurance. The glint in his eye was enough to keep her going.

"The fire at my house was not an accident. Someone deliberately turned on the gas jets. I saw them. When Daddy and J.C. walked in the back door with our groceries, it was nearly dusk and the house must have been full of gas. Wyatt says that one of them probably turned on the light, and that was what sparked the explosion."

Conway frowned. Apparently, none of this was making much sense. "If you saw someone turning on the gas, why didn't you tell your family? Why would your father knowingly go into a house set to blow?"

This was where it got rough. Glory braced herself, readying for the derision that was bound to come.

"I didn't actually *see* what had been done until the house was already burning, I just knew that something was wrong. I tried to stop them from going inside. I called out, but it was too late. They were already there."

The look on Conway's face was changing from shock to

onfusion. Afraid that he'd run her out before she got a
chance to explain, she started talking faster, anxious to get it
all said.

"I know it was a man who did it. I could see him in my
mind. I saw the back of his hands as he turned on the jets on
the stove. He even broke one of them so that it couldn't be
turned off. I saw the back of his pant legs as he ran through
the other rooms, doing the same to our heat stoves. One in
the living room…and one in the bathroom, too."

"In your mind. You saw this *in your mind.*"

She nodded.

Conway made no attempt to hide his disbelief. "Exactly
who did you see? In your mind, of course."

Glory wanted to hide. The simple fact of her father's presence in her life had prevented most people from displaying
any out-and-out derision they might have felt. This was the
first time that she'd experienced it alone. Suddenly, Wyatt's
hand slid under her hair and cupped the back of her neck. She
relaxed. *I forgot. I'm not alone.*

"No, honey, you're not," Wyatt said, still unaware that he
was reading her thoughts and answering them aloud.

Glory looked startled, but not as surprised as Anders Conway, who turned his focus to the man at her side.

"You're the fellow who was asking directions to the Dixon
place yesterday, aren't you?"

Wyatt nodded.

"Are you kin?"

Wyatt glanced down at Glory and winked, then gave the
policeman a look he couldn't ignore.

"I'm a friend. Miss Dixon saved my life last year. I'm
simply returning a favor."

"How did…?"

"None of that matters," Wyatt said. "The point is, Glory
Dixon knows that someone tried to kill her. And, obviously,
they did not succeed. The fact remains that when it's made
known that she's still alive, he will obviously try again." And
then he added, as if it were an afterthought, although he knew

what an impact his announcement would make, "you should also know that there's a U.S. marshal on his way here to help with the investigation. He's my brother-in-law. I called him this morning."

Conway's jaw dropped as Wyatt continued. "And I suppose you've already called the state fire marshal about the incident. When is he coming?"

Conway started to fidget. "Well, I...uh, I mean..." Then he slapped his hand on the desk, trying to regain control of the situation. "Look! Everyone knows that fire was an accident. A terrible accident. The coroner should be on his way out there by now to recover the bodies. They tried once yesterday and the wreckage was still too hot."

He ran a hand through his thinning hair and tried to make them see his point.

"I'm real sorry that Miss Dixon lost her family. It has to be a shock, and that's probably what's making her imagine all of this. What you need to do is get her to a doctor and..."

"You didn't answer my question," Wyatt said. "When is the fire marshal coming?"

"I didn't call him...yet," Conway added.

Wyatt gave a pointed look toward the phone and then back at the lawman's face. "We'll wait," he said shortly.

Before they had time to sit down, a dispatcher came in from the back of the department with a note in his hand.

"Chief, you won't believe this. They just radioed in from the site of the Dixon fire and said they only found two bodies in the..." At this point, he noticed the couple seated across the room and froze. The note fluttered from his fingers to the floor. "Well, my Gawd! No wonder they didn't find a third body. There you are!"

Glory felt like a bug on a pin, displayed for everyone to see, and listening to them speak of her father and brother as mere "bodies" was almost more than she could bear. She bit her lip and looked away, fighting the urge to scream. And then Wyatt unexpectedly clasped her hand and wouldn't let go. Hysteria settled as she absorbed his warmth.

"Tell them to get on back here with what they've got," Conway growled. "I'm dealing with the rest. And tell them not to do any more than remove the remains. The fire marshal is going to come out and investigate the site."

"Yes, sir!" the dispatcher said, and hurried out of the room.

Wyatt stood. "I guess we'll be going now," he said.

"How can I reach you?" Conway said.

Wyatt heard Glory's swift intake of breath, and knew that while her whereabouts wouldn't be a secret for long, she wasn't ready to reveal them just now.

"We'll be in touch," Wyatt said. "For now, I think the fewer who know where she is, the better. Don't you agree?"

Conway's face turned red. The man had all but accused him of not being able to maintain confidentiality in his own department. And then he relented. If they wanted to make a big deal out of this, he wasn't going to stop them. Everyone knew that Rafe Dixon's girl was a little bit nuts. This so-called friend of the family would learn the truth soon enough, or turn out to be just like them. Either way, it didn't matter to him.

"Yeah. Right," Conway said. "Keep in touch."

The smirk in his voice was impossible to ignore. When they walked outside, Glory wilted. "He doesn't believe me, you know," she whispered.

"I know," Wyatt said. "But I do."

His words were an anchor in Glory's unsettled world, and the touch of his hand was balm to her broken heart.

"Are you up to some shopping?" Wyatt asked. "I expect you would like some changes of clothing, and we definitely need to buy food. Is there anything else you can think of?"

Glory's lip trembled as she worked up the nerve to say it aloud.

"Funeral arrangements. I need to see about..." Her voice caught, and she knew this time, she wasn't going to be able to stop the tears.

Wyatt pulled her into his arms, cupping the back of her head as she buried her face against the front of his shirt.

"I'm sorry, Glory. I'm so sorry you're having to go through this, but you need to remember something. It's *we,* honey, not *I.* Don't forget, you're not alone in this anymore. We'll do whatever it is you want. You're calling the shots."

He seated her in the car and then slid behind the steering wheel, waiting for her to settle.

Oh, God, I don't want to be in charge. I just want this to be over, Glory thought.

Wyatt raked her pale face with a dark, brooding look. "It will be, and sooner than you think. Now then, I don't know about you, but I'm hungry as hell. Where's the best place to eat?"

"How do you do that?" Glory asked.

Wyatt grinned as he began to back out of the parking space. "Do what?"

"You're reading my thoughts, and then answering my questions, even though I haven't said them aloud."

The smile on his face stilled. "No, I'm not."

Yes, you are.

He braked in the middle of the street. Fortunately, no one was behind them. He went as pale as the shirt on his back as he looked at her face.

"What did you say?"

I said…you are reading my thoughts.

"Oh, Lord." His belly began to turn, and he could feel the muscles in his face tightening. He gripped the steering wheel until his knuckles turned white, and try as he might, he couldn't make himself move.

"You didn't know it was happening, did you?" Glory asked.

He shook his head. "It just seemed so…"

"Natural?"

His breath escaped in one long sigh. Finally he nodded. "Yes, natural. That's exactly what it feels like."

Glory nodded. "I know." Suddenly, she smiled. "You're the first person I've ever known who can understand my gift."

It wasn't much, but it was the first time he'd seen what a hint of joy could do to her face. And in that moment, before she redirected his attention to a restaurant down the street, Wyatt Hatfield feared he might be falling in love. It wasn't planned. And it definitely wasn't what he'd had in mind when he started this journey.

In the same instant that he had the revelation, he shut it out of his mind, afraid that she'd be able to see what was in his thoughts. He reminded himself that it was too soon in their relationship for anything like this. Besides, he needed to focus on keeping her alive, not finding ways to steal, then break her heart.

Carter Foster was trying to concentrate on the legal brief on which he was working, but his mind kept wandering to the different scenarios he might use to bring up his next lie. Should he say that Betty Jo had *called* and asked for a divorce, or should he just say she'd *written?* His legal mind instantly settled on the call. That way, he would never be asked to show proof of a letter. And then the moment he thought it, he scoffed. Why should he worry about ever having to showing proof? There was no one left to question his story. Not since the Dixon family perished in that terrible fire.

He'd commiserated along with the rest of the town about the tragedy, and listened to the different explanations circulating. They ranged from a faulty water heater to a leaking gas connection beneath the house. Carter didn't care what people thought. He had done what he'd intended. Glory Dixon was dead and his secret was safe, and...he had few regrets. The fact that he hadn't actually pulled a trigger kept his conscience clear enough to bear.

He had reminded himself that it wasn't his fault the Dixons hadn't detected the scent of gas in time to open some windows. It wasn't his fault that they'd come home so late that it was almost dark and automatically turned on a light upon entering the house. None of that was his fault. All he'd done was twist a few knobs. The results had been in the hands of fate. Obviously, fate was on his side.

"Oh, Mr. Carter! Did you hear?"

He frowned as his secretary flew into his office, clutching the burger and fries that he'd asked her to get.

"Hear what?" he asked, snatching the sack from her arms before she flattened the food beyond description. As he opened it, he sniffed the enticing aroma and then began unwrapping the paper from around the bun.

"Some man found that Dixon girl! She's alive!"

Mustard squeezed out from between his fingers and dripped onto the pad on his desk. A hot, burning pain shot across his chest and then down into his belly, and for a minute he thought he was going to faint.

"What do you mean...alive? How could she survive such a fire?"

"Oh, that's the best part! She wasn't inside after all. Someone said she'd spent the night in the woods, although I don't know why in the world she didn't come home with the firemen when it was over." Then she added, "Of course, you know what they say."

Carter shook his head, anxious to hear what *they* said.

"They say," the secretary said, "that she's a little off in the head. That she claims to be able to 'see things' and 'hear voices,' or some such garbage. It's a shame, too, what with her folks dead and all. Who's going to look after a grown woman whose mind is off plumb?"

Carter shrugged, pretending he didn't know and couldn't care less, and began wiping the mustard from between his fingers and then off of his desk.

"I'm sure it will all work out," he said, and handed her the notes he'd been making on the brief. "Here. Type these up please. I'll probably be out of the office for the rest of the afternoon."

"Yes, sir. Is there some place you can be reached?"

"Home. I'm going home."

She nodded, then left.

Carter stared down at the grease congealing on the paper beneath his burger and then down at the mustard that had dropped on his pants. Cursing beneath his breath, he swiped at it angrily, knowing that he'd have to take these to the cleaners again when they'd just come out. The mustard came away on the napkin, leaving behind an even darker stain on the dark fabric of his slacks.

Suddenly, another stain popped into his mind. The smear of Dixie Red lipstick across Betty Jo's face, and a matching one on the bedspread in which he'd wrapped her. His stomach rolled, and he closed his eyes and leaned back in his chair, telling himself not to panic.

Without taking a bite, he dumped his food in the sack and grabbed his briefcase. Moments later, he was on the street, inhaling the warm, spring air and telling himself to calm down. Just because one plan had failed, didn't mean he couldn't try again. He tossed the sack into a garbage can on the corner and ran across the street to the parking lot to get his car. There were things he needed to do, and they required privacy…and solitude, and a more criminal frame of mind.

A whippoorwill called from across the small clearing in front of Granny's cabin. The pup whined in its sleep, and then was silenced when Glory leaned over and gently patted it on the head.

"It will be dark in an hour or so," Glory said.

"He'll be here," Wyatt said.

"Granny's cabin is hard to find unless you know that it's here."

"Don't forget that they were still digging through the ashes when we came back from town. Chances are there will be someone at the site who Lane can ask. If not, I gave him pretty good directions over the phone." Then he smiled. "You don't know Lane Monday. If he says he'll be here, then he will, and God help the man who gets in his way."

Glory stood up, suddenly restless in the face of nothing to do, and started to go inside.

"I think I'll start supper," she said.

Wyatt caught her at the door. "Glory…"

She looked up, shocked at herself that she was aware of his thumb pressing against the side of her breast. She waited for him to finish.

Suddenly the pup began to bark. Wyatt dropped Glory's arm and thrust her behind him as he spun. In the space of a heartbeat, Glory saw him as the soldier that he'd been. His posture was defensive, his eyes raking the dense line of trees beyond the small yard, and as quickly as he stiffened, he began to relax.

"It's Lane."

Glory took a step sideways, giving herself a better view of the man who was coming out of the trees, and then gasped. *He's a giant.*

Wyatt grinned at her. "Yeah, squirt, from where you stand, I guess he is."

"You're doing it again," she muttered, and punched him on the arm. "What I'd like to know is, if I'm the psychic, why is it you're the one who keeps reading my mind? Why can't I see into yours?"

He shrugged. "Maybe it's the soldier in me. I was trained not to let down my guard." *And the day I let you into my head, I'm in trouble,* he thought, and then focused on the big man, who was coming their way.

Glory held her breath, watching the motion of man and muscle, and wondered who on earth would be brave enough to live with a man of that size.

"My sister," Wyatt answered, and then grinned. "Sorry. That slipped."

Ignoring him, Glory stepped forward and extended her hand as if welcoming Lane into a fine home, instead of a tiny cabin lost among the trees.

"Mr. Monday, I'm Glory Dixon. I thank you for coming." Then she watched as her hand disappeared in his palm.

Lane smiled, and Glory saw the gentleness in him, in spite of his size.

"Well, I sort of owe old Wyatt here," he said. "And from what he said, you're outnumbered. I thought I'd come even the odds."

"I was about to put supper on the table," she said.

"We'll help," Wyatt said, and took Lane's bag from his hand. "Follow me, and duck when you enter."

A coyote howled far in the distance and a night owl hooted from a tree in the yard, sending the puppy into a frenzy of barking that made Wyatt nervous. He knew within reason that the night sounds had set the dog off, but visions of an attacker creeping through the forest would not go away.

"Want me to check it out?" Lane asked.

"Glory says it's just the night. That if it was a man, the pup wouldn't bother to bark at all and would probably lick him to death."

Lane accepted his explanation without comment, watching intently as Wyatt paced the floor between window and chair while Glory was down the hall, taking a bath.

"Do you think she's on the up-and-up?" Lane asked.

Wyatt froze, then turned. "Yes."

"Just like that?"

"Just like that," Wyatt said.

Lane shrugged. "So tell me what you know."

Wyatt's eyes darkened, and the scar across his cheek turned red.

"She says that someone turned on the gas in her house on purpose. I know her father and brother are dead. I hear what she's thinking and I don't know how to explain it."

Lane's mouth dropped, but only slightly. "You're telling me that you can read her mind?"

"Don't look at me like that!" Wyatt growled. "I know how that sounds. But I know what I know. Blame it on the fact that I nearly died. Blame it on the fact that her blood runs in my veins. Just believe me!"

"Wyatt, don't be mad at him."

Both men turned. Glory stood in the doorway to the living room, holding a towel clutched to her breasts while her granny's nightgown lightly dusted the floor. At first glance, she looked like a child, until one noticed the swell of breast beneath the white flannel, and the curve of her hip beneath the fabric as she walked across the room.

"Your feet will get cold," Wyatt muttered, and wanted to bury his fists in the silver-blond sway of her hair brushing close to her waist.

Glory paused, then looked up at both men. The plea in her eyes was impossible to deny.

"We're not fighting, honey," Lane said gently, and watched how she moved toward Wyatt, settling within the shelter of his arms as if she'd done it countless times before. He didn't think he'd ever seen a more gentle, trusting woman in his life.

"It's not his fault he doesn't understand," Glory continued, as if Lane had not even spoken.

"I don't have to understand to help," Lane said. "And I will help. Tomorrow, I'm going to do some investigating of my own at the fire site. One of the men I talked to earlier said the fire marshal was due around nine in the morning. You can come if you want to."

Glory's voice shook, but she managed to maintain her poise. "Tomorrow I bury my family. Maybe later." And then she gave them a smile that didn't quite reach her eyes. "If you don't mind, I think I'll go on to bed. Do you have everything you need?"

Unable to let her go without touching her one last time, Wyatt brushed at a stray strand of hair that was too near her eye. "We'll manage. Just sleep. Remember, whatever happens tomorrow, you won't be alone."

She nodded, and then went into her room and shut the door.

For several minutes, neither man spoke, and when the silence was broken, it was by Lane.

"I hope you don't think that I'm sleeping with *you*," he muttered.

Wyatt grinned. "I hope you don't think that I'm giving up my bed."

Lane grinned back. "Do you know if there are any extra quilts? I'm thinking that floor looks better all the time."

The tension of the moment was past, and by the time Lane's pallet was made and Wyatt was in the shower, there was nothing to do but watch and wait to see what tomorrow would bring.

Meanwhile, Carter Foster was at home, racking his brain for a solution. Before he'd gone two blocks from the office, he'd heard enough gossip on the street to choke a horse. The fact that Glory Dixon had brought an ex-marine with her to the police department, and that a U.S. marshal was on his way, made him nervous. He was out of his element. What he needed was muscle. Hired muscle. He wondered which, if any, of his ex-clients would be capable of murder, and then wondered what the going rate on hit men was these days.

He slumped into an easy chair, contemplating the rug beneath his toes, fearing that the cost of Betty Jo's burial was bound to increase, and cursed the day he'd ever said "I do."

Chapter 5

The scent of the bacon they'd had for breakfast still lingered in the air of the cabin as Wyatt watched Lane disappear into the trees beyond the small yard, already on his way to the site of the fire. Through the dense growth of leaves overhead, sunlight dappled the ground in uneven patterns, giving an effect similar to the crazy quilt that covered his bed. The pup was in a patch of sunshine worrying a bone, while a blue jay sat on a tree branch above the pup's head, scolding it for its mere presence.

To the eye, it would seem an idyllic day, and yet today Glory was to put to rest her entire family, leaving her, virtually, alone on the face of the earth.

He could hear her moving about in her room, presumably getting dressed for the memorial services later that morning. He knew it couldn't possibly take her long to decide what to wear. She only had the one dress that she'd bought yesterday. His own clothing choices were limited, as well. When he'd left Tennessee, he'd had no inkling of what he would find. If he had, he might have planned accordingly. As it was, boots, clean jeans, a white shirt and his jacket would have to serve as proper dress. His only suit was on a hanger back at the farm above Chaney Creek.

Blindly, he looked through the window without seeing, concentrating instead on the woman he'd found at the end of his search. What was happening between them didn't make sense. It was as crazy as the fact that, seemingly, and for no apparent reason, two people had been murdered. She knew of nothing that would warrant the elimination of everyone she held dear, and yet all was gone. And she said it wasn't over.

Wyatt shuddered. Gut feeling told him she wasn't wrong, and he'd relied too many years on his instinct to ignore it now.

"Wyatt, I'm ready."

He pivoted, a half-voiced thought hanging at the edge of his lips, and then froze, forgetting what he'd been about to say as he beheld the woman before him. All images of the childlike waif were gone, hidden beneath the soft, blue folds of the dress she was wearing. The bodice molded itself to the fullness of her breasts, and the narrowness of her waist only accentuated the gentle flare of hips beneath the ankle length of her skirt. Even her hair had undergone a transformation. Forgoing her normal style of letting it fall where it may, Glory had pulled it away from her face and then anchored it all on top in a white-gold spiral. Escaping strands fell around her face and down her neck, weeping from the silky crown atop her head.

"I know it's not the standard black dress," she said. "But it was Daddy's favorite color. I did it for him, not for tradition."

Wyatt cleared his throat, moved by her beauty as well as her grace.

"I saw them once," he said softly.

"Who?"

"Your father...and your brother."

Her eyebrows arched with surprise.

"Remember, outside the hospital, the day I was being re-leased?"

Understanding dawned, and she almost smiled. "That's right! You did."

It gave her an odd sort of pleasure to know that in this, her day of greatest sorrow, he had faces to go with the names of those she loved best.

"I think they would be proud of you," he said.

She nodded, and then her chin trembled, but her voice was firm. "I wish this was over."

Her pain was so thick that he imagined he could feel it. He crossed the room and then stood before her, wanting to touch her in so many places, to test the new waters of Glory Dixon, but this wasn't the time. Today she must mourn. Tomorrow was another day.

He offered her his arm instead, and when her fingers moved across the fabric of his shirt and then locked into the bend of his elbow, Wyatt paused, savoring the contact, as well as her trust.

"Are you ready to go?" he asked.

She nodded, and together they walked out the door. It was only after she shut it behind her that Wyatt realized they were going to have to walk the quarter of a mile up the overgrown path to where his car was parked. He looked down at her shoes, worrying if she would be able to make it. The narrow strap that held the two-inch heels on her feet seemed too del-icate for the rough underbrush that had overtaken the unused road.

No sooner had the worry occurred, than a tall, dark-haired young man emerged from the woods, leading a horse behind him. His freshly starched and ironed overalls were shiny, and every button on his long-sleeved white shirt was fastened right up to the collar. Before Wyatt had time to ask, Glory gasped, her voice shaking as she quickly explained.

"Oh...oh, my! It's Edward Lee."

"He's a friend?" Wyatt asked sharply.

Glory nodded. "He lives about two miles from our house,

as the crow flies. J.C. always took him fishing. He's shy of
strangers, so don't expect much conversation. He's simple,
you see.''

"He's wh…?'' And then suddenly Wyatt understood, although it had been years since he'd heard the old hill name
for mental retardation.

Glory patted his arm. "Don't worry. Edward Lee knows
he's different. He won't embarrass you.''

That wasn't what Wyatt had been thinking, but it was too
late to explain himself now. The young man was nearly at
their feet.

"Hey, Mornin' Glory, I brought you my horse. You
shouldn't be walkin' in the brush today.''

The black gelding stood quietly at the end of the reins, as
if it understood the limitations of its master quite well. The
old saddle on its back was gleaming with polish, the metal
studs on the halter glittered in the sunlight like polished silver.
For Edward Lee, the work had been a labor of love.

Glory touched his arm in a gentle, easy manner. "Why,
Edward Lee. How did you know?''

He ducked his head as tears ran unashamedly down his
face. "I know that your pa and J.C. got burned up. Ma said
the buryin' is today and I knew where you was stayin', and
that the old road is all grown up with weeds and such.'' And
then he lifted his head, as if proud of the assumption he had
made, and continued. "I knew you'd be all pretty today, Mornin' Glory. I wanted to help you.''

Morning Glory. Somehow that fits her, Wyatt thought, and
suddenly resented Edward Lee for sharing a past with Glory
that he had not. He saw the sweetness of Glory's expression
as she accepted the young man's gift, recognized the adoration in Edward Lee's eyes, and knew that, but for a quirk of
fate that had rendered Edward Lee less than other men, he
would have been a fierce suitor for Glory Dixon's hand. Jealousy came without warning, and the moment he recognized
it for what it was, he was ashamed of having felt it.

"Edward Lee, I want you to meet my friend, Wyatt.''

Edward Lee glanced at Wyatt, his expression suddenly strained, his behavior nervous, as if expecting a negative reaction that must have happened all too many times before.

As Wyatt watched, he realized how special the bond was between Edward Lee and Glory. In their own way, they'd each experienced the judgement of a prejudiced and uneducated society. A society that seemed bound to ridicule that which it did not understand. Edward Lee was as different in his own right as Glory was in hers.

Wyatt smiled and extended his hand. "Any friend of Glory's is a friend of mine."

The grin that broke across Edward Lee's face was magnificent. He grabbed Wyatt's hand and pumped it fiercely as he started to explain.

"You can leave Rabbit in Mr. Dixon's barn," Edward Lee offered. "Then when you come home, you can ride him back here. When you don't need him no more, just lay the reins across the saddle and turn him loose. He'll come home."

Wyatt's smile widened. "Rabbit?"

Edward Lee nodded. "'Cause he runs like one."

Glory's small laugh broke the peace of the glade, and both men turned, each wearing a different expression as they gazed at the woman before them. Edward Lee's was one of devotion. Wyatt's was one of pure want.

Glory saw neither. All she knew was that two people who meant something to her seemed at ease with each other. It gave her joy in this day of distress.

"I can't thank you enough for your kindness, Edward Lee. Tell your mother I said hello," she said.

He nodded, and then turned and walked away, moving with unnatural grace for one with so crippled a mind.

"Can you ride?" Glory asked, eyeing the saddle and remembering her dress, and wondering how she was going to accomplish this feat with any amount of dignity.

Wyatt grinned, then lifted her off her feet and set her sideways in the saddle, leaving her legs to dangle off to one side.

"That's almost an insult, honey. I'm a Tennessee boy, born and bred, remember."

And with one smooth motion, he swung up on the horse, settling just behind the saddle on which Glory was perched, and slipped his long legs into the stirrups.

Glory shivered as Wyatt's breath moved across her cheek, and his arms fenced her close against his chest.

"Glory?"

"What?"

"Why did he call you Morning Glory?"

A sharp pain pierced and then settled around the region of her heart. She took a deep breath, knowing that it was something to which she must become accustomed.

"It was J.C.'s nickname for me...and they were Daddy's favorite flowers. They grow—" her breath caught on another pain as she amended "—grew, on trellises on both sides of our front porch. That's how I got my name. Daddy said when I was born my eyes were as blue as the morning glory."

Impulsively, Wyatt hugged her, and feathered a kiss near her eyebrow.

"I'm sorry. I didn't know it would cause you pain."

She looked up at him, her eyes filling with unshed tears. "It wasn't so bad," she said quietly. "In fact, it almost felt good to remember."

Wyatt watched her mouth forming around the words, and wanted to bend just a little bit closer and taste that pearly sheen of lip gloss painted on her mouth. But he couldn't...and he didn't...and the urge slowly passed. The horse moved sideways beneath them, ready for a command. He gripped the reins firmly, and settled Glory a little bit closer to his chest.

"Can you hold on?" he asked.

"As long as you're behind me," she warned, trying to find an easy way to sit without sliding too far backward or forward.

As long as I'm behind you. The words hung in Wyatt's mind, fostering another set of hopes that he didn't dare acknowledge. *What if I never left you, little Morning Glory?*

*How would you feel about that? Even more to the point, how
do I feel? Are you what I was looking for when I started on
this journey last fall...or am I just kidding myself, looking for
easy answers to the emptiness inside myself?*

He shrugged off the thoughts, unwilling to pursue them
while she was this up close and personal. He had to be careful.
The last thing he wanted to do was ruin another woman's life
as he'd ruined his and Shirley's. If he ever took a woman
again, it would be forever. Wyatt Hatfield didn't make the
same mistake twice.

The trip up the overgrown road was much easier on a horse,
and done in the bright light of day. As they passed through
the woods, Wyatt wondered how on earth they'd managed to
get through it the other night without tearing their clothing to
shreds.

For an old horse, Rabbit pranced, as if aware of his fine
appearance and the precious cargo that he carried. In spite of
the seriousness of the day, Glory smiled more than once at
what they saw as they rode.

Once her hand suddenly clutched at Wyatt's thigh and then
she pointed into the trees. He followed the direction of her
finger, and saw the disappearing tail of a tiny red fox. And
then a few minutes later, she pointed upward, watching as a
hawk rode the air currents high above their heads.

"This is a fine place to live," Wyatt said.

The words gave solace to Glory's pain. It was a sentiment
she'd heard her father offer more than once.

Wyatt felt some of the tension slipping out of her body,
and she almost relaxed against him as they rode. Almost...until her homesite came into view, and the scent of
something having been burned replaced the fresh mountain
air.

Death seemed to hover above the spot where her house
once stood. As they passed the ruins on their way to the barn
to get his car, Wyatt noticed she turned away. In spite of the
unusual activity taking place there, she was unable to look at
the place she'd once lived.

Men hard at work paused at the sight of the pair's arrival on horseback. When they realized who it was, to a man, they took off their hats, standing with eyes down, sharing her sorrow and her loss.

Glory's breath caught on a sob.

"I'm sorry, honey," Wyatt said softly.

Tears were thick in her voice as she answered. "Oh, God, Wyatt Hatfield. So am I. So am I."

A short time later, as they passed the boundary sign on the north edge of town, Wyatt began easing up on the gas. It wouldn't do to get a ticket for speeding on the way to a funeral, but he'd been lost in thought.

While Glory had been unwilling to look at the men on her property, Wyatt had looked long and hard. Satisfied that Lane was right in the middle of what was being done, he'd left with an easy conscience. Whatever was found there today, whatever conclusion they came to, it would be fair, or Lane Monday would know the reason why.

"Are you all right?" Wyatt asked.

She nodded, her eyes wide and fixed upon the road before them. And then she asked, "Do you remember the turnoff to the cemetery we took to pick out grave sites yesterday?"

"I remember."

"I thought graveside services were appropriate for Daddy and J.C., considering their…uh…their condition." And then she hesitated, suddenly unsure of the decision she'd made yesterday. "Don't you?"

"I think whatever you decided is right. They were your family. Remember?"

She sighed and covered her face with her hands. Her voice was shaky, her fingers trembling as she let them drop in her lap.

"Oh, God, just let me get through this with my dignity."

"To hell with dignity, Glory. Grief is healthy. It's what you hold back that will eat you alive. Believe me, I'm the ultimate stiff upper lip, and look what a mess I've made of my life."

"I don't see it as such a mess," she offered.

He grimaced. "Yeah, right! I got married to a perfectly good woman, and then gave my heart…and attention…to the military instead of her. It took me years to figure out why."

She listened quietly, afraid to speak for fear he'd stop the confidences he'd suddenly begun to share.

"The military didn't demand anything from me except loyalty and a strong back. What my wife wanted from me was something I didn't know how to share."

And that was…

Wyatt answered her thought before he realized it had just been a thought.

"Me. I was too big and strong and tough to let someone see inside *my* soul. I suppose I thought it wasn't manly." A corner of his mouth turned up in a wry, self-effacing grin. "I think that idiot notion came from having too many older brothers. They used to beat the hell out of me just to see how long it would take me to bleed, and then laugh. But let anyone else try the same stunt, and they'd take them apart." He shrugged as the cemetery gates came into view. "Brotherly love is a strange, strange thing. It doesn't always lay the best of groundwork for making a good husband out of a strong man."

Glory shook her head. "You're wrong," she said quietly. "It wasn't that you were the wrong kind of man. I think it was the wrong time for you to have married. Maybe if you'd waited…" She shrugged, and then unbuckled her seat belt as he pulled to a stop.

For you?

The thought came and went so quickly that Wyatt almost didn't know it had been there. But the feeling it left behind was enough to keep him close at her side as they circled tombstones, walking across the close-clipped grass toward a tent in the distance.

When they were almost there, Glory paused in midstep and stared. Wyatt followed her gaze. Realizing that she'd spotted the single casket bearing what was left of both men, he reached down and clasped her hand in his.

Her chin lifted, her eyes glittering in the midmorning sunlight as she looked up at Wyatt. A slight breeze teased the thick, dark hair above his forehead, scattering it with the temerity of an unabashed flirt. His dark eyes were filled with concern, his strong, handsome features solemn in the face of what she was about to endure. The scar on his cheek was a vivid reminder of what he'd endured, and as Glory saw, she remembered, and took hope from the fact that he'd survived.... So, then, could she.

Glory made it through the service with composure that would have made her father proud. Not once did she give way to the angry shrieks of denial that threatened to boil over. The only signs of her pain were the tears, constant and silent, that fell from her eyes and down her cheeks as the minister spoke.

It was afterward, when the people who'd come to pay their respects started to file past the chairs in which she and Wyatt were sitting, that she realized she wasn't as alone in this world as she'd thought.

The first woman who came was elderly. Her voice shook more than her hands, but her intention was plain as she paused at Glory's chair, resting her weight on the cane in one hand, while she laid a small picture in Glory's lap.

"I'm eighty-nine years old," she said. "I been burned out once and flooded out twice in my lifetime. In all them times, I never lost no family, and in that I reckon I was lucky. But I remembered the thing that I missed most of all that I'd lost, and it was my pictures. We talked about it at church last night. We've all knowed your family long before you was born, girl. The ones of us who had these, have decided to give 'em you."

Glory stared at the picture, dumbfounded. It was an old black-and-white print of a young dark-haired woman with a baby on her hip.

"It's your granny," the old woman said. "And that there's your daddy, when he was just a young'un. I don't remember how I come by it, but me and Faith Dixon are near the same age.''

Glory ran her finger lightly across the surface, absorbing the joy caught on their faces. Her voice was shaking when she looked up.

''I don't know how to thank you,'' she whispered.

''No need...no need,'' the old woman said. ''Just don't you ever be so scairt that you go and hide in no woods alone again. That plumb near broke my heart. We won't hurt you, girl. You're one of us.''

And one after the other, people filed past, giving their condolences for her loss, along with another piece of her family to treasure. A girl from her high school class gave her an annual of their senior year of school.

The man who owned the feed store had two photographs of J.C., taken years ago at a livestock show.

The newspaperman had old photos on file of the year her father had bagged a twelve-point buck.

And so they came, people and pictures of times she'd forgotten, and places to which she'd forgotten they'd been. And when they were gone, Glory sat in silence, clutching the mementos to her breast, unable to speak.

''They've made a dinner for you and your man at the church,'' the minister said, as he started to take his leave. ''I know it's hard, Miss Dixon, but letting them help you grieve will help you, as well.''

''I don't know if I can,'' she whispered, then turned her face to Wyatt's shoulder and wept.

''Just give us a bit,'' Wyatt said. ''We'll be along.''

The minister nodded. ''That's fine. Real fine. I'll let them know you're coming.''

And finally, except for the casket waiting to be lowered, they were alone.

''Oh, Wyatt. I knew that people thought a lot of Daddy and J.C., but I didn't think they liked me.''

Her pain broke his heart. ''Cry, Glory. Cry it all out, and then let it go.'' With that, he pulled her a little bit closer to his chest and held her as she mourned for all that she'd lost…and rejoiced for what she had gained.

Food was everywhere inside the tiny cabin. On the small cabinet space, overflowing in the refrigerator, stacked two deep in aluminum foil dishes on the table and waiting to be eaten.

It had been impossible to refuse the kindness of the ladies who'd prepared the meal, because when it was over, as was the custom of the country, the bereaved family had always to take home the leftover food.

Insisting that she could never use it up, Glory succumbed to their admonition that she had company to feed. They'd declared that, at the very least, she shouldn't have to cook for others in her time of grief.

Wyatt had been fully prepared to make several trips through the woods with the leftovers, because he had no intention of getting on Rabbit while trying to hold on to Glory and a handful of pies.

But when they drove into the yard, expecting Rabbit to be the next ride, they saw that while they were gone, someone had cleared the old road between their houses.

Thankful for the unexpected reprieve, Wyatt turned Rabbit loose as Edward Lee had instructed, and he and Glory drove up to Granny Dixon's cabin in comfort. It wasn't until later, when Lane was helping them unload the food from the car, that they learned one of Glory's neighbors had taken his tractor and front-end loader and done in two hours what would have taken a road crew two days to accomplish.

Glory disappeared into her room to change, and Lane dug happily through the covered dishes, eating his fill of the homemade food as he filled Wyatt in on all that had occurred while they were gone.

"She was right, you know," Lane said, as he took a second helping of scalloped potatoes. "Every gas jet in that house was opened wide. And one of the controls on the kitchen stove had been broken off. Short of turning off the gas at the propane tank, there would have been no way to stop its escape."

Wyatt shrugged. "I'm not surprised."

Lane grinned. "That Conway fellow isn't much of a cop. He wanted to suggest that Glory had turned them all on herself after the fire was over, just to back up her story. The fire marshal almost laughed in his face, and then asked him to try and turn one of the valves himself. Old Conway nearly busted a gut trying to break the knob loose."

"Did it happen?" Wyatt asked.

"Hell, no," Lane muttered, and scooped a piece of cherry pie on his fork. "The fire fused them in place. You couldn't budge one with a blowtorch."

"So, the official conclusion is in," Wyatt muttered. "Arson that resulted in two innocent deaths. The bottom line is, whoever did it is guilty of murder."

"Thank God," Glory said.

Both men turned at the sound of her voice. "At least now they *have* to believe me."

Lane grinned again. "Yes, ma'am, they do at that. Not that I didn't believe you myself...but hard proof is always good to have."

"So, where do I go from here?" she asked.

"Nowhere, unless I'm with you," Wyatt said. "Because if you're right about that, then you're right about why. Until they catch the man who's trying to hurt you, you will have twenty-four-hour protection."

Glory looked startled. *What do I do with two men the size of small horses in Granny's little cabin?*

Wyatt laughed aloud, startling Lane and making Glory flush. She'd forgotten his ability to read her thoughts.

"Well," she said, daring Wyatt to answer.

Lane wondered if he looked as lost as he felt. "I know when I've missed something, but the honest to God truth is, I never saw it go by. What's going on?"

Glory frowned, and pointed at Wyatt. "Ask him. He's Mr. Know-it-all."

Wyatt grinned even wider. "Maybe you could bed one down in your daddy's barn, and the other outside with the pup."

She raised an eyebrow, refusing to be baited by his words or his wit. "One of these days, you're going to eavesdrop on something you won't have an answer for," she said. Then she sat down beside Lane and began shuffling through the stack of pictures she'd left on the table.

The cryptic statement hit home as the smile slid off Wyatt's face. He knew she was right. Right in the middle of a new set of worries, Glory suddenly changed the subject.

"Lane, would you like to see my pictures?"

"Yes, ma'am, I would be honored."

Food and the future were forgotten as Glory led both men through her past, and as she talked, she absently caressed the pictures because it was all she had left to touch.

But while Glory was learning to heal, Carter Foster was festering into one big sore. His first choice for hit man was languishing in the state penitentiary. His second had moved to another state. He'd gone through the past seven years of his legal practice, trying without success to find a name to go with the game. It wasn't until he started on the files of his first year that he remembered Bo Marker.

It had been Carter's first big win in court. He'd successfully defended a man he knew was guilty as sin. Remembering the photographs he'd seen of Marker's victim, he was certain that this might be his man. Surely a man who was capable of killing a man with his fists was equal to pulling a trigger. He read through the file, making notes of the address and phone number he'd had at the time. He was certain that he'd have to do a little detective work on the side to find Marker, but it would all be worth it in the end.

He wrote quickly, returning the file as soon as he was through. Time was of the essence. The longer Glory Dixon remained alive, the shorter his own days of freedom. He'd lived in hell with Betty Jo long enough, and her death had, after all, been an accident. He deserved a break. Then he winced and ran his finger along his neck, loosening his collar and his tie. Just not the kind Betty Jo had gotten.

Chapter 6

Wyatt sat across the table from Glory, nursing a cup of coffee and watching the play of emotions upon her face as she went through the photographs she'd been given yesterday. At least they gave her pleasure, which was more than he could do. He'd lain in bed last night right across the hall from her door, listening for nearly an hour to her muffled sobs. It had been all he could do not to cross the hall and yank her out of that bed and into his arms. No one should have to cry like that alone.

Glory knew that Wyatt was watching her. Those dark eyes of his did things to her fantasies they had no business doing. They made her think things she shouldn't, and want things she couldn't have. She should be thinking of him as nothing but a kind stranger, yet with each passing hour, he became more of a permanent fixture in her thoughts.

She sighed.

Thinking like that could get her hurt…very, very badly, and losing her family had been hurt enough. This man had already admitted to having doubts about himself. She didn't need to be falling for a man who would be here today and gone tomorrow. Glory was a forever kind of woman. She needed a forever kind of man.

The pictures slipped from her fingers and into her lap as she closed her eyes and leaned back against the couch, letting herself imagine what forever with Wyatt Hatfield might be like.

As her eyes closed and her head tilted backward, Wyatt froze. The delicate arch of her bare neck and the flutter of those gold-tinged eyelashes upon her cheeks were a taunting temptation to a man with deep need. He set his cup aside then got up, intent on walking out of the room before he got himself in trouble, wishing he'd gone to run the errands instead of Lane. But when he reached the doorway, he made a mistake. He looked back and got caught in a silver-blue spell.

There was a question in her eyes and a stillness in her body, as if she were waiting for something to happen. Wyatt ached for her...and for himself, well aware of just what it might be if he didn't readjust his thinking.

Suddenly, some of the pictures slid out of her lap onto the floor. He reacted before he remembered his intention to keep his distance, and was on his knees at her side, scooping them up and placing them on the table, before she could move.

Glory focused her attention on his hands, seeing strength in the broad palms, tenderness in the long, supple fingers and determination in the man himself as he persisted until every picture that she'd dropped was picked up. Forgetting the fact that he could tap into her thoughts at any given moment, she pictured those hands moving upon her body instead, and softly sighed.

"Here you go," he said, and started to drop the last of the pictures in her lap when an image drifted through his mind. *Skin...smooth to the touch, dampened by a faint sheen of perspiration. A pulse racing beneath it...a heartbeat gone wild beneath his fingertips.* He rocked back on his feet and looked up at her.

Ah, God, Wyatt thought.

Glory saw the tension in his body, heard his swift intake of breath and remembered too late that, once again, she'd let him inside her mind. She held her breath, afraid to speak. How would he react, and what should she do? Ignore it…and him?

And then he lifted the pictures out of her lap and dropped them onto the cushion beside her, taking the decision out of her hands.

Mouths met. The introduction was short. It went from tentative to demanding in three short ticks of a clock.

Her lips were as soft as he'd imagined, yielding to a silent question he did not have the nerve to ask, then begging for more of the same. The sweetness of her compliance and the shock of their connection were more than he'd bargained for. Her breath was swift upon his cheek, her passion unexpected, and when he lifted his head from the kiss, as yet unfulfilled.

Oh, Wyatt!

"My sentiments exactly," he whispered, and ran his thumb across her lips where his mouth had just been. "Lord help us, Glory, but where do we go from here?"

Outside, the pup began to bark. Wyatt was on his feet in an instant, and out the door. The moment had passed.

Glory groaned, then buried her face in her hands. She'd been saved from having to respond. It was a small, but much needed, respite, because she had no answer for Wyatt. Not now, and maybe, not ever.

Lane followed Wyatt back into the house, unaware of what he'd interrupted, and blurted out what had been on his mind all night.

"Glory, can you turn that psychic business of yours on at will?"

She seemed startled by the question, yet understanding dawned as to where he was leading.

"I've never tried. In fact, it's been quite the opposite. I've tried more than once to stop what I see, but I've never tried to start it."

"Don't you think now might be a good time to practice?" he asked.

Wyatt wanted to argue. Instinct told him this was too much too soon, but it was Glory's life that was on the line. It was her family who'd died. The least he could do was let her make the decision. Yet when she nodded, he frowned.

"Are you sure?" Wyatt asked.

She looked at him with a clear gaze. "About some things, no. About this, yes."

He didn't have to be a genius to read between the lines of her answer. She wasn't sure about what had just happened between them, but she was ready to try anything in order to find the person responsible for her father's and brother's deaths. All in all, he had to admit that her answer was more than fair.

"Then let's go," Lane said.

"Where to?" she asked.

"To where it all started."

Glory blanched, and in a panic, looked to Wyatt for support.

"I'm with you all the way," he said softly. "Want to walk, or ride?"

"Ride, I think. The sooner we get there, the sooner it's over."

The drive was short, but the silence between the trio was long. When Glory got out of the car, she had to make herself look at the spot where her house had been standing. The blackened timbers and the rock foundation more resembled some prehistoric skeleton than the remnants of a home. It hurt to look at it and remember what had happened. But, she reminded herself, that was why she'd come.

Wyatt's hand cupped her shoulder. "How do you want to do this?" he asked.

"I don't know. Just let me walk around a little, maybe something will happen. I told you, I've never tried this before."

Lane had already found himself a seat in the shade. He

watched Wyatt and Glory from a distance, thinking to himself that there seemed to be a lot more between them than the simple repayment of a debt. Wyatt hovered like a watchdog, and Glory kept looking to him for more than support.

Lane's eyes narrowed thoughtfully as Wyatt caressed the crown of her head, his fingers lingering longer than necessary in the long, silvery length. When he cupped her face with the palm of his hand, an observer might have supposed it were nothing more than a comforting touch. But Lane knew better. He saw the way Glory leaned into Wyatt's hand, and even from here, he could see a glow on her face that had nothing to do with the heat of the sun. If he wasn't mistaken, there was a slow fire burning beneath those two. Only time would tell whether it caught...or whether it burned out of its own accord.

Wyatt retreated, giving Glory space and time, but watched with a nervous eye as she paused on what was left of the back porch steps.

As she stepped over the block foundation and then down onto the ground below, she stumbled. Instinctively, Wyatt started toward her, but then she caught herself, and so he paused and waited, watching as she started to move through the ash and the rubble.

Wyatt suddenly noticed that something seemed different about the site. It took a few moments for the reality to sink in. "That yellow crime scene tape is gone!"

Lane nodded. "They took it down after the fire marshal left. He said that it was impossible to preserve much of anything out in the open like this, and so he collected all of the evidence that he could. I think they took two or three of the small heating stoves in as evidence and took pictures of the rest."

"This is a hell of a deal, isn't it?" Wyatt muttered, taking consolation from Lane's comforting thump on his back.

Time passed slowly for the men, but Glory was reliving an entire lifetime as she walked through the rubble, and it was all too short a time considering what was now left.

She stood, looking out across the broken foundation, trying to picture the man who'd invaded their home, and instead saw herself as a child, running to meet her father as he came in from milking. Seeing, through her mind, the way the solemnity of his expression always broke when he smiled. Almost feeling his hands as they circled her waist, lifting her high over his head and then spinning her around. Hearing his deep, booming laughter when he set her on his shoulders and she used his ears for an anchor by which to hold.

Oh, God, Glory thought, and swayed on her feet, overwhelmed by the emotion.

Angrily, she turned away, unwilling to savor the memory because of her loss. Black soot and ash coated the legs of her jeans and the tops of her boots as she trudged through what had once been rooms. Without walls to hold the love that had abounded within, the area looked pitifully small.

Again she stumbled, and something crunched beneath her boot. She bent over, sifting through the rubble to see what it had been. When she lifted it out, she choked back a sob. "Oh, no! I broke one of J.C.'s arrowheads."

She looked back down, and then gasped. There were dozens of them everywhere, shattered into remnants of their former beauty. What the explosion and fire hadn't ruined, the men who'd conducted the investigation had.

Tears flooded her eyes, then poured down her face, streaking the faint coat of ash on her skin as rage sifted through the pain.

Damn this all to hell!

She closed her fingers around the broken bits, squeezing until they cut into the palm of her hand. Anger boiled, then spilled, rocking her with its power. On the verge of a scream, she drew back her arm and threw. The broken pieces skipped through the air like rocks on water, and then disappeared in the grass a good distance away.

She was shaking when she turned, swiping angrily at the tears on her face. Crying would get her nowhere. She'd come to try and help find out who killed her family, not feel sorry for herself.

Wyatt could tell something monumental had just occurred. Her pain was as vivid to him as if it was his own. And when she turned toward them with tears running rampant down her face, he jumped to his feet.

"Damn it, that's enough," Wyatt said, and started to go after her.

Lane grabbed him by the arm. "Don't do it, brother. She'll stop when she's ready. Don't underestimate your woman. She survived real good on her own before you came. She's tough enough to do it when you're gone."

The look Wyatt gave him would have stopped a truck. It was somewhere between anger that Lane had dared to limit the time that was between them, and fear that he might be right.

Wyatt turned, unaware that the look he was giving Glory was full of regret. "She's not *my* woman, she's... Oh hell."

He bolted across the yard just as she staggered toward them. He caught her before her legs gave way.

"Glory...sweetheart...are you all right?"

His voice was anxious, his hands gentle as he steadied her on her feet. When she looked up, her face was grim and tinged with defeat, and for the first time since he'd come, he heard surrender in the tone of her voice.

"Damn, damn, damn. Nothing worked. Absolutely nothing. I couldn't think of *him* for remembering Daddy and J.C. I'm sorry. I just couldn't do it."

"To hell with this," he muttered. "I'm taking you home."

Her face was flushed and beaded with sweat, but her mouth twisted angrily as she looked over his shoulder. The dust of death was on her clothes, up her nostrils, coating her skin. At that moment, she hated. She hated her father and brother for leaving her, and herself for having survived. Pain came out cloaked in fury as she pointed to where she'd been.

"I am home, remember?" and she tried to push him away.

Wyatt ignored her anger, understanding it for what it was, and braced her with his hand. She trembled against him like a leaf in a storm.

Lane decided it was a good time to interrupt.

"Look, Glory, don't let it worry you. It was just an idea. I think I'm going to run into town and check on a few things. You just take it easy. We'll find him the good old-fashioned way." And then Lane gave Wyatt a long, considering stare. "I trust you'll take good care of her?"

Wyatt glared at the knowing look in Lane's eyes, then ignored him. When he thought about it, his brother-in-law could be a big fat nuisance.

"You're coming with me, Glory. You need a cool bath, a change of clothes and something to eat."

His proprietary manner was too new…and at this time, too much to absorb. She pushed his hand away. "Let me be, Wyatt. Don't you understand? I just want to be left alone."

Frustration was at the source of her anger, but the fact that he'd been indirectly caught in its path, hurt. He stepped back, holding up his hands as if he'd just been arrested, and gave her the space that she obviously needed.

"You don't want help? Fine. You don't want to talk to me? That's fine, too. But you don't get to be alone. You can have distance, but you don't get alone. Not until the son of a bitch is found who set fire to your world. So, do you want to maintain your solitary state in the front seat of my car while I drive, or shall I follow at a discreet distance while you walk?"

Lane hid a grin and headed for his car, thinking he'd be better off gone when the fireworks started. He'd heard that kind of mule-headed attitude before, only it had come out of Toni's mouth, not Wyatt's. Obviously that streak ran deep in the Hatfield clan. He wondered if Glory Dixon was up to the fight.

They were still staring, eye to eye, toe to toe, when the sound of Lane's car could no longer be heard.

Wyatt's eyes glittered darkly. He'd never wanted to swing

a woman over his shoulder as badly as he did at this moment. For two cents, he'd...

I'm sorry.

"Well, hell," he grumbled, resisting the urge to kiss the droop of her lower lip. "If that's not just like a woman, expecting me to read her sweet mind for an apology."

Glory sighed, and then tried to smile. And when she held out her hand, he caught it, holding tighter than necessary as he pulled her up close.

"Apology accepted," he whispered. "I'm sorry, too."

"For what?" Glory asked. "You didn't do anything wrong."

Wyatt grinned wryly. "I'd like to get that in writing," he said. "I know people who'd beg to differ."

But despair kept pulling her deeper and deeper back into herself. "Dear God, Wyatt, there's nothing left to do but wait for him to try again."

He grabbed her by the arms and shook her, hating her for the fatalistic attitude. "Don't! Don't you even suggest that to me! You can't turn my world upside down, get into my mind and then give up on yourself without a damn fight! Do you hear me?"

After that, for a long, silent moment, neither spoke. And then Glory slowly lifted her finger and traced the path of the scar down the side of his face.

"Such a warrior."

Wyatt's confusion was obvious. "A what?"

Glory smiled, not much, but enough to let him know that he was off the hook. "You make me think of a warrior. For a while there, I forgot that you'd been a soldier. I'm sorry. I won't take you lightly, ever again."

"Well, then," he muttered, at a loss for anything else to say.

Glory nodded, glad she was forgiven, and then turned back to stare at the rubble. Long minutes passed during which the expression on her face never changed, but when she abruptly straightened and put her hands on her hips, there was a glint

in her eyes that hadn't been there before. Wyatt didn't know
whether to be glad, or get worried.

"Wyatt."

"What?"

"I am going to rebuild."

His heart surged, and then he paled. *Dear God, if only
could be that certain about my life.*

"And, since you're bound and determined to dog my steps
you're about to get as dirty as I am." She headed for the barn
with Wyatt right behind her.

"What are you going to do?" he asked, as she began to
push back the wide double doors hanging on tracks.

"I am going to clean house," she said. "Help me push this
last door back. It always sticks."

Without giving himself time to argue, he did as he was
told, and then watched her climb behind the steering wheel
of an old one-ton truck that had been parked behind the doors

"Better move," she shouted, as the starter ground and the
engine kicked to life. "The brakes aren't so good. I'll have
to coast to a stop."

"The hell you say," he muttered, and then quickly moved
aside, uncertain what to think of her newfound determination.

It was long past noon when Wyatt tossed the last board on
the truck bed that it could possibly hold. Without thinking,
he swiped at the sweat running down his face and then remembered the grime on his gloves and groaned. He yanked
them off, but it was too late.

Glory turned to see what had happened, then started to
smile. He frowned as she grinned.

"Well?" he grumbled, and she laughed aloud.

"What's so funny?" he said, knowing full well he'd probably smeared ashes all over his face.

Glory closed her eyes and grimaced, pretending to be lost
in deep thought, and then started to speak in a high singsong
voice.

"I see a man. I see dirt. I see a man with a dirty face. I *ee...*"

Her playful attitude pleased and surprised him, despite the act that he was the butt of her joke. He grinned, then without varning, scooped her off her feet, threw her over his shoulder nd stalked toward the well house near the barn.

Glory was laughing too hard to continue her taunt. The vorld hung at a crazy angle as her head dangled halfway lown his back. The ground kept going in and out of focus as he bobbed with his every step. And then her view shifted, ind a corner of her mouth tilted. She knew just how to make iim put her down.

Hey, Hatfield...nice buns!

"Lord have mercy, Glory, give a man a break," Wyatt nuttered, suddenly thankful that his face was too dirty to re-veal his blush. And while she was busy enjoying the point she had scored, he turned on the faucet, picked up the con-nected garden hose and aimed it directly at her face.

She choked on the water and a laugh, and then fought him for the nozzle. In the middle of the game, her participation suddenly ceased. Wyatt dropped the hose, letting it run into a puddle at their feet as he watched her withdrawal.

"What is it, honey?" he asked.

She started to speak and then covered her face, suddenly ashamed of what she'd been doing.

He grasped her hands and pulled them away. "Talk to me, Glory."

"I shouldn't have been... It isn't right that I..."

Understanding dawned. "You feel guilty for being happy, don't you?"

She nodded, and tried not to cry.

"Oh, honey, I'm sorry," Wyatt said, and wrapped his arms around her. "It's natural, you know. But you can't regret be-ing alive, and I don't believe that your father would have wanted you to die with him...would he?"

She shook her head.

"So, okay then." He picked up the hose, then handed it to

her. "Come on, let's wash ourselves off before we go unload
And, after I put some of that brake fluid you found in th
truck, I'm driving. You, however, will have to navigate ou
way to the city dump. It wasn't on your town's tourist map."

She held the hose, watching intently as he washed hi
hands, then lowered his head, letting the water from the hos
run over the back of his hair and down his neck. He straight
ened quickly, shaking his head and wiping water from hi
eyes with both hands.

"Now you," he offered, and held the hose while sh
washed her hands, then cupped several handfuls of water an
sluiced them on her face. "Feel better?" he asked, as h
handed her his handkerchief.

"Wyatt?"

"What, darlin'?"

"Thank you," she said, and gave the used handkerchie
back to him.

His gaze raked the contours of her body, now obviously
revealed by the wet clothes clinging to her shape, and re
minded himself of the task at hand.

"You're more than welcome."

The sign said Dump—$2.00 Per Load. But there was no
one around to collect the fee, and so they drove right in and
then backed up as near to the edge of the open pit as Wyat
dared. Taking into account the lack of decent brakes on the
truck, he had no intention of going too close and then being
unable to stop.

Glory got out of the truck with every intention of helping
unload when Wyatt stopped her.

"Let me, okay?"

She relented. Her arms already ached from the strenuous
job of loading the debris, and her legs were shaking with
weariness.

"Okay, and thanks."

He smiled. "You're welcome. Now go find yourself some
shade. This shouldn't take long."

Glory did as she was told, moving away from the side of the truck as Wyatt shed his shirt. She watched from a distance as he climbed up on top of the truck bed and began tossing the rubble, board by board, down into the pit, admiring the fluidity of his body and the grace with which he moved. After a while, she began to stroll around the area, stepping over bits of loose trash that had blown about, and kicking at pieces of metal and stone lying haphazardly about the site.

Down in the pit, a huge, black crow began cawing loudly as it suddenly took flight, and two others followed. Glory turned, watching as they moved through the air on obsidian wings. She looked back to where Wyatt was working and saw that he had paused and was scanning the area with a careful eye. It gave her courage to know that he was ever on the lookout for her welfare.

He turned to her and waved. She started to wave back when his image began to waver like a fading mirage. Believing it to be caused by heat rising from the pit, Glory started to shade her eyes, and then felt the ground go out from under her. It was reflex that sent her to her knees to keep from falling face-first, down in the dirt. And when her heart began to race, and the mirage began to reshape itself, Glory grabbed on to the grass beneath her hands and held on, afraid to let go of the ride through her mind.

Bright sunlight was suddenly gone, as was her father's flat-bed truck and Wyatt's image. Another had come to take its place. One stronger…darker…deadlier. She groaned, unaware that she was plunging her fingers deep into the dirt and grass in an effort to hold on.

Panic painted the man's movements, hastening his actions and coloring the short, uneven gasps of his breath. His rapid footsteps were muffled by the loose dirt and grass as he moved from the front of a car to the back.

A faint glow of a quarter moon glinted on the trunk lid of the car as it popped open. He bent down, then straightened, carrying something in his arms. Something heavy…something long…something white.

*He staggered to the pit and then dropped it over the edge,
watching as it fell, end over end, rolling, tumbling. Panic was
beginning to subside. His relief was palpable.*

Glory shuddered, trying to pull back from the scene in her
mind, yet caught in a web not of her making. She watched,
as if through his eyes, unable to see his face. She rode with
his thought, moved with his stride, paused with his hesitation.
But when he stood on the edge of the pit and looked down,
Glory's own horror pulled her out of the fugue. In spite of
the realization that it was all in her mind, she began to scream.

The wind tunneled through Wyatt's thick, dark hair, cooling the sweat upon his body and blowing away the ever-
present stench of burned wood. Nearly through with the job,
he paused and looked up, making certain that they were still
alone, and ever careful to keep Glory within constant view.

Watching the wind play havoc with her hair made him
smile. She'd already remarked while loading the truck that
she should have done more than just tie it at the back of her
neck, that it should have been braided to keep from whipping
in her face and eyes.

And then he watched in horror as she suddenly dropped to
her knees. Her name was on his lips as he jumped from the
truck bed. And then he was running as fast as he could run,
across the ground, past the edge of the pit, toward the sound
of her screams. He yanked her out of the dirt and into his
arms.

"Glory! Sweetheart! I'm here! I'm here. Let it go!"

She staggered, then swayed and, without thought, wrapped
her arms around Wyatt's waist and held on, because he was
her only stability in a world gone wrong.

"Dead. She's dead," Glory moaned. "All in white. And it
came undone."

The plaintive wail of her voice sent shivers up his spine.
She? Dead? What in God's name had Glory *seen* now?

He cupped her face with both of his hands, tilting it until
she had nowhere to look but at him.

"Look at me!" he shouted. "Damn it, Glory, look at *me!*"

Her gaze shifted, and he could actually see cognizance returning. Breath slid from his lungs in a deep, heavy sigh as he wrapped his arms around her shoulders and rocked her within his embrace.

"Tell me, honey. Tell me what you saw."

And as quickly as her terror had come, it passed. There was intensity in her voice, in her manners, in the way she clutched at his bare arms.

"I saw a man take something white from a trunk of a car. I saw him drop it in the pit. It rolled and tumbled and…" She shuddered, then swallowed, trying to find ways to put into words what she saw in her mind. "He watched it fall. I felt him smile. The thing that he'd thrown came open. Like a candy that had come unwrapped. I could see her face. Her eyes were open wide, as if she'd been surprised. Oh, Wyatt, he threw a woman's body into the dump!"

"Good Lord! Are you sure?"

She nodded.

He stared down into the pit, noting the few bags of garbage that had been dumped earlier in the day, and then looking more intently at the huge layers of earth that had already been pushed over weeks of refuse.

"They probably cover this site every night. There's no way of telling how long ago this happened, is there?"

Her face contorted as she tried to remember everything that she'd seen and then she slumped in dejection. "No, it was so dark, I couldn't tell…" She gasped, and then cried. "A quarter moon! There was a quarter moon."

Wyatt tensed, then turned and stared at her face. "That was less than a week ago. I know, because I sat on a porch in Tennessee, watching clouds blowing across a quarter moon and listening for the sound of your voice."

Glory shuddered. "What do we do?"

"We go tell Chief Conway."

She groaned. "He's going to laugh in our faces," she warned.

"Sticks and stones, honey. Sticks and stones. Now let's get the rest of that stuff on the truck unloaded and get back to the cabin. I think we need to look our best when we ask the chief to dig up a dump."

Chapter 7

Lane was waiting for Wyatt and Glory when they pulled up to the curb and parked in front of the police department.

"I got your message," he said. "What's up?"

"After you left, Glory wanted to haul some stuff to the dump. While we were there, she had a...uh, she saw..."

Glory sighed. Even Wyatt, who claimed to believe, had trouble putting into words what she so took for granted.

"Granny always called them *visions,*" she said.

Lane's attention piqued. "Look, Glory, you've already made a believer out of me, and that's no easy task. So what did you *see?*"

"A woman's body being tossed in the dump."

"Oh, hell," Lane muttered, thinking of the ramifications of convincing the law to act on a psychic's word. "This won't be easy."

After they went inside, he knew he'd been right. The police chief erupted as Glory started to explain, while the deputy slipped out of the room, hovering just out of sight on the other side of the door.

"You saw what?" Conway shouted, rising from his chair and circling his desk to where Glory was standing. "And I suppose you saw this incident *in your mind,* as well?"

Wyatt glared, inserting himself slightly between them. "There's no need to shout," he said.

A vein bulged near Conway's left eye as his face grew redder by the minute. "Let me get this right. You had this *vision,* during which time you saw a man throw a woman's body into the dump. Oh! And she was dressed all in white, right?"

Glory's stomach tightened. She wanted to turn and walk out and forget she'd ever seen what she'd seen. "Yes, I told you I saw her—"

Conway interrupted. "Can you explain why the man who works the bulldozer at the dump didn't see her...or why twelve men who work three different trash trucks on two different routes didn't see her while they were dumping loads?"

"No," Glory muttered.

Conway smirked. "I didn't think so." He glared at Wyatt, as if blaming him for this latest in a series of problems he felt unequipped to deal with. "Look, Hatfield. I deal in facts, and these...uh, impulses she claims to have are not facts. They're dreams. They're imagination. They're..."

The deputy slipped back in the room, unable to resist a comment. "But Chief, she was right about them gas stoves."

"Shut up," he growled, and the deputy wisely retreated again, this time to the back room.

The chief's attitude did not surprise Lane. Law enforcement dealt with rules and givens. There were no rules for what Glory Dixon could do.

"I don't suppose you've had any missing person reports filed recently," Lane asked.

Conway made no attempt to hide his surprise. He apparently couldn't believe that a U.S. marshal would actually take any of this hogwash as fact.

"No, I don't suppose I have," he muttered.

"You're also real certain that none have come in over the wire from surrounding areas."

Conway flushed. He was pretty sure, but not positive. Obviously, however, he wasn't about to say it.

"Look, you two. You think because you're from the big city that the law in a little hill town like Larner's Mill can't cut the mustard, don't you? Well, you're wrong, and I don't like anyone buttin' into *my* business." His glare was directed as much at Lane as it was at Glory.

Before Wyatt or Lane could answer, Glory interrupted.

"I said what I came to say. What you do with the information is strictly up to you. However...if I'm right...and you're wrong, you've just let a man get away with murder. And that's your business, not mine, isn't it?" She walked out, leaving Wyatt and Lane to do as they chose.

They chose to follow her, and when they were gone, Anders Conway had no one to argue with but himself. It was a brief discussion that ended on a question. Just because Glory Dixon had been right about the fire that killed her folks didn't mean that she was always going to be right about that stuff floating around in her head...did it? He ran a hand through his thinning hair in frustration as he shouted at his deputy.

The deputy came running. "Yes, sir, what do you need?"

"I want to see everything we've got on missing persons in this county, as well as recent faxes along the same line." And when the deputy grinned, Conway glared. "Just because I asked to see the files doesn't mean I believe her," he grumbled. "I'm just doing my job. That's all."

Outside, Wyatt caught Glory by the arm as she walked toward the car.

"What?" she asked, still angry with the sheriff and the world in general.

"You did good," he said quietly.

Surprise colored her expression as Lane agreed.

"Wyatt's right. You said what had to be said. If the chief fails to follow up, then he's the one who's going to look like a fool. Now, if you two think you can make it on your own for a day or two, I'm going home to check on Toni and Joy, then swing by the office. I can access more information there than we're ever going to get out of Conway. Maybe something will turn up on the computer that fits what Glory saw.''

"I'm really sorry all of this mess is taking you away from your family," Glory said.

Lane smiled. "My job always takes me away from my family, honey. We're used to it." And then his expression changed as he turned to Wyatt. "I've got some stuff I need to leave with you before I go. Why don't you pop the trunk of the car? I'll toss it in there."

"I'll do it," Glory said, and as she scooted across the seat, missed seeing the look on Wyatt's face as Lane set a handgun and several boxes of ammunition inside, then handed him his portable phone.

"Just so we can keep in touch," Lane said.

"And the other?" Wyatt asked.

"Just in case."

"Damn, I hate this," Wyatt said. "I thought I put all of this behind me when I left the military."

"Just take care of yourself," Lane said, and then gave Wyatt a quick, brotherly hug. "I'll call you as soon as I know something."

Wyatt watched him drive away, then looked back at Glory, who sat patiently inside the car, waiting for him to get in. Her profile was solemn as she stared out a window, obviously lost in thought. Wyatt glanced at the trunk lid, picturing what Lane had put inside, and then looked up at Glory, struck by her repose and innocence.

Oh, Lord, I don't know what I'm afraid of most. Trying to keep you safe, or taking you to bed.

She turned. Their eyes met, and for a second, Wyatt was afraid that she'd read his mind. But when she did nothing but smile, he got in without hesitation, satisfied that his thoughts were still his own.

"Where do we go from here?" Glory asked.

He'd asked her that same question this morning right after the kiss, and like her, he had no answer.

"It's all up to you," he finally said.

"Wyatt?"

"What, honey?"

"Have you ever had so many problems that you just wanted to run away from everything?"

"Unlike you, sweetheart, I've been running all my life. We'll find a way to work this out. Just don't quit on yourself, and better yet, don't quit on me. I would hate to wake up one morning and find you gone."

An odd light glittered in her eyes, and then she turned away. "When it comes time to leave, I won't be the one with a suitcase in hand, and we both know it."

There was no way to argue with what she said and come out on the good side of the truth. Angrily, he started the car. Having done what they came to do, they headed back to Granny Dixon's cabin.

As they drove, Wyatt fought demons of his own that kept tearing at his concentration. Okay, he told himself, he didn't have to love her, and she didn't have to love him. All he had to do was keep her safe. He thought of the gun in the trunk and the look on Lane's face when he left. His stomach turned, imagining Glory in pain or danger, and he wanted to slam on the brakes and take her in his arms. He resisted the urge and kept driving. Yet the farther he drove, the more certain he became that it was too late. He didn't *have* to love her...but he did.

Thunder rumbled beyond the valley, and a streak of lightning crossed the sky. The rocking chair in which Glory was sitting gave an occasional comforting squeak as she kept up the motion by pushing herself off with the toe of her shoe. She looked up as Wyatt came in the door and dropped the magazine she'd been reading into her lap.

"Did you find the puppy?"

He shook his head. "Maybe he's afraid of the storm. He's

probably under some bush or even gone back to the barn to a place that's familiar to him.''

''Maybe.''

But Glory couldn't shake the feeling that something was wrong. The puppy was all she had left of her life before the fire, and she couldn't bear to think of losing him, too. J.C. had adored him, and had sworn he would make a good hunting dog, but with her brother gone, the training sessions were over. If the pup came home at all, the only thing he would be hunting was biscuits. But her attention shifted from the missing pup to Wyatt as she noticed his behavior.

Rain began to pepper the glass behind the curtains, and although it wasn't really cold, she shivered, watching as Wyatt kept pacing from window to window, then to the other side of the house, ever on the lookout for something to come out of the dark. Something...or someone...that didn't belong. His every movement was that of a man on edge.

The more she watched him, the more fascinated she became. She thought back to the night of the blizzard, and the first time she'd seen him, stretched out on a gurney and covered in blood. And then again, the day he'd been released from the hospital. Who would have guessed that one day, he'd be the single person who stood between her and death?

Looking back now, it hurt to remember how good and how simple life had been. Then she'd had a home and a family and a world that made sense. Now she had nothing but her life. And how Wyatt had come to her from across the miles was still a mystery; why he stayed, an even bigger puzzle. As she rocked, he unexpectedly turned and got caught in her stare.

''Glory...what is it?''

''Why don't you doubt me? Everyone else does, except maybe Lane.''

His answer was instantaneous, as if he'd thought about it himself, time and time again, and knew all of the words by heart.

''I don't know. All I know is, from the first there's been a connection between us. I don't understand it, but I know that it's there." He looked away, unwilling to say too much.

"Everyone thinks I'm crazy, so why are you different? Why do you stay with a crazy woman, Wyatt Hatfield? Why aren't you running as fast as you can from this mess?"

Now he hesitated. Telling the truth about his growing feelings for her could ruin everything, and yet lying to her was not an option. He had to find an answer somewhere in between. When he looked up, his eyes were full of secrets.

"Maybe I'm just waiting to hear you call my name."

The rocking chair came to an abrupt halt, ending in the middle of a squeak. *Oh, Wyatt. I'm afraid to. I'm afraid to love. I'm afraid that you won't understand me, and I can't change.*

Again, as he had in the past, he tapped into her thoughts and answered without realizing she hadn't spoken them aloud.

"I wouldn't change a thing about you, even if I could," he said. "I'm the one who's all messed up. I don't have it in me to make a good woman happy, because I've already tried and failed."

"No one is perfect, Wyatt. If you wanted to try, I believe that you could make anyone happy." And then her voice faltered, and she had to clear her throat before she could continue. "Even me," she whispered.

He froze. There was no mistaking the invitation, and ignoring it was beyond him. Because she sat waiting, he went to her, then held out his hands.

Glory took them without hesitation. The magazine in her lap fell to the floor when he pulled her to her feet, and when he began threading his fingers through her hair, her focus shifted, as it did when a vision was upon her. As he cupped the back of her head, tracing his thumbs across the arch of her cheekbones, she lost her center of gravity. Had it not been for Wyatt's arms, she would have fallen.

Even though she wanted this and much more from him, yielding to his greater strength was frightening. It was as if she'd suddenly lost her sense of self and was being consumed by his power. His voice rumbled too close to her ear, and instinctively, she shivered. Wyatt read her actions as something other than desire, and began feathering small kisses across her forehead, pleading his case as he drew her closer and closer against him.

"Don't be afraid of me…or of anyone else. Being afraid of love is like hiding from life. Sometimes you have to take a chance to be happy, and taking chances is what life is all about."

When his hands moved from the back of her head to the back of her neck, she sighed, giving way to a greater need within herself.

"Oh, Wyatt, I'm not afraid *of* you, only of *losing* you."

Lord help both of us.

He lifted her off of her feet. With her lips on his mouth and her body in perfect alignment with his, he began to turn, holding her fast within his arms as her feet dangled inches above the floor. Seductively, deliberately, with nothing but passion for music, they slow danced to a tune only they could hear.

Faintly aware of the ceiling spinning above and the lights blinking in and out of focus as they moved about the floor, she wanted to laugh, and she wanted to cry. She'd never known such joy…and such fear. She was hovering on the brink of discovery in Wyatt Hatfield's arms.

Wyatt ached, wanting more, so much more than the brief, stolen kisses that he was taking. *Time, I need to take my time.* But it was all he could do to heed his own words.

Unable to resist the temptation, he traced the curve of her cheek with his mouth and groaned when he felt her shudder. When he began nuzzling the spot below her ear with his nose, then his lips, savoring the satin texture of her skin, inhaling the essence of the woman that was Glory Dixon, she sighed, whispering something he couldn't understand. Her voice was soft against his cheek, and she yielded to him like a woman, giving back more than she got.

Clutching her fingers in his short, dark hair, she hid her

face beneath the curve of his chin, ashamed of what she was about to ask, but afraid this chance would never come again.

"Oh, Wyatt, I've learned the hard way that life is too uncertain. This time tomorrow you could be gone, or I could be dead. Please make love to me. I don't want to die without knowing what that's like."

He froze in the middle of a breath, with his mouth near her lips and his hands just below the curve of her hips. Except for the blood thundering through his veins and a pulse hammering against his ear, all movement ceased.

"What did you just say?"

Glory lifted her head. She wouldn't be ashamed of what she was. Truth was better said face-to-face.

"I asked you to make love to me," she whispered.

"Not that. The part about dying."

"I've never been with a man, Wyatt. I don't know what it feels like to have a man's hands on my body, or a man inside of me."

"Oh...my...God."

There was little else he could think to say. Nearly blind with need, it was all he could do to turn her loose, yet it had to be done. He'd started something in the wrong frame of mind, and had to stop it before it was too late.

"Well, damn," he said quietly, and walked out of the room.

She could hear the front door slam from where she stood. The fire that he'd started was scalding her, from the inside out. She didn't know whether to cry or scream, to call out his name, or go after him. She was still shaking from the hunger he'd started when she heard the door reopen abruptly, and then slam shut, muting the sound of the wind accompanying the rain still pounding upon the roof. The click of a lock was loud in the sudden silence of the house. She held her breath, afraid to hope, afraid to care...and then the lights went out.

"Wyatt? Is that you?"

"Hell, yes, it's me," he growled. "Who else were you

expecting? If anyone else touched you but me right now, I'd kill them with my bare hands.''

Even in the dark, she started to smile. She wasn't going to question what had changed his mind, she would just be thankful that he had.

He found her right where he'd left her, and when his hands moved across her body in the darkness of the room, he felt her inhale, then sigh. He groaned with want as her breasts pushed against the palms of his hands.

"I didn't think you were coming back."

"I just went to my car...for these."

He caught her hands and flattened them against his rain-splattered shirt, guiding them to a shirt pocket to the right of his heartbeat.

Uncertain what was about to happen, she still followed his lead, feeling the pocket, then the flap, then at his instigation, dipping her hand inside. Thunder rattled the windowpanes as a gust of wind slapped tree limbs against the edge of the house. She gasped, spinning toward the sound behind them.

"It's all right, darlin'. It's just the wind."

And then he caught her hand and laid something into her palm.

Glory frowned as her fingers curled around the objects, unable to identify the sharp, clean edges of the flat, foil packets.

"I don't understand," she said. "What is it?"

"Your protection, sweetheart. I have never made love to a woman in my entire life without it in one form or another. I'm not about to put you at risk."

Oh!

"You guessed it," he said, and then laughed softly.

The sound of his laughter curled her toes and made her weak at the knees. Heat swept across her body, and she realized she was blushing.

"Where were we?" he muttered, and slipped his hands beneath her hips, cupping her body to his, and lowering his mouth in the darkness, searching for the sweetness of a kiss that he knew would be waiting.

The packets dropped to the bed behind them as she wrapped her arms around his neck. And then she moved against his groin, testing the bulge behind his zipper, and whispered against his mouth.

"Right about here…I think."

Moments later, Wyatt lifted her off her feet and laid her on the bed. The quilt shifted beneath her as his body pressed her deeper and deeper into the mattress.

Wyatt gritted his teeth, reminding himself that making love to Glory would be a whole new ball game, and took a long, slow breath to clear his senses. When he felt her shudder, his heart raced in sudden fear.

"Dear God, don't be afraid of me," he said. "I'll stop this right now if that's what you want."

Her hands moved up his thighs, pausing at the sides of his hips. "It's not fear that makes me tremble, Wyatt Hatfield, it's you."

"Have mercy," he said softly.

"Only if you hurry," she answered.

He did.

Clothes went flying in the darkness, landing where they'd been tossed with little care for the decorum. Now there was nothing between them but skin and need. Wyatt moved back across her body, settling the weight of himself upon her, testing the size of himself against her fragility. She was so damned tiny it scared him half to death.

Without wasted motion, he took her in his arms and rolled, taking her with him until he was flat on his back and she was lying upon him, mouth to mouth, breast to chest.

And when his hands cupped her breasts, rolling the hard aching peaks between his fingers with delicate skill, she instinctively arched, her mind blanking on everything but his touch.

Oh?

He smiled in the darkness, moving his hands upon her body, mapping the tiny bones and a waist he could circle with both hands, testing the gentle flare of her hips, then letting his thumbs slide down...down.

Oh, Wyatt!

Glory gasped, then moaned as her head fell back and her hips followed the pressure of his fingers. When her body swayed, and the long flow of her hair brushed across his thighs, teasing at the juncture of his turgid manhood, Wyatt shuddered with longing. Not yet, he warned himself.

His hands slid over the quilt top, finding, then opening one of the packets he'd brought in from the car—doing what had to be done, before it was too late to think.

The room spun and the bed tilted. Glory rode with the motion, afraid it would stop, afraid to let go of the man beneath her. He'd built too many fires with the touch of his hands and the sweep of his mouth. Something was building, tightening, spiraling inside her so deep that it had no name. There was no understanding of what would come next, only the mind-bending need for it to be.

"Oh...Wyatt."

Her cry was soft, almost unheard, but Wyatt felt it just the same. He was aware of what was happening to her and wished he could be inside of her when it happened. But he couldn't...not the first time...not until she knew that this act came with something besides pain.

"Wyyaatt?"

There was panic in her voice, riding along with a racing heart as he continued to stoke the fires he'd created.

"That's it, Glory. Don't fight it. Don't fight me. Just let it happen."

And then it did, breaking over her in swamping waves of heat, shattering in one spot and then spilling into every other part of her body.

"Ah, Wyatt," she groaned, and would have collapsed, had he not caught her in mid-slump.

"Not yet, sweet lady. There's a thing I must do, and I ask your forgiveness now, before it's too late."

Glory's mind was still swimming in the midst of pure pleasure when he rolled with her once again. Vaguely aware of the bed beneath her bare back and the weight of the man above her, she was unprepared for the spear of manhood that gently shattered the dissipating pleasure. The pain was sharp, burning and, after such joy, unexpected. Unable to stifle a cry, her fingers dug into the sides of his arms as she instinctively arched against the thrust.

"Ah, Glory, I'm sorry, so sorry," he whispered, and gritted his teeth to maintain control.

A sob caught at the back of her throat. Afraid to breathe, she braced herself for the next wave of pain. It didn't come. Only an unexpected fullness she'd never known before. One slow breath after another, she waited for him to move, and only after she began to test the theory herself, did he react.

Bracing himself above her, he shifted slightly, and then smiled in the dark when he heard a soft moan that had nothing to do with pain.

"Sweetheart, are you all right?" he whispered.

Her hands snaked around his shoulders. "I don't know yet. I'll tell you when it's over."

His laughter rocked the walls. When he lowered his head, feeling for her lips in the darkness, the smile was still upon his face. And then he started to move, slowly, tentatively, giving her time to adjust to his presence. Deeper and faster, he took her with him, driving like the rain that blew against the outer walls, losing himself in this woman who held his heart in her hands.

The end came almost without warning. One moment Wyatt was in total control, and then Glory moved unexpectedly, wrapping her legs around his hips and pulling him too far in to stop. Heat washed over him like a wave, sweeping everything from his mind but the feeling they'd created together. And then it was over, and he wanted her more.

Long silent minutes passed while he cradled her in his arms, whispering things in the dark that he could never have said in the light, stroking her body with the flat of his hand, unable to believe that this tiny, tiny woman was capable of such passion and love.

Finally he asked her again. "Glory?"

She sighed, and then slid one leg across his knees. "Hmmm?"

"Now are you all right?"

He felt her smile against his chest, and dug his hands in the long tangle he'd made of her hair.

"Oh, Wyatt...I didn't know, I didn't know."

"Know what, honey?" he whispered, as he continued to cuddle her close.

"That love came in colors."

"That it did what?"

"It's true. When we...I mean when I..."

He grinned. "It's okay, I know the moment you're trying to identify."

"I saw red...and then white."

Touched by her admission, he teased her, trying to alleviate his own emotions. "What...no blue?"

"Red was what I saw just before...when you...when we..."

His voice vibrated with laughter. "Darlin', we're going to have to find a way to get you past this mental roadblock. Just say it. When you lost your sweet mind, right?"

"I suppose it *was* right about then."

This time, he couldn't suppress a chuckle. And then her arms tightened around his chest and when he reached out to stroke her face, he felt tears on her cheeks.

"Tears? Don't tell me I was that bad," he whispered.

"No, Wyatt. I didn't cry because it was bad. I cried because it was so good."

He hugged her, too moved to respond to her praise.

A few seconds passed, and in that time, he felt her restlessness, and knew that there was something else she wanted to say. Then he remembered she hadn't explained the other color.

"So I made you see red. But what about the white?"

Excitement was in her voice as she lifted herself on one elbow and traced the lines of his face with her fingertips.

"Oh, Wyatt…just as everything within me gave way…I saw you…or at least the essence of you. There was no way to tell where I ended and you began. And the light with which you came to me was so bright…so pure…so white!" Her voice faltered, then broke. "That was when I cried."

Oh, my God!

More than once, he tried to respond, but there were no words to express what he felt, only an overwhelming sense of inevitability, as if he'd been on the course all his life, and the outcome was out of his hands.

And so they slept, wrapped in each other's arms while the storm front moved on, and morning dawned to a damp, new day.

The sharp ringing of the telephone near his ear sent Carter Foster scrambling to shut off an alarm. By the time he realized that it was the phone, and not the alarm, he had knocked a stack of papers onto the floor and cracked the plastic housing around his clock.

"Damn it," he muttered, and then picked up the phone. "Foster residence."

"It's Marker."

The skin on the back of Carter's neck crawled as his belly suddenly twisted into a knot. Hiring Bo Marker yesterday had been a last resort, but he hadn't expected to hear from him quite so soon.

"Is it over?" Carter asked.

Marker snorted loudly into the phone, his voice filled with derision. "Hell no, it ain't over. You didn't tell me she had a bodyguard *and* a watchdog."

Carter groaned. He should have known Marker would screw up.

"For all I know, she could have three of everything," Carter snarled. "You're the one who claimed to be an expert. It's up to you to find a way to accomplish what you're being paid to do.''

"I want more money," Marker argued. "I done been dog-bit, and that man who hangs on the Dixon woman's arm is no slouch. I seen him take a handful of ammo and a piece out of his trunk that could blow a hole in an elephant.''

"What did you think they would do, throw rocks at you?'' Carter yelled. "And hell no, you don't get more money. If you don't do what I paid you to do, you don't even get the last half of what I promised.''

Then he pinched the bridge of his nose, took a slow, calming breath and stared out of the window at the rising sun. Screaming at Neanderthals was not something to which he was accustomed. Someone was going to have to do the thinking, and obviously, Bo Marker was not going to be it.

"Look, just get rid of the dog and…''

"Already done it.''

Carter sighed. "Then why are you bothering me? You know what has to be done. Go the hell out and just do it. And don't call me again until it's over!''

Marker frowned. "Yeah, right,'' he muttered, and let the phone drop back onto the receiver, well aware that it would echo sharply in Carter Foster's ear.

Carter winced as he disconnected, and then fell backward onto his bed, staring up at the ceiling without seeing the fancy swirls of plaster that Betty Jo had insisted upon, and contemplating how swiftly a man's life could change.

One day he'd had a wife and a business and a fairly normal life. That he no longer had a wife was not strictly his fault. He'd firmly convinced himself that Betty Jo had brought everything upon herself. And, when he thought about it, he regretted the fact that he'd been forced to eliminate other lives in order to maintain his own…but not enough to sway himself from his chosen path. Yet thinking about that Dixon woman and what she could do to his world made him sick with fear.

"Well, damn,'' he mumbled, and rolled off the bed and headed for the bath. It was time to start another day.

Chapter 8

With daylight came restraint. Glory wasn't versed in morning-afters, and Wyatt looked even bigger and more imposing in the bright light of day as she lay in bed, watching him wake beside her.

The color of his hair was a stark contrast to the pillowcase upon which he lay. Dark to light. Black to white. His eyelashes fluttered as consciousness returned, brushing the cheeks upon which they lay like shadows moving in the night.

Glory shivered with longing as she gazed at his lips, remembering how he'd raked them across her body, and how she'd responded. He stretched, and she followed the path of muscles that contracted along his arms and chest, amazed at the size of him and of his obvious strength, yet remembering how gently he'd held her when they made love.

Nervously, she waited for those dark eyes to open, waited anxiously to see how he would respond, and reminded herself, *I'm the one who started this. I asked him to make love to me.*

Wyatt opened his eyes and turned to face her. An easy smile creased his lips as he scooped her up in his arms.

"And I will be forever grateful."

Glory blushed. "I thought you were asleep," she grumbled. "You could make a woman real nervous, sneaking in on her thoughts like that."

Wyatt grinned, then slid his hands down the length of her back, testing the softness of her skin. Stoking new fires, he began measuring the distance of his restraint between lust and passion. He wanted her to know pleasure before he knew his. But when her eyelids fluttered and her breath began to quicken, he knew it was time to ask.

"I don't want to insist, but I'd like to talk about, uh...losing our minds...just once more...before I get out of this bed."

"Talk's cheap," she said, and ran her hand down his chest, past his belly and beyond.

He grinned again as he caught her hand before she went too far in her exploration and ruined the extent of his plans, and then he paused, remembering last night had been her first time.

"But...I don't want you to do this if it's going to be uncomfortable for you," he whispered, tracing the shape of her mouth with a fingertip.

She raised up on one elbow and began digging through the tangle of bedclothes until she felt one of the flat packets beneath her hand. She handed it to Wyatt with only the faintest of blushes.

"Here. You're the one who feels uncomfortable, not me."

Again, in the midst of a most intimate moment, she had made him laugh by acknowledging that his manhood was hard and, most probably, aching. And in that moment, Wyatt knew a rare truth. Going from laughter to passion, without foreplay in between, was a rare and beautiful thing. Like the bloom of the morning glory, a thing to be treasured.

He took what she offered, and moments later he rolled across the bed, taking her with him until she was firmly in place beneath the weight of his body.

Glory looked up. The breadth of his shoulders swamped

her in size. The weight of his body was twice that of her own, and yet she knew that she was in total control.

One word.

That was all it would take to change the drift of Wyatt Hatfield's thoughts. But Glory wasn't a fool. If one word need be uttered, it would be one of compliance, not rejection. The question was in his eyes, the thrust of his body against the juncture of her thighs was all the proof that he could show of his need. The muscles in his arms jerked as he held himself above her, waiting for her decision.

"Glory...sweetheart?"

She lifted her arms and pulled him down. "Yes."

And when he slid between her legs and filled that in her that was empty, she sighed with satisfaction. "Oh, yes."

Wyatt smiled, and then it was the last thought he could manage as morning gave way to love.

Everything was wet. Last night's rain had soaked ground, grass and trees, and the creek below Granny Dixon's old cabin was frothed with mini whitecaps from the swiftly flowing stream. Wyatt stood lookout at the top of the creek bank, watching as Glory searched the thickets below, calling and calling for a missing pup that never came.

"Give it up, honey," he called. "If the pup was anywhere nearby, you know it would come to you."

She looked up, and the sorrow on her face was more than he could bear. He started down the bank toward her when she waved him away, and started up instead.

"We can go up to your house. Maybe the pup spent the night in the barn," he suggested.

She shook her head and all but fell in his arms as she reached the top. "Even if he had, he would have come back this morning begging for something to eat."

Weary in body and heart, she wrapped her arms around his waist and then suddenly gasped, jumping back in shock when her hands accidentally brushed across the pistol he had slipped in the waistband of his jeans. Her eyes widened with shock, turning more silver than blue as she looked up at Wyatt's face. It was all she could do to say his name.

"Why are you carrying a gun?"

His expression flattened. Once again, she saw the soldier that he had been.

"I want you alive. I want you safe. This is the only way I have of helping to keep you that way."

She paled, then spun away, and Wyatt watched as her hair fanned around her like a veil of pale lace. He wanted to touch her, but her posture did not invite intrusion. Instead, he waited for Glory to make the next move.

Glory stared blindly about her at the pristine beauty of the thick, piney woods that had always been her home, searching for the comfort that had always been there. Yet as she looked, the shadows that she'd once sought to play in no longer offered cool solace. Instead, they loomed, ominous by their mere presence. Trees so dense that it would be impossible to drive through no longer seemed a source of refuge. Now they seemed more like a prison. She doubled her fists and started to shake. Anger boiled up from her belly, burning and tearing as it spilled from her lips.

"I hate this," she muttered, and then turned back to Wyatt, her voice rising in increments with each word that she spoke. "I hate this! It isn't fair! My family was taken from me. I no longer have a home. And now J.C.'s puppy is gone." Her voice broke as tears began to fall. "It was the last thing I had from before."

Wyatt reached for her, but she was too fast. Before he knew it, she had started toward what was left of her home, splattering mud up the legs of her jeans and coating her boots as she stalked up the road.

He didn't argue, and he didn't blame her. Fighting mad was a hell of a lot healthier than a silent grief that never healed. He began to follow, never more than a few steps behind.

A slight mist was beginning to rise from the puddles as the midmorning sun beamed down through the trees, evaporating

the water that had not soaked into the ground. The cry of a
red-tailed hawk broke the silence between them as it circled
high above, searching for food. Wyatt shaded his eyes and
looked up, and as he did, missed seeing Glory as she suddenly
veered from the road and dashed into the edge of the trees.

But when she screamed, he found himself running toward
her with the gun in his hand before he realized that he'd even
moved. Years of training, and an instinct that had kept him
alive in places like Somalia had kicked in without thought.

By the time he reached her, she was coming back to him
on the run. He caught her in midstride, holding her close as
he trained the gun toward the place she had been, expecting
to see someone behind her. Someone who meant her great
harm.

"Talk to me," he shouted, shaking her out of hysterics
before it got them both killed. He needed to know what was
out there before he could help.

She pointed behind her, and then covered her face with her
hands and dropped to her knees in the grass.

"The puppy…back there…it's dead."

God! Wyatt ran his hand gently over the crown of her head,
then patted her shoulder, his voice was soft with regret and
concern. "Wait here, sweetheart. I'll be right back."

It had been dead for some time. That much was obvious,
due to the fact that while it had been shot, there was no blood
at the scene. Last night's rain had taken care of that…and any
other clues that might have led Wyatt to some sort of answer.
And yet he knelt near the carcass, searching the ground
around it for something, anything, that might lead to an answer.

He stared at the hole in the side of the pup's head, and
another just behind one of its front legs. For Wyatt, it was
total proof that it hadn't been some sort of hunting accident.
One shot maybe, two, no. And then he noticed something
beneath the pup's mouth and tested it with the tip of his finger.
It was soft and wet and blue. Frowning, he pulled, then rocked

back on his heels when a bit of cloth came away in his hands.
It had been caught in the pup's teeth.

"Well, I'll be damned," he muttered, fingering the small
bit of fabric. "Looks like you got a piece of him before he
got to you, didn't you, fella?"

He stuffed the fabric in his pocket, then looked back at
Glory. She was only a short distance away, and he could tell
by the way she was standing that she'd been watching every
move that he'd made.

Damn. He stood, then started toward her.

"Someone shot him, didn't they?"

He nodded.

"What was that you put in your pocket?"

He frowned, yet keeping the truth from her was dangerous.
It could very well get her killed.

"I think maybe you had the makings of a good watchdog,
honey. There was a piece of fabric caught in its teeth."

The anger that had carried her up the road simply withered
and died as she absorbed the ramifications of what that could
mean. Had the puppy died defending its territory from a tres-
passer? Maybe the same man who'd been in her house?

"So what do you think?" she finally asked.

What he was thinking didn't need to be said. He slipped
an arm around her shoulder and hugged her gently. "Just that
I need a shovel."

Her shoulders drooped. "There's one in the barn."

He held out his hand and then waited. This time, they traveled the rest of the distance hand in hand. But when they came
out of the barn, Glory groaned in dismay. Edward Lee was
walking toward them up the road, carrying the pup's limp
body dangling across his outstretched arms.

"Oh, no," she said softly.

"What?" Wyatt asked.

"Edward Lee gave J.C. the puppy for a birthday present
about six months ago. He's not going to take this well."

Sure enough, Glory was right. Edward Lee was sobbing
long before he reached them.

"Look, Mornin' Glory, someone went and killed your dog."

"We know, Edward Lee. See, we have a shovel. We were about to bury him. Would you like to pick a place?"

Tears slowed, as the idea centered within the confusion in his brain. He blinked, and then lifted his gaze from the pup to Glory.

He nodded. "I will pick a good place," he said. "A place that James Charles would like."

In spite of her pain, Glory smiled, thinking what a fit J.C. would have had if he'd heard that. Edward Lee was the only person who occasionally insisted upon calling her brother by his full given name. Everyone else had been forced to use the nickname, J.C., which he preferred.

And then Edward Lee looked at Wyatt, suddenly realizing he was there. "Wyatt is my friend," he said, assuring himself that the new relationship still held true.

Wyatt nodded. "Yes, I am, Edward Lee. Now, why don't you tell me where to dig, and we'll make a good place for the puppy to rest."

Glory watched from the shade of the barn while Edward Lee led Wyatt to a nearby lilac bush in full bloom. When he began to dig, she said a quick prayer and let go of her fear. A short time later, there was a new mound of dirt near the thick cover of lavender blossoms. It was a fitting monument for a short, but valiant, life.

They walked with Edward Lee to the end of the road, and then watched as he disappeared into the trees. A few moments later, as they were about to enter the cabin, the persistent ringing of an unanswered phone could be heard.

"Shoot." Wyatt suddenly remembered the phone that he'd tossed on the bed while getting dressed. He darted inside, and then toward the bedroom, answering it in the middle of a ring.

"Hello."

"Where have you been?" Lane growled. "And why didn't you take the damned phone with you? I left it so I could stay in touch. I was just about call out the National Guard."

"Sorry," Wyatt said, and dropped onto the side of his bed. "We were burying a dog."

"You were what?"

"The pup. Someone shot it while we were in town yesterday. We didn't find it until this morning."

"The hell you say. How's Glory taking it?"

"About like you'd imagine. It was her brother's dog."

Lane frowned. He didn't like what he was thinking, but it had to be said. "Look, Wyatt, remember when I was laid up at Toni's after the plane crash and your nephew's dog was killed?"

Wyatt grinned. "Yeah, was that before or after you got my sister pregnant?"

"Just shut up and listen," Lane muttered. "The point I'm trying to make is that the inmate we all thought was dead was actually hiding in the woods. He killed the dog to keep it quiet during one of his trips to forage for food. I'm warning you to be careful. Bad guys have a habit of eliminating all obstacles in their paths, no matter what."

Wyatt dug in his pocket and pulled out the bit of fabric.

"Don't think it hasn't already crossed my mind. The pup got a bite of whoever it was that did him in, though. I found a piece of fabric caught between his teeth."

"Well, well! That's real good detective work. Maybe there's hope for you yet," Lane drawled.

Wyatt grinned. "Is there a real reason you called, or were you just checking up on me?"

"Oh, yeah, right! Look, I've been running a check on any or all missing person reports filed in the past two months in a five-hundred-mile radius of Larner's Mill. There are only two, and both of them are males. Glory is real sure the body she visualized was a female?"

"Absolutely," Wyatt said, and heard Lane sigh in his ear.

"Okay. I'll keep searching. Meanwhile, for God's sake, carry the phone with you. You never know when you'll need to reach out and touch someone...understand?"

"Understood," Wyatt said, and disconnected. When he

looked up, Glory was standing in the doorway. She'd been listening to their conversation. There was a slight, embarrassed smile on her face, but stifling the question on her mind was impossible.

"Lane got your sister pregnant?"

Wyatt laughed. "It's a long story, honey. But don't feel sorry for my sister. She got exactly what she wanted. In fact, old Lane was the one who got caught in the Hatfield cross fire."

She smiled, trying to imagine anyone as big and forbidding as Lane Monday getting caught by anything.

"You're very lucky," she said.

Wyatt frowned as he tried to follow her line of thinking. "How so, honey?"

"You have a large family. I think it would be wonderful to be a part of that."

"I'll share mine with you," Wyatt muttered. "Sometimes they can be a royal pain in the you-know-what."

If only I could share your family, Wyatt Hatfield. But she didn't say it, and walked away.

Wyatt sat on the side of the bed, calling himself a dozen kinds of a fool for not responding to her wish. But how could he say it, when he wasn't sure what to say? All he knew was that he lived for the sound of her voice, rested easy only when she was within eyesight, and came apart in her arms from their loving. It was definitely passion. But was it true love?

He followed her into the kitchen. "Don't cook. We need to get out of here for a while. Why don't you make a list? We'll do some shopping and then eat supper out before we come home?"

Glory turned. "I have to change. I'm muddy, and my hair's a mess."

Wyatt dug his hands through the long, silky length, then buried his face in the handful he lifted to his face.

"Your hair is never a mess," he said softly. "It feels like silk, and smells like flowers." And then he leaned down and pressed a swift kiss on her mouth. "And...I love the way it feels on my skin."

And I love the way you feel on my skin, she thought.

Startled, Wyatt dropped her hair, and looked up. Glory arched an eyebrow, unashamed of having been caught.

"Did it again, didn't you?" she asked, and left him wearing a guilty expression as she went to change clothes.

Within the hour, they were in the car and on their way up the road. When they passed the old barn, Glory turned toward the new grave and impulsively pressed her hand against the glass.

"When this is all over, you could get another puppy," Wyatt said.

Glory shrugged. "If I'm still here to care for it, I might."

Wyatt was so angry he was speechless. That she kept referring to the fact that she might not live through all of this made him crazy. He couldn't shake the fear that she might be seeing something of her own future that she wasn't willing to share.

Sundown had come and gone while they were inside Milly's Restaurant on the outskirts of Larner's Mill. They exited the lively establishment into a crowded parking lot as the scent of hickory smoke from the inside grill coated the damp night air.

Glory walked silently beside Wyatt as they wove their way through the unevenly parked cars, absorbing the comfort of his presence even though she was unable to voice what she was feeling. And truth be known, she wasn't certain she could put into words the emotions swirling inside her head. All she knew was she wanted this man as she'd never wanted another.

A couple got out of a car just ahead of them, and paused and stepped aside, giving Wyatt and Glory room to pass.

Pleasantries were traded, and then they walked on just as someone shouted Wyatt's name. He turned. It was the chief of police.

Anders Conway stepped off the curb and started toward them while Glory's good mood began dissipating.

"Oh, great," she muttered. "I'm not in the mood for any more of that man's sharp-edged doubt. Wyatt, could I please have the keys? I'd rather wait for you in the car."

He slipped his hand beneath the weight of her hair, caressing the back of her neck in a gentle, soothing touch, then handed her the keys without comment.

Beneath a tree a short distance away, Bo Marker sat in a stolen car, well concealed behind the dark tinted windows as the engine idled softly. When he'd seen the Dixon woman and her man come out of Milly's, he'd been satisfied that tonight, he could quite literally kill two birds with one stone, get the rest of his money from Foster, and be out of Kentucky before this night had passed. And then the chief of police had followed them outside.

"Son of a...!" he muttered, then shifted in the seat.

But berating himself for bad luck wasn't Bo Marker's style. All he needed was a change of plans, and when Glory Dixon suddenly walked away from her watchdog companion, Marker smiled. It creased his wide, homely face like cracks down the side of a jar. He leaned forward, hunching his great bulk behind the wheel of the car, and when Glory Dixon moved into the open, he quietly shifted from Park to Drive, and then stomped on the gas.

Bo Marker had stolen wisely. The souped-up hot rod could go from zero to sixty in seconds. The engine roared, coming to life like a sleeping lion. Tires squalled, gravel flew, and the car fishtailed slightly as he shot out of a parked position, down the short driveway toward the highway beyond, and right into Glory Dixon's path.

At the sound, Glory looked up and found herself staring straight into the blinding glare of headlights on high beam. Before she could think to react, a weight caught her from behind in a flying tackle, and before she had time to panic, Wyatt's arms surrounded her as they went rolling across the gravel.

Tiny shards of rock stung her leg as the car flew past, and she heard Wyatt grunt in pain as they came to a stop against the bumper of another vehicle. His hands were moving across her body before she could catch her breath to speak. She didn't have to hear the panic in his voice to know how close that had been.

"Glory! Sweetheart! Talk to me! Are you all right?" Before she could answer, she heard a man shouting orders and remembered. Chief Conway had witnessed it all.

"How bad is she hurt?" Conway asked Wyatt, as he knelt beside them.

Wyatt's voice broke. "Oh, God, I don't..."

Glory caught Wyatt's hand as it swept up her neck in search of a pulse. In the second before she spoke, they stared straight into each other's eyes. There were no words for what they felt at that moment, nor were any necessary. He'd saved her life, as surely as she'd saved his all those months ago.

"Thanks to Wyatt, I think I'm all right."

"Damn crazy driver," the chief said. "I am in my personal car, or I'd have given chase myself." And then by way of explanation, he added, "I couldn't catch a rabbit on a hot day in that thing, but at least I had my two-way. My men are already in pursuit."

Even as Wyatt helped Glory from the ground, the sounds of fading sirens could be heard in the distance.

"Oh, damn," Wyatt whispered, as he peered through the faint glow of the security lights to the dark stain coating his hand. "Glory...you're bleeding."

She followed the trail of a burning sensation on her left arm. "I just scraped my elbow." And then she shuddered, and leaned forward, letting Wyatt enfold her within his embrace. "It wasn't an accident, Wyatt."

"I know, honey."

Conway frowned. "Now, it could have been a drunk driver, or a—"

Angry with Conway's persistent blind streak where Glory

was concerned, Wyatt interrupted. His voice rose until by the time he was finished, he was shouting in the policeman's face.

"Last week, someone blew up her house, fully expecting her to be in it. Yesterday, someone shot her dog. We found this in his teeth when we went to bury it." Wyatt dug the bit of fabric from his shirt pocket and slapped it into the chief's hand. "Now, tonight, someone tried to run her down. And before you argue, consider the fact that the car wasn't already rolling when Glory stepped into the drive. I heard the motor idling. I heard him shift gears. He was waiting for her. When he had a clear shot, he took it."

Glory shuddered and Wyatt felt it.

"Now I'm going to take her to the hospital to be checked out. If you want to talk more, feel free to come along. Otherwise, I suppose you can file this information and the bit of fabric I just gave you where you've filed the rest of Glory's case."

"No hospital, Wyatt. Just take me home. There's nothing wrong with me that you and some iodine can't fix."

"Are you sure, honey?" he asked.

"I'm sure. Just get me out of here."

Conway felt restless, even guilty, although there was little else he could do right now, other than what he'd just done. He followed them to the car as Wyatt helped Glory into her seat.

"Look, Miss Dixon. We're doing all we can to follow up on what you've told us. Maybe we'll have the man in custody before the night is out."

She didn't answer, and when they drove away, Conway was struck by the quiet acceptance he'd seen in her eyes. As if she knew that what he said was little more than whitewash for the fact that they had nothing to go on, so therefore, they were doing nothing.

"Damn it all to hell," Conway muttered. He looked down at the fabric that Wyatt had handed him, and then stuffed it in his pocket as he ran back to his car. The least he could do was get to the office and follow the pursuit from there.

As they drove through town on their way home, Wyatt couldn't quit watching the play of emotions on Glory's face.

"Honey...are you sure you don't want me to drive by the hospital?" His fingers kept tracing the knuckles of her left hand as he drove, as if he didn't trust himself to ever let her out of his grasp again. "When I took you down, I hit you hard...real hard. I just couldn't think of a quicker way to move you out of danger."

Glory turned sideways, staring at Wyatt's profile, wondering how she would bear it when he left her. Her voice was soft, just above a whisper as she reacted to his concern.

"It's all right, Wyatt. You saved my life tonight, and we both know it." She scooted across the seat and laid her head on his shoulder. "Thank you."

He exhaled slowly, finally able to shake off the panic he'd felt when he'd seen her danger. With his left hand firmly on the steering wheel, he slipped his right arm around her shoulders and held her close. "Now you know how I feel about you."

She sighed, and her breath trembled, thick with tears she wouldn't let go. "Wyatt...oh, Wyatt, what are we going to do?"

God help us, I wish that I knew, Wyatt thought, but didn't voice his own fears. Instead, he pulled her that little bit closer and stared blindly down the road, aware that their fate was as dark and uncertain as what moved through the night beyond the headlights of their car.

Marker cursed loud and long. He knew the moment he sped past that he'd missed. And all because of that man who walked at her side. Instead of the solid thump he'd expected when bumper met body, he'd got nothing for his trouble but a high-speed pursuit that had taken him hours to escape.

Thanks to the fact that the car he'd stolen was faster than the police vehicles, he finally eluded the chase. He dumped the hot rod where he'd hidden his own vehicle hours earlier.

When and if they found the car, they'd have nothing to pin it on him.

He'd made sure to leave no fingerprints behind, and he was an old hand at never leaving witnesses to his crimes. It was what had kept him out of prison this far, but cold-blooded murder was a different business and a little bit out of his class. Fed up with the hit-and-miss success of his strikes against Glory Dixon, as he drove, he made plans. New plans. Next time, he wouldn't miss.

Chapter 9

Moonlight lay across Glory's bare shoulders like a silver sheet, broken only by the presence of a long, ivory braid down the middle of her back. Covers bunched around her waist as she struggled with nightmares she couldn't escape.

Wyatt heard her moan, and turned from the window where he stood watch, sickened by the darkening bruises on her shoulder and the bloody scrapes on her elbows. It was all he could do not to crawl in that bed with her and take her in his arms. But he didn't. He'd let down his guard once and it had nearly cost her her life. It wasn't going to happen again.

Even now, the playback of the engine as it accelerated and the tires as they spun out on the gravel was all too real in his mind. He didn't remember moving, only feeling the impact of hitting Glory's body and then rolling with her across the parking lot.

As he watched, a single tear slipped from the corner of her eye and then down her cheek like a translucent pearl. Impulsively he reached out, catching it with the tip of his finger and then tracing its path with his lips, tasting the satin texture of her skin and the salt from the tear.

His breath fanned her cheek as he whispered, "Darlin', don't cry."

Her eyelids fluttered, and then she sighed. Reluctantly, he moved back to his post, took one last look out of the window by her bed, then picked up the phone and headed for the tiny living room.

The view from those windows wasn't much different from the view at the back, and yet he couldn't let go of the notion that something or someone watched them from the woods. Lightly, he ran his fingers across the gun in his waistband, waiting as his eyes adjusted to the dark, and then finally, he began to dial.

Lane Monday's voice was rough and thick with sleep, but he answered abruptly before the second ring.

"Hello?"

"It's Wyatt."

Lane rose on an elbow, leaning over Toni as she slept, to peer at the lighted dial on the alarm. It was nearly one o'clock in the morning. That, plus the tone of Wyatt's voice, gave away the urgency of the call.

"What's wrong?"

"We went out to eat this evening. Someone tried to run Glory down in the parking lot. And before you ask, no, it wasn't an accident."

Lane rolled out of bed. Taking the portable phone with him so as not to wake Toni, he went down the hallway and into the living room where his voice could not easily be heard.

"I can be there in about six hours."

Wyatt cursed softly. "And do what?" he muttered. "I was right there beside her and I was almost too late."

"Is she all right?"

"Except for bruises and scrapes...and some more nightmares to add to the ones she already has...yes." Then Wyatt started to pace. "Look, I didn't call for backup. I just wanted to let you know what's happening. The only positive thing I can tell you is that Anders Conway witnessed the whole thing."

Lane sighed, torn between wanting to help and knowing that there was nothing he could do that Wyatt wasn't already doing.

"Okay, but keep me posted," he muttered, and then added, "Remember, all you have to do is call. If it's an emergency, I can hop a copter and be there in a couple of hours."

The nervousness in Wyatt's belly started to subside, if for no other reason than the fact that someone besides him knew what was going on.

"Thanks," Wyatt said, then added, "Oh…kiss Toni and Joy for me." Then he hung up and began pacing from window to window, afraid to sleep, afraid to turn his back on Glory…ever again.

Sometime before morning, Glory woke with a start, then groaned beneath her breath when aching muscles protested the sudden movement. Seconds later, she realized what was wrong.

Wyatt was gone!

Careful not to insult her injuries, she crawled out of bed, picked up the nightgown and slipped it over her head before leaving the room.

The floor was cool beneath her feet. The old hardwood planks were smooth and polished from years of use and cleaning, and as familiar to Glory as her own home had been. The half-light between night and dawn was just below the horizon as she made her way into the kitchen. He was standing at the window.

"Wyatt?"

Startled by the unexpected sound of her voice, he spun. When she saw the gun in his hand, she wanted to cry. He was holding fast to his promise to keep her safe, even at his own expense. She crossed the room and walked straight into his arms.

"Come to bed," she whispered. "Whatever is going to

happen will happen. You can't change fate, Wyatt. No matter how much it hurts.''

He cradled her face in the palm of his hand, tracing the curve of her cheek and the edges of her lips with his fingers as a blind man would see.

''You don't understand, Glory. I don't quit. I don't give up. And one of these days, I'm going to get my hands on the bastard who's doing this to you. When it happens…''

Her fingers silenced the anger spilling out of his mouth, and in the quiet of Granny's kitchen, she took the gun from his hand and laid it on the table, then slipped her arms around his neck and whispered softly against his mouth.

''No, Wyatt, there's no room for hate in this house, only love. Now come to bed. It's my turn to take care of you.''

Unable to resist her plea, he scooped her up into his arms and carried her back to her bed, making room for himself beside her. Just when Glory thought he was settling down, he suddenly rolled, then bolted from the room, returning only moments later. When she heard a distinctive thump on the bedside table, she knew he'd gone back for the gun.

''Don't say it,'' he growled, as he crawled in beside her. ''Just let me have that much peace of mind.''

Tears shimmered across her vision, but she didn't argue. Instead, she wrapped her arms around him and cradled his head on her breasts.

Just sleep, my love. It's my turn to keep watch over you.

For a moment, he forgot to breathe.

Like all the Hatfields, Wyatt had been full grown in size by the time he was sixteen years old. At three inches over six feet, he was a very big man and had been taking care of himself for a very long time. If anything, he was the caregiver, the fixer, the doer. That a little bit of female like Glory Dixon dared suggest she could take care of him might have made him smile…if he'd been able to smile through his tears.

Long after the quiet, even sounds of his breathing were proof of his sleep, Glory still held him close. Wide-eyed and alert, she watched morning dawn and then sunlight come, as it spilled through the slightly parted curtains and onto the man in her arms.

Sunbeams danced in the air above her head, bringing hope with the new day. Wyatt stirred, and Glory shifted, giving him ease and a new place to rest. When he smiled in his sleep, the scar on his cheek shifted slightly, reminding her of what he'd endured and survived. A deep and abiding ache resurfaced. She recognized it for what it was, and while he wasn't looking or listening, let herself feel what was there in her heart.

I love you, Wyatt Hatfield. And then a small, silent prayer to a much greater power. *Dear God, please keep him safe. Don't let me be the instrument of another man's death.*

Hours later, Wyatt rolled over in bed, reached out to pull Glory closer, and then woke as suddenly as she had earlier. He was alone. But before he could panic, the scent of fresh coffee and the familiar sounds of a kitchen in use calmed his nerves.

He got out of bed and headed for the bathroom. A shower and a change of clothes later, he was entering the kitchen just as Glory set a pan of hot biscuits on the table. She looked up with a smile.

"Your timing is impeccable," she said.

Wyatt grinned. "So I've been told."

It took a second for the innuendo to sink in, and when it did, a sweet blush spread across Glory's face and neck.

"You are a menace," she muttered, and turned back to the stove just as his hands slid around her from behind and came to rest just below the fullness of her breasts.

"That, too." He chuckled, and kissed the spot just below her earlobe that he knew made her shiver.

She turned in his arms and let his next kiss center upon her mouth. It was hard and hungry, and just shy of demanding, and then he groaned, letting go as suddenly as he'd swooped.

"Glory…darlin', I almost forgot your bruises. How do you feel?"

"Like I was run over by a…"

"Don't!" His eyes darkened as he pressed a finger over her lips. "Don't joke. Not to me. I was there, remember?"

She smiled. Just a little, but just enough to let him know she was all right with the world.

"The biscuits are getting cold," she said, and aimed him toward the table. "Sit. I'm just finishing up the eggs."

"I should be cooking for you," he muttered.

"Lord help us both." When he smiled, she turned back to the eggs.

Later, Glory fidgeted as they ate, and Wyatt could tell there was something on her mind. But it wasn't until they were almost through with the dishes that she started to talk.

"Wyatt…last night at the restaurant…I nearly died, didn't I?"

"Don't remind me," he muttered, and set a clean glass in Granny's little cupboard.

"Oh…that's not what I was getting at," she explained. "What I meant was…if there had been anything left in this life I still wanted to do…it would have been too late."

"Hellfire, Glory! This is a real bad discussion right after a good meal."

She grinned. "Sorry. What I'm trying to say is…"

He tossed the dish towel on the cabinet and took her by the arm, careful not to touch the places that hurt.

"Look, girl! Just say what's on your mind."

She lifted her chin, pinning him with that silver-blue gaze that always made him feel as if he were floating.

"I need to go see my granny one more time…just in case. Chances are she might not even recognize me, but I don't want her to think that we forgot about her. Daddy always went at least once a month. It's past that time now. She's in a nursing home in Hazard. Will you take me?"

Wyatt felt the room beginning to spin. It scared the hell out of him, just hearing her admit that she might not live another week as casually as she might have announced she wasn't going to plant a garden. Unable to keep his distance, he reached out for her, and when she relaxed against him, he shuddered.

"I'll take you anywhere you want to go. I'll stand on my damned head in the woods for a week if it will make you happy. But so help me God, if you don't stop forecasting so much doom and gloom, I'm going to pack you and your stuff and take you home with me to Tennessee. Then we'll see how far this killer wants to travel to die. I've got enough kin there to mount a small army."

She could tell by the tone of his voice that he was serious. But it was an impossible suggestion.

"No, Wyatt! It's bad enough that you've put your life on the line for me. I couldn't live with myself if any more people were put in danger because of this. I'll try not to be so negative, but truth is hard to ignore."

"The only truth is...your killer is a screwup. He tried to kill you and got your family instead, and then even later your dog. The fact that he was stupid enough to try a third time, and right in front of the chief of police, doesn't say much for his brains, only his desperation. Desperate men make mistakes, Glory. Remember that!"

In the face of all she'd lost, what he said shouldn't have helped, but for some reason, it did. She relaxed in his arms.

"Okay! I promise! Now let me change my clothes so we can go. And when we go through Larner's Mill, could we stop at the bakery? Granny loves their gingersnaps."

He nodded, and as she left, he retraced his path to the window, looking out into the bright sunlight of a brand-new day, wondering what it would bring.

As nursing homes went, it wasn't so bad. Like similar institutions across the country, it offered health care and comfort to people with aging bodies and minds. But the reason for its being was still the same. It was where the old went to die.

Wyatt caught himself holding his breath as they walked down the hallway. The scent of incontinence, cleaning solvents, and medication was a blend impossible to ignore.

Somewhere ahead of them, an old man's cries for help echoed in the hall while other residents roamed at will, scooting along on walkers, thumping with their canes and wheeling the occasional wheelchair.

And then Glory touched his arm and paused at an open doorway before stepping inside. He followed. It was, after all, why they'd come.

She sat by a window, rocking back and forth in an uneven rhythm, as if sometimes forgetting to keep a motion going. Her body was withered and stooped, her snow-white hair as fluffy and sparse as wisps of cotton. The yellow robe she was wearing was old and faded to near-white, but new, fuzzy blue slippers covered her feet. She had no memory of how she'd come by them, only that they kept her warm. Her eyes were fixed on something beyond the clear glass, and her mouth was turned up in a soft, toothless smile...quite lost in happier times and happier days.

"Granny?"

At the sound of her name, the rocker stopped, and the smile slid off her face. She turned, staring blankly at the pair in the doorway and frowned.

"Comp'ny? I got comp'ny?"

Glory quickly crossed the distance between them to kneel at her side, covering the gnarled, withered hands with her own. The skirt of her only dress puddled around her as she knelt and kissed her granny's cheek. "Yes, Granny, it's me, Glory."

Wyatt watched while recognition came and went in the old woman's pale, watery eyes, and then suddenly she smiled, and ran her hand across Glory's head, fingering the long pale lengths of her hair. In that moment, he saw her as the woman she once had been.

"Well, Glory girl, it's been a while! I didn't think you was ever comin' to see your granny again. Where's your pa? I swear, that boy of mine is always late. I'm gonna give him a piece of my mind when he shows up, and that's a fact."

There was a knot in Glory's throat that threatened to choke

her. Twice she faltered before she could speak, and it was
only after Wyatt touched her shoulder that she could find the
strength to continue.

"Daddy won't be coming today, Granny. It's just me."

A frown deepened the furrow of wrinkles across her brow,
and then she cackled and slapped her knee.

"That's good! That's good! Us women gotta stick together,
don't we, little girl?"

Tears shimmered across Glory's eyes, but the smile on her
face was as bright as the sunshine warming Granny's lap.

"Yes, ma'am, we sure do."

Granny's attention shifted, as if suddenly realizing that
Glory was not alone. She looked up at Wyatt, puckering her
mouth as she considered his face, and then waved him toward
a nearby chair.

"Sit down, boy!" she ordered. "You be way too tall to
look at from down here." Then she cackled again, as if de-
lighted with her own wit.

Wyatt grinned and did as he was told.

"Who's he?" Granny asked, as if Wyatt had suddenly gone
deaf.

Glory smiled. "That's Wyatt Hatfield, Granny. He's my
friend."

And then in the blunt, tactless manner of the very old, she
looked up at Wyatt and asked, "Are you messin' with my
girl?"

Glory rolled her eyes at Wyatt, begging him to understand,
but it was a silent plea she need never have made.

"No, ma'am, I would never treat Glory lightly. I care for
her very much."

Satisfied, Granny Dixon leaned back in her rocker and
started to rock. Wyatt handed Glory the box of gingersnaps
they'd brought from the bakery in Larner's Mill.

"Look, Granny, we brought you gingersnaps."

She set the box in Granny's lap, then patted her on the
knee to remind her that she was still here.

The joy on the old woman's face was a delight to see, and

when she opened the lid, the scent of molasses and spice filled the air.

"I do love my gingersnaps," Granny said. "But I reckon I'll save 'em till I get me some milk to sop 'em in. I don't eat so good without my teeth, anymore. Glory girl, you set these by my bed, now, you hear?"

"Yes, ma'am," Glory said, and did as she was told.

When she returned, she knelt back at her Granny's knee. It was such an old, familiar place to be, that before Glory realized what she was doing, she found herself leaning forward. When the rocking chair suddenly paused, she exhaled slowly on a shaky sob and laid her head in Granny's lap, waiting for those long, crippled fingers to stroke through her hair, just as they'd done so many years ago.

Suddenly, Wyatt found himself watching through tears and feeling the isolation that Glory must be feeling. Here she was, the last of her line, caught in a hell not of her making and seeking comfort from a woman who was fighting a losing battle with reality. He had the strongest urge to take both women in his arms and hold them, but reason told him to refrain. Here he was the onlooker. He didn't belong in their world.

Long silent minutes passed while Granny Dixon combed her fingers through the silken lengths of Glory's hair, soothing old fears, calming new pain. And then in the quiet, Granny paused and tilted Glory's face. She looked long and hard, then leaned closer, peering at the tearstained gaze in her granddaughter's eyes. Knuckles swollen and locked with age stroked the soft skin on Glory's cheek, brushing lightly against the halo the sun had made on Glory's hair.

"Such a pretty little thing...Granny's little Morning Glory. You been havin' them visions again, ain't you, girl?"

Glory nodded, unable to speak of the horrors she'd recently survived, unwilling to tell this woman that her only son was dead.

"It'll be all right," Granny said. "You jest got to remember that it's God's gift to you, girl. It ain't no burden that you got to bear…it's a gift. Use it as such.''

"Yes, ma'am,'' Glory said, and when she heard Wyatt's feet shuffle behind her, she knew he was struggling with his own brand of pain.

Then the old woman's attention shifted, and once again, Wyatt found himself being grilled on the spot.

"You know 'bout Glory's gift, don't you, boy?''

"Yes, ma'am, that I do,'' Wyatt said. "It's because of her that I'm still alive. She saved my life.''

Granny beamed, and the sunlight caught and danced in her eyes, giving them life where vacancy had just been. She clapped her hands and then patted Glory on the shoulder.

"That's my girl! You see what I'm a'tellin' you, Glory? You did good with your gift, and it brought you a man. That's good fortune!''

"But Granny, he's not actually my—''

Wyatt interrupted, unwilling to hear Glory put the tenuous part of the relationship into words.

"I consider myself the fortunate one, Mrs. Dixon.''

"That's good. That's good. You got yourself a man who has the good sense to know which side his bread is done buttered on.''

When Glory blushed, Wyatt laughed, which only pleased her granny more.

"You understand your responsibilities of lovin' a woman as special as my Glory, don't you?''

Wyatt nodded. "Yes, ma'am, I believe that I do.''

"Sometimes she'll ask things of you that you'll find hard to 'cept. Sometimes she'll know things you don't want to hear. But she'll be true to you all your life and that's a fact.''

"Granny, he doesn't want to hear all about…''

Wyatt leaned forward. His brown eyes darkened, his expression grew solemn.

"Yes I do, Morning Glory, yes, I do.''

Glory held her breath as joy slowly filled her heart. She

hoped he'd meant what he said, and then suddenly turned away, unwilling to look just in case he did not.

One hour turned into two as Granny Dixon regaled them with stories from Glory's childhood as well as old times before she'd ever been born. And while Wyatt listened, absorbing the love that had spanned all the years, bonding these women in a way no family name could have done, he knew that he'd finally found what had been missing in his own life.

Love.

The love that comes with knowing another as well as you know your own heart. The quiet, certain love that is there when all else has failed. The passionate, binding love that can lift a man up, and keep him afloat all his life.

Before Glory, Wyatt had been running…always on the move…afraid of sinking before he had lived. Now the answer to his own brand of pain was sitting at his feet, and unless they caught the man who was trying to kill her, he could lose it…and her…before they were his. He believed that she loved him. He knew that he loved her. The uncertainty lay in keeping her alive.

And finally, when Granny's head began to nod, Glory motioned that it was time to go. As they stood, Granny reached out and caught Wyatt's hand.

"You'll bring my little Morning Glory back, won't you?"

"Yes, ma'am, I sure will."

Granny's mouth squinched in what might be called a flirtatious smile, although it was hard to tell with so much vacancy between her lips. "Since you're gonna be in the family, I reckon you could be callin' me by my given name."

Wyatt grinned. "I'd be honored. And what would that be?" he asked.

Granny thought and then frowned. "Why, I should be knowin' my own name, now, shouldn't I?" And then a smile spread wide. "Faith! I'm called Faith." She shook her finger in Wyatt's face. "And you'll be needin' a whole lot of faith to love a woman as special as my Glory."

"Yes, ma'am, I suppose that I will."

"Maybe you'd be inclined to name your firstborn girl after me? I'd be pleased to know that my name lived on after I'm gone."

Moved by her innocence, Wyatt knelt, and took the old woman's hands in his own.

"I'm honored, Faith Dixon. And you have my word that it will be done."

Pleased that she'd covered all the bases with her granddaughter's new beau, Granny closed her eyes. Moments later, she began to rock, forgetting that they were even still there.

Wyatt slipped an arm around Glory's shoulder.

"Are you ready?"

Glory looked up, her eyes filled with tears, her lips trembling with the weight of unvoiced love for this man who held her.

"Yes, please."

She took Wyatt's hand, and let him lead her out of this place. When they were in the parking lot, she knew there was one more place she needed to go.

"Since we're in Hazard, I suppose I should go by the lawyer's office. Daddy always said if anything ever happened to him, that J.C. and I were to come here, that Mr. Honeywell would know what to do."

"Then we will," Wyatt promised. "You direct, I'll drive."

A short time later, they were sitting in the office of Elias Honeywell, the senior partner of Honeywell and Honeywell. He was still in shock at what he'd been told. His little round face was twisted with concern.

"Miss Dixon, I'm so sorry for your loss," he said. "But you needn't worry about your position. Your father was a farseeing man. Not only did he leave a will, but there is a sizable insurance policy, of which you are the sole beneficiary."

Glory had known of the will, but had had no idea her father had indulged in life insurance. Their life had been simple. Money had never been easy to come by. That he'd used it for a future he would not participate in surprised her.

"I had no idea," she said.

Elias Honeywell nodded solemnly. "Your father wanted it that way. He was concerned about your welfare after he passed on. I believe I recall him saying something to the effect that his daughter had more to bear than most, and he wanted to make sure you would not suffer unduly."

"Oh, my." It was all Glory could say without breaking into tears. Even in death, her father was still taking care of her.

Wyatt could see that Glory was not in any shape to question him. In spite of his reticence to interfere, he thought it best to ask now, rather than after they were gone.

"Mr. Honeywell, what will you need from Glory to proceed with the probate and claims?"

The little lawyer frowned, then shuffled through the file on his desk. "Why, I believe I have nearly everything I need," he said. "Except…" He hesitated, hating to bring it up. "We will need death certificates for her father as well as her brother before I can apply for the life insurance on her behalf. I have her address. If I need anything more, I will be in touch."

Glory rose with more composure than she felt. Had it not been for Wyatt Hatfield's presence, she would have run screaming to the car. The darkness within her mind kept spreading. She kept thinking this was all a bad dream, and that most any time she would wake, and it would all be over.

But reality was a rude reminder, and when they exited the office to resume the trip home, the only thing that kept her sane was remembering the promise Wyatt made to Granny. The fact that he'd made such a claim of the heart to a woman who would never remember he'd said it, didn't matter to Glory. At least not now. He'd said she was his girl. He'd promised Granny that he would take care of her forever. Glory needed to believe that he meant every word that he'd said.

Long after they were back on Highway 421, driving south toward Pine Mountain and Larner's Mill, which nestled at its base, Glory still had no words for what Wyatt had given her this day. It wasn't until later when he stopped for gas that she managed to say what was in her heart.

"Wyatt?"

"What, darlin'?" he said absently, as he unbuckled his seat belt to get out.

"I will never forget what you said to Granny today. No matter what you really thought, you made an old woman happy."

He paused, halfway out of the car seat, and looked back at her. "What about you, Morning Glory? Did it make you happy, too?"

"What do you mean?" she asked.

"I didn't say anything that wasn't already in my heart."

"Oh, Wyatt! You don't have to pretend with..."

"If you need to go to the little girls' room, now's your time," he said quietly, aware that she looked as scared as he felt. But as Glory had said, who knew what tomorrow would bring? Denying his feelings for her seemed a careless thing to do.

She got out of the car with her head in a whirl, her heart pounding with a hope she thought had died. Was there a chance for her after all? Could she have a future with a man she'd just met? More to the point, would she even want to try it without him?

Chapter 10

Anders Conway entered his office with a beleaguered air. Having to explain to a U.S. marshal why two of his patrol cars had not been able to apprehend a hit-and-run suspect hadn't set well with his lunch. His eardrums were still reverberating from the dressing down he'd gotten over the phone from Lane Monday, and while he wanted to resent the constant interference of Glory Dixon's newfound friends, he couldn't bring himself to blame them. It was obvious they were truly worried about her welfare and afraid for her life.

What surprised him was that they believed her story without a single doubt. She'd lived in Larner's Mill all of her life and had been looked upon as something of an oddity. Why two strangers should suddenly appear in her life and take her every word as gospel was a puzzle.

But the fire marshal's report sitting on his desk was strong evidence that Glory Dixon had something going for her. After reading it, Conway been unable to deny the truth of the young woman's claim. Whether he believed her story of *how* she saw it happen was immaterial. Fact was, someone had meddled with gas stoves, causing the deaths of her father and brother.

Conway paced the room, mentally itemizing the series of events concerning her. Her claim that she'd been the target for the fire was too farfetched for him to buy, and he chalked it up to a guilt complex for not having died along with her family. And then she wanted him to believe that she was still in danger, and had used the accidental shooting of her dog as more proof.

Conway snorted softly, muttering beneath his breath. "This isn't the kind of place where people go around killin' dogs for sport."

He started to pour himself a cup of coffee and then cursed when he realized it was cold. Someone had gone and turned the darn thing off, leaving the black brew to congeal along the sides of the pot.

"To hell with dogs...and coffee," he grumbled, and slammed his cup down with a thump.

But his mind wouldn't let go of his thoughts, and he kept dwelling on the oddity of the pup being killed so soon after all of the other trauma in Glory's life. He hadn't actually viewed the carcass, but he was inclined to believe that if it *had* been shot, it was most likely by accident, and someone hadn't been man enough to own up to the deed.

He fiddled with the papers in the file on his desk, staring long and hard at the evidence bag containing the bit of fabric that was supposed to have been caught in the dog's teeth, certain that it meant nothing either.

Yet as hard as he tried to convince himself that there had to be a reasonable explanation for the things that had been happening to Glory, last night was an altogether different circumstance.

Watching that car take aim at her, and then seeing Wyatt Hatfield suddenly turn and leap, had been like watching a scene out of a bad movie. Although it was an improbable thing to be happening in Larner's Mill, he *had* seen someone purposefully try to run her down.

"But damn it, I can't take the word of a psychic to court. If only my men hadn't lost that damn hot rod on the logging road, I'd have me a bona fide suspect to question. Then maybe I could get to the bottom of this mess."

"You talkin' to me, Chief?" the dispatcher yelled from the other room.

"Hell, no, I am not!" Conway shouted, and then winced at the tone of his own voice. If he didn't get a grip, he was going to wind up a few bales short of a load and they'd be shipping him off in a straitjacket.

He cursed again, only this time beneath his breath, shoved the file back into the drawer and stomped over to his desk, slumping into his easy chair and feeling every day of his sixty-two years. If only his deputies had been able to keep up with that hit-and-run driver. Everything had hinged upon finding the suspect, and he'd gotten away.

His stomach began to hurt. The familiar burning sensation sent him digging into his desk for antacids and wishing he'd taken early retirement. But when he found the bottle, it was empty. With a muttered curse, he tossed it in the trash and then walked back to dispatch.

"I'm going to the drugstore. Be back in a few minutes," he said, and ambled out of the office without waiting for the dispatcher's reply.

As he walked down the street, a car honked. Out of habit, he turned and waved before he even looked to see who had hailed him. Across the street and directly in his line of vision, he saw Carter Foster locking his office and putting the Out to Lunch sign on the office door.

"Now there's another man with problems," Conway muttered, looking at the lawyer's rumpled suit and pale, drawn face. "Poor bastard. I wonder how much Betty Jo took him for when she left?"

Then he shrugged. He didn't have time to worry about cheating women. He had a belly on fire and an office full of trouble just waiting for him to return. Just as he was about to enter the drugstore, an odd thought hit him. He turned, staring

back down the street where the lawyer had been, but Carter
and his car were nowhere in sight.

*Well, I'll be damned. We do have one missing person…of
a sort…here in Larner's Mill, after all. Old Carter is missing
a wife, isn't he?*

But as swiftly as the thought had come, he shoved it aside.
"God Almighty, I *am* losing my grip. Everyone knows that
Betty Jo would bed a snake if it held still long enough for
her to get a grip. When her money runs out, or the old boy
she took off with runs out of steam, she'll be back. And poor
old Carter will probably be stupid enough to let her."

Satisfied with his conclusion, he entered the store, heading
straight for the aisle where antacids were stocked.

Carter drove toward the café, unaware of the chief's discarded theory. Had he known, he might have kept on driving.
As it was, he was going through the motions of normalcy
while fighting a constant state of panic. He firmly believed
that if Bo Marker didn't put Glory Dixon out of the picture,
he was a ruined man.

But, Carter kept reminding himself, there was one thing
about this entire mess that had worked to his benefit. No one
questioned his drawn countenance or his lack of attention to
details, like forgetting two court dates and missing an important appointment with a client. It *could* all be attributed to a
man who'd been dumped by his wife, and not a man who'd
tossed his wife in a dump.

He switched on the turn signal, and began to pull into the
parking lot of the café when a deputy stepped in front of his
car and waved him to a different location. Surprised by the
fact that nothing ever changes in Larner's Mill, he followed
the officer's directions. But after he had parked, he couldn't
contain his curiosity, and wandered over to the area to see
what was going on.

"Hey, buddy, what's with the yellow tape?" Carter asked,
and flipped it lightly with his finger as if he were strumming
a guitar string.

"We had ourselves a crime here last night!"

Carter watched with some interest as another deputy was measuring some sort of distance between two points.

"What kind of crime? Someone steal hubcaps or something?"

"Nope. We had ourselves a near hit-and-run, and I got in on the chase afterward." And then he frowned and turned away, unwilling to admit how it galled him that the perpetrator had escaped.

Carter grinned. "How do you have a *near* hit-and-run, as opposed to an actual one?"

"Someone deliberately tried to run that Dixon girl over. You know, the one who just buried her daddy and brother?" He was so busy telling the story, that he didn't see the shock that swept across Carter Foster's face. "Anyway...her and her friend was just comin' out of the café when some guy took aim and tried to run her down. If it hadn't been for that man who's stayin' with her, he would have done it, too."

Damn, damn, damn, Carter thought, and then worry had him prodding for more information.

"Have you considered that it might have been just a drunk driver?" he asked, hoping to steer their investigation in a different direction.

The deputy shook his head. "No way. It was deliberate! Chief Conway witnessed the whole thing. We was in fast pursuit within seconds of it happenin', and would have caught him, too, except the guy was driving a stolen car. It was that Marley kid's hot rod. Ain't no one gonna catch that car, I don't care who's drivin' it."

The hunger that had driven Carter to the café was turning to nausea. He couldn't believe what he'd just heard.

"Anders Conway witnessed the incident? He *saw* someone try to run her over?"

"Yes, sir. Now, if you'll excuse me, Mr. Foster, I'd better get back to work. We got ourselves a felon to catch."

Carter stood without moving, watching as the officers picked through the scene. The longer he stared, the more panicked he became. The thought of food turned his stomach, and the thought of Bo Marker made him want to kill all over again. The stupidity of the man, to attempt a crime in front of the chief of police, was beyond belief.

Disgusted with the whole situation, he stomped to his car then drove toward home while a slow, burning anger built steam. At least there he could eat in peace without watching his life go down the toilet.

He was already inside the kitchen, building a sandwich of mammoth proportions, when realization sank in. So Bo Marker was stupid. Carter had known that when he'd hired him. He'd counted on his dim wit to be the deciding factor when he'd offered him the job of murderer.

Carter dropped into a chair, staring at the triple-decker sandwich on the plate, as well as the knife he was holding, watching as mayonnaise dripped from it and onto his lap.

So, if I hired Bo Marker, knowing his IQ was that of a gnat, what, exactly, does that make me?

He dropped the knife and buried his face in his hands, wishing he could turn back time. A saying his mother once told him did a replay inside his head. It had something to do with how the telling of one lie could weave itself into a whole web of deceit. Carter knew he was proof of his mother's wisdom. He was caught and sinking fast. Unless Bo Marker got his act together and did what he'd been hired to do, he was done for.

Using the trees around Granny Dixon's cabin as cover for the deed he had planned wasn't unique, but Bo Marker didn't have an original thought in his head. He was still mad about missing his mark last night, but had gotten some joy out of the wild ten-mile chase afterward. Running from the cops like that made him feel young again.

He glanced down at his watch, wondering when that Dixon bitch and her lover would come back home, and cursing his luck because he'd come too late this morning to catch them as they'd left. It would have been so easy just to pick them off as they'd walked out to the car.

He sighed, shifting upon the dirt where he was sitting, searching for a softer spot on the tree against which he was leaning. That knothole behind his back was beginning to feel like a brick.

Bo was at the point of boredom with this whole procedure and kept reminding himself what he could do with the money he would get from this job. As he sat, he rested his deer rifle across his knees and then spit, aiming at a line of ants that he'd been watching for some time. It wasn't the first time he'd spit on them, and in fact, as he spit, he was making bets with himself as to which way they'd run when it splattered. But his mind quickly shifted from the game at hand when something moved in the brush behind him. He grabbed the rifle and then stilled, squinting through the brush and searching for a sign of movement.

"Don't you think that rifle's a bit big for huntin' squirrels?"

Startled, Bo rolled to his feet, aiming his gun as he moved. But the man who'd come out of the brush was ready for the action. When Bo moved, the man swung his gun downward, blocking the motion. It took Bo all of five seconds to forget about tangling with the big, bearded mountain man.

The man stood a good four inches taller, and was more than fifty pounds heavier. And while Bo's gun was more powerful, that bead the man had drawn on his belly was all the incentive Bo needed to show some restraint. Being gut-shot wasn't a good way to die.

"Who said anything about hunting squirrels?" Bo muttered, and tried taking a step back. The big man's gun followed his movement like a snake, waiting to strike.

Teeth shone, white and even through the black, bushy beard. It might have passed for a smile if one could ignore the frosty glare in the mountain man's eyes.

Bo had no option but to stand and wait while the man took the rifle from his hands and emptied the shells in the dirt, then tossed back the empty gun.

Bo caught it in midair.

The man grinned again as he spoke. "Now you're not abou
to tell me you're huntin' out of season...are you? We don'
like strangers on our mountain...especially out of season."

Bo paled. The threat was all too real to ignore.

"Well, hell, if that's the way you wanna be, then I'n
gone," he muttered, and tried a few steps of retreat.

"You know, that might be the smartest thing you did al
day," the man said.

Bo nodded, then took a deep breath. Daring to turn his back
on the man with the gun, he began to walk away. Just wher
he thought he was in the clear, a shot rang out, and he fell to
the ground in mortal fear, fully expecting to be shattered by
pain. Seconds later, something landed with a heavy thud ir
the middle of his back.

His face buried in his arms, sucking dirt and old leaves into
his mouth, he began to shriek. "God have mercy! Don't kil
me! Don't kill me!"

The man cradled his rifle in the bend of his arm and ben
over Bo's body. "Now...whatever made you think you was
in danger?" he asked.

Bo held his breath as the weight suddenly disappeared from
his back. Shocked, he slowly lifted his head and then rolled
on his back, staring up in disbelief at the big gray squirrel the
man was holding by the tail. Blood dripped from a tiny hole
in the side of its neck, and Bo had a vision of his own head
in the same condition, and shuddered.

The man waved the squirrel across Bo's line of vision,
breaking the thick swirl of his beard with another white smile.

"Got myself a good one, don't you think?"

"Oh, God, I thought you was shootin' at me," Bo groaned.
He started to crawl to his feet when the man stuck the barrel
of the gun in the middle of Bo's fat belly. "Should I have
been?" the man asked quietly.

The tip of the barrel penetrated the fat just enough to hurt.
Bo was so scared, that had he been a cat, eight of his nine
lives would have been gone on the spot.

"No, hell, no!" Bo groaned. "Now are you gonna let me up, or what?"

"Be my guest," the man said, and waved his arm magnanimously.

Five minutes later, Bo burst out of the woods on the run, sighing with relief to see his truck right where he'd left it.

Considering his bulk, he moved with great speed, his rifle in one hand, his truck keys in another. But his relief turned sour when he noticed the tires. All four were as flat as his old lady's chest, and just as useless. Fury overwhelmed him. He couldn't believe he'd let himself be bullied by some mountain man. And now this. He spun, staring back at the woods.

"For two cents," he muttered, "I'd go back in there and..."

And then the sound of breaking twigs and rustling bushes made him pause. A picture of that squirrel's bloody head and limp body made him want to retch. All of his bravado disappeared as he pivoted. Dragging the empty rifle behind him, he made a wild dash for the truck, and moments later, started down the mountain. The truck steered like a man crawling on his belly, but Bo didn't care.

Putting distance between himself and this place was all he wanted to do.

The sound of flapping rubber and bare rims grinding against the gravel on the road could be heard long after Bo had disappeared. And finally, the rustling in the underbrush ceased.

A short time later, the sounds of the forest began to revive. Birds resumed flight, a blue jay scolded from an overhead branch, and a bobcat slipped quickly across the road and into the trees on the other side.

Pine Mountain was alive and well.

It was close to sundown when Wyatt turned off the main highway and onto the one-lane road leading to the Dixon farm. A soft breeze circled through the car from the half-open windows, stirring through Glory's hair and teasing at the skirt of her blue dress like a naughty child. She'd been asleep for the better part of an hour with her head in his lap, and without thinking, Wyatt braced her to keep her from tumbling as the car took the turn.

He drove without thought, his mind completely upon the revelation that he'd had this day. It didn't matter that a week ago, he hadn't even known she'd existed. In his heart, it felt as if he'd known her for years, even from another lifetime. The years stretched out before him in his mind, and he couldn't see a future without Glory in it. But when he drove past the burned-out remnants of her home and headed down the old road toward Granny's cabin, his gut twisted. Marriage was the last thing he should be worrying about. Right now, all that mattered was keeping her alive.

His foot was on the brake when half a dozen men began coming out of the trees. They walked with the air of men who knew their place on this earth—with their heads held proud, their shoulders back. Some were bearded, some clean-shaven. Some wore jeans, others bib overalls. Some were short, while others towered heads above the rest. It was what they had in common that made Wyatt afraid. To a man, they were armed, and from where he was sitting, they definitely looked dangerous.

"God," he said softly, and braked in reflex. He was at the point of wondering whether to fight or run when Glory awoke and stirred.

"Are we home?" She rubbed sleepily at her eyes, and it was only after Wyatt grabbed her by the arm that she realized something was wrong.

She looked up. "It's all right," she said. "They're neighbors." Before Wyatt could react, she got out of the car, beckoning for him to follow.

When Edward Lee came straggling out of the trees behind them, Wyatt began to relax.

Glory smiled and motioned Wyatt to her side.

"Hey, Mornin' Glory," Edward Lee said, and barged through the men as if they were not even there. He threw his arms around her neck, hugging her in a happy, childlike way. "Me and Daddy have been waitin' for you."

Glory nodded, and then watched as Edward Lee's father took him in hand. Although Liam Fowler was a very big man, his touch and words were slow and gentle.

"That's enough, Edward Lee. We came to talk business, remember?"

Edward Lee smiled, pleased to be a part of anything his father did. And then he remembered Wyatt and pointed.

"This is Wyatt Hatfield. Wyatt is my friend," he announced.

"That's good, son." Liam Fowler's teeth were white through the thickness of his beard, as he acknowledged Wyatt with a nod. "But we need to do what we came to do, remember?"

Wyatt tensed. "And that is?"

"We came to warn you," Liam said. "There's a stranger in the woods."

Glory swayed. The shock on her face was too new to hide. She turned and fell into Wyatt's arms with a muffled moan. "Oh, God, will this never end?"

"Don't, honey," Wyatt said softly, and wrapped his arms firmly around her, willing her to feel his strength, because it was all that he had to give.

Because she was too weary and heartsick to stand on her own, she let Wyatt hold her, trusting him to face what she could not.

The men shuffled their feet, looking everywhere but at each other, uncomfortable with her fear because they had no way to stop it.

"How do you know about the stranger?" Wyatt asked. "Did you see him? Did you talk to him?"

Several of the men chuckled and then they all looked to Liam Fowler to answer. Obviously they knew more than they were telling.

Liam smiled. "You could say that," he said. "Now, back

to the business of why we're here." He gave Wyatt a long, considering look. "My son says that you're a good man."

Edward Lee almost strutted with importance. It wasn't often that grown men took anything he said to heart.

Wyatt smiled at him, and then waited.

"He says that you came to take care of Glory," Liam persisted.

"Yes, sir, I did that," Wyatt said.

"We feel right ashamed that it took a stranger to do what we should have done on our own," Liam said. "Glory sort of belongs to us now, what with her family passin' and all."

Wyatt's arms tightened around Glory's shoulders. "No, sir. She doesn't belong to you. Not anymore."

When Glory suddenly stilled then shifted within his embrace, Wyatt tightened his hold and looked down, wondering if she would challenge him here in front of everyone. To his relief, he saw nothing but surprise and a little bit of shock, and knew that she hadn't been prepared for what he'd said.

The men came to attention, each gauging Wyatt with new interest as they heard and accepted the underlying message of his words. He'd laid claim to a woman most of them feared. More than one of them wondered if he knew what he was getting into, but as was their way, no one voiced a concern. Live and let live was a motto that had served them well for several centuries, and they had no reason to change their beliefs. Not even for a stranger.

Finally, it was Liam who broke the silence. "So, it's that way, then?"

Wyatt nodded.

Liam reached out, touching the crown of Glory's head in a gentle caress. "Glory, girl, are you of the same mind?"

Without looking at Wyatt, she turned, facing the men within the safety of Wyatt's arms. "Yes, sir, I suppose that I am."

So great was his joy that Wyatt wanted to grin. But this wasn't the time, and with these somber men judging his every move, it also wasn't the place. Like dark crows on a fence, they watched, unmoving, waiting for the big, bearded man to speak for them all. So he did.

"Then that's fine," Liam said, and offered Wyatt his hand. "Know that while you're on this land, within the boundaries of our hills, you will be safe. We guarantee that to you. But when you take her away from here, her safety is in your hands."

Aware of the solemnity of the moment, Glory stepped aside as Wyatt moved forward, taking the hand that was offered. And then each man passed, sealing their vow with a firm handshake and a long hard look. When it was over, they had new respect for the stranger who'd come into their midst, and Wyatt felt relief that he was no longer in this alone. And then he noticed that Edward Lee had stayed behind.

"Edward Lee, aren't you going to shake my hand, too?"

Wyatt's quiet voice broke the awkward silence, and his request made a friend of Liam Fowler for life. Wyatt had instinctively understood how the young man wanted so badly to belong.

He looked to his father, a poignant plea in his voice. "Daddy?"

Liam nodded, then took a long, deep breath as Edward Lee mimicked the seriousness of the occasion by offering Wyatt his hand without his usual smile. But the moment the handshake was over, he threw his arms around Wyatt's neck in a boisterous hug, and when he turned back around, the smile on his face was infectious. Everyone laughed. But not at him...with him. His joy was impossible to ignore.

"Then we'll be going," Liam said, and smiled gently at Glory. "Rest easy tonight, little girl. Your man just got himself some help."

"I don't know how to thank you," Wyatt said. "But be careful. Whoever is trying to harm Glory isn't giving up."

They nodded, then walked away. They were almost into the trees when Glory called out, then ran toward them. They paused and turned, waiting for whatever she had to say.

She stopped a few feet away, unaware that she'd stopped

in a halo of late-evening sun. The blue of her dress matched the color of her eyes, and the hair drifting around her face and down her back lifted and fell with the demands of the breeze blowing through the clearing. More than one man had the notion that he was standing before an angel. Her eyes were brimming, her lips shaking with unshed emotion. But her voice was steady as she said what was in her heart.

"God bless you," she whispered. "My daddy was proud to call you his friends. Now I understand why."

Moved beyond words, they took her praise in stoic silence, and when they were certain she was through, turned and walked away without answering. Glory watched until they were gone, and then she turned.

Wyatt was waiting, and the look in his eyes made her shake. He was her man. He'd laid a claim before her people that they did not take lightly. And from the expression on his face, neither did he.

Chapter 11

Glory's eyes widened as Wyatt started toward her. Later, she would remember thinking that he moved like a big cat, powerful, but full of grace. But now, there was nothing on her mind but the look on his face and the way that his eyes raked her body.

She held her breath, wondering if she was woman enough to hold this wild, footloose man. And when he was close enough to touch her, he combed his fingers through the hair on either side of her face, and lowered his head. When his mouth moved across her face and centered upon her lips, the breath she'd been holding slipped out on a sigh. The impact of the joining was unexpected. She wasn't prepared for the reverence in his touch, or the desperation with which he held her.

Wyatt was absorbed by her love, drawn into a force that he couldn't control. It took everything he had to remember that they were standing in plain sight of whoever cared to look, and that she was still bruised and sore from yesterday's scrape with death. He groaned, then lifted his head, and when she would have protested, he silenced her plea by pressing his forefinger across her lips.

"Glory, I'm sorry. I almost forgot that you…"

"Take me to bed. Make me forget all this horror. Give me something to remember besides fear. I'm so tired of being afraid."

Ah, God.

She slipped beneath his arm, the top of her head way below his chin, and then looked up. Her silver-blue stare widened apprehensively as she waited for his response.

At that moment, Wyatt wasn't so sure that he couldn't have walked on water.

"I love you, Glory Dixon."

"I know," she said softly. "It's why I asked."

Hand in hand, they entered the cabin, for once safe in the knowledge that someone was watching their backs. The lock clicked loudly within the silence of the old rooms, and then there was nothing to be heard but the ticking of Granny's clock on the mantel, and the heartbeats hammering in their ears.

Glory was the first to move. She slid her hands beneath her hair, tugging at a zipper that wouldn't give.

"Help me, Wyatt. I think my hair's caught."

And so am I, he thought, but never voiced his fear.

He thrust his hands beneath her gold strands, moving the heavy weight of her hair aside so he could see. His fingers shook as he unwound a strand from the metal tab. When it was free, he lifted the tab and pulled.

Slowly. Lower.

Revealing the delicate body that was so much a part of the woman he loved. Impulsively, he slid his hands beneath the fabric, circling her body and coming to rest upon the gentle thrust of her breasts. Glory sighed, then moaned, arching into his palms.

He shook, burning with the need to plunge deep within the sweetness of the woman in his hands, and yet he resisted. She wasn't ready. It wasn't time. She wanted to forget, and he hoped to hell he could remember what he was supposed to do, because every breath that he took was driving sanity further and further from his mind.

"Glory."

Her name was a whisper on his lips as she moved out of his grasp. When her dress fell at her feet in a pool of blue, leaving her with nothing on but a scrap of nylon that barely covered her hips, he started to shake.

Twice he tried to unbutton his shirt, and each time, his fingers kept slipping off the buttons.

"Oh, hell," he muttered, then yanked.

Buttons popped and rolled across the floor. Boots went one direction, his blue jeans another. Before Glory had time to think, he had her in his arms and was moving toward the bed with a distinct gleam in his eye.

They fell onto the quilt in a tangle of arms and legs as the last of their clothes hit the floor. At the last minute, Wyatt remembered protection, and scrambled for the drawer in the bedside table.

There was no time for slow, easy loving, or soft, whispered promises. The passion between them was about to ignite. Glory's hands were on his shoulders, urging him down when he moved between her legs. When he slid inside, her eyelids fluttered, and then she wrapped her arms around his neck and followed where he wanted to go.

Rocking with the rhythm of their bodies, moments became endless as that sweet fire began to build. It was the time when the feeling was so good that it felt like it could go on forever. And then urgency slipped into the act, honing nerves already at the point of breaking.

One minute Wyatt was still in control, and the next thing he knew, she was arching up to meet him and crying out his name. He looked down, saw himself reflected in the pupils of her eyes, and felt as if he were drowning. A faint look of surprise was etched across her face as shock wave after shock wave ebbed and flowed throughout her body. Caught in the undertow, Wyatt couldn't pull back, and then didn't want to. He spilled all he was in the sweet act of love.

For Glory, time ceased. The problems of the world outside were momentarily forgotten. There was nothing that mattered but the man in her arms, and the love in his eyes. Seconds later he collapsed, lying with his head upon her breasts, and his fists tangled tightly in her hair.

Replete from their loving, Glory reached out with a satisfied sigh, tracing the breadth of his shoulders and combing her fingers through his hair, letting the thick, black strands fall where they might. Just as the sun sank below the horizon, she felt him relax and remembered last night, and how he'd stood watch while she slept.

Sleep, my love, she thought.

"Am I?" Wyatt asked.

Glory smiled. He'd done it again. "Are you what?" she asked, knowing full well what he was angling for.

"Your love."

"What do you think?" she whispered.

He lifted his head, his eyes still black from burned-out passion. "I think I'm in heaven."

She grinned. "No, you're in my arms, and in Granny's bed."

He rolled, moving her from bottom to top. "Like I said… I'm in heaven."

Before Glory could settle into a comfortable spot, Wyatt's hands were doing things to her that, at the moment, she wouldn't have thought it possible to feel.

She gasped, then moved against his fingers in a tantalizing circle. "I don't know about heaven," she whispered, and then closed her eyes and bit her lower lip, savoring the tiny spikes of pleasure that he'd already started. "But if you stop what you're doing anytime soon, you'll be in trouble."

He laughed, then proved that he was man enough to finish what he had started.

Carter Foster stood at the window of his darkened house, peering through the curtains and cursing beneath his breath as the patrol car moved slowly past.

It wasn't the first time it had circled his neighborhood. In fact, it was a normal patrol for the officer on duty. But in Carter's mind, he saw the police searching for clues that would destroy his world. Guilt played strange tricks on a criminal's mind.

He let the curtain drop and began to pace, wondering if he should pack and run before they got on his trail. With every day that Glory Dixon lived, his chances of getting away with murder decreased. And as a man who'd made his living on the good side of the law, he knew exactly how deep his trouble was.

He moved room by room through his house, jumping at shadows that took on sinister forms. Sounds that he'd heard all his life suddenly had ominous qualities he'd never considered. And the bed that he and Betty Jo had shared was an impossible place to rest. He sneaked by the room every night on his way to the guest room, unable to look inside, afraid that Betty Jo's ghost would be sitting on the side of that bed with lipstick smeared across her face, and a torn dress riding up her white thighs.

"When this is over, I'll sell the house and move," he reminded himself. He had started down the hallway to get ready for bed when the phone rang.

Panicked by the unexpected sound, Carter flattened against the wall, and then cursed his stupidity when he realized it was nothing but the phone. He considered just letting it ring, and then knew that with the condition his life was in, he'd better take the call. Yet when he answered, he realized that, once again, he'd made the wrong decision. He should have let it ring.

"It's me," Bo growled.

"I can hear that," Carter sneered. "Now unless you've called to tell me that you've finished something you so obviously botched last night, I don't think we have a damn thing to discuss!"

"I called to tell you that you owe me four new tires," Bo shouted.

Carter rolled his eyes. "Unless you get your butt in gear, I'm not going to owe you anything," he shouted back.

"Look, this job is more involved than you led me to believe. I ruined four tires today saving my own hide from some crazy hillbilly. You're gonna pay, or I know someone who'd be interested in my side of the incidents that have been happening to one Miss Glory Dixon."

Carter went rigid with disbelief. This was the last damned straw! The imbecile was trying to blackmail him. He took a deep breath and then grinned. Marker's gorilla brain was no match for his courtroom skills.

"Well, now, I'd be real careful before I went running to the law," Carter sneered. "They'd have nothing on me, and you have a rap sheet that dates back to your youth. You're the one who got bitten by a dog, and I'm a respectable lawyer. If some hillbilly took after you, why would they want to blame me? It wasn't my face that man saw, it was yours. And…to top that off, you're the one who stole a car and tried to run someone down, in front of the chief of police, no less. Now, you can talk all you want, but there is nothing… absolutely nothing…that links me to you. Not a dollar. Not a piece of paper. Nothing!"

Bo's response sounded nervous enough. "There's got to be a reason you want that Dixon woman dead, and I have no reason at all to care one way or another. If I tell them what I—"

Carter was so angry, he was shaking, but it didn't deter him from ending their argument with a resounding blow. One that got Bo's attention all too painfully.

"You do what you're told!" Carter screamed. "That crazy witch could ruin me. But so help me God, if you talk, I'll make it my personal responsibility to see that you spend the rest of your life behind bars."

"Now, see here," Marker growled. "You can't—"

"Oh, yes, I can," Carter said. "Now. Either do what you were hired to do, or leave me the hell alone. Understand?"

Bo frowned, then slammed the phone back on the receiver. That had not gone exactly as planned.

"Now what?" he muttered.

He frowned, cursing both Carter and bad luck, and started up the street toward his house. Somewhere between now and morning, he had to find himself four new tires, or he'd never be able to finish the job. And, if he had to steal them, which was his first choice of procedure, he could hardly be rolling the damned things down the street. He needed another pair of hands and a good pickup truck. As he walked, he wondered if his old friend, Frankie Munroe, was still around.

Anders Conway rolled over and then sat up in bed. He didn't know what hurt worse, his conscience or his belly. Grumbling beneath his breath, he crawled out from beneath the covers and started through his house in search of some more antacids. One of these days he was going to have to change his eating habits…or his job.

Today he'd faced the consequences of the law officer he'd become. With one year left to retirement, he'd let the office and himself slip. In spite of Glory Dixon's farfetched claims about her psychic abilities, the fact still remained that someone was out to do her harm.

The stolen car that they'd recovered had been wiped clean of prints…all except for a partial that they'd found along the steering wheel column. They'd already eliminated the owner and any of his friends or family. It only stood to reason that it would belong to the thief. But it was going to take days, maybe weeks, to get back a report from the state office. During that time, Glory Dixon could be dead and buried.

He'd sent the bit of fabric along to a lab with the faint hope that something could be learned, although what they could possibly glean from a bit of denim cloth was impossible to guess.

He popped a couple of effervescent tablets into a glass of

water, waiting while they fizzed, and consoled himself with the fact that at least he was doing his job.

Minutes later, he crawled back into bed, more comfortable with the situation, and with his belly. On the verge of dreams, the memory of Carter Foster's hangdog face drifted through his subconscious. But he was too far gone to wonder why, and when morning came, he wouldn't remember that it had.

Miles away, in a cabin nestled deep in the piney woods above Larner's Mill, Wyatt slept, with Glory held fast in his arms. The fear that had kept him virtually sleepless for the past two days was almost gone.

They'd gone to bed secure in the knowledge that somewhere beyond the walls of this cabin, there were six mountain men who'd sworn to a vow that he knew they would keep. He'd looked at their faces. He'd seen the men for what they were. The steadfast honesty of their expressions was all that he'd needed to see. With their help, maybe…just maybe, there would be a way out of this situation after all.

It was the quiet peace of early morning that woke Wyatt up from a deep, dreamless sleep. Or so he thought until he turned to look at Glory's face and saw it twisted into a grimace of concern.

He'd never seen horror on a face deep in sleep, but he was seeing it now. And as he watched, he knew what must be happening. Somewhere within the rest that she'd sought, another person's nightmare was taking place and taking Glory with it.

Except for the day at the city dump when she'd had the vision of the body being disposed of, he'd never witnessed this happening. His heart rate began to accelerate with fear. He wondered if this was how she'd been when she'd come to his rescue, then wondered whose life was about to take a crooked turn.

Uncertain of how to behave, or what to do, he realized the matter was out of his hands when she suddenly jerked and sat straight up in bed, her eyes wide open and staring blindly at something other than the room in which she'd slept. Her eyes moved, as if along a page, watching a drama that only she could see. She moaned softly, wadding the sheet within her hands, rocking back and forth in a terrified manner.

Still. Everything was still. No wind. Not even a soft, easy breeze. Dark clouds hovered upon the early-morning horizon, hanging black and heavy, nearly dragging on the ground.

The outer walls of the white frame house were a stark contrast to the brewing weather. Fences ranged from barns to trees without an animal in sight.

And then everything exploded before her eyes, shattering the unearthly quiet by a loud, vicious roar. Trees bent low to the ground, and then came up by the roots, flying and twisting through the air like oversized arrows.

Windows imploded. Glass shattered inward, filling the air with deadly, glittering missiles of destruction. Everything that once was, was no more.

And then as quickly as it had come, it passed. Where there had been darkness, now there was light. The house was but a remnant of its former self. The limbs of a tree protruded through a window. Beneath their deadweight, a baby's bed lay crushed on the floor. And near the doorway, a clock lay on its side, the hands stopped at five minutes past seven.

Glory shuddered, then fell forward, her head upon her knees, her shoulders shaking as she pulled herself back to reality.

"Honey...are you all right?"

Wyatt's voice was a calm where the storm had been. She threw her arms around his neck, sobbing in near hysterics.

"The storm...I couldn't stop the storm."

Wyatt held her close, smoothing the tangled hair from her face and rubbing her back in a slow, soothing motion.

"There's no storm here, honey. Maybe it was just a bad dream."

Glory's eyes blazed as she lifted her head, pinning him with the force of her glare.

"Don't!" she sobbed. "Don't you doubt me, Wyatt! Not

now! I don't *ever* dream. Either I sleep. Or these…things come into my mind. I can't make them stop, and I can't make them go away.''

She rolled out of his grasp and out of the bed, desperate to see for herself what it looked like outside. Wyatt followed her frantic race for the door, grabbing for his gun as he ran.

Sunlight hit her head-on, kissing the frown on her face with a warm burst of heat, while an easy spring breeze lifted the tail of her nightgown and then flattened it against her legs.

"Oh, Lord," she muttered, and buried her face in her hands. "I don't understand. I saw the storm. I saw the…!" Her face lit up as she remembered. "What time is it?"

He looked back inside the house at Granny's mantel clock. "A little before eight. Why?"

Glory moaned, and began pacing the dewy grass in her bare feet. "This doesn't make sense. The clock had stopped at a little after seven. That time has already come and gone."

"Come here." He caught her by the arm, gently pulling her back inside the house. "Now sit down and tell me exactly what you saw. Maybe it was happening in another part of the country, and if it did, there's not a damn thing you can do to stop it, darlin'. You can't fix the world. I'm just sorry that you get pulled into its messes."

She went limp in his arms, and at his urging, curled up on the couch, tucking her bare feet beneath the tail of her gown to warm them. When she started talking, her voice was shaky and weak.

"It was so real. The house was white. And it's set on a hill right above a creek. There was an old two-story barn just below the house, and corrals and fences behind that stretched off into the woods."

Wyatt was in the act of making coffee when something she said made him pause. He turned, listening to her as she continued, the coffee forgotten.

"What else?" he urged.

She shrugged. "The sky. It was so black. And everything

was still…you know what I mean…like the world was holding its breath?''

He nodded, although the description gave him a chill.

''And then it just exploded…right before my eyes. There was a roar, and then trees were being ripped out of the ground, and the windows…'' She closed her eyes momentarily, trying to remember what had come next. Her lips were trembling when she looked up at him. ''And then it was all over. There was a tree through a window, and a baby bed beneath it. And there was a clock on the floor that had stopped at five minutes after seven.''

Wyatt shuddered. ''Damn, honey. That's got to be hell seeing things like that and knowing you have no control of the outcome.''

''Sometimes I do,'' she whispered. ''Remember you?''

His eyes turned dark. ''How could I forget?''

But the memory was too fresh to give up, and she thumped her knees with her fists in frustration.

''I just wish I'd recognized the place,'' she muttered. ''It was so pretty. There was a rooster weather vane on the roof of the house, and it had a wide porch across the front, and a big porch swing. I love porch swings.'' And then she smiled sadly. ''And there was the prettiest bunch of pansies growing in a tin tub beneath one of those old-fashioned water wells. The kind that you had to pump.''

Wyatt paled. He listened to what she said as the air left his lungs in one hard gush. Panic sent him flying across the room. He pulled her to her feet, unaware that he was almost shaking her.

''Oh, God! Oh, God! What time did you say that clock stopped?''

Glory went still. The shock on Wyatt's face was impossible to miss. ''Five minutes after seven,'' she said. ''Why? What's wrong?''

He started to pace, looking at the mantel clock, then comparing the time that she'd stated.

''Oh, no!'' He was at the point of despair when it dawned.

"Wait! We're in a different time zone. It's not too late." Before Glory could ask what was wrong, he was running toward the bedroom, muttering beneath his breath. "The phone! The phone! I've got to find that phone."

Seconds later, she was right behind him.

His fingers were shaking as he punched in the numbers, and then he groaned as he counted the rings. Twice he looked down at his watch on the bedside table, and each time, the fear that had sent him running to call increased a thousand-fold.

And then Lane's sleepy voice echoed in his ear, and Wyatt started shouting for them to get out of the house.

"Wyatt? What the hell's wrong with you?" Lane muttered, trying to come awake. He and Toni had spent sleepless hours last night with a sick baby, and when they'd finally gotten her earache under control and her back to sleep, they had dropped into bed like zombies.

"You've got to get out of the house!" Wyatt shouted. "There's a storm coming. You have less than five minutes to get everyone into the cellar. For God's sake, don't ask me why! Just do it!"

Without question, Lane rolled out of bed, grabbing at his jeans as he nudged Toni awake.

"Was it Glory?" was all that he asked.

"Yes," Wyatt shouted. "Now run!"

The line went dead in Wyatt's ear, and he dropped onto the side of the bed, shaking from head to toe as tears shimmered across his eyes. When Glory reached out, he caught her hand, holding it to his mouth, kissing her palm, then her wrist, then pulling her down onto his lap.

"It was my home that you saw," he whispered. "I'm glad you liked it. It was where I grew up."

Glory closed her eyes against the pain in his voice. "I'm sorry. I'm so, so sorry." She wrapped her arms around his neck and held him, giving him comfort in the only way she knew how.

Minutes passed, and then a half hour, and then an hour,

during which time Glory tried to get him to eat, then gave up hoping he might talk. Wyatt sat, staring at the floor, with his hand no more than inches from a phone that wouldn't ring.

"Oh, God," he finally whispered. "What if I was too late?"

"Now you know how it feels to hold life and death in the palm of your hand," she said quietly. "I live with this every day of my life. Can you live with it, as well?"

He didn't answer, and she didn't expect one. He'd wanted to know all there was to know about her. And her heart was breaking as she realized that this might be too much to accept.

As Granny Dixon's mantel clock chimed, signaling the hour, Wyatt looked down at his watch. It was ten o'clock—nine o'clock for Toni and Lane. If they had survived, he would have heard by now…wouldn't he? He thought about calling his brother, Justin, and then couldn't remember the number. It was an excuse and he knew it. A simple call to Information would have solved that problem. But it also might have given him a truth he didn't want to face.

Seconds after he'd discarded the thought, the phone finally rang, startling them both to the point that neither wanted to answer the call. Glory held her breath and closed her eyes, saying a prayer as Wyatt picked up the phone.

"Hello?"

Lane's voice sounded weary and rough, but when it reverberated soundly in Wyatt's ear, he went weak with relief.

"It's me," Lane said.

"Thank God," Wyatt groaned. "I didn't think you would ever call. Are Toni and Joy all right? Did you—"

Lane interrupted. "I want to talk to Glory."

Wyatt handed her the phone.

"Hello?"

Lane swallowed a lump in his throat as he tried to put into words what he was feeling.

"How do I say thank-you for the only things that make my life worth living?" he asked quietly.

Glory started to smile. This must mean they were safe.

"I will never—and I mean, never—doubt a word you say to me again. Five minutes later and we would have been dead. All of us. A tree fell on Joy's crib. It smashed the—"

"I know," Glory said softly.

Lane paused, wiped a hand across his face and then smiled. "That's right, you do, don't you, girl?" He paused, then wiped a shaky hand across his face. "There's someone else who wants to talk to you." He handed the phone to Toni.

"Is this Glory?"

Glory's eyes widened. She put her hand over the phone and whispered urgently to Wyatt. "I think it's your sister."

He smiled. "So tell her hello."

Glory dropped onto the bed beside Wyatt, anxiously twisting a lock of her hair around her finger. Except for Lane, this would be her first connection with any of his people.

"Yes, this is Glory."

Toni caught her breath on a sob. "I'm Wyatt's sister, Toni. You saved our lives, you know." And then she started to cry, softly but steadily. "Thank-you is little to say for the gift that you gave me today, but I do thank you, more than you will ever know. If you knew what I went through to get this man and our child, you would understand what it means to me to know that they're safe."

A shy smile of delight spread across Glory's face as she caught Wyatt watching her. "You're very welcome," she said. "But it wasn't all me. Wyatt is the one who put two and two together. He's the one who made the call."

Toni sighed as exhaustion threatened to claim her. In another room, she could hear Joy as she started to fuss, and Justin's wife as she tried to console her. The call had to be short. With a trembling voice, she continued.

"When he comes back this way, I'd love for you to come with him. I've always wanted to hug an earthbound angel. Now put that brother of mine on, I need to tell him thank-you, too."

Glory handed Wyatt the phone.

"Sis?"

At the sound of his voice, tears sprang again. "Thank you, big brother."

"You're welcome, honey," he said, and although he hated to ask, he needed to know. "Is the house gone?"

"No. It will take a lot of work, but it can be repaired."

"That's good," Wyatt said. "Are you at Justin's?"

She rolled her eyes as Joy's cries became louder. "Yes, but not for any longer than necessary. If you need Lane, call him here, at least for the remainder of the week. As soon as we get the glass out of the house and windows back in, we'll be able to do the bulk of the repairs in residence."

Wyatt grinned. He knew what a headache it would be for two separate families to be living under one roof, especially when two of the people were as hardheaded as Toni and Justin.

"Wyatt?"

"Yes, honey?"

"Don't you hurt that girl."

Glory saw the shock on his face and heard the pain in his voice, but she didn't know why.

"Why the hell would you say that to me?" he asked.

"Because I know you. You've got a kite for a compass. You go where the wind blows, and when her troubles are over, you'll be long gone again. Don't you leave her behind with a broken heart. If I find out that you have, I don't think I'll ever forgive you."

"That was never my intention," he muttered. "And I can't thank you enough for the vote of confidence."

"You're welcome, and I love you," Toni said. "Call if you need us."

The phone went dead in his ear.

"What's wrong?" Glory asked, aware that Wyatt was more than a little out of sorts.

He tossed the phone on the bed beside them, almost afraid to look at her for fear that she'd see the truth on his face.

"Nothing. She's just being her usual bossy self. She gave me a warning...and a little advice."

"And that was?"

He shrugged, then looked up as a reluctant grin spread across his face. He took her into his arms and dropped backward onto the bed.

"Something about hanging my sorry butt from the nearest tree if I didn't treat you right."

Glory laughed, and wrapped her arms around his neck. "I like the way that woman thinks."

Chapter 12

Just after noon, the sound of a car could be heard coming down the road to Granny's cabin. Wyatt watched from his seat on the steps as a black-and-white cruiser pulled to a stop only yards from the porch. When Anders Conway got out of the car, Wyatt couldn't resist a small dig.

"Are you lost?"

Conway had to grin. From the first time they'd met, he hadn't been as accommodating as he should have been, and yet this big, dark-eyed man didn't seem to hold a grudge.

"You might think so, wouldn't you?"

Wyatt motioned toward the single cane chair against the wall. "Have a seat."

Anders shook his head. "Maybe some other time. I just came out to update you on the investigation."

Wyatt made no effort to hide his surprise. "You mean there really is one?"

Conway frowned. He had that coming. "Yeah, there really is. And I came out to tell you that, no matter what I believe about Glory Dixon's *powers,* I do believe that someone is out to do her harm." And then he scratched his head and took the chair that was offered, in spite of his earlier refusal. "The thing is, none of this makes sense. Why would anyone even *want* to hurt her? Hell, half the town is afraid of her, and the other half thinks she's a little bit..."

"Nuts?"

Both men looked startled as Glory came out of the cabin. Embarrassed at being overheard, Conway jumped up from his seat and yanked off his hat as a flush colored his skin.

"Now, Miss Dixon, I'm real sorry you heard that, and I don't mean anything personal by it," Conway said. "I was just stating a fact."

It wasn't anything she hadn't heard a hundred times before, and it wasn't what interested her. "What was that you were saying about an investigation?" she asked.

Conway relaxed, apparently thankful that the conversation had changed.

"We found a partial fingerprint on the car that tried to run you down. Course it'll take a while for any results to come back, and you understand if the fellow that left it had no priors, then we have no way of identifying him, don't you?"

She nodded.

"And for what it's worth, I sent that scrap of fabric that you gave me off to the crime lab at the capitol. Don't think we'll learn much, but we'll at least have tried, right?"

He hitched at his gun belt, and studied a knot on the plank beneath his feet. "What I came out to say is, I'm sorry. When you came to me for help, I let you down, and I can promise it won't happen again."

When the chief offered his hand, Glory didn't hesitate. And when he shook it firmly, in a small, but significant way, she felt vindicated.

"Thank you for coming," she said. "I appreciate it more than you know."

He nodded. "So, that's it, then," he said. "I suppose I'd better be getting back into town. It doesn't do to leave my two deputies alone for long. On occasion, they get ticket happy, and then I've got some angry townsfolk wondering why they could make a U-turn on Main Street one day, and then get fined for it the next. Besides that, we had ourselves a burglary last night. Someone kicked in the back door to Henley's Garage and Filling Station, waltzed in and helped themselves to a whole set of tires. From what we can tell, the thieves brought their own rims and mounted 'em right on the spot.''

Conway shook his head as he started toward the cruiser. ''I'll tell you, crooks these days either have more guts or less brains than they used to. And finding any fingerprints as evidence in that grease pit is impossible. Nearly everyone in town is in and out of there. Ain't no way to figure out who left what or when they left it, and old man Henley's fit to be tied. See you around,'' he said, and then left.

Glory turned to Wyatt, a smile hovering on her lips as Conway drove away.

''I didn't think this day would ever come,'' she said.

''What day?''

''The day when someone other than my family would bother to believe me.''

He cradled her in his arms, hugging her to him. ''After this morning, how can you forget the fifty-odd members of my immediate family who think you hung the moon?'' He tilted her chin, then kissed the tip of her nose when she wrinkled it in dismay.

''Fifty?''

He grinned. ''I underestimated on purpose so I wouldn't scare you off.''

Glory shifted within his embrace. ''As long as I have you, I'm not scared of a living thing,'' she whispered.

Joy filled him as he held her. ''Lady, you take my breath away.''

A light breeze teased at her hair, lifting, then settling long, shiny strands across his hands. Unable to resist their offer, Wyatt combed his fingers through the lengths, entranced by the sunlight caught in the depths.

"Wyatt, there's something I want to talk to you about."

Play ceased immediately. The tone of her voice was serious, as was the look in her eyes.

"Then tell me."

She moved out of his arms, then took him by the hand and started walking toward the shade trees above the creek at the back of the cabin.

Wyatt went where she led, aware that when she was ready, she would start talking. As they reached the shade, Glory dropped down onto a cool, mossy rock, and then patted the ground beside it, indicating that Wyatt join her, which he did.

As she sorted out her thoughts, she fiddled with her hair. It was sticking to her neck and in spite of the shade, hot against her shoulders. Absently, she pulled it over her shoulders, then using her fingers for a comb, separated it into three parts, and began to braid.

"I have a theory," she said, as she fastened the end of the braid with a band from her pocket. "I don't know how to explain it, but I think that the body that was buried at the dump is somehow connected to what's happening to me."

A shiver of warning niggled at Wyatt's instinct for self-preservation as he gave Glory a startled look. "I don't like this," he said.

She shrugged, then stared pensively down the bank of the creek to the tiny stream of water that continually flowed. "I don't either. But nothing else makes sense."

"What made you think like that?" he asked.

"It was something that Chief Conway said, about people being afraid of me." She turned toward Wyatt, pinning him with that clear blue stare. "What if someone thought my gift was like some, uh, I don't know…a witch's crystal ball, maybe? What if someone did something bad…really bad, and they thought that all I had to do was look at them and I'd know it?"

Wyatt's heart jumped, then settled. "You mean…something bad like committing a murder and dumping a body?"

She nodded.

His eyes narrowed thoughtfully as he considered what she'd just said. The more he thought about it, the more it made sense.

"It *would* explain why, wouldn't it?"

"It's about the only thing that does," she said. And then her chin quivered.

"Come here," he said softly, and she crawled off the rock and into his lap, settling between his outstretched legs and resting her back against the breadth of his chest. When he pulled her close, surrounding her with his arms and nuzzling his chin at the top of her head, she savored the security that came from being encompassed by the man who'd stolen her heart.

For a time, the outside world ceased to exist. For Glory and Wyatt, there was nothing but them, and the sound of the breeze rustling through the leaves, birdcalls coming from the green canopy over their heads, the ripple of the water in the creek below and the raucous complaint of a squirrel high up in a tree across the creek.

Bo Marker was back in business. He had shells for his rifle, wheels on his truck and a renewed interest in finishing the job he'd promised Carter Foster he would do. Now he didn't just *want* the money Carter had promised, he *needed* it to pay Frankie for helping him last night with the heist.

But Bo wasn't a complete fool. He had no intention of going anywhere near that Dixon farm again. He still had nightmares about that man who'd run him off, and hoped he never saw him again.

As he drove along the back roads, he kept his eye out for a good place to conceal himself and his truck. A location that would be close to the main road that led down from the mountain. That Dixon woman and her man couldn't stay up there forever. They'd have to come down sometime, if for no other reason than to get food. When they did, he'd be waiting. This time, he'd make sure that there would be no Kentucky bigfoot with a gun at his back when he took aim.

Pleased with his plan, Bo proceeded to search the roads, while Carter Foster lived each hour sinking deeper and deeper in a hell of his own making.

Carter was running. His belly bounced with each lurch of his stride, and his heart was hammering so hard against his rib cage that he feared he was going to die on the spot. With every step, the sound of his shoes slapping against the old tile floor of the courthouse echoed sharply within the high, domed ceilings.

He burst into the courtroom just as the judge was about to raise his gavel.

"I'm sorry I'm late, Your Honor. May it please the court, I have filed an injunction against the company that's suing my client."

The judge leaned over the desk, pinning Carter with a hard, frosty glare.

"Counselor…this is the third time you've been tardy in my court this week. Once more, and I'll hold you in contempt."

Carter paled. "Yes, sir. I'm sorry, sir."

And so the morning passed.

When they recessed for the day, it was nearly three o'clock. Carter's belly was growling with hunger. He'd missed breakfast, and because of his earlier dereliction, had been forced to skip lunch. Right now, he wouldn't care if his client got drawn and quartered, the only thing on his mind was food.

He came out of the courthouse, again on the run. He tossed his briefcase into his car, and was about to get in when he heard someone calling his name. With a muffled curse, he turned, and then felt all the blood drain from his face. The chief of police was walking toward him from across the street.

"Hey there, Foster," Conway said, and thumped him lightly on the back in a manly greeting.

Carter managed a smile. "Chief, I haven't seen you in a while. I guess since the last time we were in court together, right?"

Conway nodded, while gauging Foster's condition. His

supposition the other day had been right on target. Foster looked like he'd been pulled backward through a downspout. He needed a haircut. His clothes looked as if he'd slept in them, and there were bags beneath his eyes big enough to haul laundry.

"Say, I've been meaning to speak to you," Conway said.

"Oh? About what?" Carter's heart jerked so sharply that he feared he might die on the spot.

"Your wife and all," Conway said, a little uncertain how one went about commiserating with a fellow who'd just been dumped.

"What about my wife?" Carter asked, as his voice rose three octaves.

Conway shrugged and wished he'd never started this conversation. Old Foster wasn't taking this any better than he'd hoped.

"Well, you know, she's gone, and I heard that—"

"She ran off, you know," Carter interrupted. "She's been threatening to do it for years but I never believed her. I guess a man should believe his wife every so often. It might prevent problems later on, don't you think?"

The moment he said it, he gritted his teeth, wishing he had the good sense not to ramble, but when he got nervous, he always talked too much.

"I suppose you're right," Conway said. "Anyway, I just wanted to tell you I'm real sorry."

Carter sighed and even managed a smile. "Thanks. That's real nice of you, Chief."

Conway nodded, and then as Carter was about to get in his car, he asked, "Have you heard from her?"

From the look on Carter's face, the chief thought he was about to have a heart attack. Carter's mouth was working, but no words were coming out. Finally, he cleared his throat, and managed a small, shaky giggle.

"Actually, I have," he said. "I'm about to become the recipient of a Mexican divorce. Isn't that a laugh? Me a law-

yer, and she felt the need to go to Mexico to have her legal
work done.''

Conway nodded, although he couldn't see much humor in
the situation. And then he shrugged. He supposed it was every
man's right to deal with hardship in his own way.

''Well, you take care now,'' Conway said. ''I imagine I'll
be seeing you real soon.''

Carter paled. ''Why?''

''Why…in court, buddy. In court.''

Carter imagined all kinds of insinuations that were spelling
out his doom, and in a fit of panic, fell into his car and drove
off in a hurry, leaving behind a cloud of exhaust smoke and
the sounds of tires shredding on pavement.

The chief shook his head, and ambled on into the courthouse, thanking his lucky stars that he'd been the one who'd
done the divorcing all those years ago. It must play hell with
an ego when one was the dumpee.

It wasn't until later on in the afternoon that he received a
phone call that set him to thinking along a completely different line.

''Chief, line two for you,'' the dispatcher shouted, and
Conway rolled his eyes and picked up the phone. One of these
days they were going to have to invest in some sort of inter-
com. Yelling at each other from room to room didn't seem
professional.

''Chief Conway,'' he muttered, shifting files on his desk as
he searched for clean paper and pen.

''Conway, this is Lane Monday. I thought I'd call and see
how the Dixon investigation is going.''

Conway was pleased to be able to count off the number of
things that he'd done since last they'd talked. And when the
marshal seemed satisfied, it pleased him even more.

''That's good,'' Lane said. ''And it's one of the reasons I
called. I had fully intended to come back that way within a
day or two, but I've had a family emergency and a slight
change of plans.''

Conway frowned. "Nothing bad, I hope."

"No, and it's thanks to Glory Dixon," he muttered, thinking of the chaos back at their home, and then of Toni and Joy, and considered himself a fortunate man.

"How's that?" Conway said.

"All I can tell you is she knew about the tornado that hit our house this morning, even before it hit. If Wyatt hadn't called us in a panic, screaming for us to get out of the house, we wouldn't have made it to the cellar in time. I don't know how Toni and I might have fared, but a tree came through the window and crushed our baby's bed. If she'd been in it…"

He couldn't even finish the story.

"Well, I'll be damned," Conway said, and shuddered from the images the story provoked.

Unwilling to dwell on the horror still fresh in his mind, Lane quickly changed gears.

"That's not why I'm calling," he said. "It's with regards to the missing-person factor in Glory's story about the woman in the dump."

Conway fiddled with his pen, and wondered if he should admit to the marshal that he'd given that story little thought. Remembering Monday's earlier anger, he decided not.

"Yes, what do you have?" he asked.

"Well, you know how you said you had no reports of missing persons?"

"Yeah, go on," Conway said.

"I checked with the FBI. In my book, they're the experts when it comes to kidnappings and missing persons. The man I was talking to suggested that sometimes a person is actually missing for weeks, sometimes even months before it's discovered. Usually because a family member, or the community, believes them to be on a legitimate trip somewhere.

"He said they had a case once where a wife whose husband was in the oil business claimed that he'd made an unscheduled trip to South America and was then killed in a plane crash over there. Imagine their surprise when what was left of him

surfaced months later in a fisherman's net off the coast of th
Carolinas.''

"Ooh, hell," Conway said. The image was startling, to sa
the least.

"Anyway, my point is, you might keep that in mind as yo
work the case."

"Yeah, right, and thanks," Conway muttered, and then dis
connected.

He leaned back in his chair, propped his feet on the des
and locked his hands behind his neck, thinking as he did abou
what Monday just said. How did coincidence factor into
warning of impending danger? And how did...?

His feet hit the floor as his hands slapped the desk.

"Son of a..."

He jumped to his feet and stepped outside, staring acros
the street at the sign on Carter Foster's office.

Out To Lunch.

For a man who was supposed to be mourning the loss of
wife, he sure hadn't lost his appetite. "I wonder?" he mut
tered, then frowned, pivoted on his heel and stalked back int
his office.

"Hey!" he shouted.

A deputy came running.

"I want you to check the bus station, the ticket counters ir
every airport within driving distance, and anyplace else you
can think of that provides transportation."

"Yes, sir," the deputy said. "What am I checking for?"

Conway tapped the deputy on the shirt, lowering his voice
in a confidential manner. "I want you to find me a paper trail
I want to know how and from where Betty Jo Foster left town
and if possible, who with. And I don't want to walk out of
here this evening and find out that everyone in town knows
what you're doing."

The deputy's eyes widened.

"What I'm saying is...do your job and keep your trap
shut," Conway growled.

"Yes, sir," he said, and out the door he went.

* * *

Bo woke himself up when he snorted. The sound was so startling that he grabbed for his gun before he came to enough to realize that it was himself that he had heard. His legs were stiff, his butt was numb, and his belly was pushing uncomfortably against the steering wheel of his pickup truck. He yawned, then stretched as he felt nature call.

Satisfied that from where he had parked, he was perfectly concealed from the road, he opened the pickup door and then scooted out of the seat, leaving the door open for privacy's sake as he did what he needed to do. Groaning beneath his breath as his legs protested his weight, he went about his business.

At that minute, a car came flying around a corner and then headed back up the hill. Confident that he was safe from being seen, he turned to look.

His heart jerked as he cursed. In a panic, he grabbed for his rifle, forgetting that he'd been using that hand for something else. To his dismay, he was too late to take aim, and found himself watching the taillights of Wyatt Hatfield's car as it disappeared over the hill.

Disgusted with his bad luck, he kicked at the dirt. Now there was no telling how long it would be before they'd come back.

Wyatt was carrying in groceries while Glory, at his insistence, had gone to her bed to lie down. Ever since she'd had the vision about the storm, she'd had a dull, niggling headache. It wasn't uncommon for such a thing to happen, but this time, she hadn't been able to shake the feeling of malaise.

Her head had barely hit the pillow when he came into the room with a glass of water and a couple of pills in his hand.

"Here, honey," he said. "See if these will help."

Gratefully, she accepted the water and the pills and swallowed them in one quick gulp. She set the glass on the table, and then lay back down on the bed.

"Thank you for taking care of me," she said.

Wyatt leaned over and softly kissed her cheek. "It's my

pleasure," he whispered. "Now see if you can get som
sleep."

She frowned. "I don't want to sleep. It's too late in th
day. If I sleep now, then I'll never get to sleep tonight."

A cocky grin slid across his mouth. "Oh, that's okay," h
said. "I can think of a few other things we might do instead.

In spite of her pain, she laughed. And at his insistenc
rolled over and closed her eyes. *I do love the way his min
works,* she thought.

"To heck with my mind, how about the rest of me?" h
asked, and left her grinning.

In spite of Glory's determination not to sleep, she quickl
succumbed, and she was still dozing when Wyatt wandere
outside to get some air. It was hard to keep his mind occupie
with anything but Glory's safety, but he knew that he neede
to take a break from the tension under which they'd bee
living.

For a few minutes, he wandered around the immediate vi
cinity of the cabin, but he was too cautious to go far. For lac
of anything better to do, he picked up a stick, headed back t
the porch steps and then began to whittle. The activity ha
nothing to do with creativity. It was a thing to pass the time

He had a good accumulation of wood chips going when h
heard someone coming through the brush. For the first tim
since his arrival, he looked up with interest, not fear. Whe
Edward Lee came ambling out of the trees, Wyatt stood up.

"Ma said I could bring you some cookies." He hande
Wyatt the sack before adding, "They're my favorite kind."

Wyatt grinned, then opened the sack. "Would you lik
some?"

Edward Lee looked back over his shoulder. His father wa
right behind him, walking with the ease of a man who's a
peace with himself, and comfortable with the presence of th
rifle he had slung on his shoulder.

"Daddy, Wyatt says I can have some of his cookies."

Liam Fowler grinned. "Then I suppose you'd better hav
some, son."

A wide smile spread across Edward Lee's face as he thrust his hand into the sack and came up with two cookies, one for each hand, then set about eating them.

"Had yourself any more trouble?" Liam asked.

Wyatt shook his head. "No, and I suspect that's thanks to you and your friends."

Liam nodded and absently stroked his beard, rearranging the thick, black curls without care for appearance.

"What puzzles me is why Glory is suffering with this," he said.

"She has a theory," Wyatt said. "It came from something that Anders Conway said. He said that a lot of people are afraid of her."

Liam nodded. "That's true. It's a shame, but it's a fact. Lots of people fear what they don't understand."

"Are you afraid of her?" Wyatt asked.

Liam smiled, then looked down at his son. "No more than I'm afraid of Edward Lee. So, what's she getting at, anyway?"

"Not too long after I arrived, she had a vision. She *saw* someone hiding evidence of a terrible crime. But she only saw it in her mind. She believes that whoever committed this crime is afraid that, because of her gift, she will be able to point the finger at him, so to speak. And that he's trying to get rid of her to keep his secret safe."

Liam frowned. "It sounds ugly, but it makes a lot of sense. I've known that girl since the day she was born. Rafe Dixon was one of my best friends. I've seen grown men say prayers when she crosses their paths, just because she has the sight."

Wyatt shook his head in disbelief.

With cookies gone, Edward Lee's attention wandered. "Wyatt, where's my Mornin' Glory?" he asked, interrupting the seriousness of their conversation.

"She's taking a nap." As soon as he said it, he sympathized with the disappointment on the young man's face.

And then the door behind him suddenly opened, and Edward Lee bounded to his feet.

"Mornin' Glory! You woke up!" Delight was rich on his face as he threw his arms around her neck, hugging and grinning broadly as she greeted him with a kiss on the cheek.

"I thought I heard voices," she said, smiling easily at Liam and his son.

"Ma sent cookies," Edward Lee said.

Wyatt hid a grin. He could see where this was going and handed Glory the sack.

"They're my favorites," Edward Lee reminded her.

Glory laughed. "How many have you already had?"

"Only two," he said.

"Then maybe you could have two more?"

Liam laughed aloud at his boy's ingenious method of begging.

"Don't eat them all, boy!" he prodded. "Ma's got a whole cookie jar full saved for you at home."

Edward Lee nodded and chewed, unable to answer for the cookie in his mouth.

"Would you like to come inside?" Glory asked. "I could make a pot of coffee."

Liam smiled, and brushed his hand against the side of her cheek in a gentle, but testing gesture.

"No, thank you, girl. I just stopped by to say hello. We'd best be gettin' on home before my boy eats all of your food." And then he cast a long approving glance at Wyatt before tipping his hat to them both.

"You be careful now, you hear?"

Wyatt nodded. "Same to you, friend. Same to you."

When they were gone, Glory waited for Wyatt to say something, anything, to break the tension of the look he was giving her. But when he remained silent, she took the initiative.

"What?" she asked.

"I told Liam about your theory."

Her face lost all expression. She wouldn't allow herself to care if Edward Lee's father doubted her.

"So?" she asked.

"He said it made sense."

The tension in her body slowly disappeared as she dropped down to the porch steps and dug in the sack for a cookie.

"Want one?" she asked, and offered it to Wyatt.

He shook his head, then sat down beside her, slinging an arm across her shoulders.

"What I want is for you to be safe and happy. What I don't know is how to make it happen. This waiting is driving me insane."

She nodded in agreement, thoughtfully munching the cookie, savoring the spicy taste of cinnamon, oatmeal and raisin. When she was through, she brushed her hands on the sides of her jeans and then studied the toes of her shoes.

Wyatt could tell there was something on her mind, but he didn't know whether to ask, or wait for her to say it in her own time. Finally, impatience got the better of him and he tugged at her braid to get her attention.

"So are you going to say what's on your mind, or are you going to leave me hanging?" he asked.

"I think I should go back to the dump."

Wyatt flinched. He didn't like to think of what she'd endured before. Putting herself through torment again seemed more punishment than sense.

"But why, honey? You know what it did to you the first time."

She sighed, then leaned her head against his chest, relishing the comfort of his arms as he pulled her closer.

"Because if I'm right about why someone wants to harm me, then what happened there impacts my safety. When it happened before, I was so shocked by the horror that I pulled out of the vision before it had time to play out." Her voice deepened in dejection. "I don't even know, if we go back, that it *will* happen again, but if it does, maybe I will see something that will give us a face...or a name. As Chief Conway says, something solid to go on."

"I don't like it...but I'll take you."

She went limp in his arms. "Thank you, Wyatt. Thank you."

He frowned. "Don't thank me yet," he warned. "This mess isn't over."

Chapter 13

Wyatt was slipping the gun in the back of his jeans as Glory came out of the bedroom. He noticed her look of fear before she had time to hide it.

Watching him arm himself to protect her was a shock. She fiddled with the ends of her braid in embarrassment, unnecessarily tucked at the pink T-shirt already in place beneath the waistband of her jeans.

"It'll be all right," he promised, as he went to her side. "I won't take my eyes off you for a second."

"I know that." She let him hold her, relaxing against his chest, and focusing on the constant and steady beat of his heart. "It's just that the sight of that gun reminds me that I'm no longer safe."

He tilted her chin until she was forced to meet his gaze. "You say the word, and this trip to the dump is off."

Dread of what lay ahead was overwhelming, but she was firmly convinced that if her life was ever to get back to normal, it hinged upon finding the identity of the man who'd dumped that woman's body in with the garbage from Larner's Mill.

"No. I want this to be over with."

He nodded. "Then let's get started. The sooner we get there..."

He left the rest of the phrase undone as they started outside.

Glory paused in the doorway, allowing herself one last look at the inside of Granny's cabin, absorbing the familiarity of its simple decor. The old wooden floors. The papered and painted walls, peeling and faded. The pictures and knick-knacks that Faith Dixon had accumulated over her ninety-one years.

Wyatt put his hand on Glory's shoulder. When she turned, there were tears shimmering across the surface of her eyes. Her pain broke his heart.

"We'll be back, sweetheart. I swear."

Glory lifted her chin, then straightened her shoulders and nodded.

"I knew that," she said softly. "I just needed to remember my people."

There was nothing else to say as he locked the door behind her. Moments later, they were in the car and on their way down the road. When they passed the site where her home once stood, she frowned at the remaining rubble.

"This place is a mess," she muttered.

"It will get better," Wyatt said. "One of these days, every-thing will be better."

Glory sighed, then made herself relax. *This, too, shall pass.*

Wyatt heard her thought and had to restrain a shudder. He hoped to God that he wasn't destined to be part of her past. He couldn't imagine a future...his future...without Glory in it.

Bo Marker sat in the midst of the ruins of a late-night run for food that he'd made to a local convenience store. Potato chip crumbs were caught in the fabric of the truck seat, as well as hanging on the front of his shirt and jeans, leaving grease stains wherever they clung. An empty box that once held half a dozen chocolate cupcakes was on the floorboard, and the wadded wrappers from two deli sandwiches lay on the ground where he'd tossed them out the window. An empty liter of soda was on the ground beside them, and a half-empty bottle of the same was tucked safely between his backside and the butt of his gun.

His eyes were red-rimmed; his face itched from a three-day growth of whiskers. But he was determined that this time, he would not miss his chance. So when he heard the familiar sound of a car coming down the mountain, his pulse accelerated. If it was them, he was going to be ready.

He lifted the deer rifle from the seat beside him, angling it until it was pointing out the window. Adjusting the telescopic sight until the cross hairs were in perfect alignment with a tree on the opposite side of the road, he drew a deep breath and took aim at the peak of the hill down which they would come. And when the car topped the hill and started down, he squirmed with pleasure. It was them!

"All right!" he muttered. "Now it's my turn."

The speed at which they were traveling allowed him little time for error. He squinted, adjusting the scope as he followed the car's descent. Now the cross hairs were in alignment with the middle of the driver's face. The image he had was perfect, right down to the scar on the big man's face. And then he swung the barrel a few inches to the left, firmly fixing upon the woman in the seat beside the driver.

The nearer they came, the more certain he was that, in seconds, it would be over. His finger was firm upon the trigger, his breathing slow and even. He was counting his money as he squeezed.

When the car came even with his location, he was still scrambling to find the safety he'd forgotten to release. And when the car passed the trees behind which he'd hidden his truck, and then disappeared around the curve in the road beyond, he was cursing at the top of his voice and hammering his rifle against the door in unfettered fury.

"By God, you won't get away from me this time," he
screamed.

He started his engine, gunning it until blue smoke boiled
from the rear exhaust. When he launched himself from the
trees and onto the road, he left a wake of overrun bushes and
broken limbs behind him.

Potato chips flew, while discarded paper scooted from one
side of the floorboard to the other as he followed Wyatt
around the curve. The partial bottle of soda tipped over and
began to leak upon the seat. Bo couldn't have cared less. He
was on a mission, and this time, there would be no mistakes.

Their ride down the mountain had been silent. Wyatt was
concentrating on what lay ahead, and Glory was locked in the
past, trying to remember everything she could of what she'd
seen before. But when she saw the sign indicating the way to
the dump, she tensed.

Wyatt sensed her anxiety, and when he slowed to take the
turn, he gave her a quick, sidelong glance. Her face was pale,
and her hands were clenched in fists.

"Honey, don't do this to yourself," he begged. "Either
relax and let whatever comes, come, or just stop it all now."

"It's too late to stop," she said. "It was too late the day
Daddy and J.C. died." Her chin quivered as she tried to get
past the pain. "Besides, I can't stop what I didn't start. This
is someone else's game. My fear comes from the fact that I
don't know all the rules."

"Then we'll just make some rules of our own," he said,
and moments later, came sliding to a halt at the edge of the
pit.

For a time, neither moved as they stared down into the
morass. Scavengers had dug through part of the dirt covering
the latest loads. Bits of garbage were blowing around the bottom, caught in a mini-whirlwind of dust and debris, and the
usual assortment of birds were circling and landing with no
particular rhythm. Even though the windows on the car were
up, the odor of rotting garbage was invasive.

"Here goes nothing," Glory said, and got out on her side of the car as Wyatt exited on his. When he came around to get her, the gun was in his hand.

"How do you want to work this?" he asked.

She shrugged. "I don't know. I guess go back to the place where I was when it happened before." And when she started walking, Wyatt was right beside her.

She paused, then frowned as she remembered. "No, Wyatt. If this is going to work, then everyone has to be in the same position. You were on the other side of the pit with the truck."

"Damn it, Glory. I don't want you out of my sight."

Smiling, she lifted her hand, caressing the side of his face, and tracing a fingertip down the scar on his cheek.

"Then don't close your eyes," she teased.

He groaned, then pulled her into his arms and tasted her smile.

Like Glory, it was warm and light, and Wyatt held her close, demanding a response that was not long in coming.

She bent to him like a leaf to the wind. Absorbing his strength, taking courage from his presence, when he trembled beneath her touch, she knew that she was loved.

The rough squawk of an angry crow disturbed the moment, and brought them back to the task at hand.

Wyatt held her face in his hands, gazing down into those wide, all-seeing eyes, and knew a peace that he'd never known before. His voice was rough and shaky, but he was certain of his feelings. "God in heaven, but I love you, girl."

"Remember that tonight when we've nothing else to do," Glory said, and tried to laugh through an onset of tears.

And then before he could talk himself out of it, he jogged back to the place where he'd parked, then turned and waved, indicating that he was ready for her to proceed.

Glory took a deep breath, said a small prayer and started to walk, trying to remember her frame of mind that day, as well as where she'd been when she stopped and looked back at Wyatt, who'd been standing on the bed of her daddy's old truck.

The air was thick and muggy, and she wished for a breeze to stir the constant and often overpowering smell that went with this place. As she walked, she tried to let her mind go free, discarding her fears so that she would be receptive to whatever might come.

Long, anxious minutes passed, while Wyatt stood beside the car, watching her as she walked farther and farther away from him. Twice he almost called her back, but each time he resisted, remembering instead why they'd come.

And while he waited for something to happen, he constantly searched the line of trees around the dump. Now that they were off the mountain, he was solely responsible for Glory's well-being. Just when he feared this might be a wasted effort, she paused, and then her posture changed. He could tell, even from this distance, that she was lost in a world he could not see.

Glory was at the point of believing that this would be a repeat of the day she'd stood in the rubble from her home without seeing any more of the man who'd caused its destruction, when everything shifted before her eyes.

The bright light of morning faded into night. Again, a quarter moon shed a faint ivory glow on the upraised trunk of a big gray sedan. A man stood hunched over the depths of the trunk, and then he straightened and turned. Again, Glory saw the long white bundle he held in his arms.

She shuddered, then moaned in fear—afraid it would stop and afraid that it wouldn't.

She watched through his eyes as the bundle toppled, end over end, then rolled down the deep embankment before coming to a stop against a mound of dirt. And as before, the wide-eyed but unseeing gaze of a dead woman's face stared back up at her.

She screamed, but it was inside her mind. No sound escaped her lips, and she remained motionless, waiting for a revelation.

A small cloud moved across the sliver of moon. Glory knew that it was so, because for a brief time, there was little to see but the darkness in the pit itself. And then as she watched, the cloud passed, and for a second, the copper glint of the woman's red hair was highlighted against the white spread in which she'd been wrapped.

Elizabeth.

The name slid into Glory's mind, and then suddenly, her vision switched from the pit to the man who was getting into the car. She fixed upon the stoop of his shoulders, the balding spot in the back of his head. He opened the door and began to turn....

Then, as instantly as she'd been drawn into the vision, she was yanked back out.

Glory gasped as the world about her returned to normal. The glare of sun against her eyes was suddenly too harsh to bear, and she shaded them with her hand. A dark and impending sense of doom was with her that had nothing to do with what she'd just seen. It came from here! It came from the now!

Glory spun.

"Wyatt!"

His name came out in a scream as she started toward him on the run.

Wyatt knew to the moment when she came out of the trance. But when she started toward him, shouting his name, he knew that something was wrong.

Years of military training kicked in, and he ran in a crouched position with his gun drawn, searching the thick boundary of trees that surrounded the dump as he tried to get to Glory before danger got to her.

And then out of the woods to his right, he saw the flash of sun against metal, and shouted her name. He heard the gunshot at the same time that he saw Glory fall.

"No-o-o!" he raged, reaching her just seconds too late to shield her body with his own.

A heartbeat after he fell forward and then across her, the

second bullet plowed up earth only inches from his head.
Afraid to look down and see something he couldn't accept,
he scooped her into his arms, then rolled, taking them both
to a nearby stand of undergrowth. Once there, he quickly
dragged her through the trees until he was positive that they
were momentarily concealed from the shooter's eyes.

But when he started to search her body for a wound, she
gasped, then choked, and grabbed at his hand instead.

"Glory! Where are you hit?"

"Oh, God. Oh, God." It was all she could say.

Another shot pierced the limbs over their heads, and Wyatt
knew they had to move, or it would only be a matter of time
before a stray bullet hit its mark.

"Where are you hit? Answer me, honey, where are you
hit?"

Shock widened the pupils in her eyes until they appeared
almost black. "I fell. Dear God...the bullet missed me when
I fell."

He went limp with relief, and had the strongest urge to lay
his head down and cry. *Thank you, Lord.*

The sharp thump from a fourth shot hit its mark in a nearby
tree. Wyatt grabbed her hand and started moving deeper into
the woods, at an angle from where the last shot had come.

Yards away, Wyatt shoved Glory down between two large
rocks.

"Stay here, and don't move. Whatever you hear or don't
hear, don't come out until you hear me call." In fear for his
life as well as her own, Glory started to argue when Wyatt
grabbed her by the arm. "I said...don't move."

She stopped in the middle of a word. The look on his face
was one that she'd never seen before, and she realized that
this was the part of Wyatt that he'd tried to leave behind when
he'd retired from the military. This was a man trained to kill.

She nodded as a single tear rolled down her cheek. And
then he disappeared into the trees before her eyes. One minute
he was there. The next, he was gone.

Periodic shots continued from the other side of the dump,

and Glory could tell that the shooter was moving through the trees, circling the open pit. Overwhelmed by the horror of it all, Glory stretched flat in the dirt between the rocks, buried her face in her arms and prayed.

When Bo saw her fall, he was ecstatic. The fact that the man reached her seconds later was immaterial. He had a clear shot at a second hit, and took it without a qualm just as a gnat flew up his nose. One minute he was sucking air, the next, a bug. His finger twitched on the trigger, not much, but enough that it threw off his aim. And because it did, the bullet plowed into the dirt, instead of Wyatt Hatfield's head. By the time he could react, the man had rolled, taking himself and the woman's body into a cover of trees.

"Son of a hairy bitch!"

Just to prove he was still in charge, he fired another shot into the location he'd seen them last, and then waited, listening for something that would indicate that they still lived.

Sweat rolled from his hair and down between his shoulder blades as he waited, holding his breath as he sifted through the sounds on the air. He heard nothing. Not a scream. Not a groan. And more important, not a return shot.

He knew that the man had a gun. He'd seen it in his hand as he ran. That he hadn't once fired back was to Bo proof that he'd crippled, if not killed him, outright.

But while Bo's elation was high, he'd had too many misses on this job already. He was going to see for himself.

As he circled the dump, angling toward the area where he hoped to find their bodies, he continued to threaten with intermittent fire, unaware that he was no longer the hunter. He'd become the prey.

Cold reasoning took Wyatt deeper into the woods, honing instincts he had perfected years ago. He moved with the stealth of a hunter, running without disturbing the ground upon which he moved, choosing his steps and his cover with caution.

As he ran, he realized that the rifle shots were also moving in a clockwise direction. A spurt of adrenaline sent him into a higher gear. He had to get to the man before the man got to Glory.

Once he had a momentary fix on the man's location as he glimpsed a second flash of sunlight on metal. But by the time he got there, the man was already gone.

And then luck changed for them both, when Wyatt heard a loud and sudden thrashing in the underbrush ahead. Soft curses filled the air and Wyatt aimed for the sound with unerring instinct, hoping, as he ran, that the bastard had just broken his neck. It would save him the effort of doing it for him.

Bo was still trying to untangle himself from the rusting coil of barbed wire that he'd stumbled upon when he saw movement from the corner of his eye. Fear shafted, making his movements even more frantic and locking the barbs even deeper into his clothing as he staggered, trying to take aim without neutering himself in the process.

Wyatt came out of the trees at a lope. But when he saw Bo Marker struggling with the wire and the gun, he came to a stop and took aim.

"Drop the gun."

Bo gawked at the black bore of the automatic only yards from his nose, and could tell from the way the man was standing that he knew how to use it. But getting caught was not in his plan, and he feared jail almost as much as dying.

Wyatt could tell that the man was not in the mood to surrender. When he saw him shift the grip on his gun and tighten his finger on the trigger, Wyatt moved his aim a few inches to the right, then fired.

Pain exploded in Bo's arm, and his hand went numb as the rifle bounced butt first onto the ground.

"You shot me!" Bo screamed, and then fell to his knees, which considering where he was standing, was not the smartest move he could make.

"If you move, I'll do it again," Wyatt said.

Bo wasn't smart, but he knew when a man meant business.

And from the look on this one's face, he considered a broken arm a minor inconvenience. It was the barbs on which he was sitting that were causing him the misery.

The calm that had led Wyatt to this man suddenly disappeared. He was shaking with anger as he pulled him to his feet and started dragging him, wire and all, through the woods toward his car.

"You're killing me," Bo groaned, as Wyatt tightened his hold on his good arm and yanked him past a blackberry thicket.

Wyatt paused, then looked back. "Don't tempt me," he whispered. "You tried to kill my lady. It would be all too easy to return the favor."

Bo shrank from the venom in the big man's voice. Suddenly, the idea of getting to jail seemed a bit brighter than it had before.

"It wasn't personal," he whined. "I was just doing a job."

His words froze the anger in Wyatt's mind as a chill went up his spine.

"Someone hired you to do this?"

Bo nodded.

"Who?" Wyatt asked.

Bo shook his head. "Unh-uh. I ain't tellin' until I get to jail. If I tell you now, what's to keep you from shootin' me where I stand?"

Wyatt smiled, and Bo felt his potato chips curdle.

"Look," he cried. "I'll tell you who he is, I swear. But I need doctorin' first. Okay?"

"You are lucky that my father taught me to be kind to animals," Wyatt said softly. "Because I have the biggest urge to put you in the dump with the rest of the garbage."

"Oh, God," Bo said, and started to snivel. "Please, just get me to the doctor. I'll tell you everything I know."

At that moment, Wyatt hated as he'd never hated before. But he thought of Glory, who was still in hiding, and if this man was to be believed, still in danger. Without another word, he continued toward the car as if they'd not exchanged a word.

Minutes later, he dumped a bloody Bo, barbed wire and all, into the trunk of his car, and then started at a lope to the place where he'd left Glory in hiding.

She'd prayed until she'd run out of words, and cried until she'd run out of tears. The fear that held her captive between the two rocks was worse than what she'd felt when she'd witnessed her family die. Then it had been sudden and overwhelming in intensity. Now it was the waiting...the interminable waiting, that was driving her mad. But she had no choice. She'd trusted Wyatt with her life. She had to trust that he knew how to save it.

It seemed a long time before she heard the shot and the accompanying outcry. Terror for Wyatt sent her to her feet, and then fear that she'd endanger him further sent her back to her knees. She dropped between the rocks, rolling herself into a ball, and pressing her fingers against her mouth to keep from screaming.

Seconds turned to minutes, and far too many of them passed as she listened for proof that he still lived. Finally, she could bear it no more.

Wyatt...Wyatt...where are you? she thought.

"I'm here, Morning Glory. I'm here."

She caught her breath on a sob, and in spite of her fear, began crawling to her knees. When she lifted her head above the rocks where she'd been hiding, she saw him coming through the trees.

Seconds later, she was on her feet and running with outstretched arms. He caught her in midair, and then held her close, loving her with his touch, as well as his words. When he could think without wanting to cry, he took her by the hand and began leading her out of the woods.

"Is it over?" Glory asked, and then took a deep breath, trying to steady the tremble in her voice.

Wyatt frowned, and slipped an arm around her shoulders

as they came out of the woods. "Almost, sweetheart. Now if
I can get the bastard in my trunk to a doctor before he bleeds
to death, we'll find out who hired him."

Glory stumbled, as a new wave of fear crossed her face.

"Someone hired him? Oh, God! That means…"

"It means that whoever wants you dead doesn't have the
guts to do it himself," he said harshly. "Don't worry. The
loser in the trunk is going to talk, even if I have to beat it out
of him."

Glory got in the car, a little leery of riding in the same
vehicle with a man who'd been stalking her every move. But
when Wyatt took off in a cloud of dust, bouncing over ruts
and fishtailing in the loose Kentucky earth, the loud and constant shrieks of pain coming from the trunk convinced her
that, at the moment, the man was in no shape to do her any
more harm.

A short time later, Anders Conway was on his way out to
lunch when he heard the sound of a car coming around the
street corner on two wheels. He was fishing for the keys to
his patrol car, expecting that he would have to give chase,
when to his surprise, the car braked to an abrupt halt only
feet from where he stood.

"You in a hurry to spend the night in my jail?" Anders
grumbled, as he watched Wyatt Hatfield emerge from behind
the wheel.

Wyatt grinned, but the smile never reached his eyes as he
started toward his trunk. "No, but I brought someone who
is."

Anders frowned as he circled the car. But when the trunk
popped, shock replaced his earlier disgust.

"What in the world?" he muttered, missing nothing of the
man's bulk, the shattered and bloody arm and the nest of
barbed wire in which he was lying.

"That—" Wyatt pointed "—is the man who's been trying
to kill Glory."

Conway gave Wyatt a long, considering stare. "Bo
Marker…you sorry bugger…is this true?"

Bo groaned, considered lying, then looked at Wyatt's face and nodded.

Conway frowned, waving at a deputy who was just coming out of the office. "Bring me them bolt cutters from the closet," he shouted. "And then call an ambulance to this location."

The deputy pivoted, hurrying to do as he was told.

At this point, Bo began to bawl, aiming his complaints directly at Wyatt. "You nearly killed me with that crazy driving."

Wyatt leaned over the trunk. "I told you, don't tempt me, remember?"

Bo sucked up a squawk and then gave the chief a frantic look, as if begging for him to intervene.

And while no one was looking, Glory got out of the car. She was already at the trunk before Wyatt noticed her, and when he could have stopped her, realized that she needed to confront a ghost or two of her own.

Bo Marker felt the tension changing. As he tried to shift his head to see what they were looking at, she walked into his line of vision. Everything within him froze. It was the first time he'd gotten an up-close and personal look at someone he'd spent days trying to kill.

He remembered what people said about her, and when he found himself staring straight into those pale, silver-blue eyes, he started to shake. There was no accusation, no demand. No shriek of dismay, no cry of fear. Only a long, steady look that seemed to see into his soul. Every black, rotten inch of it.

He shuddered as fear overwhelmed him. When she took a step forward, he shrank back into the trunk as far as he could go.

"Who?" she said.

His mouth dropped, and he stuttered out his own name.

"No," Glory whispered. "I want to know who wants me dead."

Bo stuttered again, then swallowed a knot of panic.

"I said that I'd tell when they fixed me up," he whined. "If I tell, what's to keep all of you from letting me die?"

"The same damn thing that's keeping you alive," Wyatt said. "I want to see you hang for what you did."

Bo shrieked. "They don't hang people no more! Chief, you got to help me! Tell this crazy sucker to leave me alone!"

Conway grinned to himself. Whatever Wyatt Hatfield had said and done to this man had made a believer out of him.

"Now, Bo, it was a figure of speech." Conway eyed the barbed wire snarling around Marker's body and shook his head. And when his deputy came dashing out of the office with the bolt cutters in hand, he grumbled, "Took you long enough," and began to cut.

An hour or so later, Glory and Wyatt, with the chief for added company, were waiting impatiently for Amos Steading to come out of surgery and tell them what they wanted to hear.

And when the doors at the end of the hall suddenly swung back, and he burst through with his usual gusto, Wyatt got to his feet.

"You could have aimed a little farther to the right and made my job easier," Amos growled, and then clapped Wyatt on the arm. "But he's fine, and will be in recovery for at least another hour. After that, you can have a quick go at him."

Conway nodded. "That's fine, then," he said, and then turned to Glory. "Miss Dixon, I'll be back at that time to interrogate the suspect. Rest assured that it will soon be over. Right now, I need to check in at the office. They're towing Marker's truck from the dump as we speak, and I want to take a look inside before I talk to him. See you in a while."

They watched as he walked away, and then Amos Steading took a good long look at Glory, gauging the lingering shock in her eyes against the paleness of her skin and the way she clung to the man at her side.

"Are you all right?" he asked gently.

Glory slumped against Wyatt. "I don't know if I'll ever be all right again," she said softly. And then Wyatt's arms tightened around her shoulders, and she felt the strong steady beat of his heart against her cheek. "But I'm alive, and it's thanks to this man."

Amos shook his head in disbelief. "Well, little lady, a few months ago, I think he could have said the same thing about you."

Glory turned, her eyes wide as she gazed up at the doctor. "Amazing, isn't it?"

The doctor's laugh boomed in the confines of the hall. "That's hardly the word, girl. Hardly the word."

Chapter 14

Carter Foster was on the phone when his secretary, Bernice, burst into his office waving her hand, and mouthing for him to come look.

He covered the mouthpiece with his hand. "What? Can't you see I'm busy?"

"You've got to come see!" Her eyes were wide with excitement. "Some man just drove up in front of the police department and there's an ambulance on the way. I can hear it coming."

"So?" Carter growled. "It's the police department, for goodness' sake. Things like that happen over there."

"But that Dixon girl is there...and there's somebody screaming from inside the trunk of the car."

He blanched, and hung up the phone without excusing himself from the conversation. As he rushed to the door, he tried to pretend it was curiosity, and not horror, that made him move.

He and his secretary stood in the doorway, curbside on-lookers to the scene being enacted across the street. Even as

Carter watched, he began to sweat. He couldn't hear exactly what was being said, but that voice coming from the trunk of the car was all too familiar. When he saw the chief take a rifle out of the back seat, he started to shake. It was the same kind of gun that Bo Marker had carried in the gun rack in the cab of his truck, right down to that telescopic sight.

Oh, no.

"Look, Mr. Foster. There's a man in the trunk, and he's all tangled up in some kind of wire. What on earth do you suppose happened?"

That stupid Bo Marker got himself caught is what happened, he thought, but it wasn't what he said.

"I have no idea," he said, and made himself smile. "You know what, Bernice? It's nearly noon. Since we've been interrupted, why don't we just go ahead and break for lunch? I'll be in court all afternoon, so why don't you take the rest of the day off?"

And then the ambulance pulled up and the show was all but over. His secretary was pleased with his offer, and anxious to share the gossip of what she'd seen with the dentist's receptionist down the street. She didn't give him time to reconsider, unaware that her work schedule was the last thing Carter Foster was worried about.

As she went to get her purse, he slipped out the door and into the alley, leaving Bernice to lock up. But he wasn't going to eat. Food was the last thing on his mind. It would only be a matter of time before that idiot, Marker, started blabbing. Carter knew that if he was to have a chance of escaping, he had to be miles away when it happened.

His hands shook as he slid behind the wheel of his car, and although he wanted to race through the streets at full speed, he made himself take the trip home with his usual, poky ease.

Upon arrival, he began digging through closets, trying without success to find his big suitcase. It would hold all that he needed in the way of clothes. But the longer he looked, the more frantic he became. It was nowhere to be found.

He was at the point of hysterics when he remembered the

last time he'd used it. It was the night Betty Jo had died. He'd packed a portion of her clothes into it to back up the story of her having left him, then tossed it in the dump when he'd tossed her body.

"Okay...okay. I'll improvise," he muttered, and headed for the kitchen.

Moments later, he was back in the bedroom, stuffing shirts and underwear into a garbage bag and yanking clothes, still on their hangers from the closet. He had to get going.

Bo Marker came to in a frightening manner. One minute he'd been staring up at the bright lights of the operating room, and then everything went black. Now, light was reappearing at the periphery of his vision. A woman's voice was calling his name and urging him to wake. It was the nurse who'd put a needle in his hand earlier.

Struggling against the desire to stay where he was, he finally opened his eyes, and then wished he'd followed his own instinct. People were hovering around his bed, staring intently at his face as he awoke. In a drug-induced state, he imagined them vultures, hovering over a carcass, readying to take a first bite.

"No. Go 'way," he muttered, and tried to wave them away when he realized that one of his arms was in bandages, and the other was connected to an IV line.

"Bo, this is Chief Conway. I understand you promised Mr. Hatfield here a name."

Bo groaned. "Can't you let a man rest in peace?"

Wyatt shifted his position, leaning over the bed so that Marker could see him clearly. "If I'd known that's what you wanted, I could have aimed a little to the left and saved the county the cost of cutting on you."

Bo looked up into eyes dark with anger and then closed his eyes, partly in pain, mostly in fear.

Amos Steading stood to one side, judging his patient's capability to communicate against the need these people had to find out the truth. After learning what Glory Dixon had endured at this man's hands, he had to remind himself of the oath he'd taken to preserve life, not end it.

Wyatt leaned closer until he was directly over Marker's face. "Give me the name now…or face murder charges on your own!"

It could have been the tone of Wyatt's voice, or the fact that Bo was in too much misery to put up a fight, but when the demand was uttered, words spilled.

"I didn't murder no one," he cried. "The only thing that I put away was a dog."

Wyatt's voice was almost at a shout. "Glory Dixon's father and brother are dead because of what you did. And you tried your damnedest to send her with them today. You might also like to know that they found a partial print on that stolen car that someone used in an attempted hit and run. What do you want to bet that it's yours?"

Bo groaned.

"Just don't give me any more of your crap, Marker. I'm already wishing I'd left you in that stinking dump."

The machine monitoring Marker's heart rate began to beep in a wild and erratic pattern.

Amos Steading frowned. "That's about enough for now. You'll have to come back later for further interrogation."

"I didn't kill no one!" Bo said. "Them people was already dead before Carter Foster hired me. I didn't have anything to do with their deaths…I swear!"

The chief frowned. "Now, damn it, Bo, I don't think you're telling me the truth. Why would Carter Foster want to kill the Dixon family?"

"Who's Carter Foster?" Wyatt asked.

"He's the town lawyer," Conway said. "And as far as I know, he doesn't have a vicious bone in his body."

But as soon as he said it, he remembered the investigation he'd asked his deputy to initiate, and wondered if anything valid had turned up on the whereabouts of Betty Jo.

Wyatt spun, staring back at the doorway where Glory waited.

"Honey, what do you know about Carter Foster?"

Surprise reshaped her expression. "Who?"

"The local lawyer."

"Oh! Why, not much. I don't think Daddy ever used him. When we had to commit Granny to the nursing home in Hazard, Daddy hired a lawyer there. That's the one who's handling the probate on Daddy's will, remember?"

Wyatt nodded, then turned. He could tell by the look on the doctor's face that they were about to be ejected.

"Please," he urged. "Just one more question."

Finally, Steading nodded.

"All right, Marker, let's say you're telling the truth. Did Foster say why he wanted Glory dead?"

Consciousness was beginning to fade. Bo's attention was drifting and his tongue felt twice its normal size. He licked his lips over and over, and it took everything he had just to get the words said.

"I don't know," he muttered. "All he ever said was that the crazy witch could ruin him."

"That's enough," Steading ordered, and finally ushered the trio from the room.

Once they were in the outer hallway, Conway paused, and scratched his head. "I don't get it. This doesn't really make sense."

Wyatt grabbed the lawman by the arm, desperate to make him believe.

"Look, Chief, there's something we haven't told you. Glory thinks that there's a connection between what happened to her family and the vision she had of that body being tossed in the dump."

The argument he expected didn't come. Instead, a strange expression crossed the chief's face as he turned and stared at Glory, as if seeing her for the very first time.

"Is this true, girl?"

She nodded. "That's why we went back there today. I wanted to see if the vision I had the first time would recur. I hoped that if it did, I might *see* something that I missed seeing before, like a face, or a tag number on the car."

"Well, did you?"

"Yes, sir."

"Then who did you see?" Conway asked, and then couldn't believe he was considering the word of a psychic as an actual fact.

"I didn't see a face, but I saw the man's back," Glory said. "He was stooped and starting to go bald on the crown of his head. He also drove a dark gray sedan. And...I saw something else I hadn't seen the first time. The dead woman has red hair. And I think her name is Elizabeth."

Conway visibly staggered, then swiped a shaky hand across his face. "Good Lord, girl! Are you sure?"

"Yes, sir. Definitely sure about the red hair. Pretty sure about the name. It came to me out of nowhere, and I have no reason to believe that it is unconnected to what I was seeing."

Wyatt could tell by the look on his face that something Glory said had struck a chord. "Why? What is it you know that we don't?"

"It could be completely unrelated to what you saw. And it doesn't prove that what Bo Marker said is true. But..."

"Damn it, Glory has the right to know," Wyatt said. "Hasn't she endured enough?"

Conway looked at her where she stood, silhouetted against the bright backdrop of a wall of windows. Small in stature and fragile in appearance though she was, there was still something strangely enduring about her poise and the waiting expression on her face.

Finally, he nodded. "Yes, I suspect that she has." He made a quick decision and started talking. "A little more than a week ago, Carter Foster's wife ran off with some man. It wasn't her first indiscretion, and no one expected it to be her last. She's what you might call a loose woman."

Wyatt wasn't following this. If Foster's wife was gone, then why would he blame Glory?

"The deal is...to my knowledge, no one saw her leave. All

we know of what happened is from Foster's version of the story. What gives me pause to wonder is what Glory just said. His wife was a redhead who went by the name of Betty Jo. But I've ticketed her myself on several occasions for speeding, and I distinctly remember that the name Elizabeth was on her driver's license.''

Glory gasped, and then turned away. Wyatt came up behind her. His touch was comforting, but there was nothing he could do to ease the ugliness of what surrounded her.

''Why, Wyatt? Why did I get caught up in this?'' she cried.

''Remember when you said the two incidents were connected?''

She nodded, then leaned against his chest, as always, using his strength when her own threatened to give. Wyatt's voice was low against her ear, but the truth of what he said was too vivid to deny.

''What if his wife didn't really leave him? What if he killed her, dumped the body and then feared you would *see* it and give him away? Bo Marker said that Carter claimed you could ruin him. Marker also claimed he had nothing to do with the explosion that killed your family. If he's to be believed, then that could mean Carter caused the explosion, and when he found out you escaped, he hired Bo Marker to finish what he couldn't.''

She moaned and covered her face with her hands.

''Don't, honey,'' he said softly. ''It's just about over.''

''Look, I don't know quite know what to make of all this,'' Conway said. ''But I need to get back to the office. I want to bring Foster in for questioning.''

''I've got a cellular phone at the cabin,'' Wyatt said. ''Here's the number. I'd appreciate it if you'd keep us abreast of what goes on, but right now, I think Glory needs to go home. She's had just about all she can take.''

The trio parted company in the parking lot of the hospital, and when Wyatt seated Glory in the car, she looked like a lost child. Heartsick at what she'd endured, he was about to get in when he glanced across the street and noticed the drug-store on the corner.

Just for a moment, he had a flashback of another time when he'd been in this lot, sitting in a wheelchair and waiting for Lane to pick him up. In his mind, he could almost see the peace that had been on Glory's face that day as she'd stood between her father and brother, safe in the knowledge that she was right where she belonged. But that was then and this was now. Now they were gone, and God willing, she would soon belong to him.

She leaned across the seat, then looked out at him through the open door.

"Wyatt? Is something wrong?"

Quickly, he slid behind the wheel, then cupped the back of her head and pulled her gently toward him until their mouths were a breath apart.

"Not anymore," he whispered, "not anymore," and felt her sigh of relief as their lips connected.

Carter was at the end of the street and turning when he looked in his rearview mirror and saw a patrol car easing up his drive. There were no flashing lights or sirens squalling, but to him, the implications were all the same.

"Oh, my God," he gasped, and swerved, taking alleys instead of the streets to get out of town.

He cursed as he drove, damning everyone but himself as to blame. Once he barely missed a dog that darted across an alley, and then a few minutes later, slaughtered a pair of matching trash cans as he swerved to miss a pothole. On top of everything else, he now had a sizable dent in his left front fender.

"It's no big deal. I can handle this," he muttered, and then accelerated across a side street and into the next adjoining alley. When he realized he was on Ridge Street, he started to relax. He was almost out of town!

As if to celebrate his premature joy, a small dinging began to sound from the dash of the car. Carter looked down in dismay at the warning light near the fuel gauge. It was sitting on empty...and he had less than five dollars in cash to his name.

He slapped the steering wheel in frustration. He had credit cards he could use, but they left a paper trail. If he used them, it would be only a matter of time before they found him.

Frantic, he paused at a crossing and then saw salvation to his right. The First Federal Bank of Larner's Mill was less than a hundred yards ahead. Money was there for the taking. His money! And while he didn't dare enter, the automatic money machine in the drive-through beckoned.

Moments later, the decision made, he shot across the street and into the lane for the ATM, right behind a small brown coupé belonging to one Lizzie Dunsford, retired librarian. The moment he stopped, he realized he'd just made a mistake. Lizzie Dunsford was notorious for being unable to remember her own address. It was obvious by the way she kept punching numbers that she also could not remember her own personal identification number for her money card.

"No...oh, no," he groaned, and started to back out when a big red four-by-four pickup pulled in behind him. Although the windows were up, music could be heard as it reverberated loudly from the interior, marking time for the teenage driver and his young sweetie, who were making time of their own while they waited.

Carter waved at them to back up, but they were too busy locking lips to see him, and honking to get their attention was out of the question. Their music was so loud that they wouldn't have been able to hear, and honking his horn would only call attention to himself.

In a panic, he jumped out of his car, squeezing between it and the next car, until he was at Lizzie Dunsford's door.

"Miss Dunsford...it's me, Carter Foster. I see that you're having a little trouble. Maybe I could be of service?"

Hard of hearing, the old woman frowned. "I don't know any Arthur Fosser," she said, and started to roll up her window, certain that she was about to be the victim of a robbery.

By now, Carter was panicked. He stuck his hand in the gap between door and window, pleading his case with renewed vigor.

"I said, Foster! Carter Foster! You remember me. I'm a lawyer."

"Oh…why yes, I believe that I do," she said.

Thank God, Carter groaned inwardly. "Now…how can I be of service?"

"I just can't get this thing to work," she said. "I keep punching numbers, but nothing comes out."

Carter peered at the screen, then frowned. "I don't know what your identification number is, but this looks like a phone number to me. Are you sure you remember it right?"

She frowned, and then suddenly cackled in delight. "You know…I believe that you're right! Now, you run back to your car, boy. I'll try another. You're not supposed to watch me, you know."

"Yes, ma'am," he said, and jumped back into his car, praying that he hadn't been seen.

Afraid to kill the engine for fear there wouldn't be enough fuel to start it back up, he sat in horror as sweat rolled down his face and the gas gauge slid farther into the red. The only good thing about his location was that the patrol car cruising down the street didn't notice him sandwiched between the two cars.

In his mind, he was already preparing an argument to the court on his behalf when Lizzie's car suddenly sprang to life and bolted out of the lane and into the street, with Lizzie in less than firm control.

"It's about time," he muttered, and drove forward. Inserting his card, he began to withdraw all that he could from his account.

As Wyatt turned onto Main Street and headed out of town, he kept glancing back and forth at Glory. She was leaning against the seat with her eyes closed. More than once, he was certain that he'd seen her lips tremble. He kept watching for tears that never showed.

"Hey, little Morning Glory," he said, and slipped a hand across the seat toward her. "How about scooting a little closer to me?"

Glory opened her eyes and tried to smile, but there was too much misery inside of her to let it happen.

"What is it, baby?"

"Granny calls this…thing I can do a gift. But how can it be when it caused the deaths of my father and brother?"

"Your gift didn't cause them to die. Someone murdered them," he argued.

"Because of me," she whispered. "Because of me." Unable to accept his pity, she looked away.

There was nothing he could say to help. Only time, and a better understanding of the frailties of the human race were going to make Glory's burden easier to bear.

"Just rest," he said. "We'll be home in no time. Maybe it will make you feel better."

As they passed, the buildings seemed to blur one into the other. Glory was lost in thought and on the point of dozing, when the air inside the car suddenly seemed too close. And before she could react by rolling down a window, the skin on her body began to crawl. She went from a slump to sitting straight in the seat, searching the streets on which they drove for a reason that would explain her panic.

"Wyatt?"

Apprehension sent her scooting across the seat next to him, clutching at his arm.

"What is it?" he asked, and started to slow down, thinking she might be getting sick.

"No! No!" she shouted. "Don't stop. I think he's here!"

"You think who's h—" He swerved as understanding dawned. "Where?" he asked urgently, looking from one side of the street to another.

"I don't know," she said, and then pressed her fingers against her mouth and groaned softly. "I'm afraid."

"He can't hurt you, darlin'. I'm here."

Glory leaned even closer, her heart pounding, and let herself be pulled toward the fear. They had to find him. It was the only way she knew how to make it stop.

"Do I keep driving, or do you want me to stop?" he asked.

She closed her eyes, focusing on the fear, and then looked up with a jerk.

"Turn here!" she ordered, and Wyatt took the corner on three wheels.

Carter was stuffing money in his pockets when the sound of tires squalling on the street behind him made him look up in fright.

"Damn and blast," he groaned, and took off without retrieving his money card and receipt that were still hanging out of the machine.

"There!" Glory cried, pointing toward a dark gray car that was hurtling out of the drive-through at the bank.

Wyatt accelerated past the bank, and then swerved sharply to the right, blocking the car's only exit. Instinctively, he shoved Glory to the floor and then grabbed for his gun. He looked up just as the car came skidding to a halt. He jumped out with his gun aimed, unaware that Glory refused to stay put. The need to look into this man's face was, for her, overwhelming.

"Son of a…!" Carter's heart dropped.

But it wasn't the man with the gun who did him in. It was the sight of Glory Dixon, sitting up in the seat and staring back at him with those clear blue eyes.

"No-o-o," he screamed, and shoved his car in reverse. Rubber burned on the pavement as gears ground and tires began turning in reverse.

But no sooner had he begun to move, than the big red four-by-four that was behind them turned the corner and hit his bumper with a thump. It didn't make a dent in the big truck or its occupants, but it jerked Carter's head, popping his neck like the crack of a whip.

Whiplash!

He groaned. A lawyer's favorite injury, and here he was without a prayer of collecting on the deed. He looked out his windshield and saw the man with the gun, waving and shouting at the kids in the truck. He was vaguely aware of them getting out and running toward the bank, and then of someone dragging him out of the car.

He was choking from the hold the man had on the back of his shirt. Every time he tried to move, the hold tightened and he would be all but yanked off his feet. The reality of his situation came swiftly when he finally heard Wyatt Hatfield's angry voice.

"Glory. Is this him?"

In a daze, she stared at his face, looking past the plain appearance of an overweight and aging man, to the evil in his eyes. And when she looked, it was there. The guilt. The shame. The fear.

She looked down at his hands and, in her mind, saw the same hands turning the jets on the cookstove in her house, then breaking a knob so that it would not turn off.

"Yes," she said. "That's him. That's the man."

Carter cursed and made a desperate effort to jerk free of Wyatt's hands, but the man and his grip were too strong. In the struggle, his jacket fell open, and money dropped from his pocket and onto the ground. A draft caught the bills, shifting and fluttering them along on the pavement, farther and farther out of Carter's grasp.

"My money!" he cried. "It's blowing away!"

"You're not going to need money where you're going," Wyatt said.

Carter's mind was whirling in desperation as the sound of sirens could be heard in the distance. Moments later, when the chief himself slid to a halt and exited his car on the run, Carter started babbling.

"Conway, thank God you're here. This stranger just tried to hold me up. Look! My money! It's blowing away! You've got to help me."

Conway motioned for a deputy. "Handcuff him," he said.

"No!" Carter screeched as the steel slid and locked around his wrists. "You've got the wrong man! I didn't do anything wrong."

"That's not exactly what Bo Marker says," Conway drawled, and was satisfied with himself when all the blood seemed to drain from the lawyer's face. That was guilt showing, or his name wasn't Anders Barnett Conway.

"Who's Bo Marker?" Carter finally thought to ask, although he suspected his reaction might have come a little too late to be as believable as he'd hoped.

And then all eyes turned to Glory as she answered for them all. "He's the man you hired to kill me...isn't he, Mr. Foster?"

Carter looked away, unable to face her accusation.

But Glory wasn't through. "Why, Mr. Foster? Why would you want to harm me? I didn't even know your name."

He stared, unable to believe what she just said. She hadn't even known his name? Could that mean, if he'd let well enough alone, he would have gotten away with murder?

"Going on a trip, were you?" Conway asked, as he saw the bags and stacks of clothing in the back seat of the lawyer's car.

"Why, no," Carter muttered. "I was uh...I was going to..." He brightened. "I was about to donate all this stuff to the Salvation Army."

Wyatt picked up a handful of money from the ground and stuck it beneath Carter's nose. "What was this for? Were you going to donate all of your money, too?"

Carter glared, then focused his anger on the chief of police. "Exactly what am I being arrested for?" he muttered.

"For the murder of Rafe Dixon and James Charles Dixon. For hiring a man named Bo Marker to kill Glory Dixon. And when we get through digging in the city dump to find the body, for the murder of Elizabeth Foster."

Carter tried to fake surprise. "Betty Jo! Murdered! You can't be serious?" And then he tried another tack. "You have no proof."

"When we get through digging, I will. I'm going to go back to the office and take this little lady's statement, just like I should have done days ago. And when we get through digging through the garbage, if I find myself a redheaded woman by the name of Elizabeth, who's wrapped up in something white, then you're in serious trouble, my friend."

His eyes bugged. The description was so perfect that it made him sick. "That's impossible," he muttered, and then he thought to himself. *No one saw.*

Glory gasped, and answered before she thought. "Oh, but that's not true, Mr. Foster. I did."

Carter went weak at the knees. His mind was running on ragged, and afraid to stop for fear that hell would catch up with him while he was forced to face the truth of what she'd just said.

The witch, the witch. She'd read his damn mind.

Conway read him his rights as he dragged him away.

The ride home was quiet. Little was said until they pulled up in front of the cabin and parked. As they got out of the car, Liam Fowler and his friends walked out of the trees and into the yard.

"They've heard," Glory said.

"Already?" Wyatt asked.

She nodded. "It doesn't take long for word to get around up here."

Liam Fowler was grinning as he grabbed Wyatt's hand and gave it a fierce shake, then brushed the crown of her head with the flat of his palm.

"Glory girl, you choose your friends well," he said. "We're all glad you're safe, and if you want to rebuild, just say the word. We'll be here."

Tears shimmered on the surface of her eyes as she nodded. But the emotions of the past few hours were too much for her to speak.

"Excuse me," she said, and ran into the cabin.

"It's been a bad day," Wyatt said.

"It's been a bad week, friend. Real bad. We lost two good friends. Thanks to you, we didn't lose another. If you happen to be a mind to stay in these parts, we'd be real proud to have you."

Then without giving Wyatt time to answer, they disappeared as quickly as they had come. As soon as they were gone, Wyatt went to look for Glory.

He could hear her sobs as he walked into the room. Without pause, he locked the door, set the gun on the mantel, and followed the sound of her voice.

"It's all right, it's all right," he said gently, as he crawled onto the bed with her. "Cry all you want. I've got you." When she rolled toward him and wrapped her arms around his neck, he groaned and held her close.

"Oh, Wyatt. His face…did you see that man's face? He's not even sorry for what he did."

Wyatt felt as if his heart was breaking. If he could, he would have taken her pain twice over, just to make sure she never suffered again.

"I know, darlin', I know. Sometimes the world is an ugly place." He pulled her closer against him, comforting her in the only way he knew how. With love.

He held her until her tears dried, and only the occasional sound of a sob could be heard as she slept. And when she was fast asleep, he eased himself gently out from her bed, then went into the other room. There was something yet to be done.

Justin Hatfield leaned out the front door of his house and called to his brother-in-law, who was loading tools in the back of a truck.

"Lane! Telephone!"

Lane dropped a tool belt and a sack of nails into the bed of the truck and came running. He cleared the four steps up the porch in one leap and reached for the phone just as Toni walked into the room.

"Hello," he said, and gave Toni a wink.

"Lane, it's me, Wyatt. It's over."

Lane dropped into the chair by the phone. "What happened?"

"One of them started taking potshots at us at the dump. We caught the other one coming out of a bank. It's a long story.

"I'll fill you in on the details later."

Lane was surprised by what Wyatt just said. "There were two?"

"So it seems," Wyatt said. "At any rate, it's over. I just wanted to let you know that she's safe and everyone's in custody."

"What happens now?" Lane asked.

Wyatt rubbed his eyes wearily, then stared out the window over the kitchen sink into the nearby trees. The beauty of what was before his eyes was in direct contrast to what lay ahead.

"Tomorrow they start digging through the dump for a body."

Lane sighed with relief. He'd been living with guilt ever since the day he'd left, knowing that Wyatt was more or less on his own.

"You did a real good job, brother. Have you ever considered going into my line of work?"

Wyatt's answer was abrupt, but concise. "No. In fact, hell no!"

Lane grinned. "Just thought I'd ask."

"Anyway, thanks for all you did."

"I didn't do anything," Lane said.

"Oh, yes, you did," Wyatt argued. "When I called, you came. A man couldn't ask for anything more."

"If there's one thing that living with the Hatfields has taught me," Lane said, "it's that…that's what families are all about."

Wyatt turned toward the bedroom where Glory lay sleeping. His eyes darkened. "I guess you're right," he said. "If you can't count on family…who can you count on?"

Long after their conversation was over, the heart of it was

still with Wyatt. And as he lay beside Glory, watching her sleep, he felt the last of his uncertainties about himself slipping away.

Through a quirk of fate, he and Glory Dixon would be forever linked. He knew as surely as he knew his own name that he could not, and did not want to try to, exist without her. She was, quite literally, in his blood.

And with the acceptance of that fact, came the acceptance of his own future.

Chapter 15

Wyatt stood at the edge of the pit, watching as men scoured the dump below. With more than a week's worth of dirt and garbage to move, he did not envy them their task.

Along with the local law, officers from the state police were on the scene, and at last report, Bo Marker was recovering by the hour. The better Bo felt, the more he talked. He was perfectly willing to admit to two counts of assault with a deadly weapon, but not murder. For once, he was innocent of something vile, and fully intended that everyone know.

Wyatt knew that while Marker's testimony backed up the truth of Glory's life having been in danger, there was still only her word—the word of a psychic—as to why Carter Foster wanted her dead. Carter was sticking to his story about his wife having left him for another man. Unless they found a body, he knew her story would stand on shaky ground.

Yesterday had been bad...both for Wyatt and for Glory. But that was yesterday. This was today. And the despair that he'd expected to see on her face when she woke had been absent. In fact, she'd greeted the day with eagerness, ready to put the past behind her. *If only I was that confident about losing my ghosts,* Wyatt thought.

Someone shouted from the line of cars behind him, and as he turned to look, he realized Glory was nowhere in sight. Only moments earlier, she'd been at his side, squeezing his hand in intermittent bouts of anxiety as load after load of garbage was shifted down below. But now she was gone. A quick burst of nervousness came and then went as he reminded himself she was no longer in danger.

A hot gust of wind blew across the ground, stirring the air without cooling it as he moved away from the site. Just as he started toward the line of parked cars, he heard her calling his name.

"Wyatt!"

He spun, and when he saw her waving at him from the shade of the trees, he started toward her at an easy lope.

Glory watched him coming, looking at him as if seeing him for the first time, and marveled at the link they shared, as well as at the man himself.

In her eyes, he was as strong as the hills in which she'd been born. As brown as the earth upon which she stood. And he'd been as faithful to his promise as a man could possibly be. She wondered if after this was over, there would be anything left between them, or if he would consider this a promise made, a promise kept—and be on his way.

She said a prayer that it wouldn't be the latter. He was so deep in her blood that if he left her, he'd take part of her with him. How, she wondered, did one live with only half a heart?

Laughter was in his voice as he swung her into his arms and off her feet.

"I lost you," he said, nuzzling the spot below her ear that always made her shiver.

"No, you didn't, Wyatt Hatfield. You'll never lose me." She stroked her hand against the center of his chest. "I'm in here. All you have to do is look. I'll be waiting."

Whatever he'd been thinking died. All sense of their sur-

oundings faded. The smile slipped off his face as he lost
himself in a cool blue gaze.

"You would, wouldn't you?" he asked quietly.

But before she could answer, someone shouted his name.
He turned, still holding Glory in his arms.

"Why, it's Lane!" Glory said, and then noticed the tall,
pretty woman walking beside him. Neither the denim jeans
and shirt nor the well-worn boots she was wearing could disguise
her elegance.

"And my sister," Wyatt added.

Glory could see the resemblance in their faces, and the
proud, almost regal way in which they held themselves as they
walked. Both of them had hair the color of dark chocolate,
and eyes that matched. Along with that, there was a similar
stubborn thrust to their chins that made her smile.

Toni Hatfield Monday couldn't believe her eyes. Lane had
said Glory Dixon was small. But she wasn't prepared for that
fragile, fairy-looking waif who stood at her brother's side.
And her hair! It was a fall of silver and gold that caught and
held sunshine like a reflection on water.

But as she came closer, her opinion of helpless beauty disappeared.
In spite of the fact that Toni was nearly as tall as
Wyatt, she felt small and humbled by Glory's pure, unblinking
stare. For several seconds, she was so locked into that
gaze that she forgot why she'd come. And then Glory smiled,
and the moment passed.

"So," Toni said. "We meet." A quick sheen of tears came
and went as she spoke. "Do you remember what I said I
wanted to do when that happened?"

"About wanting to hug angels?" Glory asked.

Toni nodded.

"Good. I could use a hug today," Glory said, and let herself
heal in Toni Monday's welcoming arms.

Toni smiled at the nervous look on Wyatt's face, and then
turned and kissed him on the cheek.

"Don't worry, big brother. I won't give away your secrets.
I just came to see your lady, face-to-face."

Wyatt was playing it safe and accepted her kiss as his due.
"I have nothing to hide," he drawled.

Toni laughed aloud at her brother's audacity. "God save
us from pretty men who lie as easily as they make love," she
said, and winked at her husband as she took Glory by the
arm. "Let's walk," she said. "I came a long way to say
thank-you."

Glory held the joy that was in her heart, savoring this moment to herself. It gave her a feeling of belonging to someone
again.

"There was no need to say it again," Glory said. "I'm the
one who's thankful that Wyatt could make sense of what I'd
seen."

It was impossible for Toni to hide her amazement. "I won't
pretend to understand," she said. "But I will never doubt
your ability, of that you can be sure." And then her voice
softened as she took Glory by the hand. "Lane told me what
you've had to endure. I'm so sorry for your loss, but at the
same time, thankful that you and Wyatt have found each
other."

Glory savored the words, hoping they were true. Had she
and Wyatt truly found each other, or would he be saying
goodbye now that she was safe?

"So, what are your plans now that the worst is behind
you?" Toni asked.

Glory shrugged. "I have none, other than to rebuild my
life."

A little surprised by the singular way in which she'd expressed her plans, Toni couldn't help but ask, "You sound as
if you're planning to do this alone."

Glory paused, considering the best way to express her feelings, yet unashamed to admit what they were.

"I don't know," she finally said. "What happens between
us now is not up to me. It's up to Wyatt. He knows how I
feel." And then she smiled slightly. "In fact, most of the time
he also knows what I think. I'm supposed to be the psychic
and he reads *my* mind."

Toni's eyebrows arched, and she squeezed Glory's hand ust a little, as if in jest. "You're kidding, of course."

"No, I'm not."

Toni gasped. "Really? He can do that?"

Glory shrugged. "For some reason, we now share more han a few pints of blood."

"Good Lord!"

Toni looked back at Lane as he stood talking to her brother, rying to imagine what it would be like to live with someone and have him know her every thought. And then something occurred to her, and she started to smile.

"So…my big brother knows what you think?"

"He sure does."

Toni put her hands on her hips and gave Glory a wicked mile. "Then give him something to think about. Let him in on some…uh, innermost thoughts, then see if he's man enough to take them."

The idea was audacious, just like Toni. She couldn't help but grin. "You're a lot like Wyatt, aren't you?"

"How so?" Toni asked.

"You don't waste time on details. You just jump in with both feet?"

Toni grinned even wider. "Well now, I didn't know I was so transparent, but if you need an answer, then I guess all you need to do is look at Lane Monday. I wanted that man from the time I pulled him out of a flood." And then she paused, and grinned even broader. "I need to amend that slightly. I wanted *him,* but I was willing to settle for making a baby with him."

Glory couldn't hide her shock. "Good Lord, Wyatt was right."

"How so?" Toni asked.

"He said once Lane met you, he never had a chance…or words to that effect."

"Like I said," Toni reminded her. "If you want something but don't give it a try, you have only yourself to blame."

"Hey, you two, time's up," Wyatt shouted. "You've ha time enough to plot the fall of man."

"Just about," Toni whispered, and winked at Glory.

Glory shivered with anticipation, and then started to smile

"I'm glad you came," she said softly.

Toni hugged her. "So am I, Glory. So am I."

It was well toward evening on the second day of the di when the revelation came. Birds, disturbed from their norma scavenging, were circling the air above the pit where the gar bage was being moved. Yard by yard, earth was scooped the dumped as they continued their search.

Anders Conway stood on the precipice, wondering if he' made a mistake by putting his cards on the table too soon b calling in the state police, and wondering how he was going to explain his mistake when someone shouted, and another man started running toward him, waving him down.

Wyatt stood alone, watching from a distance away as the men began to converge upon their latest location. Even though he was high above the spot and hundreds of yards away, Wyatt could tell they'd found what they'd been looking for.

He took a long, slow breath, and said a quiet prayer, thankful that Glory wasn't here to witness it. Even from this distance, he could tell that what they found wasn't pretty. The once-white spread she'd been wrapped in was a stiff, dirty brown, and what was left of Betty Jo Foster was even worse. He turned away. He didn't need to see anymore.

"By God, Hatfield, they found her!" Conway said, as he came up and out of the pit a short time later.

Wyatt nodded. "I saw."

Conway looked around, expecting to see Glory Dixon somewhere nearby with a satisfied expression on her face.

"She didn't come with you today?"

"No," Wyatt said. "We were up late last night visiting with Lane and my sister. They left for home early this morning. Glory wanted to sleep in."

Conway nodded. "I guess it's just as well, but I thought

she'd be here…wanting to know if the body was down there after all.''

"You still don't get it, do you?" Wyatt said. "She didn't need to come for that. It was making you believe enough to look for the body that mattered. When your people started to dig, her worries were over. It was inevitable that you'd find what she already knew was there."

"You came," Conway said. "Does that mean you didn't believe her?"

Wyatt's smile never quite reached his eyes. "Oh, no. I came to make sure you didn't quit on her."

Conway flushed. "I suppose I had that coming."

"I think I'll be going now," Wyatt said. "Looks like you've got everything under control."

"Looks like," the chief said, but when Wyatt started walking away, Conway called him back.

"Hey, Wyatt!"

He paused, and then turned.

"I don't know how she does it," Conway muttered.

This time, Wyatt's smile was a little less angry. "Neither does she, Chief. Neither does she."

By the time they had Betty Jo Foster bagged and out of the pit, Wyatt was already gone.

Glory was down in the creek below the cabin, wading through the ankle-deep water with her jeans rolled up to her knees and her shoes in her hand. The soft, gentle breeze that had come with morning did not blow down here. Leaves drooped silently on heavily laden branches as an occasional dragonfly dipped and swooped only inches above the water. She moved without purpose, content only with the cool, constant flow between her toes and the ease that comes from knowing she belonged.

A squirrel scolded from somewhere in the canopy above her head, and she closed her eyes and took a slow, deep breath, realigning herself with the world in which she'd been born. Enclosed within the confines of the steep rocky banks, once again she felt safe and cleansed.

It would take longer for the anger to go away, and even longer before she learned how to live with the pain of her loss, but the guilt that had held her hostage was gone.

Something brushed against her ankle. She opened her eyes and looked down, smiling as tiny tadpoles wiggled past. And then something else, just below the surface of the water, caught her eye. As she stooped to look, her braid fell over her shoulder, baptizing the ends in the cool, Kentucky stream.

Her heart began to beat with excitement as she lifted a perfect arrowhead out of the creek.

"Oh, my gosh! J.C. is going to love..."

Realization struck. Staggered by the pain of loss, her lip trembled as she clutched it tightly in her fist. The time had come and gone for adding to her brother's beloved collection. Glory held it between her fingers, staring down at the cool gray piece and its perfect triangular shape.

Someday, there'd be another boy who was as fascinated by the past as her brother had been. The arrowhead should be there, waiting for him to find. She held her breath and let it go, watching as it turned end over end, dropping into the water and then settling, once again, into the rocks.

And then she heard someone calling her name and looked up. Wyatt was standing at the top of the bank. She could tell by the look on his face that it was over. Without looking back, she stepped out of the water and started up the bank with her shoes in her hand. He met her halfway.

"I got your mail when I came by the box," he said. "There's a letter from your lawyer. It's on the table."

Refusing to cry anymore, she stifled a sob, and just held him.

"Are you all right?"

She nodded. "I am now," she said. "Help me up the bank."

But before they moved, he tilted her chin, forcing her to look him in the face.

"Would you like to go see your granny again?"

A smile of delight spread from her eyes to her face.

"Could I?"

"Honey, you name it, it's yours."

"Be careful what you say," she warned. "I may ask for more than you want to give," then laughed at the shock on his face.

It was as if the old woman hadn't moved since they'd been there last. She sat in the same chair, in the same clothes, with the same lost expression in her eyes. Staring out a window into a world from which she'd withdrawn, she rocked without thought, moving only when the urge struck her.

"Granny."

Faith Dixon blinked, and then turned her head toward the pair at the door.

"Comp'ny? I got comp'ny?"

"It's me, Granny. It's Glory."

Identity clicked as she smiled. "Well, come on in," she said. "I've been waiting for you all day."

As before, Glory knelt at her granny's feet as Wyatt took the only other chair.

"Did you bring my gingersnaps?" she asked, and then cackled with glee when Wyatt promptly handed over a small white sack bulging with a fresh spicy batch straight from the bakery in Larner's Mill.

"I'll save some of these for your daddy," she said. "My Rafe does love cookies."

It hurt Glory just to hear his name. But she knew that keeping silent about the truth was the best thing for all concerned.

"Yes, he does, doesn't he, Granny?"

The old woman nodded, and then patted Glory's head. "He's lookin' real good, don't you think?"

A frown marred Glory's forehead as she tried to stay with her granny's train of thought. She supposed she must be referring to Wyatt, although they'd been discussing her father only seconds before.

"Who, Granny? Who looks good?"

"Why, your daddy. Who else?" She smiled to herself, and then looked up at the sky outside. "He was here jest a day or so ago," and then she began to frown. "At least I think it was then. I lose track of time, but I'm sure it warn't no longer than that."

Oh, Lord, Wyatt thought. *Maybe this wasn't such a good idea after all.*

"Honey?" He touched her shoulder, asking without saying the words.

Glory shook her head, and then whispered, "It's all right, Wyatt. It's not so bad."

Unaware of their aside, Faith was still lost in thought about her son's visit. Suddenly the frown slid off of the old woman's face.

"No! I'm right. It was only a day or so ago cause I 'member askin' him why he didn't come with you before."

Glory froze. What kind of tricks was her granny's mind playing on her?

Granny started to rock, happy that she'd settled it all in her mind. "Said he was goin' on some trip." She slapped her leg and then laughed. "I swear, that boy of mine ain't been out of Kentucky three times in his life and now he's goin' on some trip."

"Oh, God," Glory said, and rocked back on her heels. When she felt Wyatt's hand on her shoulder, she all but staggered to her feet.

Faith frowned a little, continuing to talk to herself, even forgetting that they were still there.

"I'll be seein' you soon, he said." She nodded confidently, as her tiny white topknot bobbed on her head. "Yep. That's what he said. I'll be seein' you soon."

Glory turned. Her eyes were wide, the expression on her face slightly stunned.

"Wyatt?"

There was little he could say. The implications of what Faith Dixon was saying were almost too impossible to consider. And then he thought of the connection that he and Glory shared. It was a bond stronger than love, that even death would not break.

"I heard."

"Do you suppose…?"

He pulled her to him. "It's not for us to wonder," he said. "Whatever happened is between that woman and her boy. If she believes she saw him, then who are we to question?"

Glory went limp in his arms.

"Are you all right?" he asked.

She nodded, and then looked back at her granny as she rocked. The scene was one that Glory had seen a thousand times before. But this time, she was struck by the peaceful, almost timeless quality of the sight. And as she looked, in a small way, she began to accept the inevitability of the circle of life. One was born. One died. And life still went on when yours was gone.

Suddenly, she reached out and took Wyatt by the hand.

He felt the urgency with which she held him. "What is it, sweetheart?"

"Take me home, Wyatt. I want to go home."

Moonlight slipped through the parted curtains, painting the bodies of the couple upon the bed in a white, unearthly glow. As they moved together in a dance of love, the sounds of their sighs mingled with those of the wind outside the door. Sometimes easy—just above a breath; often urgent—moving with the force that was sweeping them along.

With nothing but the night as a witness, Wyatt destroyed what was left of Glory Dixon's defenses. And when it was over, and they lay arm in arm, trembling from the power of it all, he knew that he would take the same road that he'd taken before. Risk losing his life all over again, for what he now held.

Wyatt smoothed the hair from her face, gentling her racing heart with his words and his touch. "I love you, Glory Dixon."

Weak from spent passion, Glory still clung to him, unwilling to let him go.

Ah, God, Wyatt thought. *Making love to you every night for the rest of our lives would be heaven.*

Glory gasped. She'd heard that! For the first time since their relationship really started, she'd read *his* mind. He'd said it couldn't happen. That he never let down his guard.

She turned her cheek, hiding her smile against his chest. He didn't know it yet, but he'd done more than let down his guard.

When he let her into his mind, he let her into his heart. Now she knew there were no more walls between them.

"Wyatt…"

The sound of his name on her lips was sweet music. "What, darlin'?"

"You're more than welcome to try…if you think you're able."

For a moment, he couldn't think past the shock. The little witch! She just read his mind!

"Oh, my God!" He sat straight up in bed. "What did you just do?"

She only smiled, then stretched enticingly, arching her body like a lazy cat.

"You heard what I thought…didn't you?"

"Why, yes…I believe that I did," she said.

"That does it," Wyatt said, and then pounced, pinning her with the weight of his body, and with the dark, hot fire in his eyes. "I'm done for." His words were rich with laughter, the kisses he stole from her smile were warm and sweet.

Glory shivered with longing. Even though they'd just made love, she wanted him all over again. And then she remembered his sister's advice about letting him know what was in her heart.

"Are you sure you're done?" she whispered.

"Lord, yes," he laughed.

I'm not done, Wyatt. I've only just begun.

The laughter stopped. And when he looked in her eyes, his

heart almost followed suit. Although her lips didn't move, he heard her whispers as clearly as if she were leaning next to his ear. The surge of desire that came with the words made him shake with longing. What she said…what she asked… what she wanted to do!

"Have mercy," Wyatt muttered. "Not unless you marry me."

Glory blinked slowly as she began to refocus. "Is that a proposal?"

He raised himself up on his elbows and began to grin. "Why do I feel like I've just been had?"

Her eyes widened in feigned innocence. "Oh, no, Wyatt. You're the one on top. I believe it's me who was just had."

His eyes twinkled as he scooped her into his arms, rolling until the mattress was at his back and they were lying face-to-face.

"Now, then, where were we?" he whispered. "Oh, yes, I was waiting for an answer."

"I will marry you, Wyatt Hatfield. I will love you forever. I will make babies with you and share your life until I draw my last breath."

Tears came unexpectedly. The beauty of her vow stunned him.

"And I will be forever grateful," he whispered.

"So what are we waiting for?" Glory asked.

I guess I'm just waiting for the sound of your voice.

Glory paused, gazing down at the face of the man she'd come to love, and lightly traced the path of the scar across his cheek.

Quietly…in the dark…in the tiny cabin in the deep Kentucky woods, she called his name aloud.

A single tear rolled down his cheek, following the path of the scar. It was the sweetest sound that he'd heard on earth. Someone was calling him home.

Epilogue

Spring had been a long time coming. Kentucky had wintered through more snow than it had seen in years, delaying the finishing touches that Wyatt and Glory Hatfield kept trying to put on their new home. It hadn't been so bad, wintering in that tiny cabin nestled deep in the woods, but the ground had long since thawed, and Glory had already seen the first Johnny-jump-ups beneath the trees around Granny's cabin.

Their dark, shiny green spikes with a single white flower suspended at the end of a miniature stalk were among the first woodland flowers to part the mat of rotting leaves. They were nature's signal that it was time to work the ground and plant the crops.

And for Wyatt, spring was a homecoming in more ways than one. He'd started out a child of the land, and despite a lot of lost years between then and now, it had called him home, just as his wife had done. He couldn't wait to put plow into ground, and he'd been thinking of buying some Hereford heifers to start a herd of cattle.

And then finally, three days ago, the last nail had been

driven in the house. Yesterday, two trucks from a furniture store in Hazard had delivered, and then set up, an entire houseful of brand-new furniture, which now resided in the rooms in shiny splendor, waiting to give comfort and ease.

A wide, spacious porch framed the entire front of the house, and along each side, brand-new lattice gleamed white in the noonday sun, waiting for the first tendrils of a vine…or a rose…to breach the heights. Hanging from the underside of the porch, and rocking gently in the breeze, was a white wooden swing just big enough for two.

Wyatt pulled into the yard with the last load of their clothes from the cabin and started carrying them through the back door. Inside, he could hear the frantic patter of Glory's feet as she scurried from room to room, making sure that everything was in its proper place. At any moment, the first attendees to their housewarming might arrive, and Wyatt knew that Glory would skin his hide if he wasn't dressed and waiting.

She gasped when she saw him coming through the kitchen. "Give those to me. I'll hang them up while you get dressed."

Wyatt's chin jutted as he lifted the hangers high above the reach of her hands. "No, darlin'. I've got them. I told you before, you're not carrying anything heavier for the next few months than my baby."

In spite of her anxiety, she savored the adoration in his eyes, as well as his tender care, absently rubbing the slight swell of belly barely noticeable beneath her white gauzy dress as he disappeared into the back of the house.

The dress, like the house, was new and bought especially for this day. The neckline scooped, almost revealing a gentle swell of breast. The bodice was semifitted, and hung loose and comfortable against her expanding waistline. The skirt hung midlength between knee and ankle, and moved with the sway of her body like a tiny white bell. The sides of her hair were pulled away from her face and fastened at the back of her neck with a length of white lace.

Minutes later, as Wyatt came out of the room buttoning a clean shirt and tucking it into his jeans, he looked up, saw

Glory standing in the doorway, anxiously looking down the long, winding road, and had to take a breath before he could speak. She stood silhouetted against the bright light of day. For a moment, he thought an angel had come to bless this house. And then he smiled. What was wrong with him? One already had. Her name was Glory.

She spun, her eyes wide with excitement, a smile wide upon her lips. ''Someone's coming!'' she cried.

Wyatt swung her off her feet and stole a quick kiss, aware that it would have to last him a while. ''They're supposed to, darlin','' he teased. ''We're having a party, remember?''

He clasped her hand, and together, they went out to meet the first arrival.

An hour later, the party was in full swing and the air full of laughter. A game of horseshoes was in progress over near the barn. A long picnic table had been set up underneath the shade tree at the edge of the yard and with every carful of well-wishers who arrived, more food was added to what it already held.

Children ran and climbed, shrieked and cried, and while Edward Lee was the only six-foot child in the midst of the play, he was having as much fun as the smallest.

Gifts for their new home were piled to overflowing on the porch, and Glory basked in the joy of knowing she was loved. Just when she thought there was no one left in Larner's Mill who could possibly come, more cars began to arrive.

But when the occupants started spilling from every opening, she started to smile. It was Wyatt's family.

''My goodness! Who are all of those people?'' a woman asked.

Glory smiled. ''My husband's family.''

''Well, my word,'' the lady said. ''I had no idea.'' She glanced down at Glory's belly, then back up at the brood moving like a groundswell toward the food and frivolity. ''Fruitful lot, aren't they?''

Glory laughed aloud. ''Yes, ma'am. I believe that they are.''

* * *

Babies were napping on their mothers' shoulders and the older children were playing quietly in the shade. Typical of the mountains, men sat in one spot, gathered together by the bonds that made them head of the families, while women gathered in another, secure in the knowledge that they were sheltered by more than the breadth of their husbands' shoulders. And as one, they watched while Glory and Wyatt sat side by side on the front porch steps and began opening the gifts that had been brought to bless this house.

The thoughtfulness with which each gift had been chosen was obvious. Everyone knew that the newlyweds had literally "started with nothing." The fire that had destroyed Glory's family had also destroyed everything she owned.

Stacks of new linens grew with every package they opened. Often a gasp would go up from the crowd as Wyatt would hold up a particularly fine piece of glassware meant to be put on display. Mouth-watering jars of homemade jellies and jams lined the porch like fine jewels, their colors rich and dark, like the sweets themselves, waiting for a hot biscuit to top off. From the hand-embroidered tablecloths to the colorful, crocheted afghans, everything came from the heart.

And then Justin and David Hatfield, two of Wyatt's brothers, came around the corner of the house, carrying their gift between them.

"It's been in the family for years," Justin said, setting it at Wyatt's and Glory's feet. "Nearly every one of us has used it for one baby or another, little brother. We thought it was time you had a turn."

Glory was overcome by the symbolic gesture. The rich, dark grain of the wood was smooth and warm to the touch. And when she pushed on the side, the old wooden rockers rocked without even a squeak. They hadn't just given her a cradle. They'd made room for her in their hearts.

"Oh, Wyatt, a cradle for the baby! It's fine! So fine!"

And so are you, darlin'. So are you.

Glory turned, and for just a moment, the rest of the crowd shifted out of her focus. There was nothing in the world except Wyatt's face, and the love he felt for her shining out of his eyes.

"Thank you, Wyatt."

"There she goes. She's doin' it again," Justin grumbled. "All I can say is, thank God Mary can't read my mind or I'd be in trouble from sunup to sundown."

Everyone laughed, and the moment passed as they opened their next gift. The box was small, and the crystal angel figurine even smaller, but before she ever looked at the card, Glory knew that it had come from Lane and Toni. She'd been nicknamed the family angel, and took pride in their love and the name.

"It's from Lane and Toni," she said, holding it up for the people to see. "I'm going to save it for the baby's room. He'll need a guardian angel."

"He?" Wyatt leaned over and kissed the side of her cheek. "Do you know something I don't?"

"Figure of speech," she said, and everyone laughed.

But as she set the angel back in the box, Wyatt wondered at her secretive smile. He'd already learned that the less he knew about what she was thinking, the better off he was.

The next gift was quite heavy and bulky. And when the wrapping came off and they realized it was a large sack of dog food from Liam Fowler and his wife, they tried to find a way to say thank-you for something they didn't need.

And then Liam grinned at the blank smiles on their faces and pointed toward his truck. Edward Lee was coming across the yard with a squirming black-and-white pup in his arms. He knelt at their feet, then set the pup down on the ground.

"He's a pretty one, ain't he, Mornin' Glory?" His long, slender fingers caressed the pup's ears with gentle strokes. "I'll bet he'll make a real good watchdog, too."

Glory held back tears, although it was hard to do. He was marked so like her brother's pup that she could almost hear J.C.'s shout of laughter. When Wyatt slid an arm around her shoulder, she leaned into his strength and found the courage to smile.

"Thank you, Edward Lee. It's just what we needed to make his house a home."

Pleased that his gift had been a success, he scooted back into the crowd, teasing the pup with a string of ribbon lying on the ground, while Glory and Wyatt continued to unwrap.

When all the gifts had been opened, and thanks had been given for the fellowship that they'd shared, as well as for the presents, Wyatt held up his hand. He had a gift of his own for Glory, and he'd been saving it for last.

"Wait," he said, "there's one more left to open," and ran to their car.

Surprised, Glory could only sit and wonder what he'd done now. But when he came walking back to the house, carrying a box so big that he could barely get his arms around it, she started to smile. Just like Wyatt. He did nothing halfway.

He placed it before her like gold on a platter, then stepped back, becoming one of the onlookers as he watched her shredding the ribbon and paper.

Twice she laughed and had to call for his help when the knots in the ribbon wouldn't come undone. And then finally, there was nothing left but to open the top and look in.

At first, she could see nothing for the folds of tissue paper. And then the paper finally parted and she peered inside. The smile of expectation slid sideways on her face.

"Oh, Wyatt."

It was all she could say. As hard as she tried to stop them, the tears still came, filling her eyes and running down her cheeks in silent profusion.

Stunned by her reaction, the guests shifted uneasily on their feet, uncertain whether to watch or turn away, yet wanting desperately to know what had sparked such a reaction.

And then as they watched, they saw. Handful by handful, she began to pull the contents out of the box, piling them in wild abandon into her lap. By fours and sixes, by ones and by threes. And with each handful she took, her movements became more eager, laughing through tears while they spilled

out of her lap and onto the steps beside her. As nothing else
could have ever done, they filled her hands and her heart.

And when there was nothing more to take out, she wrapped
her arms around the lot as Wyatt knelt at her feet and began
wiping the tears from her cheeks.

"I couldn't give you back what you lost," he said softly.
"But it's something to remember it by."

"Will you help me plant them?"

Wyatt grinned, and then stood. "We all will. Why do you
think I got so many?"

And then he grabbed the packets of seeds by the handful
and started tossing them to the crowd.

"Plant them anywhere. Plant them everywhere," he
shouted. "By the barns, along the fences, down by the well.
Run them up the mailbox and the old windmill. But not here."
He pointed toward the two, shiny new trellises on either side
of the porch. "Glory and I will plant here."

Caught up in the fantasy of the moment, people began
claiming their spot, and before long, the place was crawling
with gardeners on their hands and knees, planting the tiny
seeds with makeshift tools in the rich, spring earth.

Wyatt took Glory by the hand, and led her to the side of
the porch.

"I'll dig, you drop," he said.

Careful of her dress, she went to her knees, and through a
veil of tears, planted the seeds that, weeks later, would grow
into vines. And from the vines, would come flowers that gave
bloom in the mornings. Blue as a summer sky, she could
almost see the fragile little trumpets that would hang from
these walls like small bells.

They were the morning glory, her daddy's favorite flower,
and her namesake.

Like nothing else they'd been given this day, these would
make their house her home.

Glory's hands were shaking as she dropped the last of her
seeds into the ground. When she looked up at the man at her
side, she knew that she was loved.

"I wish Granny had lived to see this day," she said softly.
Tenderness colored his words and his touch as he cupped
r face with his hand.

"What makes you think she didn't?" Wyatt asked. "Re-
ember, darlin', time doesn't break the bonds of love."

*   *   *   *   *

SHADES OF A DESPERADO

To the people who have the faith
to trust in something other than what they see
before their eyes, God will bless you.
To those who act on instinct rather than rules,
God watches over you.
To those who trust with their hearts
and not with their heads, I thank God.
To those who live today with memories of a past that
won't let go, have faith in God.
To Leslie Wainger who shared a dream,
may God be with you always.

Prologue

877
he Black Hills of the Dakota Territory

The gun in Dakota's hands felt warm and familiar to him, ut the look in his eyes was as harsh and bitter as the Dakota ands for which he'd been named. Across the room, he vatched Mercy Hollister from the tiny cabin's only bed like hawk with its prey; the knot in his gut tightening with every reath that he took.

Damn her beautiful, lying face.

Twice his forefinger brushed the pistol's hair trigger as he ontemplated the hole the bullet would make in her soft white ody, and each time, the knot in his belly gave a lurch, reninding him that he'd been a fool to trust, and an even bigger ool to love.

Angry with himself and the futility of it all, he brushed a and across his face, as if wiping away what was left of a ad dream, yet when he looked up, the reality of the situation

remained. He was running from the law with the woman
now believed had betrayed him…and he still loved her.

He raised himself from a reclining position long enough
glance out the small, dusty windowpane. The plume of d
he'd seen earlier down on the flats was just that little
closer, evidence that Sheriff Ab Schuler and his posse h
found them after all.

He dropped back against the wall, only half-aware of t
soft, aimless tune Mercy was humming as she stripped dov
to wash her trail-weary body. As his gaze swept her nudi
he hated himself for the weakness of still wanting a wom:
who'd turned him in for the money, and he was certain Mer
had done just that.

If she wasn't the one who'd told where they were goin
how else had they been found? He'd been using this hideo
for more than three years, and to date, no lawman had ev
gotten close to finding it. But, Dakota reminded himself, he
never been fool enough before to tell a woman anything b
a lie. That was before Mercy—before he'd let her into h
heart and into his life. Now Ab Schuler was riding Dakota
trail like it was a marked map.

He knew the price on his head was enough to make broth
turn against brother. Why had he let himself believe a harl
would be different? Why had he let himself fall in love wi
a woman whose last lover before him had been the very she
iff who was dogging their trail? Just because she cried o
with joy when they made love, just because she swore sl
loved him more than life itself, that didn't make it so.

The gun felt heavy in his hands, almost as heavy as th
weight in his heart. With a slow, angry sigh, he laid it on h
belly, letting it balance on the flat, bare plane as he put h
hands behind his head and leaned against the wall. Using h
fists for a pillow, he angled his long legs off one side of th
narrow bunk, watching her as she washed and wondering
he had the guts to kill her.

Unaware of the drama being played out in Dakota's mind
Mercy dipped a rag in a basin of tepid water, ignoring th

sediment in the bottom of the pan. Riding the trail with an outlaw had been harder than she'd imagined, but she had no regrets. Ever since she and Dakota left Trinity three days ago, she'd been eating dirt, as well as wearing it. Washing it off her body felt like heaven.

And, for the first time in as long as she could remember, she was happy—truly happy. It had taken guts for her to leave the security of a roof over her head, a warm, dry bed and daily food on the table, even if she'd had to earn it by lying down for every sorry-ass man who passed through town.

Loving an outlaw hadn't been in Mercy's plans, but Dakota had been a hard man to resist. His black hair was only a few shades darker than his gaze, yet when he smiled at her, she saw the man he could have been...and in his eyes, she was the woman she should have been. She saw something in Dakota's face that she'd never seen before in another living soul. Trust. He not only loved her, he trusted her. She didn't know where this crazy life she'd chosen was going to lead, but as long as she was by Dakota's side, she would be happy.

She dipped the rag in the basin again, swishing it around and then wringing it out before lifting the weight of her long, dark hair to wash the back of her neck. Even though the water was less than clear, she couldn't remember ever being as glad to feel clean as she did right now.

The bunk creaked behind her, and she smiled. She could feel Dakota's gaze on her bare body. The cabin he'd brought her to was little more than a roof and four walls, yet with him at her side, it seemed like a mansion. It was going to be home...their home.

Suddenly, she could wait no longer. Clean or not, she wanted to lie in Dakota's arms, to feel his hands on her body and his mouth on her lips. She needed to hear the words he always whispered in her ear right before he took her over the edge of reason.

Sweet Mercy...have mercy....

She smiled to herself, picturing the look on his face when he said it, and dropped the rag into the basin. She turned with

anticipation in her eyes. But the smile on her lips stilled before
it became full-blown.

There was a look on Dakota's face that she'd never seen—
a cold, deadly expression that stopped her breath and very
nearly her heart. She inhaled sharply as fear sliced through
her daydreams, rudely yanking her back to the reality of loving a man who lived by the gun.

"Dakota?"

He didn't answer. He didn't move.

Mercy darted toward the bed, forgetting her sponge bath
and the fact that she was naked.

Oddly, her nudity did not raise Dakota's lust. Instead, it
seemed to enhance the innocence of the blue-eyed woman
coming toward him, as if she were proving she had nothing
to hide.

Don't fall for this again, he reminded himself, but when
she fell into his arms with tears on her face, he cursed the
surge of protective longing that swept over him.

*Even now, sweet Mercy, when I know you for what you
really are...*

"Sweetheart! What's wrong?" Mercy asked.

Angry with himself and with her, he took her and rolled,
pinning her beneath him on the dusty, narrow bunk. But when
he pressed the barrel of his gun against her temple, he broke
out in a cold sweat, unable to pull the trigger.

Mercy was in shock. Never in the six months that she'd
known Dakota had he treated her in such a fashion. Other
men had, but she thought he was different, and because this
was so unexpected, she couldn't stop her tears.

"Dakota! Talk to me! Tell me what's wrong! You know I
love you! You know I'd do anything for you! Why are you
treating me this way?"

Dakota shook his head, trying to clear his thoughts, but all
he succeeded in doing was hazing his vision of her.

Mercy couldn't believe what was happening. Even though
there were tears in Dakota's eyes, she feared for her life. None
of this was making any sense.

"Stop this!" she screamed, and began hammering on his bare chest with her fists. "You're scaring me! Whatever is wrong, I've got a right to know!"

Words ripped from his throat in harsh, angry grunts. "Why? Why did you do it?"

"Do what?" she cried. "I didn't do anything but love you!"

Dakota blinked, trying to clear his vision. The action did little except blur the fear he saw on her face.

Make her pay, he told himself, shifting his body so that she was completely immobile, pinned to the bed by his weight. With his last ounce of determination, he increased the pressure of the gun against her temple. Their gazes locked as he cocked the hammer. The small, metallic click echoed loudly in the sudden silence of the small one-room shack.

Mercy froze, her eyes widening in horror as she became aware of the desperation on Dakota's face.

"Dakota... My God...don't! I love you! Doesn't that mean anything to you anymore?"

Her words ripped through the pain in his chest, spilling the hurtful anger into every part of his body. With a cold, cruel smile, he leaned down, dragging his mouth across her face and ripping a kiss from her trembling lips. Even now, as brutally as he was treating her, he felt her respond.

Finally he tore himself away, only slightly satisfied with the small drop of blood lingering on the edge of her lower lip. With a low, guttural curse, he raked his gun down her cheek. As badly as he wanted to hate her, he caught himself regretting the fear he'd put into her eyes. But his heart wasn't the only thing breaking. His voice cracked as he spoke.

"I guess I didn't know you quite as well as I thought. You're quite a little soldier, aren't you, darlin'?"

Tears tracked down her face, only to disappear in the thick black hair pillowing her head. Her voice was weak and shaking as she lifted her hands in supplication.

"My God, my God... I don't know what you mean."

With an angry swipe of his hand, he slapped her hands away, refusing the gesture of peace.

"Since you've ridden just about every man you ever met, I guess that earns you the title."

Mercy stiffened. Not once in their entire relationship had Dakota ever alluded to her life as a prostitute, and now, when she'd given it and everything else up for him, he had thrown it in her face. Hurt by an accusation she couldn't deny, her tears fell faster, in anger now.

"Damn you!" she cried, and then choked on a sob as she hit him full force on the side of the face with the flat of her hand.

The slap ricocheted from tooth to tooth, and still Dakota kept his gun aimed at her head.

"Either pull the trigger or get off me!" Mercy screamed, and began hitting Dakota with doubled-up fists. "If you hate me this much, then do it! I dare you!"

He neither moved nor answered as his dark, angry gaze continued to burn across her features.

Groaning with disbelief, she pushed at his chest with the flat of both hands, trying to get out from under his weight.

"My God! I was such a fool! I left everything I had to ride with you! I put my own life at risk to run with a man with a price on his head. I gave you something I never gave another living soul."

The rage in her startled him. He might have expected it from an innocent…but not from Mercy. She was anything but innocent. Though he knew that, it was still all Dakota could do to meet her gaze.

"Damn you, Dakota, I thought you were different, but I was wrong! You're no better than every other man who spilled himself in me. In fact, you're worse! At least they didn't tell me a lie to get me to spread my legs. If that's all you wanted, then why didn't you say so?"

When she shifted beneath him, blatantly offering herself up to his maleness with a look in her eyes he would never forget, all the rage in him died. He eased the hammer on the pistol down without firing the shot. Choking on sobs, she went limp with relief. Dakota buried his face in the curve of her neck and swallowed a sob of his own.

A silent moment passed while Mercy struggled to get past her shock and Dakota fought to regain his sense of purpose. He was the first to act. Without speaking, he rolled himself from her body and stalked to the other end of the room, where he'd dumped his gear. He turned once, looking back at her with a longing he didn't know how to hide, then began dressing to ride.

Mercy watched in disbelief, trying to figure out what had gone so terribly wrong. But when Dakota jammed his hat on his head, slung his saddlebags over his shoulder and picked up his rifle, she jumped out of bed in sudden fright. Dear God! He was leaving her behind!

"Wait for me!" she begged, and started pulling on clothes in wild abandon.

He paused in the doorway, staring long and hard out toward the valley below, then spun abruptly, as if making a sudden decision. Without giving himself time to change his mind, he tossed her his rifle.

"Here," he drawled. "I know you can shoot, so if you love me like you say you do, then don't let Schuler take me back to hang."

Mercy caught the gun in midair as the door slammed shut behind him. Her face paled as she clutched the rifle. Suddenly she understood. The posse must have found them, and if Dakota's behavior was anything by which to judge, he believed she'd betrayed him!

"Dakota! No!"

But it was too late. She heard him riding away.

Frantic, she began grabbing at her clothing, her entire body in tremors. Buttons wouldn't go into holes, and fabric stuck to her still-damp body, hindering the haste she so desperately needed. Finally she had everything on but her boots. As she bent down to slip them on, the handgun she'd begun carrying in the pocket of her skirt shifted against her thigh. She shuddered and said a small prayer. Seconds later, she was out of the cabin, with the rifle in her hand and the handgun bumping against her leg as she ran.

Sensing her panic, her horse shied, dancing sideways, nickering and tossing its head as she tried to mount.

"Whoa, whoa…easy, boy," she muttered, trying to calm the horse, as well as her own racing heart, but it wasn't to be.

As she was in the midst of trying to get her toe in the stirrup, the sounds of gunfire echoed from the canyon below. Startled by the abrupt and unexpected noise, the horse reared, then bolted, dumping her in the dirt and leaving her unable to ride to Dakota's aid.

"Oh, no," Mercy groaned.

Picking herself and the rifle up out of the dirt as the horse disappeared, she started running down the long, winding path, with the sound of gunfire slamming into her body as it echoed from rim to rim.

She came to a sliding halt at the crest of the hill and looked down into the canyon, staring in mute despair. She was too late! Dakota was pinned down, with no way out. Using his dead horse for a shield, he continued to fire at the men in the posse with cold precision.

Mercy groaned. She had to help him!

With shaking hands, she dropped to one knee and aimed the rifle, adjusting her shot to the downward slant in elevation. But when she realized the rifle Dakota had tossed her had only two rounds remaining, hope died.

"Damn you, Dakota, why? You never carry unloaded guns. Why now?"

Her finger slid from the trigger as she lowered the rifle to her side. Even if she hit her target both times, it would not be enough to stop the posse from capturing him. And if that happened, then she would be helpless to do as he'd asked. He already believed she'd betrayed him. No matter what, she couldn't let him hang.

It seemed like hours, but it was only a matter of minutes

before the shooting stopped, as abruptly as it had started. Even where she was standing, the smell of gunpowder filled the air, and the silence after the endless barrage was almost as frightening as the inevitable arrest she saw coming. She stifled a sob. Dear God, Dakota was out of ammunition!

She watched as Ab Schuler stepped out from behind a rock, calling for Dakota to surrender. When Dakota stood, Mercy's spirit sank. And when he tossed his empty gun in the dirt and lifted his arms above his head, she panicked.

This couldn't be happening! Only minutes earlier she'd been planning the rest of their lives, and now it was over.

But Mercy hadn't survived this long in the Dakota Territory by being weak, and she couldn't ignore Dakota's last request. She got to her feet. Still clutching the rifle Dakota had given her, she walked to the edge of the rim. Schuler was putting handcuffs on her man. Panic resurfaced.

"Nooo!" she screamed, and the sound of her voice echoed down into the belly of the canyon like the eerie wail of a she-panther that had just lost its mate.

Momentarily surprised by the sound of her voice, the men down below paused in their jubilant actions, then stared around in confusion. When they saw the woman standing poised on the rim above them with a rifle in her hands, to a man they began grabbing for weapons and scrambling for cover.

Dakota looked up. Forgetting the handcuffs that Schuler had just placed around his wrists, he stared, fixing the image of Mercy Hollister one last time within his mind. The distance between them seemed to shrink, and he almost believed he could see the tears on her face. He turned until he was facing her squarely, offering her a full view of his chest.

Do it, girl. If you ever loved me, for God's sake, do it now!

Even from where she was standing, Mercy recognized Dakota's move. But he was asking her for something she wasn't sure she knew how to give. How could she end the life of the only man she'd ever loved?

From the corner of her eye, she saw Ab Schuler grabbing

for his rifle. She shifted her stance. There was no more time. She lifted the rifle to her shoulder, taking aim the way her brother had taught her years ago.

God help me.

She cocked the hammer.

God forgive me.

Everything seemed to happen in slow motion. The sound of the gunshot cracked like winter ice on a spring-thawing river. Loud and clear, the echo bounced from rim to rim and into Mercy's heart, piercing her as sharply as the bullet that struck Dakota square in the chest.

Mercy watched as Dakota dropped, and from where she was standing, it was like watching snow fall, soundless, and so inevitably final. Pain tore through her body in waves as nausea nearly sent her to her knees. With a wild cry of ungovernable rage for what she'd done, she drew back the rifle and sent it spinning out into the vast space below, then thought about following it down. Sick at heart, and staggering from an onslaught of emotion, she fell to the ground, unable to look at Dakota again.

It hurt to breathe and she wondered if he'd felt the same pain when her bullet ripped through his chest and into his heart. A wave of vertigo sent her grabbing for dirt, and as she did, the handgun in her pocket slid between her knees. Seconds later, she was clutching it in one hand and staring up into the wide expanse of the midday sky, remembering that only yesterday she and Dakota had made love beneath that same bowl of blue.

The steel warmed to her touch, offering comfort and the answer she needed. She took a deep breath, then lifted the gun.

Ab Schuler spun with gun in hand as the outlaw dropped at his feet. A surge of anger washed over him. He'd been cheated out of watching the son of a bitch hang. He looked up in time to see Mercy's rifle go flying into space. Along with his men, he stared in mute fascination as it seemed to hang in the air before spinning end over end, then shattering on the rocks below. But when Mercy dropped to the ground and pulled a pistol from her skirt, fear for her stunned him as he realized her intent. He started up the path, screaming her name as he ran.

The second shot came before he'd gone ten yards, and he paused, unable to believe what she'd done. As before, the single gunshot echoed, but when it had passed, an unearthly stillness seemed to come over the canyon. The men in the posse looked away, as if they felt guilt for having been a part of what had just taken place, despite being fully within the boundaries of the law.

Up until now, the day had been hot and still, but a sharp wind suddenly sprang up, wailing through the mouth of the canyon like the sound of someone crying. The high-pitched moan grew louder and louder as the wind continued in force. One man quickly dropped to his knees in prayer, while another scrambled for his horse and rode out without ever looking back. Years later, as the story was told and retold, one thing never changed. To a man, the posse swore they'd felt the hot wrath of God that day as He came sweeping through the canyon to reclaim the two lost souls.

Chapter 1

Present Day
The Kiamichi Mountains of southeastern Oklahoma

A small branch slapped Boone MacDonald across the nose, bringing quick tears to his eyes that he blinked away. Silently he cursed the thickness of the undergrowth through which he was creeping, as well as the weak light from the three-quarter moon filtering through the dense thicket of trees. Skulking in woods as heavy as those on the Kiamichi Mountains was next to impossible. Not even a possum could move through here without making some sort of noise.

A low murmur of voices from the men up ahead drifted on the air, reminding him of the urgency of his task. Working as an undercover agent for the Drug Enforcement Administration was nothing new for him, but working this deep under cover was not something he liked. It wasn't the first time he'd insinuated himself into a gang, but it *was* the first time it had taken him so long to find out who was running the show.

He'd been living a lie for nearly six weeks, and he had yet to meet the man behind the money.

For the past half hour, success had been less than fifteen yards ahead. Each time the silhouette of a tall, well-built man was briefly outlined against the moonlight, Boone could almost see his face. But it never happened. They were moving too quickly for him to get close enough for an identification.

Frustration mounted. Intent on the task at hand, he unintentionally walked into a spider web and stifled a curse as he swiped at the sticky, clinging strands on his face.

Suddenly he froze, part of the web still stuck to his hand. They'd stopped! His instinct for survival was at an all-time high as he stood with one ear cocked to the wind while the hapless spider escaped up a branch. Boone slowed his breathing, concentrating instead on the sounds around him.

In his mind, there could be only two reasons for the quiet. Either he'd been made and someone was at this moment circling his position, or they'd reached their destination. Forced to wait for answers he might not like, Boone took a quiet step back, moving deeper into the darkness of the trees.

Above him, an owl suddenly took flight, and he cursed his luck in having stopped beneath its roost. If the men were on to him, the bird's flight alone would indicate his position. He pulled a .357 Magnum from the holster beneath his black denim jacket, then squatted within the dense undergrowth, making himself less of a target.

All his senses were keying on sound and movement, sorting what he recognized from what he did not. His face was a study in darkness, both in spirit and in fact. Black eyes glittered dangerously from beneath hooded lids, giving away nothing of what was going on inside his mind.

He was a man who lived on the edge—a man who played by his own set of rules and, by doing so, had kept himself alive. His friends were few, his family none. As far back as he could remember, he'd answered to no one but himself, which, as a child, had been the reason for his constant movement through the welfare system. The way he'd looked at it, no one had wanted him. In self-defense, he had refused to care.

But that attitude had put him on the wrong side of the law at an early age. When he was sixteen, he had watched his best friend die from a gunshot wound to the head. At that moment, something inside of him had snapped. When the shock of it was over, he'd made a vow that ultimately changed his life.

Becoming a cop might have been his salvation. But even if he was now on the side of right, he was still living on the wrong side of the law, and it had seared his soul. He'd run with the bad boys for so long that being an outlaw had become the norm. He'd forgotten everything about the real world, including how to trust. The only thing Boone trusted was himself, his instincts, and they were telling him now to stay still.

While he watched, the owl he'd startled flew silently out of sight. His grip shifted on the .357 as a sharp burst of laughter broke the quiet in which he was waiting. He frowned. From his point of view, there wasn't a damn thing funny about the situation.

As he continued to listen, the unmistakable sound of car doors opening and closing brought him to his feet.

"Damn it," he muttered, and bolted through the trees, hoping for one last chance to ID his man. All he saw was the disappearing taillights of two separate vehicles. Once again, he'd missed his chance!

His face mirrored disgust as he holstered his gun, reminding himself that there was always a next time. Peering at the luminous dial of his digital watch to check the hour, he started back through the trees. The way he figured it, he was a couple of miles from his truck, and it was all uphill.

Habit sent him up the mountain at a different angle from the one he'd come down. Like the men with whom he ran, he moved with stealth, searching shadows and choosing his paths with caution. Fifteen minutes later, he was telling himself that he was too far east when he heard an indistinct sound.

Eyes narrowing, he felt for the bulge of his gun beneath his jacket. But when the sound came again, he knew what he'd heard, and he started running with no thought of stealth.

Bathed in moonlight, the woman stood without moving while the water from the creek in which she was standing tugged at the hem of her long, wet gown. Plastered to her trembling body, the pale, fragile fabric made her appear like alabaster, rather than a living, breathing soul, and yet Boone knew that she was real. No statue had hair that fluid and dark, or breasts that lifted and fell with each indrawn breath.

The soft, helpless sobs that he'd heard still wracked her body. Her beauty was haunting, but her pain was palpable, plowing into subconscious memories of his own that were better left alone.

Riveted by her presence, he hesitated, wanting to go to her, but afraid to interrupt something he didn't understand.

"I love you. I've always loved you," she whispered, then reached out in front of her, clutching at air.

Boone took a quick step back into the trees, using the shelter of darkness as he trained his gaze on the scene, searching for the man who must surely be there. To his surprise, no one came forward.

Again the woman swayed where she stood, choking on her own sobs, as if in terrible pain.

"Why?" she cried. "Why didn't you believe me before it was too late?"

When she went to her knees in the cold mountain stream, Boone stalked out of the trees, heading toward her with single-minded intent. It was September. At night, the water in that creek had to be freezing. He called out to her, anxious not to frighten her, but knowing he had to help all the same.

Rachel Brand groaned as the pain in her head shattered, spilling through her body and sending her into the same black, numbing void that always preceded cognizance. Yet when sanity came, she knew without doubt that she'd sleepwalked again. This time she was in the creek, wet and cold, with no memory of how she'd gotten there. All she knew was that the episodes were becoming more frequent and, if tonight was any indication, life-threatening. Pulling a stunt like this in the Kiamichis in autumn was risky; repeating it in mid-winter could be deadly.

She got up, thumping her knee in helpless frustration. Tossing back the braid hanging over her shoulder, then grabbing at the wet, clinging fabric of the gown wrapped around her legs, she started to climb out of the water. But disgust gave way to terror when a deep, quiet voice broke the solitude of the night.

"Lady... are you all right?"

Horrified, Rachel froze. She was no longer alone! She spun, unaware of how the gown had plastered itself to her body, delineating a slender build, a fullness of breast, the gentle flare of slim hips and long, trim legs.

In fear for her life, she began backing up as a tall, dark stranger came out of the trees. When he paused within the pale glow of moonlight in the clearing near the edge of the stream, she took one look at the strength in his body and the length of his legs and knew she could not outrun him.

"Don't hurt me," she begged, taking several tentative steps backward, as if testing the man's intent.

Boone wished he could pull out a badge and assure her that he meant her no harm. He knew how she would perceive his appearance. The outlaw look was in vogue when you were running with a pack like Denver Cherry's.

"Lady, be careful!" he said, his voice low and urgent, as she stumbled on the rocks hidden beneath the cold, icy waters. "Don't be afraid. I don't mean you any harm. I heard you crying and came to see if you needed help."

"No, I'm fine!" she cried, motioning to him to stay back. "Just leave me alone. Please!"

Rachel's heart was thundering, and her legs were shaking.

Frantic, raked the dense forest behind him with her gaze, wondering how many more like him might come creeping out of the shadows.

Boone winced at the panic in her voice. This was getting him nowhere. Instinct told him to get out while the getting was good. The longer he stayed here, the more likely it was that some man would show up, and then there would be hell to pay explaining why he was alone in the woods with a half-dressed and terrified woman. But she looked so lost, and something inside him couldn't let go. He took a deep breath and gave it one last try.

"I swear to God, I would never hurt you."

The sound of his voice…and those words… They struck a chord of memory in Rachel that she'd never known was there. Her gaze focused on the cut of his shoulders and the tilt to his head, and she forgot what she'd been about to say. She had the strangest sensation of having heard that voice say those same words before.

Good sense was telling her to run, but her feet wouldn't move. His presence frightened and at the same time compelled her.

As she stood there trying to make sense of it all, the sensation of numbing cold disappeared. Before her eyes, the night began to turn backward, and Rachel watched in quiet defeat as the brilliant rays of a pink-and-gold sunset suddenly framed a man standing before her. He seemed to be the same man as the one in the forest, and yet in the ways that mattered, he was not.

This is it, she thought. *I'm either losing my mind, or going to die.*

The man now standing before her smiled, and to her disbelief, she felt herself smiling back. When he started toward her with a bounce in his step and a gleam in his eye that she seemed to know all too well, everything spun out of control.

* * *

He laughed. "God, woman, but you're too beautiful to be believed."

She threw her arms around his neck and lifted her face for his kiss. It came as she'd expected, hard and swift and with an ever-present sense of urgency. "If you mean that, I'll love you forever," she whispered.

Fear tied hard warning knots in his belly. He wasn't prepared for her openness, or for the loving, trusting look on her face. Now was the time to stop this madness before he got himself in too deep.

"Women don't love men like me," he growled, as his fingers dug into her arms.

She smiled up at him, flirting in spite of the hard-edged glitter in his eyes.

"You don't mean that," she said. "There isn't a woman in Trinity who wouldn't trade places with me right now if they thought you'd give them the time of day."

He laughed, a short, brittle bark of self-deprecating mirth that made her shudder. The smile on his face was just shy of cruel, but the look in his eyes told it all. He was just as scared of this thing between them as she was. Ordinarily, men didn't love women like her, either. She gave nothing away. They paid for what they got. At least, they did until you, she thought, and reached up, tunneling her fingers through the thick black length of his hair.

"And just what kind of a man are you, if not a man to love?"

A bitter expression tore the smile from his face as he turned her loose.

"I'm a loser, darlin'. A man on the wrong side of the law. I've killed before, and I'll very likely kill again. I'm a badlands desperado who's forgotten how to pray and you'd be well advised to leave me alone."

She laid her hand gently against the edge of his cheek. "I would if I could," she said, and then stepped into his embrace and rested her head upon his shoulder. "Besides, haven't you heard that a woman's love can make a bad man good?"

Pain drilled a hole through his heart, piercing all the way to his soul. He looked down, then tilted her chin until she was staring him straight in the face.

"Sweet, sweet Mercy, don't you understand? Once a desperado, always a desperado."

A cloud passed between earth and the moon, casting everything on the Kiamichis into an abrupt darkness. At the apex of total density, Rachel gasped. Just like that, the sunset and the dream man were gone. She had no idea how long she'd been standing there watching the scene unfold inside her mind, but the world had shifted back to nighttime and reality.

Her awareness returned to the cold, flowing water on her bruised and numbing feet, and then to the stranger who'd come out of the dark. The first thought in her head was that if she couldn't see him, he couldn't see her. Grabbing at the tail of her gown, she bolted from the creek and back up the hill, running away from a waking nightmare more horrible than those that haunted her sleep.

Boone heard water splashing. His heart sank. She was running away.

"Wait!" he called, afraid that she would hurt herself by running full tilt through the woods in the darkness. But when the cloud passed and the mountains were once again bathed in moonglow, he found himself standing alone at the edge of the stream.

With a sense of having somehow failed her, he turned and started back the same way he'd come. A long while later, he slid into the seat of his truck and then sat without moving, contemplating the sequence of events that had taken place this night.

He'd started out with one mystery and wound up with two. He still didn't know the identity of the man behind Denver Cherry's operation, and he'd found a woman who seemed as lost as he felt. Even worse, he didn't know her name.

"And that's the way you'd better leave it," he reminded

himself. "You were out to catch a thief, not mess with some one else's woman."

Startled by a car's sudden appearance around a bend in the road below, he started his engine, then let it idle as the vehicle passed by. When it was gone, he turned on the headlights and pulled out of his place of concealment and drove away.

By the time he got into bed and pulled up the covers, it was past 3:00. The silent rooms of the dilapidated trailer that was his undercover home seemed to mock him. They were empty, just like his life.

Long after the lights were out, his jangled nerves were still rocking, on edge. Tonight was the closest he'd come to finding the brains behind Denver Cherry's operation. But he'd failed again, and until he knew all there was to know about this drug operation, he was still a man living a lie.

With a curse, he rolled over on his belly. Jamming his hands beneath his pillow, he closed his eyes and willed himself to sleep. But when sleep finally came, there was little rest. Instead, he dreamed of a tall, slender woman with long black hair who called out his name and then ran screaming from him in fright.

Chapter 2

Rachel twisted the band on the end of her braid and then tossed it over her shoulder. It fell between her shoulder blades with a thump. Dressed for the day, she headed to the kitchen as the welcome scent of fresh-brewed coffee wafted through the rooms.

Working as an emergency medical technician for the town of Razor Bend was often stressful and sometimes hazardous, but to Rachel, it was a fulfilling career. She couldn't remember a time in her life when she hadn't wanted to be in some field of medicine.

She hadn't really chosen the job of EMT. It had chosen her. Years ago she'd witnessed firsthand the dramatic difference that on-the-spot medical help could make in saving someone's life.

After seeing the quick wit and skill of an EMT bringing a nearly drowned child back to life, her decision was made.

While her vocation had been planned, settling in Razor Bend had not. That had been an accident. Two years ago, while driving back from Galveston, Texas, where she'd spent a summer vacation from her job in St. Louis, Missouri, her car had blown a head gasket. It had taken the mechanic in Razor Bend a day and a half to get the parts to fix it. By the time it was ready to go, she'd fallen in love with the small mountain community.

That day, when she drove out of town, she'd left behind the beginnings of some good friendships, as well as her résumé. Less than a month later, she'd gotten a call that changed her life. Now she was a full-fledged employee of the town of Razor Bend. And, except for the recent onset of her sleep-walking episodes, everything was just about perfect.

Rachel entered the kitchen, aiming for the coffee brewing in the pot, and poured herself a cup. What was left of last night's headache lingered at the base of her neck. Coffee in hand, she turned to look out the kitchen window, giving careful attention to the wide expanse of yard that sloped downward toward the trees surrounding the house. As she lifted the mug to her mouth, blowing gently before taking a sip, she took note of the weather, gauging what she was wearing against what she might need before her shift was over. The sun was coming up. The sky looked clear. After the rain they'd had all last week, they could use a picture-perfect day.

It didn't take long for the jolt of caffeine to settle Rachel's nerves, but as she let herself relax, memories came flooding into her mind, and with them a return of the fear and the panic that had come with the stranger who caught her sleep-walking.

With a groan, she turned from the window, her heart pounding, her hands trembling as she clasped them around the cup. She closed her eyes, remembering the sound of his voice coming out of the darkness, and with it the fear that had momentarily shattered what was left of her sanity. He'd seemed so big and menacing, yet he'd made no overture toward her that she could call threatening. His voice had been filled with concern, but Rachel had known such an overwhelming sense of dread that she'd lost all rational thought.

Tired of worrying over things she could not change, she

pulled herself out of the past to focus on matters at hand. Such as a grocery list she needed to fill. Taking a jacket to work, just in case it would rain. Things that mattered. Things that she could control.

But even though her mind had moved on, her body was still in the same place, standing before the window with a cup of coffee held tight in her hand.

Why? Why is this happening to me?

She'd moved up the mountain exactly four weeks ago tomorrow. She'd never had an episode of sleepwalking in her life until a little over six weeks ago. That had been at the end of July. Now it was September, and their frequency was increasing by the week. If only she could remember what was going on in her head when they happened, then maybe she could figure out what it all meant—and, better yet, find a way for them to stop.

The first time she came to in her nightgown on a back street in Razor Bend, she'd panicked. The second time it happened, she'd woken up on the edge of town in a downpour and crept back to her bed, certain that she would be found out and fired.

Luck had been with her, but Rachel didn't trust her luck to hold and had decided that finding a secluded house to rent outside of town might be safer…at least until she could figure out what had triggered this behavior.

This house was about as secluded as it got. Her nearest neighbor was down the mountain and more than two miles away, with acres and acres of dense woods between them. But after last night, she wondered if she'd made a mistake. Last night she'd come close to losing more than a job. What if she hadn't gotten away from that man? What might he have done to her? Worse yet, was he still out there…watching?

A muscle in her arm jerked, sending coffee sloshing over the side of the cup. It was only luck that kept her from spilling it on the navy blue pant legs of her last clean uniform.

With a sigh of disgust, she put her coffee on the counter and then reached for a paper towel to clean up the mess she'd made on the floor. Moments later, she tossed the towel in the trash and then glanced at her watch. Her shift started at eight. It was time to go.

Grabbing her purse and jacket, Rachel exited her house just as the sun was brimming on the horizon. She paused, inhaling the fresh, piney scent of cool, clean air as a squirrel took a flying leap from the edge of her roof to the overhanging branches of a nearby tree. Laughter was rich in her voice as she chided his daring, but the smile on her face stilled as she looked east, past the limbs of the tree, to the sunrise in progress.

Her mouth went dry, and she choked on a breath. Her face flushed, then blanched, as she stared at the rich, vivid hues spreading across the sky. She reached toward the porch railing to steady herself.

It was all coming back. Only now was she remembering what happened before she broke and ran. Last night, the world had shifted before her eyes. She'd watched time move backward from night to day and let a dark-eyed, dangerous man take her in his arms.

Last night she'd tried to convince herself that her encounter with the stranger had been had been part of the dream that had taken her from her bed and into the woods, but now, in the bright light of day, she had to face the truth. She hadn't been asleep. She'd been wide awake and begging a stranger not to hurt her.

Rachel stared at the sunrise, shaking with a sick kind of fear.

"I'm going crazy."

Without warning, she bolted for her car. After she was safely inside, with the door locked and the engine running, she started to rationalize.

"I'm imagining things," she muttered. "Maybe it's because I'm so isolated up here. My mind is starting to play tricks on me, that's all."

She put the car into gear and started to work. A short while later, she turned the last curve on the mountain road and saw Razor Bend in the distance. Relaxing at the familiarity of it, she took her foot from the brake and accelerated. It wasn't until she passed the city-limit's sign that something else occurred to her. Something she hadn't let herself consider all through the night.

If the man who'd caught her in the creek was real, but the outlaw in her dream was not, then how had she known before the outlaw spoke that he was going to call her Mercy?

Late that same afternoon, Rachel was on her knees inside the ambulance, putting clean linen on the gurney and restocking supplies. Charlie Dutton, a resident paramedic and also her partner for the past sixteen months, was in the office, filling out the paperwork on the run they'd just made. The rollicking rhythms of country music were playing on a nearby radio, a welcome interruption to Rachel's train of thought.

All day she'd been haunted by last night's events—another sleepwalking episode—the fear she'd felt at being caught in the woods by a stranger, and then the dream that had become mixed up in it all.

Only when she and Charlie were on an actual call was she able to put the memory behind her. But there was something different about her work today. Though her hands were busy, it seemed as if her mind were moving in slow motion. On one level she was doing everything right, but on another, she felt out of place, as if she were seeing the world through someone else's eyes.

Replace gauze pads.

Dark eyes searched her face as he lowered his head.

Check oxygen level in tank.

Sweet, sweet Mercy.

Need a new box of disposable syringes.

Once a desperado, always a desperado.

Her hands paused above a shelf as she let her mind roll backward. The feel of the outlaw's mouth on hers had been so real...so familiar. She shuddered, then sighed. None of what was happening to her made any sense. She yearned for someone to talk to, someone in whom she could confide, yet there was no one she could trust.

She couldn't talk to Charlie. He would think she was crazy. The idea of talking to a psychiatrist had already crossed her mind, but not in a small rural community like Razor Bend. It was asking for trouble. Someone would find out, and then that same someone—or another like him—would decide she didn't have what it took to work under stress. It could very well cost her the job she loved so well.

She'd already faced the fact that telling her best friend, Joanie Mills, wouldn't be smart. The old saying "Telegraph, telephone, tell a woman" could be directly applied to Joanie. She owned a beauty shop called Curlers, and it was a known fact in town that her place was a better source for current news than CNN.

Therefore, Rachel would not be telling Joanie that she sleepwalked, and she would certainly not mention the fact that, in her mind, the thin line of demarcation between fact and fantasy was starting to fade. Frustration was turning to anxiety. If only there was someone... She shoved the last box of disposable syringes into place and frowned.

Oh, God, what am I going to do?

No sooner had the thought crossed her mind than she realized the light in which she'd been kneeling was gone. She looked up as her heart took a nosedive. It was Griffin Ross.

She managed a smile. "I didn't hear you walk up."

Griffin Ross grinned and leaned inside, pulling her down from the ambulance.

"I know I should have announced myself, but when you're working, you get this intense, adorable expression on your face. I couldn't resist playing voyeur. I'm sorry I frightened you. Forgive me?" Before she could answer, he'd kissed her cheek. Uncomfortable with what he'd just done, Rachel took a quick step back and managed to smile.

"You're forgiven."

Griff wanted to shake her. She said one thing, but he could see another in her eyes. Frustration was mounting over their situation. He'd been dating her for months, and if he was honest with himself, he had to admit that the only way he'd gotten to first base with her was on a walk. Rachel hadn't given him a moment of encouragement. As always, she smiled nervously, then turned away.

Griff must have come for a reason, Rachel thought as she tugged at the edge of a sheet covering the gurney, tucking it in place. He wouldn't be here during business hours unless he wanted something. She kept telling herself that if she stayed busy, she wouldn't have to make small talk with a man she wished would leave her alone.

As president of Ross Savings and Loan, Griffin was Razor Bend's most eligible bachelor. He'd been relentlessly pursuing her for the better part of six months, yet she knew that when he kissed her just now, she'd flinched.

It wasn't the first time she'd objected to Griffin Ross's interest in her, though Joanie saw fit to remind her on a daily basis that he was handsome, well-to-do, single—and interested. If she had a brain in her head, Joanie claimed, she would already have snatched him up. But Rachel didn't want him.

There had been more than one occasion during the past few months when she wondered if something was wrong with her feminine radar. She knew she should be thanking her lucky stars that a man like Griffin was pursuing her so diligently, but she wasn't.

Griff frowned as Rachel turned away. By nature, he wasn't a masochist, but he was beginning to realize that the only relationship he and Rachel Brand had was the one in his mind. Yes, they dated, and on more than one occasion they'd shared what he liked to call a passionate kiss, but nothing more. And the passion that existed between them was definitely one-sided.

But Griffin Ross hadn't risen to his level of success with a defeatist attitude. As his father had always said, the show wasn't over until the fat lady sang. He laid his hand on Rachel's shoulder, ignoring the flinching of muscle beneath hi palm.

"Rachel?"

She looked up.

"The Elks lodge is sponsoring a fund-raising dance thi weekend. Would you like to go?"

The pause between his question and her answer was too long. Griff hid his impatience behind an open smile, but whe Rachel's partner, Charlie Dutton, came out of the office call ing her name, he fought the urge to wring the man's neck.

Thankful that she'd been spared from answering, Rachel turned. "I'm here!" she shouted. "What's up?"

Charlie Dutton's walk was closer to a bounce than a stride but when he saw Griffin Ross standing at her side, he came to an abrupt halt. It was all he could do not to frown.

"Sorry. I didn't know you had company. You left your keys on the desk." He handed them to her with an easy grin. "What's the deal with putting nail polish on them?"

"The keys to the front and back door look alike, but they're not, so I painted an *F* on this one, for *Front,* and a *B* on this one, for *Back,*" she said.

Charlie grinned. "So, what's on the key to your car? *C* for *Car,* or *D* for *Drive?*"

"Very funny," she said, dropping her keys in her pocket. "Don't you have something else to do?"

"No."

Rachel rolled her eyes. When pushed, Charlie Dutton was impossible.

"I was going to tell you that I'm through with the paper-work and ready to go to lunch," he offered, purposely ignor-ing the fact that Griff was there.

Rachel felt torn. She was all too aware that Charlie's feel-ings for her went beyond friendship, and while she admired and respected him, she felt nothing romantic for him in return. But they were partners, and on the job, where one went, the other followed.

"Just give me a minute," she said.

Charlie nodded, then gave Griffin Ross another cool glance
nd walked away.

Rachel waited until Charlie was gone before addressing
riffin's request. "About the dance... I'm not sure about my
chedule. Can I get back to you?"

Griff's smile felt frozen on his face. "Of course. I'll give
ou a call at home in a few days, okay?"

Rachel braced herself for the kiss she saw coming, but
vhen Griff's mouth touched her lips, she had to hide her
listaste. His lips were too hot, too soft, and too demanding.
)ut of nowhere came the thought... *The outlaw's lips had
een cool and hard...but so beguiling.*

A car honked on the street and Rachel jerked with embar-
assment and took a quick step back. Distinguished citizen or
1ot, she shouldn't be letting Griffin Ross kiss her while she
vas on duty.

"Griff, please don't," she said quickly. "Someone will
ee."

But as she looked across the street, to her dismay, she realized her caution had come too late. Three of the most dis-
eputable-looking men she'd ever seen were coming out of
he Adam's Rib Café.

One was short. Another seemed as broad as he was tall.
They were unshaven and unkempt. Their clothing ranged from
black leather to worn and faded denim. The short, skinny one
actually had the audacity to grin at her, then wink. But it was
the tall one wearing black, dusty denim and a three-day
growth of whiskers who caught her eye.

He stood a head above the others in stature, and even from
where she was standing, she felt his eyes raking her body
from her head to her toes. Neither by word or by deed did he
reveal what he might be thinking, yet Rachel felt the impact
of his gaze as if she'd been gut-kicked. Breathless, and more
than a little bit nervous, she tried to break his stare, but instead
found herself unable to move. Griff's presence was forgotten,
and there was a fleeting sensation of having stood beneath
this man's gaze once before.

Griff frowned, for once refusing to hide his displeasure. "Damn it, Rachel..."

But his comment was forgotten when he realized that Rachel was no longer looking at him but at a point past his shoulder. Her eyes were wide and fixed, and her mouth was slightly parted. Startled by the intensity of her gaze, he turned, following the direction of her stare.

"Oooh, Lordy, wouldya look at the tits on her?"

Tommy Joe Smith followed the direction of Snake Martin's stare to the couple who were standing in the doorway of the EMS station. Snake's grin was lost behind a thick brush of brown, curly beard, but his leer was unmistakable. Tommy Joe had to admit Snake seemed to have an eye for the finer things in life, but he kept thinking of Denver Cherry, sitting at home waiting for them to come back with his food.

"Now, Snake, we got more important things to do today. Denver's waitin' on us, remember?"

The mention of Denver Cherry's name was enough to suck the smile off Snake's face. He glanced back at Tommy Joe, then over his shoulder, to the third man in their trio.

"I still say she's got some real pretty tits. Ain't that what you say, Boone?"

Boone MacDonald stifled the urge to put his fist all the way down Snake's throat. Damn him, and damn this situation. To his dismay, the woman they were ogling was none other than the one he'd found crying in the stream. The one whose voice had trembled with fear at his arrival—the same one who'd chosen to take her chances by running through the woods in the dark rather than risk another moment alone with him.

For the first time since he'd taken his oath of office, he hated what he was doing. People judged by appearances, and he knew how he appeared. He'd worked long and hard at perfecting his image...and his cover. And should someone be inclined to check, they would find out that one Boone Mac-Donald had a very dirty rap sheet, that he'd done time in and

ut of state, and that, when riled, he had more than a tendency
ıward violence.

On the job, his real name and true existence were kept
idden in an unused part of his mind. For Boone MacDonald,
ecent women did not exist. It had been so dark last night,
ven with the moonlight, that he'd believed himself safe. But
rom the expression on her face, he feared she'd recognized
im as the man from the woods.

The only thing he could think of doing was to move, and
nove now. The last thing he needed was for her to point him
ıut to that fancy man beside her. He didn't want anyone
nowing where he'd been last night. Snake and Tommy Joe
ıelieved he'd been in Kansas, just what he'd led them to
hink. Having someone accuse him of sneaking around up on
he Kiamichis last night could get him shot.

"Damn it, Boone, I asked you a question," Snake mut-
ered.

Boone blinked, breaking the stare between himself and the
woman, then glared down at Snake.

"She's not my type," Boone drawled. "I like my women
ılond and crazy, with long legs and red nails."

Snake's grin broke through the thick bush of his beard,
revealing a mouthful of yellowing teeth. The image Boone
ıad put in his mind made him giggle.

"Yeah, yeah," he said, his head flopping up and down on
his scrawny neck like a cork bobbing on water. "I know just
the kind you mean."

Tommy Joe waved a greasy sack in Snake's face. "Oh,
man, if Denver could hear you two, he'd puke. Now come
on, we gotta be going. The boss is waitin'. for his ribs, and
you know how Denver gets when he's hungry."

Relieved that the conversation had taken a turn away from
the woman, Boone started toward his truck without waiting
for the motley pair to follow.

From the corner of his eye, Boone saw the man beside her
take her by the arm, then heard him call her name aloud. He
paused, letting the sound soak into his mind. As he slid behind

the steering wheel, a small, satisfied smile spread across his face.

So her name is Rachel.

Chapter 3

In the fall, dark came early in the mountains. By the time Rachel got off work and picked up a few groceries, it was already night. As she drove home, the headlights of her car beamed brightly on the narrow blacktop road, scaring away a rabbit and spotlighting a deer that had just started to cross. The big buck froze in the oncoming glare, and Rachel hit the brakes, fishtailing slightly to keep from hitting it. But when the tires started squealing, the buck jumped as if someone had prodded it from behind, then bounded off the road and out of sight.

Rachel breathed a sigh of relief, her fingers curling around the steering wheel as she stared past the yellow beams of light, searching the darkness to make sure it was gone. But while she was looking, she thought of the man who'd walked out of the trees last night, and in a fit of panic she stomped on the accelerator, leaving behind a wake of flying leaves and burnt rubber.

A few minutes later, when she pulled into the driveway,

anxiety was still with her. Grabbing her bag of groceries, sh
slung her purse over her shoulder and bolted for the door.

Only after she was inside, with the door shut and locke
did she start to relax. As she passed through the rooms, sh
turned on light after light. By the time she got to the kitche
her nervousness was almost gone. After changing out of he
uniform and into an old pair of jeans and a loose long-sleeve
shirt, she began preparing her food.

Somewhere beyond the ring of trees that surrounded he
place, dogs yipped and then bayed as they did when treein
prey. At that moment, an idea came that filled her with relie.

A hunter! That was probably who found me last night!

Pleased that she'd given herself an answer she could liv
with, she went on preparing her dinner.

Yet all during her solitary meal, and even afterward, sh
fought a lingering hint of anxiety. Disgusted with herself fo
being faint of heart, she started to turn off the lights to ge
ready for bed.

The first switch Rachel turned sent the living room int
darkness, and for a moment, before reality returned, she fel
just as disoriented as she had when waking up in the stream
Shadows seemed to shift before her eyes. She stared until th
familiar shapes of her couch and matching chairs becam
more than hulking figures in a dark, quiet room.

"You're losing it, Rachel," she muttered, and went to tur
out the light still burning in the kitchen.

The scent of supper lingered in the air, the tantalizin
aroma of broiled ham, the homey scents of butter beans an
thick, crusty yellow corn bread. She gave the room a quick
last glance, making sure everything was neatly in place, ther
flipped that switch as well.

But when those lights went out, her throat tightened. She
stood in the darkened room, glancing nervously toward the
back of the house. The light from her bedroom spilled out
into the hall beyond, marking a place on the floor. In her
mind, the warm yellow glow spelled safety.

She had to stop this craziness. This was her home...her

haven. But even as she was listening to the voice of her rational self, she found herself walking back to the kitchen windows for a last, lingering look.

Outside, the lawn was heavy with dew. Moonlight glimmered on the glistening water droplets holding fast to the grass, giving the yard the appearance of frost, although Rachel knew it was not cold enough to freeze. A slight breeze pushed and tugged at the empty swing hanging from the limb of a gnarled oak. Something clattered out on the porch, and she leaned forward, peering toward the corner of the house, where the racket continued.

Inner tension melted as an empty bucket rolled into view, its bail flopping from one side to the other as it bounced off the porch, then along the grass. Weak at the knees, she sighed with relief.

"Another big deal out of nothing," she mumbled, then frowned as the bucket continued to roll farther and farther away from the house. That was her best bucket! If she let it go until morning, there was no telling where it might end up if some animal got hold of it.

Darn it all.

Ignoring the nervous jerk of her heart when the tumblers of the door lock clicked loudly in the silence, she took a deep breath and stepped onto the porch, pausing on the broad stone steps to survey the scene before her. Glancing nervously at bushes, she looked beyond the obvious, to what might be waiting for her, unseen.

As she stood, the brisk breeze began playing with wayward bits of her hair that had escaped its braid. Satisfied that all was normal, she took a deep breath and closed her eyes, letting herself become one with the darkness, instead of fearing it.

Off to her right, the low, mournful call of a dove soon brought an answer from its mate somewhere up ahead.

I'm not the only one who feels lost and nervous tonight.

When she opened her eyes and looked up, a black-velvet sky shot through with pinpoints of lights winked down at her

with timeless persistence. She smiled. The panic was gone
As she started down the steps, a night moth fluttered past her
hand.

"Watch where you're going, buddy. You're not the only
traveler out here tonight."

Blithely unaware of anything except the backyard security
light toward which it was heading, the moth rode the breeze,
safely out of her reach.

Now that Rachel was out, she didn't want to go back. She
retrieved the bucket, setting it safely out of the wind, then
returned to the porch, loath to give up her unexpected rapport
with the night.

As she sat down on the old stone steps, the lingering heat
they'd absorbed during the day still felt warm to her hands.
Absently she undid her braid and, in lieu of a brush, began
combing her fingers through the thick, dark lengths. The
weight of hair on her back was just a little bit less than the
weight in her heart, and out of nowhere came a longing for
someone with whom she could share this time.

Just not Griffin Ross.

The knowledge was sudden, but too sure to be denied. The
image of his handsome, smiling face popped into her head.
Ashamed, she buried her face in her hands.

*I don't love him. I'm not even certain I really like him. But
why? What's wrong with me? What's wrong with him, that
I can't give my heart away?*

Unbidden, the outlaw from her dream superimposed himself over Griff's face, changing light hair to dark and blue
eyes to black. One man's smile died, becoming a solemn expression in another's face—a face filled with longing too
strong to be denied.

Rachel gasped. The image was so strong, so sure! She was
certain that when she looked up, the man from her dream
would be standing before her. But when she looked, there was
no one there.

Stifling an odd sense of disappointment, she gazed across
the yard and down the slope to the trees below, almost holding

her breath. Everything seemed normal. Nothing was out of place.

Again she thought of going to bed, and then feared that if she did, another sleepwalking episode might occur. She thought of last night and the state in which she'd returned to the house, long hair flying and dripping wet, wearing nothing but a nightgown stuck fast to her body, and groaned.

"I probably frightened that hunter as badly as he did me."

But the assumption didn't lighten her mood. Like a bad penny, her thoughts returned to Griff. She didn't know what she was going to do about him, but a decision needed to be made, and soon. It wasn't fair to keep leading him on, letting him believe that she felt something for him that wasn't there.

Saturday night was only days away, yet it loomed in her conscience like doomsday. A dance. Griff had asked her to a dance. It wasn't as if he'd asked to spend the night, although she'd seen that desire in his eyes more than once. And if Charlie hadn't interrupted, she also knew she would already have said yes to the dance, simply for lack of a reason to say no.

A swift gust of wind suddenly cornered the house, shifting the neck of her shirt and cooling the skin beneath like the urgent breath of an anxious lover. Sighing with pent-up longing, she finally accepted the truth of her life. She didn't know what her future held, but Griffin Ross did not belong anywhere in it.

Still on the steps and now one with the night, she wished for a man like the man from her dreams.

Outlaw or not, he was loving and gentle with me.

Rachel jerked. Mentally she'd just put herself in the shoes of a woman called Mercy. Panicked by a warning she didn't understand, she wrapped her arms around herself, shivering, though not from cold.

But Rachel was not the kind of woman to live in a dream world. Today the reality of life had metaphorically slapped her in the face. A real-life outlaw had been standing on the streets of Razor Bend, staring at her and making no attempt to hide his interest or apologize for the company he kept.

A shiver of warning came over her, and she wished he had not witnessed her kissing Griffin Ross. She could have dismissed the incident without thought if it hadn't been for him. But he'd seen, and she couldn't forget. In fact, he'd stared so intently that she'd begun to imagine his breath upon her face. In spite of his needing a shave, his dark, handsome looks had intrigued her…reminded her of someone…someone she'd once known. If only she could remember who…

She stood up with a jerk. Thoughts like that were dangerous for lonely women, and Rachel knew it.

"He didn't intrigue me. Not at all. It was…it was curiosity, and nothing more."

Aggravated at herself and at the flight of fancy her mind had taken, she stomped across the grass to the empty swing dancing alone in the breeze. Scooting onto the old board seat, she pushed off, setting sail in the moonlight with a satisfied sigh.

Thinking of her partner, Charlie, she chuckled. "If he could see me now, he'd call me crazy for playing in the dark."

But she didn't care. The wind felt good on her face. The feeling of weightlessness lifted her spirits, and before she knew it, she was flying up and back, her legs pumping with each swing, caught up in a wayward joy not unlike that of the night moth that had swooped past her hand.

While waiting for his call to go through, Boone watched a cockroach crawling up the wall of the tin can he called home. It was past time to check in with his contact, and while he had nothing new to report, he knew that Waco still wanted to hear her sweet boy's voice. That was the order given, tongue in cheek, by Captain Susan Cross, who was not only Boone's contact, but also his immediate superior.

The phone number Boone used was a dedicated phone line in the captain's office. And if she wasn't there in person, the message on her answering machine was as low and sexy and as atypical as the code name that hid her true identity.

The rings came, one after the other, and on the fourth ring, when the machine should have kicked on, Boone's expression lightened as Waco's low, husky voice purred in his ear.

"This is Waco. Talk to me. It's been a long, lonely night."

"Hey, sweetheart, what's happening?"

"Boone...darling, it's about time you gave me a call."

Waco's sweet, sexy voice was her only physical asset, in direct opposition to her thick, stocky body, her short, graying hair and the gold-rimmed half glasses she wore down on her nose.

In spite of the fact that she was his boss, Boone never had to fake a smile when he heard her speak. He was hearing her call him "darling," but in his mind, he could just see that intent bulldog expression she always got when business was at hand.

"Sweet thing!" Waco cooed. "You've been a bad, bad boy again, haven't you? Why didn't you call me last night like you promised?"

Boone grinned as he leaned over and picked up a dirty yellow tennis ball from the floor near his boot. With unerring aim, he drew back and threw it, nailing the cockroach on the first throw, then retrieving the ball as it bounced back his way.

Captain Cross frowned at the thump she heard over the phone.

"What was that?"

"Bug patrol," Boone drawled, and tossed the tennis ball into a nearby chair.

Ignoring his insinuating reference to the dive in which he was living, she focused on the business at hand.

"So, when are you coming to see me, handsome? It's been a long, long time since I've kissed your sweet face."

Boone grinned. "Yes, ma'am, I'd venture to say it has."

At the word *ma'am*, Susan Cross leaned back in her chair and then grinned. "I take it you're alone."

"Affirmative, Captain."

Her voice sharpened. "Okay, then the gloves are off. Why didn't you check in last night? I had visions of having to send out the troops to comb those damned mountains for your body."

Boone shifted his cell phone to the other ear and then leaned forward, staring at the floor as he sifted through what he could tell her, as opposed to what was better left unsaid.

"I started to, and then things changed. I almost got lucky."

Cross rolled her eyes. "Well, that's just dandy, but I don't want to hear about your prowess in bed. I need facts. You've been under too long now as it is. I'm considering pulling you out and coming at this bunch from a different angle."

Boone jumped to his feet, and when he spoke again, his voice was deep and demanding. "No way." And then he imagined Cross thrusting out her chin as she always did when readying for a verbal battle.

"No way, Captain...ma'am."

Cross sighed. She was all too aware of how determined this agent could be. He was one of her best, and yet she knew less about him personally than any agent on the force.

"Okay, then talk to me."

"Last night I trailed Cherry and two of his boys through the mountains. They had a meeting with a man I suspect is the real power behind Denver Cherry's tawdry little throne. I think they'd been to the new lab, but I didn't get on their tail in time to find the location, or ID the man."

Cross doodled on a pad on her desk as she listened. The news was not what she needed to hear. Boone had been under cover in Razor Bend for more than six weeks, and still it seemed he hadn't made a close enough connection with this bunch to gain their trust. They kept moving their drug lab, and although he was technically in the gang, they kept him apart from the funny business they were conducting. The most he'd seen and could swear to was the chemicals they used to cook up the methamphetamine.

"Okay, you missed a chance, that's all. One missed chance does not a failure make."

Boone grinned. "Where did you learn that bit of wisdom?"

"Fortune cookies."

He laughed aloud, and realized it felt good.

And just because he couldn't see her, Cross allowed herself a wide grin in return. It wouldn't do to let the men know her heart of stone was actually made of glass.

"So, tell me what you're thinking," she barked.

Boone relaxed. He should have known she was just testing his frame of mind. Yet, when she asked, he realized he wasn't thinking of the job, but of a woman named Rachel and how she'd looked in wet white flannel.

"It wouldn't do to repeat it," Boone drawled.

Cross rolled her eyes. "Go get yourself laid, and call me when your head's on straight."

A crooked smile broke the angles of his face.

"I couldn't cheat on you, darlin' Waco. You're the love of my life."

A sharp snort prefaced the distinct click in Boone's ear. He grinned again. Although Captain Cross had hung up on him, she'd fueled the fire of a need Boone was trying to ignore. He knew damn good and well that getting laid was out of the question, but if he was careful, he told himself he could see Rachel again. Not enough to get himself in trouble—just enough to sleep on.

He was telling himself no even as he was getting into his truck. He wasn't going to do anything but look. She wouldn't see him again—not unless he wanted her to. In his mind, there was only one place to start—the stream where he'd seen her last night.

When he finally found the location, he stopped in the moonlight, remembering the way the wet white gown had molded itself to her body, picturing the gentle thrust of her breasts and the imprint of long, slim legs beneath the fabric.

Long minutes passed while he wrestled with his conscience.

Finally, with an undisguised groan of disgust, he stalked through the cold, shallow water and started walking uphill, in the direction she'd disappeared.

The house was shining in the darkness, lit from within like a church on Sunday. Her car, the same car he'd seen on the street near the EMS station, was now parked beneath a tree. A light in the house was on, and the warm, yellow glow bleeding through the curtains was a balm to his solitary heart. To Boone, it was a beacon inviting him to come in from the cold.

But he couldn't. This picket-fence, happy-ever-after life was not for him. Not now, maybe not ever, and especially not with a woman who feared the very sight of his face. Living a lie was easier for Boone than living with the truth of his own life. In reality, he was a lonely man. Under cover, he was simply a loner.

And then she came out of her house, and he forgot everything he'd told himself on the walk up the mountain.

Now, ten minutes later, he stood in the darkness, deep enough in the trees not to be seen, while he stared at the woman in the swing. Her head was thrown back, and her arms were straight and outstretched as she clung to the ropes, pumping her legs with each ebb and flow of her flight through the air. Her braid had come undone, and the long black hair now hanging down her back lifted and billowed around her face like a widow's veil blowing in the wind.

He ached with a longing he didn't understand. What he'd done tonight by coming here was way past stupid. He'd wanted to know her name, and now he did. Yet after he'd learned it, it hadn't been enough. Now he stood in the dark with his heart in his mouth, listening to her laughter ringing out in the night. Somewhere between ten o'clock and midnight, Boone fell quietly in love. It made no sense. He'd only seen her twice before. Once on her knees in a stream, crying for a man who was nowhere in sight, and again in another man's arms. But it didn't seem to matter. He knew her name was Rachel, and he knew he loved her.

Denver Cherry rocked back on his heels, absently rubbing his paunch with the flat of his hand as he paced the floor in front of his television, his cell phone held close to his ear. Nearing sixty, the aging biker still sported long, graying hair with a beard to match. The tattoos on his arms and his belly were all the remnants he had left of a woman he'd once known in Seattle. Just under six feet tall, he carried fifty pounds of excess weight on legs that had been broken more times than he could remember. It was only after the last set of casts had come off that he traded his hog for a short-bed pickup and his biker leathers for jeans. While Denver's mode of travel and appearance might have taken on a new look, his occupation had not. Denver lived by a motto he wouldn't give up: Life is greener on the wrong side of the law.

Ignoring the intermittent static from the police scanner on a nearby counter, as well as the traffic on the CB base in the nearby kitchen, he stared intently at the big-screen TV on the other side of the room.

In deference to the call he was taking, the television was on mute, yet he was still able to follow the play-by-play of "Monday Night Football." When the 49ers suddenly fumbled the ball, he winced, then cursed beneath his breath and grabbed an empty beer can from a nearby table. Crumpling it with one beefy hand, he threw it across the room, where it landed with a tinny-sounding clink. He had a twenty-dollar bet on this game, and now there was no time for them to recover. Added to that, the boss was bitching in his ear about stuff that was out of Denver's control.

"Look, I know what I'm doing," Denver muttered. "It's not my fault that big shipment you sent out went down in the ocean off Padre Island. I told you that pilot was a user and a loser."

There was a moment of total silence, and Denver wondered if he'd overstepped his bounds.

Over the years, he'd worked with plenty of men who considered the profits they made secondary to the power they could achieve. Denver wasn't picky about the jobs he took. Shy of murder, if it paid good, he'd do it. But there was something about the boss that made him nervous. Something that didn't set quite right. More than once, he'd had the feeling that the man would just as soon gut him as look at him. He swallowed nervously as a low, angry voice growled in his ear.

"I remember everything, Cherry, but you better remember something, too. I don't like screwups, and those two fools you've got working for you aren't pulling their weight."

Denver frowned. There was no denying the truth. After the mess Tommy Joe made of the last delivery, he'd been ready to shoot him himself. If Snake hadn't popped the watchman who caught them in the act, they would have gone down for sure.

"I've got a new man," Denver muttered. "Been breaking him in all slow-like. If he shows up today, maybe I'll send him on the run with the boys."

"No way, Cherry. I don't like *new*."

Denver dropped into a chair, gauging the depth of his daring against what he was about to say. Boss or no boss, he'd had just about enough. His voice lowered warningly. "Listen here—you hired me to run it from this end, so either fire me or get the hell out of my face."

There was a moment of complete silence, then a warning whisper sent shivers down Denver's fat back. "Fine. The new man is on your head."

The line went dead in Denver's ear. He shrugged. What was done was done. He disconnected, then traded the phone for the remote. The instant roar of the crowd drowned out the sound of Tommy Joe's arrival. It was only after a shadow crossed his television screen that he realized he was no longer alone.

Denver glanced over his shoulder, waving for Tommy Joe to take a seat. When he refused, Denver knew something was wrong. By the look on Tommy Joe's face, losing twenty bucks might be the least of his worries. He began to curse.

Once again the television was silenced as Denver got up from his chair. He wasn't sure what was wrong, but the absence of Tommy Joe's other half was a good place to start.

"Where's Snake?"

Tommy Joe shuffled his feet, then looked at the floor rather than face Denver Cherry's wrath. His voice was barely above a whisper when he finally answered. "Jail."

Denver's face turned red. "Like hell! Then get him out. We've got a delivery to make tonight."

"Can't. Judge is out of town till tomorrow. The cops said arraignment will be sometime Tuesday afternoon."

Denver doubled his fists, resisting the urge to slam one into Tommy Joe's face for nothing more than relief.

"What did he do this time?"

Tommy Joe shrugged, and for Denver, it was the last straw in a day long gone wrong. He grabbed him by the throat and shoved him hard against the wall.

"You talk to me, you piece of sh—"

"Looks like I'm too late for the dance."

Both men looked up in surprise, to see Boone MacDonald leaning against the doorway with his arms folded across his chest. The black denim he was wearing went well with the cold, taunting smirk on his face.

Unlike Denver, Tommy Joe was more than happy for the interruption.

Denver frowned. Seeing that hard-eyed loner lounging in his doorway as if he owned the place didn't set too well with him, especially with the boss's warning still ringing in his ears.

"Don't mess with me, Boone, I'm not in the mood," Denver warned, but the worst of his anger was already subsiding. With a curse, he shoved Tommy Joe aside and dropped back in his chair.

Pretending disinterest in the whole affair, Boone shrugged while breathing an inward sigh of relief. Tommy Joe was his ticket to this party, and had been from the start. Snake didn't make friends, only enemies. If Denver got mad enough to run one of them off, Boone wanted it to be Snake, not Tommy Joe. Mixing with this crew for the past six weeks had been bad enough, but having it all blow up in his face without identifying the man behind the money would play hell with his conscience.

But while Boone was counting his blessings, Denver was gauging Boone's cold expression with satisfaction. At least this man had something between his ears besides the hair on his head.

"What brought you over?" Denver asked.

Boone tilted his head toward Tommy Joe. "I was looking for him. He told me the next time I went to Oklahoma City, he wanted to go. I'm on my way."

Denver straightened in his chair. This could be the answer to his immediate problem. He'd already warned the boss he was going to try the new man, and now here he was, heading in the direction Denver needed him to go.

"What's so great about O.K. city?" he asked.

Boone shrugged. "My old lady. I check in on her every now and then, just to make sure she hasn't slipped somebody else into my spot on her bed."

Denver's eyes narrowed thoughtfully. "I didn't know you were married. I don't like none of my men too tied down."

Boone's pulse rate accelerated slightly. *My men? Am I about to get that break?*

Boone cocked his eyebrow and then smoothed his hand down the front of his fly, playing his part to the hilt. "I'm not. But a smart man doesn't leave a woman like Waco alone for too long. She starts getting ideas about being better off without me...and you can't be having a woman get too independent, if you know what I mean."

When Denver laughed, Boone relaxed, and then glanced at the man cowering near the far wall.

"So, Tommy Joe, you still itching to take a ride?"

Tommy Joe glanced at Denver, then slumped. He knew the responsibility of delivering the haul would fall on his shoulders, now that Snake was out of commission.

"Guess not. I promised Snake I'd come by tonight. Maybe next time."

Pretending disinterest, Boone nodded, but his senses were

on edge. He'd already figured out that when Snake and Tommy Joe were "busy," there was a load going out or coming in.

"Whatever."

He was halfway off the porch when Denver's shout halted his progress. He paused, then turned, watching the fat man hobble toward him.

"What?" he asked.

"How would you feel about doing me a favor?" Denver asked.

Boone stood his ground, giving nothing of his underlying excitement away.

"Depends," he said.

Denver's eyes narrowed as he watched Boone's face for signs of too much interest. To his satisfaction, there was nothing visible but an impatience the man made no attempt to hide.

"I've got a little shipment of goods to be delivered tonight. With Snake in jail, I might be needing someone to help me out."

Boone pretended to frown and glanced at his watch, then up at Tommy Joe.

"What about him?" Boone asked.

Denver Cherry's voice was a mirror of his disposition. He sounded out of patience and purely put out. "His license is still suspended. I can't take a chance on him getting stopped for some violation and having some gung ho cop confiscate my stuff."

Boone shifted his stance. "Look, Cherry, I'm no saint, and I'm damn sure not stupid. I don't do anyone a favor until I know what I'm hauling." And then he grinned. "I've done too much time as it is. If I'm going down, I want it to be my choice."

At that moment, Denver wished he hadn't started this conversation unarmed, but it was too late to pull back now. "Meth."

Boone nodded. "Then I want to know something."

"Yeah, what?" Denver muttered.

"What's in it for me?"

Denver laughed. It was a short bark of delight that sounded more like a shout than a chuckle, but it was proof of the satisfaction he was feeling. He knew he'd been right about this man.

"Enough," Denver said, still chuckling beneath his breath. "So, you interested or not?"

"Where's the drop going to be?"

"I'll draw you a map."

Boone stood in the yard, glancing at his watch and playing his hesitation to the hilt.

"What's wrong?" Denver asked.

"Waco. She's going to give me hell for not showing up."

Denver grinned. "No she's not. The party is on your way."

Boone started back up the steps. "Okay, boss, you've got yourself a deal."

The word *boss* was setting real good with Denver Cherry as he hunted through a drawer for a pad and pen. He liked a man who was willing to stay in his place.

Chapter 4

Traffic was moderate to heavy on Interstate 35-A. Boone had his pickup truck set on cruise control, careful not to risk a stop by some ticket-happy highway patrolman. As drug deals went, the shipment Boone was carrying was small. If something went bad, Cherry wouldn't lose enough to hurt him. And if Boone did as he was told and the buyer came away happy, then so much the better.

But there was one thing about the trip that kept bothering him. Why hadn't Cherry sent Tommy Joe with him? It would have made sense, even if as nothing more than a gesture of good faith to the man he was supposed to meet. He shrugged, then relaxed. Cherry was probably testing him on this run.

He glanced up in the rearview mirror, absently checking the lights behind him, then hit the turn signal and moved into the fast lane to pass an eighteen-wheeler. Moments later, a vehicle several cars back did the same. He thought nothing of it until it happened again...and then again...and then again. Within the space of half an hour, Boone knew he was being tailed.

The first adrenaline surge quickly passed as he recognized a familiar feature about the car. One headlight beam was yellow and one was white. Boone grinned, remembering the day he'd watched Tommy Joe and Snake replacing the bulbs. Snake had put in one kind of bulb, Tommy Joe another. It wasn't until that night that they'd realized their mistake and, typically, they had left the lights the way they were, claiming they burned, which was really all that mattered. But at night it gave the headlights a wall-eyed appearance, not unlike that of an animal with one blue eye and one black.

"So, fat boy, you decided not to trust me after all," Boone muttered.

Cherry had launched himself a spy. Boone eased back into the right-hand side of the lane and picked up the cell phone in the seat beside him.

A few moments later, a low, husky voice growled softly in his ear.

"Talk to me, baby," Waco said.

"I'm in," Boone said, and heard a deep sigh of relief.

"How so?"

"I'm northbound I-35 with a load behind the seat. It's not big, but I'm being tailed."

"I assume you're alone."

"Affirmative, Captain, except for the tick on my ass."

"You think they're testing you?"

"Yes."

"And if not?" the captain asked.

"Then I'll tell them if they can't play fair, I'm going home to tell Mama."

"Damn it, Boone, don't get smart with me. None of this is worth risking your life for."

Boone's smile faded. "Better men have died for less."

"The point is not debatable," the captain barked. "If you suspect a trap, then get the hell out."

"Why, Waco, darlin', I think you really care."

"You heard me," Cross muttered, pushing her glasses up

er nose with the tip of her finger as she swiveled her chair
o face a map on the wall behind her desk.

"Where's the buy going down?"

Boone mentioned a county road a few miles south of the
ity of Norman. Cross stood up and leaned forward, poking
red pin on the map to mark the drop, then calculating the
ime it would take to get some agents in place.

"It's too late for backup to get there ahead of you," she
nuttered. "You should have called sooner."

"I don't want backup, I want Cherry's boss. This deal
eeds to go through without incident."

Cross frowned and rubbed at a pain shooting up her temple.
he already knew that. It just didn't make her job any easier.

"So what you're telling me is, you only called because you
vanted to 'reach out and touch someone,' right?"

Boone grinned. His captain had a way with words. "No
vay, Waco. I called to tell you to put a light in the window.
Daddy's coming home."

A soft snort that sounded suspiciously like a chuckle was
ll Boone heard before the line went dead. He disconnected,
hen, out of habit, punched in a few random numbers, then
lisconnected again. It was an old trick he'd learned early on.
ven though his contact was supposedly secure, there was no
vay he was giving anyone a free ride to his source by letting
hem pick up his phone and hit redial to find out who he had
alled.

He looked into the rearview mirror again. White and yellow
yes were bearing down upon him. The smile on his face was
leadly.

"Okay, Cherry, let's see how good your boy really is."

Boone stomped the accelerator, ignoring the needle on the
peedometer when it moved past eighty, then ninety, then into
he red. Climbing…climbing…then off the dial.

Everything to his right was a blur. The vehicles he was
assing became nothing more than a flicker of shape, light
nd color. His gaze was focused on the darkness ahead and
he narrow beam of light cutting through it.

A short time later, he glanced up in the rearview mirro
The reflection of headlights from the cars he was passing ra
together like a bright yellow ribbon, but the wall-eyed head
lights of his tail were no longer in sight.

Only after he began to ease up on the gas did he realiz
that he was gritting his teeth against an impact that neve
came. His jaw was clenched, but his hands were steady, hi
nerves calm. With one smooth, easy motion, he moved bac
into the right-hand lane, sliding in between a bull hauler an
an eighteen-wheeler, where he continued to ride until his ex
appeared.

Again he moved to the right, taking the off-ramp like a bir
going home to roost. With nothing but guts for backup, h
took the county-road bridge that arched over I-35 and heade
for the location of the buy.

Within the hour he'd found the place Cherry had marke
on the map and pulled off the road and into the driveway o
the abandoned farm house. Off to his right was a faint tra
leading toward what appeared to have once served as a ha
barn.

Just as Cherry had directed, Boone circled around behin
the barn, coming to a stop out of sight of the road. He kille
the lights but left the engine running.

Five, ten, then thirty, seconds passed while his eyes grev
accustomed to the dark. An overcast sky kept moonglow at
minimum. Only now and then was he able to detect anythin
more than the subtle shapes of trees and bushes. He reache
down, feeling for the butt of his gun, protruding above th
holster at his waist. The hard, familiar shape was comfortin
to a man who had no one to depend on but himself. Anothe
minute passed, and then another, stretching nerves alread
humming with nervous energy.

And then, without warning, three men emerged from th
old barn and started walking toward him. Adrenaline surged
They were carrying guns! He took a deep breath, pulled ou
the .357 and got out of the truck with it ready to fire. It wa
time to party.

One man growled. "Where's Snake?"

"In jail," Boone answered. "Cherry sent me instead."

Someone cocked the hammer on a rifle, and Boone's senses went on alert. He moved a step closer, making sure they could see that they weren't the only ones armed.

He heard one man mutter, "Watch it, Slick. He's packin'."

"Who the hell are you?" Slick asked.

"Name's Boone MacDonald. If you got a problem doing business with me, then let's call the whole deal off now, before someone makes a mistake they can't fix."

Feet shuffled, voices whispered, one to the other. Boone stood with his back to his truck and his finger on the trigger. The rest of the deal was out of his hands.

A few moments later Slick lowered his rifle. "You tell Cherry if his plans change again, he'd better let us know. Strange faces make us antsy."

Boone snorted softly. "I'd say that just about makes us even. So...show me some green."

Again whispers cut through the silence. Finally one of the men split from the pack and headed inside the barn.

Guns lowered. The other men started forward. Boone still held his gun.

"Let's just wait on your buddy," he said softly.

They stopped. Still muttering, they waited. Moments later, the man returned, carrying a sack.

"Nothing personal," Boone said, "but I'd like to see what you brought for lunch."

Someone snickered as the sack was tossed to Boone. He caught it in midair and opened it. Moonlight revealed large stacks of the used twenties and hundreds he'd been led to expect. He started backing toward his truck, without taking his eyes off the trio.

"No fancy moves now," Slick warned.

Boone paused. "It's behind the seat. Help yourself."

Once again Slick was in control. "Go get it, Donny," he ordered.

Boone stepped aside, giving way to a tall, lanky man wear-

ing baggy jeans and tennis shoes. The cap on Donny's head
bore the Dallas Cowboys logo, and the chew in his mouth
was bigger than his nose. Even in the half-light, Boone could
see it pushing at the interior of his cheek. As Boone moved
aside, the man spat before leaning in to retrieve the package,
then handed it over.

"You don't mind waiting a bit longer now, do you?" Slick
asked as he dug inside the package to make sure he had what
he was paying for.

"No skin off of my nose," Boone said. "Just so everybody's happy."

He watched for smiles of satisfaction. When they came, he
was ready to go. Lingering too long around a buy could get
a man killed.

"It was real nice meeting you boys," Boone said, and slid
behind the wheel of his truck. To his relief, the trio seemed
as willing to part company as he did.

He watched while they disappeared into the barn. Less than
a minute later, an engine started. Lights came on, and a dirty
black four-by-four bounced out of the doorway, heading toward anonymity with speed.

Only after they were gone did Boone start to relax. At least
the first half of this night was over. He pulled his truck inside
the barn, using it for cover the same way Slick and his boys
had done earlier, then settled down to wait for the long-
distance burr still stuck to his tail.

More than ten minutes passed, and he was beginning to
wonder if he'd guessed wrong about Cherry. Maybe he hadn't
sent Tommy Joe after all. But no sooner had he thought it
than his nerves went on alert.

A car on the road beyond was beginning to slow down.
Boone sat up straight. When he saw the headlights turning
into the overgrown driveway, he grinned. The car and its lopsided leer came toward the back of the barn. When it stopped,
the lights went out with a drunken wink. And when Tommy
Joe's familiar figure rolled out from behind the steering wheel,

Boone eased out of his truck with Denver's money in hand, careful not to make any noise.

Tommy Joe was sick with worry. Denver was going to be real mad. Not only had he lost sight of Boone on I-35, but now he'd gotten here too late to see if the buy had gone down as planned.

He got out of the car and circled it twice, eyeing the surrounding countryside with a nervous stare.

Dang old Snake, anyway. If he hadn't gone and gotten himself tossed in jail, none of this would be happening.

Tommy Joe kicked at a tuft of grass and then groaned when his toe connected with a half-buried rock. It was a perfect ending to a washed-out night. There was nothing left for him to do but go back and tell Denver Cherry the truth. He was starting to get back in his car when he looked at the barn. In his mind, the black, yawning maw of the open doorway was like a big, wide mouth laughing at him for his mistakes.

The barn! He'd better take a look around. If he didn't and Denver asked him if he had, he'd catch hell again. Tommy Joe wasn't good at much of anything, not even lying. Cursing beneath his breath, he began heading toward the barn for a last-minute check.

The hand squeezing his windpipe moments later was only half as frightening to Tommy Joe as the voice whispering in his ear.

"Looking for something?" Boone asked.

Tommy Joe gasped, his hands flailing as his air flow began to shut down.

"Damn you, Boone," he squeaked. "Let me go!"

Boone turned loose, but with a last, warning push. Tommy Joe slumped against the wall, rubbing at his neck and trying not to quake at the hard, angry glitter in Boone MacDonald's eyes.

"No need getting all riled," Tommy Joe grunted. "I was just following orders."

He started to duck as Boone tossed a sack in his face, then

caught it in reflex. His good humor returned when he looked inside. But his grin died when he looked up. There was no mistaking that Boone MacDonald was thoroughly pissed.

"Damn it, Boone. Don't get all high-and-mighty with me! You know what Denver's like. He gives the orders. We follow."

The flat of Boone's hand slammed into the middle of Tommy Joe's chest, pinning him against the wall.

"Tommy Joe…"

"What?" he muttered, while wishing himself a thousand miles away.

"Since you're so damn good at following orders, then I've got some for you."

Tommy Joe nodded, then feared Boone might not be able to see in the dark and added a nervous "Okay."

"I want you to take Cherry his money, and I want you to tell him something for me when you do. You tell him that I don't lie…and I don't trust people who do. Now, when I leave here, I'm going to see my woman, and I'd better not see that damned car on my tail again."

"Sure thing," Tommy Joe muttered, trying to get free of Boone's grip. It didn't work. To his horror, he felt the cold end of a gun barrel pressing against his temple. "Oh, God!" he muttered. "Don't shoot me, man! Don't shoot! It ain't my fault!"

"Shut up!" Boone muttered. "I'm not through with you. I also want you to tell Cherry I'll be back in a couple of days to get what's owed me."

"Will do," Tommy Joe said quickly, anxious to appease the big man's anger.

With a muffled curse, Boone spun and stalked out of the barn toward Tommy Joe's car.

Seconds later the gun went off, and Tommy Joe fell to the ground. When he found the guts to look up, he realized that it wasn't him that Boone had shot at, it was his right front tire.

He scrambled to his feet, crawling and then running, the sack of money clutched tight to his chest.

"Are you crazy?" he screamed, staring at the shattered rubber. The tire was ruined. Angrily he tossed the sack on the front seat before scrambling to open his trunk.

Boone shoved the gun into its holster and then turned.

"You'd better hurry," he said. "Someone might just get curious about that gunshot and come to look." With that, he walked away.

Tommy Joe was cursing loudly as he scrambled through the trunk, pulling out his jack and lug wrench. But when he went back for the spare, it was nowhere to be found.

"Boone! Wait!" Tommy Joe yelled. "A spare. I don't have a spare!"

Boone grinned, and even at that distance, Tommy Joe shivered. It was a cold, mirthless smile that made his guts knot.

"Denver told me you didn't have a driver's license, either, but that didn't stop you from driving. There's an all-night station about seven or eight miles back. Guess you'll have to drive on the rim, huh?"

Tommy Joe started to curse. "Wait, damn it. You can't leave me here like this." He was digging through his pockets in panic, well aware of the lack of cash in the wallet he was carrying. "I don't have enough money to buy a new tire."

Boone's smile broadened as he pointed toward the car. "Sure you do. There's a sack full of bills in the front seat of your car."

Tommy Joe groaned. Denver would kill him for sure if he spent a penny of unlaundered drug money. To add insult to injury, as the taillights of Boone MacDonald's truck disappeared, it began to rain.

The day dawned gray and gloomy. Rain threatened on an hourly basis, but a drop had yet to fall. Rachel hadn't been at work two hours when elation hit. She was handed a gold-plated excuse not to go to the dance with Griff, and she couldn't even bring herself to feel guilty that it had come at

the expense of one of her fellow workers. Ken Wade's family
emergency had changed the week's work schedule for every
one. After volunteering to take her co-worker's shift, she fel
ashamed of the thanks that he heaped on her head.

"You would do it for me," she'd said swiftly, and ther
made herself scarce.

She bolted for the office and shut herself inside before
heading to the phone. Now she had a good excuse to turn
down Griffin Ross's invitation to the dance. She dialed his
number, then counted the rings.

His secretary picked up. "Ross Savings and Loan."

"Hi, Lois, this is Rachel. Is Griff busy?"

The pleasant smile on Lois Klein's face froze in place. She
knew it wasn't Christian to envy, but she envied Rachel
Brant's place in her boss's life with every ounce of her being.

Glancing across the floor to the glassed-in walls of Griffin
Ross's office, where he sat at his desk, deep in a mountain of
paperwork, she toyed with the idea of lying, then relented.

"He's always busy," she said. "But he's alone...and, of
course, he's in to you. Just a moment, please, while I ring
you through."

There was tension in Lois's voice, and Rachel felt sorry to
be the cause. It was common knowledge that Lois Klein was
very much enamored of her boss.

"Wait!" Rachel said, almost shouting into the phone to
keep Lois from putting her on hold.

Lois frowned. "Yes, was there something else I could do
for you?"

Rachel took a deep breath; she had to be careful not to say
too much. "Uh...about the fund-raiser Saturday night."

Disappointment stilled the expression on Lois's face.
"What about it?"

"Are you going?"

"No, I'm not," Lois said.

Her answer was too swift and abrupt. Rachel knew she'd
been right about Lois's feelings toward Griff.

"Gee, that's too bad, but I know how you feel. Neither am I."

The secretary's eyebrows arched with interest as she glanced at Griff. "But I thought you and…"

"Have to work," Rachel said, and then pretended to sigh in disappointment. "It's too bad that Griff might have to go alone. Unless he can find someone who hasn't already made plans, I suppose he'll just have to go stag."

This time the corners of the secretary's mouth tilted up to match her eyebrows' arch.

"Indeed!" she said, unable to believe the underlying hint she was picking up in Rachel's conversation.

"Yes," Rachel said. "So…if Griff's not busy, I guess you'd better put me through. I've got to give him the bad news."

"Sure thing," Lois said brightly. "Please hold."

One small click sounded in Rachel's ear, and the next thing she heard were the deep, resonant tones of Griffin Ross's voice.

"This is Griffin Ross."

Rachel stiffened. Just the sound of his voice made her nervous. In the past, no matter how many times she tried to dissuade him from further pursuit, he'd outtalked and outmaneuvered her every time. But this time she had to be strong.

"Griff, it's me, Rachel. Sorry to bother you at work, but—"

"You're never a bother!" he said brightly, and kicked back in his chair, ready to chat.

"About Saturday night," she began.

"I'll pick you up around six. We can grab a bite to eat beforehand. Nothing too heavy, though. I expect they'll have—"

"I can't go."

He straightened, unaware that his secretary was eyeing him from across the room.

"I have to work," Rachel added. "Ken Wade had a family emergency, and everyone's shifts have changed."

Griff wanted to argue, but he knew it would be futile. He could hardly have a fit in front of the customers and staff of Ross Savings and Loan. The finality of her announcement was obvious, and he knew her excuse was valid. He'd already heard about the Wade family's trouble, yet he couldn't help adding, "This is unfortunate, Rachel. You know, if you'd consider *us* once in a while, and let our relationship grow instead of being so self-centered, you wouldn't have to be working at that damned gory job."

Ignoring the other slights to her character, Rachel frowned as she stood up for the thing she loved most. "Griff, you don't know me at all, or you wouldn't say that. I like my job."

Griff panicked. He'd never heard such authority in her voice. "Darling, I'm sorry. I was just disappointed. How about if I call you tonight, after you get home? We'll make plans for another—"

"No, I don't think so."

He started to sweat. "I didn't mean to make you mad," he whispered, and spun around so that no one in the outer part of the building could see his face. "Please, Rachel. You know how I feel about you."

She sighed. "Yes, I think I do," she said. "And that's why I think it's time to put a stop to this, before it goes any further. I *like* you, Griff, and that's as far as it goes."

"But in time, I'm sure, you'll come to—"

"That's just it," Rachel said. "I'm just as sure I won't."

Griff couldn't believe what he was hearing. Never in his entire privileged life had he been thwarted so royally, or turned down so succinctly.

The skin of his face turned pale, and when the color came back, it was a dark, angry red. It took him every ounce of his control to keep his voice calm and his thoughts collected.

"I can't say I'm happy about this," he said. "But, as I always say, life isn't fair. I suppose I have to understand your feelings as clearly as I understand mine."

Rachel went weak with relief. This had been easier than

ne'd imagined, and because the load of guilt was off her houlders, her voice was lighter than she might have intended vhen she said, "I'm really sorry, Griff."

"Yes, so am I," he said.

"Thanks for being so understanding," she added, and when he disconnected, she practically danced a little jig of delight t having conquered something that had been weighing on her nind.

I don't understand anything yet, Griff thought, as he hung p the phone. *But before I'm through, I will.*

When Boone awoke, rain was hammering against the window. He yawned, then stretched, savoring the feel of clean heets and his own king-size bed. Last night had been a close ne. Walking cold into a buy where the odds were three to ne wasn't smart, but it had happened just the same. His expression darkened as he faced having to go back to Razor 3end. He was sick and tired of that roach-infested trailer, of istening to Snake and Tommy Joe's incessant chatter, and, nost of all, he was sick of being Boone MacDonald.

But leaving Razor Bend also meant leaving Rachel Brant, and he wasn't sure how he felt about that. As long as he vorked under cover, he could never go back as himself, and even if he did, what would it gain him? She had a boyfriend and a life that didn't include him, and that was the way it would have to be.

Angry with himself and the fact that he'd let hormones interfere with business, he rolled over, then got out of bed, walking to the window to stare out at the busy traffic on the Northwest Expressway just visible beyond the rooftops below.

Water was running swift and deep on the pavement and in the gutters. Experience warned him that some streets were bound to be flooded. It was all the excuse he needed to stay indoors, rather than check in at the office with Captain Cross, and going in and out of DEA headquarters in his undercover guise was risky, at best.

The thought of coffee, strong and black, pulled him away

from the window and sent him into the kitchen to start a po
brewing. A short time later, when he exited his shower, th
fresh-brewed scent filled the rooms.

He took a cup with him to the desk and sipped as h
thumbed through his notes, making corrections as he wen
before he made his call. There wasn't a lot to tell the captai
apart from what she already knew, but she was his connectio
with reality, and accepting his reality was what was keepin
him alive.

Chapter 5

A night and two days had passed since Boone had sent Tommy Joe home on three wheels. The way he figured it, he'd given Denver Cherry something to think about and Tommy Joe time to get over his mad. If he'd guessed wrong and Denver kicked him out of the gang, he almost didn't care. He was tired of playing cat and mouse with the entire bunch.

And the weather wasn't any better than Boone's mood. A cool front had stalled over the entire southern half of the state. For the past two days it had seemed that every time the hour changed, so did the weather. He'd driven south out of Oklahoma City in sunshine, but for the past two hours he had been driving in and out of rain.

He glanced at the mile marker and frowned. Only minutes away from Razor Bend; it was time to crawl back inside the head of a drug runner. No more Mr. Nice Guy. Boone Mac-Donald was back in town.

Puddles shimmered in the uneven roadbed, splattering the underside of his truck as he drove through them. A slight mist still lingered in the air, enough for him to keep the windshield

wipers on low. The day was gray and showed no signs c
getting better. Low-hanging clouds, heavy with rain that ha
yet to fall, darkened the sky, bringing an early end to a mis
erable day.

Boone was driving on autopilot. His body was in perfec
control of his truck, but his mind was sifting through possibl
scenarios for his coming confrontation with Denver Cherry
When a small compact car suddenly came out of nowhere
passing his truck at high speed, it startled him.

"Crazy kid," he muttered as the car sailed through a pud
dle of water, showering both sides of the road with displace
spray. "If he isn't careful, he'll hydroplane that thing."

The couple in the front seat were laughing and talking
seemingly unaware of any danger. Boone continued along be
hind, watching the way the young woman would reach out t
the driver, as if talking to him weren't enough, as if sh
needed to touch him, as well. Although the couple were sittin
apart, their affection for each other was impossible to miss.

It kindled a longing in Boone to have someone like that o
his own. Someone who cared when he was sick. Someon
who could laugh with him. Someone who was willing to wak
up beside him every morning for the rest of their lives.

At that moment, an odd sensation came over him. He fel
lost, as if the road he was on had nowhere to go. Yes, he wa
going to Razor Bend, where he had a meeting with Denve
Cherry that he knew could get sticky. But after that...wha
came next? Another bad guy? Another gang to be taker
down? Another town, another identity, another lie to be told
For the first time in his life, Boone thought past tomorrow
and he didn't like what he saw. He didn't want to wake ur
one morning and find out that while he'd been living his lie
life had passed him by.

Rachel Brant.

The woman's name came unexpectedly. Boone snorted
softly beneath his breath and shifted in the seat.

What about her? Why did he persist in fabricating the mere
idea of a relationship with a woman who didn't know he

xisted? He'd never thought of himself as a masochist, but he vas beginning to wonder. He'd either been under too long, r alone too many nights.

"Forget about a woman you can't have," he muttered. He ad reached down to turn up the radio when everything before im began to come undone.

The first thing he saw was a quick flash of brake lights on he car in front of him, a bright red warning that something vas wrong. In response, he tapped his own brakes and began o slow down, but unlike the driver in the car up ahead, he it them easy to decrease his speed.

Boone had seen the aftermaths of plenty of wrecks and had ven been involved in a couple himself, but he'd never been a witness to what he was seeing now.

The little car spun completely around more than twice be- ore it started to roll, and when it did, Boone winced and then groaned. Even though his windows were up and he was still a distance away, he heard the small car literally coming apart. Metal crunched; glass cracked, then shattered. One wheel came off and rolled down into the woods, out of sight, as the car settled upside down. Smoke and steam began to boil from under the hood as hoses popped and wiring was torn.

Boone felt shock and then a fleeting sorrow that happiness could so easily be destroyed. But there was no time left for emotion, only a reaction to the tragedy he'd seen. He grabbed for the phone lying next to him in the seat.

Because he was a cop, he made it his business to always know the number of the police department within his under- cover operation. For him, it was nothing more than a little added insurance, but right now he was thankful he knew who to call.

As he punched in the numbers, his mind began to focus. When the dispatcher answered, Boone's words were clipped, but his information was concise.

"There's a wreck just off the highway about four miles northwest of Razor Bend. Two people inside. Need an am- bulance and a wrecker, stat!"

The dispatcher's voice faded in and out as Boone came t
a sliding stop. He repeated the information at the top of hi
voice as he left his truck.

"No, no other cars involved!" he shouted, and when th
dispatcher signed off, he tossed the phone into the seat an
leaped from the pavement to the grassy slope and started run
ning and sliding toward the upended car.

By the time he'd reached the wreck, he'd already made
mental inventory of what he could possibly do before medica
personnel arrived.

The car was on its top. The right front wheel was stil
spinning as steam poured out from beneath the hood, fillin
the inside of the car and eliminating what visibility Boon
might have had. The silence was eerie. Except for escapin
steam, the only sound he heard was the rapid pounding of hi
own heart.

"Hey in there, can you hear me?" he shouted.

When no one answered, he circled the car on the run, mak
ing sure that the steam he saw was coming from the radiato
and not an impending explosion or fire.

At the passenger's side, he got down on his hands an
knees and thrust a hand through a shattered window, remem
bering that they would very probably be upside down, an
began feeling for the woman he knew should be there. At firs
he felt nothing. He scooted closer to the car, extending hi
arm farther into the space. Seconds later, his fingers touche
fabric, then hair, then warm, damp flesh. In spite of his year
of training, he jerked in reflex.

"Lady! Lady, can you hear me?" he shouted.

She didn't answer. He leaned forward, accidentally thrust
ing his fingers into a mop of wet, matted hair. He shuddered
Dear God. Seconds ago she was laughing.

Gently he traced the curve of a cheek, then the slende
column of her throat. To his relief, he felt a pulse, faint bu
sure. When he did, he jumped to his feet and began pulling
at the bent and folded metal. Seconds felt like an eternity a

He struggled, trying unsuccessfully to dislodge the door. It was no use. He gritted his teeth, then leaned down again.

"Help is coming," he shouted, then ran to the other side of the car, thinking maybe he could get to them from that side.

That window was gone, too. Steam billowed out of the opening in long, cloudlike puffs, sending signals of peril spiraling up into the gray, misty sky. Boone dropped to his knees, trying to crawl inside, but the driver's inert and pinned body was blocking the exit.

It didn't take long to see that the driver was dead, pinned in place by a crumpled piece of the dash. Through the smoke and steam, Boone had a fleeting glimpse of the young man's face, of his eyes, wide open, frozen in the horror of his last sight on earth.

"Damn," he muttered. He had started to back out of the window when, out of the smoke and steam, a small hand emerged, locking onto his fingers in a surprisingly firm grip. A tiny bracelet slid down a fragile wrist, and Boone felt what seemed to be charms dangling against his skin.

Oh my God! There's a child in here...a little girl!

He wrapped his hand around her grasping fingers then gave an easy, reassuring tug. As he did, he realized that she was strapped into some sort of child seat, because she was hanging upside down.

"Hey there, baby," he said gently, trying to keep the urgency out of his voice. "Are you hurt?"

At the question, the child started to cry. Not a loud, frightened wail, but a soft, helpless sob that tore at Boone's heart.

"It's okay, sweetheart," he said quickly. "We're going to get you out. I promise. Yes, we are, we're going to get you out."

"Mommy. Want Mommy," the little girl sobbed, and tugged even tighter on Boone's hand, as if trying to pull herself out of confinement.

Boone thought of the woman and her faint, fading pulse and prayed for the ambulance to get there in time.

"Mommy's resting right now," he said quickly. "Don'
cry, sweetheart…we might wake her up…okay?"

"Daddy…want Daddy."

Boone's heart ached. She was so small. Chances were she
would never remember the daddy who'd brought her into this
world. He would be nothing more than a name and a face in
some old family pictures. Damn it all to hell, he thought.
There was no justice in any of this.

"Daddy's asleep, too, honey."

Her grip tightened, almost as if she sensed that this man
was her only line to safety. He began to wish she would
scream or shriek from the fear she was bound to be feeling.
She was too passive, too quiet. At that point, he realized that
she very well might have internal injuries. He didn't even
know her name, but for him, her living had suddenly become
paramount.

Please, God. Don't let her die.

To his overwhelming relief, he began to hear a siren. It was
a distance away, but it was the first sign he'd had that help
was truly on the way.

"Do you hear that, baby girl? They're coming to help us.
Don't be afraid.… They're going to help us all."

Then the tiny fingers started to slip from his hand, and
Boone knew a moment of panic.

"Hey!" he said loudly, and his fear eased when she tightened her grip. He didn't even mind that he'd made her cry
again. As long as he could hear her, he knew she was still
alive. Gently, so as not to hurt what might turn out to be a
broken or dislocated bone, he gave her fingers a soft but urgent tug.

"What's your name, honey? Can you tell me your name?"

"Out. Want out," she sobbed.

"I'll tell you my name if you'll tell me yours," he urged.
"My name is…" He paused. Lying at a time like this almost
seemed unholy, but then he shrugged off the thought. Names
didn't count. It was the sound of his voice that she needed to

near. "My name is Boone. Can you say that? Can you say, Boone?"

"Boo," she repeated.

He didn't bother to correct her. She could call him anything she pleased. Then he heard her choke, and his heart nearly stopped. He had no way of knowing if she was gasping for breath or just choking on sobs.

"Sweetheart...can you tell me your name?"

She didn't answer.

"Honey...it's Boone, remember? Can you tell me your name?"

And then she spoke, and to Boone it was the sweetest sound in the world.

"Punkin."

His throat swelled and his eyes began to burn.

"Punkin, huh? That's a real pretty name. I'll bet you're a real pretty girl. Are you, baby? Are you a real pretty girl?"

"Daddy's girl," she said softly, and Boone lowered his head on his outstretched arm, fighting back tears.

"Come on, come on," he muttered to himself, praying for the ambulance to hurry.

More than once he tried to crawl past the man to get to her. He needed to see her. He wanted to feel her breath on his face and know that she was going to live long past this rainy September day. But the car had caved in, and the man was wedged between them like a block in a vise. Without help, Boone had gone as far as he could go.

And then the ambulance was suddenly there, lights flashing red and blue atop the boxy white truck, while the dying sounds of a siren choked into silence.

For the past few minutes Rachel Brant had been the farthest thing from his mind, but now, suddenly, she was on her knees beside him, grabbing his arm and asking for information. He started talking in shorthand, wanting them to know everything he knew before it was too late.

"Driver's dead. Woman on the passenger side. Alive...or

was when I first got here. Can't open the door. Child trapped
between them.''

Rachel put her hand on his shoulder, her eyes wide and
fixed on his face. ''Sir, I'll need you to move back,'' she said
quickly, and started to move him aside.

Boone frowned, afraid to let go of that small, trusting hand
''She won't let me go.''

''Please, sir,'' Rachel said, pushing her way past his bulk.
''I can't get to her with you in the way.''

Reluctantly Boone turned loose of the little girl's fingers,
and when he did, he felt a part of himself going with her.
And when he did let go, the scream he'd wanted to hear earlier came, and in full, panicked force. The baby's shrieks echoed within the confines of the small, crumpled cab, and Boone
could only imagine how afraid she must feel, losing touch
with her last and only lifeline, while hanging upside down in
a world filled with smoke.

In spite of her smaller size, Rachel couldn't get past the
driver's body, either, and despite several attempts, she
couldn't communicate with the child, because she was
screaming with every breath she took. Rachel backed out the
same way she'd crawled in. Her touch on Boone's arm was
brief, but her instructions were to the point.

''Sorry,'' she said quickly. ''See if you can calm her down.
We'll have to get to her from the other side.''

Boone went to his knees and thrust his arm into the car,
more than willing to reach out to a child in fear.

''Hey, Punkin, it's me, Boone. Don't cry, sweetheart. I'm
here. I'm still here.''

To his relief, the small, flailing arm came into contact with
his hand. He caught her, feeling the bracelet, then the tiny
fingers that had been clutching at nothing but smoke.

The child latched on to his hand in desperation, and moments later her shrieks had subsided to thick choking sobs.

''Boo...want out. Want out,'' she begged.

''Damn it, hurry up!'' he shouted. ''She's hanging upside
down in here.''

The tone of his voice was angry, but Rachel knew that ame from fear. She was well aware of the little girl's posiion, and the danger she could be in. Neck and head injuries vere always serious. In a child that small, dangling in an nsecure position could easily make things worse.

She circled the wreck, running to where Charlie was working on the other side, trying to focus on the task at hand and not the fact that she'd recognized the man on the other side of the car. He was the man from the Adam's Rib Café.

"Can't get this door open," Charlie said between grunts, tugging at the frame.

"The rescue squad was right behind us," Rachel said. "They should be here any minute. I'll get the KED, and a collar. We'll have to stabilize her before we can pull her out."

"I'll get it," Charlie said, and ran to the ambulance.

Rachel thrust her hand past the shattered glass, reaching down toward the woman inside. Thankfully, the steam was starting to subside and the victims were becoming visible. She felt for a pulse. It was there, but faint.

Charlie came back with the small backboard to stabilize her for removal. "What about the driver?" he asked as he dropped to his knees.

Rachel shook her head. "There's a child in an infant seat trapped between them. Can't ascertain her condition, other than that she's still alert enough to cry and has bonded with the man who stopped to help. He seems to be able to communicate with her. I sure couldn't."

To their relief, another siren was blasting around the winding curves. The arrival of the rescue squad was imminent. Seconds later, Rachel was on her feet and running to meet them.

"Bring the Jaws," she shouted, indicating the powerful Jaws of Life, which they would need to extricate the victims from the crumpled metal.

Men in uniform began swarming around what was left of the small car. Everything was being done that could possibly be done, yet Boone couldn't find it within himself to care

about anything but the child who had, strangely, entruste
herself to him.

The steam was nearly gone, baring what was left of the ca
to a clear view. There was a spilled juice box lying on a film
of shattered glass. The scent of grape mixed with the smel
of burning rubber and spilled fuel, giving added poignancy t
the truth of how quickly a life could end. A rag doll dangled
from what was left of a rearview mirror. A woman's purse
and its contents were strewn all over the ceiling of the car
Boone made himself focus on something other than the con
dition of the young driver's body. He looked past him to the
child beyond, and for the first time he had a clear, perfec
view of her face.

Even upside down, with her cheeks flushed and her eyes
swollen from crying, she was beautiful. Thick brown curls
framed a face just starting to lose its fat baby shape. Tiny
scratches on her cheeks and forehead, probably from flying
glass, had already stopped bleeding. She had a turned-up nose
and a rosebud mouth, and there were creases in her cheeks
that he suspected just might be dimples. Boone tugged at her
fingers and smiled.

"Hey there, Punkin. It's me, Boone."

Unbelievably, she tried to smile back. Then he watched as
her gaze slowly moved to her father, then her mother, as if
she, too, was seeing for the first time the aftermath of what
had happened. He didn't know what to say. Could a child that
small understand what she was seeing?

"Punkin…?"

She looked back at Boone. "Sleepin'," she said softly.
"Daddy sleepin'."

Tears shattered what was left of Boone's view. "Yes, baby,
your daddy is sleeping."

Rachel was rechecking the injured woman's pulse when she
heard the little girl's voice. Her gaze shifted to the man on
the opposite side of the car. He was smiling at the child, but
there were tears shimmering in his eyes, eyes so black she
couldn't even see the pupils. The grip he had on the baby's

and was gentle, so gentle. She took a deep breath and went back to her work, aware that this was no time to join him in grief.

And then Charlie tapped her on the back. "Rachel, you've got to pull back. They're going to use the Jaws.

Metal crunched and popped as the hydraulic claw did what it had been designed to do. Moments later, they had the door on the passenger side open. Rachel pushed her way past the firemen to the young mother inside. To Rachel's relief, the woman's eyelids began to flutter. Charlie was on his knees beside her, the neck brace in his hand. They began to do what they'd been trained to do.

Before Boone knew it, the ambulance holding Punkin and her mother was flying down the road, with lights flashing and the wail of a siren to accompany them home. He shuddered. It sounded too much like a little girl's scream. And while he watched, another vehicle arrived. The name emblazoned in gold paint on both doors said it all. County Coroner. They'd come for Punkin's daddy.

Oh, God.

His mind went blank. He looked down at his scratched and bloodstained hands. The pale blue T-shirt he'd put on this morning was blood-spattered. His black leather jacket was wet and muddy. And while he stood, rain started to fall again. The urge to cry was so close at hand that he couldn't focus on what to do next. He closed his eyes and lifted his face to the sky, wishing it would wash away the memories of what he'd just seen.

With weariness in every movement, he turned toward his truck just as the familiar black and white of an Oklahoma Highway Patrol car pulled up to the scene. In a gesture of defeat, he leaned against the fender, waiting for the officer to emerge.

Rain was coming down faster now, plastering his hair to his head and his clothes to his body. Impulsively he held out his hands, welcoming the cold, bulletlike droplets that fell

upon his bloodstained skin. For once the thought of solitude
inside that run-down trailer house in the Kiamichis seemed
inviting, but he couldn't leave. Not now. He took a deep
breath. It wasn't quite over yet.

He drove through Razor Bend in a daze, not stopping until
he found himself in Denver Cherry's front yard. He'd come
back to Razor Bend to finish a job. Either he would finish
it…or it would finish him. He walked onto the porch and into
the house without knocking.

One look at Boone MacDonald and Denver forgot any notion he'd had about putting him in his place. There was blood
on his shirt, and his clothes were wet clear through. He didn't
know what had happened to him, but the look in Boone's
eyes made Denver nervous.

"I suppose you came for your money," he said, trying to
maintain the upper hand.

Boone didn't have to pretend to be angry. Denver Cherry
was a man who didn't care who he hurt or how it happened,
as long as he got what he wanted. The world would be better
off without Cherry's kind, and yet he lived and a young man
had died. Boone swallowed his rage. He couldn't get the
sound of a little girl's sobs out of his mind.

"We never did agree on how much," Denver said, then
looked away when Boone's hands doubled into fists. He'd
known sending Tommy Joe to tail Boone might tick him off,
but he'd never figured Boone would take it so hard.

"Just pay me. I've got things to do," Boone said.

Denver shrugged, then handed over a wad of bills that
Boone didn't even bother to count. He shoved them in his
pocket and turned on his heel, aware that if he didn't put some
space between them, someone was going to get hurt.

"Hey, Boone."

Boone stopped in midstride, without turning around.

Denver stared at the angry set to Boone's shoulders, wondering what kind of response he was about to get.

"You did a real good job. I might have some more work or you, if you're interested."

Boone swallowed, then closed his eyes, letting himself remember why he was here.

"Sure, why not," he muttered. "But next time, either send your bird dog with me, or keep him tied on a leash. Understand?"

Denver grinned. "You're a hard nut, aren't you?"

Boone blinked. Today he'd cried. Tonight he just might get drunk. That made him a nut, all right, but he wasn't hard enough to ignore the pain.

"You know where to find me," Boone said, and slammed the door shut behind him.

Hours later, he lay in bed, wide-eyed and sleepless, ignoring a line of cockroaches running up the wall, while he listened to the rain running off the tin roof. An unopened bottle of Jack Daniel's sat right where he'd put it hours ago. He'd taken one look at it and known that drowning this pain wouldn't make it go away. A notion was pushing at him, urging him up, moving past reason to a need he couldn't stop. He wanted to know what had happened to those people from the wreck…and he needed to see Rachel Brant.

Watching her in action today had intrigued him. The helpless, crying woman he'd found in the dark was not the woman who'd taken charge at the wreck. The woman she'd been today was cool, collected and competent. She'd done everything right, and with skill and ease. She hadn't folded once at the sight of blood and death, and he knew seasoned officers who wouldn't have been able to say the same.

It wouldn't take long, he reminded himself. All he had to do was just knock on her door and ask about the victims' conditions. She was bound to know something.

He rolled out of bed and reached for his boots. Before he slept, he needed to hear the sound of her voice.

Rachel puttered through the last of her evening chores, only half-aware that the rain had finally subsided. Water dripped

from the leaves onto the roof, soft, gentle sprinkles hardl
detectable from indoors. It was only after she went outside t
toss coffee grounds beneath her rosebush that she becam
aware of the slight trickle running through the gutter and ou
the downspout at the end of the house. There was a much
needed gentleness to the night that the day had not held.

Pictures kept flashing into her mind. A young father, gon
from this earth too soon. A young mother, hanging on to life
A small child who'd held even tighter to a wet rag doll, he
only familiar object in a world gone awry.

Rachel sat down on the back porch steps and buried he
face in her hands. Losing a patient was the downside of he
job. She'd thought she'd learned to live with the knowledge
that sometimes, even when they'd done everything possible
it still wasn't enough. But tonight she wasn't sure.

Music drifted out through the screen door and into the
night, blending man-made notes with those of Mother Nature.
In a fanciful way, the raindrops sounded a little like teardrops,
which fit well with the songs being sung. Her taste in music
was eclectic, but tonight, sad country songs fit her mood.

She looked up just as the moon emerged from behind a
cloud. There on the lawn, standing in the shadows next to her
swing, was the tall, unmistakable, silhouette of a man. She
gasped. Heart pounding, she jumped to her feet. All she could
think was to get inside and lock the door.

"Please, lady, wait!"

She froze. She couldn't see his face, but she knew that
voice and the straight set of those shoulders as he stood with
his legs slightly apart, as if bracing himself for a blow. It was
the same man who'd found her standing in the stream!

He'd come through the woods as he had before, telling
himself with every step he took that he was doing this all
wrong, that if he kept this up, he might as well put a gun to
his head and pull the trigger. Everything he was doing was
in direct opposition to what an undercover officer should do.

Personal wanting was supposed to take a back seat to the job, but that wasn't happening tonight.

And then he'd seen her come out of the house, and while his mind was shouting, *No!* his feet had been moving ever closer to her house, to her. When she sat down on the steps, he'd wanted to join her, and when she buried her face in her hands, his heart had gone out to her in empathy.

So, he'd thought, *you do feel the pain.*

Music had drifted out of the house, coming to him on the night. At first it had been nothing more than background to the woman who'd captured his focus. But somewhere between one breath and the next, he'd heard the voice, then the words, and they'd taken his breath away.

It was an old song from the Eagles. Once, years ago, he'd stood in the back of a crowded concert hall and heard them sing this very same song.

Desperado.

Then, the words hadn't meant anything more than any lyrics, but now they came to him as a warning that struck deep in his heart.

He swayed where he stood, as if wounded. Love somebody before it was too late? It was already too late for him. By virtue of his life-style, and in society's eyes, he *was* a desperado…an outlaw who didn't belong in a good woman's life.

"I'll call the police!" Rachel shouted.

Boone's heart hurt at the knowledge he kept putting that fear in her voice.

"Please don't. I came to ask you a question."

Rachel's hand was on the doorknob, and if the man had taken a single step farther, she would have been inside in a instant. But he never moved, so neither did she.

"What?"

"Today you worked a wreck outside of town."

To say Rachel was surprised at the man's choice of topic was putting it mildly. She'd been expecting something personal, even something sexual, that would fit the dark anonym-

ity of his coming and going. She stood without answering
waiting for him to make a wrong move.

"There was a little girl who called herself Punkin."

Rachel's eyes widened. How had he known that?

"Is she all right?" Boone persisted.

She could see no danger in answering, but her voice wa:
still shaking when she spoke. "Yes, I believe so."

"And her mother?"

Rachel's hand fell from the doorknob to her side. "We lef
her in good hands. Last I heard, she was stable."

Boone exhaled slowly in relief. "Good," he said softly
"That's good."

"How did you know?" Rachel asked.

But Boone answered her question with another of his own.

"The little girl...Punkin...was she still crying when you
left?"

Rachel's eyebrows arched. *Still? How did he know she'd
been crying at all? Unless...*

"No. Some of the family had arrived. When I saw her last,
she was sound asleep in her grandmother's arms."

"Thank you," Boone said, and his voice was so quiet that
Rachel had to strain to hear his answer.

"Who are you?" she asked, just as the last notes of the
song faded into the night.

"No one."

The emptiness in his voice was unmistakable. In spite of
herself, Rachel felt empathy instead of fear.

And then he moved. But instead of coming toward her, he
turned and started back toward the woods. When he moved
out from beneath the tree and into the moonlight, it fell upon
his shoulders, enhancing their breadth and his height. Once
again Rachel was struck by his strength and his size. But this
time, as he walked, something struck her as familiar. Impulsively she ran to the edge of the porch and called out.

"Wait!"

Surprised, Boone turned before he thought, and then realized that he was no longer concealed by the shadows of night.

Although the distance between them was real, there was no way he could hide the sight of his face.

Oh, God… Dear God… Rachel thought, as her hands curled tightly into fists.

Neither spoke. Neither moved. A lingering rain cloud passed between moonlight and earth. A few moments later, it was gone…and so was the man.

A nervous chill ran up Rachel's back. She turned and bolted for the door, shutting it and locking it firmly behind her. Yet even after she was safely inside and sitting in the dark with the phone in her hand, she couldn't get past the fact that the man who'd found her sleepwalking…the man who kept coming to her out of the dark…the man who'd cared about a small child's tears…was the same man who ran with that gang.

That night, when at last she slept, she dreamed. But not the same dream as before. This time she dreamed of a man with dark, laughing eyes, a man who killed with the same passion as he made love.

Chapter 6

When the alarm went off in Rachel's ear, she rolled over and out of bed in the same smooth motion. Only after she hit the button to shut off the alarm did she realize that she'd set it last night out of habit. She groaned in disbelief. She didn't have to go to work today or tomorrow. It was six in the morning, and she'd gotten up for nothing.

"Good grief," she muttered, and crawled back between the covers.

But habit was a hard thing to break. In spite of burying her nose in the pillow and squeezing her eyes tight against a burgeoning dawn, sleep wouldn't come.

Finally she flopped onto her back, scrunched her pillow beneath her neck and contemplated the luxury of two entire days to herself.

No one to answer to.

No sitting around waiting for an emergency to happen.

Today, she could make things happen for herself. She glanced toward the window. It wasn't raining, but wind was whipping the azalea bushes beneath the window near her bed.

Every now and then, an elongated branch hit the pane with a thump, then a scratch, as if someone, or something, were begging to get in.

Goose bumps peppered the skin on her arms as her imagination took flight. And even though she knew she was safe, she got up and headed toward the kitchen.

Two cups of coffee later, she was still pondering the identity of the man who'd found her in the stream. For all she knew, he was a criminal. He certainly looked like one. At any rate, he was a man who didn't belong in her world. She shuddered, remembering the men he ran with and the way he'd watched Griff kissing her with no sense of shame.

Yet, even in her dismay, she was forced to give credit where credit was due. If he hadn't happened upon that wreck yesterday, more than likely that mother would have died, and God knew what might have happened to the baby before anyone found them.

She would never have believed a man who presented himself as a modern-day outlaw could be as empathetic and compassionate as he had been with that small, frightened child. But he had.

In fact, Rachel knew that if that had been their first meeting, she would have come away from that wreck with a completely different impression of the man. She'd seen him reluctant to move from danger, eager to go back to the child who was trapped. And not only that, he'd been concerned enough to come last night and ask about her condition.

"Oh, for Pete's sake," Rachel muttered, and dumped the last of her coffee down the drain. "I'm romanticizing about some probable felon, just because he hasn't lost the ability to shed tears for someone else's pain."

Angry with herself and what she considered "flights of fancy," she made a list of things she wanted to do today, then went to get dressed. Casual would be the order of the day.

But just as she was walking out the door, the phone began to ring. Conscience told her to answer. Instead, she stood, listening to the second, then the third, shrill ring. When it rang for the fourth time, her answering machine clicked on, and Rachel stood in the doorway, listening to Griffin Ross's voice.

An odd sensation of dread settled in the pit of her stomach as he rambled through his monologue, with a reason for calling that she didn't believe. He was still talking when she walked out the door, locking it behind her. As she drove away, she had the strangest sensation of having made an escape, then told herself she was being silly. Griff wasn't the man she should be worrying about. He wasn't the one who'd been showing up in all the wrong places.

After a long, enjoyable day in Broken Bow, Rachel entered the city limits of Razor Bend. It was fifteen minutes to four, and school was letting out. A line of yellow buses was at a stoplight, waiting for it to turn green, while teenagers barely old enough to drive were cruising the streets in their cars, honking and waving as if they hadn't seen one another in weeks, when they'd just spent the day together in class.

She turned off the main thoroughfare and pulled up to the self-serve pump outside Jimmy's Place. He sold diesel and gas and the greasiest made-to-order burgers in town. Saturday nights, when the town all but died, Jimmy's Place was usually packed. The draw? A well-worn pool table in a small back room, four video games, of which only three worked, and the only place in town that fixed flats. She didn't need a flat fixed, but she could use a tank of gas. It was the perfect excuse to get off the streets until the worst of the traffic had passed.

Rachel put her car in park and killed the engine, then glanced over her shoulder to the sacks of groceries sitting in the back seat. There was nothing inside that warranted refrigeration, so they should be fine. Shopping in Broken Bow had netted her more than a week's worth of groceries, plus a couple of rental movies she'd been wanting to see. She got out with a smile on her lips, thinking about solitude, popcorn and Patrick Swayze in drag as she unscrewed the gas cap and set it aside.

But when she turned toward the pump, she stifled a gasp. A weasel of a man with a brown, shaggy beard was blocking her path. He grinned, then winked, adding a slow, appreciative whistle to the leer he was wearing.

"Well, hello, now..." Snake said.

His audacity took Rachel by surprise, and then, to her dismay, she realized where she'd seen him before. He was one of the trio of men who'd ogled her and Griff from the street in front of the Adam's Rib Café.

She refused to be bullied. She would not be afraid. She lifted her chin, her eyes glittering with anger as she waited for him to give way.

"Excuse me, but you're in my way."

Snake Martin grinned. "Now...there ain't no need to be actin' that way. I see you're needin' you some gas. How 'bout lettin' old Snake do that for you, honey? You don't want to be gettin' your pretty self all dirty doin' man's work, do you?"

Her stare was unwavering, and her words were cool and clipped. "I don't need any help," she said, and tried to step around him to get to the pump.

But Snake wasn't through playing. He moved with her, once again positioning himself between her and the gas. When he saw her pupils widen, he took advantage of her panic and grabbed her by the arm.

The contact was so sudden, so abhorrent, that Rachel panicked and tried to yank herself free.

"Let me go!" she cried.

But Snake still wasn't done. He knew who she was. He made it his business to know things about beautiful women. He also knew she was no longer anyone's property. The way he heard it, the banker had himself another girlfriend, which, to Snake's way of thinking, made this one free game.

"Now, now, you need to take it easy, sugar," Snake whispered.

"A pretty thing like you shouldn't be alone. You need a

man...a man like me. I'd take real good care of— Ouch!
Ow...ow... Damn it, Boone, let me go."

Rachel jerked, then looked over her shoulder to the man
who'd come up behind her...and to the rage on his face.

Now she *was* afraid.

Boone's hand tightened around Snake's bony wrist until he
was forced to turn Rachel loose.

"What the hell are you doing?" Boone asked, and if Snake
had had the good sense he'd been born with, he would have
known to be scared.

"Mind your own damned business," Snake said, then doubled up his free fist and took a wild swing.

Boone didn't bother to duck. At the moment of Snake's
swing, he turned him loose and stepped aside. With nothing
to check the forward momentum of his own body, Snake fell
to the ground.

But when he would have come up fighting, he found himself on the underside of a very large boot, staring up into the
face of a cold, angry man.

"Keeping you out of jail is my business," Boone said
softly.

Snake winced. That boot on his neck was beginning to hurt.

"Damn you, Boone. I wasn't hurtin' her none. Was I,
lady?"

Both pairs of eyes turned to Rachel, one begging to be
absolved of an intended sin, the other pinning her in place
with a cold, dark stare. She had half a mind to get in her car
and drive away, leaving the two toughs to fight it out on their
own, but she feared her exit would be less than effective. With
a gas gauge on empty and nowhere to go, she struggled to
find an answer that would put an end to the entire fiasco.

A gust of warm air whipped a wayward strand of hair toward her face, bringing with it the scent of old grease from
the french fries Jimmy's Place served, as well as the gas in
the pumps. But before she could answer either man's unspoken plea, something started to change.

The awning beneath which she was standing seemed to

melt in her mind. Instead of shade, she felt sun on her face and the sting of dust in her eyes. The sound of cars on the busy street behind her faded, and to her right a horse nickered, then stomped fretfully as it pulled at its tether.

Someone ran past her, shouting. She turned to look, and Razor Bend had disappeared. The paved streets had turned to dust. The busy downtown business district was nothing but an odd, ramshackle assortment of unpainted clapboard buildings and weather-worn tents, popping in the wind.

A man called out a name that made her blood run hot, then cold with fear.

"Dakota! I'm callin' you out!"

Dakota stood in the middle of the street, his legs braced, his fingers taut and curled above the butt of the gun riding low on his hip. His voice was low, his demeanor deadly.

"For the last damn time, I did not steal your gold," Dakota growled.

Mercy moaned. She recognized the miner who'd called Dakota out. It was Rufus Stampler. He'd been drinking and gambling for the better part of a week. If his gold was gone, chances were he'd wagered it and lost when he was too drunk to know.

And then the miner made his move.

She screamed. "Dakota, look out!"

She could have saved her breath. Rufus had announced his intent when he went for his gun.

Dakota's draw was as deadly as the look on his face. He'd already known that it would come to this. It always did. For him, there was no other way.

Fire spewed from the end of Dakota's gun. The sound of the shot was still ringing in the onlookers' ears when the miner fell. His gun had never cleared the holster.

Weak with relief, Mercy thought if a man had to die, thank God it hadn't been hers.

The wind lifted the skirt of her red satin dress, plastering it indecently to her slim, shapely body. But Mercy Hollister had long ago given up decency for a dry bed and a full belly.

*And if asked, she would give those up, too, for the love of
this man who lived by the gun.*

She needed to touch him…to feel the heartbeat still strong
in his chest. Blindly she started toward him, but someone
grabbed her by the shoulder, yanking her rudely around.

Sunlight hit the tin badge pinned to the front of Ab Schuler's
shirt. Mercy's heart sank. Ab couldn't arrest him. It hadn't
been Dakota's fault.

"It was a fair fight. Rufus called him out. We all saw it,"
she said.

Ab Schuler frowned. He'd never known it was possible to
love a woman and hate her all at the same time, but that was
what he felt now, knowing that a gunman had replaced him
in Mercy Hollister's heart.

"What's wrong with you?" he snarled, twisting her arm in
an effort to make her see sense, but his anger turned to fear
when a cold, deadly voice called his name.

He turned, still holding her arm. Dakota was standing not
six feet away, with his gun drawn and aimed at Ab's belly.

"Let her go," Dakota warned, and then cocked his gun.

Mercy fell free.

Rachel staggered, then covered her face with her hands. *Oh,
my God… Oh, my God…*

Boone saw her sway, and before she could fall, he caught
her close. For a heartbeat—but no longer—he knew what it
felt like to hold Rachel Brant in his arms. The instant she felt
steady, he let her go. When he looked back at Snake, the
threat in his voice brought Snake to his feet.

"Get!" he said hoarsely.

Snake didn't have to be told twice. What had started out
as a little bit of fun had turned into a great big stinking deal.
He glared at Rachel as he stomped past her.

Boone turned, noting Rachel's lack of color, as well as the
odd, flat stare in her eyes. Something didn't set right. She was
a woman who dealt with life and death every day; he wouldn't
have expected her to react so emotionally to an act of sexual

harassment. Punch Snake out? Yes, definitely yes! But pass out on him? No.

"Are you all right?" he asked, wishing he could take her in his arms again and make that fear on her face go away. But the man he was pretending to be could not be touching a woman like her. It would only make things worse.

Rachel shuddered. That voice. His voice. It was so like… She looked up. Reality checked in with a jolt as she realized she had a name to go with the face.

Boone. Your name is Boone.

For some reason, it didn't quite fit. There was a cold, almost cruel, expression on his face, but his eyes, those dark, fathomless eyes, had changed. If she hadn't known better, she might have believed there was love shining there.

Boone was getting nervous. Why didn't she answer? Was there something he was missing?

"Lady, are you all right?" he repeated.

It wouldn't do to let him know she was scared. Her hand was shaking as she lifted it to her face, smoothing away the windblown tendrils that had escaped from her braid. Her voice was as calm as she could make it. "I'm fine, thank you."

Stifling an urge to continue this fruitless conversation, he walked away before he could change his mind.

Rachel stared after him, once again wondering why she kept thinking she'd seen him before. Before Razor Bend. There was something about that slow, careless walk. He reminded her of someone, but she couldn't think who.

"Who in the world could I possibly know who would be anything like—?"

Her heart skipped a beat, and she had to steady herself by hanging on to the pump.

Dakota! Dear God, he walks like the man in my dreams.

"Hey, Rachel. Need any help?"

She turned. The owner of Jimmy's Place was leaning out the door, waiting for her answer.

And where were you when I needed you? "No. No, I've got it," she muttered, and pulled the hose from the pump.

The tank began to fill, and as it did, Rachel was forced to accept a fact that she should have acknowledged long ago.

Just now, when the world as she knew it and the one in her mind had separated, she hadn't been dreaming. She'd been wide awake and part of an ugly confrontation. Yet in the midst of it all, reality had slipped, just as it had that night in the stream. No longer could she tell herself it was the aftermath of sleepwalking. Something was happening to her that she didn't understand. Even worse, it was something she couldn't control.

Denver Cherry was sprawled in his favorite easy chair, with the television remote in one hand and his third longneck of the hour in the other. He squinted at the set, watching Debbie do Dallas, as well as several other men in between, all the while wondering if his satellite dish was as steamy as the show on the screen.

Right in the middle of him wishing he had a little female company, the front door of his house flew back with a bang, rattling nearby windows and setting his teeth on edge. He turned, then glared. This was not the company he'd had in mind.

"Don't you people ever knock?" he growled, giving Boone a hard-edged stare.

Boone pointed toward Snake, who, like his namesake, was slithering toward a chair on the opposite side of the room.

"I've had it," Boone said. "Either I'm in all the way, or I'm out for good!"

Denver frowned. He didn't like ultimatums. He was the boss. He made the decisions.

"Now you listen here...." he growled. But he never got a chance to finish what he'd been going to say.

Boone jabbed a finger in Denver's fat belly. "No, you listen. The whole lot of you are nothing but a bunch of penny-ante thugs. You told me when I signed on that I could work my way up in this organization...that there would be something for me if I was willing to wait." He took a deep breath.

There was a lot riding on what he said next, and it had to come out just right. "But I just figured something out."

"Like what?" Denver said.

Sarcasm colored his voice. "Like I think I've been lied to. You told me you had backing. You said there would be big money in it for me. Well, hell, Denver, except for that run the other night, all I've done is pick up after your two stooges."

Denver glared, first at Boone, then at Snake. Something had happened to precipitate this explosion. He would bet money on it. And it was forcing an issue he wasn't ready to face, namely bringing an outsider into the fold. Yes, Boone had made an unplanned delivery for him with no hitches. But he was an unknown. Until six weeks ago, Denver hadn't known the man existed, and now he wanted in. Well, he didn't think so. He'd known Snake Martin and Tommy Joe Smith nearly all their lives. Granted, they were stupid, but they followed orders and kept their mouths shut.

Denver glared at Snake. "What the hell did you do?"

"Not a damned—"

"Shut up!" Boone muttered.

Snake did as he was told. Boone started to pace in a jumpy, nervous manner, as if he expected the cops to burst in on them at any moment. To add to the drama, static from the police scanner broke the momentary silence in the room as a dispatcher's voice came in loud and clear behind them.

"See the woman at 1022 Main about a disturbance."

Boone relaxed. That wasn't the address of Jimmy's Place, but it very well could have been. He pointed at Snake, but his comments were directed to Denver.

"He accosted a very unwilling woman in a very public place. I'd venture to say any number of people saw what he was doing. I yanked his ass away before he wound up back in jail, and left the woman standing by the gas pumps at Jimmy's Place. For all I know, she still might press charges."

Denver's face turned a mottled purple. He stared at Snake,

wondering, if he killed him right now, how he could dispose of the body without being caught.

"You fool!" His voice was shaking with rage. The boss was already on his ass about the messes Snake was making. "Do you ever think?"

Snake glared, although he was starting to realize the implications of what he'd just done.

"I didn't hurt her none," he muttered.

Denver stalked toward Snake, who was scrambling to his feet and looking for the quickest way out. He grabbed him by the throat and slammed him up against the wall, stopping Snake's exit.

"She better not have been someone's wife."

Snake slapped at Denver's hand, trying unsuccessfully to free himself from the angry man's grasp.

"Hell, no," he grumbled. "She's free and legal. She ain't married, and she ain't nobody's girl. I know that for a fact."

"You're lying," Boone said softly. "You know as well as I do that she belongs to that banker. We all saw him kiss her at the EMS headquarters where she works."

Denver's face paled. He gawked at Snake, as if seeing him for the reptile he really was. There was only one banker who counted in Razor Bend, and only one female EMT. Boone had to be talking about Griffin Ross and Rachel Brant.

"Is Boone telling the truth? Did you mess with Griffin Ross's woman?"

When Snake looked away, Denver exploded.

"You idiot! You fool! You stepped out of your league, and I will not put my neck on the line for you with the boss this time. He's already on your case for offing that guard. If he finds out about this, too, you're gone! Get that?"

"That guard wasn't supposed to be there," Snake whined. "It's not my fault. He pulled a gun on me first."

Boone froze. Snake had killed a guard? What guard? Every lawman's instinct he had said he should arrest them now and forget the boss, whoever the hell he was. And yet he stood without moving, aware that he couldn't say a thing. He'd just witnessed a confession to murder and was unable to act upon it.

"That does it," Boone muttered, and spun on his heel. "I'm outa here. I've done time, and I'll probably do some more before I die, but I don't plan on lethal injection as my method of passing. You people are out of my league. I don't hire on with killers."

Denver paled. He couldn't lose Snake *and* Boone. There was no way he and Tommy Joe could handle the business alone. The boss had too many irons in the fire already.

"Wait!" Denver shouted.

Boone turned.

"You're in."

Whatever elation Boone should have been feeling was masked by a slow-burning rage. "In how?"

Denver didn't like to be put on the spot. He shrugged. "You haul, just like Snake and Tommy Joe. You get paid when I get paid."

"And if something goes wrong?"

Denver sighed. "We take care of our own. If you get caught, you'll be bailed out."

"Who do I call if that happens? You?"

"No! If it happens, just bide your time. The boss handles that."

"But how will he know?"

Denver shrugged. "He just knows, that's all."

"I like to know who I'm working for," Boone said, aware that he might be pushing his luck.

This time Denver balked. "It's not my story to tell. If the boss wants to meet you, then you'll be the first to know. Otherwise, do what you're told and keep your mouth shut."

"I'm not baby-sitting that fool again," Boone said. "I work alone, or not at all." He glared at Snake again to reiterate his point.

Denver held up his hands, as if in surrender. "Fine...fine. Just check back with me in a day or so. We've got a load of crystal meth that's overdue from the lab. When it shows, we've got to get rid of it fast, understand?''

Boone nodded, then left. When he was several miles down the road, he reached for his phone. Moments later, he was unloading what he'd learned to Captain Cross. They'd spread a net to catch some thieves, and caught a killer, as well.

Pain shattered the dream within Rachel's head. She woke up facedown in the yard. As always, she had a blinding head-ache and tears on her cheeks. She scrambled to her feet. Unaware of the rain-soaked ground coming up between her toes, she swayed slightly as she stared into the night. This time, to her relief, she was alone.

''Dear God, this has got to stop,'' she muttered, and stag-gered up the steps and into the house.

Once inside, she stripped off her muddy gown as she headed for the bath, anxious to wash away more than the mud clinging to her skin and clothes.

The water was warm and welcoming as she stepped beneath the spray. She lifted her face, letting the heat soak into her chilled, shaking body. Long after she was out and dry, wrapped in a clean robe, she was afraid to sleep, for fear it would happen again. But she'd been forced to accept a truth she'd been ignoring before. She needed help—professional help. She would deal with it tomorrow.

And then she looked at the clock. Tomorrow was already here.

Griffin Ross had a new suit. Lois Klein spotted it the mo-ment he walked in. Her hand automatically went to her hair, checking to make sure it was all in place. She didn't want to rush things, yet she was determined not to miss her chance. One dance did not a relationship make, and although they'd had what she considered a wonderful time, there had been nothing between them since then but cordial smiles and polite conversation.

Griff walked like a man who knew his place on this earth. He had everything he'd ever wanted...except Rachel Brant, and he hadn't completely given up on changing that fact. He saw his secretary fidget, and knew that taking her to the dance had been a mistake. Lois was a nice woman, and more than attractive, but she wasn't Rachel. He nodded and smiled as he walked past her desk.

"Morning, Lois."

She preened. "Good morning, Griff...." She blushed, then glanced at the customers waiting outside his office. "I mean, Mr. Ross."

Griff winced. He'd been right. Taking Lois to the dance had been a great big mistake.

Lois handed Griff a file. "Mr. Dutton is waiting to see you, sir."

Griff glanced at Charlie Dutton and smiled. "Come in, Charlie." As Charlie entered the office, Griff closed the door and then took a seat behind his desk.

Charlie slid into the guest chair and then sat forward, leaning toward the desk.

Griffin Ross was of the opinion that body language told more about a customer than what they might say about themselves. From the way Charlie was behaving, he was expecting him to ask for an extension on his loan. He couldn't have been more wrong.

"I came to pay off my note," Charlie said, and pulled a cashier's check from his pocket, already made out and signed.

For a moment Griff was taken aback, but then he smiled broadly. "Well, now, that's fine, just fine! But that's quite a sizable amount, isn't it?"

Charlie grinned and slid the check across the desk to Griffin.

"Thirty-three thousand dollars and forty-four cents, interest and all."

"My goodness," Griff said. "You must have a whale of a second job." He grinned. "What are you doing, making moonshine on the side?"

Charlie's eyes narrowed, but his smile stayed fixed. "I jus
had myself a little luck," he said quickly. "I don't like to be
in debt any more than the next man."

Griff nodded. "Good. That's good. Now you wait here
while I have Lois pull your note. We'll have you free and
clear in no time."

Down the street, Rachel pulled her car up to the curb, righ
in front of Curlers. Joanie Mills looked up, then waved at her
through the window as she gave her client's hair a final pat.

The doorbell jangled as Rachel walked in.

"Be right with you," Joanie said, making change for Mavis
Bealer, who was paying for her perm.

"Nice hairdo, Mavis," Rachel said, and was rewarded with
a wide grin as Mavis prissed herself out of the door.

Joanie turned to Rachel, and her smile faded. "What's
wrong?"

Rachel sat down and ran her hands through her long, dark
hair.

"I need the ends trimmed."

Joanie frowned. "I wasn't talking about your hair. I haven'
seen circles that dark under anyone's eyes since New Year's
Day. Have you had a bad week?"

Rachel shrugged. She could lie and blame her mood on her
job, and Joanie would believe her. Joanie all but fainted a
the sight of her own blood, and considered Rachel something
between an angel and a masochist.

"I've had better," she said.

Joanie patted her on the shoulder and then flopped a wa-
terproof cape around her shoulders, fastening it firmly at the
neck. "Let's get you washed. You close your eyes and relax."
She wiggled her fingers in Rachel's face. "I give the bes
scalp massages in town."

Rachel grinned as Joanie angled her head beneath a flow
of warm water. "That's because you give the *only* scalp massages in town."

Joanie pretended to leer, and then lowered her voice to a

whisper. "That's not what I hear. Someone told me that ColaBelle Prather was doing all right for herself on Saturday nights."

Rachel laughed, then closed her eyes and started to relax. Her friend's outrageous gossip was just what she'd needed to hear. She shifted in the chair and then settled, letting her mind wander in and out of focus as Joanie washed and rambled. It was only when Joanie's hands suddenly stilled in the act of scrubbing that she started to listen more closely.

When Joanie groaned and then sighed, Rachel opened her eyes and looked up. The look on her friend's face was close to rapture.

"What?" Rachel asked, wishing she could see more than the flyspecks on the ceiling above.

"Oh…my…Gawd!" Joanie gasped. Joanie quickly washed the soap out of Rachel's hair, then swathed her head in a towel and sat her up. "Take a look out there!"

Rachel rolled her eyes and grinned, then looked in the direction Joanie was pointing. The grin froze on her face as Joanie continued.

"I'd say about a hundred and ninety-something pounds. At least two or three inches over six feet…and good grief, Granny, the longest legs and the cutest butt I've ever seen on a man."

Rachel had no comment to make about Joanie's raves. There was nothing to say. She'd been up close and personal with this man far too many times as it was. Even ogling him from behind plate glass seemed risky.

"Just look at that face!" Joanie gasped, and pretended to shiver with ecstasy. "Isn't he just to die for?"

Judging by who he hangs out with, you very well might.

Joanie elbowed Rachel. "Wouldn't you just love to get him alone in the dark?"

A nervous twinge pulled at Rachel's belly. What on earth would Joanie think if she knew that had already happened?

"I don't know," Rachel said, feeling her way through the unexpected conversation. "He looks pretty rough to me."

Joanie grinned. "The better to love you with, my dear. Sh
giggled.

But Rachel wasn't laughing. She was too busy trying t
hang on to the chair. In spite of the fact that she could se
her own reflection in the window before her, another shape—
another face—was again superimposing itself over hers. I
was her…and yet it wasn't. She wanted to shriek. She wante
to cry. But she couldn't move. By the time she took her nex
breath, her reflection was gone and Mercy Hollister had take
her place.

It was happening all over again!

An off-key piano was being played downstairs. Short burst
of laughter drifted to the floor above, floating down the hal
and under the door of Mercy's private room. A coal-oil lamp
burned on the washstand nearby, highlighting the passion on
Dakota's face as he slid into Mercy's soft body.

Mercy sighed and wrapped her arms around his neck.

"Dakota…Dakota… I love you so. Promise you'll never
leave me."

He stilled, his eyes black and glittering. Caught in sweet
Mercy's warmth, he looked down at her, A smile broke the
hard, embittered expression he normally wore as he leaned
down and kissed the side of her face.

"Only when I die. Only when I die."

Rachel jerked and, to her horror, nearly pitched forward out
of the chair. If Joanie hadn't grabbed her, she might have
fallen facedown on the floor.

"Good grief, girl. I know he's gorgeous, but this is no time
to be falling at his feet. Besides, he's not the type to take
home to Mama. That's a look-but-don't-touch man. They're
pretty…but way too dangerous for a good woman's heart."

Rachel wanted to cry. She felt an overwhelming urge to
tell Joanie what had just happened. But how could she explain
something she didn't understand herself?

"Sorry," she muttered, and closed her eyes, trying to come to terms with the transition she'd just made from one world to another. "I got dizzy, but I'm fine now."

Joanie frowned and pressed her hand against Rachel's forehead to test for a fever.

"I'm not sick," Rachel said, and managed a smile. "Maybe you just sat me up too fast."

Joanie wasn't buying it, but she had no explanation to replace the one Rachel had given her. Still frowning, she turned Rachel toward the mirror to begin the trim she'd asked for; the man on the street forgotten.

But Rachel hadn't forgotten him. More than once, as Joanie combed and snipped, Rachel's gaze drifted to the mirror, and to the reflection of what—and who—she could see on the street behind her.

Boone was still there, leaning against the front of his truck, obviously waiting for someone in a store nearby. His face was a study in repose; she had the oddest sensation she was watching two different men.

Whenever someone passed by, Boone's face underwent an odd transformation. His eyes narrowed, his mouth turned up at one corner in a cold, mirthless smirk, and his slouch went from careless to careful. It was only when he believed he was unobserved that he let down his guard. Only then did Rachel see the man who'd been at the scene of the wreck, the man who'd crawled into a wreck to hold a little girl's hand, the one who'd shed tears for a dead man and his child.

Something inside her started to hurt. It was a pain she couldn't locate and had no way to heal. Blinking back tears, she tore her gaze from his face and made herself watch what Joanie was doing.

She was getting scared. Every time she saw that man, she also saw Mercy and her outlaw. Why? What on earth was the connection between them? Or was it all in her head?

She closed her eyes and sighed, absorbing the pleasure of the comb gently biting into her scalp as Joanie combed

through her hair. But try as she might, she couldn't get th
words of an outlaw out of her mind.

Only when I die. Only when I die.

Chapter 7

Rachel stepped off the elevator and turned left, as she'd been instructed to do by the downstairs receptionist, then paused outside a door halfway down the hall.

Doctors of Psychiatry
E. G. Ealey
Steven Milam
H. A. Smith

Her fingers were trembling as she took a deep breath and entered. The receptionist behind the counter looked up, nodding a welcome. Rachel returned it with a shaky smile.

"Rachel Brant to see Dr. Ealey."

The woman handed Rachel a clipboard with a blank form attached. "We'll need some information for our records. Fill out this form and give it back to me as soon as you've finished."

Rachel stared at the page. If she took the next step, there

would be no turning back. It would be the final admission
that her life was out of control.

Choosing a chair in the far corner of the room, she ventured
a quick glance at the other people waiting to be seen and
hoped there was no one present she knew. To her relief, they
were all strangers.

Before she could change her mind, she filled out the form,
but when she looked up to return it, the receptionist was no
longer at her desk. Leaning the clipboard against the leg of
her chair, she reached for a magazine.

Two magazines later, and well into her third, she turned to
a page that brought her from a slump to upright, her attention
focused on the subject matter of the article before her.

"Dreams: Imagination or Reincarnation?"

Curiosity turned to interest, and interest to shock. The more
she read, the faster her heart raced. There were too many
similarities between what had been happening to her and the
case studies mentioned in the article to ignore.

Yet as she finished the piece, she knew that what she was
thinking was way off the wall. Granted, the article was in the
doctor's office, but that didn't mean he would adhere to such
farfetched theories. The doctors she knew preferred to deal in
specifics; specific symptoms were treated with specific pro-
cedures. And while psychiatrists dealt with mental instabilities
and stress-related problems, she knew the chances were slim
of finding one who would easily buy into the idea that one of
his patients had memories of having lived before.

So what do I do now?

Rachel set the magazine aside, then looked up. The receptionist was back, but busy at her desk. The longer Rachel sat,
the more convinced she became that the answers to her problems would not come from a doctor. Without giving herself
time for second thoughts, she got up and started out the door,
then paused.

What am I forgetting?

She looked back at where she'd been sitting. The clipboard
with the form with all her personal information on it was

leaning next to the chair where she'd left it. She removed the sheet of paper from the clipboard and put it in her purse.

"Miss Brant, the doctor will see you now."

"I'm sorry, but I've changed my mind."

Rachel walked out without looking back. Her step was lighter, her mind already focused. She glanced down at her watch. *Good. There's still plenty of time for what I want to do.*

It was late in the afternoon when Rachel left Lawton and started home. The drive to Razor Bend was long and boring, but after the time she'd just spent in the Lawton Public Library, she had plenty to think about.

The articles and books she'd found on the subjects of past-life regression and reincarnation were verifications of her own situation. But while she was beginning to think there could be truth in the theory, she had no idea as to why it was happening, or how to fix it.

What she did know was that the single continuing thread between her reality and insanity was an outlaw called Boone. The first experience of déjà vu had come the night she woke up in the stream. He'd been mere yards away, reaching out to her. At that moment she'd lost her identity in what she thought was a dream. His reappearances in her life were always unpredictable, yet the end result was always the same. Every time she saw him, she slipped back into Mercy Hollister's world. And therein lay her dilemma. She couldn't live out the rest of her life slipping in and out of reality. There had to be a reason why this was happening to her now, and she was determined to find it.

Her medical training gave her no background support for a hypothesis such as the one she was considering. Medicine was based on cause and effect—symptoms and treatments for specific illnesses and diseases.

In Razor Bend, as well as in most of the world, past life experiences meant what had happened yesterday, or last week, or last year…not in another lifetime. But Rachel was begin-

ning to believe that maybe—just maybe—she'd walked on
this earth in another time…in another place…in another
life…and with another man.

Mile after mile she drove, drawing closer to home. About
five miles outside Razor Bend, she began to relax. The sun
at her back was close to setting. But when she took the next
curve in the road, it didn't take her long to realize her plans
for the evening were about to change.

In the distance, Rachel could see a man standing at the edge
of the highway beside an obviously disabled pickup truck.
Even from here, she could see the lopsided angle at which
the truck bed was leaning. He'd had a flat. A few seconds
later, she jerked with recognition. It was Boone!

Her fingers tightened on the steering wheel. *Why does he
keep turning up everywhere I go?*

Panic fought with conscience as she drew nearer. Only a
day or so earlier, he'd stopped on this very same road to give
assistance to the injured and dying. Did she have the nerve
to pass him by? Even worse, was she so lacking in brains as
to stop?

She came closer, all the while warning herself not to look,
but as she drew even with where he was standing, her gaze
locked with his, as if drawn by a magnet.

In spite of his obvious need for help, he made no move to
try to flag her down. Instead, his dark, silent gaze tore through
her conscience, bit by bit. And as she drove past, a relentless
warning kept up a replay inside her mind.

*If you want to find out what's going on in your head, now's
your chance. Stop, stupid, stop!*

But she didn't. Afraid of feelings she couldn't control, she
looked away, unwilling to let him see her weakness. But it
was too late. She'd already seen his face, and it was the expression he was wearing that helped her make up her mind.
He didn't expect her to stop…and for that very reason, she
did.

The blowout had come without warning. One minute
Boone had been driving with ease, thinking of picking up

ome barbecue at the Adam's Rib Café to take home for sup-
er, and the next thing he knew, he'd been skidding all over
he road. It had taken all his skill to come to a halt without
hitting a nearby stand of trees. And as he got out of his truck,
he'd realized he was less than a mile from where the wreck
had occurred.

"This stretch of road must be jinxed," he muttered as he
circled his truck, checking for damage. Luckily for him, the
only thing ruined was a tire.

But his disgust turned to anger when he realized his jack
was missing, and not only that, his spare was flat. He glanced
up at the setting sun, judging the time he had left before darkness set in, and faced the fact that he'd be after dark walking
into Razor Bend. Yet no sooner had he looked up than a car
came around the far curve, heading his way.

"Talk about luck," he said. He was about to wave the
driver down when he recognized the car.

His luck had just gone from bad to worse. It was Rachel
Brant, and judging from the way she looked at him each time
they met, there was no way she was going to stop. He stood
like a man waiting for the other shoe to drop, watching as she
drove past.

And then her brake lights came on and, to his disbelief, she
started backing up. Moments later, her window came down.
With only a trace of a tremor in her voice, she spoke. "Need
any help?"

He couldn't think what to say. He'd been so certain that
she would leave him standing there that it took him a moment
to gather his thoughts.

"Had a blowout," he finally muttered.

Rachel nodded. "Do you have a spare?"

"It's flat."

Rachel took a deep breath. "I have room in my trunk. Toss
it in. I'll be glad to drop you off at Jimmy's Place. It's the
only place in town that…"

Boone finished her sentence. "…fixes flats."

Rachel grinned, more to herself than at him, but it brok
the ice. She got out of the car with her key in her hand whil
Boone turned to get the spare.

Before she could get the key in the hole, wind whippe
around the curve where she'd parked, blasting grit and dus
in her face and into her eyes.

"Oh!" she gasped, and covered her face with her hands
but it was too late. The damage had already been done.

At the sound of her cry, Boone spun, just as she covered
her face. Seconds later, he was at her side. He had no way o
knowing what had caused her to cry out, but he could see
that she was hurting.

"What's wrong?"

"My eyes," Rachel mumbled, and then staggered up
against her own car, disoriented by the pain.

"Let me see," he urged, trying to pull her hands from
her face.

At first Rachel wouldn't budge. She'd covered her face in
reflex, and although it had been too late to prevent the damage, the dark felt better than the light. And then his soft plea
broke through her resolve.

"Please, honey…let me see."

Rachel froze at the familiarity, but his voice compelled her
to obey. When he laid his hands on top of hers, gently urging
them aside, her legs went weak, but from want, not panic.
He'd stirred a longing within her that she'd been trying to
deny. It wasn't fear that he made her feel. It was fascination.

"Easy now," he said softly, as her hands dropped to her
sides.

And when she tilted her head back, her eyes still closed,
awaiting his ministrations, it was all Boone could do not to
kiss the invitation he saw on her lips. Then she started to
speak, and he gritted his teeth, trying to remember what he'd
been about to do.

"Dirt. In my eyes. My eyes."

To his dismay, healing tears were already seeping out from
beneath her dark lashes.

"I'm sorry," he said. "This wouldn't have happened if you hadn't stopped to help. Will you let me help you?"

Her hesitation was momentary. She was already blinded and helpless. He'd had his chance to do her harm, and once again, all he'd done was offer her aid.

She nodded.

Boone exhaled, only then realizing he'd been holding his breath. "One eye at a time, okay?"

His hands were cupping her face. Gently…so gently. It was all she could do not to lean into them, into him. "Okay."

"We need to rinse that grit out. I've got a nearly full bottle of spring water in my truck."

"That will work," Rachel said, and when he turned her loose to go back to his truck, she felt adrift in a dark, empty sea. Only after she felt his hand on her arm did she feel rooted once again to the earth.

"I need you to tilt your head back. Easy now…a little more…a little more."

She did as she was told.

"That's good. Hold it there."

She felt him put something in her hand.

"Here's a handkerchief to catch the drip."

Her fingers curled around the fabric and, in doing so, caught the tips of his fingers with it.

Boone inhaled slowly, reminding himself of the business at hand, and slipped out from beneath her touch.

Rachel sighed. She had every reason in the world to distrust him, and yet the feeling just wasn't there. He was too gentle to be frightening.

"Pour away," she said, and when the tepid water began washing away the dirt, she knew an overwhelming feeling of relief. "That feels so good."

Boone's imagination hit overdrive. If things had been different, he could have envisioned her saying that very same thing in his ear as they made love.

"Easy does it," he cautioned, staying her hand as she

started to scrub at her eye. "Let's do the other one. Then, if we need to, we'll give them both a second dose."

Again the water ran free, washing the last of the grit out and freeing her sight.

"Hallelujah! I was blind and now I see," she said, half laughing and half crying with relief as she opened her eyes fully. It broke the tension of the moment.

A smile tilted the corner of his mouth. "Would you believe in another life I walked on water?"

Rachel laughed. "No."

"I didn't think so," he drawled, and handed her the bottle of water. "Here, trade you this for your keys. You get back in the car before any more damage is done. I'll load the tire."

Gratefully she handed over the keys and reached for the door.

"Can you see okay to drive?" Boone asked.

Rachel turned, gazing intently past his hard-bitten look to the gentle depths of his dark eyes.

"I'm fine...thanks to you."

Time stood still. Neither moved, neither spoke, both of them absorbing the fact that, for the moment, they were the only two people in the world. And then, off in the distance, the sound of an eighteen-wheeler pulling up a distant steep grade could be heard. Boone was the first to look away.

"I'd better get this tire loaded, or we'll have to drive behind that rig all the way into town."

Rachel slipped behind the wheel. Seconds later the trunk lid shut with a thump, and Boone slid inside, bringing a new kind of tension with him.

The space inside the car suddenly shrank. Rachel fiddled with her seat belt and tried to pretend he wasn't there. But it was useless. His presence was overpowering, and it was all she could do not to stare. She took the keys from him and started the car.

She'd never known his legs were so long or his shoulders so wide. She hadn't noticed that his eyebrows were as black as his eyes, or that his eyelashes threw shadows on the planes

f his cheeks. Afraid that he would catch her staring, she
ripped the steering wheel like a hungover bull rider on an
ight-second ride and sped away.

Silence had never been so loud.

Neither spoke, and then both spoke at once, stepping all
ver each other's conversation in the act of trying to end the
ngoing standoff.

Rachel flushed and then shrugged, waiting for him to con-
inue, but Boone had other ideas.

"Sorry," he said.

"No," Rachel said. "You first."

He looked intently at her face. "How are your eyes?"

She smiled. "Much better."

He nodded, then looked away to keep from revealing his
eelings. Dear God, being this close without being able to hold
er was driving him mad.

Rachel glanced at him as the car took a curve. "Have we
ever met before? I mean, before the other night?"

He panicked. It was the last thing he had expected her to
say, and it was an undercover cop's worst fear, that someone
from his past would walk up and call him by a name other
than the one under which he was living. It could not only
blow his cover all to hell, it was what got people killed. His
gaze was cool and fixed as he answered. "No way. I would
have remembered."

Rachel flushed, uncomfortable with the entire situation. But
she kept thinking of the mess she was in, and that it was
getting deeper by the day. For that reason, she persisted.

"So the first time we met was the other night…on the
mountain?"

"I didn't mean to snoop. I heard you crying, you know."

She knew she shouldn't, but she was starting to believe
him.

After all, he would have had no way of knowing that she
was going to wander around the Kiamichis in her sleep.

"I know that," she said quietly.

"But I frightened you."

A slight grin split the seriousness of her expression. "Th₂
you did."

Boone's tension started to ease. Damn, but she was prett₂
when she smiled. He gave himself permission to stare, an₂
then almost wished he hadn't. Her hair was down, just as ₂
had been the night he saw her in the swing. It reminded hir₂
of some black satin sheets he'd once seen, rich, glossy an₂
shining. He remembered the ebb and flow of it against he₂
body as she'd taken flight in the night. Her clothes were sim₂
ple, nothing more than blue jeans and a thick white sweater₂
but they were the perfect foil for that slim body and beautifu₂
face. He wasn't sure, but he didn't think he'd ever seen eye₂
that blue or skin so fair. And then she ended his musing witł₂
another pointed question he would have preferred to ignore.

"So, what brought you to Razor Bend?"

"A job."

She nodded. Obviously she'd opened a subject he woulc₂
rather not discuss. And when she thought of his buddies, she₂
decided *she* would rather not know. "Been in town long?"

This time, at least, he could answer with complete truth₂
"Six weeks or so."

Rachel's heart thumped. The timeline coincided with the₂
onset of her sleepwalking episodes. Another clue to add tc₂
the mental list she was making. For lack of anything else tc₂
say, she started to introduce herself.

"I suppose I should have done this before. My name is—"₂

Boone finished the sentence for her. "Rachel Brant." And₂
then he was the one to look embarrassed. "Someone told₂
me."

She glanced at the scenery, aware that she was less than₂
three miles outside town. If there was anything more to learn,₂
she was going to have to act fast. "And you're Boone?"

He nodded.

"First name or last?

This time he grinned, and as he did, Rachel felt herself₂
sliding back in time.

"No…no," she muttered. "Not now. Not now."

Boone frowned. She wasn't making any sense, but when her gaze went out of focus and the car began to swerve, he shouted, "Rachel, look out!" then grabbed the steering wheel and set the car back on track.

Rachel jerked. The sensation was gone.

"Sorry. I'm… I keep seeing… Uh, I guess I must be tired."

He sighed. Something was going on with her, and had been from the moment he saw her standing in the water, talking to someone who wasn't really there. Just like now.

"Boone MacDonald."

Rachel was still lost in thought. "What?"

"My name is Boone MacDonald."

"Oh."

As they stopped at a crossroads outside town, she gave him another long, considering stare, then decided that after what had just transpired between them, she owed him at least this much. "I'm pleased to meet you, Boone MacDonald."

If he hadn't been already sitting, he would be now. That was the last thing he'd expected her to say.

Stay cool, damn it. Stay focused…and for God's sake stay away from this woman.

But he'd wasted a good pep talk on himself. Instead of turning a cold eye, he found himself with a half-assed grin and a lighter heart. "Have mercy," he drawled. "But the pleasure is mine."

Rachel froze. The smile on her face tilted as her mind began to race.

Have mercy? Did he just say, 'Have mercy'? Oh, my God! Oh, my God!

She heard Mercy's outlaw saying the very same words.

Have mercy, sweet Mercy.

"It's your turn to go," Boone said, pointing out the clear four-way stop and the fact that no one else was in sight.

"Oh! Right!"

Rachel accelerated, shooting through the intersection and on into town. When Jimmy's Place appeared on her left, she signaled her turn, pulled to a stop between the building and the pumps, then popped the trunk lid and killed the engine.

"We're here," she said.

Once again, he grinned, and at that moment Rachel knew that she'd seen that same smile before—but on another man's face.

Boone leaned toward her, not much, but just enough to make Rachel's heart jump with an odd sort of longing.

"Thank you," he said softly.

"For what?" she muttered, lost in the depths of a pair of dark eyes.

He grinned again. For some reason, this very capable woman seemed incapable of following a single train of thought.

"For the ride," he said.

Rachel blinked, then sat upright. "Oh! Oh, yes! You're welcome, of course."

"You sure your eyes are okay?"

"Yes." *Just don't ask me about my heart.*

Boone nodded. "Then I'll just get my tire and get out of your life." He got out of the car and headed toward the trunk to remove the spare.

"If only," Rachel muttered, then jumped when Boone slammed the trunk lid shut.

"Thanks again," he called.

She watched as he rolled the tire toward the garage and once again was struck by the familiarity of his slow, careless stride. Before she could think to move, he suddenly turned and caught her watching.

Embarrassed, she looked away, only to come eye-to-eye with Charlie Dutton's inquiring stare. He was standing in the doorway of Jimmy's Place with a can of pop, a bag of chips and an expression on his face that might have been described as one of disbelief.

It struck a defensive chord in Rachel that she couldn't have explained. What she did on her own time was no one's busi-

ress, and yet living in a town the size of Razor Bend, she
was constantly subjected to everyone's scrutiny.

She waved at Charlie, then glanced once again toward the
garage. Boone was nowhere in sight. It was just as well. She
started her car and drove away.

The road home was long and winding, but the path was
well marked by a sunset of remarkable hues. This evening,
the heavenly artwork was wasted on Rachel. Her mind was
still locked on the facts she'd unearthed. But were they real
facts, she wondered, or just figments of a wild imagination?
Or, worse—was she truly losing her mind?

Griffin Ross was coming out of the bakery as Rachel pulled
into Jimmy's Place. Unable to believe his eyes, he stood with
his mouth agape. There was Rachel—*his* Rachel—and she
was with another man. They were smiling and talking as if
they'd known each other forever.

He stepped back into the lengthening shadows before she
could see him and watched as she parked in the drive by the
self-serve pumps. He saw the trunk pop up, then saw the man
get out and remove a flat tire. A long, telling glance passed
between them before Rachel suddenly waved and drove away.

The whole thing seemed innocent enough. And it was just
like Rachel to help someone out.

But it was the man himself who was giving Griffin such
pause for thought. He wasn't exactly one of Razor Bend's
most admirable citizens. In fact, he looked as if he'd stepped
off a Wanted poster. And he was staring after Rachel like a
starving man looking at a feast. Even worse, Griffin had seen
something very near longing on Rachel Brant's face. That was
what really galled him.

Jealousy turned to rage. *She didn't want me. How dare she
yearn for a loser like him?*

He stared until the man had disappeared into the garage
with the tire, then stomped to his car with new determination.
He didn't know who the hell that man was, but he was going
to find out.

* * *

By the time Boone got home, it was way after dark. He was tired. He was cold. And he was hungry. The message light was blinking on his answering machine, but the urge to ignore it was great. The scent of the barbecued ribs he'd brought home seeped from the sack in his hand, enticing him. But his training overcame everything else. He set the sack aside, then punched the button, listening closely as Denver Cherry's voice came into the room.

All he said was "Call me," but Boone knew who it was and his adrenaline surged. There was only one reason for Cherry to be calling him. He picked up the phone and made the call. Denver answered on the second ring.

Boone's words were as clipped as Denver's had been. "It's me," Boone said. "What's up?"

Denver muttered beneath his breath, then grumbled, "What time is it?"

Boone glanced at his watch. "Ten minutes until twelve."

Denver groaned, and Boone could hear the bed springs giving beneath his weight.

"Don't you ever sleep?" Denver grumbled.

"I had a blowout coming home this evening. My jack was gone, and my spare was flat, and I take better care of my gear than that. You can tell that son of a bitch Snake I want my jack back. I'll deal with him on my own about the spare."

Denver's eyes narrowed. "Damn it! I want you and Snake to make peace, not start another war. We've got our hands full as it is. Come by tomorrow evening. Got a job for you."

Boone grinned. He'd been right in assuming the gang was about to make another big move. The shipment must be in. Denver sounded antsy, the way he always did when the stuff was on hand.

"I'll be there," Boone said.

"You'd better," Denver muttered, then disconnected.

Boone set the receiver back in the cradle, then glanced at his late-night supper and knew it would have to wait a little while longer. The captain needed to know what was going on. He picked up the phone and started to dial, then paused and hung it back up. Cautious as ever, he used his cell phone to make the call. Ignoring the time, he listened as the phone at the other end began to ring. A few moments later, a low, husky voice, somewhat sleepy-sounding but nevertheless alert, answered. "This better be good."

Boone grinned. Obviously the captain was at home and had put a transfer order on the safe line.

"It's me, darlin' Waco," he drawled.

"Talk to me, good-looking."

"You better be sleeping alone."

In spite of the late hour and the tone of her agent's voice, Susan Cross grinned. The man was outrageous. "And you better have some sweet words to whisper in my ear," she retorted.

Boone felt himself beginning to relax, and knew that part of it came from being able to share the burden of what he knew with someone else.

"Something big is going down tomorrow night."

Cross sat up on the side of the bed, grabbing for her glasses and turning on the light, all at the same time.

"Like what?"

"There was a big shipment due. I think it's in. Cherry wants me over there tomorrow evening. Said he had a 'job' for me."

"So you think they're going to move it out?"

"Yes."

"Will the boss be there?"

Boone tensed. "I doubt it," he muttered. "I pushed my luck the other day by insisting that I meet the man I work for, and Cherry balked."

Cross frowned. "Okay, here's what I want you to do. See if you can find out the distribution points. And after you've got your load, call me. We'll decide where to go from there."

Boone frowned. "Damn it, Waco, don't mess it up for me by taking them in yet. I'm getting close.... I can feel it."

Cross sighed. She was walking a fine line between the law and her subordinate's renegade ways as it was. Knowingly

letting a huge shipment of methamphetamine onto the streets
didn't set well with her, but neither did pulling in a man
before he'd done what he set out to do.

"Just call me," she said, and hung up.

Boone sat with his head in his hands, his food forgotten.
The whole situation stank to high heaven. He felt like a bug
caught between a hungry crow and a big flat shoe. Whichever
way he turned, he was bound to be had.

The image of Rachel Brant's face drifted through his mind,
and he groaned. "Not now, lady, not now."

Yet long after he'd gone to bed, his thoughts were still of
her—the sound of her laugh, the way her eyes crinkled up at
the corners when she smiled, the scent of her perfume…even
the way her breathing quickened when she looked at him. She
was eating him up from within.

He rolled over in bed, angrily punching his pillow and then
burrowing his nose into it. Moments later, he tossed it aside.
Smothering himself wouldn't accomplish a damn thing except
to take himself out of the fray, and Boone MacDonald wasn't
the kind of man to run.

Long after midnight had come and gone, Rachel was still
awake, rereading the articles on reincarnation that she'd cop-
ied at the library, as well as excerpts from books that pertained
to the same subject. She went to bed around 3:00 a.m., convinced that she was on the right track. But even though her
instincts said yes, there was a common thread among the articles that she had yet to verify in relation to her own situation.

She needed to know if a woman named Mercy Hollister
had ever existed. If she hadn't, then Rachel was facing an
entirely different problem.

But where to start? Finding something as simple as a birth
certificate was an easy task now, but back before the territo-
ries became states, births had rarely been recorded. It hadn't
been unusual for a person to live out their entire life with no
written record of having existed.

And then she thought of the outlaw, Dakota. Maybe he

would be the link. If he'd been real, then history might have made note of his name and deeds.

Again her doubts returned. What to do first? All she knew was what she'd seen in her dream...or whatever one called the state of losing one's mind. And then she remembered!

Trinity. Mercy had lived in a town called Trinity.

Find Trinity, or find out if it had ever existed. If so, she could start from there.

With a sigh of relief, Rachel rolled over on her stomach, shifted the pillow until it felt just right beneath her chin and closed her eyes. Sleep came, and with it the dream.

When she awoke, it was just before dawn, and she was facedown in the grass beneath her swing. Her head was splitting, and there were tears on her cheeks. She couldn't remember a thing about what she'd dreamed or what it was that had made her cry. Disgusted and disheartened, she crawled to her feet and staggered back indoors.

This had been the last straw. She'd made up her mind. When she went in to work today, she was going to ask for time off. Until this mess was cleared up, she didn't trust herself to care for anyone else, when she couldn't even take care of herself.

Charlie Dutton pulled up to the station just ahead of Rachel, giving her both front and back views of his shiny new car. As he got out, she couldn't help but grin as he took out his handkerchief and polished a spot on the lacquered blue surface.

She honked as she parked. Charlie turned, then went to meet her with a sheepish grin on his face.

"Wow, Charlie, you're going to have to beat the girls off with a stick."

His grin stilled. "So, are you telling me you might be susceptible?"

When Rachel flushed, Charlie hid his hurt behind a chuckle. "Calm down," he said softly. "It never hurts to ask, right?"

Just for a moment, she'd been afraid he was serious. Relaxing as he slipped back into his easygoing manner, she thumped him lightly on the arm as they headed for the door.

But Charlie had something else on his mind besides showing off his new car. He hadn't been able to get past the sight of Rachel and that modern-day outlaw riding together in her car. Charlie being Charlie, he circled the issue of what he wanted to know by making a joke out of the question.

"So, are you giving old Griffin a run for his money?"

Rachel stumbled, and Charlie grabbed her before she fell on her face.

"What did you mean by that?" she asked, fixing him with a cool, judging stare.

"Oh...not much. It's just that I never knew your tastes in men were so varied."

She gritted her teeth. "Not that it's any of your business, but Griffin Ross and I are old news. As for my passenger last night, all I did was give him a ride. He had a blowout, and his spare was flat."

"His kind is bad news, Rachel."

She flushed, angry because he wasn't saying anything she didn't already know. "I gave him a ride, not the key to my house."

"Little steps will take a man the same place big ones do. The only difference is, it just takes a little longer to get there."

"Just what are you saying?"

From the chill of her glare, Charlie realized he'd already overstepped his bounds. There was no use making the situation worse.

"Oh, nothing," he said, and looked back at his car, absently admiring the high-gloss sheen.

Rachel sighed. Charlie was her friend. She should have expected him to at least voice his opinion.

"It's okay," she said, and patted his arm. "I don't think he's as bad as he's made out to be. Remember how he was with those people the day of that wreck. They were lucky he was there."

Charlie rolled his eyes. "I must have been out of my mind

to complain about a hero. I keep forgetting how women love them.''

Rachel hit him on the arm and pointed toward the car, determined to change the subject.

''That last raise they gave you must have been a doozie.''

Charlie's expression underwent a dark metamorphosis, but Rachel didn't notice. As they entered the garage, they stopped short, staring in disbelief at the crumpled fender, missing bumper and shattered windshield of one of Razor Bend's two working ambulances.

''Oh, no!'' she moaned, and grabbed Charlie by the arm.

''It's the new one, too,'' he said, eyeing the dented hood. ''Because of an accident we'll have to make do with the old one until this is fixed. Man, I hope the good citizens of Razor Bend don't have themselves a run of bad luck.''

As they entered the office, Rachel couldn't help thinking that while the ambulance's condition was unfortunate for the town, it was quite convenient for her. With only one ambulance to run, and two paramedics and three EMTs besides herself, she wouldn't be missed.

Chapter 8

The bass boat slid into the bed of Boone's pickup truck as if it had been made to fit. With Tommy Joe on one side and Boone on the other, they walked the length of the truck, tying the boat down as they went. As he tied the last knot, Boone gave the rope a sharp tug, just to make sure it was holding. The last thing he needed was to lose that boat and its belly full of meth along the highway.

The false bottom should work. Oklahoma was full of people who lived for the great outdoors. About half the residents of the state either owned or rented boats. And at this time of year, die-hard fishermen everywhere were making last-minute runs to the lakes, rivers and creeks, taking advantage of the good fishing weather before winter set in. There wouldn't be a cop on the road who thought anything unusual of his rig.

"I guess I'm ready to roll," Boone said, and looked around for Denver. "Where's Cherry?"

Tommy Joe shrugged. "He'll be here directly. Want a beer?" Without waiting for Boone to answer, he tossed him a cold, dripping can.

Boone's hard-ass mode was in place as he caught the can in midair. "No thanks," he drawled, and tossed it right back. "Tonight I'm the designated driver, remember?"

Tommy Joe snickered, then popped the top, unmindful of the froth that spewed and spilled out of the hole and down the sides of the can, coating his fingers, then dripping onto his shoes.

Boone leaned against the bed of his truck and took a slow, deep breath as he settled down to wait.

Come on, come on, he fumed, wondering where Denver Cherry had gone. The man was like a caged cat until the meth was moved off his place, and now that the moment was at hand, he'd disappeared.

A short distance away, Denver was making last-minute plans with the boss. Their conversation ceased in midstream as the boss started to curse.

"What the hell is he doing here?"

"Who?" Denver asked.

"That *cowboy.*"

Denver winced. The derision in the boss's voice was impossible to miss.

"That's my new man, Boone MacDonald."

"You're not serious."

Denver nodded.

"Can you trust him?"

Denver nodded, then backed off, reluctant to be blamed should something go wrong. "Well, as best as I can tell, he's okay. You know, there's no surefire way to tell until a deal goes down."

The boss grunted, and Denver got nervous, watching the way his eyes narrowed and his jaw clenched.

"Something wrong?" Denver asked.

"No. Which route is he taking?"

Denver told him and when he made no comment, added, "I'd better get going. I need to send them on their way."

"Them?"

Denver shifted his stance, readjusting his belly above the

belt buckle poking into his soft flesh. "Yeah, Tommy Joe is going with him, just to make sure everything goes okay."

"Send him alone."

"But I—"

An ominous quality infiltrated the boss's voice. "I said... send him alone."

"Yes, sir," Denver muttered.

"Now. Do it now."

Denver scuttled away. He'd heard enough to know that the boss was mad; he just wasn't sure why.

"Hey, here comes Denver," Tommy Joe said, pointing off to their right.

Boone turned just as the old biker waddled out of a thick stand of trees. His eyes narrowed thoughtfully; he wondered exactly what the man had been doing in there besides taking a leak.

"We're ready," Tommy Joe said. He started toward the passenger side of the truck, but Denver stopped him cold.

"You're not going," he muttered, and waved him away.

Boone went from a careless slouch to a careful stance. Sudden changes in plans made him nervous. He gave Denver a calculated stare. "Why not?"

"Yeah, why not?" Tommy Joe echoed.

"Because I said so," Denver shouted. "Now get back inside."

Tommy Joe scuttled away.

"Are there any other changes I need to know about?" Boone asked.

Denver met him stare for hard stare. "No."

Boone glanced over Denver's shoulder into the darkness of the trees. Then he grinned. "You're the boss," he said softly, and crawled into his truck. "See you when I see you."

Denver shuddered as Boone drove out of sight. Something didn't feel right, but there was no way of stopping things now.

Boone wasn't wasting any time waiting to be shot in the back of the head. Instinct told him he was being tested again, only this time he sincerely doubted it was Denver who'd set up the test.

As he started down the mountain, he passed the road leading to Rachel's house and had a sudden urge to ditch the whole night and hide within the shelter of Rachel Brant's embrace.

But it was a wild, impossible thought, and Boone wasn't the type to waver from what he'd set out to do. Instead, he picked up the phone. He'd promised Waco a call.

"Talk to me, baby," Waco crooned.

Boone grinned. "You can turn off the heat, sugar. I'm all alone."

Captain Cross reached for a pen. "What do you know?"

Boone swerved to miss an armadillo waddling across the road and then glanced back at the boat, making sure it was still in place.

"I know I wish it was Christmas and I was under your tree, sweet thing."

"Shut up and get down to business," she muttered, then grinned in spite of herself. "Did the whole load go out?"

Boone sighed. She wasn't going to like this one bit. "Yeah, but I couldn't say where. Denver made a run earlier that I didn't expect, and Snake was already gone when I got there."

"Damn."

"My sentiments exactly," Boone said, knowing he hadn't been quite honest with her.

If the captain had known all three locations, chances were she would have opted for the busts, arresting him along with the perps. It wouldn't have blown his cover, but it would have ended his quest to find the man behind Denver Cherry's operation.

"Where is he sending you?"

"Dallas."

"Where in Dallas?"

"Some joint called ReBob's Boat Repair, just off I-35, on the freeway."

"I'll let the proper authorities know."

"Damn it, Waco, don't get me busted. I'm not ready to quit this town."

Susan Cross frowned. "What do you mean…not ready?"

Boone took a deep breath. He'd said the wrong thing, and like the bulldog she was, the captain had jumped on his slip of the tongue.

"I don't mean anything," he muttered.

"I told you to get laid and get over it," she said sharply. "You damn well better not be messing around with some woman. It'll all blow up in your face and you know it."

"I'm not." And then he muttered, more to himself than to her, "Besides, she's not the laying type."

The captain groaned. "Why couldn't you go find some bimbo? What on earth possessed you to get mixed up with Snow White?"

Boone sighed. "It wasn't by choice. I couldn't help myself."

"God help us all," she groaned. "I ought to pull you out now, before you ruin the entire operation, and send Wayland in instead."

"Like hell," he said sharply, disconnecting before she could make any more threats.

An hour passed. Boone guessed he was no farther than five miles from the state line when his cell phone rang. The sound startled him. The only person who knew this number was…

"Waco?"

"You've been set up."

Her words jolted through him like a bolt of heat lightning. Now it made sense. This was why Tommy Joe had been pulled off the run. But why would Denver risk losing this load?

"How did you find out?"

"Don't question me, just listen. Where are you now?"

Boone gave his location.

"Good," she muttered. "Then there's still time to make the switch."

''What switch?''

''You aren't listening,'' she said sharply.

He listened, and hours later, when he pulled into ReBob's Boat Repair, he was driving a rickety old Jeep with a canoe ied on top. The meth was in backpacks under a tarp on the back seat, along with a motley assortment of camping equipment. It took less than fifteen minutes to do what he'd been sent to do, and when he was finished, he lit out of Dallas without looking back.

Just across the border into Oklahoma, he switched back to his own truck, thanking the pair of sheriff's deputies who'd patiently waited for his return. But his truck wasn't the only thing they traded. He headed toward Denver Cherry's house with the payoff. A bag full of marked bills.

A new sun was just coming over the treetops as Boone pulled into Denver's front yard. Denver came to meet him, with a cup of coffee in one hand and a sausage biscuit in the other. For once, he seemed amiable, even jovial.

''Trade you coffee and a biscuit for what's in the case,'' Denver said, grinning around the oversize bite he'd just taken.

Boone set the case down at Denver's bare feet and then gave him a cool, studied stare.

''I think I'll pass.''

Denver frowned. ''Something wrong?''

''You tell me,'' Boone said, and started back to his truck.

''Hey, don't go off mad!'' Denver shouted.

Boone turned, and the cold, hard glare on his face startled Denver enough that he sloshed hot coffee on his feet.

''What makes you think I should be mad?'' Boone asked.

Having left that cryptic statement hanging in the air, Boone drove away, leaving Denver with scalded toes and a hundred thousand dollars in marked money.

Denver grabbed the money and then hurried inside. The boss wasn't going to like being called on the job, but Denver didn't much care.

* * *

Sunlight ricocheted off highly polished chrome, momentarily blinding the man behind the wheel as he came to a four way stop just inside the city limits of Razor Bend. When the car phone rang, he answered without thought, unprepared for the sound of Denver Cherry's voice.

"Hello?"

"It's me," Denver said.

The driver's face underwent a dark change, from bland observation of the roadway to cold anger.

"What?"

"I just thought I'd let you know my new man did all right last night. Everything went off without a hitch. He just left."

A rough curse slipped out of the driver's mouth before he thought, but it was enough to let Denver know he'd been right in suspecting that something bad had gone down last night.

"Whatever you did, don't do it again," Denver warned. "You do, and I'm out." Having said what he'd called to say, he hung up, then dropped into the chair. "Hell's bells," he muttered. "Am I the only one left with any sense?"

While Denver was making his call, Boone was making a side trip of his own. Although he was exhausted and needed to sleep, there was something else he needed much more. Whatever the captain had averted last night could have cost him his life.

All the way back from Dallas, his thoughts had been about Rachel. If he had died, would she have cared? He'd held her but briefly. He'd touched her face, but he wanted to touch her soul. He needed to know if her lips were as soft as they looked. He'd made love to her, but only in dreams. The urge to know her in the true sense of the word was making him crazy. The thought of losing her was worse than losing his own life.

And yet, as he turned off the road and into the driveway leading to her house, he knew he was losing his grip. He couldn't lose someone he'd never had. Coming up here was wrong. It was dumb. It was dangerous. And yet, God help him, it had to be done. He wanted just to see her face, hear her voice. After that, maybe he could rest.

But when he got there she was gone.

Rachel boarded a plane in Oklahoma City and made a connection in Denver that took her straight into South Dakota. When she disembarked, instead of going for her luggage, she paused at the windows outside the skyline surrounding the terminal.

She stared until her eyes burned and the glare of the sun against the plate glass made her flesh damp with perspiration. As she stood at the window looking out on the horizon, a stocky middle-aged man in business attire paused beside her, noting her intense expression.

"I know how you feel," he said. "It's always good to get home, isn't it?"

Rachel turned, her eyes wide and a little stunned. "Oh, I don't live here," she said. "In fact, this is my first visit."

"My mistake," he said, and then added as he started to walk away, "You just had that look."

"What look?" Rachel asked.

"Oh…you know…the kind of look soldiers have when they get pictures from home. Like they've left a piece of themselves behind with those they love. I just assumed…" He shrugged. "Anyway, have a nice day, miss."

He walked away, leaving Rachel to wonder if what he'd said was true. On the surface, everything around her seemed foreign. But was there a part of her, a subconscious part, that was rejoicing in a long-awaited return? She shuddered. At this point, the thought didn't bear contemplation.

A day later, she learned one irrefutable fact: Trinity was no more.

But it had been there once, a small but thriving boomtown located somewhere between Lead and Deadwood. That it had ever existed was a shock in itself. She'd been braced for defeat, and instead she was getting answers she hadn't been prepared to find.

But her search for any sort of trail to Mercy Hollister or an outlaw named Dakota was fruitless, until the curator at a wild West museum showed her into a room filled with memorabilia of Wild Bill Hickok and his days in Deadwood. Even then, she almost missed it.

An old, fragile and very yellowed newspaper had been put on display behind a glass frame. The headlines were all about Hickok and a gunfight he'd had. But it was an item in the lower right-hand corner of the paper that caught her eye. And it was the lead line that sent her to her knees, her nose pressed against the glass as she read.

Outlaw dies at lover's hands

When she was through, it was all she could do to get up.

"Dear, sweet Lord," Rachel whispered, and wanted to run as far and as fast as her legs could carry her. She'd come hundreds of miles for the truth, and now that it was staring her in the face, she felt nothing but panic.

Not only had Mercy Hollister been real, but, according to this article, she'd been responsible for the death of an outlaw called Dakota Blaine. It didn't make sense. The visions she'd been having were of a man and a woman in the deep throes of love, not a woman in fear for her life—or afraid of the man. How had this happened? What could possibly have changed between them to bring them to such a sorrowful end?

Rachel flushed, then turned pale as she fought to keep from passing out. Only the fact there were other people in the room kept her sane and silent.

"Okay, okay. So they were real. That doesn't tie me to them," she muttered, then went limp with defeat.

The very fact that she'd been reliving their lives tied her firmly to them, whether she liked it or not. When she finally trusted herself to walk, she went outside and caught a cab back to her hotel. It was time to go home.

* * *

And home she was. When Rachel landed in Oklahoma City nce again, it was raining. The damp, dreary day went well /ith her state of mind. When she boarded the plane in Rapid 'ity, she'd been in shock. The flight back home had been ell, as she struggled with what she had learned. The past iree days had changed her perception of the world. She iidn't want to be anyone but herself, but what she wanted night have to take a back seat to who she had been.

Granted, she was back in Oklahoma, but the facts she'd rought home still gave her no answers. Yet as she started he long drive to Razor Bend, there was one fact she couldn't gnore. Boone MacDonald's appearance in her life had triggered everything that was happening to her. Therefore, he nust also be the key to making it stop.

The next morning she entered her boss's office with a letter equesting an indefinite leave of absence. Not only was her equest granted, but his unexpected concern and offer of help ent her out of the office with tears in her eyes.

Which was exactly how Charlie Dutton first saw her. He grabbed her by the arm and spun her around as she started to oass him by.

"Hey! Is that any way to treat your partner?"

Rachel looked away, unwilling for him to see her tears, but she was too late.

"You're crying."

Rachel gave him a lopsided grin. "No, my eyes are leaking."

"Same thing," he muttered. "What's wrong?"

"Nothing. Really."

"The same nothing that prompted the three-day absence?"

"Sort of."

"Look, it's probably none of my business, so if you don't want me to butt in, just say so."

"So."

He glowered. "Damn it, Rachel, you're my partner. Consider yourself butted. I want to know what's going on."

His mangled grammar made her laugh. "Charlie, yo
sweet-talking charmer. You have such a way with words."

He glowered, refusing to be deterred. "What's wrong? An
why aren't you in uniform?"

This was going to be rough. "I've decided to take a leav
of absence."

"I knew it! Something is really wrong. You wouldn't b
doing this if…" His face darkened. "It's a guy, isn't it?"

She flushed.

"It can't be that stupid banker, because you were the dump
er, and he was the dump-*ee.* It's not him, is it?"

"No, Griffin has nothing to do with my decision to—"

"Son of a—" Her grabbed her by the arm in sudden anger
pinning her until she had nowhere to look but at him.

Rachel struggled. "Charlie, let me go!"

"It's that man I saw you with. That…that…damned out
law, isn't it?"

Rachel glared. She wouldn't answer, because she couldn'
lie, and if she said it was true, Charlie would have Boone's
head before she could explain what was wrong. And, dea
God, how to explain what was going on?

"I'm going to kill him," Charlie muttered, and dragged
Rachel out of the hall to a secluded part of the station. "Did
he hurt you? Are you, uh… Is there any way you could
be…?"

Rachel gasped, her eyes wide with shock. "Good Lord,
no!"

Charlie flushed, then looked away. "Well," he muttered,
"I had to know."

"He doesn't have anything to do with it," Rachel said, and
then bit her tongue at the lie. "I've been having some personal
problems. Until I get them all worked out, I don't feel it's in
my patients' best interest that I be less than focused, do you?"

"Is that the best excuse you could come up with?"

"Just about."

He slumped, his hands shoved in his pockets. "I have a

ew car, a new haircut, I even have a new suit. Who am I
oing to impress if you're not here?''

Tears came again, and Charlie groaned when he saw them
n her eyes.

"Well, damn it, I was just kidding,'' he muttered. ''I al-
eady have too many girls as it is. Practically have to beat
nem off with a stick.''

Rachel laughed, then caught her breath on a sob. ''Take
are of yourself,'' she said. ''I'll be seeing you.'' Then she
valked out the door.

"Yeah, right,'' Charlie muttered. ''See you around.''

Rachel exited the station with her head down, blinking back
ears with fierce intent. She needed a hole to crawl into and
. shoulder to cry on, but she didn't think the pair would com-
ute. Not unless she found a willing gopher or a very small
nan. Unfortunately for her, before she reached her car, she
ad her man—just not the one she wanted.

"Rachel, I've been trying to catch you for...''

Griffin Ross paused, at a sudden loss for words, when he
aw the tears in Rachel Brant's eyes.

"Why, sweetheart, what on earth is wrong?''

His sympathy was her undoing. She shook her head and
ried to duck into her car, but he would have none of it. To
er dismay, he took her in his arms.

"Griff, don't,'' she muttered, and ducked out from under
his grasp, then out of his reach.

"You've been crying!''

She rolled her eyes. The men she knew were *so* astute.

"People do that sometimes, you know.''

"But why?'' he asked.

"Frankly, Griff, it's none of your business,'' Rachel said,
and got into her car and drove away, leaving him to think
what he would of it all.

Boone came out of the auto supply store carrying a new
jack. Snake had proclaimed an innocence that Boone didn't
buy, but he'd made a believer out of Snake, just the same.

Now, when the gang was all together at Denver's house
Snake gave him a wide, cautious berth, which was fine wit
Boone. The less he had to do with the man, the better of
they would both be.

A flash of color caught his eye as he put the jack in th
bed of the truck. He turned. Relief surged. It was Rachel. Sh
was back!

He glanced at his watch, noting the time, and wondering
why she wasn't in uniform. Then he shrugged and got int
his truck.

I'm making a big deal out of nothing. Shifts change.

And yet, as he drove down the street to the Adam's Rit
Café to have lunch, he couldn't help remembering the look
on her face. She'd seemed upset.

Tonight I'll go see. She won't even have to know I'm there

The night was clear and dark. The threat of rain had passed.
Countless stars dappled the dense black sky as a breeze rustled leaves just starting to turn color.

Rachel slept warm and snug beneath her covers, uncon-
cerned that, outside, an oncoming frost was dropping the tem-
perature by degrees. Her sleep was deep and dreamless. She
never knew when it began to change.

She rolled onto her back, her eyes wide open and fixed on
a scene only she could see. Panicked, she shoved the covers
aside and bolted from the bed, running through the house on
bare feet, once nearly tripping on the tail of her white flannel
gown. Her subconscious mind was in total control. Locks
turned. Doors were opened, then closed behind her, as if
someone else were performing the acts.

Rachel ran from the house, unmindful of the dew-damp
grass or the growing chill in the air. She moved as a woman
in terror, struck dumb by the sight of what lay before her. In
her mind she was shouting, but no sound ever came from her
lips.

All she could see was the man in the canyon below her.
The scent of gunpowder filled her nostrils. The sun beamed

own upon her head. She lifted her arm and screamed. It came
rom so far within her that it moved past her mind and into
he present, breaking the silence of the Kiamichis. Moments
ater, pain shattered the dream. She fell to her knees in the
grass, with tears streaming down her face.

Boone braked as his headlights flashed on a deer racing
across the narrow ribbon of blacktop. Its magnificence was
illuminated as it paused, momentarily stunned by the bright
glare of the lights in which it had been caught. The rack of
antlers spreading out from its head gleamed, a bejeweled
crown on the king of the mountain. Then the animal moved
and, like a shadow, was gone.

Boone accelerated carefully, cognizant of the fact that another deer could be waiting just around the next bend.

A mile farther up the mountain, that caution saved him
from hitting the woman who ran from the trees and straight
into the glare of his lights. She ran with eyes wide open and
tears on her face.

It was Rachel.

He hit the brakes, jamming the truck into park as he
grabbed for the door. Within seconds, he was out of his truck
and running toward her with his weapon drawn. Convinced
that she was fleeing for her life, he crouched with his gun
aimed into the darkness behind her, aiming at an unknown
foe as she let out a scream and fell onto her knees in the ditch
at the side of the road.

Chapter 9

Gritting her teeth, Rachel clutched at her head, only vaguely aware of the cold and the damp and a blinding white light.

"Oh, God, make it stop," she begged, rocking back and forth on her knees and digging her fingers into her hair as the pain ripped through her brain like grasping tentacles.

But when she was lifted from the ground and held fast against a wild, beating heart, she went limp, absorbing the warmth of a body and the strength from the arms in which she was held.

She sighed as a low, urgent voice murmured near her ear. "Rachel! What happened to you?"

She couldn't focus, and even as she spoke, the sound of her own voice in her ears wracked her head with a fresh wave of pain. "Who—?"

"It's me. Boone."

She blinked, her head lolling against his arm. She tried hard to focus on the dark, shadowy face silhouetted above her, but the light from behind him was too bright and the pain in her ead still too great. She clutched weakly at the front of his acket, her voice barely above a whisper.

"Home...I want to go home."

Boone turned, holding her tight. Seconds later, she was on he seat beside him. By the time he reached her house, tears vere streaming down her face. In all his years on the force, 1e'd never been this scared. Hesitancy was in his voice as he eached for her, wanting to hold her. "Rachel?"

She leaned toward him, and it was all the invitation he 1eeded.

"Come here, baby," he said softly. "Let's get you in the 1ouse."

She went into Boone's arms as if she'd been doing it all her life. As he carried her up the walk, something hard and cold and hidden way deep inside him began to unfold. And when he carried her into her house and kicked the door shut behind him, he had an overwhelming sense of having finally come home.

The rooms were warm, a safe shelter from the cold and the night. He sat her on the side of her bed, and she stayed, like a misbehaving child who'd been put in a corner. Then he tossed his jacket on a nearby chair and knelt down before her.

"Rachel...can you tell me what's wrong?"

Speech was impossible. All she could do was hang on to the bed as the light in her room changed from bulb to wick and the covers from patchwork and cotton to red velvet and white satin.

Dakota looked up at Mercy with a smile on his face and a promise in his eyes. His fingers were soft and gentle as his hand moved up her thigh.

Mercy shivered with longing and leaned back on the bed, waiting for this man to work his magic.

He hooked his forefinger in the top of her stocking and started pulling it down, inch by agonizing inch.

Mercy sighed and then groaned as he lowered his head, fervently kissing a dimple near the bend of her knee. Digging

her fingers into his thatch of black hair, she urged him bac
up until he was kissing her mouth instead.

Rachel blinked, as if refocusing her gaze, and for the firs
time since she'd been lifted from the middle of the road, sh
knew her rescuer for who he was. The dark eyes, the hard
edged features in a cold, handsome face. Black hair an
leather, Levi's and boots.

"Boone?" Her eyes grew round. Her voice started t
shake.

"Why…? How?" Helpless to say more, she waited for hin
to explain.

Tenderly he brushed the long black tangles of her hair from
her face and ran his thumb lightly near a scratch on her chin
catching the small streak of blood running down before i
dripped on her gown.

"You were out on the mountain. I almost hit you with my
truck."

"Oh, my God," Rachel groaned, and hid her face in her
hands.

"You need to get into something warm and dry. Will you
let me help you?"

Only after he remarked on her condition did she begin to
feel the cold. She shivered, then dropped her hands in her lap
and looked up.

"Well?" he persisted.

"I have a robe in the bathroom. If you'll just give me a
minute…"

Boone stood up and stepped away, but when she put her
feet on the floor, she winced and dropped back onto the bed.
He followed her descent. Back on his knees, he saw the deep,
ugly gash in the arch of one foot.

"Damn, Rachel, you need to see a doctor."

"No!" she said, clutching at his arm as he reached for the
phone.

"Why not?"

She didn't answer.

"Rachel?"

She turned away.

He cupped her face, forcing her to look back at him.

"Talk to me, woman. Why not?"

To his surprise, she seemed angry. "Because then I'd have to explain how it happened, and I don't have an explanation to give."

It didn't make sense. When he saw her, he would have sworn that she'd also seen him. After all, she'd been running toward him with her eyes wide open.

"So, you're telling me you don't remember what happened."

Her expression darkened. "That's what I said."

"I'm sorry. I didn't mean to sound so persistent." He laid his hand on her knee, waiting until she looked back at him.

"It's happened before, hasn't it? That first time I saw you, in the creek, you were talking to someone who wasn't there."

She bit her lip.

Fear for her, coupled with a frustration he couldn't deny, sharpened his voice. "What, Rachel? Talk to me, damn it!"

This time her anger was real. "And say what, Boone? That I guess I'm losing my mind? Don't think it hasn't already occurred to me."

Regretting the way he'd raised his voice, he tried to smooth things over, but her temper had already been lit, like a short, burning fuse.

"I go to bed. I close my eyes. I sleep. But I don't always wake up in my bed!" The more she talked, the faster the words came, often harsh, sometimes shrill, as if she were on the brink of breaking down. "Sometimes I wake up standing in water. Sometimes I'm facedown in the dirt. It happens. I don't know why. I can't control it." Then she swayed and once again covered her face with her hands. "Oh, God…I can't control it."

"Damn."

It was all he could say. With a groan, he went from his

knees to her side, then lifted her in his arms and set her down in his lap, holding her close until her shaking had stopped.

Rachel felt like a thief, absorbing his strength to replace her own. For some reason, she wanted to explain how destructive these episodes had become.

"I took a leave of absence from work."

Boone held her just that little bit tighter. "I noticed you've been gone. Figured you'd gone to visit your folks or something."

"No, I was on a...trip. My parents are dead. Have been for several years."

"Sorry."

She sighed. "Me too."

"Are you okay now?"

"Yes, just help me to the bathroom, will you? There's some peroxide in the medicine chest I can use on my foot."

The fluorescent lights were unkind to the damage she'd done to herself. In the bright white light, all was revealed, from the scratches on her face to the rip in her gown. Even more, her womanly shape was too easy to see beneath the soft white flannel.

Desire for more than her smile made Boone's hand shake as he held her foot over the edge of the tub. Following her instructions, he poured antiseptic on the wound, then applied a bandage. He gave her another long look as he put away the supplies.

"Now what?"

She almost blushed. "If you'll give me a minute..."

He walked out of the bathroom, shutting the door behind him. He clenched his hands as he stared around Rachel's room. The essence of her was everywhere, from a lacy slip hanging on a hook on the closet door to the tumbled covers of the bed she'd been sleeping in. He stared at the sheets and the pillow still bearing the indentation of her head until something inside him snapped. Gritting his teeth, he stalked out of the room. Not only had he reached the limit of his self-denial, he was pretty sure he'd passed it.

When Rachel came out, she was alone. Surprised, she stood for a moment, listening to the quiet in her small frame house. And then a pot banged somewhere down the hall. He was in the kitchen and, from the sounds of it, trying to cook something. Probably for her. She smiled to herself. For a bad boy, he had a remarkable bedside manner.

As she hobbled to the kitchen, it never once crossed her mind to thank him kindly and send him packing. Somewhere between the time she went to bed and the moment when she returned to consciousness in his arms, she'd come to terms with the fact that her life and Boone MacDonald's were somehow intertwined.

Even though she made no sound, Boone seemed to know he was no longer alone. When he turned, she was staring at him from the doorway. She'd gone from the white gown to a pink one with a robe to match. He didn't know whether to stand his ground or run for cover. Either way, he'd lost the last of his control. For better or worse, it was a given fact that he loved her.

Have mercy, he thought. "Feeling better?" he asked.

She smiled. "Yes, thanks."

"I'm making coffee."

She pointed. "Works better when it's plugged in."

He looked down. "Well, damn," he muttered, and shoved the plug into the outlet.

"Boone."

"Hmm?"

"Thank you."

He could see her out of the corner of his eye. All it would take was a couple of steps and she could be in his arms. He didn't move.

"You're welcome."

To his relief, the coffee started to brew.

She didn't budge from the doorway, continuing to stare at him for long, agonizing minutes, until Boone felt ready to explode. Finally he gave her an angry glare and pointed toward the table and chairs.

"Either sit the hell down or suffer the consequences."

She sat.

He poured coffee and joined her.

Another minute passed while she blew on her cup and Boone gulped from his. Silence grew. And grew. And grew. It was Boone who broke first.

"If you don't need me anymore, I'm out of here," he said, disregarding the fact that he sounded rude. But his patience had long since run its course, and desire for this woman was eating him alive.

Need you? I think I'll always need you, Rachel thought, and then it scared her so much that she didn't argue when he stood up to leave.

"Are you finished?" he asked, pointing to her half-empty cup.

Rachel nodded and shoved it aside. But before she could help herself up, he once again lifted her into his arms, then paused, giving her a look she was afraid to believe.

"What do you think you're doing?" she asked, and hated the nervous tremor she heard in her own voice. It wouldn't do to let him know she was scared.

"Tucking you into bed?"

It was the hesitation in his voice that gave her comfort. If she wasn't the only one unsure about the ground on which they were standing, then it helped to balance the confusion she was feeling. There was a tinge of despair in her voice as he carried her down the hall. "Maybe you should just tie me down while you're at it. I'm not real good at staying tucked."

He grinned, and once again Rachel was reminded that this was no altar boy she was messing with. The smile on his face was pure devil, the glitter in his eyes far too bright for her peace of mind.

To her relief, he kept quiet until he was in the act of pulling up her covers. At that point, he reached out and traced the arch of her upper lip with the tip of his finger.

"The last time I tied a woman up in bed, it was not with the intention of putting her to sleep."

Rachel gasped. The image was too vivid to ignore.

Desire for her was so strong that Boone couldn't deny himself any longer. Before he could talk himself out of the deed, he bent down.

She tasted better than he'd dreamed. Soft, slightly surprised lips parted beneath his demand. He groaned, and she sighed, and the pressure increased. At the point of lying down beside her, he drew back, his nostrils flaring, his eyes dark and wild with unfulfilled need.

"Don't expect me to apologize for that."

"I don't expect anything of the sort from a man like you," Rachel said, then could have kicked herself. After all he'd done for her, all she seemed able to do was hurt him, and she knew that she had. It was there in his eyes.

He grinned, but it was not a happy smile. "Well, darlin', it seems you've got me pegged, and that's a fact. If you value your sweet head and your hide, you'll keep yourself locked inside this house, where a desperado like me can't get to you."

Desperado!

The constant similarities she kept seeing between this man and Dakota gave her a chill of warning. Rachel shivered and pulled the covers up to her chin, her eyes wide and fixed in shock.

"Have mercy, Rachel, don't give me that look."

Have mercy. Once again, another echo of the long-dead outlaw. Rachel stared, searching for more than a familiar phrase to tell her that she was on the right track.

"I'll lock myself out," Boone said.

He had started toward the door when she stopped him with a whisper so soft it went almost unheard. "I'm not afraid of you anymore."

He froze, and when he turned, there was a look on his face that she knew she would never forget.

"You should be, sweet Rachel. You surely should be."

And then she was listening to the sound of his footsteps

moving through her house and the soft, distinct click of the lock falling into place. He was gone.

She relaxed, then, moments later, leaned over and turned off the light by her bed. Only after the house was dark did she hear him start up his truck and drive away. She closed her eyes, wondering if he'd looked back, and then she slept. When she woke, it was morning and the sun was streaming in upon her face.

Joanie Mills darted into the bakery just as Rachel was in the act of going out.

"Rachel! Just the gal I want to see!" she cried. "Wait for me. We need to talk."

Rachel rolled her eyes and leaned against the wall. If only she'd been a little bit earlier, she might have escaped Joanie's third degree. A minute or so later, Joanie was back at the door, with a jelly doughnut in one hand and a soda in the other.

"Get the door for me, sugar, will you?"

Rachel obliged.

"Follow me," Joanie ordered, as she started down the street toward her shop. "We've got to hurry. Melvina Woodruff is due in fifteen minutes for her monthly rinse. I swear, that woman's roots grow faster than mold on bread."

In spite of the grilling she knew was forthcoming, Rachel had to laugh.

Joanie grinned, then noticed Rachel's limp and pointed with the straw poking out of her soda cup.

"What happened to you?"

"I, uh…I stepped on a root."

Joanie's painted-on eyebrows arched toward her bright red hair. "You were barefoot? Lord A-mighty, girl, it's too late in the year for such stuff." She opened her door by backing into it, using her blue-jeaned behind for leverage. "Get in here *now*. You've got some explaining to do."

Rachel knew she didn't have to go. But as she followed

oanie inside, deep down she knew she'd been wanting to do
nis from day one.

"Sit," Joanie ordered, and inhaled the last of her doughnut
n one gulp, washing it down with a long slurp of soda. "You
alk, I'll listen. I've got to get Melvina's rinse mixed before
he gets here. She always wants it too black. I tried to tell her
hat a woman her age shouldn't have hair darker than the
noles on her arms, but she just won't listen."

Rachel grinned. Melvina would hate to know her moles had
been the topic of such a discussion.

"I'm waiting," Joanie said.

"For what?"

"For why you didn't see fit to tell me you've taken a leave
of absence from work, and why you left the state and didn't
bother to tell me you were gone. I had to hear it from Char-
ie." She frowned as she poured and measured, all the while
keeping one eye on the clock and the other on Rachel. "You
know how I hate hearing second-hand news."

"There's not much to tell," Rachel said. "I went to South
Dakota to—"

Joanie shrieked. "South Dakota! Girl! What on earth were
you thinking? There's nothing up there but—" She took a
deep breath and started over. "Sorry."

"As I was saying," Rachel muttered, "there were some
things I needed to find out, and going there was the best way
to do it."

Joanie paused, the bottle of rinse held tight in her hand.

"So...did you find out whatever it was you needed to
know?"

Rachel sighed and nodded. "Probably even more than I
wanted to know."

"Rachel?"

"What?"

"You know you're the best friend I have in Razor Bend,
probably my best friend in the entire world, don't you?"

Rachel looked a little embarrassed, although pleased by
what Joanie had said. "I guess."

"Then know this. We both know I gossip a little, but swear to God—even on my sweet mother's grave, and she' not even dead—that I would never, ever, reveal anything you told me in confidence."

This is it, Rachel thought. Now's my time. "Joanie?"

"Yeah?"

"Do you believe in reincarnation?"

Melvina Woodruff's rinse hit the floor with a splat, coating Joanie's white tennies in a dark, malevolent color, as well as a goodly portion of the floor on which she was standing. To her credit, she never looked down.

"Rachel Brant...are you just askin' for something to talk about, or are you serious?"

"Do you see me laughing?"

Joanie's eyes grew round with interest. "Tell me."

"You swear?" Rachel asked, reminding her of her vow.

Joanie nodded, then sighed. "Who would believe me, any-way?"

Rachel began to relax. It felt good to be able to talk, even if what she said made no sense.

"It's like this. Over the past six weeks I've come to a conclusion. Either I'm losing my mind, or my mind is no longer my own."

"Rachel...you're scaring me."

"*You're* scared?" Rachel's fingers curled around the arms of the chair as she leaned forward. "Joanie, you have no idea. I'm remembering things that never happened to me. I'm see-ing things that aren't there. I wake up in the present, but right when I'm least expecting it, it's as if the world turns backward and I'm still in it, but I'm not me anymore."

To Joanie's credit, she didn't laugh or tell Rachel that she was crazy. Instead, she stepped over the black puddle on the floor and hugged her.

"I'm here, honey. You just talk away. Tell me whatever you want, however you feel like saying it, while I clean up this mess."

Rachel went limp, only then realizing she was still holding

the sack of cookies she'd bought from the bakery. She set them aside and, to her dismay, felt a lump come into her throat.

Her chin quivered as she voiced her worst fear. "Do you think I'm crazy?"

Joanie's face crumpled as she gave Rachel a handful of tissues and then took one for herself and blew noisily before answering. "Lord, no, honey. You're the most together person I know. You have to be, to do the things you do."

"Then explain it to me," Rachel said. "Tell me why this is happening. Tell me how to make it stop."

"I can't," Joanie said, and then lowered her voice. "But I'll tell you one thing my granny used to say—and my granny knew about things that other folks made fun of. She always said, 'There's many a thing twixt earth and heaven that man's not supposed to understand.'"

Rachel grabbed for her purse as Joanie groaned.

"Darn, here comes Melvina."

"I'd better go," Rachel said, unwilling for anyone but Joanie to see her distress.

She had started out the door when Joanie called out. "Rachel, wait!"

She turned.

Joanie pointed to her sack. "Forgot your cookies."

Rachel rolled her eyes and managed a grin. "Oh, that. I thought you were about to say I'd lost my marbles."

Joanie was still laughing when Rachel walked out the door. All the way to her car, Rachel kept thinking that she shouldn't have said anything. Yet, even though she'd done little more than skim over the facts, she knew she would do it again. The relief that she felt was overwhelming. Secrets were a burden to carry and a good thing to share.

It was nearing noon. Rachel was sitting in a chair outside Jimmy's Place, waiting for an oil-and-lube job to be finished on her car before starting home, when Charlie Dutton and Ken Wade pulled the ambulance into the station to refuel.

Charlie jumped out, a wide grin on his face, as Ken winked and went inside to sign the charge ticket that would be billed to the city.

"Loafing already?" Charlie teased.

"I'm waiting for Stu to get through with my car."

Charlie snorted softly beneath his breath. "Hope you're not in any big hurry," he muttered. "Stu doesn't exactly set the world on fire."

"He may be slow, but he's sure," Rachel said.

"The only thing he's sure about is that he's going to get his five-fifty an hour, no matter how much work he puts out."

Rachel laughed. "Who put the bee in your bonnet?"

"You," Charlie said, and pointed at Ken as he came out of the store. "Damn it, Rachel, I miss smelling your wild-flower perfume. *He* doesn't smell like wildflowers."

Ken laughed. "And may I say my wife is heartily thankful for that. You might also like to know I don't wrap bandages right, and I hit all the holes in the road, and I—"

Charlie threw up his hands. "So I've been griping a bit."

Rachel grinned. "Charlie always gripes. The trick is not to pay any attention until it matters." Her grin widened. "I know. Maybe you should just buy a bottle of my perfume. That way, when he gets testy, you can just sprinkle a little bit on him to sweeten him up."

"Okay, that does it," Charlie said. "Get in. We're taking you for a ride."

Rachel looked startled. "No, I think I'd better…"

"Oh, for Pete's sake," Charlie muttered. "We're only going to the Adam's Rib to eat lunch. You still eat, don't you?"

"Only if you're paying."

"You asked for that, buddy," Ken said, as he opened the door and crawled inside first, stepping between the seats and into the back, where the patients were transported, leaving the empty seat for her.

"Hey," Charlie said. "How come you're limping?"

"I cut the bottom of my foot. It's nothing."

"Want me to take a look at it for you?"

Rachel grinned as she slid into the seat. "No thanks, I still know how to doctor my own boo-boos, thank you. Besides, I know an excuse to play with my feet when I hear one."

"Can't blame a guy for trying," Charlie said, and took off for the café with a grin on his face and the wind in his hair.

Rachel glanced down at his hand, her eyes widening at the ornate gold ring he was wearing. Impulsively she started to remark about its sudden appearance, but Ken caught her eye and shook his head, warning her away from that tack.

She shrugged and let the thought go, but as they parked and got out, it crossed her mind that her life wasn't the only one undergoing drastic changes. Lois Klein had told Joanie, and Joanie had told her, that Charlie had paid off the note on his house. Add to that the new car he'd just bought and the ring on his hand, and either Charlie had a fairy godmother he'd wasn't talking about, or he'd won the lottery and was hoping to hide the fact from the IRS.

They entered the café, laughing and talking as old friends do, only to come face-to-face with Griff and Lois having lunch. Griff's face turned red, while Lois's glowed. All Rachel felt was relief.

"Hi, guys," Rachel said brightly. "What's good today?"

"*We're* having the special," Lois said, adding extra emphasis on the *we*.

Griff stood and started pulling out an empty chair for her. "We'd be glad to share a table. It's pretty crowded in here today."

But Charlie was having none of that. "Thanks," he said, "but there's an empty one over there."

There was nothing for Griffin to do but watch Rachel disappear through the crowd with the two men. He sat down, his food forgotten, and tried not to glare at the woman sitting at his table. *Why? Why couldn't Rachel be as pliable as Lois?*

Lois beamed under his tense observation, unaware of the turn his thoughts had taken.

A little while later, the bell over the front door jingled again and, out of curiosity, Rachel looked up—and came close to choking. Hoping Charlie hadn't noticed, she looked down at her plate; then, like a magnet, her gaze was drawn up again, and she stared, unable to take her eyes from the men who'd entered.

Snake never saw her. Tommy Joe, too, was focused on food. But Boone seemed to know she was there before the door swung shut behind him. Like a heat-seeking missile, his gaze locked on hers, and a wry smile tilted the right-hand corner of his mouth. The look he gave her was intimate, the smile secretive.

Griffin Ross saw the whole thing, from Boone's entry into the café to Rachel's blush and smile. He stared in disbelief, clutching his table knife as if it were a switchblade and fighting the urge to plunge it into the big man's back as he passed their table.

My God, Rachel, how could you?

Rage shook him as he flung down the knife and a handful of bills and stalked out the door, Lois hustling along behind in mute confusion.

The three men came nearer, and Rachel caught herself holding her breath and watching the changing expressions on Boone's face. Once again their gazes met, and his moved first, from her eyes to her mouth. She felt hot and at the same time cold as she realized he was remembering their kiss. Embarrassed and a little bit panicked, she looked away.

As they neared the table where she was sitting, his footsteps slowed and then stopped. Certain he was about to make a big scene, she kept her eyes on her plate and clutched at the napkin in her lap. Moments later, she realized he'd stepped aside to let a busboy pass, and tried to relax. But with him standing only inches away, it was impossible.

Keep your eyes on your plate, she told herself. It was no use. She could no more have looked away than she could have stopped breathing. She raised her head and got caught in the dark, silent power of his gaze.

"Excuse us," he said softly, and then moved on, well aware of the flush he'd left staining her face.

Charlie saw enough to worry about, but never got a chance to inquire. At that moment, his pager went off. He and Ken started digging in their pockets.

"Sorry, Rachel, duty calls," Charlie said, as he and Ken tossed their money on the table and bolted out the door, leaving her behind to finish alone.

She fiddled with her tea, sipping and stirring until the hair on the back of her neck started to rise. She didn't have to turn around to know Boone was staring. His spirit was all around her.

The urge to get out from under the weight of his presence was overwhelming. She stood up too fast, stumbling as she put too much weight too suddenly on her sore foot. All the way to the door, she kept reminding herself, *I'm not afraid. I'm not afraid.*

And, in a way, it was true. Alone, Boone MacDonald posed no threat, but when she saw him with the company he kept, she was reminded of who and what he really was—a man who undoubtedly lived on the wrong side of the law.

When she was halfway out the door, someone gripped her shoulder, and she didn't have to look back to know who it was.

"Need a ride?" he asked softly, glancing down at her foot.

She looked over his shoulder, expecting Snake and Tommy Joe to be at his heels.

"I'm alone," Boone said, answering her unspoken question as to the other men's whereabouts.

"Thanks, but I think I can—"

"You gave me a ride. I'm only returning the favor."

Rachel thought of the half-mile trek to get back to her car and the pain already throbbing in her foot.

"Okay."

It would have been impossible for Boone to describe his relief. It wasn't much, but it was a great big first step in trusting him. He hurried ahead to open the truck door for her.

In the act of trying to seat herself, Rachel was suddenly lifted and scooted inside before she could argue the fact.

"Don't fuss. Last night I carried you, and you didn't complain. You can't begrudge a small boost."

She refused to look at him all the way to Jimmy's Place. He pulled up and parked, then jumped out before she could move. In seconds he'd come around to her door and was helping her out.

"Easy does it," he said gently, taking both her hands and easing her out of the seat.

It was only after she was firmly standing on both feet that he realized they were still holding hands. This time he was the one who started to panic.

"Boone?"

Let her go, you fool. Mesmerized by the look in her eyes, he wasn't strong enough to follow his own advice.

"Hmm?"

"Have you ever been to South Dakota?"

Gut-shot by the question, and scared to death of why she'd asked, he froze. Boone MacDonald hadn't been there, but *he* was born there. It took everything Boone had not to panic. Instinctively he stepped back, putting some distance between himself and the shock. Shoving his hands in his pockets, he gave her a cold, questioning stare.

"No, I haven't. Why do you ask?"

Rachel shrugged. "No reason. It's just that while I was there last week, I saw some—"

He grabbed her by the arm, and this time he made no attempt to hide the anger in his voice. "You were there? Why?"

"You're hurting me," Rachel said.

The accusation shocked him. He turned her loose as quickly as he'd grabbed her, and wondered if he was losing his mind. He'd known better than to do this. Rule one in undercover work was to stay focused on the assumed identity. Never let a piece of your real self show through. Boone MacDonald wouldn't have had a damn thing to do with a woman like Rachel Brant. It was the man he was who'd been drawn to her. *I'm the one who keeps coming back, time after time. And I'm the one who will suffer if anything goes wrong.*

"As I was saying," Rachel said, "the state historical society has a wonderful display on Deadwood. You know…all the gold-rush stuff, and Wild Bill Hickok and—" she shrugged "—and things. I wondered if you'd ever seen it."

Too stunned to speak, all he could do was shake his head.

Accepting the disappointment, all Rachel could do was try to smile. "Then that's that," she said. "Thanks for the ride. I guess I'd better go see if Stu is through with my car."

She limped away, and he tried to tell himself that it didn't matter. People took trips. Trips to anywhere they chose. But why, he wondered? Of all the places in the world to see, why on earth South Dakota? Unless…

He got in his truck and drove out of town, leaving Snake and Tommy Joe to get back to their vehicles as best they could. He had a sudden need to find out all he could about Rachel Brant.

Chapter 10

Boone wasted no time in digging into Rachel Brant's past. To his relief, it seemed she was all she claimed to be. Orphaned at the age of twenty-one. A certified EMT. Dedicated to her work. And, up until a short time ago, rumored to be about to become Mrs. Griffin Ross.

But no more. Griffin Ross was dating his secretary, although some said it was more for show than for love, at least on his part. And Boone knew that Rachel Brant was combing the Kiamichi Mountains at night like a woman possessed, crying out to a man who wasn't really there. It made no sense to Boone that she'd taken a leave from her job, and even less that she seemed drawn to him, rather than afraid. While there were questions that remained unanswered, he wanted to believe her trip to South Dakota had been a coincidence. And because he wanted it so badly, he let it be so.

Two days passed in which Boone rarely went home. Instead, he prowled the streets of Razor Bend in the hope of seeing Rachel again, but it didn't happen. And while there was nothing going on at Denver Cherry's but the nightly drink-till-you-drop routine, Boone couldn't completely absent himself from the group, not when it had taken him so long to be called to the fold.

Never before had he wanted to call it quits as badly as he did now, and it was because of Rachel. He was beginning to think of this job as his last. Once an undercover cop began to think more of who he was, than of who he was pretending to be, things always went wrong. He wanted out before that started to happen.

It was midnight when Boone drove up to the trailer and parked. He sat in silence with the engine running and the radio playing, letting himself unwind before going inside to bed. And as he stared at the darkened windows and the rusting trailer, the solitude of his existence overwhelmed him.

He hit the steering wheel with angry force. "Why am I doing this? We lock them up, the system lets them go."

On impulse, he picked up his cell phone. Leaning his head against the back of the seat, he closed his eyes, waiting for the link to the outside world that kept his head on straight.

"This is Waco. Is this you?"

Boone exhaled in an angry grunt. "I don't know," he muttered. "You tell me."

Susan Cross hit the mute button on her remote and shoved her bowl of popcorn aside. Something was wrong. "Talk to me, darlin'," she said softly.

"I want this over."

"Has something happened?"

"Hell, no. If it had, we wouldn't be having this conversation."

"I don't understand," she said.

Boone sighed and shoved a hand through his hair, massaging the back of his neck as he did.

"Me either, Captain. I shouldn't have called."

It took Susan a moment to think, and when she did, the first thing that came to mind was the woman.

"It's her, isn't it?"

His heart sank as the futility of the situation struck him. *Dear God, it will always be her.* But admitting to his captain that he was losing his edge didn't come easy.

"I don't know what you mean," he muttered.

A short, succinct epithet rang in his ear.

He arched an eyebrow, then grinned. "Why, Waco, I didn't know you knew words like that."

"Say the word and I'll pull you in," she said.

Boone sighed. That wasn't why he'd called, and it damn sure wasn't what he wanted.

"Look, Captain, like I said, I'm sorry I called. Let's just call it a bad-hair day and let it go at that, okay?"

"I have some news that might cheer you up," she said.

Boone stiffened. "I'm listening."

"Marked drug money has been circulating in Razor Bend like flies on honey."

This was definitely good news. "Have you been able to trace it to the source?"

"We're working on it," she said. "One thing's for sure, if it showed up there, then our boy is there, too. We're checking to see if it's being laundered through a business or major purchases of some kind. Either way, I hope to know something within the week."

"Thanks, Captain," Boone said.

"No, Boone, thank you," she said quietly, and hung up.

Boone disconnected, then, out of habit, entered a series of random numbers and disconnected again.

It was warm inside his truck. The heater was working at a neat little clip. He glanced up at the trailer, thinking of cold sheets and the lonely bed waiting for him inside.

"Suck it up," he reminded himself, and was reaching to turn off the engine when a song on the radio stopped his intent.

To his regret, it was the same lonely song he'd heard playing once before at Rachel's place.

"Desperado."

And in that moment, he knew what he was.

A longing swept over him that he couldn't control. Blind as he was to everything but the words of the song hammering at his heart, the need to see Rachel was too strong to deny. He put the truck in gear and took off down the mountain.

Rachel couldn't sleep. Truth be told, she was afraid to close her eyes. She'd paced inside her house until she wore out the floors, as well as her patience. The night was cool, but calm. The Kiamichis beckoned, promising peace if only she would come. Rachel walked out her back door, then stretched and inhaled slowly. Like a piper playing a seductive, sweet song, the dark enfolded her. Even as she sat down on the steps, the tension inside her was beginning to unwind.

Long minutes passed as she sat there, one with the night, listening to an owl hoot from a nearby tree, watching a possum as it waddled to and fro beneath a nearby bush, feeling the moisture on her face as it came down through the air, soon to become dewdrops on the lush mountain grass. Crickets chirped; night birds called. And then, while she wasn't listening, everything went silent. It was only after the possum suddenly scuttled away that Rachel realized what had happened.

She stood, alert now to a presence that, at this point, she could only feel. It took several moments for her eyesight to penetrate the darkness beyond the perimeter of the security light outside her house, but when it did, her heart started to pound.

She could see him now, coming toward her like some dark mountain cat, long and lean, dressed in black, blending with the shadows through which he was moving. There was a purpose in his step that she'd never seen before, an intent that created an ache deep inside of her.

Oh, God.

Waiting…waiting…she felt her legs begin to tremble, and she reached out toward the porch post to steady herself.

He came on without words, his intention obvious in the tilt of his head and the rhythm of his walk. He was closer now.

She imagined she could hear his heart thundering in his chest, feel the rush of his blood as it coursed through his veins. Somehow, before it happened, she knew what the weight of his body would feel like as he drove deep inside her. She shuddered, then swallowed a moan. The time was past for sampling. What was between them was ripe; about ready to burst.

When he reached the bottom of the steps, he looked up, blistering Rachel with a single dark stare.

"Turn loose of me, woman, or suffer the consequences."

His demand was raw, like the need on his face.

Rachel took a deep breath. "I can't. I don't know how."

"Then God help us both, because neither do I."

Seconds later, she was in his arms.

Urgently, desperately, Boone's mouth swept her face, then her lips, then down the curve of her neck, drinking in the essence of the woman called Rachel.

When she moaned against his mouth, he lost the last of his control. He pulled her off her feet and into his arms, shoving aside a screen door, then kicking the wooden one shut behind them.

"Turn them off," he ordered, tilting his head toward the lights.

Rachel reached for the switch. As it clicked, dark replaced light, and she was aware of the sound of his breath as it flowed against her cheek. How ragged, how deep...

As if she'd done this all her life, Rachel locked her hands behind his neck and pulled his head down until there was nothing between them but a hurt waiting to be healed.

Boone could hardly think, yet there were things that had to be said.

"I want you, Rachel. I'm going to make love to you, and once I start, I won't stop." He didn't want to do it, but he took a deep breath and gave her an out. "If you don't want the same thing, tell me now."

He could feel the tension winding in her body like the

springs of a clock. Her whisper brushed past his face, settling deep in his soul. It was the last thing that either of them said.

"Oh, God, Boone MacDonald, just don't let me go."

There was a trail of clothing on the floor, scattered from the kitchen down the hall to the end of her bed. The covers were torn back, with fresh sheets exposed. Completely revealed, Rachel lay waiting, her skin burning from the fiery sweep of his mouth, as he tossed the last of his clothes aside. He came to her without words or excuse, wasting no time in foreplay or sweet whispers and lies. And when he moved between her legs and drove himself deep inside, there was an intensity of feeling Rachel couldn't deny. She'd known all along what this ride would be like.

Once he was inside her, Boone paused, his jaw clenched, muscles jerking in his arms as he raised himself up to look down at her face. He never wanted to forget the way she looked making love.

Passion gave a sultry expression to Rachel's face. Her eyes were hooded, as if she were waking from a deep, restful sleep. Her eyelashes fluttered like butterflies in the wind. Her neck was arched, her lips were slightly parted, and with each soft gasp of air she inhaled, she clutched him tight, for fear he would disappear like the man from her dreams.

He groaned, then bent down, his mouth only inches from her damp, swollen lips. Rolling his hips against her belly, he moved himself deeper inside.

"Look at me, Rachel. Look at *me*."

She sighed and then shuddered, trying to do as he asked, but his face kept blurring in and out of her sight. From Dakota to Boone, from Boone to Dakota, as if she were looking into a bad mirror in a carnival sideshow.

The urge to move was coming upon him like a powerful wave. But he wanted her to know, when she fell over the edge of reason, that it was because he'd sent her there.

Resting his weight on his elbows, he put a hand on either side of her face and pulled her focus toward him. Centering her gaze so that she saw nothing but his face, he started to rock. For a brief span, time stood still.

Thoughts tumbled, one after the other, from her to him, from him to her. They read them in each other's eyes. Saw them in each other's faces.

She was soft where he was hard, giving against his need to take, gentle when he was strong. She filled him, completed him.

Watching a man like Boone come undone in her arms was, for Rachel, more than a joy. It was at once a satisfaction and a pleasure, knowing that she'd been made for this…for him. And of that she had no doubt. In spite of what and who he was now, they belonged.

Flesh against flesh, their bodies hammering with an unfinished need, Rachel felt the end beginning and knew a quick moment of relief. Soon, soon, it would happen. It had to. A woman could withstand only so much sweet pain. Mesmerized by the power of the man above her, Rachel couldn't look away. Making love with him was unlike anything she'd ever experienced.

And then it came upon her, a rush of blood, a pounding heart, a blinding flash. When she would have closed her eyes from the pleasure, he wouldn't let her go to that place all alone.

And then it was over.

Spent and shaking, they lay in each other's arms and cherished the loving they had shared. Rachel exhaled softly and closed her eyes, only now aware that she'd been crying.

He heard her sigh and lifted his hand to her cheek. It came away wet. With a groan, he pulled her closer, pillowing his head on her breast. The security of her heartbeat, the satin feel of her skin, all were a balm to a lonely soul.

Just before his eyes closed in sleep, the last lines of the song he'd heard earlier drifted into his mind. It gave him comfort to think that maybe it wasn't too late for him after all. He'd let her love him…even better, he'd let himself return hat love. Maybe he would be the exception to the rule. Maybe his desperado could find the way to a good woman's heart.

Dawn was imminent when Boone slipped out of bed. He dressed as he'd undressed last night. Room by room, item by item, taking his clothes from the floor as he went. His boots were the last to be put on. Last night they'd been the first to go. But when he was dressed, he found it wasn't as easy to walk out as it had been to come in. He went back to her room, then stood in the doorway, watching her sleep.

He'd made tangles of her hair. Her shoulder was bare, a reminder that he'd taken everything from her last night, including her clothes.

When she was asleep, the animation that was so much a part of her face was missing. Only now, while she was still, was he fully aware of her near-perfect features and heart-shaped face. He looked at her, and his breath caught from the intensity of his feelings.

Last night he'd been swept away by passion. Today his mind was clear, his focus intent. He'd thought he knew about love, but that had been before Rachel. He'd never known that love could hurt so deeply, or heal so completely. The bond between them was more than he'd expected, and not enough to count on. How was she going to feel in the bright light of day? Would she be sorry? And, what was worse…even if she was sorry, he couldn't wait around to see.

Taking a pad and pencil from her bedside table, he scribbled a note and dropped it on the pillow. Resisting the urge for a goodbye kiss, he walked out of the house without looking back.

By the time he got home, the sun was just coming up over the horizon. He entered the trailer with no small amount of regret. Going from her place to his was like walking out of the light into the dark. It was a rude reminder of who he still had to be.

* * *

Rachel woke up one eye at a time, stretching slowly as she rolled over on her back. She couldn't remember the last time she'd slept this soundly or felt as refreshed. She glanced at the clock and groaned. It was almost 10:00 a.m. She yawned and as she did, she realized her lower lip felt tight. Tracing her finger against the edge, she winced, and then the reason for its condition slammed into her with force. Boone! Ravaging her mouth…her body…her soul.

"Oh, my God!"

She sat up in bed. Last night, and everything that had happened, came back to her in a rush.

Her pink gown was still hanging on the closet door by a hook. She'd never put it on. Her clothes were all over the floor. There was nothing between her and God but a white cotton sheet…and Boone was nowhere in sight.

The fact that he was gone was multiplied a hundredfold by the fact that he hadn't bothered to say goodbye. And then she saw the note lying on the pillow and picked it up. It was brief. But the message was more than she'd expected from a man like Boone.

Vaya con Dios, Rachel, till we meet again.

She fell back on her pillow, clutching the note to her breast. *Till we meet again.* It was all she needed to know.

Rachel came down off the mountain with a purpose in mind. She wanted to know more about the man with whom she was falling in love, and that wasn't going to happen if they wound up in bed as quickly as they had last night. Not, she reminded herself, that she didn't want to be there again.

There were other things they could do in between. She desperately wanted to find out more about him and, in doing so, get some much-needed answers about herself, as well. But she had no idea how to go about finding him or finding out, so she let the thought ride.

Shopping. She could shop for food. She didn't know a man who wouldn't slow down for a home-cooked meal. Her mind was filled with thoughts of how she could get him to unwind.

Yet by the time she'd wheeled an empty shopping cart up and down the aisles for a good fifteen minutes without making a single choice, the headway she'd planned to make was nowhere in sight.

As bad luck would have it, Joanie came up aisle two as Rachel was going down. For some reason, she feared Joanie would be able to see the change in her. Rachel shifted gears, trying to think of meat and potatoes instead of Boone Mac-Donald, and hoped her expression wouldn't give her away.

Joanie parked herself near the canned peas and carrots and pointed to Rachel's empty cart.

"Hi, girl. I see you're just starting."

"Sort of," Rachel said. "I didn't make a list. Can't remember what I needed."

"Don't you hate it when that happens?"

Rachel nodded and started to smile, but the cut on her lip pulled, causing her to wince instead.

Joanie being Joanie didn't miss a thing, from the glow in Rachel's eyes to the small bruise Boone's loving had left on her lip. Her eyebrows rose as her eyes began to twinkle. "So...I guess it's pretty lonesome up there on the mountain all by yourself."

Joanie's drawl didn't fool Rachel one bit. *I should have known.* She gave her friend a cool, unwavering glare. "I don't suppose it would do any good to tell you to mind your own business?"

Joanie scooted closer until they were head to head. "I don't suppose it would," she drawled. "Now, fess up. Who's got your head in a whirl? Don't tell me you've made up with Griff?"

Rachel frowned. "We didn't ever fight, so we had nothing to make up."

"But I thought... Then, if you never..." Joanie sighed. "Just tell me this. He's handsome. He's solvent. He's single. What was wrong with him?"

"Nothing was wrong with him," Rachel muttered, and took off down the aisle.

Joanie cut her off at the milk case. For once, the giggle was gone from her voice. "Don't do this, Rachel. You're scaring me, okay? First you ask me if I believe in *you-know what....*" She glanced over her shoulder, making certain there was no one in sight, although she'd never said the word *reincarnation* aloud. "You said nothing was wrong with Griff which means you think something might be wrong with you instead." Joanie grabbed her by the arm, her face full of concern, and all but pinned Rachel to the milk case as she waited for an answer. "Well...I'm waiting."

But Rachel didn't answer. She was looking over Joanie's shoulder to the aisle beyond, at the tall, dark man who was sauntering down the aisle with a loaf of bread dangling from one hand and a three-liter bottle of pop in the other.

His hair was windblown, his black jeans were soft and faded. He wore a dark blue T-shirt and a black denim jacket. His boots were worn and dusty, as if he'd been out in the woods, and from the way he was walking, he'd seen her long before she spotted him.

It was Boone.

There was no expression on his face, but his eyes were alive with a message she couldn't misinterpret.

Remember last night?

How could I forget?

It didn't take Joanie long to realize that she'd lost her friend's attention. Rachel had a faraway look in her eyes, and a smile on her lips that shouldn't have been there.

"So, you think what I just said was funny, do you?"

To her surprise, Rachel still didn't answer, and judging from the way she was staring over Joanie's shoulder, she'd completely forgotten Joanie was here. She spun around, ready to attack.

"I'd like to know what's so all-fired interesting behind my—" Joanie took a deep breath. The answer was literally staring her in the face. "Oh...my...Gawd."

It only lasted a few seconds, but within that space of time, Rachel felt as if all the bones in her body had just turned to nush. Before she could think what to say, Boone turned a corner and disappeared up another aisle.

Joanie grabbed her by the arm, and this time she had Rachel's full attention. "Please, Rachel, tell me that didn't mean what I thought it meant."

Rachel winced at the fear in Joanie's voice. But what on earth could she say that would make any sense? "I don't know what you mean," she muttered, and looked away.

"Is he why you dumped Griffin Ross?"

"No," Rachel said. "He came after."

Joanie exhaled slowly. "Then there *is* something between you two?"

Rachel looked up, but she didn't have to answer. The truth was there for Joanie to see.

"Oh, honey, I hope you know what you're doing," she said softly.

Rachel sighed as she looked in the direction Boone had gone. "That's just it, Joanie," she said, her voice quiet and shaking. "I don't have a clue, yet in spite of how this may seem, it still feels right."

Joanie shook her head and started to walk away when Rachel called out, "Joanie, you won't say any…"

There was a look of high indignation on Joanie's face. "I can't believe you felt the need to ask."

You can't believe it? I can't believe I've put myself in the position of having to ask.

"Thank you," Rachel said.

"You're welcome," Joanie replied, and left Rachel standing.

Rachel shoved her cart forward, but didn't get very far. She was so shaken that for a few minutes all she did was stare blindly at a display of fruits and vegetables. She didn't know anyone was behind her until a low, husky voice whispered near her ear, "What's the matter, lady, can't you make up your mind?"

She jumped, but she didn't have to turn around to know who it was. Boone was back.

She glanced over her shoulder just long enough to confirm her suspicions. "You're making me crazy," she snapped.

He grinned. "Welcome to the club, darlin'," he said, and dropped a pint of out-of-season strawberries in her cart. "These look good, don't you think? Sweet and juicy...but not too soft. Just firm enough to sink your teeth right into."

A chill ran up Rachel's spine that had nothing to do with fright. She stared down at the strawberries, thinking of what he'd said—and the way he'd said it.

Ignoring Rachel's slight state of shock, Boone picked up a long, dark green cucumber, hefting it in his hands as if testing it for length and weight.

"Hey, how about one of these? It feels just about right. Plenty long and smooth...and firm. They have to be firm, or the dish is ruined. Here, what do you think?"

Before Rachel could answer, he tossed it toward her. She caught the cucumber in midair, then looked up at him in shock. There was a grin on his face she couldn't believe.

"So," he asked. "Do you think it's hard enough?"

If it had been a rat, she couldn't have been any more shocked by it. She dropped it into the basket. It landed next to the strawberries, then rolled into a corner.

By now, her face was definitely flushed. Somewhere in the back of her mind, she knew she should make a run for the door, but there was a part of her that was far too intrigued by this man to do anything but see what came next.

Boone moved down the display case, sorting and feeling. "Say, the celery looks good. You know how to pick the best?"

Rachel had no idea, but from the way Boone was grinning, it was plain he was about to let her know.

"See the leaves on the end of the stalk?"

Her gaze moved up the stalk as if magnetized.

Boone held the stalk upside down, dangling the celery like a baited hook over a pond full of fish. Unbeknownst to her, Rachel's eyes were widening and her lips were slightly agape.

"What I always do is dangle this over my hand...sort of like a feather duster...see?"

Rachel saw.

"Sometimes the leaves will be all soft and limp. That means you need to put that stalk back. But if the leaves feel crisp, and the sensation makes your toes curl in your shoes, then that means..."

Rachel snatched the celery out of his hand and slapped it in her basket. "For God's sake, Boone, what are you trying to—?"

"Oh, wow! Look here," he said, and grabbed her cart, pulling her farther down the aisle to the end, where a large display of oranges had been arranged.

These look safe enough, Rachel thought. She was wrong.

He took one off the top of the pile and tossed it up in the air a time or two, like a baseball, as if getting the feel of it in his hand.

"Now, choosing these is completely opposite of the rest of the stuff we have in the basket."

"Why am I not surprised?" Rachel muttered.

Boone looked at her and winked. "Pay attention, woman. You might learn something."

All I have to do is take control of this situation and he'll stop. But that meant she would have to leave him, and there was a great big piece of Rachel Brant that knew she didn't ever want to leave this man again.

"Unlike other fruits, which need to be firm to be good, an orange should have plenty of juice and plenty of flavor." He held it under her nose, offering it up to be smelled. "Even if it smells like an orange, it could still be a fake." There was an odd tilt to the corner of his lips. "You can't be too careful about fakes, you know."

Rachel couldn't have moved if she wanted to.

"The true test is to squeeze it."

She watched as Boone wrapped his long fingers around the fleshy orange globe and then, ever so slowly, began tightening them. Her heart jerked as she remembered last night and the feel of his hands as he'd cupped her hips, tilting her body up to meet his advance.

She swallowed nervously as his voice lowered. When i was just above a whisper, she caught herself leaning forward anxious not to miss a single word of his lecture.

Boone continued, well aware that he had his one and only student…and the orange…in the palm of his hand.

"But you can't be sure with just one squeeze. Sometimes you have to squeeze it over and over and…"

Rachel groaned.

Boone swallowed a chuckle and dropped the single orange into her cart.

"Now that we've got salad and dessert out of the way, what kind of meat do you like?"

"Not wieners."

Boone threw back his head and laughed. And when he did, for a moment, Rachel saw Dakota's face slide between them. He, too, seemed to be laughing aloud, and she could almost hear a soft, indistinct giggle, as if Mercy were sharing his mirth.

"Oh, God," Rachel said, and grabbed the cart for support.

"Just when I think you're gone…you come back."

She didn't realize until she'd spoken that Boone could misinterpret what she said. But when the laughter died, she knew what had happened. Back came the old, angry Boone. The one with no smile and cold eyes.

"Wait," Rachel said, and took him by the arm as he turned. "I wasn't talking to you."

"Yeah, right," Boone said, and made a big pretense of looking around, although they both knew there was no one else in sight.

"You don't understand," Rachel said.

"Then make me," he said quietly. When she didn't answer, he walked away.

Rachel hurt too much to cry. *What have I done?* But there were no answers for her, and she'd suddenly lost her appetite for everything, including shopping.

Long, empty minutes passed while she stared at the oranges like a woman in mourning. When a lady with two noisy children headed her way, she reacted by pushing her near-empty cart to a checkout stand, then waiting with dull, lifeless eyes while the clerk rang up her groceries. She hadn't bought much as such things normally went—one small pint of strawberries, a long, smooth cucumber, the green, leafy celery and a single orange, slightly squeezed.

"Will that be all, Rachel?" the clerk asked.

She nodded, then dug out her money as the young boy who sacked groceries for the store began to bag her purchases.

"Wait! That's not mine," she said, as the boy dangled a large plastic bottle of lilac-scented bubble bath above the sack.

"Oh, yes, ma'am, it is," the kid said. "A man paid for it a few minutes ago and then left. He said you would be along to pick it up."

Bubble bath?

Weight lifted from the region of her heart. All might not be forgiven, but it would seem he was willing to give her another try at explaining...as well as washing his back.

Chapter 11

Evening came, and with it anxiety about the night that lay ahead. After the way Boone had walked out of the store, Rachel was scared to death he might not come back. The only thing giving her courage was the bottle of bubble bath he'd left at the checkout stand.

The strawberries had long ago been cleaned and bagged, and now they were chilling in the refrigerator. The celery and cucumber had gone into a salad. T-bone steaks were in the refrigerator, still thawing after having been removed from the freezer a few hours ago. The bottle of lilac-scented bubble bath was sitting on the side of the tub. The orange was on hold until breakfast.

She kept telling herself that she had to eat, whether he came or not, and that she'd been taking baths alone for a good many years. She didn't need the appearance of some modern-day desperado to make her wash behind her ears. She was perfectly capable of feeding and bathing herself. All she'd done was plan ahead. Just in case.

Rachel walked through the house one last time, checking

to see if there was something she'd forgotten. Pale blue throw pillows were neatly arranged on her floral-print sofa; magazines were in place. Dark green easy chairs were turned at just the right angle for conversation, and there was a mini-bouquet of bright orange marigolds on the cherrywood coffee table in the center of the room. The table was laid, but not with good china. Something told her that Boone wasn't the kind of man to sit easy at a table with too much fuss.

There was nothing left to do but wait. Rachel passed the hall mirror, then stopped and went back for a last-minute check. Her slacks were old but neat, charcoal gray. Her sweater was a soft rose pink, matching the color on her cheeks. Her hair was down, but pulled back from the sides and fastened at the crown of her head. A cascade of long, loose curls tumbled from the clip holding it in place. Reluctantly she met her own gaze, comparing what she saw with the way her heart ached. Her eyes seemed to be a perfect match to her mood; dark and blue.

She turned away and walked out the back door as a heartfelt sigh escaped her lips. Glancing toward the sunset spreading across the western sky, she thought to herself that Mother Nature was rather fanciful tonight. Only a western sky in evening would dare wear such bold slashes of orange, or such vivid shades of hot pink coupled with the dark, somber hue of deep purple.

But not even the glorious sunset could hold her attention. Not tonight. Rachel's gaze turned toward the forest beyond her backyard. The shade it was casting was already turning from blue to darker gray. Before long, it would be impossible to tell where the trees started and shadow ended.

Please let him come, she prayed. She stood with her hands folded in front of her like a penitent child, but there was a tense, expectant tilt to her stance.

The sunset came and went.

Out on the road beyond her house, she heard the gears of a pickup truck shifting as the driver started up the steep, winding blacktop. That wouldn't be Boone. He would come when she was least expecting it. She never asked why he chose to appear and disappear in such secrecy, because she was afraid of what he might say. She was falling in love with a man who couldn't give her a future, yet she was willing to accept what he *could* give. If love was all he had to offer, then she would take it.

She stood without moving until the chill wind that came up began to seep through her clothes. When her teeth began to chatter and her eyes began to tear, she told herself it was because of the wind and not from disappointment. With a tilt of her chin, she turned to enter the house.

Her hand was on the doorknob when the skin on the back of her neck began to crawl. Her heart missed a beat as she turned around. She walked off the porch and then farther, moving past the glow of the security light, then past the old rope swing dancing in the brisk night wind.

With nothing but instinct to guide her, she kept moving toward the forest with swift, certain strides. And then she saw him coming out of the trees in a long, easy lope.

Joy surged. She went from a walk to a run, and seconds later found herself in his arms, her feet dangling from the ground as he enfolded her within his embrace.

Laughter mixed with tears as she pressed cold welcoming kisses all over his face. He smelled of pine, and of soap and a musk-scented cologne that made her senses swirl.

"You're here! You're here! I was afraid you wouldn't come!"

Boone could think of nothing but the feel of her breasts against his chest, the tiny span of her waist as he'd lifted her up, and the gentle swell of her hips beneath the palms of his hands as he held her close. She was everything he'd ever wanted, and he was the last thing that should have happened to her.

If the good people of Razor Bend knew she was consorting with a man like him, her reputation would be on the rocks. He couldn't live without her, but the least he could do was keep his distance until dark.

"Darlin', wild horses couldn't have kept me away," he whispered, and feathered a kiss near the bottom of her ear, then laughed when she shuddered and moaned.

"Oh, Boone, Boone..." Her voice was soft, and her words were broken.

She met his kiss in the dark, felt his hands in her hair, and accepted the fact that he made her complete. Desperation tinged her every thought, her every motion, until she was shaking with need. With her heart in her eyes, she took him by the hand and led him toward the house.

Boone went willingly, stunned by the way she'd run into his arms. He didn't know a thing about what made her tick, but he knew how to detonate the woman in her. He wondered if she felt as off balance in the face of the passion that hung between them as he did. It scared him to think how much she meant to him, and with that thought came the knowledge that he might be putting her in danger simply by associating with her. His stride slowed, and as they neared the old swing, he stopped.

Puzzled, Rachel turned. "What's wrong?"

"Slow down, darlin'," he said softly. "We're moving too fast."

His meaning was all too clear, and she knew it had nothing to do with the speed of their walk.

The smile on her face dimmed, and Boone felt it go out like a light in the dark.

"Have mercy, Rachel. Don't look at me that way." He took her hand and led her to the swing. "I've got eight hours to get this right, okay?"

She smiled but didn't really mean it. She'd been so happy to see him. What if he didn't feel the same way? What if he'd come to tell her it was over?

"I'm so stupid," she muttered, and was starting to turn away when she heard him curse beneath his breath, then grab her by the hand. She had nowhere to look but at him.

"No! You're not stupid, but you're damn sure missing the point. I didn't say what I did to hurt you."

"Then why are you hesitating?" she asked, and hated the tremor in her voice. "Are you sorry for what we did last night? Because if you are, I can promise you I won't hold you to a—"

"Being with me could get you hurt."

She froze. Now it was out in the open. She could no longer ignore his life-style, because he'd thrown it in her face. Yet hearing it from his own lips couldn't change what she felt. She loved him.

She reached out, cupping the side of his face with the palm of her hand. A day-old growth of whiskers tickled her fingers as she traced the shape of his mouth. A muscle jerked at the side of his jaw as she brushed her thumb across his lower lip.

"Did you ever think of changing?" she whispered.

He groaned and dropped down to the swing, then pulled her onto his lap. Rachel tried to face him, but he stopped her, so she sat with her back to his front as he held her hard against him.

Boone buried his nose in her hair, inhaling the sweet, clean scent of Rachel's shampoo, as well as the woman herself. Dear God, what had he done? Part of him needed to tell her the truth...at least as much as he could.

"They say a nurse found me in a cardboard box on the doorstep of a hospital when I was less than a day old. It was snowing. I'd been wrapped in two army blankets, both old, both dirty. They also told me I was howling at the top of my lungs. When she took me inside and dug me out of the box, the only thing I had on was an adult-size T-shirt with a note pinned to it. There was a name. They had no way of knowing if it was my first name or my last, so the nurse improvised."

Rachel's heart began to break for the little boy he'd been and for the hurt she still heard in the man.

"Oh, Boone, I'm so sorry." She leaned against him, giving him her warmth and her strength.

He swallowed the knot in his throat and then hugged her tight. "I didn't tell you that for sympathy, but you've got to understand, I didn't grow up like you did. I didn't have any-

ne who gave a damn whether I lived or died...or cared if I
tayed in school, or whether I got in trouble. It's not an ex-
use...but it's an explanation. Right or wrong, that's who I
m."

"Surely you had friends while you were growing up?"

She felt him shrug.

"You don't make many friends when you're constantly be-
ng moved within the system."

The image of a little boy with big eyes and no smile hurt
er heart. Rachel slid from his lap and turned. "I'll be your
riend."

Before he could think to react, she'd run behind him as he
at in the swing.

"Rachel, wait," Boone said quickly, embarrassed, when
she started to push.

"Pick up your feet," she chided. "Good grief, a body
would think you'd never been in a swing before."

He did as he'd been told.

"Now hold on," she said, as his momentum began to build.
"You're going to love this. Once you get going real good, it
almost feels as if you could fly."

And there in the Kiamichis, on a dark September night,
they fell the rest of the way into love. Boone MacDonald had
taught Rachel Brant how to love; now she was teaching him
how to play.

For a while time stood still as she pushed and he sailed
high off the ground. The muted sounds of laughter drifted
into the quiet as the rope yielded to Boone's weight, squeak-
ing and rasping on the massive limb over which it was tied.
Leaves rustled overhead as he dipped and swayed, and somewhere in the middle of it all, Rachel quit pushing and stepped
back to watch.

There were tears in her eyes, but the delight on his face
was there to see. At that moment Rachel made herself a vow.
His childhood might not have been worth remembering, but
if he would let her, from this day forward she would give him
a life he would never forget.

"I love you, Boone."

Right in the middle of an arc leading up toward the sky, Boone heard her. When he came down, he bailed out and walked into her arms. All he could do was hold her tight and pray that what he'd done wouldn't ruin them both.

"Love? God, Rachel, do you know what you're saying?"

"Only what I feel."

He took her hand and held it over his heart. "Feel that?" he asked.

Her eyes widened as the thunder reverberated beneath her palm.

"Yes...oh, yes."

"I don't have the words to explain what you mean to me, but I can honestly say that I would lie down and die for you and not ask why."

Dakota's face began to drift between them.

Don't let them hang me. Don't let them hang me.

Rachel choked on a cry of dismay and threw her arms around Boone's neck.

"No, no," she muttered, and hid her face against his chest as she held on tight. "Don't ever say that! Never, ever say die!"

Something inside him began to ache. He'd never felt a pain such as this before, but he was pretty sure it was regret. Their whole relationship was built on a lie. What scared him most was wondering, if she learned the truth, would she still feel the same?

He smiled, then hugged her close.

"Come on, darlin', you feel cold. I think it's time we went inside."

Rachel shuddered. She was chilled, all right, but only on the inside, and from fear, not the cold.

Rachel lay on her side, watching Boone as he slept. A lock of hair had fallen over his forehead, giving him a little-boy look. But that was as far as it went. There was nothing child-ish about Boone MacDonald, including the way he made love.

he inhaled softly, and even in sleep, Boone seemed attuned
> her every move. He reached out, pulling her closer against
im, relaxing only when her head was beneath his chin and
er cheek pillowed on his chest. Rachel let herself be snug-
led. Tonight had been a long night of firsts.

Lesson number one: Real men *can* smell like lilacs and still
rive a woman out of her mind.

Just thinking of the bubble bath they'd shared made her
rin. Her bathtub was old and deep, but not nearly big enough
> accommodate a man with legs as long as Boone's, espe-
ially with Rachel sitting between them.

They'd made hats with the bubbles, fake smiles with the
ubbles, transparent bras with the bubbles, even large, bul-
ous noses with the bubbles, and they'd laughed so hard they
accidentally swallowed some bubbles. When the water got
:old and the bubbles began to go flat, there was nothing left
o hide the circumstance they were in. Wet, naked, and yearn-
ng to belong to each other, Boone drained the water out of
he tub and took her to bed with minuscule bubbles still cling-
ng to her skin.

"I'm all wet," she cried as he pulled back the bedspread
and laid her on the blue patchwork quilt beneath.

His smile was wicked, and his eyes were dark and dancing,
as he slid between her legs and into her body like a well-
oiled machine.

"That just makes it better," he whispered.

Rachel laughed. He'd deliberately misunderstood what she
meant, but she didn't care. This playful side of him was an
unexpected joy.

Lesson number two: Making love naked on patchwork
quilts is highly erotic. Making love on the floor is plain cold.

Now Boone slept while Rachel gazed her fill, and sometime
during her musing, her own eyes closed and she slept. And,
God help her, she started to dream.

* * *

"You promised you'd love me forever, but yc cheated...you lied. You never said forever would be over s fast."

Boone sat up in bed, wide awake and staring about in suc den confusion. He could have sworn he'd heard a woman voice.

Rachel twisted and turned beneath the covers, reaching ou to someone who wasn't there. But it wasn't her behavior tha made Boone start to shake. Rachel was talking, but in a di ferent voice. It was higher-pitched and had a different inflec tion.

"Oh, man," Boone muttered and reached out to her.

"No...don't go...don't go!" Rachel cried, and threw bac the covers, unintentionally shoving his hand aside as she di

Before Boone could think, Rachel was out of the room an running down the hall, moving through the darkened room as if they were swathed in full light. He reached for his jean and pulled them on in a panic, grabbing a blanket as he fo lowed her out of the house.

The front door was ajar. He stood on the porch, searchin the night to see which way she'd gone. Already out of rang of her security light, it was a flash of pale flesh in the distanc that caught his eye. She was heading for the forest. He bolte off the porch in a flat-out run. If he didn't reach her befor she got to the trees, he would lose her for sure.

Ignoring the pricking of the rough ground on his bare fee he ran as he'd never run before, catching up with her jus outside the boundary of the forest.

But when he tried to put the blanket over her chilled, nake body, she fought him like a woman possessed.

"Rachel, don't!" he begged.

When he was at the point of wrestling her to the ground Rachel suddenly stilled, and the blanket he'd just put on he slid off her shoulders, pooling around her bare feet. Boon stared as she dropped to her knees, then cried out and fe facedown upon the ground.

"Have mercy," he whispered, and picked her up. This time, she made no move to stop him.

Like a baby, he wrapped her in the blanket and started back toward the house with her limp body dangling from his arms. Though the price had been the trauma of seeing Rachel in such a state, he now had an explanation for the strange behavior he'd been witnessing.

Rachel wasn't dreaming. She was sleepwalking. Up until the moment she passed out, her eyes had been wide open. It seemed as though she was reliving some incident out of her past.

Unaware of what she'd done, Rachel was inside the house and tucked in bed before she began coming around. When she did, two things brought her rudely awake. The lights were on, and the shock in Boone's eyes was something she'd hoped never to see. It must have happened again...and he'd witnessed it! She covered her face with her hands.

Boone crawled into the bed beside her and pushed her hands aside.

"Don't hide from me, sweetheart," he said softly. "What happened to you?"

"I think you can answer that better than I can," she said, and then winced at the sound of her own voice. Her head was throbbing.

Boone's touch was gentle as he rubbed at the frown on her forehead. "Have you seen a doctor?"

"No."

This didn't make sense. She was trained in the medical field. Surely she wouldn't have a reluctance to trust a fellow professional.

"Why not?" he persisted.

Oh, Boone. How can I make you understand? "Because pills can't fix what's wrong with me."

Rachel's face was filled with despair. He ached to make her better, and he had never felt so lost. This couldn't be fixed with his fists or a gun, and he feared not even his love was strong enough to make this go away.

"Then what will?" he asked.

Rachel's eyes widened, and her chin began to quiver. "I don't know."

"God," he muttered, and lay down beside her, holding her close. "You scared me, Rachel."

"I know," she whispered. "I scare myself."

Neither of them slept again. About an hour before dawn, Boone got out of bed and began putting on his clothes.

"I wish you didn't have to go."

In the act of tucking his shirt into his jeans, he turned. There was a calm, watchful look on his face that she'd never seen before. "Maybe one day I won't," he said.

She sat up.

"But today's not the day."

She flopped back down on the pillow with a mutinous look in her eyes. "Will I see you tomorrow?"

He grinned slightly. "Honey girl, it's already tomorrow."

"You know what I meant," she muttered, as he started for the door.

He turned. "Don't wait up," he said. "I might be late."

Rachel jumped out of bed. Unmindful of her nudity, she raced for the bureau. "Here," she said, and tossed him a key.

He caught it in midair, then looked down. "What's this?" he asked, pointing to the red *B* she'd put on it.

"Fingernail polish. The *B* stands for *Back,* as in *Back Door.*"

He grinned and slipped it on his key ring. "Why, Rachel, I thought you were giving me the key to your heart."

She threw her arms around his neck. "I already did," she said softly. "Don't you remember?"

Lesson number three: There is nothing quite as sensual as being completely naked and being made love to by a fully dressed man.

Charlie Dutton and Ken Wade were coming down the mountain after an early-morning run to Latisha Belmon's home. It wasn't the first time they'd been called out to put her back in bed, and it very likely wouldn't be the last.

Latisha was seventy-two and nearly four hundred pounds, and the strength in her legs was just about gone. And her husband, Clyde, at seventy-four and weighing in at 128, was no match for her weight or her girth. When Latisha went down, Ken and Charlie went up...the mountain, that is.

Sharing a sack of doughnuts and finishing the last of his cold coffee, Charlie came around a corner in the ambulance, taking his half of the road out of the middle.

"Son of a—!" He dropped the coffee in his lap and grabbed the wheel with both hands, narrowly missing the pickup that was in the act of pulling out of the trees and onto the road.

"Oh, man!" Charlie muttered, swiping at his lap and glaring in his rearview mirror at the same time. "Look what he made me do!"

Ken was still choking on the doughnut he'd been trying to swallow when the near accident occurred.

"Well, now, Charlie, you were a little bit too far to the left, and we weren't running lights or siren, so he couldn't have known we'd be coming. Besides, I'd a whole lot rather have to change uniforms than go back and explain to the boss why we just wrecked the last ambulance in Razor Bend."

Charlie paled. "You're right," he muttered, then stared thoughtfully as they passed the cutoff that led to Rachel's house. "Still, I wonder what he was doing up in there."

Ken shrugged and dug in the sack for the last doughnut. "Oh, who knows. Probably hunting or something."

"More likely something," Charlie muttered, remembering where he'd seen that man before. It was the same man who'd hitched a ride into town with Rachel. His stomach turned as a thought skittered through his mind. He frowned. He didn't like what he was thinking one bit. At that moment, he made up his mind—first chance he got, he was going to stop by and visit Rachel. Just to say hello.

* * *

Boone was still white-knuckled from the near miss with the ambulance when he pulled into the yard at his trailer. Seeing Tommy Joe sprawled out on the front steps didn't do his disposition one bit of good. He got out with a scowl on his face.

"Hey, Boone," Tommy Joe said, as he pushed his bulk up from the steps. "I didn't think you was ever coming back. Where you been?"

"None of your damned business," Boone muttered, and pushed his way past Tommy Joe and into the trailer, leaving him to follow behind at his will.

Tommy Joe grinned. "You got a girl? I bet anything you got yourself a girl. I told Snake the other day, I think old Boone's got hisself a girl."

Boone turned around. All expression was gone. His eyes glittered angrily as he pushed a finger in Tommy Joe's chest.

"You and Snake stay out of my face, and I'll stay out of yours," he said softly.

Tommy Joe paled. "Hey, man, I didn't mean anything by it. I was just making small talk, you know."

"So you came for a *chat?*"

"No…no. I came to deliver a message. Denver wants all of us at his house tonight."

"What's up?"

"I don't know. I just follow orders, I don't give 'em."

Damn it, Boone thought. After what he'd witnessed last night, he didn't want to leave Rachel alone in a bed ever again. Now, here he was, faced with a choice between the job he'd been sent to do and being with the woman he'd come to love.

"I'll be there," Boone said, and looked at the door. "Don't let it hit you on the way out."

Tommy Joe scuttled out, leaving Boone alone with an ever-increasing sense of doom.

Chapter 12

Daylight had come and gone when Boone pulled into Denver Cherry's front yard.

"What took you so long?" Denver muttered as Boone walked in the door.

"You need to get your money back. The printer left the time off the engraved invitation," Boone drawled.

Denver grinned, revealing broken teeth through his brush of gray beard.

"You're a real wiseass, aren't you?" he asked, then chuckled. "Reminds me of myself in my younger days," he muttered, then scratched beneath his armpit as he pointed toward the kitchen. "Ribs and beer on the table, if you're hungry."

Boone frowned. "Not hungry. What's up?"

"No need to get in a huff," Denver said. "We're waiting on the boss to show."

Boone's heart went into overdrive, but, to his credit, he never blinked an eye.

"Maybe I'll get that beer after all," he muttered, and saun-

tered into the kitchen as if he didn't have a care in the world
when he really wanted to kick up his heels. *It's about time.*

Another football game was blasting from Denver's living
room, and from the sounds of it, Boone decided, Denver must
be raising the volume on every down. The noise was so loud
that when he opened the can of beer he never heard it pop
although it fizzed over the top and down the side of his hand.
A double order of barbecued ribs lay uncovered on the take-
out tray, while a couple of flies ate their fill. Boone looked
around the kitchen in disgust. He tossed the can of beer in
the sink, wiped his hands on his jeans and stalked out of the
kitchen just as Snake Martin walked into the house. He was
muddy and winded and looked as if he'd been running.

"What's wrong with you?" Denver asked.

Snake ran a shaky hand through his hair, then scratched at
his face where his beard began.

"Durn near had myself a wreck. Ran off in a ditch tryin'
to miss a deer."

Boone could almost sympathize. He'd come close to having
the same thing happen to him only days earlier.

"Well, you're here, and that's what counts," Denver said.

"I'm not here to stay," Snake said. "I need a jack." He
shuffled his feet, unable to look Boone in the face.

"What happened to mine?" Boone asked.

"Someone stole it," Snake muttered, then flushed as he
realized he'd finally admitted to the theft after all.

Boone grinned. "Well, well, what goes around comes
around."

"My jack won't work on your four-by-four," Denver said.
"Not big enough."

Snake cast a quick glance at Boone, who was grinning more
broadly by the minute.

"You're going to have to ask," Boone said.

"Can I borrow your jack?" Snake mumbled.

"I didn't hear you say 'please.'"

Snake was livid. "Damn it, Denver, make him—"

"Oh, shut up and do as he says," Denver grumbled. "You got yourself into this mess. Now get yourself out."

If Snake had had a gun, he would gladly have emptied it in Boone MacDonald's belly, but since he didn't, he saved the image of the act for another day.

"Please, Boone, can I borrow your jack?"

"How about 'pretty please with sugar on it'?"

Snake's face mottled in anger. "I'm gonna…"

Boone laughed, then took the keys from his pocket and tossed them to Snake, who caught them just before they hit the floor.

"Here. You know where it is, so help yourself. Bring back my keys when you bring back my jack, or I'll take it out of your miserable hide."

"Ain't someone gonna take me back to my truck?"

Denver took one look at Boone and knew that ordering him to go wouldn't work. Not this time.

"Wait for me outside," Denver said. "I gotta get my shoes."

Snake was still muttering as he walked out the door.

"You better not mess with him," Denver warned as he pulled on some sneakers, minus their strings. "If he gets mad at someone, he can be real mean."

Boone didn't blink. "I've seen mean before." Then he picked up Denver's remote and hit the mute button. "That's too damned loud," he said softly, and walked into the kitchen and out the back door as Denver went out the front.

A mile and a half down the road, Denver saw Snake's red-and-yellow four-by-four nose down in a shallow ditch. He pulled over, then let Snake out, aiming the lights so Snake could see to set the jack.

At that moment a car topped the hill, then began slowing down. Denver squinted against the oncoming glare, waving his arms to alert the driver not to run over them.

"Hey, look," Snake said. "It's the boss."

The big car came to a stop, and Denver called back Snake as the door began to open, "I know who it is. Now get on with what you're doing. The boss won't like having to wait on us."

Snake went to his knees. Setting the lug wrench in place he began loosening the bolts one at a time.

The man was nothing but a dark silhouette against the glare of his own headlights. "What's going on?"

Denver held out his hands, as if to say it was out of his control. It seemed the boss was in no mood to talk.

"Just get it over with and get on up to the house. I haven't got all night."

"You bet, boss. Be right there," Denver said. "I'll move my car so you can get by."

Snake suddenly remembered the borrowed keys in his pocket. While he wouldn't have admitted he was afraid of a thing, in truth, Boone MacDonald made him nervous. He saw Denver get in the car and panicked. He didn't want Boone coming after him alone in the dark.

"Uh... Hey, boss!" Snake yelled, and started running toward the long, shiny car. "Take these keys back to the house for me and tell him I'm not through with the jack." He dropped them in the boss's hand and hurried back to his truck.

The keys slid through the boss's fingers into the dust. Cursing, he leaned over to pick them up, then saw something he didn't want to believe. There, highlighted in the twin beams from his headlights and angling from the ring, was an oddly marked key. The letter *B* had been painted on it with red fingernail polish. He held it closer to the light, and as he did, shock began to seep throughout his system.

Son of a... It couldn't be! But it was, and it was marked just like the one on Rachel Brant's key ring. He'd seen her with it dozens of times in the past.

"Snake!"

The little man looked up from his work. "Yeah, boss?"

"Who do these keys belong to?"

"Boone MacDonald."

Rage struck him hard and fast. Unable to trust himself to speak, he clutched the keys until they left an imprint in the palm of his hand. He'd even seen Rachel and Boone together, and still he'd ignored the implications, choosing to believe the worst was all in his mind. But to know it had come to this! A cold smile broke across his face.

Now I know why the interest between us was never there. You little bitch, who would have thought your tastes ran so rough?

The importance of tonight's meeting had taken a back seat to revenge. Now he had another objective. One far more serious, far more deadly. Boone MacDonald was going to pay for messing with a woman out of his league. For that matter, Rachel needed to be taught a lesson, too. They wanted to be together? Fine. For all he cared, they could spend eternity in each other's arms.

"Denver!"

Denver came on the run. "Yes, boss?"

"I've changed my mind about tonight," he said.

"But I thought…"

"I said, I changed my mind." He slapped the keys in Denver's hand and drove off without another word of explanation.

"What set him off?" Snake muttered.

Denver shrugged, his mind locked on the football game playing on without him. "Who knows? Just hurry up, will you? I'm gonna miss the whole last half."

Last night had been the longest night of Rachel's life. She'd fallen asleep on the sofa waiting for Boone, waking up just before morning with cold feet and a crick in her neck. It was a far cry from lilac-scented bubble baths and a warm embrace.

In the back of her mind, she couldn't help thinking that her actions had scared him off. And in a way, she could hardly blame him. What man wanted to be saddled with a woman who went off half-cocked in the middle of the night, ranting and raving about something she couldn't explain?

Halfway through breakfast, Rachel made a decision. She couldn't spend the rest of her life hiding in a house in the Kiamichis, waiting for dark. What she needed was a little reorganization. She picked up the phone and punched in the numbers, hoping that her friendship with Joanie was still of good standing. She waited as the phone began to ring.

"Curlers."

Rachel grinned. From the abrupt manner in which Joanie answered the phone, she must have been be up to her elbows in shampoos and sets.

"Hi, Joanie, it's me. Got any free time today?"

"Rachel! I was going to call you when I had a minute. Are you wanting an appointment or a friend?"

Thank goodness Joanie didn't hold a grudge. "How about both?" she asked, and heard papers shuffling as Joanie leafed through her appointment book.

"Hmmm…Shirley Jo just called and canceled a perm, so I've got anywhere from eleven this morning until three this afternoon free. You name it."

"How about a manicure and then lunch?"

"Eleven okay?"

"Put me down," Rachel said. "We need to talk."

"It's a date," Joanie said. "See you later."

Rachel hung up, satisfied that she was moving in the right direction. Just because she'd fallen in love with a social outcast, that didn't mean she had to remove *herself* from society, as well.

"Red is a good color on you."

Rachel frowned as she held her forefinger up to the light, squinting to judge the shade of nail polish Joanie was applying. "You think so?" she asked.

Joanie grabbed her hand and yanked it back down to the table. "I *think* you don't care what color I put on, just as long as I listen." She shifted the gum she was chewing to the opposite side of her cheek, cracking and popping it as she went. "Well? What's the big scoop?" she asked, as she bent to her task.

"Joanie, have you ever been in love?"

Joanie's jaw went slack. Red fingernail polish dripped unattended on Rachel's thumb.

"Oh, shoot, look what you made me do!" she said, dabbing at the blob with polish remover.

Rachel sighed. She should have known this wasn't a good idea.

Joanie couldn't bring herself to look up, but she had to ask. "Rachel?"

"Hmm?"

"Is it that man who runs with Denver Cherry's men... Are you in love with him?"

There was no way Rachel could deny the fact and ever face herself in a mirror again, but she was afraid. Afraid of being rejected. Afraid of losing her very best friend.

"What would you say if I said yes?"

Joanie jerked. When she looked up, what she saw in Rachel's face frightened her. "I don't know, sugar...maybe a prayer?"

Rachel's eyes teared, and when Joanie saw her reaction, she groaned and set the polish aside.

"Honey...don't cry," she said softly. "Look, I don't pretend to understand why people fall in and out of love, but you and him...I don't get it. What on earth does he have that Griffin Ross didn't have, or, for that matter, Charlie Dutton? You know Charlie's got a big crush on you."

It took a moment for Rachel to find the words to explain, and even then, it was almost impossible to express how she felt. "It's not what he has, Joanie. It's what he gives me."

"Okay, so he's good in bed. I could tell that from looking at him." She rolled her eyes and then shivered. "Gawd... have you ever seen eyes like that on a man in your life? They just about look through you, don't they?"

"You don't understand. It isn't about sex. It's like... Oh, never mind." Rachel laid her hand down on the manicure table again. She should have known this would be a mistake. "Here, either take the stuff off or make me match. I can't go out of here with one hand done and the other bare."

Joanie sighed. It was obvious Rachel was hurt by her inability to understand. She dabbed the brush back in the polish, then paused.

"Look, sugar. If you love him, then there must be more to the man than good looks and a bad reputation, okay? All I'm saying is...be careful."

"Okay."

Moments passed, and just when Rachel thought the worst was over, Joanie started up all over again.

"Rachel, make me understand."

Rachel took a deep breath and then started naming reasons, as if she were reading from a list. "He makes me whole. He fills my heart. He makes me laugh."

"He'll make you cry."

Rachel frowned, then glanced up at the clock. "Are we nearly through? If we get to the café after twelve, the best tables will all be full."

Joanie wilted. "Sorry. I never did know when to keep my big mouth shut."

"That's okay," Rachel said. "Actually, you reacted just about like I thought you would."

"Then why did you tell me?" Joanie asked.

Rachel shrugged. "I don't know. Maybe I just wanted one person to know what was going on in my life, in case..."

Joanie paled. "In case of what?"

There was a strange look on Rachel's face as she spoke. "Just in case, that's all."

The subject was promptly dropped. A short time later, they entered the Adam's Rib Cafe just ahead of the noon-hour rush, and took a table toward the back, so that Joanie had a bird's-eye view of everything that went on.

"We're having the special," Joanie said, waving away the menus. "She's having iced tea. I'm having a cola with no ice and a slice of lemon."

Rachel grinned. Some things never changed.

Halfway into their meal, Rachel looked up in dismay. Griffin Ross was coming their way.

"Rats," she muttered.

Joanie glanced up, then back at Rachel. "Gee, honey, I'm orry. If we'd thought, we could have ordered this to go and ated it back at the shop."

"It's too late now," Rachel said. "The vulture's descending."

"Rachel! Darling! Long time no see!" Griff cried, and, without waiting to be asked, seated himself at their table. 'You don't mind, do you? It's a little crowded in here, and 've got to eat and run."

There was little they could do but acquiesce with as much grace as possible.

"This is a bit of good fortune," Griff said, as the waitress hurried away with his order. He thrust his hand inside his suit coat. "I just picked these up at the drugstore. You and Joanie made quite a splash at the Labor Day picnic, remember?"

He handed over a packet of newly developed pictures, which Joanie began sifting through in delight. In no time at all they were grinning and laughing as they relived the memories of the day, the three-legged race, the marshmallow roll, and the sack race that had resulted in both Rachel and Joanie falling into the duck pond at the park. Even Rachel had to admit it had been a good day. Griff had been full of fun, and a very good sport.

The café was doing such a brisk business that Rachel never noticed when Boone walked in, pausing near the door. She never saw the shock, then the disbelief, spreading over his face, and even if she had, she would have been hard-pressed to find a way to explain without making a scene.

Without saying a word, Boone spun and walked back out the door the same way he'd come in—hungry and alone. He was still discouraged by the cancellation of last night's meeting with the boss, and this only added to the frustration he was feeling.

Just for a while he'd been convinced his time as Boone MacDonald was nearly over. Then Denver had come wad-

dling into the house with Snake right behind him. All he'
gotten out of the night were his keys back and his jack intac

He glanced at the café, then headed for his truck. *Th*
doesn't have to mean a thing, Boone kept reminding himsel.
The room was full. They were just sharing a table. But eve
though he thought it, he couldn't force himself to believe i
Betrayal was a hard image to lose.

Later that same day, Rachel was on her way home when
on impulse, she wheeled into the parking lot outside EM:
headquarters. Ken Wade was in knee-high fireman's boots
with a hose in one hand and a soapy cloth in the other as h
washed down the ambulance. He grinned and waved as sh
started up the sidewalk.

"Hey there!" he called. "Coming back to get your nam
in the pot?"

"Not yet," Rachel said. "But soon."

He grimaced. "Not soon enough for Charlie. He thinks you
can do no wrong."

"And I suppose you can do no right?"

He laughed. "You said it."

"Sorry," Rachel said. "I didn't take him to raise. He was
like this when we met, remember?"

In playful retaliation, Ken waved the spray of water in her
direction. Not too close, but close enough to send her scur-
rying inside.

Because she was looking over her shoulder as she went,
she ran full tilt into Charlie. Her purse went flying, spilling
its contents all over the floor and under a chair near the door.

"Whoa!" Charlie said, laughter filling his voice. "I always
knew you couldn't stay away from me, but you didn't have
to run. I would have come if you'd called."

"Good grief," Rachel muttered as she went down on all
fours, grabbing at a lipstick, then a pen, then her wallet.

Charlie bent to help. "What was the big rush?" he asked,
as he handed her a comb.

"I was about to get hosed down."

Charlie grinned. "Yeah, Ken's mean with that soap and
ater."

"My keys...I can't find my keys," Rachel muttered as she
oked around on the floor.

They both began to search. Seconds later, Charlie spied
em beneath the front bumper of the spare ambulance, parked
side the station.

"There they are," he said. Before he handed them back,
e fingered through them in a nosy but friendly sort of way.
hen he looked up, he was grinning. "Hey, Rachel, let me
e the bottoms of your shoes."

She did as he asked without thinking why, assuming that
e must have walked in grease or the like without noticing.

"No," Charlie muttered. "I guess I was wrong."

"About what?"

"Well, you mark your keys to tell which goes to the front
oor and which goes to the back. Thought you might have
our shoes marked, as well. You know...one for the left and
e for the right."

The grin on his face was too broad to resist. She laughed.
"You worm. Give me my keys."

"It's gonna cost you," he teased, dangling them over her
ead.

"Like what?"

An odd expression spread over his face. "Like a kiss?"

Suddenly the fun had gone out of the game. Rachel froze,
nable to find a way out of the embarrassment she was feel-
ng. Charlie was her friend. He was her peer. But he would
ever be anything more.

"Oh, good grief," Charlie said, and dropped the keys in
er hand. "I was just kidding."

"I knew that," Rachel muttered, and put the keys into her
urse, along with everything else they'd retrieved.

"So, if you didn't come for a little loving, what's up?
Please tell me you're coming back to work."

She shook her head. "Not just yet, Charlie...but soon."

He rolled his eyes in an overdramatic gesture of defeat.
will not survive Ken Wade.''

"That's funny. He says the same thing about you.''

To his credit, Charlie grinned, and Rachel began to rela
The worst was over.

"I see they got the ambulance fixed.''

"Yep.''

Rachel eyed Charlie, trying to figure out what was so di
ferent about him. Suddenly, she knew.

"Your hair!''

Charlie flushed beet red and swiped his hand across th
back of his neck.

"What's wrong with my hair?'' he muttered.

"Odie Waters didn't cut your hair. It's been styled.''

He thrust his chin out in a righteous show of defense. "Sc
Lots of guys do that.''

"I know.... I didn't mean it didn't look good. What I mear
was…it looks *good*. You know Odie. He's a dear, but he'
been cutting hair the same way since the forties.''

Charlie didn't answer, and his reticence made Rachel re
member other changes in Charlie that had recently take
place.

"I wonder what will be next,'' she said, and poked him i
the arm, trying to tease him out of his mood. "New car..
fancy ring. New hairstyle. The next thing we know, Razo
Bend will be too small for you.''

"Well, a man's got to look to his future,'' Charlie said. "'
might actually want to settle down one day. Can't do it o
this salary alone, that's for sure.''

It was the word *alone* that worried her. What else wa:
Charlie doing to allow him such a major change in life-style'
But as soon as she thought it, she let the thought go. Who
was she to tell anyone what to do with his life? Hers was in
chaos.

"Whatever you're doing, it must be right,'' Rachel said.

Charlie grinned, although a bit of guilt had started to rise
within him. It *was* right, he thought. And it was no one else':

usiness what he did with his money...no matter how he'd ome by it.

"Well, I just came to say hi," Rachel said. "I'd better get ut of here before the boss snags me and makes me feel guilty ll over again."

"I'll walk you to the door," Charlie said.

"How about walking me past the madman of the car wash, nstead?"

"Deal."

Together they walked to her car. As she was getting inside, Charlie leaned down.

"Hey, Rachel, if you ever want to talk about anything— nything at all—I'm your man. I don't gossip. I don't judge. And I don't lie."

A wave of fear washed over Rachel, leaving her face hocked and pale. She didn't know how or why, but for some eason, she suspected he knew about Boone.

"Why...thank you, Charlie." It was all she could think of o say.

She looked up in her rearview mirror as she drove away. Charlie was standing right where she'd left him, watching her ;o.

Chapter 13

"He'll come tonight."

Rachel figured if she said it often enough, it would happen. But it was nearing sundown, and the time for hoping would soon be past. One thing had become clear to her after talking to Joanie. If she didn't trust her feelings for Boone, no one else would, and she'd come too far in accepting this relationship to quit on him at the first hint of trouble.

She walked out on the porch and sat down on the steps to begin her wait. But to her dismay, she realized that a thunderstorm was brewing. Heavy clouds were building in the southwest. And although the storm was too far away for her to hear thunder, the intermittent lightning strikes could be seen silhouetted against the navy blue sky above the Kiamichi peaks.

Shivering, she pulled her knees up to her chin. The wind began to quicken as she looked toward the forest beyond her back yard.

"Oh, Boone, hurry, please hurry!"

And as she waited, darkness swept over the land, lending a ominous quality to the oncoming storm.

Driven inside sometime later by blowing rain, Rachel fially gave up hope that Boone would come tonight. She sat a her living room with the television on, watching weather ulletins as they crawled across the bottom of the screen.

Half dozing in her chair, she was suddenly awakened by a ud clap of thunder that rocked the house on its foundation, ollowed by a bolt of lightning so close and so bright that she eard the crack as it hit. She hit the mute button on the TV nd ran for the door.

All she had time to see was the gust of blowing rain as it it her in the face. She ducked her head in reflex, and when he turned around, Boone was standing at the edge of the orch.

Startled more by his sudden appearance than by the man imself, she screamed. He ran toward her just as the second ust came, grabbing her close and propelling her backward nto the house, out of the storm.

The door slammed shut behind them, and the silence of the oom was overwhelming as Rachel looked up.

"You came!" she said, and threw her arms around his neck n a joyful welcome.

Boone told himself she wouldn't play games with him, but he couldn't forget how she she'd laughed and talked to Griffin Ross as if there had never been a break in their relationship.

Rachel caressed the side of his cheek, feeling the rough growth of a two-day beard and remembering how it felt on her skin.

"You didn't come last night. I didn't think you would come tonight, either."

Boone lifted his head, as if bracing himself for a blow.

Was that why you went back to Griffin Ross? Did a couple of nights in the sack with an outlaw satisfy your sense of adventure?

Rachel began to worry. He looked so lost and so hurt, and she didn't understand why. His hand was at the back of her

head, as if cushioning it from an unseen blow, but he seeme
locked in some silent war with himself that she didn't unde
stand.

"Boone, if there's something you want to talk about, a
you—"

He interrupted before she could finish. He seemed angr
and at the same time despairing. "I love you so damned muc
it scares me to death."

"Oh, Boone…"

He unsnapped his jacket and dropped it on the floor by th
door. It fell with a sodden squish.

"My truck is parked on the far side of your house. If yo
don't want anyone to know I'm here, say so now and I'ı
gone."

Rachel didn't know why there was so much anger in th
love he'd just professed, but she wasn't about to let him leav
until he'd told her what was wrong. She pushed past him t
the door, turned the lock and turned out the light. Except fo
the mute and flickering television, the house was now in dark
ness. She turned and faced him.

"Something is wrong, so don't insult my intelligence b
lying. Besides, if I had my way, you'd never leave me again.'

Boone came toward her, then quietly enfolded her withiı
his embrace.

"God help us both, Rachel Brant, because I don't have th
good sense to let you go."

*Dakota's hands dug into Mercy's shoulders with painfu
intensity.*

*"Come away with me, Mercy. Come with me now, before
it's too late."*

Rachel shuddered, clutching at Boone's shirt in sudden desperation. Why did this keep happening to her? Was it some
kind of warning? Was the past about to repeat itself in more
ways than one? Fear gripped her as she tried to imagine her
life without this man in it. She couldn't. Not anymore. She
fisted her hands in the front of his shirt, feeling the cold, damp
fabric give way to her demand.

''You can make the world go away. Make love to me, Boone. Do it now.''

Passion shattered the last of his control. Right now he didn't care if she'd cheated and he wouldn't accept that she'd lied. She belonged to him in a way she would never understand. He couldn't give her assurances or promises of a happy-ever-after kind of life. All he could give her was love.

He lowered his head. She met him. His mouth was cold, the demand in his kiss almost frightening until she heard a soft, muffled groan.

With desperation in every movement, he shoved their clothing aside and himself inside her. With no promise of heaven other than the look in his eyes, he pinned her between the door and his heart and drove them both crazy with love.

Light flickered on the opposite wall as the television continued to play with no sound. Every now and then lightning shattered the darkness outside, just as Boone was shattering the last of Rachel's control.

The force with which he took her was gentled by each touch of his hand on her body, his lips on her face and his sharp, ragged breaths on her cheek. Rachel had long ago lost contact with reality. Boone was her anchor, her center of gravity. As long as his arms were holding her in place, she couldn't fall off the world.

In the midst of too much pleasure, it all came undone. One minute Rachel was living for the next thrust of his body, and then heat spilled within her, leaving her weak and limp and hanging on to his shoulders to keep from falling. But each breath Boone was taking was longer and deeper than the last. She could tell the end was near for him, as well.

''God, Rachel... Oh, God...'' His voice was less than a whisper, more like a prayer.

Rachel buried her face against the curve of his neck and felt him tremble. There was little she could do to help the inevitable, other than bring him closer. With her last ounce of strength, she wrapped her legs around his waist and held on for dear life.

A short while later, when Boone could remember to think and breathe at the same time, he sank to the floor on his knees, with Rachel still in his arms. At a loss for anything to say that wouldn't give himself away, Boone held her close, showing her in the only way he could that she was loved.

Rachel rubbed her face gingerly against his whisker-rough cheek, then leaned forward, tenderly kissing a small scar she felt on his chin.

"What was that for?" Boone whispered.

"The boo-boo I suspect no one kissed."

Remembering the knife and the man who'd put the scar there, he tried to grin, but it just wouldn't come.

"I wish to hell I'd met you years ago," Boone growled.

Oh, but, my darling, you did. Rachel traced the scar with the tip of her finger and smiled.

"It's never too late for love," she said.

"You'd better be right," he said, as he rolled, pinning her beneath him on the floor.

She grinned. "First thing you should learn about loving a woman. When it counts, we're always right."

"Did you leave any bubble bath for me?" Boone asked.

"You liked that? My, my, have I created a monster? I don't believe I've ever known a lilac-scented, bubble-blowing monster before."

This time, Boone found his grin. It was right behind the tears in his eyes.

"So sue me," he said. "Thanks to you, I'm weak as a kitten and cold as a frog. Right now, I'll take smelling like a lilac bush over these wet clothes any day."

Once again, they left a trail of clothing from the front door to the back of the house.

It was getting to be a habit.

The storm had passed. The air smelled fresh, and the bushes beneath the glow of the security light glistened as if they'd been dressed in white diamonds.

Somewhere in another part of the house, her clothes dryer

rumbled as Boone's clothing tossed within the drum. Rachel stood at the window overlooking the back yard, listening to the runoff from the rain flowing downward toward the trees. Ultimately, she knew, it would wind up in the small creek far below her house. The one where she and Boone had first met.

"Come to bed, Rachel. You're going to freeze."

She turned. Boone lay sprawled upon her bed. Although there was a sheet covering the lower half of his body, the thin covering did little to hide the length of his legs or his underlying strength.

She bit her lip, hesitant to speak of what she was thinking.

"I love the way things look after a rain. Everything is fresh and clean and shining. It always makes me think of new beginnings."

She clasped her hands beneath her chin, then let them drop to her sides, and Boone could tell by the way she was standing that she hadn't said what she wanted to say.

"What are you thinking, honey?"

Her voice was soft and full of hope. "Of new beginnings."

He stifled a groan. God help him, no one would like that more than he would.

"Come here," he said gruffly. Rachel came without hesitation.

"Do you believe me when I say I love you more than my own life?" he asked.

Rachel's throat began to close. She couldn't discuss this with him without feeling an odd sort of panic. She kept thinking of the old newspaper clipping she'd found in South Dakota. The one claiming a woman named Mercy Hollister had been responsible for an outlaw's death.

"Well, do you?" Boone asked.

She nodded.

"Okay, then listen, and try to read between the lines. I wish to God I could tell you what's going on in my life, but I can't...at least, not right now."

"That's okay," she said softly.

"No, it's not okay," Boone retorted. "In fact, it's a great

big mess. But if I promise you it will get better, will you wait for me?''

Her heart soared. It was the first hint of anything between them resembling a future.

''I've been waiting forever,'' she said. ''A few more lifetimes won't make that much difference.''

He laughed softly and held her close. But Rachel couldn't find much humor in what she'd said. What frightened her most was being pretty sure they'd already messed up once. She didn't want to think about going through all this turmoil only to find they'd failed again to get it right.

Just before daylight, she helped him dress. His clothes were still warm from the dryer.

''I could get used to this,'' Boone said, as Rachel handed him his shirt. He put it on, then absently tucked it into the waistband of his Levi's before sitting down on the bed to pull on his boots.

''So could I,'' Rachel said, combing her fingers through his thick black hair.

''So what are you going to do today?'' Boone asked.

Rachel plopped down on the bed. ''I don't know. I've thought about going back to work. I feel so useless just sitting up here waiting to run amok.''

He frowned. ''I know some people in Oklahoma City,'' he said, and then added, before she could bring up the fact, ''They aren't anything like Snake and Tommy Joe, trust me.''

She looked away, hating that he'd brought the reality of his life into their own little world.

He was already saying more about himself than he should, but he couldn't stop talking.

''I could ask around. Find out if they know a good shrink.'' It was obvious from the way she was behaving that she didn't want to hear what he was saying. ''Please, honey…there's got to be a reason why this is happening to you. I just want you well. It scares the hell out of me when I think how close you've come to real danger.''

"Do you think it doesn't scare me, too?" she said, and tried to pull away.

He pulled her onto his lap, kissing the side of her cheek and her chin until she was forced to look at him.

"We've never talked about life before *us,* have we?" he asked.

She shook her head. There wasn't much to tell about hers, and she'd been afraid to ask about his.

"Rachel…"

She wouldn't answer. He sighed. This was getting them nowhere, and it was almost daylight. Although her house was far enough from the road to hide his car, he didn't want to push his luck. He had to be out of here before sunrise.

"Never mind," he said softly. "Just remember, anything broken can always be fixed."

She threw her arms around his neck and then clung to him in fear. "No, Boone, you're wrong. Remember what I do for a living?"

He knew what was coming.

"I've seen too many broken bodies and too many broken homes. Sometimes life just isn't fair."

He held her tight and closed his eyes. If he didn't think about losing her, then maybe it wouldn't happen. Moments later, he looked up and out the window. The thick brew of night was swiftly diluting.

"Rachel, sweetheart, I've got to go."

"I know," she said, and lifted her lips for one last kiss.

It came, and with it all the reluctance Boone was feeling. He tore himself away with a groan, then headed for the door. Yet in spite of the urgency, something kept pulling at him, warning him…. *If you leave, you may never come back.* He turned, wanting to remember her all soft from sleep, wearing a well-loved smile and little else.

He got what he wanted.

"If you love me…trust me," he said.

Rachel never saw him go. The last thing she heard was his plea, and then the air began to thicken and the light began to shift, breaking into refractions and angles that didn't make sense. She groaned and clutched the bed for support as Dakota turned and looked at Mercy from the doorway of a dusty cabin.

He tossed a rifle toward her as she sat on the bed. "If you love me like you say you do…then don't let me hang."

Mercy caught the gun in midair, then screamed out his name. It was too late. He was already gone.

Rachel came too with a groan, then looked around for Boone. He was nowhere in sight.

"Dear God, dear God," she muttered, and jumped to her feet.

The coincidence between Boone's parting and what she'd just seen was too much to bear. She ran through the house, calling his name. When he didn't answer, she ran out of the house, onto the porch. The taillights of his pickup truck were just disappearing around the bend in the drive.

She dashed into the yard, waving frantically at him. "Boone! Wait! Come back! Come back!"

It was too late. He was already gone.

Water dripped from the leaves and down onto the man's hooded coat. He hunched his shoulders against the cold and took a step backward, although he was well hidden behind the trees in which he stood. His purpose: watching the driveway leading to Rachel Brant's home.

Driven by a jealousy he could no longer contain, he'd followed Boone MacDonald out of town, then all the way up the mountain, taking care to stay at least a quarter of a mile behind him. But when the taillights of Boone's pickup suddenly disappeared, it meant either the driver had parked to wait out the storm, or he was taking shelter elsewhere in a lying woman's arms. To his dismay, when he topped the hill where he'd last seen the truck, it was nowhere in sight.

Now, as he shifted from one leg to the other, tired of the cold and of the hatred eating at him from inside, he waited to see if he'd been right all along.

The sun was minutes from the horizon when a dark blue pickup suddenly appeared at the end of the drive, the driver momentarily pausing to check the main road. Even from where he was standing, he could see the driver's face. Rage rattled the edge in his voice as he watched Boone MacDonald turn up the mountain and drive out of sight.

"I'll kill them both," he muttered. "So help me God, I will kill them both."

Boone paced the trailer with nervous intent. He'd been in this business too long not to trust his own instincts, and they were warning him that something was going to happen. He could feel it. But he was ready. He wanted this job to be over. What worried him was Rachel. If Denver's boys found out about her, he shuddered to think what they might do, especially after he'd called Snake down for making a pass at her. The little weasel was still holding a grudge. And because he knew better than to ignore his own intuition, he picked up the phone. It was time to confess—at least up to a point—about what he had done.

"This is Waco. Is this you?"

"It's me, Captain. I don't have much time."

Susan Cross shoved aside the file on which she'd been working, giving Boone her full attention. "What's up?"

"I need you to do something for me," he said quickly.

"Name it."

"There's a woman. Her name is Rachel Brant."

A soft curse slipped into the one-sided conversation, settling on Boone's nerves like a slap.

"Just listen," he muttered. "You can give me hell later."

"I'm listening," she said.

"If anything should happen to me, I want your promise that you'll make sure she's protected in any way necessary."

"Boone, what the hell have you done?"

"Fallen in love."

"Dear God," Susan said, and rubbed at a pain shooting up the back of her neck. "Does she know anything?"

"No, she loves Boone. She doesn't know I exist."

"Do you know what you've done?"

"Yes, ma'am," Boone said sharply. "Why the hell do you think I called you?"

Susan sighed. "To fix another one of your messes, I assume."

"I knew there was a reason I loved you," he said softly.

"Oh shut up," Susan said. "I'm immune to your charm."

"You love me and you know it," Boone said.

"I want your ass back here at headquarters in the morning, or I'll know the reason why," she ordered.

He sighed. It was to be expected. "I'll see what I can do," he said.

"No! You do what *I* said," Susan said.

The click at the other end of the line did not make her happy. She swiveled around in her chair and picked up her other phone.

"Bennet, get Wayland in here on the double, and tell him to pack a bag. He might be staying a while."

Susan Cross's angry voice was still ringing in Boone's ear as he walked into Jimmy's Place. The place was crawling with customers. It seemed as if every other citizen of Razor Bend had come to town all at once, and half of them were gathering here.

"What's going on?" Boone asked, as a man hurried by.

"Jimmy's having a drawing. Every hour, on the hour. You have to be present to win."

Boone looked around the room, absently fiddling with his key ring as he realized the impact of what was taking place. Jimmy was a smart man. If people had to wait to win a prize, they spent money while they waited. Candy and chips were flying off the shelves, and the door to the cooler was banging on a regular basis as customers reached for cans and bottles of pop to wash it all down. The air was thick with smoke from burgers cooking on the grill, and people were laughing d talking among themselves as they waited for the hour to me around.

Boone frowned. From the looks of things, it was going to e longer than he'd expected to buy a couple of quarts of otor oil, but it didn't really matter. His days were all the me. He felt as if he were caught in the middle of a long, rk tunnel and all he could do was wait for a light to appear d show him the way out.

He took a step back and knew it was a mistake by the body--body impact he made with the man behind him. The ring keys slipped out of his hands, hitting the floor with a loud, stinct clink.

Boone reached down at the same time as the man he had mped.

"Sorry, buddy," Charlie Dutton said, as he picked up the ys. "It's pretty crowded in…"

The keys were splayed, and one in particular stood out from e rest. It was shiny and new and marked with the letter *B* red fingernail polish. The implication of that key on this ng stunned him, and the urge to put his fist in the big man's ce was overwhelming.

I only gave him a ride, not the key to my house.

Rachel's words rang in Charlie's ears like a death knell. *ly God, girl, what have you done?*

Boone straightened, his fists doubled, readying himself for e blow he sensed was coming. Instead, Charlie took a deep reath, then dropped the keys in Boone's hand.

Time seemed to stop. Eye-to-eye, they stood without mov-ig, gauging each other's intent. Charlie was the first to speak. Ie pointed to the keys he'd just handed Boone.

"A man needs to be real careful about his keys."

Boone looked down at the ring in the palm of his hand. here, shining out from the others, was a small gold key with bright red *B*. His heart stopped.

Rachel.

He looked at Charlie again. An intense stare passed be-

tween them again, and this time it was Boone who broke t
silence.

"You don't need to worry," he said quietly. "I'm re
careful about all my things."

Charlie wanted to hate him, but there was something abc
the look in Boone MacDonald's eyes that led him down a
other emotional path. "You take care now," Charlie said, a
moved away through the crowd.

When the man was gone, Boone started to shake. He did
have to wonder what that was all about. It had been obvio
from the start. Rachel had worked with that man. He kne
her habits, and he'd obviously seen her mark keys like th
before. And with that knowledge came another thought, eve
worse than what had just occurred. Charlie Dutton wasn't t
only one who might have noticed the marked key. Witho
giving it a second thought, he'd handed his keys over to Sna
Martin as if he were handing him a match.

What in hell have I done?

A middle-aged couple barreled past him, laughing and wa
ing to a man on the other side of the room. Boone steppe
aside to let them pass, and as he did, he felt a touch on th
back of his hand. It was little more than a brush of fles
against flesh, but it was enough to get his attention. He looke
down. His heartbeat jerked, then kicked back in at an irregula
pace. He knew that face, those curls, those beseeching blu
eyes.

He squatted down until he was level with her gaze.

"Well, hello, Punkin," he said softly and held out on
hand.

She ducked her head, then looked back again, this tim
wearing a smile.

"Already learning to flirt, are you?" he asked.

Although his meaning was lost on her, she giggled, please
to have been noticed.

Boone wondered if she could possibly remember him, an
then decided she couldn't. All that smoke and steam, and the
hanging upside down, it was a wonder she'd remembered he

n name. He searched her face for remnants of the wreck.
e bruises were gone, as were the scratches and cuts. The
ly visible sign of what she'd endured was a small red mark
ar her temple. The scar would fade with time, as would her
s.

He winked and started to tousle her curls. But Punkin had
her ideas. She grabbed his finger, just as she had the day of
e wreck. Her grip was firm, her jaw determined.

"Boo," she said clearly.

"So, pretty baby, you do remember me."

"Melissa Ann, you leave that man alone!"

Boone jerked as if he'd been slapped as the little girl was
ddenly yanked away. The middle-aged woman staring down
him wore a fearful expression on her face. He couldn't
ame her. Boone MacDonald wasn't the kind of man to trust
ith any woman, no matter their age. He stood.

"I'm sorry, ma'am. I wasn't…" he began, but Charlie Dut-
n suddenly appeared once again at his side.

"Hey, Esther, how are things going? I see you and Boone
e finally getting to meet."

Esther Worlie looked puzzled. Losing her son-in-law had
en shock enough, and her daughter was just now able to
ove about on her own. When she turned around in the crowd
d realized the baby was nowhere in sight, her heart had
opped. Seeing Melissa with this man had set off a new kind
f panic.

When Boone would have walked off into the crowd without
xplaining himself, Charlie halted his exit with an unexpected
troduction.

"Esther, this is the man who witnessed Paul and Sally's
reck. He called it in and stayed with them until we got
ere." An odd look passed between Charlie and Boone, as
neither of them could believe they were still talking to each
ther. "Boone MacDonald, isn't it?" Charlie asked.

Wordlessly Boone nodded.

Esther Worlie looked back at Boone, seeing him in a whole
ther light. A dark red flush spread over her face.

"Why…I had no idea," she muttered, then looked dov
at her granddaughter, who was cowering behind her le
"Come here, Melissa, it's all right." When the child did
budge, she bent down and picked her up. "I guess I scar
her," she said. "It doesn't take much these days to set h
off."

Boone hurt for the fear on the little girl's face. "I'm ve
sorry for your loss," he said softly. "I hope Punkin's moth
is doing all right."

Esther looked even more surprised by Boone's use of h
granddaughter's nickname than by his concern for her daug
ter's well-being.

"Why, yes, she is…thank you."

Boone needed to get away. This conversation was becon
ing dangerous. It was too congenial—too ordinary—for a m;
like him to be having.

"I guess I'll get my motor oil another day," he said quietl
and started to walk away when Esther Worlie stopped him.

"Mr. MacDonald?"

"Yes, ma'am?"

"You called my granddaughter Punkin."

He frowned. "Yes, ma'am."

"That was what Paul called her. No one else in the famil
ever calls her that." She looked at her granddaughter agaii
hesitant about how much to say in front of the child. "Ho
did you know?" she asked. "I mean…Paul was already…"

Suddenly Boone understood. Her daughter had been ur
conscious. Her son-in-law dead. Who'd told him?

Boone ran his hand over the top of the little girl's head
gently tousling the abundant and unruly curls.

"I asked this pretty thing her name…and she told m
didn't you, Punkin?"

Esther Worlie's face fell. Her eyes teared, and her lips be
gan to tremble. "She told you her name was Punkin?"

Boone nodded. "Yes, ma'am, she did. I guess the wrecl
cost her more than a daddy, didn't it? If no one ever calls he
Punkin anymore, then she lost her identity, as well."

Esther Worlie had a lot to consider as she walked away
ith her grandchild in her arms.

Boone watched until they disappeared in the crowd, then
rned to Charlie, who'd remained a silent bystander during
e odd conversation. Boone's eyes narrowed as he studied
e intent expression on the man's face.

"I owe you," Boone said.

Charlie shrugged. "One of these days I'll collect."

There was too much tension between them for Boone to
ay any longer. "I'm out of here," he said, and walked away.

Chapter 14

Although Boone was nowhere in sight, Agent B. J. Waylan wasn't bashful. He wasted no time in checking his old friend messages. He'd been sent to find him and bring him out, an that wouldn't happen unless he knew where he'd gone.

A cockroach scuttled across the floor beside his tennis sho as he considered his options. He stepped on the bug and re played the message.

"Boone, Denver says come on over around eight. He's g someone he wants you to meet."

B.J. checked his watch and frowned. It was five minute until eight. Having been briefed on the situation, he knew a about Denver Cherry, as well as his cohorts. He took a ce phone out of his jacket pocket and made a call.

"Captain, he's not here, but there's a message on his ma chine that leads me to think something's about to go down Didn't you tell me he's never met the man behind th scenes?"

"That's right," Susan Cross said.

"I think he's about to," B.J. said.

"Do you know where?"

"Denver Cherry's…I think."

"You have the location," Susan said. "Get over there now. From the way Boone was talking earlier today, I think he expects trouble."

Wayland grinned, "Want me to go in shooting or wait for someone else to fire the first shot?"

Susan rolled her eyes. "You hotshots are all alike. You know the routine. I'm sending down backup…just in case. They'll have your number. You coordinate."

"All right," Wayland said.

"And, Wayland…"

"Yes, Captain?"

"Just get him out of there alive, okay?"

Wayland's smile turned cold. "Yes, ma'am…I'll do my best."

Boone's nerves were on edge. When he pulled up in front of Denver Cherry's house, he noticed Denver's vehicle was missing. Snake and Tommy Joe came out of the house as he parked and got out, and with every step he took, his gut instinct was to duck and run. This didn't feel right.

"Where's Denver?" he asked.

As always, Tommy Joe deferred to Snake, letting him answer.

"At the lab," Snake said, and then glanced at his watch.

Boone's hopes fell. Not only had he never met the boss, he'd been unable to find the new location of the lab. "Then the meeting is off?"

"Nope," Snake said. "You're coming with us. The boss is already there."

Boone felt torn. This was what he'd been waiting for, but it wasn't the way he'd wanted it to happen. "I'll follow you," he said, and started toward his truck.

"No way," Snake said. "We can't have no damned parac on the way up. You go with us. Boss's orders."

Tommy Joe was as nervous as Boone had ever seen him That alone gave Boone food for thought. While Boone was pretending disinterest in the entire affair, in reality his min was in overdrive. Something was up besides a meeting, an as he slid onto the seat between Snake and Tommy Joe, h had a sudden sense of his own mortality. As they drove away the last thought in his mind was of Rachel. He'd never gotte to tell her goodbye.

The narrow blacktop highway up this side of the Kiamichi was unmarked and unlit. At night, unless you were familia with its twists and turns, it could be deadly. Snake drove with his usual disregard for oncoming traffic and the laws of grav ity, while Boone took comfort in the small loaded handgu concealed inside the top of his boot.

The radio was blaring a sad country song with which Snak felt compelled to sing along. Tommy Joe rode with his lef elbow in Boone's ribs and his other one hanging out the ope window. The wind whipped through the cab, drowning ou the worst of Snake's voice and easing the stench of swea from the two men's unwashed bodies. Boone never took hi eyes from Snake's hands. Of the two men, he trusted him th least. It was his first mistake.

Snake slammed on his brakes without warning and shot of the road to the right, barreling down the driveway leading to Rachel Brant's house before Boone had time to react.

"What the hell are you—?"

The familiar feel of a gun in his ribs ended his question He looked at Tommy Joe with surprise.

"Sorry," Tommy Joe said. "Just following orders."

Snake hit the brakes near the front porch steps, coming to a halt right beside a dark, shiny car. Boone's heart stopped. He recognized the car, even knew the man who drove it, and at this point, he didn't even want to consider what all this meant.

"Get out," Snake ordered, and grabbed Boone by the arm, dragging him beneath the steering wheel and out of the truck.

Boone didn't argue. Tommy Joe's gun was too close to the small of his back.

Their footsteps were loud on the old wooden porch, and Snake shoved Boone through the door first without bothering to knock.

From the first, Boone had faced the dangers of living life as an undercover cop. Over the years, he'd prepared himself for just about any situation that could possibly have occurred. But there was no way in hell he could have predicted he would find the woman he loved in another man's arms.

Despair gave way to a ballooning, white-hot pain, and for a moment Boone wondered if he'd been shot. But when he took a deep breath, he realized the only thing shot was his faith. The expression in his eyes went flat. A muscle jerked in his jaw as a cold, derisive smile spread across his face.

Rachel was still reeling from the shock of opening her door, expecting to see Boone, and finding Griffin Ross waiting instead. He'd asked to use her phone, but that had been three minutes ago, and he had yet to make a move toward it, or the table on which it was sitting. Instead, he kept glancing nervously out the window, then back at her, muttering things that made no sense.

Just when Rachel thought this night couldn't get any worse, more car lights suddenly appeared, and instead of curiosity about who it could be, Griffin Ross was all but jumping up and down in an odd kind of delight.

"Griff, what on earth...?"

He spun, grabbing her by the arm. She didn't know what shocked her most, the grip with which he was holding her, or the crazy grin on his face.

"What's wrong with you?" Rachel cried, trying to yank free from his hand.

Instead of being set free, she was attacked. He slammed her up against the wall, grinding his lower body against her hips and his mouth against her lips. Shock passed swiftly into disbelief. This couldn't be happening...not to her...and not with Griff.

She tried to scream, but when she opened her mouth, he thrust his tongue inside. All but gagging at the unexpected intrusion, Rachel hammered helplessly at his chest with her hands.

And then the front door opened. Her freedom was as sudden as her violation had been. Stunned, she watched Griffin turn, then smile at the men who came through the door.

"Oh, my God," she groaned, and wiped her hand across her face. Everything she'd been experiencing up to this point had prepared her for an understanding she wasn't ready to face. Something told her this was the beginning of the end.

The look on Boone's face broke her heart. She knew how this would look. Her first thought was to explain.

She started toward him, but Griffin grabbed her, yanking her roughly against him, then sliding his arm beneath her breasts and holding her fast.

The shock was so sudden and so rough that it left her momentarily breathless, and in that moment, when she couldn't speak, she realized that Boone had not come in of his own accord. There was a gun in his back. Her hesitation was just long enough for Boone to say what was on his mind.

"Well, hell, Rachel. You're quite a little trooper, aren't you? That must be some man you've got, to let him talk you into sleeping with his enemies."

"You're quite a little soldier, aren't you, Mercy? Since you've ridden every man you rode with, I guess you..."

"No!" she screamed, struggling to get free of Griffin's clutch. It *was* happening all over again, just as she'd feared, and unless she could figure out a way to change it, she was going to be responsible for another outlaw's death.

Griff splayed his hands across her breasts in a rude but possessive gesture. "What's wrong, little Rachel? Did you get a little too attached to this pig?"

"You're the pig!" she cried, and kicked backward at his shins, trying to free herself from his grasp.

"You can cut the play," Boone said. "You won, Rachel. I hope you and your socially correct boyfriend live a long and miserable life on other people's money."

Rachel didn't know what he was talking about, but she knew how this must look. Boone wasn't going to help her. It was up to her to save them both. Then, to her dismay, Griffin Ross pulled a gun out of his pocket and jammed it into her throat.

"Take him out back," he ordered. "Before we let these two lovers follow each other to hell, there's some unfinished business sweet Rachel and I have between us, isn't there, darling?"

Boone froze. Two lovers? Follow each other to hell? He stared at Rachel, at the shock on her face and the fear in her eyes, and wondered if he'd read this all wrong.

"Rachel, I…"

She moved like a wildcat thrown into a den of pups. Screaming at the top of her lungs, she spun and lunged, leaving claw marks down Griffin Ross's face before she kicked him in the crotch. He dropped the gun to grab his face, falling backward over the only light in the room. As if in answer to a prayer, the room went dark.

Snake never saw the kick coming. One minute he was in control; the next thing he felt was his supper coming up uninvited as Boone's boot hit him square in the belly. Tommy Joe ducked and fired the gun at the same time, and because he did, the shot went wild. It was all the chance Rachel needed. She grabbed Boone by the arm.

"Run!" she screamed, and started through the house, moving on instinct and memory around furniture and walls, pulling him with her.

As they reached the kitchen, she paused long enough to throw the main switch on the breaker box. Boone yanked her by the arm.

"What are you trying to prove?"

"That I love you!" Rachel screamed. "Now run, damn it, run!"

He didn't have to be told twice. They bolted out the back door and into the yard, running past the shrubs and the swing, out into the wide-open space between her house and the woods beyond.

Just let me get her out of range of that damned security light and into the trees, Boone thought.

Gunfire suddenly erupted behind them. The lights were back on. Someone had found the switch. Boone heard the screen door slam and then a rash of wild, angry shouts.

He shoved Rachel in front of him, not wanting her to be an easy target at his side.

"Keep going!" he yelled.

She ran without looking back, confident from the sound of his footsteps at her heels that he would follow.

"There they go!" someone shouted.

Rachel winced at the sound of Griffin's voice. He must be crazy!

Fear lent speed to her steps, although she was getting winded. A stitch was pulling in her side, and her legs felt like rubber. No matter how fast they ran, the trees didn't seem any closer.

Gunfire came again, like firecrackers going off on the Fourth of July, and Rachel had a fleeting thought that she would never like fireworks again. She wanted to look back, to see if Boone was still behind her, but she was afraid that if she stopped she wouldn't be able to take another step.

Again the sound of gunshots shattered the silence, echoing from one side of the Kiamichis to the other, until Rachel couldn't tell where the shots had originated.

Then she looked up, and to her relief, the trees were right before them. Elation lent a fresh spurt of energy to her stride. Because she was so certain that they were safe, she didn't see Boone stagger and then pull himself upright. All she knew was that when they moved into the shelter of the forest, he was behind her all the way.

Wayland cursed his bad luck four ways to Sunday. He'd gotten to Denver Cherry's house just in time to see the taillights of a vehicle in the distance. Boone's truck was parked in the yard, but it didn't take more than a quick glance at the house to see that no one was there. Moving on instinct rather than knowledge, B. J. Wayland took after the taillights and hoped to hell he wasn't following some couple who were going off to the woods to neck. He would have some difficulty explaining if he caught them peeled down and going at it.

Twice he feared he'd lost them, but then he would catch a glimpse of the lights disappearing around another bend in the road.

"Damn roads aren't much better than a goat path," he muttered as he took a curve at high speed. Give him a flat road and a hot car any day over this hide-and-seek.

He flew past the small dirt road on his left like a blind bat coming out of hell with his tail on fire, moving with no sense of direction except fast and forward. It was pure luck and a good angle in the road that made him realize the car he'd been following had turned off. He glanced up in his rearview mirror just as Snake Martin hit the brakes in front of Rachel Brant's house.

B.J. stomped on his own brakes and went into a slide. The car spun sideways. When B.J. came to a stop, the smell of hot rubber drifted up through the heating system into the interior of his car, and the headlights were pointing in the direction from which he'd just come.

"Just like in the movies," he drawled, and gunned the car forward.

He parked in the trees at the end of the driveway and then got out, intending to go the rest of the way on foot. But he never made it past thc front of his car before all the lights in the house went out. At the first sounds of gunfire, he grabbed his cell phone and hit redial as he started to run.

"Cross here."

"It's going down!" Wayland said as he ran. "Get me some backup, Captain. It doesn't sound pretty."

"What's your location?" she asked.

"Damned if I know!" Wayland yelled. "About five miles below Boone's trailer and into the trees. Just follow the sound of gunfire. You can't miss us."

"Wayland, don't do—"

"Gotta go, Captain. Catch you later."

The line went dead in Susan Cross's ear. She slammed the phone down as she bolted from the room. God save them all.

Boone hadn't planned on getting shot. But then, a sane man never actively searched for different ways to die. His shoulder felt numb, and the farther they ran, the lighter his head was getting. They had to find a place to hide, at least until he got his second wind. He hadn't come this far to fall flat on his face. And then he staggered as a tree suddenly jumped into his path. It was luck that kept him upright and moving…that and Rachel. To his overwhelming relief, she began to slow down and seemed to be searching the area for a specific location.

"Over here," she said, and took him by the hand.

He went where she led him, weaving around trees and staggering through bushes until they entered a tiny clearing, little more than six feet in diameter. Completely surrounded by a dense stand of evergreens, their location seemed safe...at least for the time being.

Rachel stopped, her heart pounding as she drew harsh, aching breaths through burning lungs. She peered back through the trees, unable to see anything beyond the branches in front of her face, and exhaled slowly.

Safe. Now they were safe. She turned. Even in the darkness, the expression on Boone's face was too plain to conceal. Fear for what he'd seen...for what he'd so terribly misunderstood washed over her.

"Boone...darling, you've got to understand. I didn't know...."

He swayed, and she caught him. A new fear surfaced as she steadied him where he stood. His breath came in short, aching grunts. His shirt was wet with sweat. And then a terrible thought dawned. Despite their frantic race to safety, it was too cold for him to be sweating to this degree. She looked at her hand. Even in the darkness, the bloodstain was impossible to miss.

"Dear God! Boone, why didn't you tell me?"

He went down on his knees to keep from falling.

Instead of an answer, he threw a question back in her face.

"Why did you change your mind?" he muttered, and dropped his head between his knees, trying desperately to keep from passing out.

Rachel groaned. With all the medical skill in her head, she had none of it at her fingertips.

"About what?" she asked as she undid his shirt, searching by feel, rather than sight, to test for damage.

"About your boyfriend. You already had me cold. What made you change your mind?"

She attributed his rambling questions to shock as she felt along his back for an entrance wound. And then she found it and breathed a small sigh of relief. It seemed to be safely away from his heart and spinal column, although she had no way of knowing what the angle of the trajectory had been. She closed her eyes, picturing in her mind the internal workings of the human body and what damage the bullet could have done. There were too many variables to assume anything.

"Oh, God, what I wouldn't give for Charlie Dutton now," she muttered.

"He's in love with you," Boone said, and then slumped forward.

Determined to keep panic out of her voice, she eased Boone down on his side. "And I'm in love with you," she said. "That would make for quite an odd group, don't you think?"

Shoving back the front of his shirt, she moved her examination to the front of his chest, searching for a point of exit, and then groaned. There was none. She checked his back again and stifled new panic. Blood was no longer seeping. It was starting to flow.

Pressure. She needed packing and pressure. Without hesitation, she yanked off her shirt and began folding it up.

"Rachel, I..."

"Hush," she whispered. "I need to stop the bleeding."

She stuffed the thick pad she'd made beneath his shirt, centering it on the hole in his back.

"Easy, sweetheart," she said as she eased him onto his back, using his own body weight for pressure on her makeshift bandage. For now, it was all she could do.

Boone looked up. Rachel's face was wavering in and out of focus, as if she were a dark angel hovering above him. Consciousness was slipping fast. He didn't know whether he was just passing out or about to die, but there was something she needed to know. He grabbed her hand with surprising force.

"In my boot...there's a gun."

She gasped. "I don't know how to shoot."

"Get it," he said, and then groaned. "All you have to do aim and fire. The bullet will do the rest."

"Oh, my God," she muttered, and pulled the thing out with mbling hands.

"Rachel."

She leaned down, her breath just a whisper above his face. Yes, darling."

"I'm not who you think I am."

Tears blurred her vision of his face as she rested her fore-ad against his chest.

"You're going to get well," she said, focusing her energy this man who'd stolen her heart. "I'll go anywhere with ou. Live anywhere you say. I don't care who you are or hat you do, just don't leave me, Boone. Dear God, don't ave me again."

He frowned. She wasn't making sense. He'd never left her efore, so how could he leave her again? But one thing she'd id soaked into his fuzzy brain. She still believed he was an utlaw, and was willing to run with him if that was what it ook for them to be together.

He went weak; and he didn't know if it was from lack of lood or the wash of emotion flooding him. He'd waited all is life for a woman like her, and now it might be too late.

"You don't understand," he kept saying. "I'm not the bad uy, Griffin Ross is the bad guy."

Though she still misunderstood what he was trying to say, he would have agreed with him about anything.

"I know that," she said softly, smoothing the hair away rom his face, then clenched her teeth to keep from raging vith helplessness. His skin was cold and clammy. Symptoms of shock.

She thrust her hand beneath his back to make sure the ban-dage was still in place, and then stifled a scream. It was al-ready soaked.

"Rachel, I want you to leave me here. If you head towa━
the road, you can go for help."

She leaned forward until he could feel her breath on ┝
face. "Just shut up and rest," she said. "We're in this t━
gether, and we're going to come out of it the same way."

He swallowed a groan. It was too damned ironic to believ
He'd thought for sure when he walked into her house that h━
cover had been blown. Rachel had gone to South Dakot━
She'd told him so without blinking an eye. He'd been bo━
in South Dakota. Rachel had dumped her boyfriend, the
fallen for *him*. Then the boyfriend had turned out to be tʰ
man behind Denver Cherry's operation. Finally Rachel ha━
turned up in the boyfriend's arms. It had all been so neat. An
he'd been so very wrong.

He clutched at Rachel's hand, but she kept slipping away
Panic began to spread. This wasn't fair. He couldn't die. N━
when he'd just found her.

"Denver Cherry wasn't the real boss. I never knew wh━
my boss was," he muttered. "They were taking me to mee
the boss."

Rachel groaned. She'd suspected that Boone was mixed u━
with drugs, but refused to consider the possibility. Hearin━
Denver Cherry's name confirmed her worst suspicions. Hi━
reputation had long preceded him, although the authorities ha━
yet to prove a thing that could put him in prison. Now Boon━
was admitting what she'd refused to believe.

"Rachel…damn it, are you listening?" Boone said, and
then broke out in a wave of cold sweat. "Hell," he mutterec
weakly.

Rachel pressed her hand above his heart; the beat was faint
almost too faint to be felt. Frantic, she thrust her fingers
against his neck, searching for a pulse. It was there
Thready…but there.

His eyelids fell shut, and his head rolled sideways. In thaᵗ

>ment, Rachel knew true terror. Clutching the front of his

›rt with both hands, she gave him a vicious jerk.

"Boone! Damn you, don't die on me, do you understand?"

His eyes came open. "What's it take to get a little sleep

)und here?" he muttered.

"You talk to me," she said.

"Where's the gun?"

She glanced around. It was by her knee, where she'd

›opped it.

"Here," she said.

"Don't put it down again," he said, and for some reason

·e quiet authority in his voice moved past her panic to a

ality she suddenly understood.

"I won't," she said, and set it in her lap, one hand on it

all times.

He started to talk, and at first Rachel thought he was ram-

·ing. But the longer she listened, the clearer it finally became.

"They were taking me to meet the boss. Denver wasn't the

)ss. They were taking me to meet the boss."

"Oh…my…God!" She leaned forward, cupping Boone's

·eek until he finally focused again on her face.

"Rachel…I love you. Did I tell you I loved you?"

"Yes, darling, and you told me so much more, didn't you?

ou were trying to tell me Griff is the real boss, weren't

ou?"

A smile broke through the pain. He relaxed. She finally

nderstood.

"I'm just going to rest now," he said. "Be right back,

·kay?"

But before Rachel could answer, sounds outside the trees

n which they were hiding brought her to a new level of fear.

Before she could react, the branches of the evergreens parted

nd Griffin Ross came staggering through, cursing as the thick

›ranches slapped and stung at his face. She swallowed a

noan. They'd been found!

If you love me, don't let me hang.

For Rachel, the message was loud and clear. She grabb
the gun from her lap and then stood with one foot on eith
side of Boone's prone body. Griff was going to have to cor
through her to get to Boone.

Griffin's gun was dangling from his hand as he shoved t
last branch aside. When he saw Boone sprawled out on t
ground, seemingly lifeless—just the way he wanted him—
smile of pure evil spread across his face. The fact that Rach
was only half dressed made it all the better.

There was still a cold smile on his face as he kicked at tl
toe of Boone's boot.

"Did I interrupt your little tryst?" Griff sneered.

Rachel's head started to throb.

"Get away from him!" she muttered.

"And what if I don't want to?" Griff asked, and starte
toward her.

Pain shafted from the back of her head and then spirale
down her neck. Her heart was racing, her hands were shakin,
but there was a newfound resolve that she didn't understan
She didn't even know how to hold a gun, and yet she foun
it light, even comfortable in the palm of her hand.

*"I know that you can shoot...so if you love me...don't le
me hang."*

Understanding dawned. That was it! She couldn't shoot, bu
Mercy could. *Okay, girl, you've been haunting my sleep, s
help me now, or forever hold your peace.*

"Then I guess I'll just have to make you," Rachel said
and lifted her arm. Steadying the gun with both hands, she
aimed at the biggest target she could see, which was the dea
center of Griffin Ross's chest.

He stopped in midstep as shock spread across his face. He
hadn't expected the gun. When it bloomed at the barrel, he
wasn't prepared for the jolt of bullet to flesh, or for the numb-
ness to spread so fast.

"You bitch!" he gasped, and tried to aim his own gun. But something was the matter with his arm. He stared down at his hand, watching in disbelief as the gun fell to the ground at his feet.

The ground was coming at him in waves. He looked up. "No fair," he mumbled.

"You already told me life wasn't fair, Griff. Don't you remember?"

He hated her for throwing his own words back in his face.

"I'll kill you," he said, and reached toward her.

The second shot knocked him flat on his back. "No, you won't," she said in a quiet, shaky voice. "Because you're already dead."

It might have been seconds. It might have been minutes. But a short time later, Rachel heard someone shouting as he ran through the trees. She didn't recognize the voice, but what he said sent her out to meet him.

"MacDonald! Where the hell are you, buddy? It's me. B.J.! Come on, man, answer me."

B. J. Wayland wasn't prepared for the woman who burst out of the trees. The gun she was waving made him nervous, but he took one look at her face, then registered the fact that she was minus a shirt, and decided to trust her.

"In here!" Rachel screamed, waving him to come inside. "He's been shot. We need an ambulance!"

B.J. blanched. Following her guidance, he pushed his way past the trees and stumbled on Griffin Ross's prone body as he entered the clearing.

"What the—?"

"He's dead," she said, and then her voice changed pitch as she let go of the panic she'd been holding in place. "Please! Oh, God, help me! Boone needs help!"

B.J. whipped out his cell phone and called for an ambulance while Rachel sank to her knees, back at Boone's side.

Moments later, he knelt beside her, doing his own test run
Boone's injuries and vitals. The weak pulse scared him.

"It won't take them long to get here," he promised. "T
ambulance and local authorities were already at the house.

"But...how?"

"I called them to come pick up those two losers in y
flower bed. I hope you don't mind. The fat one's in the yell
mums, and there's a skinny one who's taking himself a l
swing."

Rachel shuddered. The image of what had taken place
her home was horrible. She'd believed it to be her haven, a
instead it had become a place of death.

"But who are you?" she asked. "And how do you kno
Boone?"

B.J. shrugged. "Men like us stick together."

She didn't understand and, at this point, she didn't rea
care. All she wanted was for Boone to wake up. She lean
down, patting his cheek in a gentle, constant motion.

"Boone, can you hear me? It's over. All you have to do
wake up and get well." Her voice broke. "Please, Boon
don't leave me."

B.J. couldn't keep his eyes off her. Even in the darknes
even with her hair disheveled and tiny scratches all over h
face and nearly bare upper body, the woman was stunnin
He took off his jacket and slipped it over her shoulders. Sh
hardly acknowledged the act.

"Are you Rachel?"

She nodded.

He looked down at Boone, remembering what the captai
had told him about the situation. An odd grin broke the som
berness of his face.

"He won't die, honey," he said softly. "He's too damne
hardheaded to leave you behind for someone else."

Chapter 15

Rachel was hanging on to sanity by a thin, fragile thread. The halls of Comanche County Memorial in Lawton, Oklahoma, were well-lit and busy, but she couldn't see them for the darkness within her heart.

She looked up as Charlie Dutton slid into the seat beside her.

"Joanie sends her love. She says not to worry about a thing at your house. She'll get it all cleaned up before you get home."

Rachel blanched. Cleaned up? She'd forgotten the mayhem that had been done after she and Boone made a break for the door.

"Tell her thank-you," Rachel muttered, and couldn't bring herself to care if all four walls had fallen in. There was only one thing that mattered, and that was keeping Boone alive.

"Charlie?"

"Yeah?"

"Is he going to die?"

Charlie winced. Rachel looked so lost, so unsure, so unli
the Rachel he knew. She was wearing the blue long-sleev
shirt he'd had on under his uniform when they took Boc
out of the woods. In a dark, selfish part of his soul, Char
had already let himself consider what might happen if Boc
did die. Rachel would be free. But the thought hadn't be
there long. When you cared for someone, you put her ha
piness ahead of your own all the way. He took her har
squeezing it between his palms in a gesture of comfort.

"I don't know, honey. They're working on him now."

She shuddered, then swayed in the chair. Charlie slipp
an arm around her shoulder and pulled her close.

"Lean on me, Rachel."

She accepted the offer. Silence stretched into endle
minutes.

"Charlie."

"Yeah?"

"I'm sorry."

Her hair tickled the edge of his chin. Her shoulders we
trembling. But what hurt most was the finality of it all. H
couldn't kid himself any longer about her ever changing h
mind. For better or worse, she was in love with another ma
It was the tears on her face that broke his heart.

"I know, honey. So am I." *Oh, God...so am I.*

An hour passed, and then another. The sound of footstep
made Rachel look up each time someone passed, always hop
ing it was the doctor...and at the same time, afraid for hir
to come.

This time it wasn't the doctor. This time it was B. J. Way
land, and a middle-aged woman Rachel didn't know. Rache
straightened, slipping out from under the shelter of Charlie'
arms as the woman stopped abruptly in front of where sh
was sitting.

"Rachel Brant?"

There was something in the woman's voice that demanded attention. Without asking herself why, Rachel stood.

"Yes, I'm Rachel Brant."

The woman held out her hand. "Captain Cross, DEA." She glanced at B.J., then back at Rachel. Arching an eyebrow, she told Rachel, "*You* can call me Susan."

DEA?

Rachel wasn't the only one who was impressed. Charlie got to his feet and extended his hand.

"Charlie Dutton, paramedic out of Razor Bend," and then added, "Rachel is my partner."

Susan nodded. She understood about partners.

Rachel was afraid. If Denver Cherry had been running drugs and Boone had been working for Denver, then that meant these people were going to arrest Boone. She took a deep breath, lifted her chin and stared Susan Cross straight in the eyes.

"I don't know what Boone's done," she said quietly. "But I want you to know I plan to testify on his behalf as to the admirable qualities I had occasion to witness. Since I've known him, he's helped save a woman's and a child's lives, and he saved my life at the risk of his own."

Susan's eyebrow arched even farther.

"Told you, Captain," B.J. muttered. "She's the real thing. Blaine's a lucky SOB and that's a natural fact."

Susan Cross glared at B.J.'s slip of the lip and then gave Rachel a thoughtful look, although it seemed as if Rachel had missed the connection between Boone and Blaine. It was obvious to Susan that Rachel Brant was in severe distress about Boone MacDonald's health. It wasn't fair to let her think that if he lived, he would be imprisoned, as well.

"Come with me, Miss Brant. We need to talk."

Rachel hesitated.

"We won't go far," Susan said. "Just over there, by the windows. We can still see the doctor if he comes."

Rachel did as she asked. At this point, she would have don anything Susan Cross suggested.

But when they got there, instead of talking, Susan turne and stared out the windows overlooking the city of Lawton She hadn't reached the age of fifty-five without facing som truths of her own. She was short, she was dumpy, and he hair was gunmetal gray. The only things she had going fo her were her years on the force, her brains and her voice. Tha commanded authority. She demanded respect. For the mos part, she got it. Her men trusted her, because she backed then one hundred percent.

She didn't want to lose the man in surgery, but when she saw Rachel Brant waiting with her heart in her eyes, she'c known the fight was already lost. She'd lost him to a woman who would never give him back.

Boone MacDonald was one of her toughest undercover agents. He would survive the surgery, of that she was convinced. But she'd taken one look at Rachel's beauty and heard her plea for clemency on his behalf and known that Boone would not survive losing Rachel Brant. And because of that, she divulged a truth she'd sworn to protect.

"He's one of ours, you know."

At first Rachel didn't understand. "He's one of your what?"

Susan turned, her eyes cool, always judging…constantly gauging.

"Boone—at least, that's the name by which you know him—is one of our best undercover agents."

The room started to spin. Rachel turned and leaned against the cold glass, relishing the coolness against her feverish forehead.

"Are you all right?" Susan asked.

Rachel closed her eyes, then swallowed a lump in her throat, remembering the things that had seemed so out of character for the man she'd believed him to be. He'd asked her o trust him. Offered her help when she was certain none was here. She caught her breath on a sob. He'd even told her at the last that he was one of the good guys, but she hadn't understood what he meant. Rachel took a deep breath, then let it out on a sigh.

"Yes, Susan, I'm all right. I'm very all right...now."

Susan Cross nodded. It felt good to break a rule. Maybe she should do it more often.

"Well, then," she said quietly, "you understand I'm telling you this under the strictest confidence. It wouldn't do to let some of his enemies know he was flat on his back and virtually defenseless, would it?"

The tone of Rachel's voice went flat, ominous in its lack of emotion. "No one will hurt him while he's defenseless, I promise you that."

To say that Susan was startled by Rachel's statement was putting it mildly, but then she remembered what B.J. had told her about finding Griffin Ross dead. It was obvious from the shape Boone had been in when they hauled him out of the Kiamichis that he couldn't have done it. That left Rachel as the triggerman. It was hard to look at her now and see a woman who'd drilled two holes into the front of Griffin Ross's shirt.

"Sometimes it's dangerous to make such a promise unless you're ready to back it up."

Rachel flushed but refused to admit to what the captain was implying. What had happened back there in the mountains was thanks to Mercy, not her.

There was no way a by-the-book kind of woman like Susan Cross would understand about a past life taking hold of the one happening now, and when Rachel thought about it, neither did she. All she knew was that, when it counted, she'd aimed and fired, just as Boone had told her to do, and hit a target she hadn't expected to hit.

Convinced that she'd accomplished what she'd set out to do, Susan started to leave, but Rachel caught her by the arm.

"Susan?"

"Yes?"

"What's his name?"

"Daniel Blaine."

Rachel nodded, trying to match the man she knew with a new identity. "What do they call him?"

Susan grinned. "Other than mule-headed?"

Rachel's heart lifted. The name might be strange, but the personality was not. "Yes, other than that."

"Just Daniel. He's not much for nicknames."

There was a note pinned to the T-shirt. Just one name. Didn't know if it was my first name or my last.

"No, I guess he's not," Rachel agreed.

"He's going to be all right," Susan said. "If you'd known him as long as I have, you'd believe me."

And then Rachel smiled. "It seems like I've known him forever."

Susan touched Rachel's arm. It was a brief, almost clumsy gesture. She wasn't used to showing her emotions.

"I'd better be going. We've got a lot of cleaning up to do. When he comes to, tell him we smashed the lab and took Cherry into custody. Griffin Ross had been laundering drug money out of his savings and loan, and with the aid of his secretary, who's agreed to cooperate fully by helping us with the paperwork to prove it, we can seize his personal assets. The rest of the bunch is history, thanks to you and B.J."

"Poor Lois," Rachel said, and then it dawned on her what Susan had just said. She gave the DEA captain a wary look. *Thanks to me and B.J.? So they know how Griffin died after all.*

"Don't worry," Susan said. "It was Boone's gun, and quite obviously self-defense. There will be no problem with who pulled the trigger."

Rachel lifted her chin. "I wasn't hiding the fact," she said quietly. "Put whatever you have to in the records. I just did what I had to do to keep him alive."

Susan's eyebrow arched again. "You know, there's something about you I didn't expect. Have you ever thought of going into law enforcement?"

Rachel didn't bother to hide her shudder. "No! I don't like guns. That was my first time to hold one, and I hope my last. I'm trained to save people's lives, not take them."

"I think you're looking at us from the wrong side of the road," Susan said. "We're trained to do the very same thing."

That was food for thought as Susan Cross walked away, taking B. J. Wayland with her. Rachel stared after them until the elevator swallowed them whole.

She turned and looked back out the window. It was almost morning.

Daniel Blaine. His name is Daniel....

Rachel straightened. A memory hovered at the back of her mind. There was something she needed to remember. Something about her trip to South Dakota. Something connected to the newspaper story about Dakota's demise.

"Oh, my God!" Blaine! That was it! Mercy Hollister had been responsible for the death of an outlaw named Dakota Blaine.

Charlie's reflection appeared in the glass as he came to stand behind her. "Rachel, is anything wrong?"

It was the last little link in her connection to the past that made a crazy kind of sense out of it all.

"No, oh, no. In fact, it's just the opposite. Everything is very all right."

Charlie didn't know what had made her so happy, but at this point, as he hugged her close, he didn't really care. He was willing to take what he could get, when he could get it.

Another half hour passed, and the earlier elation Rachel had experienced was beginning to pass. She was back to pacing and worrying, and Charlie was hard-pressed to find something to occupy her mind. A notion did occur to him, and as he considered telling her, he also considered the consequences if his secret went past her.

"Hey, Rachel, if I tell you something, will you swear not to tell a living, breathing soul, especially Joanie Sue Miller?"

Rachel nodded. "I promise, especially about Joanie."

"You remember Ida Mae Frawley?"

"Widow Frawley? The old recluse who died a few months back?"

"Yeah, that's the one."

"What about her?" Rachel asked.

"I used to mow her yard when I was a kid, did you know that?"

Rachel shook her head.

"Yeah, I did. As I got older, I did all kinds of odd jobs for her. She was almost ninety when she died. Someone had to help her."

"That was good of you, Charlie."

He ducked his head. "I guess she liked me a lot."

Rachel smiled. "You're an easy man to like, Charlie Dutton."

He gave her a long, judging look. "Remember, you promised."

"Oh, for Pete's sake. You'd think we were five years old and you just stole the last piece of pie. What are you trying to say?"

"Well, hell, how would you feel if you were minding your own business and then found out one day that someone had died and left you seven hundred thousand dollars?"

"Seven hundred thousand..." She gasped. "You're kidding!"

"No, I am not," Charlie said. "And keep your voice down."

Rachel was stunned. ''That explains your ring and your car and your hairstyle,'' she said. ''But not why you want to keep it a secret.''

Charlie blushed, then looked away, and at that moment Rachel came as close to loving him as she ever would.

''I didn't want anyone to know because I want to be loved for who I am, not what I've got.''

Rachel's voice trembled. ''Oh, Charlie, I don't know what to say.''

''Now, don't go all squishy-eyed on me. This is a secret, remember?'' Then he grinned. ''Besides, it's too late for you now, baby. Even if you swear, I won't believe you love me.''

Rachel had to laugh, which was exactly what he had wanted, and before anything else could be said, Charlie grabbed her and spun her around. A doctor was coming toward them in surgery greens. Rachel went to meet him.

For the rest of her life, Rachel would remember the first sight she'd had of Daniel Blaine in ICU. She'd fallen in love with Boone, and she'd been prepared to love him in spite of himself. Now she was face-to-face with an unconscious man in a hospital bed and learning all over again what love and sacrifice were about.

She could only imagine the risks he'd taken by letting their relationship grow. Only now, since she'd learned his true identity, did she understand what he must have thought when he saw her in Griffin Ross's arms. She made a promise to herself then and there that she would never give him cause to doubt her again.

Four days later, Daniel Blaine was moved from ICU to a private room. When he moved, Rachel went with him. She'd been home only once, and that had been to get her own car and several changes of clothes. She wasn't letting him out of her sight until he was able to leave on his own. She knew now the selfless act of love he'd shown by shoving her in front of him as they ran through the night, putting himself between her and danger, willing to take the bullet that might have hit her instead. The doctors were doing their part in healing Daniel's body, but it was Rachel's quiet, steady presence that began the healing of a desperado's heart.

She thought he was asleep. Daniel could tell by the quiet way in which she moved around the room, adding water to the flowers the agency had sent, folding the extra blanket at the foot of his bed, easing the sheet from beneath his arm to keep from jostling the IV.

The sounds around him hadn't changed much in the past five days. Nine altogether, taking into consideration the four he'd spent in ICU. He didn't remember much from that time, but he'd always known she was there. Her presence filled some long-empty part of him.

Just outside the doorway, life went on, but inside his room, his world consisted of Rachel. Doctors' and nurses' intrusions were tolerated. Only Rachel was welcomed into the private space of his heart.

The sounds of glasses and dishes being rattled told him it must be suppertime. Food odors drifted amid the scents of medicine and disinfectant, an unappetizing combination.

Daniel shifted slightly where he lay, easing the pressure on the healing wound on his back, and as he did, he sensed Rachel's instant appraisal.

His eyelids fluttered as he hid a smile. God help him, but when he gave his heart to Rachel Brant, he'd also given up the last of his secrets. The joke on her was that he didn't mind at all. If they'd been his secrets to tell, he would have shared them with her long ago.

He had but the vaguest of memories of what had happened after she took off her shirt in the forest and used it to stanch the flow of his blood. They were little more than flashes of

ages, of voices, of smells. The fear mirrored on Rachel's
ce. The gun he'd put in her hand. The smell of rotting leaves
d cold night air…of pine and cedar…and gunpowder.

But there was one image that had stayed sure and strong
his mind, and that was Rachel standing over him like an
venging angel with his gun aimed straight at Griffin Ross's
est. He remembered feeling hopeless and helpless, and he
membered a complete and total fear that he'd brought her
this end.

It had been days later before he learned what she'd done,
nd even then he had been unable to picture the Rachel he
new, the healer, the caregiver, as being able to shoot a man
vice, point-blank. But he was living proof that she had.

"Daniel, darling…"

She'd had nine days to get used to the change in his iden-
ty, but it felt good to hear his name on her lips. Her hand
vas on his forehead. He felt her lips brush his cheek. He
pened his eyes.

"They're bringing supper around."

"I don't want food. I want you."

Rachel stifled a smile. "Hmm…what was that word Susan
Cross used? Oh yes, I remember…*mule-headed*. I believe she
aid you were mule-headed. Darling, are you? Mule-headed,
mean?"

Daniel grinned. "Probably, but that doesn't change what I
want."

Rachel straightened his covers and stepped back just as a
nurse entered the room with his meal. She leaned close and
warned him in a none-too-gentle tone of voice, "What you
want and what you're about to get are two entirely different
things."

"Good evening, Mr. Blaine, how are we doing?"

Daniel glared. He hated the communal *we*. The last time
he looked, he'd been the only one in this room stuck in a bed.

"You tell me. How are we?" he grumbled.

The nurse slid the tray onto the table and lifted the warmin covers off the food, then hit a button on the bed that sat Dani abruptly upright.

He cursed as the stitches pulled his skin.

"We're a little testy this evening, aren't we? That's alway a good sign. We'll be ready to go home before we know it.

"You're damn sure not going with me," Daniel mutteree glaring at the food, which was sitting there on his plate in a its unappetizing glory.

"This looks wonderful," Rachel said, as she went to g him a warm, wet cloth so that he could wash before eating Her voice was lower as she dropped the cloth in his hand "Will one washcloth be enough, sweetheart, or should I g another one, with soap for your mouth?"

He got the message and took the washcloth without furthe comment.

"I'll be back later to get your tray, Mr. Blaine. Enjoy."

Daniel shoved the tray and table aside, then glared at Ra chel, daring her to argue with his decision.

"You eat it," he said.

"No, thank you," she said brightly. "I had a snack while you were asleep." Then she picked up his fork and handed i to him without batting an eye. "Oh, look, darling, they've pu cucumber in your salad. I seem to remember you're quite an authority on cucumbers."

His mouth quirked at one corner. The little witch! She was taunting him just as he'd teased her that day in the grocery store.

Rachel sat at the foot of the bed, with her hand on his leg, rubbing gently...but still, rubbing just the same. She leaned forward only slightly—but there was a definite and unex-pected sexual tension in her voice.

"Is it good?"

He blinked. All sorts of images came to mind that might

t that question much better than the damned cucumber in his
ılad.

"Is what good?" he mumbled.

"The salad, sweetheart. Is it crisp? You know how you like
ıings to have a certain texture. None of that limp, floppy
.uff for you, right?"

He had to grin. She'd won that round. He jammed the fork
ı the salad and took a big bite. To his chagrin, it didn't taste
alf-bad.

Rachel slipped off the bed and went to get her nail file.
Moments later, she climbed back to her spot and began to file
t a tear on her nail as if it were the most important thing she
ıad to do. And because she wasn't paying attention, he fin-
shed his salad in spite of himself.

She looked up. "Ummm…the scalloped potatoes and ham
.mell good. How do they taste?"

Daniel stared at the conglomeration piled on his plate and
wished for a greasy take-out burger instead.

Rachel wasn't to be deterred. "I *love* sauces, don't you?
Especially cheese—the way it melts…and blends. It adds just
hat right touch to plain food. It's so…so…fluid, and warm,
and…"

"Have mercy, Rachel. I'll eat the stuff, just give me a
break!"

Rachel smiled and moved on to another nail while Daniel
dug into his dinner.

"Would you look at that!" she said a little while later,
when he'd finished the ham and potatoes. "There are strawberries in the mixed fruit! Remember when—"

"Don't even start," Daniel muttered, and picked up his
spoon. "I'm eating. I'm eating."

Hours later, the hospital had undergone its daily metamorphosis. The shift had changed, and the nurses on duty were
readying everyone for the night. Vitals had been taken; med-

icine rounds were over. The muted sounds of visitors takin
their leave from other patients could be heard out in the hal

Daniel was absorbing the quiet while absently watching th
television. After being coaxed to come up beside him, Rach
now lay on the edge of his bed, her back aligned with th
length of his leg, dozing in snatches.

Every time she jerked, or sighed a little more than he'
expected, Daniel would lay his hand upon her hair, or strok
the softness of her cheek, anything it took to gentle her slum
ber and reassure himself that she was going to be all righ
He'd had nightmares about Rachel sleepwalking off the edg
of the world and him not being able to catch her. Even now
though she was wide-awake and within reach of his hand, th
thought scared him to death. She was his life.

He heard her sigh and knew that she was awake again. Tha
was good. There were things that needed to be said.

"Rachel?" he whispered. "Are you awake?"

She stretched. "Umm-humm."

"There's something I've been wanting to say."

She heard a tone in his voice that hadn't been there in days
She went still.

"Thank you for saving my life."

Horror flashed, then quickly disappeared. She would not le
the memory of Griffin Ross's evil ruin their lives. She sat up
to face him, wearing a small, unusual smile.

Daniel had no way of knowing that, for Rachel, the act had
been twofold. Mercy Hollister had been responsible for the
death of the man she loved. It had been up to Rachel to see
that history did not repeat itself. She would have done whatever it took to keep this man alive—for herself, as well as for
him.

"You're welcome."

His jaw clenched nervously as he debated with himself as
to the best way to pursue what was on his mind.

"You know…we haven't known each other very long, although I feel as if I've known you all my life."

Oh, my darling, Daniel…if only you knew. Rachel smiled and reached for his hand. "I love you, sweetheart. Always have. Always will."

Daniel's eyebrow arched as a smile crooked the corner of his mouth. "You were scared of me, and you know it."

"Not of *you*. Never of you. Only what you represented."

He nodded. "I can accept that. What I'm trying to say is, I know in my heart how I feel, but I'm willing to wait as long as it takes until you're—"

"No."

He looked startled. "No, what?"

"I'm not willing to wait."

His grin widened as his black eyes glittered with promises he could hardly wait to keep. Then he took a deep breath, trying to remember where he'd been going with this thought. "I have a couple of things I need to tell you."

"Okay."

"This was my last undercover assignment."

She looked slightly startled. "Not because of me?"

A wry smile cocked the corner of his mouth. "Of course it's because of you. You think I'm going to go off half-cocked the rest of my life and leave you within reach of someone like Charlie Dutton?"

Rachel frowned. "I would never cheat on our love."

He caught her hand. "I was only teasing," he said quietly. "I knew this job would be my last one before you and I ever met. I've had enough of it, honey, and it's had enough of me."

Never in her life had Rachel wanted to throw herself into someone's arms as badly as she did right then, but they were too confined by tubes and needles to give it a thought. Instead, she leaned forward until mere inches separated their lips and whispered, "I'll never have enough of you. Just remember that."

Emotion came swiftly, blinding Daniel to all but the love shining out of Rachel's eyes.

"Rachel, if I asked you real nice, would you marry me?"

To his surprise, she started to cry.

He grimaced, swallowing a few tears of his own. "Come here, you."

She went willingly. Time passed as she settled in his good arm.

"Rachel."

"What, darling?"

"You never answered me."

She sighed. After all they'd been through, how on earth could he doubt? She moved, needing to look him in the eye when she said what she had to say.

"Yes, a thousand times yes, I will marry you. For the love we have now, and for all the love we once shared."

He groaned and pulled her back into his arms. What she'd said made no sense, but he was too happy a man to care.

"Daniel, be careful," she warned him, as he urged her into his lap.

"Now, darlin', I'm always careful, don't you remember?"

One last time, the image of Dakota's face slid between them. Black hair blowing in the wind as he mounted a horse in a flying leap. The laughter she could see on his lips as he yanked Mercy up behind him.

Rachel closed her eyes, waiting for the kiss to come, and when it did, there was no mistaking the man who was in control. Daniel's breath was soft against her skin. The touch of his hand ever gentle against her cheek.

"Open your eyes, Rachel. See who loves you, baby."

She complied, although she knew before she did as he asked.

Through the centuries, all kinds of men had walked the

earth. Some of their spirits had been dark, their souls black and hell-bent against redemption before they were ever born. But not her Daniel. He *was* a desperado...but in a subtle shade of gray.

Epilogue

It was spring in South Dakota. When Daniel and Rachel landed in Rapid City, it was just after noon. The rental car was waiting, as they'd requested, and by the time they loaded their bags and headed toward Deadwood, Rachel's anxiety was at an all-time high.

It hadn't been until after their wedding that Rachel learned where Daniel was born. That surprised him. Up until that moment, he'd still believed that was why she'd gone to South Dakota in the first place.

But now they were here—together—and for reasons he still didn't understand. Rachel had been oddly reticent with explanations, and adamant that they should go, and so he'd come—because she'd asked.

She didn't sleepwalk anymore. She claimed the episodes had stopped as abruptly as they'd appeared. There were a lot of things Rachel didn't explain and Daniel didn't care to ask. As long as she was well, nothing else mattered.

They drove into Deadwood as the sun was setting in the

~est.

Tomorrow their mission would begin.

Rachel walked among the tombstones, clutching a small plastic bag, her gaze focused downward, reading each epitaph, one by one. It was here. It had to be.

"Rachel, I know there's a real good reason why we came all the way to Deadwood for a belated honeymoon, and an even better one for dragging me through Boot Hill, but I have yet to figure it out."

"I love you, too," she said absently, and kept moving without looking back.

There was an abstracted look Rachel got on her face when she was concentrating real hard that made his toes curl in his boots. It always made him want to take her to bed and give her something else to think about. Daniel grinned to himself as he watched the sway of her hips in those tight blue jeans. These old outlaws would probably rise up and cheer if he followed his instincts right now.

"Hey, Rachel, don't you think it's sort of early on in our relationship for you to be ignoring me?"

Rachel paused and stifled a grin. Some of the verses on these tombstones were a hoot. This one in particular.

Red Fred
Died in bed

"What did you say?" she asked, suddenly realizing Daniel was a distance away and looking as if he were waiting for some sort of answer.

He laughed and threw up his arms. "Nothing, honey. Just wait for me."

Joy surged anew as Rachel stood in the warm Dakota sunshine while a cool spring breeze played with the ends of her hair. Love for this man...for her husband...was overwhelming.

His wind-tossed hair gleaming a sleek seal black, Daniel
Blaine came toward her with a long, careless stride. His head
was up, and his chin was thrust forward in the same way he
met life: straight on. There was a power in him even clothes
couldn't hide. The wide set of strong shoulders, the determination on his face that rarely wavered, and, always, a dark
carefree glitter in his eyes.

Rachel smiled as he drew near. In some ways he was like
those who lay buried here, but in the ways that counted, he
was so much more. He'd made the most of himself instead
of letting life drag him down. She loved him, and her respect
for him knew no bounds.

He swooped, lifting her off her feet and into his arms, kissing her grandly and with no sense of embarrassment for the
dozens of other tourists who were sharing their day.

"Daniel Blaine! What will all these people think?" Rachel
said, as he put her back down.

He threw his head back and laughed. "Honey, I don't care
what they think. You're my woman. I'll kiss you any place I
damn well please." He glanced down and then grinned.
"Even in front of Red Fred."

She laughed and then took him by the hand. "You're impossible, but I love you. Now come help me look."

He rolled his eyes and let her lead him away. "I'd be glad
to help, if I only knew what I was looking for."

Rachel ignored his complaint as, once again, her attention
was focused on the tombstones scattered all around.

Few voices shattered the silence within the cemetery
grounds as people walked about. Even though these men had
been hell on earth, they'd been buried in hallowed ground.
Preachers had spoken over their graves. Friends had shed tears
for their passing. They'd gained a stature in death that they'd
missed in life.

It wasn't until sometime later that Rachel paused, then
dropped to her knees.

Daniel was a few feet ahead before he realized she wasn't behind him. He turned, a smile on his face and laughter in his voice as he started to chide her for dawdling again. But his jest was never voiced, because he saw her reach out and trace the letters on a gray, weathered headstone.

Her head was bowed, and even from where he was standing, he could see a tremor in her chin. Within seconds, he was at her side. Curiosity drew his gaze to the stone that had so captured Rachel's fancy, but curiosity changed to surprise when he read the name on the stone.

Dakota Blaine
Deserved No Mercy

"Well, I'll be darned," Daniel said. "We have the same last name."

Rachel's eyes were filled with tears as she lifted the tiny bouquet of flowers from the sack she'd been carrying. When she'd seen them displayed among the florist's array, she'd picked them up without a second thought.

They were bluebells, tiny bell-like flowers that grew on fragile-looking stems that even the strongest of winds could not break. Their pure blue was also the color of Mercy Hollister's eyes. As she laid them on the grave, Rachel knew Dakota would have approved of her choice.

"How did you know this was here?" Daniel asked, as he watched Rachel place the flowers with care.

She looked up at him. Tears shimmered on the surface of her eyes—blue eyes, just like the bluebells she'd laid on the grave.

"I guess you could say I saw it in my dreams."

Daniel gave her a sharp, studied look. "Are you all right?"

Rachel smiled and held out her hand. "Let's go. I've done what I came here to do."

He helped her up without pressing her further. Rachel had

loved him without question; the least he could do was return the favor.

They walked away without looking back, but Rachel felt no need to linger. Only one more stop and her mission in coming this far would be over.

The day was drawing to a close, but Rachel had been firm in her convictions that this stop was truly necessary. The church was old and long since abandoned, yet the tiny nearby cemetery was well kept and mowed—proof to passersby that, while the parishioners had moved on, the care of those left behind still continued.

Daniel was beginning to worry. Combing cemeteries seemed an unhealthy pastime. The tension on Rachel's face was showing, and her actions seemed frantic, as if she were racing against some deadline of her own. This behavior was too symptomatic of her sleepwalking episodes for his peace of mind.

But she wasn't talking, and he didn't know how to intrude. For the time being, he stayed at her side, keeping careful watch over the lady who was his wife.

Months earlier, Rachel had enlisted the aid of a service designed for genealogists in search of missing ancestors. The letter she held contained the name of this church and the approximate location of the grave marker she'd come to find. One fact had come out in the search that she hadn't expected. Mercy Hollister had taken her own life. She had not been buried in hallowed ground.

For Rachel, it was the last piece of the puzzle she'd been trying to find. Maybe this was why Mercy Hollister's search for love on earth had not ended with her death. By taking her own life, she'd lost her chance to follow Dakota Blaine into eternity.

Rachel stumbled. Daniel caught her, then pulled her to him,

caressing the side of her face with his hand as he gauged the fever of her intent.

"Rachel, darlin', you're beginning to scare me. Can't you tell me what's wrong? I promise you, there's nothing you can say that I won't understand."

Rachel was tired. She'd been fighting this thing alone for so long. She caught his hand, feathering a gentle kiss upon the palm, then looked up, searching the beloved features she'd come to know so well.

How to tell you, my love? How to explain where we've been...what we've done? She sighed.

"It's almost over," she said, pleading with him to persevere with her a while longer.

He bowed his head and then held her close, feeling her tremble with fatigue. He fought with himself and his instincts, but his love for her won out.

"Tell me what to do," he said.

"Do you have my flowers?"

He held up the second small florist's sack. She nodded in satisfaction.

"Then come with me. It should be right over here."

She took him by the hand, and together they traversed the neat, narrow rows between headstones, to a small section of markers set aside from the rest. They were outside the old picket fence, beyond the neat rows and well-clipped grass.

The grass was taller here, obscuring the stones that were less prominent in height. A small brown rabbit suddenly darted from behind an old tombstone, while tiny wildflowers, only inches high, blew to and fro with the breeze. Rachel leaned down to read the names.

"Help me," she said.

Daniel came to her side. "Who are you looking for?" he asked.

"Mercy. Her name is Mercy."

A chill of foreboding swept across Daniel's senses, almost

the same sensation as when a bust was about to go down. A sense of knowing that within moments everything was going to come apart and there was no way of knowing the outcome until it was over and done. But then it passed, and he took her hand.

Together they walked, stooping every now and then to brush away leaves and read names, to toss away brush caught against the stones.

It was Daniel who found it. And, as Rachel had done at Boot Hill, he found himself down on his knees, tracing the weathered, hand-carved letters in an old piece of stone.

But as he touched it, he rocked back on his heels, startled by an overwhelming wave of sadness. He shook his head in disbelief and chalked it up to the fact that they'd been in too many graveyards.

"Rachel."

She was at his side in moments. She knelt beside him, and as his finger traced the letters in Mercy's name, her throat swelled with the ache of unshed tears.

"Oh, Daniel," she said, and laid her head against his shoulder.

Mercy Hollister
1853-1877
Dakota took her
Gone but not forgotten

Only Rachel knew the subtlety of the Dakota reference. It wasn't the Dakota Territory that had taken her away; it was the man who'd taken his name from the land.

Rachel began pulling grass and weeds away from the stone, clearing a small place for the flowers to go. But when Daniel handed Rachel the sack, she rejected it with tear-filled eyes.

"No, sweetheart, I think this would be better if it came from you."

He shrugged. "Whatever makes you happy, darlin'."

No, Daniel. It's you...or who you were...that will make Mercy happy, wherever she is.

The nosegay was small and round and tied at the bottom with baby-fine ribbons. White ones. Purple ones. Sky-blue scalloped ones.

"Put it there, I think," Rachel said, pointing to a sheltered spot against the small stone.

Daniel leaned the flowers there, firmly shoving the end of the bouquet into the soft, loamy earth until they appeared to have sprouted on the spot.

The blossoms dipped and bounced with the South Dakota breeze. Rachel reached out and touched them, testing the fresh, tender petals with the palm of her hand. They felt cool and soft, like Daniel's lips on her face when they made love in the dark.

And as they knelt, a feeling of peace settled deep in Rachel's heart.

"It's over...isn't it?" she said softly.

"What did you say?" Daniel asked, and then realized Rachel wasn't talking to him.

His nerves skittered, reminding him suddenly that they were a long, long way from home. He put his arm around her and urged her to stand.

"Rachel, honey. It's getting late."

She looked up at him. "No, Daniel. We were just in time."

They stood, looking down at the flowers on the shamefully small grave.

"The flowers are pretty," Daniel said. "Wonder what kind they are?"

"Forget-me-nots."

He nodded, rereading the verse on the grave one last time.

"They seem to fit real well, don't they? You know...gone but not forgotten?"

There was a hard knot in her throat as Daniel took her by the hand. *Rest in peace, Mercy Hollister.*

Just for a moment, the steady blowing breeze seemed to stop, as if God were holding his breath. A small cloud passed between the earth and the sun, casting the place in which they were standing into sudden shadow. And then, slowly, as clouds have a way of doing, it moved on and, as it did, left sunlight behind to mark its passing.

Rachel watched the small shadow moving across the face of the land, across the cemetery beyond, and then along the road on which they'd traveled.

It was a fanciful thought, and one she knew had no real foundation, but she could almost believe the receding shadow was Mercy Hollister's spirit, going home to rest.

"Daniel?"

"Yes, darlin'?"

"Take me home."

*   *   *   *   *

Silhouette ®

Where love comes alive ™

SILHOUETTE *Romance* ™

From first love to forever, these love stories are
for today's woman with traditional values.

Silhouette ® *Desire*

A highly passionate, emotionally powerful
and always provocative read.

Silhouette ®

SPECIAL EDITION ™

Emotional, compelling stories that capture the
intensity of living, loving and creating a family in
today's world.

Silhouette ®

INTIMATE MOMENTS ™

A roller-coaster read that delivers romantic thrills
in a world of suspense, adventure and more.

Visit Silhouette at www.eHarlequin.com

SDIR2